The Two A

James Fenimore Cooper

Alpha Editions

This edition published in 2024

ISBN : 9789362516602

Design and Setting By
Alpha Editions
www.alphaedis.com
Email - info@alphaedis.com

Contents

PREFACE.

It is a strong proof of the diffusive tendency of every thing in this country, that America never yet collected a fleet. Nothing is wanting to this display of power but the will. But a fleet requires only one commander, and a feeling is fast spreading in the country that we ought to be all commanders; unless the spirit of unconstitutional innovation, and usurpation, that is now so prevalent, at Washington, be controlled, we may expect to hear of proposals to send a committee of Congress to sea, in command of a squadron. We sincerely hope that their first experiment may be made on the coast of Africa.

It has been said of Napoleon that he never could be made to understand why his fleets did not obey his orders with the same accuracy, as to time and place, as his *corps d'armée*. He made no allowances for the winds and currents, and least of all, did he comprehend that all important circumstance, that the efficiency of a fleet is necessarily confined to the rate of sailing of the dullest of its ships. More may be expected from a squadron of ten sail, all of which shall be average vessels, in this respect, than from the same number of vessels, of which one half are fast and the remainder dull. One brigade can march as fast as another, but it is not so with vessels. The efficiency of a marine, therefore, depends rather on its working qualities, than on its number of ships.

Perhaps the best fleet that ever sailed under the English flag, was that with which Nelson fought the battle of the Nile. It consisted of twelve or thirteen small seventy-fours, each of approved qualities, and commanded by an officer of known merit. In all respects it was efficient and reliable. With such men as Hallowell, Hood, Trowbridge, Foley, Ball, and others, and with such ships, the great spirit of Nelson was satisfied. He knew that whatever seamen could do, his comparatively little force could achieve. When his enemy was discovered at anchor, though night was approaching and his vessels were a good deal scattered, he at once determined to put the qualities we have mentioned to the highest proof, and to attack. This was done without any other order of battle than that which directed each commander to get as close alongside of an enemy as possible, the best proof of the high confidence he had in his ships and in their commanders.

It is now known that all the early accounts of the man[oe]uvring at the Nile, and of Nelson's reasoning on the subject of anchoring inside and of doubling on his enemies, is pure fiction. The "Life" by Southey, in all that relates to this feature of the day, is pure fiction, as, indeed, are other portions of the work of scarcely less importance. This fact came to the writer, through the late Commodore (Charles Valentine) Morris, from Sir Alexander Ball, in the early part of the century. In that day it would not have done to proclaim it, so tenacious is public opinion of its errors; but since that time, naval officers of rank have written on the subject, and stripped the Nile, Trafalgar, &c., of their poetry, to give the world plain, nautical, and probable accounts of both those great achievements. The truth, as relates to both battles, was just as little like the previously published accounts, as well could be.

Nelson knew the great superiority of the English seamen, their facility in repairing damages, and most of all the high advantage possessed by the fleets of his country, in the exercise of the assumed right to impress, a practice that put not only the best seamen of his own country, but those of the whole world, more or less, at his mercy. His great merit, at the Nile, was in the just appreciation of these advantages, and in the extraordinary decision which led him to go into action just at nightfall, rather than give his enemy time to prepare to meet the shock.

It is now known that the French were taken, in a great measure, by surprise. A large portion of their crews were on shore, and did not get off to their ships at all, and there was scarce a vessel that did not clear the decks, by tumbling the mess-chests, bags, &c., into the inside batteries, rendering them, in a measure, useless, when the English doubled on their line.

It was this doubling on the French line, by anchoring inside, and putting two ships upon one, that gave Nelson so high a reputation as a tactician. The merit of this man[oe]uvre belongs exclusively to one of his captains. As the fleet went in, without any order, keeping as much to windward as the shoals would permit, Nelson ordered the Vanguard hove-to, to take a pilot out of a fisherman. This enabled Foley, Hood, and one or two more to pass that fast ship. It was at this critical moment that the thought occurred to Foley (we think this was the officer) to pass the head of the French line, keep dead away, and anchor inside. Others followed, completely placing their enemies between two fires. Sir Samuel Hood anchored his ship (the Zealous) on the inner bow of the most weatherly French ship, where he poured his fire into, virtually; an unresisting enemy. Notwithstanding the great skill manifested by the English in their mode of attack, this was the only two-decked ship in the English fleet that was able to make sail on the following morning.

Had Nelson led in upon an American fleet, as he did upon the French at the Nile, he would have seen reason to repent the boldness of the experiment. Something like it *was* attempted on Lake Champlain, though on a greatly diminished scale, and the English were virtually defeated before they anchored.

The reader who feels an interest in such subjects, will probably detect the secret process of the mind, by which some of the foregoing facts have insinuated themselves into this fiction.

CHAPTER I.

"Then, if he were my brother's.
My brother might not claim him; nor your father,
Being none of his, refuse him: This concludes—
My mother's son did get your father's heir;
Your father's heir must have your father's land."

KING JOHN.

The events we are about to relate, occurred near the middle of the last century, previously even to that struggle, which it is the fashion of America to call "the old French War." The opening scene of our tale, however, must be sought in the other hemisphere, and on the coast of the mother country. In the middle of the eighteenth century, the American colonies were models of loyalty; the very war, to which there has just been allusion, causing the great expenditure that induced the ministry to have recourse to the system of taxation, which terminated in the revolution. The family quarrel had not yet commenced. Intensely occupied with the conflict, which terminated not more gloriously for the British arms, than advantageously for the British American possessions, the inhabitants of the provinces were perhaps never better disposed to the metropolitan state, than at the very period of which we are about to write. All their early predilections seemed to be gaining strength, instead of becoming weaker; and, as in nature, the calm is known to succeed the tempest, the blind attachment of the colony to the parent country, was but a precursor of the alienation and violent disunion that were so soon to follow.

Although the superiority of the English seamen was well established, in the conflicts that took place between the years 1740, and that of 1763, the naval warfare of the period by no means possessed the very decided character with which it became stamped, a quarter of a century later. In our own times, the British marine appears to have improved in quality, as its enemies, deteriorated. In the year 1812, however, "Greek met Greek," when, of a verity, came "the tug of war." The great change that came over the other navies of Europe, was merely a consequence of the revolutions, which drove experienced men into exile, and which, by rendering armies all-important even to the existence of the different states, threw nautical enterprises into the shade, and gave an engrossing direction to courage and talent, in another quarter. While France was struggling, first for independence, and next for the mastery of the continent, a marine was a secondary object; for Vienna, Berlin, and Moscow, were as easily entered without, as with its aid. To these, and other similar causes, must be referred the explanation of the seeming invincibility of the English arms at sea, during the late great conflicts of Europe; an invincibility that was more apparent than real, however, as many well-established defeats were, even then, intermingled with her thousand victories.

From the time when her numbers could furnish succour of this nature, down to the day of separation, America had her full share in the exploits of the English marine. The gentry of the colonies willingly placed their sons in the royal navy, and many a bit of square bunting has been flying at the royal mast-heads of King's ships, in the nineteenth century, as the distinguishing symbols of flag-officers, who had to look for their birth-places among ourselves. In the course of a chequered life, in which we have been brought in collision with as great a diversity of rank, professions, and characters, as often falls to the lot of any one individual, we have been thrown into contact with no less than eight English admirals, of American birth; while, it has never yet been our good fortune to meet with a countryman, who has had this rank bestowed on him by his own government. On one occasion, an Englishman, who had filled the highest civil office connected with the marine of his nation, observed to us, that the only man he then knew, in the British navy, in whom he should feel an entire confidence in entrusting an important command, was one of these translated admirals; and the thought unavoidably passed through our mind, that this favourite commander had done well in adhering to the conventional, instead of clinging to his natural allegiance, inasmuch as he might have toiled for half a century, in the service of his native land, and been rewarded with a rank that would merely put him on a level with a colonel in the army! How much longer this short-sighted policy, and grievous injustice, are to continue, no man can say; but it is safe to believe, that it is to last until some legislator of influence learns the simple truth, that the fancied reluctance of popular constituencies to do right, oftener exists in the apprehensions of their representatives, than in reality.— But to our tale.

England enjoys a wide-spread reputation for her fogs; but little do they know how much a fog may add to natural scenery, who never witnessed its magical effects, as it has caused a beautiful landscape to coquette with the eye, in playful and capricious changes. Our opening scene is in one of these much derided fogs; though, let it always be remembered, it was a fog of June, and not of November. On a high head-land of the coast of Devonshire, stood a little station-house, which had been erected with a view to communicate by signals, with the shipping, that sometimes lay at anchor in an adjacent roadstead. A little inland, was a village, or hamlet, that it suits our purposes to call Wychecombe; and at no great distance from the hamlet itself, surrounded by a small park, stood a house of the age of Henry VII., which was the abode of Sir Wycherly Wychecombe, a baronet of the creation of

King James I., and the possessor of an improveable estate of some three or four thousand a year, which had been transmitted to him, through a line of ancestors, that ascended as far back as the times of the Plantagenets. Neither Wychecombe, nor the head-land, nor the anchorage, was a place of note; for much larger and more favoured hamlets, villages, and towns, lay scattered about that fine portion of England; much better roadsteads and bays could generally be used by the coming or the parting vessel; and far more important signal-stations were to be met with, all along that coast. Nevertheless, the roadstead was entered when calms or adverse winds rendered it expedient; the hamlet had its conveniences, and, like most English hamlets, its beauties; and the hall and park were not without their claims to state and rural magnificence. A century since, whatever the table of precedency or Blackstone may say, an English baronet, particularly one of the date of 1611, was a much greater personage than he is to-day; and an estate of £4000 a year, more especially if not rack-rented, was of an extent, and necessarily of a local consequence, equal to one of near, or quite three times the same amount, in our own day. Sir Wycherly, however, enjoyed an advantage that was of still greater importance, and which was more common in 1745, than at the present moment. He had no rival within fifteen miles of him, and the nearest potentate was a nobleman of a rank and fortune that put all competition out of the question; one who dwelt in courts, the favourite of kings; leaving the baronet, as it might be, in undisturbed enjoyment of all the local homage. Sir Wycherly had once been a member of Parliament, and only once. In his youth, he had been a fox-hunter; and a small property in Yorkshire had long been in the family, as a sort of foothold on such enjoyments; but having broken a leg, in one of his leaps, he had taken refuge against *ennui*, by sitting a single session in the House of Commons, as the member of a borough that lay adjacent to his hunting-box. This session sufficed for his whole life; the good baronet having taken the matter so literally, as to make it a point to be present at all the sittings; a sort of tax on his time, which, as it came wholly unaccompanied by profit, was very likely soon to tire out the patience of an old fox-hunter. After resigning his seat, he retired altogether to Wychecombe, where he passed the last fifty years, extolling England, and most especially that part of it in which his own estates lay; in abusing the French, with occasional inuendoes against Spain and Holland; and in eating and drinking. He had never travelled; for, though Englishmen of his station often did visit the continent, a century ago, they oftener did not. It was the courtly and the noble, who then chiefly took this means of improving their minds and manners; a class, to which a baronet by no means necessarily belonged. To conclude, Sir Wycherly was now eighty-four; hale, hearty, and a bachelor. He had been born the oldest of five brothers; the cadets taking refuge, as usual, in the inns of court, the church, the army, and the navy; and precisely in the order named. The lawyer had actually risen to be a judge, by the style and appellation of Baron Wychecombe; had three illegitimate children by his housekeeper, and died, leaving to the eldest thereof, all his professional earnings, after buying commissions for the two younger in the army. The divine broke his neck, while yet a curate, in a fox-hunt; dying unmarried, and so far as is generally known, childless. This was Sir Wycherly's favourite brother; who, he was accustomed to say, "lost his life, in setting an example of field-sports to his parishioners." The soldier was fairly killed in battle, before he was twenty; and the name of the sailor suddenly disappeared from the list of His Majesty's lieutenants, about half a century before the time when our tale opens, by shipwreck. Between the sailor and the head of the family, however, there had been no great sympathy; in consequence, as it was rumoured, of a certain beauty's preference for the latter, though this preference produced no *suites*, inasmuch as the lady died a maid. Mr. Gregory Wychecombe, the lieutenant in question, was what is termed a "wild boy;" and it was the general impression, when his parents sent him to sea, that the ocean would now meet with its match. The hopes of the family centred in the judge, after the death of the curate, and it was a great cause of regret, to those who took an interest in its perpetuity and renown, that this dignitary did not marry; since the premature death of all the other sons had left the hall, park, and goodly farms, without any known legal heir. In a word, this branch of the family of Wychecombe would be extinct, when Sir Wycherly died, and the entail become useless. Not a female inheritor, even, or a male inheritor through females, could be traced; and it had become imperative on Sir Wycherly to make a will, lest the property should go off, the Lord knew where; or, what was worse, it should escheat. It is true, Tom Wychecombe, the judge's eldest son, often gave dark hints about a secret, and a timely marriage between his parents, a fact that would have superseded the necessity for all devises, as the property was strictly tied up, so far as the lineal descendants of a certain *old* Sir Wycherly were concerned; but the present Sir Wycherly had seen his brother, in his last illness, on which occasion, the following conversation had taken place.

"And now, brother Thomas," said the baronet, in a friendly and consoling manner; "having, as one may say, prepared your soul for heaven, by these prayers and admissions of your sins, a word may be prudently said, concerning the affairs of this world. You know I am childless—that is to say,—"

"I understand you, Wycherly," interrupted the dying man, "you're a *bachelor.*"

"That's it, Thomas; and bachelors *ought* not to have children. Had our poor brother James escaped that mishap, he might have been sitting at your bed-side at this moment, and *he* could have told us all about it. St. James I used to call him; and well did he deserve the name!"

"St. James the Least, then, it must have been, Wycherly."

"It's a dreadful thing to have no heir, Thomas! Did you ever know a case in your practice, in which another estate was left so completely without an heir, as this of ours?"

"It does not often happen, brother; heirs are usually more abundant than estates."

"So I thought. Will the king get the title as well as the estate, brother, if it should escheat, as you call it?"

"Being the fountain of honour, he will be rather indifferent about the baronetcy."

"I should care less if it went to the next sovereign, who is English born. Wychecombe has always belonged to Englishmen."

"That it has; and ever will, I trust. You have only to select an heir, when I am gone, and by making a will, with proper devises, the property will not escheat. Be careful to use the full terms of perpetuity."

"Every thing was so comfortable, brother, while you were in health," said Sir Wycherly, fidgeting; "you were my natural heir—"

"Heir of entail," interrupted the judge.

"Well, well, *heir*, at all events; and *that* was a prodigious comfort to a man like myself, who has a sort of religious scruples about making a will. I have heard it whispered that you were actually married to Martha; in which case, Tom might drop into our shoes, so readily, without any more signing and sealing."

"A *filius nullius*," returned the other, too conscientious to lend himself to a deception of that nature.

"Why, brother, Tom often seems to me to favour such an idea, himself."

"No wonder, Wycherly, for the idea would greatly favour him. Tom and his brothers are all *filii nullorum*, God forgive me for that same wrong."

"I wonder neither Charles nor Gregory thought of marrying before they lost their lives for their king and country," put in Sir Wycherly, in an upbraiding tone, as if he thought his penniless brethren had done him an injury in neglecting to supply him with an heir, though he had been so forgetful himself of the same great duty. "I did think of bringing in a bill for providing heirs for unmarried persons, without the trouble and responsibility of making wills."

"That would have been a great improvement on the law of descents—I hope you wouldn't have overlooked the ancestors."

"Not I—everybody would have got his rights. They tell me poor Charles never spoke after he was shot; but I dare say, did we know the truth, he regretted sincerely that he never married."

"There, for once, Wycherly, I think you are likely to be wrong. A *femme sole* without food, is rather a helpless sort of a person."

"Well, well, I wish he had married. What would it have been to me, had he left a dozen widows?"

"It might have raised some awkward questions as to dowry; and if each left a son, the title and estates would have been worse off than they are at present, without widows or legitimate children."

"Any thing would be better than having no heir. I believe I'm the first baronet of Wychecombe who has been obliged to make a will!"

"Quite likely," returned the brother, drily; "I remember to have got nothing from the last one, in that way. Charles and Gregory fared no better. Never mind, Wycherly, you behaved like a father to us all."

"I don't mind signing cheques, in the least; but wills have an irreligious appearance, in my eyes. There are a good many Wychecombes, in England; I wonder some of them are not of our family! They tell me a hundredth cousin is just as good an heir, as a first-born son."

"Failing nearer of kin. But we have no hundredth cousins of the *whole blood*."

"There are the Wychecombes of Surrey, brother Thomas—?"

"Descended from a bastard of the second baronet, and out of the line of descent, altogether."

"But the Wychecombes of Hertfordshire, I have always heard were of our family, and legitimate."

"True, as regards matrimony—rather too much of it, by the way. They branched off in 1487, long before the creation, and have nothing to do with the entail; the first of their line coming from old Sir Michael Wychecombe, Kt. and Sheriff of Devonshire, by his second wife Margery; while we are derived from the same male ancestor, through Wycherly, the only son by Joan, the first wife. Wycherly, and Michael, the son of Michael and Margery, were of the half-blood, as respects each other, and could not be heirs of blood. What was true of the ancestors is true of the descendants."

"But we came of the same ancestor, and the estate is far older than 1487."

"Quite true, brother; nevertheless, the half-blood can't take; so says the perfection of human reason."

"I never could understand these niceties of the law," said Sir Wycherly, sighing; "but I suppose they are all right. There are so many Wychecombes scattered about England, that I should think some one among them all might be my heir!"

"Every man of them bears a bar in his arms, or is of the half-blood."

"You are quite sure, brother, that Tom is a *filius nullus*?" for the baronet had forgotten most of the little Latin he ever knew, and translated this legal phrase into "no son."

"*Filius nullius*, Sir Wycherly, the son of nobody; your reading would literally make Tom nobody; whereas, he is only the son of nobody."

"But, brother, he is your son, and as like you, as two hounds of the same litter."

"I am *nullus*, in the eye of the law, as regards poor Tom; who, until he marries, and has children of his own, is altogether without legal kindred. Nor do I know that legitimacy would make Tom any better; for he is presuming and confident enough for the heir apparent to the throne, as it is."

"Well, there's this young sailor, who has been so much at the station lately, since he was left ashore for the cure of his wounds. 'Tis a most gallant lad; and the First Lord has sent him a commission, as a reward for his good conduct, in cutting out the Frenchman. I look upon him as a credit to the name; and I make no question, he is, some way or other, of our family."

"Does he claim to be so?" asked the judge, a little quickly, for he distrusted men in general, and thought, from all he had heard, that some attempt might have been made to practise on his brother's simplicity. "I thought you told me that he came from the American colonies?"

"So he does; he's a native of Virginia, as was his father before him."

"A convict, perhaps; or a servant, quite likely, who has found the name of his former master, more to his liking than his own. Such things are common, they tell me, beyond seas."

"Yes, if he were anything but an American, I might wish he were my heir," returned Sir Wycherly, in a melancholy tone; "but it would be worse than to let the lands escheat, as you call it, to place an American in possession of Wychecombe. The manors have always had English owners, down to the present moment, thank God!"

"Should they have any other, it will be your own fault, Wycherly. When I am dead, and that will happen ere many weeks, the human being will not be living, who can take that property, after your demise, in any other manner than by escheat, or by devise. There will then be neither heir of entail, nor heir at law; and you may make whom you please, master of Wychecombe, provided he be not an alien."

"Not an American, I suppose, brother; an American is an alien, of course."

"Humph!—why, not in law, whatever he may be according to our English notions. Harkee, brother Wycherly; I've never asked you, or wished you to leave the estate to Tom, or his younger brothers; for one, and all, are *filii nullorum*—as I term 'em, though my brother Record will have it, it ought to be *filii nullius*, as well as *filius nullius*. Let that be as it may; no bastard should lord it at Wychecombe; and rather than the king; should get the lands, to bestow on some favourite, I would give it to the half-blood."

"Can that be done without making a will, brother Thomas?"

"It cannot, Sir Wycherly; nor with a will, so long as an heir of entail can be found."

"Is there no way of making Tom a *filius somebody*, so that *he* can succeed?"

"Not under our laws. By the civil law, such a thing might have been done, and by the Scotch law; but not under the perfection of reason."

"I wish you knew this young Virginian! The lad bears both of my names, Wycherly Wychecombe."

"He is not a *filius Wycherly*—is he, baronet?"

"Fie upon thee, brother Thomas! Do you think I have less candour than thyself, that I would not acknowledge my own flesh and blood. I never saw the youngster, until within the last six months, when he was landed from the roadstead, and brought to Wychecombe, to be cured of his wounds; nor ever heard of him before. When they told me his name was Wycherly Wychecombe, I could do no less than call and see him. The poor fellow lay at death's door for a fortnight; and it was while we had little or no hope of saving him, that I got the few family anecdotes from him. Now, that would be good evidence in law, I believe, Thomas."

"For certain things, had the lad really died. Surviving, he must be heard on his *voire dire*, and under oath. But what was his tale?"

"A very short one. He told me his father was a Wycherly Wychecombe, and that his grandfather had been a Virginia planter. This was all he seemed to know of his ancestry."

"And probably all there was of them. My Tom is not the only *filius nullius* that has been among us, and this grandfather, if he has not actually stolen the name, has got it by these doubtful means. As for the Wycherly, it should pass for nothing. Learning that there is a line of baronets of this name, every pretender to the family would be apt to call a son Wycherly."

"The line will shortly be ended, brother," returned Sir Wycherly, sighing. "I wish you might be mistaken; and, after all, Tom shouldn't prove to be that *filius* you call him."

Mr. Baron Wychecombe, as much from *esprit de corps* as from moral principle, was a man of strict integrity, in all things that related to *meum* and *tuum*. He was particularly rigid in his notions concerning the transmission of real estate, and the rights of primogeniture. The world had taken little interest in the private history of a lawyer, and his sons having been born before his elevation to the bench, he passed with the public for a widower, with a family of promising boys. Not one in a hundred of his acquaintances even, suspected the fact; and nothing would have been easier for him, than to have imposed on his brother, by inducing him to make a will under some legal mystification or other, and to have caused Tom Wychecombe to succeed to the property in question, by an indisputable title. There would have been no great difficulty even, in his son's assuming and maintaining his right to the baronetcy, inasmuch as there would be no competitor, and the crown officers were not particularly rigid in inquiring into the claims of those who assumed a title that brought with it no political privileges. Still, he was far from indulging in any such project. To him it appeared that the Wychecombe estate ought to go with the principles that usually governed such matters; and, although he submitted to the dictum of the common law, as regarded the provision which excluded the half-blood from inheriting, with the deference of an English common-law lawyer, he saw and felt, that, failing the direct line, Wychecombe ought to revert to the descendants of Sir Michael by his second son, for the plain reason that they were just as much derived from the person who had acquired the estate, as his brother Wycherly and himself. Had there been descendants of females, even, to interfere, no such opinion would have existed; but, as between an escheat, or a devise in favour of a *filius nillius*, or of the descendant of a *filius nullius*, the half-blood possessed every possible advantage. In his legal eyes, legitimacy was everything, although he had not hesitated to be the means of bringing into the world seven illegitimate children, that being the precise number Martha had the credit of having borne him, though three only survived. After reflecting a moment, therefore, he turned to the baronet, and addressed him more seriously than he had yet done, in the present dialogue; first taking a draught of cordial to give him strength for the occasion.

"Listen to me, brother Wycherly," said the judge, with a gravity that at once caught the attention of the other. "You know something of the family history, and I need do no more than allude to it. Our ancestors were the knightly possessors of Wychecombe, centuries before King James established the rank of baronet. When our great-grandfather, Sir Wycherly, accepted the patent of 1611, he scarcely did himself honour; for, by aspiring higher, he might have got a peerage. However, a baronet he became, and for the first time since Wychecombe was Wychecombe, the estate was entailed, to do credit to the new rank. Now, the first Sir Wycherly had three sons, and no daughter. Each of these sons succeeded; the two eldest as bachelors, and the youngest was our grandfather. Sir Thomas, the fourth baronet, left an only child, Wycherly, our father. Sir Wycherly, our father, had five sons, Wycherly his successor, yourself, and the sixth baronet; myself; James; Charles; and Gregory. James broke his neck at your side. The two last lost their lives in the king's service, unmarried; and neither you, nor I, have entered into the holy state of matrimony. I cannot survive a month, and the hopes of perpetuating the direct line of the family, rests with yourself. This accounts for all the descendants of Sir Wycherly, the first baronet; and it also settles the question of heirs of entail, of whom there are none after myself. To go back beyond the time of King James I.: Twice did the elder lines of the Wychecombes fail, between the reign of King Richard II. and King Henry VII., when Sir Michael succeeded. Now, in each of these cases, the law disposed of the succession; the youngest branches of the family, in both instances, getting the estate. It follows that agreeably to legal decisions had at the time, when the facts must have been known, that the Wychecombes were reduced to these younger lines. Sir Michael had two wives. From the first *we* are derived—from the last, the Wychecombes of Hertfordshire— since known as baronets of that county, by the style and title of Sir Reginald Wychecombe of Wychecombe-Regis, Herts."

"The present Sir Reginald can have no claim, being of the half-blood," put in Sir Wycherly, with a brevity of manner that denoted feeling. "The half-blood is as bad as a *nullius*, as you call Tom."

"Not quite. A person of the half-blood may be as legitimate as the king's majesty; whereas, a nullius is of *no* blood. Now, suppose for a moment, Sir Wycherly, that you had been a son by a first wife, and I had been a son by a second—would there have been no relationship between us?"

"What a question, Tom, to put to your own brother!"

"But I should not be your *own* brother, my good sir; only your *half* brother; of the *half*, and not of the *whole* blood."

"What of that—what of that?—your father would have been my father—we would have had the same name—the same family history—the same family *feelings*—poh! poh!—we should have been both Wychecombes, exactly as we are to-day."

"Quite true, and yet I could not have been your heir, nor you mine. The estate would escheat to the king, Hanoverian or Scotchman, before it came to me. Indeed, to *me* it could never come."

"Thomas, you are trifling with my ignorance, and making matters worse than they really are. Certainly, as long as you lived, you would be *my* heir!"

"Very true, as to the £20,000 in the funds, but not as to the baronetcy and Wychecombe. So far as the two last are concerned, I am heir of blood, and of entail, of the body of Sir Wycherly Wychecombe, the first baronet, and the maker of the entail."

"Had there been no entail, and had I died a child, who would have succeeded our father, supposing there had been two mothers?"

"I, as the next surviving son."

"There!—I knew it must be so!" exclaimed Sir Wycherly, in triumph; "and all this time you have been joking with me!"

"Not so fast, brother of mine—not so fast. I should be of the *whole* blood, as respected our father, and all the Wychecombes that have gone before him; but of the *half*-blood, as respected *you*. From our father I might have taken, as his heir-at-law: but from *you*, never, having been of the *half*-blood."

"I would have made a will, in that case, Thomas, and left you every farthing," said Sir Wycherly, with feeling.

"That is just what I wish you to do with Sir Reginald Wychecombe. You must take him; a *filius nullius*, in the person of my son Tom; a stranger; or let the property escheat; for, we are so peculiarly placed as not to have a known relative, by either the male or female lines; the maternal ancestors being just as barren of heirs as the paternal. Our good mother was the natural daughter of the third Earl of Prolific; our grandmother was the last of her race, so far as human ken can discover; our great-grandmother is said to have had semi-royal blood in her veins, without the aid of the church, and beyond that it would be hopeless to attempt tracing consanguinity on that side of the house. No, Wycherly; it is Sir Reginald who has the best right to the land; Tom, or one of his brothers, an utter stranger, or His Majesty, follow. Remember that estates of £4000 a year, don't often escheat, now-a-days."

"If you'll draw up a will, brother, I'll leave it all to Tom," cried the baronet, with sudden energy. "Nothing need be said about the *nullius*; and when I'm gone, he'll step quietly into my place."

Nature triumphed a moment in the bosom of the father; but habit, and the stern sense of right, soon overcame the feeling. Perhaps certain doubts, and a knowledge of his son's real character, contributed their share towards the reply.

"It ought not to be, Sir Wycherly," returned the judge, musing, "Tom has no right to Wychecombe, and Sir Reginald has the best moral right possible, though the law cuts him off. Had Sir Michael made the entail, instead of our great-grandfather, he would have come in, as a matter of course."

"I never liked Sir Reginald Wychecombe," said the baronet, stubbornly.

"What of that?—He will not trouble you while living, and when dead it will be all the same. Come—come—I will draw the will myself, leaving blanks for the name; and when it is once done, you will sign it, cheerfully. It is the last legal act I shall ever perform, and it will be a suitable one, death being constantly before me."

This ended the dialogue. The will was drawn according to promise; Sir Wycherly took it to his room to read, carefully inserted the name of Tom Wychecombe in all the blank spaces, brought it back, duly executed the instrument in his brother's presence, and then gave the paper to his nephew to preserve, with a strong injunction on him to keep the secret, until the instrument should have force by his own death. Mr. Baron Wychecombe died in six weeks, and the baronet returned to his residence, a sincere mourner for the loss of an only brother. A more unfortunate selection of an heir could not have been made, as Tom Wychecombe was, in reality, the son of a barrister in the Temple; the fancied likeness to the reputed father existing only in the imagination of his credulous uncle.

CHAPTER II.

——"How fearful
And dizzy 'tis, to cast one's eyes so low!
The crows, and choughs, that wing the midway air,
Show scarce so gross as beetles! Half-way down
Hangs one that gathers samphire! dreadful trade!"

KING LEAR.

This digression on the family of Wychecombe has led us far from the signal-station, the head-land, and the fog, with which the tale opened. The little dwelling connected with the station stood at a short distance from the staff, sheltered, by the formation of the ground, from the bleak winds of the channel, and fairly embowered in shrubs and flowers. It was a humble cottage, that had been ornamented with more taste than was usual in England at that day. Its whitened walls, thatched roof, picketed garden, and trellised porch, bespoke care, and a mental improvement in the inmates, that were scarcely to be expected in persons so humbly employed as the keeper of the signal-staff, and his family. All near the house, too, was in the same excellent condition; for while the head-land itself lay in common, this portion of it was enclosed in two or three pretty little fields, that were grazed by a single horse, and a couple of cows. There were no hedges, however, the thorn not growing willingly in a situation so exposed; but the fields were divided by fences, neatly enough made of wood, that declared its own origin, having in fact been part of the timbers and planks of a wreck. As the whole was whitewashed, it had a rustic, and in a climate where the sun is seldom oppressive, by no means a disagreeable appearance.

The scene with which we desire to commence the tale, opens about seven o'clock on a July morning. On a bench at the foot of the signal-staff, was seated one of a frame that was naturally large and robust, but which was sensibly beginning to give way, either by age or disease. A glance at the red, bloated face, would suffice to tell a medical man, that the habits had more to do with the growing failure of the system, than any natural derangement of the physical organs. The face, too, was singularly manly, and had once been handsome, even; nay, it was not altogether without claims to be so considered still; though intemperance was making sad inroads on its comeliness. This person was about fifty years old, and his air, as well as his attire, denoted a mariner; not a common seaman, nor yet altogether an officer; but one of those of a middle station, who in navies used to form a class by themselves; being of a rank that entitled them to the honours of the quarter-deck, though out of the regular line of promotion. In a word, he wore the unpretending uniform of a master. A century ago, the dress of the English naval officer was exceedingly simple, though more appropriate to the profession perhaps, than the more showy attire that has since been introduced. Epaulettes were not used by any, and the anchor button, with the tint that is called navy blue, and which is meant to represent the deep hue of the ocean, with white facings, composed the principal peculiarities of the dress. The person introduced to the reader, whose name was Dutton, and who was simply the officer in charge of the signal-station, had a certain neatness about his well-worn uniform, his linen, and all of his attire, which showed that some person more interested in such matters than one of his habits was likely to be, had the care of his wardrobe. In this respect, indeed, his appearance was unexceptionable; and there was an air about the whole man which showed that nature, if not education, had intended him for something far better than the being he actually was.

Dutton was waiting, at that early hour, to ascertain, as the veil of mist was raised from the face of the sea, whether a sail might be in sight, that required of him the execution of any of his simple functions. That some one was near by, on the head-land, too, was quite evident, by the occasional interchange of speech; though no person but himself was visible. The direction of the sounds would seem to indicate that a man was actually over the brow of the cliff, perhaps a hundred feet removed from the seat occupied by the master.

"Recollect the sailor's maxim, Mr. Wychecombe," called out Dutton, in a warning voice; "one hand for the king, and the other for self! Those cliffs are ticklish places; and really it does seem a little unnatural that a sea-faring person like yourself, should have so great a passion for flowers, as to risk his neck in order to make a posy!"

"Never fear for me, Mr. Dutton," answered a full, manly voice, that one could have sworn issued from the chest of youth; "never fear for me; we sailors are used to hanging in the air."

"Ay, with good three-stranded ropes to hold on by, young gentleman. Now His Majesty's government has just made you an officer, there is a sort of obligation to take care of your life, in order that it may be used, and, at need, given away, in his service."

"Quite true—quite true, Mr. Dutton—so true, I wonder you think it necessary to remind me of it. I am very grateful to His Majesty's government, and—"

While speaking, the voice seemed to descend, getting at each instant less and less distinct, until, in the end, it became quite inaudible. Dutton looked uneasy, for at that instant a noise was heard, and then it was quite clear some heavy object was falling down the face of the cliff. Now it was that the mariner felt the want of good nerves, and experienced the sense of humiliation which accompanied the consciousness of having destroyed them by his excesses. He trembled in every limb, and, for the moment, was actually unable to rise. A light step at his side, however, drew a glance in that direction, and his eye fell on the form of a lovely girl of nineteen, his own daughter, Mildred.

"I heard you calling to some one, father," said the latter, looking wistfully, but distrustfully at her parent, as if wondering at his yielding to his infirmity so early in the day; "can I be of service to you?"

"Poor Wychecombe!" exclaimed Dutton. "He went over the cliff in search of a nosegay to offer to yourself, and—and—I fear—greatly fear—"

"What, father?" demanded Mildred, in a voice of horror, the rich color disappearing from a face which it left of the hue of death. "No—no—no—he *cannot* have fallen."

Dutton bent his head down, drew a long breath, and then seemed to gain more command of his nerves. He was about to rise, when the sound of a horse's feet was heard, and then Sir Wycherly Wychecombe, mounted on a quiet pony, rode slowly up to the signal-staff. It was a common thing for the baronet to appear on the cliffs early in the morning, but it was not usual for him to come unattended. The instant her eyes fell on the fine form of the venerable old man, Mildred, who seemed to know him well, and to use the familiarity of one confident of being a favourite, exclaimed—

"Oh! Sir Wycherly, how fortunate—where is Richard?"

"Good morrow, my pretty Milly," answered the baronet, cheerfully; "fortunate or not, here I am, and not a bit flattered that your first question should be after the groom, instead of his master. I have sent Dick on a message to the vicar's. Now my poor brother, the judge, is dead and gone, I find Mr. Rotherham more and more necessary to me."

"Oh! dear Sir Wycherly—Mr. Wychecombe—Lieutenant Wychecombe, I mean—the young officer from Virginia—he who was so desperately wounded—in whose recovery we all took so deep an interest—"

"Well—what of him, child?—you surely do not mean to put him on a level with Mr. Rotherham, in the way of religious consolation—and, as for anything else, there is no consanguinity between the Wychecombes of Virginia and my family. He may be a *filius nullius* of the Wychecombes of Wychecombe-Regis, Herts, but has no connection with those of Wychecombe-Hall, Devonshire."

"There—there—the cliff!—the cliff!" added Mildred, unable, for the moment, to be more explicit.

As the girl pointed towards the precipice, and looked the very image of horror, the good-hearted old baronet began to get some glimpses of the truth; and, by means of a few words with Dutton, soon knew quite as much as his two companions. Descending from his pony with surprising activity for one of his years, Sir Wycherly was soon on his feet, and a sort of confused consultation between the three succeeded. Neither liked to approach the cliff, which was nearly perpendicular at the extremity of the head-land, and was always a trial to the nerves of those who shrunk from standing on the verge of precipices. They stood like persons paralyzed, until Dutton, ashamed of his weakness, and recalling the thousand lessons in coolness and courage he had received in his own manly profession, made a movement towards advancing to the edge of the cliff, in order to ascertain the real state of the case. The blood returned to the cheeks of Mildred, too, and she again found a portion of her natural spirit raising her courage.

"Stop, father," she said, hastily; "you are infirm, and are in a tremour at this moment. My head is steadier—let me go to the verge of the hill, and learn what has happened."

This was uttered with a forced calmness that deceived her auditors, both of whom, the one from age, and the other from shattered nerves, were certainly in no condition to assume the same office. It required the all-seeing eye, which alone can scan the heart, to read all the agonized suspense with which that young and beautiful creature approached the spot, where she might command a view of the whole of the side of the fearful declivity, from its giddy summit to the base, where it was washed by the sea. The latter, indeed, could not literally be seen from above, the waves having so far undermined the cliff, as to leave a projection that concealed the point where the rocks and the water came absolutely in contact; the upper portion of the weather-worn rocks falling a little inwards, so as to leave a ragged surface that was sufficiently broken to contain patches of earth, and verdure, sprinkled with the flowers peculiar to such an exposure. The fog, also, intercepted the sight, giving to the descent the appearance of a fathomless abyss. Had the life of the most indifferent person been in jeopardy, under the circumstances named, Mildred would have been filled with deep awe; but a gush of tender sensations, which had hitherto been pent up in the sacred privacy of her virgin affections, struggled with natural horror, as she trod lightly on the very verge of the declivity, and cast a timid but eager glance beneath. Then she recoiled a step, raised her hands in alarm, and hid her face, as if to shut out some frightful spectacle.

By this time, Dutton's practical knowledge and recollection had returned. As is common with seamen, whose minds contain vivid pictures of the intricate tracery of their vessel's rigging in the darkest nights, his thoughts had flashed athwart all the probable circumstances, and presented a just image of the facts.

"The boy could not be seen had he absolutely fallen, and were there no fog; for the cliff tumbles home, Sir Wycherly," he said, eagerly, unconsciously using a familiar nautical phrase to express his meaning. "He must be clinging to the side of the precipice, and that, too, above the swell of the rocks."

Stimulated by a common feeling, the two men now advanced hastily to the brow of the hill, and there, indeed, as with Mildred herself, a single look sufficed to tell them the whole truth. Young Wychecombe, in leaning forward to pluck a flower, had pressed so hard upon the bit of rock on which a foot rested, as to cause it to break, thereby losing his balance. A presence of mind that amounted almost to inspiration, and a high resolution, alone saved him from being dashed to pieces. Perceiving the rock to give way, he threw himself forward, and alighted on a narrow shelf, a few feet beneath the place where he had just stood, and at least ten feet removed from it, laterally. The shelf on which he alighted was ragged, and but two or three feet wide. It would have afforded only a check to his fall, had there not fortunately been some shrubs among the rocks above it. By these shrubs the young man caught, actually swinging off in the air, under the impetus of his leap. Happily, the shrubs were too well rooted to give way; and, swinging himself round, with the address of a sailor, the youthful lieutenant was immediately on his feet, in comparative safety. The silence that succeeded was the consequence of the shock he felt, in finding him so suddenly thrown into this perilous situation. The summit of the cliff was now about six fathoms above his head, and the shelf on which he stood, impended over a portion of the cliff that was absolutely perpendicular, and which might be said to be out of the line of those projections along which he had so lately been idly gathering flowers. It was physically impossible for any human being to extricate himself from such a situation, without assistance. This Wychecombe understood at a glance, and he had passed the few minutes that intervened between his fall and the appearance of the party above him, in devising the means necessary to his liberation. As it was, few men, unaccustomed to the giddy elevations of the mast, could have mustered a sufficient command of nerve to maintain a position on the ledge where he stood. Even he could not have continued there, without steadying his form by the aid of the bushes.

As soon as the baronet and Dutton got a glimpse of the perilous position of young Wychecombe, each recoiled in horror from the sight, as if fearful of being precipitated on top of him. Both, then, actually lay down on the grass, and approached the edge of the cliff again, in that humble attitude, even trembling as they lay at length, with their chins projecting over the rocks, staring downwards at the victim. The young man could see nothing of all this; for, as he stood with his back against the cliff, he had not room to turn, with safety, or even to look upwards. Mildred, however, seemed to lose all sense of self and of danger, in view of the extremity in which the youth beneath was placed. She stood on the very verge of the precipice, and looked down with steadiness and impunity that would have been utterly impossible for her to attain under less exciting circumstances; even allowing the young man to catch a glimpse of her rich locks, as they hung about her beautiful face.

"For God's sake, Mildred," called out the youth, "keep further from the cliff—I see you, and we can now hear each other without so much risk."

"What can we do to rescue you, Wychecombe?" eagerly asked the girl. "Tell me, I entreat you; for Sir Wycherly and my father are both unnerved!"

"Blessed creature! and *you* are mindful of my danger! But, be not uneasy, Mildred; do as I tell you, and all will yet be well. I hope you hear and understand what I say, dearest girl?"

"Perfectly," returned Mildred, nearly choked by the effort to be calm. "I hear every syllable—speak on."

"Go you then to the signal-halyards—let one end fly loose, and pull upon the other, until the whole line has come down—when that is done, return here, and I will tell you more—but, for heaven's sake, keep farther from the cliff."

The thought that the rope, small and frail as it seemed, might be of use, flashed on the brain of the girl; and in a moment she was at the staff. Time and again, when liquor incapacitated her father to perform his duty, had Mildred bent-on, and hoisted the signals for him; and thus, happily, she was expert in the use of the halyards. In a minute she had unrove them, and the long line lay in a little pile at her feet.

"'Tis done, Wycherly," she said, again looking over the cliff; "shall I throw you down one end of the rope?—but, alas! I have not strength to raise you; and Sir Wycherly and father seem unable to assist me!"

"Do not hurry yourself, Mildred, and all will be well. Go, and put one end of the line around the signal-staff, then put the two ends together, tie them in a knot, and drop them down over my head. Be careful not to come too near the cliff, for—"

The last injunction was useless, Mildred having flown to execute her commission. Her quick mind readily comprehended what was expected of her, and her nimble fingers soon performed their task. Tying a knot in the ends of the line, she did as desired, and the small rope was soon dangling within reach of Wychecombe's arm. It is not easy to make a landsman understand the confidence which a sailor feels in a rope. Place but a frail and rotten piece of twisted hemp in his hand, and he will risk his person in situations from which he would otherwise recoil in dread. Accustomed to hang suspended in the air, with ropes only for his foothold, or with ropes to grasp with his hand, his eye gets an intuitive knowledge of what will sustain him, and he unhesitatingly trusts his person to a few seemingly slight strands, that, to one unpractised, appear wholly unworthy of his confidence. Signal-halyards are ropes smaller than the little finger of a man of any size; but they are usually made with care, and every rope-yarn tells. Wychecombe, too, was aware that these particular halyards were new, for he had assisted in reeving them himself, only the week before. It was owing to this circumstance that they were long enough to reach him; a large allowance for wear and tear having been made in cutting them from the coil. As it was, the ends dropped some twenty feet below the ledge on which he stood.

"All safe, now, Mildred!" cried the young man, in a voice of exultation the moment his hand caught the two ends of the line, which he immediately passed around his body, beneath the arms, as a precaution against accidents. "All safe, now, dearest girl; have no further concern about me."

Mildred drew back, for worlds could not have tempted her to witness the desperate effort that she knew must follow. By this time, Sir Wycherly, who had been an interested witness of all that passed, found his voice, and assumed the office of director.

"Stop, my young namesake," he eagerly cried, when he found that the sailor was about to make an effort to drag his own body up the cliff; "stop; that will never do; let Dutton and me do that much for you, at least. We have seen all that has passed, and are now able to do something."

"No—no, Sir Wycherly—on no account touch the halyards. By hauling them over the top of the rocks you will probably cut them, or part them, and then I'm lost, without hope!"

"Oh! Sir Wycherly," said Mildred, earnestly, clasping her hands together, as if to enforce the request with prayer; "do not—do not touch the line."

"We had better let the lad manage the matter in his own way," put in Dutton; "he is active, resolute, and a seaman, and will do better for himself than I fear we can do for him. He has got a turn round his body, and is tolerably safe against any slip, or mishap."

As the words were uttered, the whole three drew back a short distance and watched the result, in intense anxiety. Dutton, however, so far recollected himself, as to take an end of the old halyards, which were kept in a chest at the foot of the staff, and to make, an attempt to stopper together the two parts of the little rope on which the youth depended, for should one of the parts of it break, without this precaution, there was nothing to prevent the halyards from running round the staff, and destroying the hold. The size of the halyards rendered this expedient very difficult of attainment, but enough was done to give the arrangement a little more of the air of security. All this time young Wychecombe was making his own preparations on the ledge, and quite out of view; but the tension on the halyards soon announced that his weight was now pendent from them. Mildred's heart seemed ready to leap from her mouth, as she noted each jerk on the lines; and her father watched every new pull, as if he expected the next moment would produce the final catastrophe. It required a prodigious effort in the young man to raise his own weight for such a distance, by lines so small. Had the rope been of any size, the achievement would have been trifling for one of the frame and habits of the sailor, more especially as he could slightly avail himself of his feet, by pressing them against the rocks; but, as it was, he felt as if he were dragging the mountain up after him. At length, his head appeared a few inches above the rocks, but with his feet pressed against the cliff, and his body inclining outward, at an angle of forty-five degrees.

"Help him—help him, father!" exclaimed Mildred, covering her face with her hands, to exclude the sight of Wychecombe's desperate struggles. "If he fall now, he will be destroyed. Oh! save him, save him, Sir Wycherly!"

But neither of those to whom she appealed, could be of any use. The nervous trembling again came over the father; and as for the baronet, age and inexperience rendered him helpless.

"Have you no rope, Mr. Dutton, to throw over my shoulders," cried Wychecombe, suspending his exertions in pure exhaustion, still keeping all he had gained, with his head projecting outward, over the abyss beneath, and his face turned towards heaven. "Throw a rope over my shoulders, and drag my body in to the cliff."

Dutton showed an eager desire to comply, but his nerves had not yet been excited by the usual potations, and his hands shook in a way to render it questionable whether he could perform even this simple service. But for his daughter, indeed, he would hardly have set about it intelligently. Mildred, accustomed to using the signal-halyards, procured the old line, and handed it to her father, who discovered some of his professional knowledge in his manner of using it. Doubling the halyards twice, he threw the bight over Wychecombe's shoulders, and aided by Mildred, endeavoured to draw the body of the young man upwards and towards the cliff. But their united strength was unequal to the task, and wearied with holding on, and, indeed, unable to support his own weight any longer by so small a rope, Wychecombe felt compelled to suffer his feet to drop beneath him, and slid down again upon the ledge. Here, even his vigorous frame shook with its prodigious exertions; and he was compelled to seat himself on the shelf, and rest with his back against the cliff, to recover his self-command and strength. Mildred uttered a faint shriek as he disappeared, but was too much horror-stricken to approach the verge of the precipice to ascertain his fate.

"Be composed, Milly," said her father, "he is safe, as you may see by the halyards; and to say the truth, the stuff holds on well. So long as the line proves true, the boy can't fall; he has taken a double turn with the end of it round his body. Make your mind easy, girl, for I feel better now, and see my way clear. Don't be uneasy, Sir Wycherly; we'll have the lad safe on *terra firma* again, in ten minutes. I scarce know what has come over me, this morning; but I've not had the command of my limbs as in common. It cannot be fright, for I've seen too many men in danger to be disabled by *that*; and I think, Milly, it must be the rheumatism, of which I've so often spoken, and which I've inherited from my poor mother, dear old soul. Do you know, Sir Wycherly, that rheumatism can be inherited like gout?"

"I dare say it may—I dare say it may, Dutton—but never mind the disease, now; get my young namesake back here on the grass, and I will hear all about it. I would give the world that I had not sent Dick to Mr. Rotherham's this morning. Can't we contrive to make the pony pull the boy up?"

"The traces are hardly strong enough for such work, Sir Wycherly. Have a little patience, and I will manage the whole thing, 'ship-shape, and Brister fashion,' as we say at sea. Halloo there, Master Wychecombe—answer my hail, and I will soon get you into deep water."

"I'm safe on the ledge," returned the voice of Wychecombe, from below; "I wish you would look to the signal-halyards, and see they do not chafe against the rocks, Mr. Dutton."

"All right, sir; all right. Slack up, if you please, and let me have all the line you can, without casting off from your body. Keep fast the end for fear of accidents."

In an instant the halyards slackened, and Dutton, who by this time had gained his self-command, though still weak and unnerved by the habits of the last fifteen years, forced the bight along the edge of the cliff, until he had brought it over a projection of the rocks, where it fastened itself. This arrangement caused the line to lead down to the part of the cliffs from which the young man had fallen, and where it was by no means difficult for a steady head and active limbs to move about and pluck flowers. It consequently remained for Wychecombe merely to regain a footing on that part of the hill-side, to ascend to the summit without difficulty. It is true he was now below the point from which he had fallen, but by swinging himself off laterally, or even by springing, aided by the line, it was not a difficult achievement to reach it, and he no sooner understood the nature of the change that had been made, than he set about attempting it. The confident manner of Dutton encouraged both the baronet and Mildred, and they drew to the cliff, again; standing near the verge, though on the part where the rocks might be descended, with less apprehension of consequences.

As soon as Wychecombe had made all his preparations, he stood on the end of the ledge, tightened the line, looked carefully for a foothold on the other side of the chasm, and made his leap. As a matter of course, the body of the young man swung readily across the space, until the line became perpendicular, and then he found a surface so broken, as to render his ascent by no means difficult, aided as he was by the halyards. Scrambling upwards, he soon rejected the aid of the line, and sprang upon the head-land. At the same instant, Mildred fell senseless on the grass.

CHAPTER III.

"I want a hero:—an uncommon want,
When every year and month send forth a new one;
'Till, after cloying the gazelles with cant,
The age discovers he is not the true one;—"

BYRON.

In consequence of the unsteadiness of the father's nerves, the duty of raising Mildred in his arms, and of carrying her to the cottage, devolved on the young man. This he did with a readiness and concern which proved how deep an interest he took in her situation, and with a power of arm which showed that his strength was increased rather than lessened by the condition into which she had fallen. So rapid was his movement, that no one saw the kiss he impressed on the palid cheek of the sweet girl, or the tender pressure with which he grasped the lifeless form. By the time he reached the door, the motion and air had begun to revive her, and Wychecombe committed her to the care of her alarmed mother, with a few hurried words of explanation. He did not leave the house, however, for a quarter of an hour, except to call out to Dutton that Mildred was reviving, and that he need be under no uneasiness on her account. Why he remained so long, we leave the reader to imagine, for the girl had been immediately taken to her own little chamber, and he saw her no more for several hours.

When our young sailor came out upon the head-land again, he found the party near the flag-staff increased to four. Dick, the groom, had returned from his errand, and Tom Wychecombe, the intended heir of the baronet, was also there, in mourning for his reputed father, the judge. This young man had become a frequent visiter to the station, of late, affecting to imbibe his uncle's taste for sea air, and a view of the ocean. There had been several meetings between himself and his namesake, and each interview was becoming less amicable than the preceding, for a reason that was sufficiently known to the parties. When they met on the present occasion, therefore, the bows they exchanged were haughty and distant, and the glances cast at each other might have been termed hostile, were it not that a sinister irony was blended with that of Tom Wychecombe. Still, the feelings that were uppermost did not prevent the latter from speaking in an apparently friendly manner.

"They tell me, Mr. Wychecombe," observed the judge's heir, (for this Tom Wychecombe might legally claim to be;) "they tell me, Mr. Wychecombe, that you have been taking a lesson in your trade this morning, by swinging over the cliffs at the end of a rope? Now, that is an exploit, more to the taste of an American than to that of an Englishman, I should think. But, I dare say one is compelled to do many things in the colonies, that we never dream of at home."

This was said with seeming indifference, though with great art. Sir Wycherly's principal weakness was an overweening and an ignorant admiration of his own country, and all it contained. He was also strongly addicted to that feeling of contempt for the dependencies of the empire, which seems to be inseparable from the political connection between the people of the metropolitan country and their colonies. There must be entire equality, for perfect respect, in any situation in life; and, as a rule, men always appropriate to their own shares, any admitted superiority that may happen to exist on the part of the communities to which they belong. It is on this principle, that the tenant of a cock-loft in Paris or London, is so apt to feel a high claim to superiority over the occupant of a comfortable abode in a village. As between England and her North American colonies in particular, this feeling was stronger than is the case usually, on account of the early democratical tendencies of the latter; not, that these tendencies had already become the subject of political jealousies, but that they left social impressions, which were singularly adapted to bringing the colonists into contempt among a people predominant for their own factitious habits, and who are so strongly inclined to view everything, even to principles, through the medium of arbitrary, conventional customs. It must be confessed that the Americans, in the middle of the eighteenth century, were an exceedingly provincial, and in many particulars a narrow-minded people, as well in their opinions as in their habits; nor is the reproach altogether removed at the present day; but the country from which they are derived had not then made the vast strides in civilization, for which it has latterly become so distinguished. The indifference, too, with which all Europe regarded the whole American continent, and to which England, herself, though she possessed so large a stake on this side of the Atlantic, formed no material exception, constantly led that quarter of the world into profound mistakes in all its reasoning that was connected with this quarter of the world, and aided in producing the state of feeling to which we have alluded. Sir Wycherly felt and reasoned on the subject of America much as the great bulk of his countrymen felt and reasoned in 1745; the exceptions existing only among the enlightened, and those whose particular duties rendered more correct knowledge necessary, and not always among them. It is said that the English minister conceived the idea of taxing America, from the circumstance of seeing a wealthy Virginian lose a large sum at play, a sort of *argumentum ad hominem* that brought with it a very dangerous conclusion to apply to the sort of people with whom he had to deal. Let this be as it might, there is no more question, that at the period of our tale, the profoundest ignorance concerning America existed generally in the mother country, than there is that the profoundest respect existed in America for nearly every thing English. Truth compels us to add, that in despite of all that has passed, the cis-atlantic portion of the weakness has longest endured the assaults of time and of an increased intercourse.

Young Wycherly, as is ever the case, was keenly alive to any insinuations that might be supposed to reflect on the portion of the empire of which he was a native. He considered himself an Englishman, it is true; was thoroughly loyal; and was every way disposed to sustain the honour and interests of the seat of authority; but when questions were raised between Europe and America, he was an American; as, in America itself, he regarded himself as purely a Virginian, in contradistinction to all the other colonies. He understood the intended sarcasm of Tom Wychecombe, but smothered his resentment, out of respect to the baronet, and perhaps a little influenced by the feelings in which he had been so lately indulging.

"Those gentlemen who are disposed to fancy such things of the colonies, would do well to visit that part of the world," he answered, calmly, "before they express their opinions too loudly, lest they should say something that future observation might make them wish to recall."

"True, my young friend—quite true," put in the baronet, with the kindest possible intentions. "True as gospel. We never know any thing of matters about which we know nothing; that we old men must admit, Master Dutton; and I should think Tom must see its force. It would be unreasonable to expect to find every thing as comfortable in America as we have it here, in England; nor do I suppose the Americans, in general, would be as likely to get over a cliff as an Englishman. However, there are exceptions to all general rules, as my poor brother James used to say, when he saw occasion to find fault with the sermon of a prelate. I believe you did not know my poor brother, Dutton; he must have been killed about the time you were born— St. James, I used to call him, although my brother Thomas, the judge that was Tom's father, there—said he was St. James the Less."

"I believe the Rev. Mr. Wychecombe was dead before I was of an age to remember his virtues, Sir Wycherly," said Dutton, respectfully; "though I have often heard my own father speak of all your honoured family."

"Yes, your father, Dutton, was the attorney of the next town, and we all knew him well. You have done quite right to come back among us to spend the close of your own days. A man is never as well off as when he is thriving in his native soil; more especially when that soil is old England, and Devonshire. You are not one of us, young gentleman, though your name happens to be Wychecombe; but, then we are none of us accountable for our own births, or birth-places."

This truism, which is in the mouths of thousands while it is in the hearts of scarcely any, was well meant by Sir Wycherly, however plainly expressed. It merely drew from the youth the simple answer that—"he was born in the colonies, and had colonists for his parents;" a fact that the others had heard already, some ten or a dozen times.

"It is a little singular, Mr. Wychecombe, that you should bear both of my names, and yet be no relative," continued the baronet. "Now, Wycherly came into our family from old Sir Hildebrand Wycherly, who was slain at Bosworth Field, and whose only daughter, my ancestor, and Tom's ancestor, there, married. Since that day, Wycherly has been a favourite name among us. I do not think that the Wychecombes of Herts, ever thought of calling a son Wycherly, although, as my poor brother the judge used to say, *they* were related, but of the half-blood, only. I suppose your father taught you what is meant by being of the half-blood, Thomas?"

Tom Wychecombe's face became the colour of scarlet, and he cast an uneasy glance at all present; expecting in particular, to meet with a look of exultation in the eyes of the lieutenant. He was greatly relieved, however, at finding that neither of the three meant or understood more than was simply expressed. As for his uncle, he had not the smallest intention of making any allusion to the peculiarity of his nephew's birth; and the other two, in common with the world, supposed the reputed heir to be legitimate. Gathering courage from the looks of those around him, Tom answered with a steadiness that prevented his agitation from being detected:

"Certainly, my dear sir; my excellent parent forgot nothing that he thought might be useful to me, in maintaining my rights, and the honour of the family, hereafter. I very well understand that the Wychecombes of Hertfordshire have no claims on us; nor, indeed, any Wychecombe who is not descended from my respectable grandfather, the late Sir Wycherly."

"He must have been an *early*, instead of a *late* Sir Wycherly, rather, Mr. Thomas," put in Dutton, laughing at his own conceit; "for I can remember no other than the honourable baronet before us, in the last fifty years."

"Quite true, Dutton—very true," rejoined the person last alluded to. "As true as that 'time and tide wait for no man.' We understand the meaning of such things on the coast here. It was half a century, last October, since I succeeded my respected parent; but, it will not be another half century before some one will succeed me!"

Sir Wycherly was a hale, hearty man for his years, but he had no unmanly dread of his end. Still he felt it could not be very distant, having already numbered fourscore and four years. Nevertheless, there were certain phrases of usage, that Dutton did not see fit to forget on such an occasion, and he answered accordingly, turning to look at and admire the still ruddy countenance of the baronet, by way of giving emphasis to his words.

"You will yet see half of us into our graves, Sir Wycherly," he said, "and still remain an active man. Though I dare say another half century will bring most of us up. Even Mr. Thomas, here, and your young namesake can hardly hope to run out more line than that. Well, as for myself, I only desire to live through this war, that I may again see His Majesty's arms triumphant; though they do tell me that we are in for a good thirty years' struggle. Wars *have* lasted as long as *that*, Sir Wycherly, and I don't see why this may not, as well as another."

"Very true, Dutton; it is not only possible, but probable; and I trust both you and I may live to see our flower-hunter here, a post-captain, at least—though it would be wishing almost too much to expect to see him an admiral. There has been *one* admiral of the name, and I confess I should like to see another!"

"Has not Mr. Thomas a brother in the service?" demanded the master; "I had thought that my lord, the judge, had given us one of his young gentlemen."

"He thought of it; but the army got both of the boys, as it turned out. Gregory was to be the midshipman; my poor brother intending him for a sailor from the first, and so giving him the name that was once borne by the unfortunate relative we lost by shipwreck. I wished him to call one of the lads James, after St. James; but, somehow, I never could persuade Thomas to see all the excellence of that pious young man."

Dutton was a little embarrassed, for St. James had left any thing but a godly savour behind him; and he was about to fabricate a tolerably bold assertion to the contrary, rather than incur the risk of offending the lord of the manor, when, luckily, a change in the state of the fog afforded him a favourable opportunity of bringing about an apposite change in the subject. During the whole of the morning the sea had been invisible from the head-land, a dense body of vapour resting on it, far as eye could reach; veiling the whole expanse with a single white cloud. The lighter portions of the vapour had at first floated around the head-land, which could not have been seen at any material distance; but all had been gradually settling down into a single mass, that now rose within twenty feet of the summit of the cliffs. The hour was still quite early, but the sun was gaining force, and it speedily drank up all the lighter particles of the mist, leaving a clear, bright atmosphere above the feathery bank, through which objects might be seen for miles. There was what seamen call a "fanning breeze," or just wind enough to cause the light sails of a ship to swell and collapse, under the double influence of the air and the motion of the hull, imitating in a slight degree the vibrations of that familiar appliance of the female toilet. Dutton's eye had caught a glance of the loftiest sail of a vessel, above the fog, going through this very movement; and it afforded him the release he desired, by enabling him to draw the attention of his companions to the same object.

"See, Sir Wycherly—see, Mr. Wychecombe," he cried, eagerly, pointing in the direction of the sail; "yonder is some of the king's canvass coming into our roadstead, or I am no judge of the set of a man-of-war's royal. It is a large bit of cloth, too, Mr. Lieutenant, for a sail so lofty!"

"It is a two-decker's royal, Master Dutton," returned the young sailor; "and now you see the fore and main, separately, as the ship keeps away."

"Well," put in Sir Wycherly, in a resigned manner; "here have I lived fourscore years on this coast, and, for the life of me, I have never been able to tell a fore-royal from a back-royal; or a mizzen head-stay from a head mizzen-stay. They are the most puzzling things imaginable; and now I cannot discover how you know that yonder sail, which I see plain enough, is a royal, any more than that it is a jib!"

Dutton and the lieutenant smiled, but Sir Wycherly's simplicity had a cast of truth and nature about it, that deterred most people from wishing to ridicule him. Then, the rank, fortune, and local interest of the baronet, counted for a good deal on all such occasions.

"Here is another fellow, farther east," cried Dutton, still pointing with a finger; "and every inch as big as his consort! Ah! it does my eyes good to see our roadstead come into notice, in this manner, after all I have said and done in its behalf—But, who have we here—a brother chip, by his appearance; I dare say some idler who has been sent ashore with despatches."

"There is another fellow further east, and every inch as big as his consort," said Wychecombe, as we shall call our lieutenant, in order to distinguish him from Tom of the same name, repeating the very words of Dutton, with an application and readiness that almost amounted to wit, pointing, in his turn, at two strangers who were ascending to the station by a path that led from the beach. "Certainly both these gentlemen are in His Majesty's service, and they have probably just landed from the ships in the offing."

The truth of this conjecture was apparent to Dutton at a glance. As the strangers joined each other, the one last seen proceeded in advance; and there was something in his years, the confident manner in which he approached, and his general appearance, that induced both the sailors to believe he might be the commander of one of the ships that had just come in view.

"Good-morrow, gentlemen," commenced this person, as soon as near enough to salute the party at the foot of the flag-staff; "good-morrow to ye all. I'm glad to meet you, for it's but a Jacob's ladder, this path of yours, through the ravine in the cliffs. Hey! why Atwood," looking around him at the sea of vapour, in surprise, "what the devil has become of the fleet?"

"It is lost in the fog, sir; we are above it, here; when more on a level with the ships, we could see, or fancy we saw, more of them than we do now."

"Here are the upper sails of two heavy ships, sir," observed Wychecombe, pointing in the direction of the vessels already seen; "ay, and yonder are two more—nothing but the royals are visible."

"Two more!—I left eleven two-deckers, three frigates, a sloop, and a cutter in sight, when I got into the boat. You might have covered 'em all with a pocket-handkerchief, hey! Atwood!"

"They were certainly in close order, sir, but I'll not take it on myself to say quite as near together as that."

"Ay, you're a dissenter by trade, and never will believe in a miracle. Sharp work, gentlemen, to get up such a hill as this, after fifty."

"It is, indeed, sir," answered Sir Wycherly, kindly. "Will you do us the favour to take a seat among us, and rest yourself after so violent an exertion? The cliff is hard enough to ascend, even when one keeps the path; though here is a young gentleman who had a fancy just now to go down it, without a path; and that, too, merely that a pretty girl might have a nosegay on her breakfast-table."

The stranger looked intently at Sir Wycherly for a moment, then glanced his eye at the groom and the pony, after which he took a survey of Tom Wychecombe, the lieutenant, and the master. He was a man accustomed to look about him, and he understood, by that rapid glance, the characters of all he surveyed, with perhaps the exception of that of Tom Wychecombe; and even of that he formed a tolerably shrewd conjecture. Sir Wycherly he immediately set down as the squire of the adjacent estate; Dutton's situation he hit exactly, conceiving him to be a worn-out master, who was employed to keep the signal-station; while he understood Wychecombe, by his undress, and air, to be a sea-lieutenant in the king's service. Tom Wychecombe he thought it quite likely might be the son, and heir of the lord of the manor, both being in mourning; though he decided in his own mind that there was not the smallest family likeness between them. Bowing with the courtesy of a man who knew how to acknowledge a civility, he took the proffered seat at Sir Wycherly's side without farther ceremony.

"We must carry the young fellow to sea with us, sir," rejoined the stranger, "and that will cure him of looking for flowers in such ticklish places. His Majesty has need of us all, in this war; and I trust, young gentleman, you have not been long ashore, among the girls."

"Only long enough to make a cure of a pretty smart hurt, received in cutting out a lugger from the opposite coast," answered Wychecombe, with sufficient modesty, and yet with sufficient spirit.

"Lugger!—ha! what Atwood? You surely do not mean, young gentleman, la Voltigeuse?"

"That was the name of the craft, sir—we found her in the roads of Groix."

"And then I've the pleasure of seeing Mr. Wychecombe, the young officer who led in that gallant attack?"

This was said with a most flattering warmth of manner, the stranger even rising and removing his hat, as he uttered the words with a heartiness that showed how much his feelings were in unison with what he said.

"I am Mr. Wychecombe, sir," answered the other, blushing to the temples, and returning the salute; "though I had not the honour of leading; one of the lieutenants of our ship being in another boat."

"Yes—I know all that—but he was beaten off, while you boarded and did the work. What have my lords commissioners done in the matter?"

"All that is necessary, so far as I am concerned, sir, I do assure you; having sent me a commission the very next week. I only wish they had been equally generous to Mr. Walton, who received a severe wound also, and behaved as well as man could behave."

"That would not be so wise, Mr. Wychecombe, since it would be rewarding a failure," returned the stranger, coldly. "Success is all in all, in war. Ah! there the fellows begin to show themselves, Atwood."

This remark drew all eyes, again, towards the sea, where a sight now presented itself that was really worthy of a passing notice. The vapour appeared to have become packed into a mass of some eighty or a hundred feet in height, leaving a perfectly clear atmosphere above it. In the clear air, were visible the upper spars and canvass of the entire fleet mentioned by the stranger; sixteen sail in all. There were the eleven two-deckers, and the three frigates, rising in pyramids of canvass, still fanning in towards the anchorage, which in that roadstead was within pistol-shot of the shore; while the royals and upper part of the topgallant sails of the sloop seemed to stand on the surface of the fog, like a monument. After a moment's pause, Wychecombe discovered even the head of the cutter's royal-mast, with the pennant lazily fluttering ahead of it, partly concealed in vapour. The fog seemed to settle, instead of rising, though it evidently rolled along the face of the waters, putting the whole scene in motion. It was not long ere the tops of the ships of the line became visible, and then living beings were for the first time seen in the moving masses.

"I suppose we offer just such a sight to the top-men of the ships, as they offer to us," observed the stranger. "They *must* see this head-land and flag-staff, Mr. Wychecombe; and there can be no danger of their standing in too far!"

"I should think not, sir; certainly the men aloft can see the cliffs above the fog, as we see the vessels' spars. Ha! Mr. Dutton, there is a rear-admiral's flag flying on board the ship farthest to the eastward."

"So I see, sir; and by looking at the third vessel on the western side of the line, you will find a bit of square bunting at the fore, which will tell you there is a vice-admiral beneath it."

"Quite true!" exclaimed Wychecombe, who was ever enthusiastic on matters relating to his profession; "a vice-admiral of the red, too; which is the next step to being a full admiral. This must be the fleet of Sir Digby Downes!"

"No, young gentleman," returned the stranger, who perceived by the glance of the other's eye, that a question was indirectly put to himself; "it is the southern squadron; and the vice-admiral's flag you see, belongs to Sir Gervaise Oakes. Admiral Bluewater is on board the ship that carries a flag at the mizzen."

"Those two officers always go together, Sir Wycherly," added the young man. "Whenever we hear the name of Sir Gervaise, that of Bluewater is certain to accompany it. Such a union in service is delightful to witness."

"Well may they go in company, Mr. Wychecombe," returned the stranger, betraying a little emotion. "Oakes and Bluewater were reefers together, under old Breasthook, in the Mermaid; and when the first was made a lieutenant into the Squid, the last followed as a mate. Oakes was first of the Briton, in her action with the Spanish frigates, and Bluewater third. For that affair Oakes got a sloop, and his friend went with him as his first. The next year they had the luck to capture a heavier ship than their own, when, for the first time in their service, the two young men were separated; Oakes getting a frigate, and Bluewater getting the Squid. Still they cruised in company, until the senior was sent in command of a flying squadron, with a broad pennant, when the junior, who by this time was post, received his old messmate on board his own frigate. In that manner they served together, down to the hour when the first hoisted his flag. From that time, the two old seamen have never been parted; Bluewater acting as the admiral's captain, until he got the square bunting himself. The vice-admiral has never led the van of a fleet, that the rear-admiral did not lead the rear-division; and, now that Sir Gervaise is a commander-in-chief, you see his friend, Dick Bluewater, is cruising in his company."

While the stranger was giving this account of the Two Admirals, in a half-serious, half-jocular manner, the eyes of his companions were on him. He was a middle-sized, red-faced man, with an aquiline nose, a light-blue animated eye, and a mouth, which denoted more of the habits and care of refinement than either his dress or his ordinary careless mien. A great deal is said about the aristocracy of the ears, and the hands, and the feet; but of all the features, or other appliances of the human frame, the mouth and the nose have the greatest influence in producing an impression of gentility. This was peculiarly the case with the stranger, whose beak, like that of an ancient galley, gave the promise of a stately movement, and whose beautiful teeth and winning smile, often relieved the expression of a countenance that was not unfrequently stern. As he ceased speaking, Dutton rose, in a studied manner, raised his hat entirely from his head, bowed his body nearly to a right angle, and said,

"Unless my memory is treacherous, I believe I have the honor to see Rear-Admiral Bluewater, himself; I was a mate in the Medway, when he commanded the Chloe; and, unless five-and-twenty years have made more changes than I think probable, he is now on this hill."

"Your memory is a bad one, Mr. Dutton, and your hill has on it a much worse man, in all respects, than Admiral Bluewater. They say that man and wife, from living together, and thinking alike, having the same affections, loving the same objects, or sometimes hating them, get in time to look alike; hey! Atwood? It may be that I am growing like Bluewater, on the same principle; but this is the first time I ever heard the thing suggested. I am Sir Gervaise Oakes, at your service, sir."

The bow of Dutton was now much lower than before, while young Wychecombe uncovered himself, and Sir Wycherly arose and paid his compliments cordially, introducing himself, and offering the admiral and all his officers the hospitality of the Hall.

"Ay, this is straight-forward and hearty, and in the good old English manner!" exclaimed the admiral, when he had returned the salutes, and cordially thanked the baronet. "One might land in Scotland, now, anywhere between the Tweed and John a'Groat's house, and not be asked so much as to eat an oaten cake; hey! Atwood?—always excepting the mountain dew."

"You will have your fling at my poor countrymen, Sir Gervaise, and so there is no more to be said on the subject," returned the secretary, for such was the rank of the admiral's companion. "I might feel hurt at times, did I not know that you get as many Scotsmen about you, in your own ship, as you can; and that a fleet is all the better in your judgment, for having every other captain from the land o' cakes."

"Did you ever hear the like of that, Sir Wycherly? Because I stick to a man I like, he accuses me of having a predilection for his whole country. Here's Atwood, now; he was my clerk, when in a sloop; and he has followed me to the Plantagenet, and because I do not throw him overboard, he wishes to make it appear half Scotland is in her hold."

"Well, there are the surgeon, the purser, one of the mates, one of the marine officers, and the fourth lieutenant, to keep me company, Sir Gervaise," answered the secretary, smiling like one accustomed to his superior's jokes, and who cared very little about them. "When you send us all back to Scotland, I'm thinking there will be many a good vacancy to fill."

"The Scotch make themselves very useful, Sir Gervaise," put in Sir Wycherly, by way of smoothing the matter over; "and now we have a Brunswick prince on the throne, we Englishmen have less jealousy of them than formerly. I am sure I should be happy to see all the gentlemen mentioned by Mr. Atwood, at Wychecombe Hall."

"There, you're all well berthed while the fleet lies in these roads. Sir Wycherly, in the name of Scotland, I thank you. But what an extr'ornary (for so admirals pronounced the word a hundred years ago) scene this is, hey! Atwood? Many a time have I seen the hulls of ships when their spars were hid in the fog; but I do not remember ever to have seen before, sixteen sets of masts and sails moving about on vapour, without a single hull to uphold them. The tops of all the two-decked ships are as plainly to be seen, as if the air were without a particle of vapour, while all below the cat-harpings is hid in a cloud as thick as the smoke of battle. I do not half like Bluewater's standing in so far; perhaps, Mr. Dutton, they cannot see the cliffs, for I assure you we did not, until quite close under them. We went altogether by the lead, the masters feeling their way like so many blind beggars!"

"We always keep that nine-pounder loaded, Sir Gervaise," returned the master, "in order to warn vessels when they are getting near enough in; and if Mr. Wychecombe, who is younger than I, will run to the house and light this match, I will prime, and we may give 'em warning where they are, in less than a minute."

The admiral gave a ready assent to this proposition, and the respective parties immediately set about putting it in execution. Wychecombe hastened to the house to light the match, glad of an opportunity to inquire after Mildred; while Dutton produced a priming-horn from a sort of arm-chest that stood near the gun, and put the latter in a condition to be discharged. The young man was absent but a minute, and when all was ready, he turned towards the admiral, in order to get the signal to proceed.

"Let 'em have it, Mr. Wychecombe," cried Sir Gervaise, smiling; "it will wake Bluewater up; perhaps he may favour us with a broadside, by way of retort."

The match was applied, and the report of the gun succeeded. Then followed a pause of more than a minute; when the fog lifted around the Cæsar, the ship that wore a rear-admiral's flag, a flash like lightning was seen glancing in the mist, and then came the bellowing of a piece of heavy ordnance. Almost at the same instant, three little flags appeared at the mast-head of the Cæsar, for previously to quitting his own ship, Sir Gervaise had sent a message to his friend, requesting him to take care of the fleet. This was the signal to anchor. The effect of all this, as seen from the height, was exceedingly striking. As yet not a single hull had become visible, the fog remaining packed upon the water, in a way to conceal even the lower yards of the two-deckers. All above was bright, distinct, and so near, as almost to render it possible to distinguish persons. There every thing was vivid, while a sort of supernatural mystery veiled all beneath. Each ship had an officer aloft to look out for signals, and no sooner had the Cæsar opened her three little flags, which had long been suspended in black balls, in readiness for this service, than the answers were seen floating at the mast-head of each of the vessels. Then commenced a spectacle still more curious than that which those on the cliff had so long been regarding with interest. Ropes began to move, and the sails were drawn up in festoons, apparently without the agency of hands. Cut off from a seeming communication with the ocean, or the hulls, the spars of the different ships appeared to be instinct with life; each machine playing its own part independently of the others, but all having the same object in view. In a very few minutes the canvass was hauled up, and the whole fleet was swinging to the anchors. Presently head after head was thrown out of the fog, the upper yards were alive with men, and the sails were handed. Next came the squaring of the yards, though this was imperfectly done, and a good deal by guess-work. The men came down, and there lay a noble fleet at anchor, with nothing visible to those on the cliffs, but their top-hamper and upper spars.

Sir Gervaise Oakes had been so much struck and amused with a sight that to him happened to be entirely novel, that he did not speak during the whole process of anchoring. Indeed, many a man might pass his life at sea, and never witness such a scene; but those who have, know that it is one of the most beautiful and striking spectacles connected with the wonders of the great deep.

By this time the sun had got so high, as to begin to stir the fog, and streams of vapour were shooting up from the beach, like smoke rising from coal-pits. The wind increased, too, and rolled the vapour before it, and in less than ten minutes, the veil was removed; ship after ship coming out in plain view, until the entire fleet was seen riding in the roadstead, in its naked and distinct proportions.

"Now, Bluewater is a happy fellow," exclaimed Sir Gervaise. "He sees his great enemy, the land, and knows how to deal with it."

"I thought the French were the great and natural enemies of every British sailor," observed Sir Wycherly, simply, but quite to the point.

"Hum—there's truth in that, too. But the land is an enemy to be feared, while the Frenchman is not—hey! Atwood?"

It was, indeed, a goodly sight to view the fine fleet that now lay anchored beneath the cliffs of Wychecombe. Sir Gervaise Oakes was, in that period, considered a successful naval commander, and was a favourite, both at the admiralty and with the nation. His popularity extended to the most distant colonies of England, in nearly all of which he had served with zeal and credit. But we are not writing of an age of nautical wonders, like that which succeeded at the close of the century. The French and Dutch, and even the Spaniards, were then all formidable as naval powers; for revolutions and changes had not destroyed their maritime corps, nor had the consequent naval ascendency of England annihilated their navigation; the two great causes of the subsequent apparent invincibility of the latter power. Battles at sea, in that day, were warmly contested, and were frequently fruitless; more especially when fleets were brought in opposition. The single combats were usually more decisive, though the absolute success of the British flag, was far from being as much a matter of course as it subsequently became. In a word, the science of naval warfare had not made those great strides, which marked the career of England in the end, nor had it retrograded among her enemies, to the point which appears to have rendered their defeat nearly certain. Still Sir Gervaise was a successful officer; having captured several single ships, in bloody encounters, and having actually led fleets with credit, in four or five of the great battles of the times; besides being second and third in command, on various similar occasions. His own ship was certain to be engaged, let what would happen to the others. Equally as captains and as flag-officers, the nation had become familiar with the names of Oakes and Bluewater, as men ever to be found sustaining each other in the thickest of the fight. It may be well to add here, that both these favourite seamen were men of family, or at least what was considered men of family among the mere gentry of England; Sir Gervaise being a baronet by inheritance, while his friend actually belonged to one of those naval lines which furnishes admirals for generations; his father having worn a white flag at the main; and his grandfather having been actually ennobled for his services, dying vice-admiral of England. These fortuitous circumstances perhaps rendered both so much the greater favourites at court.

CHAPTER IV.

——"All with you; except three
On duty, and our leader Israel,
Who is expected momently."

MARINO FALIERO.

As his fleet was safely anchored, and that too, in beautiful order, in spite of the fog, Sir Gervaise Oakes showed a disposition to pursue what are termed ulterior views.

"This has been a fine sight—certainly a very fine sight; such as an old seaman loves; but there must be an end to it," he said. "You will excuse me, Sir Wycherly, but the movements of a fleet always have interest in my eyes, and it is seldom that I get such a bird's-eye view of those of my own; no wonder it has made me a somewhat unreflecting intruder."

"Make no apologies, Sir Gervaise, I beg of you; for none are needed, on any account. Though this head-land does belong to the Wychecombe property, it is fairly leased to the crown, and none have a better right to occupy it than His Majesty's servants. The Hall is a little more private, it is true, but even that has no door that will close upon our gallant naval defenders. It is but a short walk, and nothing will make me happier than to show you the way to my poor dwelling, and to see you as much at home under its roof, as you could be in the cabin of the Plantagenet."

"If any thing could make me as much at home in a house as in a ship, it would be so hearty a welcome; and I intend to accept your hospitality in the very spirit in which it is offered. Atwood and I have landed to send off some important despatches to the First Lord, and we will thank you for putting us in the way of doing it, in the safest and most expeditious manner. Curiosity and surprise have already occasioned the loss of half an hour; while a soldier, or a sailor, should never lose half a minute."

"Is a courier who knows the country well, needed, Sir Gervaise?" the lieutenant demanded, modestly, though with an interest that showed he was influenced only by zeal for the service.

The admiral looked at him, intently, for a moment, and seemed pleased with the hint implied in the question.

"Can you ride?" asked Sir Gervaise, smiling. "I could have brought half-a-dozen youngsters ashore with me; but, besides the doubts about getting a horse—a chaise I take it is out of the question here—I was afraid the lads might disgrace themselves on horseback."

"This must be said in pleasantry, Sir Gervaise," returned Wychecombe; "he would be a strange Virginian at least, who does not know how to ride!"

"And a strange Englishman, too, Bluewater would say; and yet I never see the fellow straddle a horse that I do not wish it were a studding-sail-boom run out to leeward! We sailors *fancy* we ride, Mr. Wychecombe, but it is some such fancy as a marine has for the fore-topmast-cross-trees. Can a horse be had, to go as far as the nearest post-office that sends off a daily mail?"

"That can it, Sir Gervaise," put in Sir Wycherly. "Here is Dick mounted on as good a hunter as is to be found in England; and I'll answer for my young namesake's willingness to put the animal's mettle to the proof. Our little mail has just left Wychecombe for the next twenty-four hours, but by pushing the beast, there will be time to reach the high road in season for the great London mail, which passes the nearest market-town at noon. It is but a gallop of ten miles and back, and that I'll answer for Mr. Wychecombe's ability to do, and to join us at dinner by four."

Young Wychecombe expressing his readiness to perform all this, and even more at need, the arrangement was soon made. Dick was dismounted, the lieutenant got his despatches and his instructions, took his leave, and had galloped out of sight, in the next five minutes. The admiral then declared himself at liberty for the day, accepting the invitation of Sir Wycherly to breakfast and dine at the Hall, in the same spirit of frankness as that in which it had been given. Sir Wycherly was so spirited as to refuse the aid of his pony, but insisted on walking through the village and park to his dwelling, though the distance was more than a mile. Just as they were quitting the signal-station, the old man took the admiral aside, and in an earnest, but respectful manner, disburthened his mind to the following effect.

"Sir Gervaise," he said, "I am no sailor, as you know, and least of all do I bear His Majesty's commission in the navy, though I am in the county commission as a justice of the peace; so, if I make any little mistake you will have the goodness to overlook it, for I know that the etiquette of the quarter-deck is a very serious matter, and is not to be trifled with;—but here is Dutton, as good a fellow in his way as lives—his father was a sort of a gentleman too, having been the attorney of the neighbourhood, and the old man was accustomed to dine with me forty years ago—"

"I believe I understand you, Sir Wycherly," interrupted the admiral; "and I thank you for the attention you wish to pay my prejudices; but, you are master of Wychecombe, and I should feel myself a troublesome intruder, indeed, did you not ask whom you please to dine at your own table."

"That's not quite it, Sir Gervaise, though you have not gone far wide of the mark. Dutton is only a master, you know; and it seems that a master on board ship is a very different thing from a master on shore; so Dutton, himself, has often told me."

"Ay, Dutton is right enough as regards a king's ship, though the two offices are pretty much the same, when other craft are alluded to. But, my dear Sir Wycherly, an admiral is not disgraced by keeping company with a boatswain, if the latter is an honest man. It is true we have our customs, and what we call our quarter-deck and forward officers; which is court end and city, on board ship; but a master belongs to the first, and the master of the Plantagenet, Sandy McYarn, dines with me once a month, as regularly as he enters a new word at the top of his log-book. I beg, therefore, you will extend your hospitality to whom you please—or—" the admiral hesitated, as he cast a good-natured glance at the master, who stood still uncovered, waiting for his superior to move away; "or, perhaps, Sir Wycherly, you would permit *me* to ask a friend to make one of our party."

"That's just it, Sir Gervaise," returned the kind-hearted baronet; "and Dutton will be one of the happiest fellows in Devonshire. I wish we could have Mrs. Dutton and Milly, and then the table would look what my poor brother James—St. James I used to call him—what the Rev. James Wychecombe was accustomed to term, mathematical. He said a table should have all its sides and angles duly filled. James was a most agreeable companion, Sir Gervaise, and, in divinity, he would not have turned his back on one of the apostles, I do verily believe!"

The admiral bowed, and turning to the master, he invited him to be of the party at the Hall, in the manner which one long accustomed to render his civilities agreeable by a sort of professional off-handed way, well knew how to assume.

"Sir Wycherly has insisted that I shall consider his table as set in my own cabin," he continued; "and I know of no better manner of proving my gratitude, than by taking him at his word, and filling it with guests that will be agreeable to us both. I believe there is a Mrs. Dutton, and a Miss—a—a—a—"

"Milly," put in the baronet, eagerly; "Miss Mildred Dutton—the daughter of our good friend Dutton, here, and a young lady who would do credit to the gayest drawing-room in London."

"You perceive, sir, that our kind host anticipates the wishes of an old bachelor, as it might be by instinct, and desires the company of the ladies, also. Miss Mildred will, at least, have two young men to do homage to her beauty, and *three* old ones to sigh in the distance—hey! Atwood?"

"Mildred, as Sir Wycherly knows, sir, has been a little disturbed this morning," returned Dutton, putting on his best manner for the occasion;

"but, I feel no doubt, will be too grateful for this honour, not to exert herself to make a suitable return. As for my wife, gentlemen—"

"And what is to prevent Mrs. Dutton from being one of the party," interrupted Sir Wycherly, as he observed the husband to hesitate; "she sometimes favours me with her company."

"I rather think she will to-day, Sir Wycherly, if Mildred is well enough to go; the good woman seldom lets her daughter stray far from her apron-strings. She keeps her, as I tell her, within the sweep of her own hawse, Sir Gervaise."

"So much the wiser she, Master Dutton," returned the admiral, pointedly. "The best pilot for a young woman is a good mother; and now you have a fleet in your roadstead, I need not tell a seaman of your experience that you are on pilot-ground;—hey! Atwood?"

Here the parties separated, Dutton remaining uncovered until his superior had turned the corner of his little cottage, and was fairly out of sight. Then the master entered his dwelling to prepare his wife and daughter for the honours they had in perspective. Before he executed this duty, however, the unfortunate man opened what he called a locker—what a housewife would term a cupboard—and fortified his nerves with a strong draught of pure Nantes; a liquor that no hostilities, custom-house duties, or national antipathies, has ever been able to bring into general disrepute in the British Islands. In the mean time the party of the two baronets pursued its way towards the Hall.

The village, or hamlet of Wychecombe, lay about half-way between the station and the residence of the lord of the manor. It was an exceedingly rural and retired collection of mean houses, possessing neither physician, apothecary, nor attorney, to give it importance. A small inn, two or three shops of the humblest kind, and some twenty cottages of labourers and mechanics, composed the place, which, at that early day, had not even a chapel, or a conventicle; dissent not having made much progress then in England. The parish church, one of the old edifices of the time of the Henrys, stood quite alone, in a field, more than a mile from the place; and the vicarage, a respectable abode, was just on the edge of the park, fully half a mile more distant. In short, Wychecombe was one of those places which was so far on the decline, that few or no traces of any little importance it may have once possessed, were any longer to be discovered; and it had sunk entirely into a hamlet that owed its allowed claims to be marked on the maps, and to be noted in the gazetteers, altogether to its antiquity, and the name it had given to one of the oldest knightly families in England.

No wonder then, that the arrival of a fleet under the head, produced a great excitement in the little village. The anchorage was excellent, so far as the bottom was concerned, but it could scarcely be called a roadstead in any other point of view, since there was shelter against no wind but that which blew directly off shore, which happened to be a wind that did not prevail in that part of the island. Occasionally, a small cruiser would come-to, in the offing, and a few frigates had lain at single anchors in the roads, for a tide or so, in waiting for a change of weather; but this was the first fleet that had been known to moor under the cliffs within the memory of man. The fog had prevented the honest villagers from ascertaining the unexpected honour that had been done them, until the reports of the two guns reached their ears, when the important intelligence spread with due rapidity over the entire adjacent country. Although Wychecombe did not lie in actual view of the sea, by the time the party of Sir Wycherly entered the hamlet, its little street was already crowded with visiters from the fleet; every vessel having sent at least one boat ashore, and many of them some three or four. Captain's and gun-room stewards, midshipmen's foragers, loblolly boys, and other similar harpies, were out in scores; for this was a part of the world in which bum-boats were unknown; and if the mountain would not come to Mahomet, Mahomet must fain go to the mountain. Half an hour had sufficed to exhaust all the unsophisticated simplicity of the hamlet; and milk, eggs, fresh butter, soft-tommy, vegetables, and such fruits as were ripe, had already risen quite one hundred per cent. in the market.

Sir Gervaise had called his force the southern squadron, from the circumstance of its having been cruising in the Bay of Biscay, for the last six months. This was a wild winter-station, the danger from the elements greatly surpassing any that could well be anticipated from the enemy. The duty notwithstanding had been well and closely performed; several West India, and one valuable East India convoy having been effectually protected, as well as a few straggling frigates of the enemy picked up; but the service had been excessively laborious to all engaged in it, and replete with privations. Most of those who now landed, had not trod terra firma for half a year, and it was not wonderful that all the officers whose duties did not confine them to the vessels, gladly seized the occasion to feast their senses with the verdure and odours of their native island. Quite a hundred guests of this character were also pouring into the street of Wychecombe, or spreading themselves among the surrounding farm-houses; flirting with the awkward and blushing girls, and keeping an eye at the same time to the main chance of the mess-table.

"Our boys have already found out your village, Sir Wycherly, in spite of the fog," the vice-admiral remarked, good-humouredly, as he cast his eyes around at the movement of the street; "and the locusts of Egypt will not come nearer to breeding a famine. One would think there was a great dinner *in petto*, in every cabin of the fleet, by the number of the captain's stewards that are ashore, hey! Atwood? I have seen nine of the harpies, myself, and the other seven can't be far off."

"Here is Galleygo, Sir Gervaise," returned the secretary, smiling; "though *he* can scarcely be called a captain's steward, having the honour to serve a vice-admiral and a commander-in-chief."

"Ay, but *we* feed the whole fleet at times, and have some excuse for being a little exacting—harkee, Galleygo—get a horse-cart, and push off at once, four or five miles further into the country; you might as well expect to find real pearls in fishes' eyes, as hope to pick up any thing nice among so many gun-room and cock-pit boys. I dine ashore to-day, but Captain Greenly is fond of mutton-chops, you'll remember."

This was said kindly, and in the manner of a man accustomed to treat his domestics with the familiarity of humble friends. Galleygo was as unpromising a looking butler as any gentleman ashore would be at all likely to tolerate; but he had been with his present master, and in his present capacity, ever since the latter had commanded a sloop of war. All his youth had been passed as a top-man, and he was really a prime seaman; but accident having temporarily placed him in his present station, Captain Oakes was so much pleased with his attention to his duty, and particularly with his order, that he ever afterwards retained him in his cabin, notwithstanding the strong desire the honest fellow himself had felt to remain aloft. Time and familiarity, at length reconciled the steward to his station, though he did not formally accept it, until a clear agreement had been made that he was not to be considered an idler on any occasion that called for the services of the best men. In this manner David, for such was his Christian name, had become a sort of nondescript on board of a man-of-war; being foremost in all the cuttings out, a captain of a gun, and was frequently seen on a yard in moments of difficulty, just to keep his hand in, as he expressed it, while he descended to the duties of the cabin in peaceable times and good weather. Near thirty years had he thus been half-steward, half-seaman when afloat, while on land he was rather a counsellor and minister of the closet, than a servant; for out of a ship he was utterly useless, though he never left his master for a week at a time, ashore or afloat. The name of Galleygo was a *sobriquet* conferred by his brother top-men, but had been so generally used, that for the last twenty years most of his shipmates believed it to be his patronymic. When this compound of cabin and forecastle received the order just related, he touched the lock of hair on his forehead, a ceremony he always used before he spoke to Sir Gervaise, the hat being removed at some three or four yards' distance, and made his customary answer of—

"Ay-ay-sir—your honour has been a young gentleman yourself, and knows what a young gentleman's stomach gets to be, a'ter a six months' fast in the

Bay of Biscay; and a young gentleman's *boy's* stomach, too. I always thinks there's but a small chance for us, sir, when I sees six or eight of them light cruisers in my neighbourhood. They're som'mat like the sloops and cutters of a fleet, which picks up all the prizes."

"Quite true, Master Galleygo; but if the light cruisers get the prizes, you should recollect that the admiral always has his share of the prize-money."

"Yes, sir, I knows we has our share, but that's accordin' to law, and because the commanders of the light craft can't help it. Let 'em once get the law on their side, and not a ha'pence would bless our pockets! No, sir, what we gets, we gets by the law; and as there is no law to fetch up young gentlemen or their boys, that pays as they goes, we never gets any thing they or their boys puts hands on."

"I dare say you are right, David, as you always are. It wouldn't be a bad thing to have an Act of Parliament to give an admiral his twentieth in the reefers' foragings. The old fellows would sometimes get back some of their own poultry and fruit in that way, hey! Atwood?"

The secretary smiled his assent, and then Sir Gervaise apologized to his host, repeated the order to the steward, and the party proceeded.

"This fellow of mine, Sir Wycherly, is no respecter of persons, beyond the etiquette of a man-of-war," the admiral continued, by way of further excuse. "I believe His Majesty himself would be favoured with an essay on some part of the economy of the cabin, were Galleygo to get an opportunity of speaking his mind to him. Nor is the fool without his expectations of some day enjoying this privilege; for the last lime I went to court, I found honest David rigged, from stem to stern, in a full suit of claret and steel, under the idea that he was 'to sail in company with me,' as he called it, 'with or without signal!'"

"There was nothing surprising in that, Sir Gervaise," observed the secretary. "Galleygo has sailed in company with you so long, and to so many strange lands; has been through so many dangers at your side, and has got so completely to consider himself as part of the family, that it was the most natural thing in the world he should expect to go to court with you."

"True enough. The fellow would face the devil, at my side, and I don't see why he should hesitate to face the king. I sometimes call him Lady Oakes, Sir Wycherly, for he appears to think he has a right of dower, or to some other lawyer-like claim on my estate; and as for the fleet, he always speaks of *that*, as if we commanded it in common. I wonder how Bluewater tolerates the blackguard; for he never scruples to allude to him as under *our* orders! If any thing should befal me, Dick and David would have a civil war for the succession, hey! Atwood?"

"I think military subordination would bring Galleygo to his senses, Sir Gervaise, should such an unfortunate accident occur—which Heaven avert for many years to come! There is Admiral Bluewater coming up the street, at this very moment, sir."

At this sudden announcement, the whole party turned to look in the direction intimated by the secretary. It was by this time at one end of the short street, and all saw a man just entering the other, who, in his walk, air, attire, and manner, formed a striking contrast to the active, merry, bustling, youthful young sailors who thronged the hamlet. In person, Admiral Bluewater was exceedingly tall and exceedingly thin. Like most seamen who have that physical formation, he stooped; a circumstance that gave his years a greater apparent command over his frame, than they possessed in reality. While this bend in his figure deprived it, in a great measure, of the sturdy martial air that his superior presented to the observer, it lent to his carriage a quiet and dignity that it might otherwise have wanted. Certainly, were this officer attired like an ordinary civilian, no one would have taken him for one of England's bravest and most efficient sea-captains; he would have passed rather as some thoughtful, well-educated, and refined gentleman, of retired habits, diffident of himself, and a stranger to ambition. He wore an undress rear-admiral's uniform, as a matter of course; but he wore it carelessly, as if from a sense of duty only; or conscious that no arrangement could give him a military air. Still all about his person was faultlessly neat, and perfectly respectable. In a word, no one but a man accustomed to the sea, were it not for his uniform, would suspect the rear-admiral of being a sailor; and even the seaman himself might be often puzzled to detect any other signs of the profession about him, than were to be found in a face, which, fair, gentlemanly, handsome, and even courtly as it was, in expression and outline, wore the tint that exposure invariably stamps on the mariner's countenance. Here, however, his unseaman-like character ceased. Admiral Oakes had often declared that "Dick Bluewater knew more about a ship than any man in England;" and as for a fleet, his mode of man[oe]uvring one had got to be standard in the service.

As soon as Sir Gervaise recognised his friend, he expressed a wish to wait for him, which was courteously converted by Sir Wycherly into a proposition to return and meet him. So abstracted was Admiral Bluewater, however, that he did not see the party that was approaching him, until he was fairly accosted by Sir Gervaise, who led the advance by a few yards.

"Good-day to you, Bluewater," commenced the latter, in his familiar, off-hand way; "I'm glad you have torn yourself away from your ship; though I must say the manner in which you came-to, in that fog, was more like instinct, than any thing human! I determined to tell you as much, the moment we met;

for I don't think there is a ship, half her length out of mathematical order, notwithstanding the tide runs, here, like a race-horse."

"That is owing to your captains, Sir Gervaise," returned the other, observing the respect of manner, that the inferior never loses with his superior, on service, and in a navy; let their relative rank and intimacy be what they may on all other occasions; "good captains make handy ships. Our gentlemen have now been together so long, that they understand each other's movements; and every vessel in the fleet has her character as well as her commander!"

"Very true, Admiral Bluewater, and yet there is not another officer in His Majesty's service, that could have brought a fleet to anchor, in so much order, and in such a fog; and I ask your leave, sir, most particularly to thank you for the lesson you have given, not only to the captains, but to the commander-in-chief. I presume I may admire that which I cannot exactly imitate."

The rear-admiral merely smiled and touched his hat in acknowledgment of the compliment, but he made no direct answer in words. By this time Sir Wycherly and the others had approached, and the customary introductions took place. Sir Wycherly now pressed his new acquaintance to join his guests, with so much heartiness, that there was no such thing as refusing.

"Since you and Sir Gervaise both insist on it so earnestly, Sir Wycherly," returned the rear-admiral, "I must consent; but as it is contrary to our practice, when on foreign service—and I call this roadstead a foreign station, as to any thing we know about it—as it is contrary to our practice for both flag-officers to sleep out of the fleet, I shall claim the privilege to be allowed to go off to my ship before midnight. I think the weather looks settled, Sir Gervaise, and we may trust that many hours, without apprehension."

"Pooh—pooh—Bluewater, you are always fancying the ships in a gale, and clawing off a lee-shore. Put your heart at rest, and let us go and take a comfortable dinner with Sir Wycherly, who has a London paper, I dare to say, that may let us into some of the secrets of state. Are there any tidings from our people in Flanders?"

"Things remain pretty much as they have been," returned Sir Wycherly, "since that last terrible affair, in which the Duke got the better of the French at—I never can remember an outlandish name; but it sounds something like a Christian baptism. If my poor brother, St. James, were living, now, he could tell us all about it."

"Christian baptism! That's an odd allusion for a field of battle. The armies can't have got to Jerusalem; hey! Atwood?"

"I rather think, Sir Gervaise," the secretary coolly remarked, "that Sir Wycherly Wychecombe refers to the battle that took place last spring—it was fought at Font-something; and a font certainly has something to do with Christian baptism."

"That's it—that's it," cried Sir Wycherly, with some eagerness; "Fontenoï was the name of the place, where the Duke would have carried all before him, and brought Marshal Saxe, and all his frog-eaters prisoners to England, had our Dutch and German allies behaved better than they did. So it is with poor old England, gentlemen; whatever *she* gains, her allies always *lose* for her— the Germans, or the colonists, are constantly getting us into trouble!"

Both Sir Gervaise and his friend were practical men, and well knew that they never fought the Dutch or the French, without meeting with something that was pretty nearly their match. They had no faith in general national superiority. The courts-martial that so often succeeded general actions, had taught them that there were all degrees of spirit, as well as all degrees of a want of spirit; and they knew too much, to be the dupes of flourishes of the pen, or of vapid declamation at dinner-speeches, and in the House of Commons. Men, well led and commanded, they had ascertained by experience, were worth twice as much as the same men when ill led and ill commanded; and they were not to be told that the moral tone of an army or a fleet, from which all its success was derived, depended more on the conventional feeling that had been got up through moral agencies, than on birth-place, origin, or colour. Each glanced his eye significantly at the other, and a sarcastic smile passed over the face of Sir Gervaise, though his friend maintained his customary appearance of gravity.

"I believe le Grand Monarque and Marshal Saxe give a different account of that matter, Sir Wycherly," drily observed the former; "and it may be well to remember that there are two sides to every story. Whatever may be said of Dettingen, I fancy history will set down Fontenoï as any thing but a feather in His Royal Highness' cap."

"You surely do not consider it possible for the French arms to overthrow a British army, Sir Gervaise Oakes!" exclaimed the simple-minded provincial—for such was Sir Wycherly Wychecombe, though he had sat in parliament, had four thousand a year, and was one of the oldest families in England—"It sounds like treason to admit the possibility of such a thing."

"God bless us, my dear sir, I am as far from supposing any such thing, as the Duke of Cumberland himself; who, by the way, has as much English blood in his veins, as the Baltic may have of the water of the Mediterranean—hey! Atwood? By the way, Sir Wycherly, I must ask a little tenderness of you in behalf of my friend the secretary, here, who has a national weakness in favour of the Pretender, and all of the clan Stuart."

"I hope not—I sincerely hope not, Sir Gervaise!" exclaimed Sir Wycherly, with a warmth that was not entirely free from alarm; his own loyalty to the new house being altogether without reproach. "Mr. Atwood has the air of a gentleman of too good principles not to see on which side real religious and political liberty lie. I am sure you are pleased to be jocular, Sir Gervaise; the very circumstance that he is in your company is a pledge of his loyalty."

"Well, well, Sir Wycherly, I would not give you a false idea of my friend Atwood, if possible; and so I may as well confess, that, while his Scotch blood inclines him to toryism, his English reason makes him a whig. If Charles Stuart never gets the throne until Stephen Atwood helps him to a seat on it, he may take leave of ambition for ever."

"I thought as much, Sir Gervaise—I thought *your* secretary could never lean to the doctrine of 'passive obedience and non-resistance.' That's a principle which would hardly suit sailors, Admiral Bluewater."

Admiral Bluewater's line, full, blue eye, lighted with an expression approaching irony; but he made no other answer than a slight inclination of the head. In point of fact, *he* was a Jacobite: though no one was acquainted with the circumstance but his immediate commanding officer. As a seaman, he was called on only to serve his country; and, as often happens to military men, he was willing to do this under any superior whom circumstances might place over his head, let his private sentiments be what they might. During the civil war of 1715, he was too young in years, and too low in rank to render his opinions of much importance; and, kept on foreign stations, his services could only affect the general interests of the nation, without producing any influence on the contest at home. Since that period, nothing had occurred to require one, whose duty kept him on the ocean, to come to a very positive decision between the two masters that claimed his allegiance. Sir Gervaise had always been able to persuade him that he was sustaining the honour and interests of his country, and that ought to be sufficient to a patriot, let who would rule. Notwithstanding this wide difference in political feeling between the two admirals—Sir Gervaise being as decided a whig, as his friend was a tory—their personal harmony had been without a shade. As to confidence, the superior knew the inferior so well, that he believed the surest way to prevent his taking sides openly with the Jacobites, or of doing them secret service, was to put it in his power to commit a great breach of trust. So long as faith were put in his integrity, Sir Gervaise felt certain his friend Bluewater might be relied on; and he also knew that, should the moment ever come when the other really intended to abandon the service of the house of Hanover, he would frankly throw up his employments, and join the hostile standard, without profiting, in any manner, by the trusts he had previously enjoyed. It is also necessary that the reader should understand that Admiral Bluewater had never communicated his political opinions to any person but his friend; the Pretender and his counsellors being as ignorant of them, as George II. and his ministers. The only practical effect, therefore, that they had ever produced was to induce him to decline separate commands, several of which had been offered to him; one, quite equal to that enjoyed by Sir Gervaise Oakes, himself.

"No," the latter answered to Sir Wycherly's remark; though the grave, thoughtful expression of his face, showed how little his feelings chimed in, at the moment, with the ironical language of his tongue. "No—Sir Wycherly, a man-of-war's man, in particular, has not the slightest idea of 'passive obedience and non-resistance,'—that is a doctrine which is intelligible only to papists and tories. Bluewater is in a brown study; thinking no doubt of the manner in which he intends to lead down on Monsieur de Gravelin, should we ever have the luck to meet that gentleman again; so we will, if it's agreeable to all parties, change the subject."

"With all my heart, Sir Gervaise," answered the baronet, cordially; "and, after all, there is little use in discussing the affair of the Pretender any longer, for he appears to be quite out of men's minds, since that last failure of King Louis XV."

"Yes, Norris rather crushed the young viper in its shell, and we may consider the thing at an end."

"So my late brother, Baron Wychecombe, always treated it, Sir Gervaise. He once assured me that the twelve judges were clearly against the claim, and that the Stuarts had nothing to expect from *them*."

"Did he tell you, sir, on what ground these learned gentlemen had come to this decision?" quietly asked Admiral Bluewater.

"He did, indeed; for he knew my strong desire to make out a good case against the tories so well, that he laid all the law before me. I am a bad hand, however, to repeat even what I hear; though my poor brother, the late Rev. James Wychecombe—St. James as I used to call him—could go over a discourse half an hour long, and not miss a word. Thomas and James appear to have run away with the memories of the rest of the family. Nevertheless, I recollect it all depended on an act of Parliament, which is supreme; and the house of Hanover reigning by an act of Parliament, no court could set aside the claim."

"Very clearly explained, sir," continued Bluewater; "and you will permit me to say that there was no necessity for an apology on account of the memory. Your brother, however, might not have exactly explained what an act of Parliament is. King, Lords, and Commons, are all necessary to an act of Parliament."

"Certainly—we all know that, my dear admiral; we poor fellows ashore here, as well as you mariners at sea. The Hanoverian succession had all three to authorize it."

"Had it a king?"

"A king! Out of dispute—or what we bachelors ought to consider as much better, it had a *queen*. Queen Anne approved of the act, and that made it an act of Parliament. I assure you, I learned a good deal of law in the Baron's visits to Wychecombe; and in the pleasant hours we used to chat together in his chambers!"

"And who signed the act of Parliament that made Anne a queen? or did she ascend the throne by regular succession? Both Mary and Anne were sovereigns by acts of Parliament, and we must look back until we get the approval of a prince who took the crown by legal descent."

"Come—come, Bluewater," put in Sir Gervaise, gravely; "we may persuade Sir Wycherly, in this manner, that he has a couple of furious Jacobites in company. The Stuarts were dethroned by a revolution, which is a law of nature, and enacted by God, and which of course overshadows all other laws when it gets into the ascendant, as it clearly has done in this case. I take it, Sir Wycherly, these are your park-gates, and that yonder is the Hall."

This remark changed the discourse, and the whole party proceeded towards the house, discussing the beauty of its position, its history, and its advantages, until they reached its door.

CHAPTER V.

"Monarch and ministers, are awful names:
Whoever wear them, challenge our devoir."

YOUNG.

Our plan does not require an elaborate description of the residence of Sir Wycherly. The house had been neither priory, abbey, nor castle; but it was erected as a dwelling for himself and his posterity, by a Sir Michael Wychecombe, two or three centuries before, and had been kept in good serviceable condition ever since. It had the usual long, narrow windows, a suitable hall, wainscoted rooms, battlemented walls, and turreted angles. It was neither large, nor small; handsome, nor ugly; grand, nor mean; but it was quaint, respectable in appearance, and comfortable as an abode.

The admirals were put each in possession of bed-chambers and dressing-rooms, as soon as they arrived; and Atwood was *berthed* not far from his commanding-officer, in readiness for service, if required. Sir Wycherly was naturally hospitable; but his retired situation had given him a zest for company, that greatly increased the inborn disposition. Sir Gervaise, it was understood, was to pass the night with him, and he entertained strong hopes of including his friend in the same arrangement. Beds were ordered, too, for Dutton, his wife, and daughter; and his namesake, the lieutenant, was expected also to sleep under his roof, that night.

The day passed in the customary manner; the party having breakfasted, and then separated to attend to their several occupations, agreeably to the usages of all country houses, in all parts of the world, and, we believe, in all time. Sir Gervaise, who had sent a messenger off to the Plantagenet for certain papers, spent the morning in writing; Admiral Bluewater walked in the park, by himself; Atwood was occupied with his superior; Sir Wycherly rode among his labourers; and Tom Wychecombe took a rod, and pretended to go forth to fish, though he actually held his way back to the head-land, lingering in and around the cottage until it was time to return home. At the proper hour, Sir Wycherly sent his chariot for the ladies; and a few minutes before the appointed moment, the party began to assemble in the drawing-room.

When Sir Wycherly appeared, he found the Duttons already in possession, with Tom doing the honours of the house. Of the sailing-master and his daughter, it is unnecessary to say more than that the former was in his best uniform—an exceedingly plain one, as was then the case with the whole naval wardrobe—and that the last had recovered from her illness, as was evident by the bloom that the sensitive blushes constantly cast athwart her lovely face. Her attire was exactly what it ought to have been; neat, simple, and becoming. In honour of the host, she wore her best; but this was what became her station, though a little jewelry that rather surpassed what might have been expected in a girl of her rank of life, threw around her person an air of modest elegance. Mrs. Dutton was a plain, matronly woman—the daughter of a land-steward of a nobleman in the same county—with an air of great mental suffering, from griefs she had never yet exposed to the heartless sympathy of the world.

The baronet was so much in the habit of seeing his humble neighbours, that an intimacy had grown up between them. Sir Wycherly, who was anything but an acute observer, felt an interest in the melancholy-looking, and almost heart-broken mother, without knowing why; or certainly without suspecting the real character of her habitual sadness; while Mildred's youth and beauty had not failed of producing the customary effect of making a friend of the old bachelor. He shook hands all round, therefore, with great cordiality; expressing his joy at meeting Mrs. Dutton, and congratulating the daughter on her complete recovery.

"I see Tom has been attentive to his duty," he added, "while I've been detained by a silly fellow about a complaint against a poacher. My namesake, young Wycherly, has not got back yet, though it is quite two hours past his time; and Mr. Atwood tells me the admiral is a little uneasy about his despatches. I tell him Mr. Wycherly Wychecombe, though I have not the honour of ranking him among my relatives, and he is only a Virginian by birth, is a young man to be relied on; and that the despatches are safe, let what may detain the courier."

"And why should not a Virginian be every way as trustworthy and prompt as an Englishman, Sir Wycherly?" asked Mrs. Dutton. "He *is* an Englishman, merely separated from us by the water."

This was said mildly, or in the manner of one accustomed to speak under a rebuked feeling; but it was said earnestly, and perhaps a little reproachfully, while the speaker's eye glanced with natural interest towards the beautiful face of her daughter.

"Why not, sure enough, my dear Mrs. Dutton!" echoed the baronet. "They *are* Englishmen, like ourselves, only born out of the realm, as it might be, and no doubt a little different on that account. They are fellow-subjects, Mrs. Dutton, and that is a great deal. Then they are miracles of loyalty, there being scarcely a Jacobite, as they tell me, in all the colonies."

"Mr. Wycherly Wychecombe is a very respectable young gentleman," said Dutton; "and I hear he is a prime seaman for his years. He has not the honour of being related to this distinguished family, like Mr. Thomas, here, it is true; but he is likely to make a name for himself. Should he get a ship, and do as handsome things in her, as he has done already, His Majesty would probably knight him; and then we should have *two* Sir Wycherly Wychecombes!"

"I hope not—I hope not!" exclaimed the baronet; "I think there must be a law against *that*. As it is, I shall be obliged to put Bart. after my name, as my worthy grandfather used to do, in order to prevent confusion; but England can't bear two Sir Wycherlys, any more than the world can bear two suns. Is not that your opinion, Miss Mildred?"

The baronet had laughed at his own allusion, showing he spoke half jocularly; but, as his question was put in too direct a manner to escape general attention, the confused girl was obliged to answer.

"I dare say Mr. Wychecombe will never reach a rank high enough to cause any such difficulty," she said; and it was said in all sincerity; for, unconsciously perhaps, she secretly hoped that no difference so wide might ever be created between the youth and herself. "If he should, I suppose his rights would be as good as another's, and he must keep his name."

"In such a case, which is improbable enough, as Miss Mildred has so well observed," put in Tom Wychecombe, "we should have to submit to the *knighthood*, for that comes from the king, who might knight a chimney-sweep, if he see fit; but a question might be raised as to the *name*. It is bad enough as it is; but if it really got to be *two* Sir Wycherlys, I think my dear uncle would be wrong to submit to such an invasion of what one might call his individuality, without making some inquiry as to the right of the gentleman to one or both his names. The result might show that the king had made a Sir Something Nobody."

The sneer and spite with which this was uttered, were too marked to escape notice; and both Dutton and his wife felt it would be unpleasant to mingle farther in the discourse. Still the last, submissive, rebuked, and heart-broken as she was, felt a glow on her own pale cheek, as she saw the colour mount in the face of Mildred, and she detected the strong impulses that urged the generous girl herself to answer.

"We have now known Mr. Wychecombe several months," observed Mildred, fastening her full, blue eye calmly on Tom's sinister-looking face; "and we have never known any thing to cause us to think he would bear a name—or names—that he does not at least think he has a right to."

This was said gently, but so distinctly, that every word entered fairly into Tom Wychecombe's soul; who threw a quick, suspicious glance at the lovely speaker, as if to ascertain how far she intended any allusion to himself. Meeting with no other expression than that of generous interest, he recovered his self-command, and made his reply with sufficient coolness.

"Upon my word, Mrs. Dutton," he cried, laughing; "we young men will all of us have to get over the cliff, and hang dangling at the end of a rope, in order to awaken an interest in Miss Mildred, to defend us when our backs are turned. So eloquent—and most especially, so lovely, so charming an advocate, is almost certain of success; and my uncle and myself must admit the absent gentleman's right to our name; though, heaven be praised, he has not yet got either the title or the estate."

"I hope I have said nothing, Sir Wycherly, to displease *you*," returned Mildred, with emphasis; though her face was a thousand times handsomer than ever, with the blushes that suffused it. "Nothing would pain me more, than to suppose I had done so improper a thing. I merely meant that we cannot believe Mr. Wycherly Wychecombe would willingly take a name he had no right to."

"My little dear," said the baronet, taking the hand of the distressed girl, and kissing her cheek, as he had often done before, with fatherly tenderness; "it is not an easy matter for *you* to offend *me*; and I'm sure the young fellow is quite welcome to both my names, if you wish him to have 'em."

"And I merely meant, Miss Mildred," resumed Tom, who feared he might have gone too far; "that the young gentleman—quite without any fault of his own—is probably ignorant how he came by two names that have so long pertained to the head of an ancient and honourable family. There is many a young man born, who is worthy of being an earl, but whom the law considers—" here Tom paused to choose terms suitable for his auditor, when the baronet added,

"A *filius nullius*—that's the phrase, Tom—I had it from your own father's mouth."

Tom Wychecombe started, and looked furtively around him, as if to ascertain who suspected the truth. Then he continued, anxious to regain the ground he feared he had lost in Mildred's favour.

"*Filius nullius* means, Miss Mildred, exactly what I wish to express; a family without any legal origin. They tell me, however, that in the colonies, nothing is more common than for people to take the names of the great families at home, and after a while they fancy themselves related."

"I never heard Mr. Wycherly Wychecombe say a word to lead us to suppose that he was, in any manner, connected with this family, sir," returned Mildred, calmly, but quite distinctly.

"Did you ever hear him say he was *not*, Miss Mildred?"

"I cannot say I ever did, Mr. Wychecombe. It is a subject that has seldom been introduced in my hearing."

"But it has often been introduced in his! I declare, Sir Wycherly, it has struck me as singular, that while you and I have so very frequently stated in the presence of this gentleman, that our families are in no way connected, he has never, in any manner, not even by a nod or a look of approbation, assented to what he must certainly know to be the case. But I suppose, like a true colonist, he was unwilling to give up his hold on the old stock."

Here the entrance of Sir Gervaise Oakes changed the discourse. The vice-admiral joined the party in good spirits, as is apt to be the case with men who have been much occupied with affairs of moment, and who meet relaxation with a consciousness of having done their duty.

"If one could take with him to sea, the comforts of such a house as this, Sir Wycherly, and such handsome faces as your own, young lady," cried Sir Gervaise, cheerfully, after he had made his salutations; "there would be an end of our exclusiveness, for every *petit maître* of Paris and London would turn sailor, as a matter of course. Six months in the Bay of Biscay gives an old fellow, like myself, a keen relish for these enjoyments, as hunger makes any meat palatable; though I am far, very far, indeed, from putting this house or this company, on a level with an indifferent feast, even for an epicure."

"Such as it is, Sir Gervaise, the first is quite at your service, in all things," rejoined the host; "and the last will do all in its power to make itself agreeable."

"Ah—here comes Bluewater to echo all I have said and feel. I am telling Sir Wycherly and the ladies, of the satisfaction we grampuses experience when we get berthed under such a roof as this, with woman's sweet face to throw a gleam of happiness around her."

Admiral Bluewater had already saluted the mother, but when his eye fell on the face and person of Mildred, it was riveted, for an instant, with an earnestness and intentness of surprise and admiration that all noted, though no one saw fit to comment on it.

"Sir Gervaise is so established an admirer of the sex," said the rear-admiral, recovering himself, after a pause; "that I am never astonished at any of his raptures. Salt water has the usual effect on him, however; for I have now known him longer than he might wish to be reminded of, and yet the only mistress who can keep him true, is his ship."

"And to that I believe I may be said to be constant. I don't know how it is with you, Sir Wycherly, but every thing I am accustomed to I like. Now, here I have sailed with both these gentlemen, until I should as soon think of going to sea without a binnacle, as to go to sea without 'em both—hey! Atwood? Then, as to the ship, my flag has been flying in the Plantagenet these ten years, and I can't bear to give the old craft up, though Bluewater, here, would have turned her over to an inferior after three years' service. I tell all the young men they don't stay long enough in any one vessel to find out her good qualities. I never was in a slow ship yet."

"For the simple reason that you never get into a fast one, that you do not wear her fairly out, before you give her up. The Plantagenet, Sir Wycherly, is the fastest two-decker in His Majesty's service, and the vice-admiral knows it too well to let any of us get foot in her, while her timbers will hang together."

"Let it be so, if you will; it only shows, Sir Wycherly, that I do not choose my friends for their bad qualities. But, allow me to ask, young lady, if you happen to know a certain Mr. Wycherly Wychecombe—a namesake, but no relative, I understand, of our respectable host—and one who holds a commission in His Majesty's service?"

"Certainly, Sir Gervaise," answered Mildred, dropping her eyes to the floor, and trembling, though she scarce knew why; "Mr. Wychecombe has been about here, now, for some months, and we all know something of him."

"Then, perhaps you can tell me whether he is generally a loiterer on duty. I do not inquire whether he is a laggard in his duty to you, but whether, mounted on a good hunter, he could get over twenty miles, in eight or ten hours, for instance?"

"I think Sir Wycherly would tell you that he could, sir."

"He may be a Wychecombe, Sir Wycherly, but he is no Plantagenet, in the way of sailing. Surely the young gentleman ought to have returned some hours since!"

"It's quite surprising to me that he is not back before this," returned the kind-hearted baronet. "He is active, and understands himself, and there is not a better horseman in the county—is there, Miss Mildred?"

Mildred did not think it necessary to reply to this direct appeal; but spite of the manner in which she had been endeavouring to school her feelings, since the accident on the cliff, she could not prevent the deadly paleness that dread of some accident had produced, or the rush of colour to her cheeks that followed from the unexpected question of Sir Wycherly. Turning to conceal her confusion, she met the eye of Tom Wychecombe riveted on her face, with an expression so sinister, that it caused her to tremble. Fortunately, at this moment, Sir Gervaise turned away, and drawing near his friend, on the other side of the large apartment, he said in an under tone—

"Luckily, Atwood has brought ashore a duplicate of my despatches, Bluewater, and if this dilatory gentleman does not return by the time we have dined, I will send off a second courier. The intelligence is too important to be trifled with; and after having brought the fleet north, to be in readiness to serve the state in this emergency, it would be rare folly to leave the ministry in ignorance of the reasons why I have done it."

"Nevertheless, they would be almost as well-informed, as I am myself," returned the rear-admiral, with a little point, but quite without any bitterness of manner. "The only advantage I have over them is that I *do* know where the fleet is, which is more than the First Lord can boast of."

"True—I had forgot, my friend—but you must feel that there *is* a subject on which I had better not consult you. I have received some important intelligence, that my duty, as a commander-in-chief, renders it necessary I should—keep to myself."

Sir Gervaise laughed as he concluded, though he seemed vexed and embarrassed. Admiral Bluewater betrayed neither chagrin, nor disappointment; but strong, nearly ungovernable curiosity, a feeling from which he was singularly exempt in general, glowed in his eyes, and lighted his whole countenance. Still, habitual submission to his superior, and the self-command of discipline, enabled him to wait for any thing more that his friend might communicate. At this moment, the door opened, and Wycherly entered the room, in the state in which he had just dismounted. It was necessary to throw but a single glance at his hurried manner, and general appearance, to know that he had something of importance to communicate, and Sir Gervaise made a sign for him not to speak.

"This is public service, Sir Wycherly," said the vice-admiral, "and I hope you will excuse us for a few minutes. I beg this good company will be seated at table, as soon as dinner is served, and that you will treat us as old friends— as I should treat you, if we were on board the Plantagenet. Admiral Bluewater, will you be of our conference?"

Nothing more was said until the two admirals and the young lieutenant were in the dressing-room of Sir Gervaise Oakes. Then the latter turned, and addressed Wycherly, with the manner of a superior.

"I should have met you with a reproof, for this delay, young gentleman," he commenced, "did I not suspect, from your appearance, that something of moment has occurred to produce it. Had the mail passed the market-town, before you reached it, sir?"

"It had not, Admiral Oakes; and I have the satisfaction of knowing that your despatches are now several hours on their way to London. I reached the office just in season to see them mailed."

"Humph! On board the Plantagenet, it is the custom for an officer to report any important duty done, as soon as it is in a condition to be thus laid before the superior!"

"I presume that is the usage in all His Majesty's ships, Sir Gervaise Oakes: but I have been taught that a proper discretion, when it does not interfere with positive orders, and sometimes when it does, is a surer sign of a useful officer, than even the most slavish attention to rules."

"That is a just distinction, young gentleman, though safer in the hands of a captain, perhaps, than in those of a lieutenant," returned the vice-admiral, glancing at his friend, though he secretly admired the youth's spirit. "Discretion is a comparative term; meaning different things with different persons. May I presume to ask what Mr. Wycherly Wychecombe calls discretion, in the present instance?"

"You have every right, sir, to know, and I only wanted your permission to tell my whole story. While waiting to see the London mail start with your despatches, and to rest my horse, a post-chaise arrived that was carrying a gentleman, who is suspected of being a Jacobite, to his country-seat, some thirty miles further west. This gentleman held a secret conference with another person of the same way of thinking as himself; and there was so much running and sending of messages, that I could not avoid suspecting something was in the wind. Going to the stable to look after Sir Wycherly's hunter, for I knew how much he values the animal, I found one of the stranger's servants in discourse with the ostler. The latter told me, when the chaise had gone, that great tidings had reached Exeter, before the travellers quitted the town. These tidings he described as news that 'Charley was no longer over the water.' It was useless, Sir Gervaise, to question one so stupid; and, at the inn, though all observed the manner of the traveller and his visiter, no one could tell me any thing positive. Under the circumstances, therefore, I threw myself into the return chaise, and went as far as Fowey, where I met the important intelligence that Prince Charles has actually landed, and is at this moment up, in Scotland!"

"The Pretender is then really once more among us!" exclaimed Sir Gervaise, like one who had half suspected the truth.

"Not the Pretender, Sir Gervaise, as I understand the news; but his young son, Prince Charles Edward, one much more likely to give the kingdom trouble. The fact is certain, I believe; and as it struck me that it might be important to the commander of so fine a fleet as this which lies under Wychecombe Head, to know it, I lost no time in getting back with the intelligence."

"You have done well, young gentleman, and have proved that discretion *is* quite as useful and respectable in a lieutenant, as it can possibly prove to be in a full admiral of the white. Go, now, and make yourself fit to take a seat by the side of one of the sweetest girls in England, where I shall expect to see you, in fifteen minutes. Well, Bluewater," he continued, as soon as the door closed on Wycherly; "this *is* news, of a certainty!"

"It is, indeed; and I take it to be the news, or connected with the news, that you have sent to the First Lord, in the late despatches. It has not taken you altogether by surprise, if the truth were said?"

"It has not, I confess. You know what excellent intelligence we have had, the past season, from the Bordeaux agent; he sent me off such proofs of this intended expedition, that I thought it advisable to bring the fleet north on the strength of it, that the ships might be used as the exigency should require."

"Thank God, it is a long way to Scotland, and it is not probable we can reach the coast of that country until all is over! I wish we had inquired of this young man with what sort of, and how large a naval force the prince was accompanied with. Shall I send for him, that we may put the question?"

"It is better that you remain passive, Admiral Bluewater. I now promise you that you shall learn all I hear; and that, under the circumstances, I think ought to content you."

The two admirals now separated, though neither returned to the company for some little time. The intelligence they had just learned was too important to be lightly received, and each of these veteran seamen paced his room, for near a quarter of an hour, reflecting on what might be the probable consequences to the country and to himself. Sir Gervaise Oakes expected some event of this nature, and was less taken by surprise than his friend; still he viewed the crisis as exceedingly serious, and as one likely to destroy the prosperity of the nation, as well as the peace of families. There was then in England, as there is to-day, and as there probably will be throughout all time, two parties; one of which clung to the past with its hereditary and exclusive privileges, while the other looked more towards change for anticipated advantages, and created honours. Religion, in that age, was made the stalking-horse of politicians; as is liberty on one side, and order on the other, in our own times; and men just as blindly, as vehemently, and as regardlessly of principle, submitted to party in the middle of the eighteenth century, as we know they do in the middle of the nineteenth. The mode of acting was a little changed, and the watchwords and rallying points were not exactly the same, it is true; but, in all that relates to ignorant confidence, ferocious denunciation, and selfishness but half concealed under the cloak of patriotism, the England of the original whigs and tories, was the England of conservatism and reform, and the America of 1776, the America of 1841.

Still thousands always act, in political struggles, with the fairest intentions, though they act in bitter opposition to each other. When prejudice becomes the stimulant of ignorance, no other result may be hoped for; and the experience of the world, in the management of human affairs, has left the upright and intelligent, but one conclusion as the reward of all the pains and penalties with which political revolutions have been effected—the conviction that no institutions can be invented, which a short working does not show will be perverted from their original intention, by the ingenuity of those entrusted with power. In a word, the physical constitution of man does not more infallibly tend to decrepitude and imbecility, imperiously requiring a new being, and a new existence, to fulfil the objects of his creation, than the moral constitutions which are the fruits of his wisdom, contain the seeds of abuses and decay, that human selfishness will be as certain to cultivate, as human indulgence is to aid the course of nature, in hastening the approaches of death. Thus, while on the one hand, there exists the constant incentive of abuses and hopes to induce us to wish for modifications of the social structure, on the other there stands the experience of ages to demonstrate their insufficiency to produce the happiness we aim at. If the world advances in civilization and humanity, it is because knowledge will produce its fruits in every soil, and under every condition of cultivation and improvement.

Both Sir Gervaise Oakes and Admiral Bluewater believed themselves to be purely governed by principles, in submitting to the bias that each felt towards the conflicting claims of the houses of Brunswick and Stuart. Perhaps no two men in England were in fact less influenced by motives that they ought to feel ashamed to own; and yet, as has been seen, while they thought so much alike on most other things, on this they were diametrically opposed to each other. During the many years of arduous and delicate duties that they had served together, jealousy, distrust, and discontent had been equally strangers to their bosoms; for each had ever felt the assurance that his own honour, happiness, and interests were as much ruling motives with his friend, as they could well be with himself. Their lives had been constant scenes of mutual but unpretending kindnesses; and this under circumstances that naturally awakened all the most generous and manly sentiments of their natures. When young men, their laughing messmates had nick-named them Pylades and Orestes; and later in life, on account of their cruising so much in company, they were generally known in the navy as the "twin captains." On several occasions had they fought enemies' frigates, and captured them; on these occasions, as a matter of course, the senior of the two became most known to the nation; but Sir Gervaise had made the most generous efforts to give his junior a full share of the credit, while Captain Bluewater never spoke of the affairs without mentioning them as victories of the commodore. In a word, on all occasions, and under all circumstances, it appeared to be the aim of these generous-minded and gallant seamen, to serve each other; nor was this attempted with any effort, or striving for effect; all that was said, or done, coming naturally and spontaneously from the heart. But, for the first time in their lives, events had now occurred which threatened a jarring of the feelings between them, if they did not lead to acts which must inevitably place them in open and declared hostility to each other. No wonder, then, that both looked at the future with gloomy forebodings, and a distrust, which, if it did not render them unhappy, at least produced uneasiness.

CHAPTER VI.

"The circle form'd, we sit in silent state,
Like figures drawn upon a dial-plate;
Yes ma'am, and no ma'am, uttered softly show,
Every five minutes how the minutes go."

COWPER.

It is scarcely necessary to tell the reader that England, as regarded material civilization, was a very different country a hundred years since, from what it is to-day. We are writing of an age of heavy wagons, coaches and six, post-chaises and four; and not of an era of MacAdam-roads, or of cars flying along by steam. A man may now post down to a country-house, some sixty or eighty miles, to dinner; and this, too, by the aid of only a pair of horses; but, in 1745 such an engagement would have required at least a start on the previous day; and, in many parts of the island, it would have been safer to have taken two days' grace. Scotland was then farther from Devonshire, in effect, than Geneva is now; and news travelled slowly, and with the usual exaggerations and uncertainties of delay. It was no wonder, then, that a Jacobite who was posting off to his country-house—the focus of an English landlord's influence and authority—filled with intelligence that had reached him through the activity of zealous political partisans, preceded the more regular tidings of the mail, by several hours. The little that had escaped this individual, or his servants rather, for the gentleman was tolerably discreet himself, confiding in only one or two particular friends at each relay, had not got out to the world, either very fully, or very clearly. Wycherly had used intelligence in making his inquiries, and he had observed an officer's prudence in keeping his news for the ears of his superior alone. When Sir Gervaise joined the party in the drawing-room, therefore, he saw that Sir Wycherly knew nothing of what had occurred at the north; and he intended the glance which he directed at the lieutenant to convey a hearty approval of his discretion. This forbearance did more to raise the young officer in the opinion of the practised and thoughtful admiral, than the gallantry with which the youth had so recently purchased his commission; for while many were brave, few had the self-command, and prudence, under circumstances like the present, that alone can make a man safe in the management of important public interests. The approbation that Sir Gervaise felt, and which he desired to manifest, for Wycherly's prudence, was altogether a principle, however; since there existed no sufficient reason for keeping the secret from as confirmed a whig as his host. On the contrary, the sooner those opinions, which both of them would be apt to term sound, were promulgated in the neighbourhood, the better it might prove for the good cause. The vice-admiral, therefore, determined to communicate himself, as soon as the party was seated at table, the very secret which he so much commended the youth for keeping. Admiral Bluewater joining the company, at this instant, Sir Wycherly led Mrs. Dutton to the table. No alteration had taken place among the guests, except that Sir Gervaise wore the red riband; a change in his dress that his friend considered to be openly hoisting the standard of the house of Hanover.

"One would not think, Sir Wycherly," commenced the vice-admiral, glancing his eyes around him, as soon as all were sealed; "that this good company has taken its place at your hospitable table, in the midst of a threatened civil war, if not of an actual revolution."

Every hand was arrested, and every eye turned towards the speaker; even Admiral Bluewater earnestly regarding his friend, anxious to know what would come next.

"I believe my household is in due subjection," answered Sir Wycherly, gazing to the right and left, as if he expected to see his butler heading a revolt; "and I fancy the only change we shall see to-day, will be the removal of the courses, and the appearance of their successors."

"Ay, so says the hearty, comfortable Devonshire baronet, while seated at his own board, favoured by abundance and warm friends. But it would seem the snake was only scotched; not killed."

"Sir Gervaise Oaken has grown figurative; with his *snakes* and *scotch*ings," observed the rear-admiral, a little drily.

"It is *Scotch*-ing, as you say with so much emphasis, Bluewater. I suppose, Sir Wycherly—I suppose, Mr. Dutton, and you, my pretty young lady—I presume all of you have heard of such a person as the Pretender;—some of you may possibly have *seen* him."

Sir Wycherly now dropt his knife and fork, and sat gazing at the speaker in amazement. To him the Christian religion, the liberties of the subject—more especially of the baronet and lord of the manor, who had four thousand a year—and the Protestant succession, all seemed to be in sudden danger.

"I always told my brother, the judge—Mr. Baron Wychecombe, who is dead and gone—that what between the French, that rogue the Pope, and the spurious offspring of King James II., we should yet see troublesome times in England! And now, sir, my predictions are verified!"

"Not as to England, yet, my good sir. Of Scotland I have not quite so good news to tell you; as your namesake, here, brings us the tidings that the son of the Pretender has landed in that kingdom, and is rallying the clans. He has come unattended by any Frenchmen, it would seem, and has thrown himself altogether on the misguided nobles and followers of his house."

"'Tis, at least, a chivalrous and princely act!" exclaimed Admiral Bluewater.

"Yes—inasmuch as it is a heedless and mad one. England is not to be conquered by a rabble of half-dressed Scotchmen."

"True; but England may be conquered by England, notwithstanding."

Sir Gervaise now chose to remain silent, for never before had Bluewater come so near betraying his political bias, in the presence of third persons. This pause enabled Sir Wycherly to find his voice.

"Let me see, Tom," said the baronet, "fifteen and ten are twenty-five, and ten are thirty, and ten are forty-five—it is just thirty years since the Jacobites were up before! It would seem that half a human life is not sufficient to fill the cravings of a Scotchman's maw, for English gold."

"Twice thirty years would hardly quell the promptings of a noble spirit, when his notions of justice showed him the way to the English throne," observed Bluewater, coolly. "For my part, I like the spirit of this young prince, for he who nobly dares, nobly deserves. What say you, my beautiful neighbour?"

"If you mean to address me, sir, by that compliment," answered Mildred, modestly, but with the emphasis that the gentlest of her sex are apt to use when they feel strongly; "I must be suffered to say that I hope every Englishman will dare as nobly, and deserve as well in defence of his liberties."

"Come—come, Bluewater," interrupted Sir Gervaise, with a gravity that almost amounted to reproof; "I cannot permit such innuendoes before one so young and unpractised. The young lady might really suppose that His Majesty's fleet was entrusted to men unworthy to enjoy his confidence, by the cool way in which you carry on the joke. I propose, now, Sir Wycherly, that we eat our dinner in peace, and say no more about this mad expedition, until the cloth is drawn, at least. It's a long road to Scotland, and there is little danger that this adventurer will find his way into Devonshire before the nuts are placed before us."

"It would be nuts to us, if he did, Sir Gervaise," put in Tom Wycherly, laughing heartily at his own wit. "My uncle would enjoy nothing more than to see the spurious sovereign on his own estate, here, and in the hands of his own tenants. I think, sir, that Wychecombe and one or two of the adjoining manors, would dispose of him."

"That might depend on circumstances," the admiral answered, a little drily. "These Scots have such a thing as a claymore, and are desperate fellows, they tell me, at a charge. The very fact of arming a soldier with a short sword, shows a most bloody-minded disposition."

"You forget, Sir Gervaise, that we have our Cornish hug, here in the west of England; and I will put our fellows against any Scotch regiment that ever charged an enemy."

Tom laughed again at his own allusion to a proverbial mode of grappling, familiar to the adjoining county.

"This is all very well, Mr. Thomas Wychecombe, so long as Devonshire is in the west of England, and Scotland lies north of the Tweed. Sir Wycherly might as well leave the matter in the hands of the Duke and his regulars, if it were only in the way of letting every man follow his own trade."

"It strikes me as so singularly insolent in a base-born boy like this, pretending to the English crown, that I can barely speak of him with patience! We all know that his father was a changeling, and the son of a changeling can have no more right than the father himself. I do not remember what the law terms such pretenders; but I dare say it is something sufficiently odious."

"*Filius nullius*, Thomas," said Sir Wycherly, with a little eagerness to show his learning. "That's the very phrase. I have it from the first authority; my late brother, Baron Wychecombe, giving it to me with his own mouth, on an occasion that called for an understanding of such matters. The judge was a most accurate lawyer, particularly in all that related to names; and I'll engage, if he were living at this moment, he would tell you the legal appellation of a changeling ought to be *filius nullius*."

In spite of his native impudence, and an innate determination to make his way in the world, without much regard to truth, Tom Wychecombe felt his cheek burn so much, at this innocent allusion of his reputed uncle, that he was actually obliged to turn away his face, in order to conceal his confusion. Had any moral delinquency of his own been implicated in the remark, he might have found means to steel himself against its consequences; but, as is only too often the case, he was far more ashamed of a misfortune over which he had no possible control, than he would have been of a crime for which he was strictly responsible in morals. Sir Gervaise smiled at Sir Wycherly's knowledge of law terms, not to say of Latin; and turning good-humouredly to his friend the rear-admiral, anxious to re-establish friendly relations with him, he said with well-concealed irony—

"Sir Wycherly must be right, Bluewater. A changeling is *nobody*—that is to say, he is not the *body* he pretends to be, which is substantially being nobody—and the son of nobody, is clearly a *filius nullius*. And now having settled what may be called the law of the case, I demand a truce, until we get our nuts—for as to Mr. Thomas Wychecombe's having *his* nut to crack, at least to-day, I take it there are too many loyal subjects in the north."

When men know each other as well as was the case with our two admirals, there are a thousand secret means of annoyance, as well as of establishing amity. Admiral Bluewater was well aware that Sir Gervaise was greatly superior to the vulgar whig notion of the day, which believed in the fabricated tale of the Pretender's spurious birth; and the secret and ironical allusion he had made to his impression on that subject, acted as oil to his own chafed spirit, disposing him to moderation. This had been the intention of the other; and the smiles they exchanged, sufficiently proved that their usual mental intercourse was temporarily restored at least.

Deference to his guests made Sir Wycherly consent to change the subject, though he was a little mystified with the obvious reluctance of the two admirals to speak of an enterprise that ought to be uppermost, according to his notion of the matter, in every Englishman's mind. Tom had received a rebuke that kept him silent during the rest of the dinner; while the others were content to eat and drink, as if nothing had happened.

It is seldom that a party takes its seat at table without some secret man[oe]uvring, as to the neighbourhood, when the claims of rank and character do not interfere with personal wishes. Sir Wycherly had placed Sir Gervaise on his right and Mrs. Dutton on his left. But Admiral Bluewater had escaped from his control, and taken his seat next to Mildred, who had been placed by Tom Wychecombe close to himself, at the foot of the table. Wycherly occupied the seat opposite, and this compelled Dutton, and Mr. Rotherham, the vicar, to fill the other two chairs. The good baronet had made a wry face, at seeing a rear-admiral so unworthily bestowed; but Sir Gervaise assuring him that his friend was never so happy as when in the service of beauty, he was fain to submit to the arrangement.

That Admiral Bluewater was struck with Mildred's beauty, and pleased with her natural and feminine manner, one altogether superior to what might have been expected from her station in life, was very apparent to all at table; though it was quite impossible to mistake his parental and frank air for any other admiration than that which was suitable to the difference in years, and in unison with their respective conditions and experience. Mrs. Dutton, so far from taking the alarm at the rear-admiral's attentions, felt gratification in observing them; and perhaps she experienced a secret pride in the consciousness of their being so well merited. It has been said, already, that she was, herself, the daughter of a land-steward of a nobleman, in an adjoining county; but it may be well to add, here, that she had been so great a favourite with the daughters of her father's employer, as to have been admitted, in a measure, to their society; and to have enjoyed some of the advantages of their education. Lady Wilmeter, the mother of the young ladies, to whom she was admitted as a sort of humble companion, had formed the opinion it might be an advantage to the girl to educate her for a governess; little conceiving, in her own situation, that she was preparing a course of life for Martha Ray, for such was Mrs. Dutton's maiden name, that was perhaps the least enviable of all the careers that a virtuous and intelligent female can run. This was, as education and governesses were appreciated a century ago; the world, with all its faults and sophisms, having unquestionably made a vast stride towards real civilization, and moral truths, in a thousand important interests, since that time. Nevertheless, the education was received, together with a good many tastes, and sentiments, and opinions, which it may well be questioned, whether they contributed most to the happiness or unhappiness of the pupil, in her future life. Frank Dutton, then a handsome, though far from polished young sea-lieutenant, interfered with the arrangement, by making Martha Ray his wife, when she was two-and-twenty. This match was suitable, in all respects, with the important exception of the educations and characters of the parties. Still, as a woman may well be more refined, and in some things, even more intelligent than her husband; and as sailors, in the commencement of the eighteenth century, formed a class of society much more distinct than they do to-day, there would have been nothing absolutely incompatible with the future well-being of the young couple, had each pursued his, or her own career, in a manner suitable to their respective duties. Young Dutton took away his bride, with the two thousand pounds she had received from her father, and for a long time he was seen no more in his native county. After an absence of some twenty years, however, he returned, broken in constitution, and degraded in rank. Mrs. Dutton brought with her one child, the beautiful girl introduced to the reader, and to whom she was studiously imparting all she had herself acquired in the adventitious manner mentioned. Such were the means, by which Mildred, like her mother, had been educated above her condition in life; and it had been remarked that, though Mrs. Dutton had probably no cause to felicitate herself on the possession of manners and sentiments that met with so little sympathy, or appreciation, in her actual situation, she assiduously cultivated the same manners and opinions in her daughter; frequently manifesting a sort of sickly fastidiousness on the subject of Mildred's deportment and tastes. It is probable the girl owed her improvement in both, however, more to the circumstance of her being left so much alone with her mother, than to any positive lessons she received; the influence of example, for years, producing its usual effects.

No one in Wychecombe positively knew the history of Dutton's professional degradation. He had never risen higher than to be a lieutenant; and from this station he had fallen by the sentence of a court-martial. His restoration to the service, in the humbler and almost hopeless rank of a master, was believed to have been brought about by Mrs. Dutton's influence with the present Lord Wilmeter, who was the brother of her youthful companions. That the husband had wasted his means, was as certain as that his habits, on the score of temperance at least, were bad, and that his wife, if not positively broken-hearted, was an unhappy woman; one to be pitied, and admired. Sir Wycherly was little addicted to analysis, but he could not fail to discover the superiority of the wife and daughter, over the husband and father; and it is due to his young namesake to add, that his obvious admiration of Mildred was quite as much owing to her mind, deportment, character, and tastes, as to her exceeding personal charms.

This little digression may perhaps, in the reader's eyes, excuse the interest Admiral Bluewater took in our heroine. With the indulgence of years and station, and the tact of a man of the world, he succeeded in drawing Mildred out, without alarming her timidity; and he was surprised at discovering the delicacy of her sentiments, and the accuracy of her knowledge. He was too conversant with society, and had too much good taste, to make any deliberate parade of opinions; but in the quiet manner that is so easy to those who are accustomed to deal with truths and tastes as familiar things, he succeeded in inducing her to answer his own remarks, to sympathize with his feelings, to laugh when he laughed, and to assume a look of disapproval, when he felt that disapprobation was just. To all this Wycherly was a delighted witness, and in some respects he participated in the conversation; for there was evidently no wish on the part of the rear-admiral to monopolize his beautiful companion to himself. Perhaps the position of the young man, directly opposite to her, aided in inducing Mildred to bestow so many grateful looks and sweet smiles, on the older officer; for she could not glance across the table, without meeting the admiring gaze of Wycherly, fastened on her own blushing face.

It is certain, if our heroine did not, during this repast, make a conquest of Admiral Bluewater, in the ordinary meaning of the term, that she made him a friend. Sir Gervaise, even, was struck with the singular and devoted manner in which his old messmate gave all his attention to the beautiful girl at his side; and, once or twice, he caught himself conjecturing whether it were possible, that one as practised, as sensible, and as much accustomed to the beauties of the court, as Bluewater, had actually been caught, by the pretty face of a country girl, when so well turned of fifty, himself! Then discarding the notion as preposterous, he gave his attention to the discourse of Sir Wycherly; a dissertation on rabbits, and rabbit-warrens. In this manner the dinner passed away.

Mrs. Dutton asked her host's permission to retire, with her daughter, at the earliest moment permitted by propriety. In quitting the room she cast an anxious glance at the face of her husband, which was already becoming flushed with his frequent applications of port; and spite of an effort to look smiling and cheerful, her lips quivered, and by the time she and Mildred reached the drawing-room, tears were fast falling down her cheeks. No explanation was asked, or needed, by the daughter, who threw herself into her mother's arms, and for several minutes they wept together, in silence. Never had Mrs. Dutton spoken, even to Mildred, of the besetting and degrading vice of her husband; but it had been impossible to conceal its painful consequences from the world; much less from one who lived in the bosom of her family. On that failing which the wife treated so tenderly, the daughter of course could not touch; but the silent communion of tears had got to be so sweet to both, that, within the last year, it was of very frequent occurrence.

"Really, Mildred," said the mother, at length, after having succeeded in suppressing her emotion, and in drying her eyes, while she smiled fondly in the face of the lovely and affectionate girl; "this Admiral Bluewater is getting to be so particular, I hardly know how to treat the matter."

"Oh! mother, he is a delightful old gentleman! and he is so gentle, while he is so frank, that he wins your confidence almost before you know it. I wonder if he could have been serious in what he said about the noble daring and noble deserving of Prince Edward!"

"That must pass for trifling, of course; the ministry would scarcely employ any but a true whig, in command of a fleet. I saw several of his family, when a girl, and have always heard them spoken of with esteem and respect. Lord Bluewater, this gentleman's cousin, was very intimate with the present Lord Wilmeter, and was often at the castle. I remember to have heard that he had a disappointment in love, when quite a young man, and that he has ever since been considered a confirmed bachelor. So you will take heed, my love."

"The warning was unnecessary, dear mother," returned Mildred, laughing; "I could dote on the admiral as a father, but must be excused from considering him young enough for a nearer tie."

"And yet he has the much admired profession, Mildred," said the mother, smiling fondly, and yet a little archly. "I have often heard you speak of your passion for the sea."

"That was formerly, mother, when I spoke as a sailor's daughter, and as girls are apt to speak, without much reflection. I do not know that I think better of a seaman's profession, now, than I do of any other. I fear there is often much misery in store for soldiers' and sailors' wives."

Mrs. Dutton's lip quivered again; but hearing a foot at the door, she made an effort to be composed, just as Admiral Bluewater entered.

"I have run away from the bottle, Mrs. Dutton, to join you and your fair daughter, as I would run from an enemy of twice my force," he said, giving each lady a hand, in a manner so friendly, as to render the act more than gracious; for it was kind. "Oakes is bowsing out his jib with his brother baronet, as we sailors say, and I have hauled out of the line, without a signal."

"I hope Sir Gervaise Oakes does not consider it necessary to drink more wine than is good for the mind and body," observed Mrs. Dutton, with a haste that she immediately regretted.

"Not he. Gervaise Oakes is as discreet a man, in all that relates to the table, as an anchorite; and yet he has a faculty of *seeming* to drink, that makes him a boon companion for a four-bottle man. How the deuce he does it, is more than I can tell you; but he does it so well, that he does not more thoroughly get the better of the king's enemies, on the high seas, than he floors his friends under the table. Sir Wycherly has begun his libations in honour of the house of Hanover, and they will be likely to make a long sitting."

Mrs. Dutton sighed, and walked away to a window, to conceal the paleness of her cheeks. Admiral Bluewater, though perfectly abstemious himself, regarded license with the bottle after dinner, like most men of that age, as a very venial weakness, and he quietly took a seat by the side of Mildred, and began to converse.

"I hope, young lady, as a sailor's child, you feel an hereditary indulgence for a seaman's gossip," he said. "We, who are so much shut up in our ships, have a poverty of ideas on most subjects; and as to always talking of the winds and waves, that would fatigue even a poet."

"As a sailor's daughter, I honour my father's calling, sir; and as an English girl, I venerate the brave defenders of the island. Nor do I know that seamen have less to say, than other men."

"I am glad to hear you confess this, for—shall I be frank with you, and take a liberty that would better become a friend of a dozen years, than an acquaintance of a day;—and, yet, I know not why it is so, my dear child, but I feel as if I had long known you, though I am certain we never met before."

"Perhaps, sir, it is an omen that we are long to know each other, in future," said Mildred, with the winning confidence of unsuspecting and innocent girlhood. "I hope you will use no reserve."

"Well, then, at the risk of making a sad blunder, I will just say, that 'my nephew Tom' is any thing but a prepossessing youth; and that I hope all eyes regard him exactly as he appears to a sailor of fifty-five."

"I cannot answer for more than those of a girl of nineteen, Admiral Bluewater," said Mildred, laughing; "but, for her, I think I may say that she does not look on him as either an Adonis, or a Crichton."

"Upon my soul! I am right glad to hear this, for the fellow has accidental advantages enough to render him formidable. He is the heir to the baronetcy, and this estate, I believe?"

"I presume he is. Sir Wycherly has no other nephew—or at least this is the eldest of three brothers, I am told—and, being childless himself, it *must* be so. My father tells me Sir Wycherly speaks of Mr. Thomas Wychecombe as his future heir."

"Your father!—Ay, fathers look on these matters with eyes very different from their daughters!"

"There is one thing about seamen that renders them at least safe acquaintances," said Mildred, smiling; "I mean their frankness."

"That is a failing of mine, as I have heard. But you will pardon an indiscretion that arises in the interest I feel in yourself. The eldest of three brothers—is the lieutenant, then, a younger son?"

"*He* does not belong to the family at all, I believe," Mildred answered, colouring slightly, in spite of a resolute determination to appear unconcerned. "Mr. Wycherly Wychecombe is no relative of our host, I hear; though he bears both of his names. He is from the colonies; born in Virginia."

"*He* is a noble, and a noble-looking fellow! Were I the baronet, I would break the entail, rather than the acres should go to that sinister-looking nephew, and bestow them on the namesake. From Virginia, and not even a relative, at all?"

"That is what Mr. Thomas Wychecombe says; and even Sir Wycherly confirms it. I have never heard Mr. Wycherly Wychecombe speak on the subject, himself."

"A weakness of poor human nature! The lad finds an honourable, ancient, and affluent family here, and has not the courage to declare his want of affinity to it; happening to bear the same name."

Mildred hesitated about replying; but a generous feeling got the better of her diffidence. "I have never seen any thing in the conduct of Mr. Wycherly Wychecombe to induce me to think that he feels any such weakness," she said, earnestly. "He seems rather to take pride in, than to feel ashamed of, his being a colonial; and you know, we, in England, hardly look on the people of the colonies as our equals."

"And have you, young lady, any of that overweening prejudice in favour of your own island?"

"I hope not; but I think most persons have. Mr. Wycherly Wychecombe admits that Virginia is inferior to England, in a thousand things; and yet he seems to take pride in his birth-place."

"Every sentiment of this nature is to be traced to self. We know that the fact is irretrievable, and struggle to be proud of what we cannot help. The Turk will tell you he has the honour to be a native of Stamboul; the Parisian will boast of his Faubourg; and the cockney exults in Wapping. Personal conceit lies at the bottom of all; for we fancy that places to which *we* belong, are not places to be ashamed of."

"And yet I do not think Mr. Wycherly at all remarkable for conceit. On the contrary, he is rather diffident and unassuming."

This was said simply, but so sincerely, as to induce the listener to fasten his penetrating blue eye on the speaker, who now first took the alarm, and felt that she might have said too much. At this moment the two young men entered, and a servant appeared to request that Admiral Bluewater would do Sir Gervaise Oakes the favour to join him, in the dressing-room of the latter.

Tom Wychecombe reported the condition of the dinner-table to be such, as to render it desirable for all but three and four-bottle men to retire. Hanoverian toasts and sentiments were in the ascendant, and there was every appearance that those who remained intended to make a night of it. This was sad intelligence for Mrs. Dutton, who had come forward eagerly to hear the report, but who now returned to the window, apparently irresolute as to the course she ought to take. As both the young men remained near Mildred, she had sufficient opportunity to come to her decision, without interruption, or hindrance.

CHAPTER VII.

———"Somewhat we will do.
And, look, when I am king, claim thou of me
The earldom of Hereford, and all the moveables
Whereof the king my brother was possessed."

RICHARD III.

Rear-Admiral Bluewater found Sir Gervaise Oakes pacing a large dressing-room, quarter-deck fashion, with as much zeal, as if just released from a long sitting, on official duty, in his own cabin. As the two officers were perfectly familiar with each other's personal habits, neither deviated from his particular mode of indulging his ease; but the last comer quietly took his seat in a large chair, disposing of his person in a way to show he intended to consult his comfort, let what would happen.

"Bluewater," commenced Sir Gervaise, "this is a very foolish affair of the Pretender's son, and can only lead to his destruction. I look upon it as altogether unfortunate."

"That, as it may terminate. No man can tell what a day, or an hour, may bring forth. I am sure, such a rising was one of the last things *I* have been anticipating, down yonder, in the Bay of Biscay."

"I wish, with all my heart, we had never left it," muttered Sir Gervaise, so low that his companion did not hear him. Then he added, in a louder tone, "*Our* duty, however, is very simple. We have only to obey orders; and it seems that the young man has no naval force to sustain him. We shall probably be sent to watch Brest, or l'Orient, or some other port. Monsieur must be kept in, let what will happen."

"I rather think it would be better to let him out, our chances on the high seas being at least as good as his own. I am no friend to blockades, which strike me as an un-English mode of carrying on a war."

"You are right enough, Dick, in the main," returned Sir Gervaise, laughing.

"Ay, and *on* the main, Oakes. I sincerely hope the First Lord will not send a man like you, who are every way so capable of giving an account of your enemy with plenty of sea-room, on duly so scurvy as a blockade."

"A man like *me*! Why a man like *me* in particular? I trust I am to have the pleasure of Admiral Bluewater's company, advice and assistance?"

"An inferior never can know, Sir Gervaise, where it may suit the pleasure of his superiors to order him."

"That distinction of superior and inferior, Bluewater, will one day lead you into a confounded scrape, I fear. If you consider Charles Stuart your sovereign, it is not probable that orders issued by a servant of King George will be much respected. I hope you will do nothing hastily, or without consulting your oldest and truest friend!"

"You know my sentiments, and there is little use in dwelling on them, now. So long as the quarrel was between my own country and a foreign land, I have been content to serve; but when my lawful prince, or his son and heir, comes in this gallant and chivalrous manner, throwing himself, as it might be, into the very arms of his subjects, confiding all to their loyalty and spirit; it makes such an appeal to every nobler feeling, that the heart finds it difficult to repulse. I could have joined Norris, with right good will, in dispersing and destroying the armament that Louis XV. was sending against us, in this very cause; but here every thing is English, and Englishmen have the quarrel entirely to themselves. I do not see how, as a loyal subject of my hereditary prince, I can well refrain from joining his standard."

"And would *you*, Dick Bluewater, who, to my certain knowledge, were sent on board ship at twelve years of age, and who, for more than forty years, have been a man-of-war's-man, body and soul; would you now strip your old hulk of the sea-blue that has so long covered and become it, rig yourself out like a soldier, with a feather in your hat,—ay, d——e, and a camp-kettle on your arm, and follow a drummer, like one of your kinsmen, Lord Bluewater's fellows of the guards?—for of sailors, your lawful prince, as you call him, hasn't enough to stopper his conscience, or to whip the tail of his coat, to keep it from being torn to tatters by the heather of Scotland. If you *do* follow the adventurer, it must be in some such character, since I question if he can muster a seaman, to tell him the bearings of London from Perth."

"When I join him, he will be better off."

"And what could even *you* do alone, among a parcel of Scotchmen, running about their hills under bare poles? Your signals will not man[oe]uvre regiments, and as for man[oe]uvring in any other manner, you know nothing. No—no; stay where you are, and help an old friend with knowledge that is useful to him.—I should be afraid to do a dashing thing, unless I felt the certainty of having you in my van, to strike the first blow; or in my rear, to bring me off, handsomely.

"You would be afraid of nothing, Gervaise Oakes, whether I stood at your elbow, or were off in Scotland. Fear is not your failing, though temerity may be."

"Then I want your presence to keep me within the bounds of reason," said Sir Gervaise, stopping short in his walk, and looking his friend smilingly in the face. "In some mode, or other, I always need your aid."

"I understand the meaning of your words, Sir Gervaise, and appreciate the feeling that dictates them. You must have a perfect conviction that I will do nothing hastily, and that I will betray no trust. When I turn my back on King George, it will be loyalty, in one sense, whatever he may think of it in another; and when I join Prince Charles Edward, it will be with a conscience that he need not be ashamed to probe. What names he bears! They are the designations of ancient English sovereigns, and ought of themselves, to awaken the sensibilities of Englishmen."

"Ay, Charles in particular," returned the vice-admiral, with something like a sneer. "There's the second Charles, for instance—St. Charles, as our good host, Sir Wycherly, might call him—he is a pattern prince for Englishmen to admire. Then his father was of the school of the Star-Chamber martyrs!"

"Both were lineal descendants of the Conqueror, and of the Saxon princes; and both united the double titles to the throne, in their sacred persons. I have always considered Charles II. as the victim of the rebellious conduct of his subjects, rather than vicious. He was driven abroad into a most corrupt state of society, and was perverted by our wickedness. As to the father, he was the real St. Charles, and a martyred saint he was; dying for true religion, as well as for his legal rights. Then the Edwards—glorious fellows!—remember that they were all but one Plantagenets; a name, of itself, to rouse an Englishman's fire!"

"And yet the only difference between the right of these very Plantagenets to the throne, and that of the reigning prince, is, that one produced a revolution by the strong hand, and the other was produced by a revolution that came from the nation. I do not know that your Plantagenets ever did any thing for a navy; the only real source of England's power and glory. D——e, Dick, if I think so much of your Plantagenets, after all!"

"And yet the name of Oakes is to be met with among their bravest knights, and most faithful followers."

"The Oakes, like the pines, have been timbers in every ship that has floated," returned the vice-admiral, half-unconscious himself, of the pun he was making.

For more than a minute Sir Gervaise continued his walk, his head a little inclined forward, like a man who pondered deeply on some matter of interest. Then, suddenly stopping, he turned towards his friend, whom he regarded for near another minute, ere he resumed the discourse.

"I wish I could fairly get you to exercise your excellent reason on this matter, Dick," he said, after the pause; "then I should be certain of having secured you on the side of liberty."

Admiral Bluewater merely shook his head, but he continued silent, as if he deemed discussion altogether supererogatory. During this pause, a gentle tap at the door announced a visiter; and, at the request to enter, Atwood made his appearance. He held in his hand a large package, which bore on the envelope the usual stamp that indicated it was sent on public service.

"I beg pardon, Sir Gervaise," commenced the secretary, who always proceeded at once to business, when business was to be done; "but His Majesty's service will not admit of delay. This packet has just come to hand, by the arrival of an express, which left the admiralty only yesterday noon."

"And how the devil did he know where to find me!" exclaimed the vice-admiral, holding out a hand to receive the communication.

"It is all owing to this young lieutenant's forethought in following up the Jacobite intelligence to a market-town. The courier was bound to Falmouth, as fast as post-horses could carry him, when he heard, luckily, that the fleet lay at anchor, under Wychecombe Head; and, quite as luckily, he is an officer who had the intelligence to know that you would sooner get the despatches, if he turned aside, and came hither by land, than if he went on to Falmouth, got aboard the sloop that was to sail with him, for the Bay of Biscay, and came round here by water."

Sir Gervaise smiled at this sally, which was one in keeping with all Atwood's feelings; for the secretary had matured a system of expresses, which, to his great mortification, his patron laughed at, and the admiralty entirely overlooked. No time was lost, however, in the way of business; the secretary having placed the candles on a table, where Sir Gervaise took a chair, and had already broken a seal. The process of reading, nevertheless, was suddenly interrupted by the vice-admiral's looking up, and exclaiming—

"Why, you are not about to leave us, Bluewater?"

"You may have private business with Mr. Atwood, Sir Gervaise, and perhaps I had better retire."

Now, it so happened that while Sir Gervaise Oakes had never, by look or syllable, as he confidently believed, betrayed the secret of his friend's Jacobite propensities, Atwood was perfectly aware of their existence. Nor had the latter obtained his knowledge by any unworthy means. He had been neither an eavesdropper, nor an inquirer into private communications, as so often happens around the persons of men in high trusts; all his knowledge having been obtained through native sagacity and unavoidable opportunities. On the present occasion, the secretary, with the tact of a man of experience, felt that his presence might be dispensed with; and he cut short the discussion between the two admirals, by a very timely remark of his own.

"I have left the letters uncopied, Sir Gervaise," he said, "and will go and finish them. A message by Locker"—this was Sir Gervaise's body-servant—"will bring me back at a moment's notice, should you need me again to-night."

"That Atwood has a surprising instinct, for a Scotchman!" exclaimed the vice-admiral, as soon as the door was closed on the secretary. "He not only knows when he *is* wanted, but when he is *not* wanted. The last is an extraordinary attainment, for one of his nation."

"And one that an Englishman may do well to emulate," returned Bluewater. "It is possible my company may be dispensed with, also, just at this important moment."

"You are not so much afraid of the Hanoverians, Dick, as to run away from their hand-writing, are ye? Ha—what's this?—As I live, a packet for yourself, and directed to 'Rear-Admiral Sir Richard Bluewater, K.B.' By the Lord, my old boy, they've given you the red riband at last! This is an honour well earned, and which may be fitly worn."

"'Tis rather unexpected, I must own. The letter, however, cannot be addressed to me, as I am not a Knight of the Bath."

"This is rank nonsense. Open the packet, at once, or I will do it for you. Are there two Dick Bluewaters in the world, or another rear-admiral of the same name?"

"I would rather not receive a letter that does not strictly bear my address," returned the other, coldly.

"As I'll be sworn this does. But hand it to me, since you are so scrupulous, and I will do that small service for you."

As this was said, Sir Gervaise tore aside the seals; and, as he proceeded rather summarily, a red riband was soon uncased and fell upon the carpet. The other usual insignia of the Bath made their appearance, and a letter was found among them, to explain the meaning of all. Every thing was in due form, and went to acquaint Rear-Admiral Bluewater, that His Majesty had been graciously pleased to confer on him one of the vacant red ribands of the day, as a reward for his eminent services on different occasions. There was even a short communication from the premier, expressing the great satisfaction of the ministry in thus being able to second the royal pleasure with hearty good will.

"Well, what do you think of that, Richard Bluewater?" asked Sir Gervaise, triumphantly. "Did I not always tell you, that sooner or later, it *must* come?"

"It has come too late, then," coldly returned the other, laying the riband, jewels, and letters, quietly on the table. "This is an honour, I can receive, *now*, only from my rightful prince. None other can legally create a knight of the Bath."

"And pray, Mr. Richard Bluewater, who made you a captain, a commander, a rear-admiral? Do you believe me an impostor, because I wear this riband on authority no better than that of the house of Hanover? Am I, or am I not, in your judgment, a vice-admiral of the red?"

"I make a great distinction, Oakes, between rank in the navy, and a mere personal dignity. In the one case, you serve your country, and give quite as much as you receive; whereas, in the other, it is a grace to confer consideration on the person honoured, without such an equivalent as can find an apology for accepting a rank illegally conferred."

"The devil take your distinctions, which would unsettle every thing, and render the service a Babel. If I am a vice-admiral of the red, I am a knight of the Bath; and, if you are a rear-admiral of the white, you are also a knight of that honourable order. All comes from the same source of authority, and the same fountain of honour."

"I do not view it thus. Our commissions are from the admiralty, which represents the country; but dignities come from the prince who happens to reign, let *his* title be what it may."

"Do you happen to think Richard III. a usurper, or a lawful prince?"

"A usurper, out of all question; and a murderer to boot. His name should be struck from the list of English kings. I never hear it, without execrating him, and his deeds."

"Pooh—pooh, Dick, this is talking more like a poet than a seaman. If only one-half the sovereigns who deserve to be execrated had their names erased, the list of even our English kings would be rather short; and some countries would be without historical kings at all. However much Richard III. may deserve cashiering in this summary manner, his peers and laws are just as good as any other prince's peers and laws. Witness the Duke of Norfolk, for instance."

"Ay, that cannot be helped by me; but it *is* in my power to prevent Richard Bluewater's being made a knight or the Bath, by George II.; and the power shall be used."

"It would seem not, as he is already created; and I dare to say, gazetted."

"The oaths are not yet taken, and it is, at least, an Englishman's birth-right, to decline an honour; if, indeed, this can be esteemed an honour, at all."

"Upon my word, Rear-Admiral Sir Richard Bluewater, you are disposed to be complimentary, to-night! The unworthy knight present, and all the rest of the order, are infinitely indebted to you!"

"Your case and mine, Oakes, are essentially different," returned the other, with some emotion in his voice and manner. "Your riband was fairly won, fighting the battles of England, and can be worn with credit to yourself and to your country; but these baubles are sent to me, at a moment when a rising was foreseen, and as a sop to keep me in good-humour, as well as to propitiate the whole Bluewater interest."

"That is pure conjecture, and I dare say will prove to be altogether a mistake. Here are the despatches to speak for themselves; and, as it is scarcely possible that the ministry should have known of this rash movement of the Pretender's son, more than a few days, my life on it, the dates will show that your riband was bestowed before the enterprise was even suspected."

As Sir Gervaise commenced, with his constitutional ardour, to turn over the letters, as soon as his mind was directed to this particular object, Admiral Bluewater resumed his seat, awaiting the result, with not a little curiosity; though, at the same time, with a smile of incredulity. The examination disappointed Sir Gervaise Oakes. The dates proved that the ministers were better informed than he had supposed; for it appeared they had been apprised about the time he was himself of the intended movement. His orders were to bring the fleet north, and in substance to do the very thing his own sagacity had dictated. So far every thing was well; and he could not entertain a doubt about receiving the hearty approbation of his superiors, for the course he had taken. But here his gratification ended; for, on looking at the dates of the different communications, it was evident that the red riband was bestowed after the intelligence of the Pretender's movement had reached London. A private letter, from a friend at the Board of Admiralty, too, spoke of his own probable promotion to the rank of admiral of the blue; and mentioned several other similar preferments, in a way to show that the government was fortifying itself, in the present crisis, as much as possible, by favours. This was a politic mode of procedure, with ordinary men, it is true; but with officers of the elevation of mind, and of the independence of character of our two admirals, it was most likely to produce disgust.

"D—n 'em, Dick," cried Sir Gervaise, as he threw down the last letter of the package, with no little sign of feeling; "you might take St. Paul, or even Wychecombe's dead brother, St. James the Less, and put him at court, and he would come out a thorough blackguard, in a week!"

"That is not the common opinion concerning a court education," quietly replied the friend; "most people fancying that the place gives refinement of manners, if not of sentiment."

"Poh—poh—you and I have no need of a dictionary to understand each other. I call a man who never trusts to a generous motive—who thinks it always necessary to bribe or cajole—who has no idea of any thing's being done without its direct *quid pro quo*, a scurvy blackguard, though he has the airs and graces of Phil. Stanhope, or Chesterfield, as he is now. What do you think those chaps at the Board, talk of doing, by way of clinching my loyalty, at this blessed juncture?"

"No doubt to get you raised to the peerage. I see nothing so much out of the way in the thing. You are of one of the oldest families of England, and the sixth baronet by inheritance, and have a noble landed estate, which is none the worse for prize-money. Sir Gervaise Oakes of Bowldero, would make a very suitable Lord Bowldero."

"If it were only that, I shouldn't mind it; for nothing is easier than to refuse a peerage. I've done *that* twice already, and can do it a third time, at need. But one can't very well refuse promotion in his regular profession; and, here, just as a true gentleman would depend on the principles of an officer, the hackneyed consciences of your courtiers have suggested the expediency of making Gervaise Oakes an admiral of the blue, by way of sop!—me, who was made vice-admiral of the red, only six months since, and who take an honest pride in boasting that every commission, from the lowest to the highest, has been fairly earned in battle!"

"They think it a more delicate service, perhaps, for a gentleman to be true to the reigning house, when so loud an appeal is made to his natural loyalty; and therefore class the self-conquest with a victory at sea!"

"They are so many court-lubbers, and I should like to have an opportunity of speaking my mind to them. I'll not take the new commission; for every one must see, Dick, that it is a sop."

"Ay, that's just my notion, too, about the red riband; and I'll not take *that*. You have had the riband these ten years, have declined the peerage twice, and their only chance is the promotion. Take it you ought, and must, however, as it will be the means of pushing on some four or five poor devils, who have been wedged up to honours, in this manner, ever since they were captains. I am glad they do not talk of promoting *me*, for I should hardly know how to refuse such a grace. There is great virtue in parchment, with all us military men."

"Still it must be parchment fairly won. I think you are wrong, notwithstanding, Bluewater, in talking of refusing the riband, which is so justly your due, for a dozen different acts. There is not a man in the service, who has been less rewarded for what he has done, than yourself."

"I am sorry to hear you give this as your opinion; for just at this moment, I would rather think that I have no cause of complaint, in this way, against the reigning family, or its ministers. I'm sure I was posted when quite a young man, and since that time, no one has been lifted over my head."

The vice-admiral looked intently at his friend; for never before had he detected a feeling which betrayed, as he fancied, so settled a determination in him to quit the service of the powers that were. Acquainted from boyhood with all the workings of the other's mind, he perceived that the rear-admiral had been endeavouring to persuade himself that no selfish or unworthy motive could be assigned to an act which he felt to proceed from disinterested chivalry, just as he himself broke out with his expression of an opinion that no officer had been less liberally rewarded for his professional services than his friend. While there is no greater mystery to a selfish manager, than a man of disinterested temperament, they who feel and submit to generous impulses, understand each other with an instinctive facility. When any particular individual is prone to believe that there is a predominance of good over evil in the world he inhabits, it is a sign of inexperience, or of imbecility; but when one acts and reasons as if *all* honour and virtue are extinct, he furnishes the best possible argument against his own tendencies and character. It has often been remarked that stronger friendships are made between those who have different personal peculiarities, than between those whose sameness of feeling and impulses would be less likely to keep interest alive; but, in all cases of intimacies, there must be great identity of principles, and even of tastes in matters at all connected with motives, in order to ensure respect, among those whose standard of opinion is higher than common, or sympathy among those with whom it is lower. Such was the fact, as respected Admirals Oakes and Bluewater. No two men could be less alike in temperament, or character, physically, and in some senses, morally considered; but, when it came to principles, or all those tastes or feelings that are allied to principles, there was a strong native, as well as acquired affinity. This union of sentiment was increased by common habits, and professional careers so long and so closely united, as to be almost identical. Nothing was easier, consequently, than for Sir Gervaise Oakes to comprehend the workings of Admiral Bluewater's mind, as the latter endeavoured to believe he had been fairly treated by the existing government. Of course, the reasoning which passed through the thoughts of Sir Gervaise, on this occasion, required much less time than we have taken to explain its nature; and, after regarding his friend intently, as already related, for a few seconds, he answered as follows; a good deal influenced, unwittingly to himself, with the wish to check the other's Jacobite propensities.

"I am sorry not to be able to agree with you, Dick," he said, with some warmth. "So far from thinking you *well* treated, by any ministry, these twenty years, I think you have been very *ill* treated. Your rank you have, beyond a question; for of that no brave officer can well be deprived in a regulated service; but, have you had the *commands* to which you are entitled?—I was a commander-in-chief when only a rear-admiral of the blue; and then how long did I wear a broad pennant, before I got a flag at all!"

"You forget how much I have been with you. When two serve together, one must command, and the other must obey. So far from complaining of these Hanoverian Boards, and First Lords, it seems to me that they have always kept in view the hollowness of their claims to the throne, and have felt a desire to purchase honest men by their favours."

"You are the strangest fellow, Dick Bluewater, it has ever been my lot to fall in with! D——e me, if I believe you know always, when you *are* ill treated. There are a dozen men in service, who have had separate commands, and who are not half as well entitled to them, as you are yourself."

"Come, come, Oakes, this is getting to be puerile, for two old fellows, turned of fifty. You very well know that I was offered just as good a fleet, as this of your own, with a choice of the whole list of flag-officers below me, to pick a junior from; and, so, we'll say no more about it. As respects their red riband, however, it may go a-begging for me."

Sir Gervaise was about to answer in his former vein, when a tap at the door announced the presence of another visiter. This time the door opened on the person of Galleygo, who had been included in Sir Wycherly's hospitable plan of entertaining every soul who immediately belonged to the suite of Sir Gervaise.

"What the d——l has brought *you* here!" exclaimed the vice-admiral, a little warmly; for he did not relish an interruption just at this moment. "Recollect you're not on board the Plantagenet, but in the dwelling of a gentleman, where there are both butler and housekeeper, and who have no occasion for your advice, or authority, to keep things in order."

"Well, there, Sir Gervaise I doesn't agree with you the least bit; for I thinks as a ship's steward—I mean a *cabin* steward, and a good 'un of the quality— might do a great deal of improvement in this very house. The cook and I has had a partic'lar dialogue on them matters, already; and I mentioned to her the names of seven different dishes, every one of which she quite as good as admitted to me, was just the same as so much gospel to *her*."

"I shall have to quarantine this fellow, in the long run, Bluewater! I do believe if I were to take him to Lambeth Palace, or even to St. James's, he'd thrust his oar into the archbishop's benedictions, or the queen's caudle-cup!"

"Well, Sir Gervaise, where would be the great harm, if I did? A man as knows the use of an oar, may be trusted with one, even in a church, or an abbey. When your honour comes to hear what the dishes was, as Sir Wycherly's cook had never heard on, you'll think it as great a cur'osity as I do myself. If I had just leave to name 'em over, I think as both you gentlemen would look at it as remarkable."

"What are they, Galleygo?" inquired Bluewater, putting one of his long legs over an arm of the adjoining chair, in order to indulge himself in a yarn with his friend's steward, with greater freedom; for he greatly delighted in Galleygo's peculiarities; seeing just enough of the fellow to find amusement, without annoyance in them. "I'll answer for Sir Gervaise, who is always a little diffident about boasting of the superiority of a ship, over a house."

"Yes, your honour, that he is—that is just one of Sir Jarvy's weak p'ints, as a body might say. Now, I never goes ashore, without trimming sharp up, and luffing athwart every person's hawse, I fall in with; which is as much as to tell 'em, I belongs to a flag-ship, and a racer, and a craft as hasn't her equal on salt-water; no disparagement to the bit of bunting at the mizzen-topgallant-mast-head of the Cæsar, or to the ship that carries it. I hopes, as we are so well acquainted, Admiral Bluewater, no offence will be taken."

"Where none is meant, none ought to be taken, my friend. Now let us hear your bill-of-fare."

"Well, sir, the very first dish I mentioned to Mrs. Larder, Sir Wycherly's cook, was lobscous; and, would you believe it, gentlemen, the poor woman had never heard of it! I began with a light hand, as it might be, just not to overwhelm her with knowledge, at a blow, as Sir Jarvy captivated the French frigate with the upper tier of guns, that he might take her alive, like."

"And the lady knew nothing of a lobscous—neither of its essence, nor nature?"

"There's no essences as is ever put in a lobscous, besides potaties, Admiral Bluewater; thof we make 'em in the old Planter"—*nautice* for Plantagenet—"in so liquorish a fashion, you might well think they even had Jamaiky, in 'em. No, potaties is the essence of lobscous; and a very good thing is a potatie, Sir Jarvy, when a ship's company has been on salted oakum for a few months."

"Well, what was the next dish the good woman broke down under?" asked the rear-admiral, fearful the master might order the servant to quit the room; while he, himself, was anxious to get rid of any further political discussion.

"Well, sir, she knowed no more of a chowder, than if the sea wern't in the neighbourhood, and there wern't such a thing as a fish in all England. When I talked to her of a chowder, she gave in, like a Spaniard at the fourth or fifth broadside."

"Such ignorance is disgraceful, and betokens a decline in civilization! But, you hoisted out more knowledge for her benefit, Galleygo—small doses of learning are poor things."

"Yes, your honour; just like weak grog—burning the priming, without starting the shot. To be sure, I did, Admiral Blue. I just named to her burgoo, and then I mentioned duff (*anglice* dough) to her, but she denied that there was any such things in the cookery-book. Do you know, Sir Jarvy, as these here shore craft get their dinners, as our master gets the sun; all out of a book as it might be. Awful tidings, too, gentlemen, about the Pretender's son; and I s'pose we shall have to take the fleet up into Scotland, as I fancy them 'ere sogers will not make much of a hand in settling law?"

"And have you honoured us with a visit, just to give us an essay on dishes, and to tell us what you intend to do with the fleet?" demanded Sir Gervaise, a little more sternly than he was accustomed to speak to the steward.

"Lord bless you, Sir Jarvy, I didn't dream of one or t'other! As for telling you, or Admiral Blue, (so the seamen used to call the second in rank,) here, any thing about lobscous, or chowder, why, it would be carrying coals to New Market. I've fed ye both with all such articles, when ye was nothing but young gentlemen; and when you was no longer young gentlemen, too, but a couple of sprightly luffs, of nineteen. And as for moving the fleet, I know, well enough, that will never happen, without our talking it over in the old Planter's cabin; which is a much more nat'ral place for such a discourse, than any house in England!"

"May I take the liberty of inquiring, then, what *did* bring you here?"

"That you may, with all my heart, Sir Jarvy, for I likes to answer your questions. My errand is not to your honour this time, though you are my master. It's no great matter, after all, being just to hand this bit of a letter over to Admiral Blue."

"And where did this letter come from, and how did it happen to fall into your hands?" demanded Bluewater, looking at the superscription, the writing of which he appeared to recognise.

"It hails from Lun'nun, I hear; and they tell me it's to be a great secret that you've got it, at all. The history of the matter is just this. An officer got in to-night, with orders for us, carrying sail as hard as his shay would bear. It seems he fell in with Master Atwood, as he made his land-fall, and being acquainted with that gentleman, he just whipped out his orders, and sent 'em off to the right man. Then he laid his course for the landing, wishing to get aboard of the Dublin, to which he is ordered; but falling in with our barge, as I landed, he wanted to know the where-away of Admiral Blue, here; believing him to be afloat. Some 'un telling him as I was a friend and servant of both admirals, as it might be, he turned himself over to me for advice. So I promised to deliver the letter, as I had a thousand afore, and knowed the way of doing such things; and he gives me the letter, under special orders, like; that is to say, it was to be handed to the rear-admiral as it might be under the lee of the mizzen-stay-sail, or in a private fashion. Well, gentlemen, you both knows I understand that, too, and so I undertook the job."

"And I have got to be so insignificant a person that I pass for no one, in your discriminating mind, Master Galleygo!" exclaimed the vice-admiral, sharply. "I have suspected as much, these five-and-twenty years."

"Lord bless you, Sir Jarvy, how flag-officers will make mistakes sometimes! They're mortal, I says to the people of the galley, and have their appetites false, just like the young gentlemen, when they get athwart-hawse of a body, I says. Now, I count Admiral Blue and yourself pretty much as one man, seeing that you keep few, or no secrets from each other. I know'd ye both as young gentlemen, and then you loved one another like twins; and then I know'd ye as luffs, when ye'd walk the deck the whole watch, spinning yarns; and then I know'd ye as Pillardees and Arrestee, though one pillow might have answered for both; and as for Arrest, I never know'd either of ye to got into that scrape. As for telling a secret to one, I've always looked upon it as pretty much telling it to t'other."

The two admirals exchanged glances, and the look of kindness that each met in the eyes of his friend removed every shadow that had been cast athwart their feelings, by the previous discourse.

"That will do, Galleygo," returned Sir Gervaise, mildly. "You're a good fellow in the main, though a villanously rough one—"

"A little of old Boreus, Sir Jarvy," interrupted the steward, with a grim smile: "but it blows harder at sea than it does ashore. These chaps on land, ar'n't battened down, and caulked for such weather, as we sons of Neptun' is obligated to face."

"Quite true, and so good-night. Admiral Bluewater and myself wish to confer together, for half an hour; all that it is proper for you to know, shall be communicated another time."

"Good-night, and God bless your honour. Good-night, Admiral Blue: we three is the men as can keep any secret as ever floated, let it draw as much water as it pleases."

Sir Gervaise Oakes stopped in his walk, and gazed at his friend with manifest interest, as he perceived that Admiral Bluewater was running over his letter for the third time. Being now without a witness, he did not hesitate to express his apprehensions.

"'Tis as I feared, Dick!" he cried. "That letter is from some prominent partisan of Edward Stuart?"

The rear-admiral turned his eyes on the face of his friend, with an expression that was difficult to read; and then he ran over the contents of the epistle, for the fourth time.

"A set of precious rascals they are, Gervaise!" at length the rear-admiral exclaimed. "If the whole court was culled, I question if enough honesty could be found to leaven one puritan scoundrel. Tell me if you know this hand, Oakes? I question if you ever saw it before."

The superscription of the letter was held out to Sir Gervaise, who, after a close examination, declared himself unacquainted with the writing.

"I thought as much," resumed Bluewater, carefully tearing the signature from the bottom of the page, and burning it in a candle; "let this disgraceful part of the secret die, at least. The fellow who wrote this, has put 'confidential' at the top of his miserable scrawl: and a most confident scoundrel he is, for his pains. However, no man has a right to thrust himself, in this rude manner, between me and my oldest friend; and least of all will I consent to keep this piece of treachery from your knowledge. I do more than the rascal merits in concealing his name; nevertheless, I shall not deny myself the pleasure of sending him such an answer as he deserves. Read that, Oakes, and then say if keelhauling would be too good for the writer."

Sir Gervaise took the letter in silence, though not without great surprise, and began to peruse it. As he proceeded, the colour mounted to his temples, and once he dropped his hand, to cast a look of wonder and indignation towards his companion. That the reader may see how much occasion there was for both these feelings, we shall give the communication entire. It was couched in the following words:

"DEAR. ADMIRAL BLUEWATER:

"Our ancient friendship, and I am proud to add, affinity of blood, unite in inducing me to write a line, at this interesting moment. Of the result of this rash experiment of the Pretender's son, no prudent man can entertain a doubt. Still, the boy may give us some trouble, before he is disposed of altogether. We look to all our friends, therefore, for their most efficient exertions, and most prudent co-operation. On *you*, every reliance is placed; and I wish I could say as much for *every flag-officer afloat*. Some distrust—unmerited, I sincerely hope—exists in a very high quarter, touching the loyalty of a certain commander-in-chief, who is so completely under your observation, that it is felt enough is done in hinting the fact to one of your political tendencies. The king said, this morning, 'Vell, dere isht Bluevater; of *him* we are shure asht of ter sun.' You stand excellently well *there*, to my great delight; and I need only say, be watchful and prompt.

"Yours, with the most sincere faith and attachment, my dear Bluewater, &c., &c.

"REAR-ADMIRAL BLUEWATER.

"P. S.—I have just heard that they have sent you the red riband. The king himself, was in this."

When Sir Gervaise had perused this precious epistle to himself, he read it slowly, and in a steady, clear voice, aloud. When he had ended, he dropped the paper, and stood gazing at his friend.

"One would think the fellow some exquisite satirist," said Bluewater, laughing. "*I* am to be vigilant, and see that *you* do not mutiny, and run away with the fleet to the Highlands, one of these foggy mornings! Carry it up into Scotland, as Galleygo has it! Now, what is your opinion of that letter?"

"That all courtiers are knaves, and all princes ungrateful. I should think my loyalty to the good *cause*, if not to the *man*, the last in England to be suspected."

"Nor is it suspected, in the smallest degree. My life on it, neither the reigning monarch, nor his confidential servants, are such arrant dunces, as to be guilty of so much weakness. No, this masterly move is intended to secure *me*, by creating a confidence that they think no generous-minded man would betray. It is a hook, delicately baited to catch a gudgeon, and not an order to watch a whale."

"Can the scoundrels be so mean—nay, dare they be so bold! They must have known you would show me the letter."

"Not they—they have reasoned on my course, as they would on their own. Nothing catches a weak man sooner than a pretended confidence of this nature; and I dare say this blackguard rates me just high enough to fancy I may be duped in this flimsy manner. Put your mind at rest; King George knows he may confide in *you*, while I think it probable *I* am distrusted."

"I hope, Dick, you do not suspect *my* discretion! My own secret would not be half so sacred to me."

"I know that, full well. Of *you*, I entertain no distrust, either in heart or head; of myself, I am not quite so certain. When we *feel*, we do not always *reason*; and there is as much feeling, as any thing else, in this matter."

"Not a line is there, in all my despatches, that go to betray the slightest distrust of me, or any one else. You are spoken of, but it is in a manner to gratify you, rather than to alarm. Take, and read them all; I intended to show them to you, as soon as we had got through with that cursed discussion"

As Sir Gervaise concluded, he threw the whole package of letters on the table, before his friend.

"It will be time enough, when you summon me regularly to a council of war," returned Bluewater, laying the letters gently aside. "Perhaps we had better sleep on this affair; in the morning we shall meet with cooler heads, and just as warm hearts."

"Good-night, Dick," said Sir Gervaise, holding out both hands for the other to shake as he passed him, in quitting the room.

"Good-night, Gervaise; let this miserable devil go overboard, and think no more of him. I have half a mind to ask you for a leave, to-morrow, just to run up to London, and cut off his ears."

Sir Gervaise laughed and nodded his head, and the two friends parted, with feelings as kind as ever had distinguished their remarkable career.

CHAPTER VIII.

"Look to't, think on't, I do not use to jest.
Thursday is near; lay hand on heart, advise;
An' you be mine, I'll give you to my friend;
An' you be not, hang, beg, starve, die i' the streets."

ROMEO AND JULIET.

Wychecombe Hall, had most of the peculiarities of a bachelor's dwelling, in its internal government; nor was it, in any manner, behind, or, it might be better to say, before, the age, in its modes and customs connected with jollifications. When its master relaxed a little, the servants quite uniformly imitated his example. Sir Wycherly kept a plentiful table, and the servants' hall fared nearly as well as the dining-room; the single article of wine excepted. In lieu of the latter, however, was an unlimited allowance of double-brewed ale; and the difference in the potations was far more in the name, than in the quality of the beverages. The master drank port; for, in the middle of the last century, few Englishmen had better wine—and port, too, that was by no means of a very remarkable delicacy, but which, like those who used it, was rough, honest, and strong; while the servant had his malt liquor of the very highest stamp and flavour. Between indifferent wine and excellent ale, the distance is not interminable; and Sir Wycherly's household, was well aware of the fact, having frequently instituted intelligent practical comparisons, by means of which, all but the butler and Mrs. Larder had come to the conclusion to stand by the home-brewed.

On the present occasion, not a soul in the house was ignorant of the reason why the baronet was making a night of it. Every man, woman, and child, in or about the Hall, was a devoted partisan of the house of Hanover; and as soon as it was understood that this feeling was to be manifested by drinking "success to King George, and God bless him," on the one side; and "confusion to the Pretender, and his mad son," on the other; all under the roof entered into the duty, with a zeal that might have seated a usurper on a throne, if potations could do it.

When Admiral Bluewater, therefore, left the chamber of his friend, the signs of mirth and of a regular debauch were so very obvious, that a little curiosity to watch the result, and a disinclination to go off to his ship so soon, united to induce him to descend into the rooms below, with a view to get a more accurate knowledge of the condition of the household. In crossing the great hall, to enter the drawing-room, he encountered Galleygo, when the following discourse took place.

"I should think the master-at-arms has not done his duty, and dowsed the glim below, Master Steward," said the rear-admiral, in his quiet way, as they met; "the laughing, and singing, and hiccupping, are all upon a very liberal scale for a respectable country-house."

Galleygo touched the lock of hair on his forehead, with one hand, and gave his trowsers a slue with the other, before he answered; which he soon did, however, though with a voice a little thicker than was usual with him, on account of his having added a draught or two to those he had taken previously to visiting Sir Gervaise's dressing-room; and which said additional draught or two, had produced some such effect on his system, as the fresh drop produces on the cup that is already full.

"That's just it, Admiral Blue," returned the steward, in passing good-humour, though still sober enough to maintain the decencies, after his own fashion; "that's just it, your honour. They've passed the word below to let the lights stand for further orders, and have turned the hands up for a frolic. Such ale as they has, stowed in the lower hold of this house, like leaguers in the ground-tier, it does a body's heart good to conter'plate. All hands is bowsing out their jibs on it, sir, and the old Hall will soon be carrying as much sail as she can stagger under. It's nothing but loose-away and sheet-home."

"Ay, ay, Galleygo, this may be well enough for the people of the household, if Sir Wycherly allows it; but it ill becomes the servants of guests to fall into this disorder. If I find Tom has done any thing amiss, he will hear more of it; and as your own master is not here to admonish *you*, I'll just take the liberty of doing it for him, since I know it would mortify him exceedingly to learn that his steward had done any thing to disgrace himself."

"Lord bless your dear soul, Admiral Blue, take just as many liberties as you think fit, and I'll never pocket one on 'em. I know'd you, when you was only a young gentleman, and now you're a rear. You're close on our heels; and by the time we are a full admiral, you'll be something like a vice. I looks upon you as bone of our bone, and flesh of our flesh,—Pillardees and Arrestees— and I no more minds a setting-down from your honour, than I does from Sir Jarvy, hisself."

"I believe that is true enough, Galleygo; but take my advice, and knock off with the ale for to-night. Can you tell me how the land lies, with the rest of the company?"

"You couldn't have asked a better person, your honour, as I've just been passing through all the rooms, from a sort of habit I has, sir; for, d'ye see, I thought I was in the old Planter, and that it was my duty to overlook every thing, as usual. The last pull at the ale, put that notion in my head; but it's gone now, and I see how matters is. Yes, sir, the mainmast of a church isn't stiffer and more correct-like, than my judgment is, at this blessed moment. Sir Wycherly guv' me a glass of his black-strap, as I ran through the dining-room, and told me to drink 'Confusion to the Pretender,' which I did, with hearty good-will; but his liquor will no more lay alongside of the ale they've down on the orlop, than a Frenchman will compare with an Englishman. What's your opinion, Admiral Blue, consarning this cruise of the Pretender's son, up in the Highlands of Scotland?"

Bluewater gave a quick, distrustful glance at the steward, for he knew that the fellow was half his time in the outer cabin and pantries of the Plantagenet, and he could not tell how much of his many private dialogues with Sir Gervaise, might have been overheard. Meeting with nothing but the unmeaning expression of one half-seas-over, his uneasiness instantly subsided.

"I think it a gallant enterprise, Galleygo," he answered; too manly even to feign what he did not believe; "but I fear as a *cruise*, it will not bring much prize-money. You have forgotten you were about to tell me how the land lies. Sir Wycherly, Mr. Dutton, Mr. Rotherham, are still at the table, I fancy—are these all? What have become of the two young gentlemen?"

"There's none ashore, sir," said Galleygo, promptly, accustomed to give that appellation only to midshipmen.

"I mean the two Mr. Wychecombes; one of whom, I had forgot, is actually an officer."

"Yes, sir, and a most partic'lar fine officer he is, as every body says. Well, sir, *he's* with the ladies; while his namesake has gone back to the table, and has put luff upon luff, to fetch up leeway."

"And the ladies—what have they done with themselves, in this scene of noisy revelry?"

"They'se in yonder state-room, your honour. As soon as they found how the ship was heading, like all women-craft, they both makes for the best harbour they could run into. Yes, they'se yonder."

As Galleygo pointed to the door of the room he meant, Bluewater proceeded towards it, parting with the steward after a few more words of customary, but very useless caution. The tap of the admiral was answered by Wycherly in person, who opened the door, and made way for his superior to enter, with a respectful obeisance. There was but a single candle in the little parlour, in which the two females had taken refuge from the increasing noise of the debauch; and this was due to a pious expedient of Mildred's, in extinguishing the others, with a view to conceal the traces of tears that were still visible on her own and her mother's cheeks. The rear-admiral was, at first, struck with this comparative obscurity; but it soon appeared to him appropriate to the feelings of the party assembled in the room. Mrs. Dutton received him with the ease she had acquired in her early life, and the meeting passed as a matter of course, with persons temporarily residing under the same roof.

"Our friends appear to be enjoying themselves," said Bluewater, when a shout from the dining-room forced itself on the ears of all present. "The loyalty of Sir Wycherly seems to be of proof."

"Oh! Admiral Bluewater," exclaimed the distressed wife, feeling, momentarily, getting the better of discretion; "*do* you—*can* you call such a desecration of God's image enjoyment?"

"Not justly, perhaps, Mrs. Dutton; and yet it is what millions mistake for it. This mode of celebrating any great event, and even of illustrating what we think our principles, is, I fear, a vice not only of our age, but of our country."

"And yet, neither you, nor Sir Gervaise Oakes, I see, find it necessary to give such a proof of your attachment to the house of Hanover, or of your readiness to serve it with your time and persons."

"You will remember, my good, lady, that both Oakes and myself are flag-officers in command, and it would never do for us to fall into a debauch in sight of our own ships. I am glad to see, however, that Mr. Wychecombe, here, prefers such society as I find him in, to the pleasures of the table."

Wycherly bowed, and Mildred cast an expressive, not to say grateful, glance towards the speaker; but her mother pursued the discourse, in which she found a little relief to her suppressed emotion.

"God be thanked for that!" she exclaimed, half-unconscious of the interpretation that might be put on her words; "All that we have seen of Mr. Wychecombe would lead us to believe that this is not an unusual, or an accidental forbearance."

"So much the more fortunate for him. I congratulate you, young sir, on this triumph of principle, or of temperament, or of both. We belong to a profession, in which the bottle is an enemy more to be feared, than any that the king can give us. A sailor can call in no ally as efficient in subduing this mortal foe, as an intelligent and cultivated mind. The man who really *thinks* much, seldom *drinks* much; but there are hours—nay, weeks and months of idleness in a ship, in which the temptation to resort to unnatural excitement in quest of pleasure, is too strong for minds, that are not well fortified, to resist. This is particularly the case with commanders, who find themselves isolated by their rank, and oppressed with responsibility, in the privacy of their own cabins, and get to make a companion of the bottle, by way of seeking relief from uncomfortable thoughts, and of creating a society of their own. I deem the critical period of a sailor's life, to be the first few years of solitary command."

"How true!—how true!" murmured Mrs. Dutton. "Oh! that cutter—that cruel cutter!"

The truth flashed upon the recollection of Bluewater, at this unguarded, and instantly regretted exclamation. Many years before, when only a captain himself, he had been a member of a court-martial which cashiered a lieutenant of the name of Dutton, for grievous misconduct, while in command of a cutter; the fruits of the bottle. From the first, he thought the name familiar to him; but so many similar things had happened in the course of forty years' service, that this particular incident had been partially lost in the obscurity of time. It was now completely recalled, however; and that, too, with all its attendant circumstances. The recollection served to give the rear-admiral renewed interest in the unhappy wife, and lovely daughter, of the miserable delinquent. He had been applied to, at the time, for his interest in effecting the restoration of the guilty officer, or even to procure for him, the hopeless station he now actually occupied; but he had sternly refused to be a party in placing any man in authority, who was the victim of a propensity that not only disgraced himself, but which, in the peculiar position of a sailor, equally jeoparded the honour of the country, and risked the lives of all around him. He was aware that the last application had been successful, by means of a court influence it was very unusual to exert in cases so insignificant; and, then, he had, for years, lost sight of the criminal and his fortunes. This unexpected revival of his old impressions, caused him to feel like an ancient friend of the wife and daughter; for well could he recall a scene he had with both, in which the struggle between his humanity and his principles had been so violent as actually to reduce him to tears. Mildred had forgotten the name of this particular officer, having been merely a child; but well did Mrs. Dutton remember it, and with fear and trembling had she come that day, to meet him at the Hall. The first look satisfied her that she was forgotten, and she had struggled herself, to bury in oblivion, a scene which was one of the most painful of her life. The unguarded expression, mentioned, entirely changed the state of affairs.

"Mrs. Dutton," said Bluewater, kindly taking a hand of the distressed wife; "I believe we are old friends; if, after what has passed, you will allow me so to consider myself."

"Ah! Admiral Bluewater, my memory needed no admonisher to tell me *that*. Your sympathy and kindness are as grateful to me, now, as they were in that dreadful moment, when we met before."

"And I had the pleasure of seeing this young lady, more than once, on that unpleasant occasion. This accounts for a fancy that has fairly haunted me throughout the day; for, from the instant my eye fell on Miss Mildred, it struck me that the face, and most of all, its expression, was familiar to me. Certainly it is not a countenance, once seen, easily to be forgotten."

"Mildred was then but a child, sir, and your recollection must have been a fancy, indeed, as children of her age seldom make any lasting impression on the mind, particularly in the way of features."

"It is not the features that I recognize, but the expression; and that, I need not tell the young lady's mother, is an expression not so very easily forgotten. I dare say Mr. Wychecombe is ready enough to vouch for the truth of what I say."

"Hark!" exclaimed Mrs. Dutton, who was sensitively alive to any indication of the progress of the debauch. "There is great confusion in the dining-room!—I hope the gentlemen are of one mind as respects this rising in Scotland!"

"If there is a Jacobite among them, he will have a warm time of it; with Sir Wycherly, his nephew, and the vicar—all three of whom are raging lions, in the way of loyalty. There does, indeed, seem something out of the way, for those sounds, I should think, are the feet of servants, running to and fro. If the servants'-hall is in the condition I suspect, it will as much need the aid of the parlour, as the parlour can possibly—"

A tap at the door caused Bluewater to cease speaking; and as Wycherly threw open the entrance, Galleygo appeared on the threshold, by this time reduced to the necessity of holding on by the casings.

"Well, sir," said the rear-admiral, sternly, for he was no longer disposed to trifle with any of the crapulous set; "well, sir, what impertinence has brought you here?"

"No impertinence at all, your honour; we carries none of *that*, in the old Planter. There being no young gentlemen, hereabouts, to report proceedings, I thought I'd just step in and do the duty with my own tongue. We has so many reports in our cabin, that there isn't an officer in the fleet that can make 'em better, as myself, sir."

"There are a hundred who would spend fewer words on any thing. What is your business?"

"Why, sir, just to report one flag struck, and a commander-in-chief on his beam-ends."

"Good God! Nothing has happened to Sir Gervaise—speak, fellow, or I'll have you sent out of this Babel, and off to the ship, though it were midnight."

"It be pretty much that, Admiral Blue; or past six bells; as any one may see by the ship's clock on the great companion ladder; six bells, going well on to seven—"

"Your business, sir! what has happened to Sir Gervaise?" repeated Bluewater, shaking his long fore-finger menacingly, at the steward.

"We are as well, Admiral Blue, as the hour we came over the Planter's side. Sir Jarvy will carry sail with the best on 'em, I'll answer for it, whether the ship floats in old Port Oporto, or in a brewer's vat. Let Sir Jarvy alone for them tricks—he wasn't a young gentleman, for nothing."

"Have a moment's patience, sir," put in Wycherly, "and I will go myself, and ascertain the truth."

"I shall make but another inquiry," continued Admiral Bluewater, as Wycherly left the room.

"Why, d'ye see, your honour, old Sir Wycherly, who is commander-in-chief, along shore here, has capsized in consequence of carrying sail too hard, in company with younger craft; and they're now warping him into dock to be overhauled."

"Is this all!—that was a result to be expected, in such a debauch. You need not have put on so ominous a face, for this, Galleygo."

"No, sir, so I thought, myself; and I only tried to look as melancholy as a young gentleman who is sent below to report a topgallant-mast over the side, or a studding-sail-boom gone in the iron. D'ye remember the time, Admiral Blue, when you thought to luff up on the old Planter's weather-quarter, and get between her and the French ninety on three decks, and how your stu'n-sails went, one a'ter another, just like so many musherrooms breaking in peeling?"

Galleygo, who was apt to draw his images from his two trades, might have talked on an hour, without interruption; for, while he was uttering the above sentence, Wycherly returned, and reported that their host was seriously, even dangerously ill. While doing the honours of his table, he had been seized with a fit, which the vicar, a noted three-bottle man, feared was apoplexy. Mr. Rotherham had bled the patient, who was already a little better, and an express had been sent for a medical man. As a matter of course, the *convives* had left the table, and alarm was frightening the servants into sobriety. At Mrs. Dutton's earnest request, Wycherly immediately left the room again, forcing Galleygo out before him, with a view to get more accurate information concerning the baronet's real situation; both the mother and daughter feeling a real affection for Sir Wycherly; the kind old man having won their hearts by his habitual benevolence, and a constant concern for their welfare.

"*Sic transit gloria mundi*," muttered Admiral Bluewater, as he threw his tall person, in his own careless manner, on a chair, in a dark corner of the room. "This baronet has fallen from his throne, in a moment of seeming prosperity and revelry; why may not another do the same?"

Mrs. Dutton heard the voice, without distinguishing the words, and she felt distressed at the idea that one whom she so much respected and loved, might be judged of harshly, by a man of the rear-admiral's character.

"Sir Wycherly is one of the kindest-hearted men, breathing," she said, a little hurriedly; "and there is not a better landlord in England. Then he is by no means addicted to indulgence at table, more than is customary with gentlemen of his station. His loyalty has, no doubt, carried him this evening farther than was prudent, or than we could have wished."

"I have every disposition to think favourably of our poor host, my dear Mrs. Dutton; and we seamen are not accustomed to judge a *bon vivant* too harshly."

"Ah! Admiral Bluewater, *you*, who have so wide-spread a reputation for sobriety and correct deportment! Well do I remember how I trembled, when I heard your name mentioned as one of the leading members of that dreadful court!"

"You let your recollections dwell too much on these unpleasant subjects, Mrs. Dutton, and I should like to see you setting an example of greater cheerfulness to your sweet daughter. I could not befriend you, *then*, for my oath and my duty were both against it; but, *now*, there exists no possible reason, why I should not; while there does exist almost every possible disposition, why I should. This sweet child interests me in a way I can hardly describe."

Mrs. Dutton was silent and thoughtful. The years of Admiral Bluewater did not absolutely forbid his regarding Mildred's extreme beauty, with the eyes of ordinary admiration; but his language, and most of all, his character, ought to repel the intrusive suspicion. Still Mildred was surpassingly lovely, and men were surpassingly weak in matters of love. Many a hero had passed a youth of self-command and discretion, to consummate some act of exceeding folly, of this very nature, in the decline of life; and bitter experience had taught her to be distrustful. Nevertheless, she could not, at once, bring herself to think ill of one, whose character she had so long respected; and, with all the rear-admiral's directness of manner, there was so much real and feeling delicacy, blended with the breeding of a gentleman-like sailor, that it was not easy to suppose he had any other motives than those he saw fit to avow. Mildred had made many a friend, by a sweetness of countenance, that was even more winning, than her general beauty of face and form was attractive; and why should not this respectable old seaman be of the number.

This train of thought was interrupted by the sudden and unwelcome appearance of Dutton. He had just returned from the bed-side of Sir Wycherly, and now came to seek his wife and daughter, to bid them prepare to enter the chariot, which was in waiting to convey them home. The miserable man was not intoxicated, in the sense which deprives a man of the use of speech and limbs; but he had drunk quite enough to awaken the demon within him, and to lay bare the secrets of his true character. If any thing, his nerves were better strung than common; but the wine had stirred up all the energies of a being, whose resolutions seldom took the direction of correct feeling, or of right doing. The darkness of the room, and a slight confusion which nevertheless existed in his brain, prevented him from noticing the person of his superior, seated, as the latter was, in the dark corner; and he believed himself once more alone with those who were so completely dependent on his mercy, and who had so long been the subjects of his brutality and tyranny.

"I hope Sir Wycherly is better, Dutton," the wife commenced, fearful that her husband might expose himself and her, before he was aware of the presence in which he stood. "Admiral Bluewater is as anxious, as we are ourselves, to know his real state."

"Ay, you women are all pity and feeling for baronets and rear-admirals," answered Dutton, throwing himself rudely into a chair, with his back towards the stranger, in an attitude completely to exclude the latter from his view; "while a husband, or father, might die a hundred deaths, and not draw a look of pity from your beautiful eyes, or a kind word from your devilish tongues."

"Neither Mildred nor I, merit this from *you*, Dutton!"

"No, you're both perfection; like mother, like child. Haven't I been, fifty times, at death's door, with this very complaint of Sir Wycherly's, and did either of you ever send for an apothecary, even?"

"You have been occasionally indisposed, Dutton, but never apoplectic; and we have always thought a little sleep would restore you; as, indeed, it always has."

"What business had you to *think*? Surgeons think, and medical men, and it was your duty to send for the nearest professional man, to look after one you're bound both to honour and obey. You are your own mistress, Martha, I do suppose, in a certain degree; and what can't be cured must be endured; but Mildred is my child; and I'll have her respect and love, if I break both your hearts in order to get at them."

"A pious daughter always respects her parent, Dutton," said the wife, trembling from head to foot; "but love must come willingly, or, it will not come at all."

"We'll see as to that, Mrs. Martha Dutton; we'll see as to that. Come hither, Mildred; I have a word to say to you, which may as well be said at once."

Mildred, trembling like her mother, drew near; but with a feeling of filial piety, that no harshness could entirely smother, she felt anxious to prevent the father from further exposing himself, in the presence of Admiral Bluewater. With this view, then, and with this view only, she summoned firmness enough to speak.

"Father," she said, "had we not better defer our family matters, until we are alone?"

Under ordinary circumstances, Bluewater would not have waited for so palpable a hint, for he would have retired on the first appearance of any thing so disagreeable as a misunderstanding between man and wife. But, an ungovernable interest in the lovely girl, who stood trembling at her father's knee, caused him to forget his habitual delicacy of feeling, and to overlook what might perhaps be termed almost a law of society. Instead of moving, therefore, as Mildred had both hoped and expected, he remained motionless in his seat. Dutton's mind was too obtuse to comprehend his daughter's allusions, in the absence, of ocular evidence of a stranger's presence, and his wrath was too much excited to permit him to think much of any thing but his own causes of indignation.

"Stand more in front of me, Mildred," he answered, angrily. "More before my face, as becomes one who don't know her duty to her parent, and needs be taught it."

"Oh! Dutton," exclaimed the afflicted wife; "do not—do not—accuse Mildred of being undutiful! You know not what you say—know not her obliga—you cannot know her *heart*, or you would not use these cruel imputations!"

"Silence, Mrs. Martha Dutton—my business is not with *you*, at present, but with this young lady, to whom, I hope, I may presume to speak a little plainly, as she is my own child. Silence, then, Mrs. Martha Dutton. If my memory is not treacherous, you once stood up before God's altar with me, and there vow'd to love, honour, and *obey*. Yes, that was the word; *obey*, Mrs. Martha Dutton."

"And what did *you* promise, at the same time, Frank?" exclaimed the wife, from whose bruised spirit this implied accusation was torn in an agony of mental suffering.

"Nothing but what I have honestly and manfully performed. I promised to provide for you; to give you food and raiment; to let you hear my name, and stand before the world in the honourable character of honest Frank Dutton's wife."

"Honourable!" murmured the wife, loud enough to be heard by both the Admiral and Mildred, and yet in a tone so smothered, as to elude the obtuse sense of hearing, that long excess had left her husband. When this expressive word had broken out of her very heart, however, she succeeded in suppressing her voice, and sinking into a chair, concealed her face in her hands, in silence.

"Mildred, come hither," resumed the brutalized parent. "*You* are my daughter, and whatever others have promised at the altar, and forgotten, a law of nature teaches you to obey me. You have two admirers, either of whom you ought to be glad to secure, though there is a great preference between them—"

"Father!" exclaimed Mildred, every feeling of her sensitive nature revolting at this coarse allusion to a connection, and to sentiments, that she was accustomed to view as among the most sacred and private of her moral being. "Surely, you cannot mean what you say!"

"Like mother, like child! Let but disobedience and disrespect get possession of a wife, and they are certain to run through a whole family, even though there were a dozen children! Harkee, Miss Mildred, it is *you* who don't happen to know what you say, while I understand myself as well as most parents. Your mother would never acquaint you with what I feel it a duty to put plainly before your judgment; and, therefore, I expect you to listen as becomes a dutiful and affectionate child. You can secure either of these young Wychecombes, and either of them would be a good match for a poor, disgraced, sailing-master's daughter."

"Father, I shall sink through the floor, if you say another word, in this cruel manner!"

"No, dear; you'll neither sink nor swim, unless it be by making a bad, or a good choice. Mr. Thomas Wychecombe is Sir Wycherly's heir, and must be the next baronet, and possessor of this estate. Of course he is much the best thing, and you ought to give him a preference."

"Dutton, *can* you, as a father and a Christian, give such heartless counsel to your own child!" exclaimed Mrs. Dutton, inexpressibly shocked at the want of principle, as well as at the want of feeling, discovered in her husband's advice.

"Mrs. Martha Dutton, I can; and believe the counsel to be any thing but heartless, too. Do you wish your daughter to be the wife of a miserable signal-station keeper, when she may become Lady Wychecombe, with a little prudent management, and the mistress of this capital old house, and noble estate?"

"Father—father," interrupted Mildred, soothingly, though ready to sink with shame at the idea of Admiral Bluewater's being an auditor of such a conversation; "you forget yourself, and overlook my wishes. There is little probability of Mr. Thomas Wychecombe's ever thinking of me as a wife— or, indeed of anyone else's entertaining such thoughts."

"That will turn out, as you manage matters, Milly. Mr. Thomas Wychecombe does not think of you as a *wife*, quite likely, just at this moment; but the largest whales are taken by means of very small lines, when the last are properly handled. This young lieutenant would have you to-morrow; though a more silly thing than for you two to marry, could not well be hit upon. He is only a lieutenant; and though his name is so good a one, it does not appear that he has any particular right to it."

"And yet, Dutton, you were only a lieutenant when *you* married, and your name was *nothing* in the way of interest, or preferment," observed the mother, anxious to interpose some new feeling between her daughter, and the cruel inference left by the former part of her husband's speech. "We *then* thought all lay bright before us!"

"And so all would lie to this hour, Mrs. Dutton, but for that one silly act of mine. A man with the charges of a family on him, little pay, and no fortune, is driven to a thousand follies to hide his misery. You do not strengthen your case by reminding me of *that* imprudence. But, Mildred, I do not tell you to cut adrift this young Virginian, for he may he of use in more ways than one. In the first place, you can play him off against Mr. Thomas Wychecombe; and, in the second place, a lieutenant is likely, one day, to be a captain; and the wife of a captain in His Majesty's navy, is no disreputable birth. I advise you, girl, to use this youngster as a bait to catch the heir with; and, failing a good bite, to take up with the lad himself."

This was said dogmatically, but with a coarseness of manner that fully corresponded with the looseness of the principles, and the utter want of delicacy of feeling that alone could prompt such advice. Mrs. Dutton fairly groaned, as she listened to her husband, for never before had he so completely thrown aside the thin mask of decency that he ordinarily wore; but Mildred, unable to control the burst of wild emotion that came over her, broke away from the place she occupied at her father's knee, and, as if blindly seeking protection in any asylum that she fancied safe, found herself sobbing, as if her heart would break, in Admiral Bluewater's arms.

Dutton followed the ungovernable, impulsive movement, with his eye, and for the first time he became aware in whose presence he had been exposing his native baseness. Wine had not so far the mastery of him, as to blind him to all the consequences, though it did stimulate him to a point that enabled him to face the momentary mortification of his situation.

"I beg a thousand pardons, sir," he said, rising, and bowing low to his superior; "I was totally ignorant that I had the honour to be in the company of Admiral Bluewater—Admiral Blue, I find Jack calls you, sir; ha-ha-ha—a familiarity which is a true sign of love and respect. I never knew a captain, or a flag-officer, that got a regular, expressive ship's name, that he wasn't the delight of the whole service. Yes, sir; I find the people call Sir Gervaise, Little Jarvy, and yourself, Admiral Blue—ha-ha-ha—an infallible sign of merit in the superior, and of love in the men."

"I ought to apologize, Mr. Dutton, for making one, so unexpectedly to myself, in a family council," returned the rear-admiral. "As for the men, they are no great philosophers, though tolerable judges of when they are well commanded, and well treated.—But, the hour is late, and it was my intention to sleep in my own ship, to-night. The coach of Sir Wycherly has been ordered to carry me to the landing, and I hope to have your permission to see these ladies home in it."

The answer of Dutton was given with perfect self-possession, and in a manner to show that he knew how to exercise the courtesies of life, or to receive them, when in the humour.

"It is an honour, sir, they will not think of declining, if my wishes are consulted," he said. "Come, Milly, foolish girl, dry your tears, and smile on Admiral Bluewater, for his condescension. Young women, sir, hardly know how to take a joke; and our ship's humours are sometimes a little strong for them. I tell my dear wife, sometimes—'Wife,' I say, 'His Majesty can't have stout-hearted and stout-handed seamen, and the women poets and die-away swains, and all in the same individual,' says I. Mrs. Dutton understands me, sir; and so does little Milly; who is an excellent girl in the main; though a little addicted to using the eye-pumps, as we have it aboard ship, sir."

"And, now, Mr. Dutton, it being understood that I am to see the ladies home, will you do me the favour to inquire after the condition of Sir Wycherly. One would not wish to quit his hospitable roof, in uncertainty as to his actual situation."

Dutton was duly sensible of an awkwardness in the presence of his superior, and he gladly profited by this commission to quit the room; walking more steadily than if he had not been drinking.

All this time, Mildred hung on Admiral Bluewater's shoulder, weeping, and unwilling to quit a place that seemed to her, in her fearful agitation, a sort of sanctuary.

"Mrs. Dutton," said Bluewater, first kissing the cheek of his lovely burthen, in a manner so parental, that the most sensitive delicacy could not have taken the alarm; "you will succeed better than myself, in quieting the feelings of this little trembler. I need hardly say that if I have accidentally overheard more than I ought, it is as much a secret with me, as it would be with your own brother. The characters of all cannot be affected by the mistaken and excited calculations of one; and this occasion has served to make me better acquainted with you, and your admirable daughter, than I might otherwise have been, by means of years of ordinary intercourse."

"Oh! Admiral Bluewater, do not judge him *too* harshly! He has been too long at that fatal table, which I fear has destroyed poor dear Sir Wycherly, and knew not what he said. Never before have I seen him in such a fearful humour, or in the least disposed to trifle with, or to wound the feelings of this sweet child!"

"Her extreme agitation is a proof of this, my good madam, and shows all you can wish to say. View me as your sincere friend, and place every reliance on my discretion."

The wounded mother listened with gratitude, and Mildred withdrew from her extraordinary situation, wondering by what species of infatuation she could have been led to adopt it.

CHAPTER IX.

——"Ah, Montague,
If thou be there, sweet brother, take my hand,
And with thy lips keep in my soul awhile!
Thou lov'st me not; for, brother, if thou didst,
Thy tears would wash this cold congealed blood
That glues my lips, and will not let me speak.
Come quickly, Montague, or I am dead."

KING HENRY VI.

Sir Wycherly had actually been seized with a fit of apoplexy. It was the first serious disease he had experienced in a long life of health and prosperity; and the sight of their condescending, good-humored, and indulgent master, in a plight so miserable, had a surprising effect on the heated brains of all the household. Mr. Rotherham, a good three-bottle man, on emergency, had learned to bleed, and fortunately the vein he struck, as his patient still lay on the floor, where he had fallen, sent out a stream that had the effect not only to restore the baronet to life, but, in a great measure, to consciousness. Sir Wycherly was not a *hard* drinker, like Dutton; but he was a *fair* drinker, like Mr. Rotherham, and most of the beneficed clergy of that day. Want of exercise, as he grew older, had as much influence in producing his attack as excess of wine; and there were already, strong hopes of his surviving it, aided as he was, by a good constitution. The apothecary had reached the Hall, within five minutes after the attack, having luckily been prescribing to the gardener; and the physician and surgeon of the family were both expected in the course of the morning.

Sir Gervaise Oakes had been acquainted with the state of his host, by his own valet, as soon as it was known in the servants'-hall, and being a man of action, he did not hesitate to proceed at once to the chamber of the sick, to offer his own aid, in the absence of that which might be better. At the door of the chamber, he met Atwood, who had been summoned from his pen, and they entered together, the vice-admiral feeling for a lancet in his pocket, for he, too, had acquired the art of the blood-letter. They now learned the actual state of things.

"Where is Bluewater?" demanded Sir Gervaise, after regarding his host a moment with commiseration and concern. "I hope he has not yet left the house."

"He is still here, Sir Gervaise, but I should think on the point of quitting us. I heard him say, that, notwithstanding all Sir Wycherly's kind plans to detain him, he intended to sleep in his own ship."

"That I've never doubted, though I've affected to believe otherwise. Go to him, Atwood, and say I beg he will pull within hail of the Plantagenet, as he goes off, and desire Mr. Magrath to come ashore, as soon as possible. There shall be a conveyance at the landing to bring him here; and he may order his own surgeon to come also, if it be agreeable to himself."

With these instructions the secretary left the room; while Sir Gervaise turned to Tom Wychecombe, and said a few of the words customary on such melancholy occasions.

"I think there is hope, sir," he added, "yes, sir, I think there is hope; though your honoured relative is no longer young—still, this early bleeding has been a great thing; and if we can gain a little time for poor Sir Wycherly, our efforts will not be thrown away. Sudden death is awful, sir, and few of us are prepared for it, either in mind, or affairs. We sailors have to hold our lives in our hands, it is true, but then it is for king and country; and we hope for mercy on all who fall in the discharge of their duties. For my part, I am never unprovided with a will, and that disposes of all the interests of this world, while I humbly trust in the Great Mediator, for the hereafter. I hope Sir Wycherly is equally provident as to his worldly affairs?"

"No doubt my dear uncle could wish to leave certain trifling memorials behind him to a few of his intimates," returned Tom, with a dejected countenance; "but he has not been without a will, I believe, for some time; and I presume you will agree with me in thinking he is not in a condition to make one, now, were he unprovided in that way?"

"Perhaps not exactly at this moment, though a rally might afford an opportunity. The estate is entailed, I think Mr. Dutton told me, at dinner."

"It is, Sir Gervaise, and I am the unworthy individual who is to profit by it, according to the common notions of men, though Heaven knows I shall consider it any thing but a gain; still, I am the unworthy individual who is to be benefited by my uncle's death."

"Your father was the baronet's next brother?" observed Sir Gervaise, casually, a shade of distrust passing athwart his mind, though coming from what source, or directed to what point, he was himself totally unable to say. "Mr. Baron Wychecombe, I believe, was your parent?"

"He was, Sir Gervaise, and a most tender and indulgent father, I ever found him. He left me his earnings, some seven hundred a year, and I am sure the death of Sir Wycherly is as far from my necessities, as it is from my wishes."

"Of course you will succeed to the baronetcy, as well as to the estate?" mechanically asked Sir Gervaise, led on by the supererogatory expressions of

Tom, himself, rather than by a vulgar curiosity, to ask questions that, under other circumstances, he might have thought improper.

"Of course, sir. My father was the only surviving brother of Sir Wycherly; the only one who ever married; and I am *his* eldest child. Since this melancholy event has occurred, it is quite fortunate that I lately obtained this certificate of the marriage of my parents—is it not, sir?"

Here Tom drew from his pocket a soiled piece of paper, which professed to be a certificate of the marriage of Thomas Wychecombe, barrister, with Martha Dodd, spinster, &c. &c. The document was duly signed by the rector of a parish church in Westminster, and bore a date sufficiently old to establish the legitimacy of the person who held it. This extraordinary precaution produced the very natural effect of increasing the distrust of the vice-admiral, and, in a slight degree, of giving it a direction.

"You go well armed, sir," observed Sir Gervaise, drily. "Is it your intention, when you succeed, to carry the patent of the baronetcy, and the title-deeds, in your pocket?"

"Ah! I perceive my having this document strikes you as odd, Sir Gervaise, but it can be easily explained. There was a wide difference in rank between my parents, and some ill-disposed persons have presumed so far to reflect on the character of my mother, as to assert she was not married at all."

"In which case, sir, you would do well to cut off half-a-dozen of their ears."

"The law is not to be appeased in that way, Sir Gervaise. My dear parent used to inculcate on me the necessity of doing every thing according to law; and I endeavour to remember his precepts. He avowed his marriage on his death-bed, made all due atonement to my respected and injured mother, and informed me in whose hands I should find this very certificate; I only obtained it this morning, which fact will account for its being in my pocket, at this melancholy and unexpected crisis, in my beloved uncle's constitution."

The latter part of Tom's declaration was true enough; for, after having made all the necessary inquiries, and obtained the hand-writing of a clergyman who was long since dead, he had actually forged the certificate that day, on a piece of soiled paper, that bore the water-mark of 1720. His language, however, contributed to alienate the confidence of his listener; Sir Gervaise being a man who was so much accustomed to directness and fair-dealing, himself, as to feel disgust at any thing that had the semblance of cant or hypocrisy. Nevertheless, he had his own motives for pursuing the subject; the presence of neither at the bed-side of the sufferer, being just then necessary.

"And this Mr. Wycherly Wychecombe," he said; "he who has so much distinguished himself of late; your uncle's namesake;—is it true that he is not allied to your family?"

"Not in the least, Sir Gervaise," answered Tom, with one of his sinister smiles. "He is only a Virginian, you know, sir, and cannot well belong to us. I have heard my uncle say, often, that the young gentleman must be descended from an old servant of his father's, who was transported for stealing silver out of a shop on Ludgate Hill, and who was arrested for passing himself off, as one of the Wychecombe family. They tell me, Sir Gervaise, that the colonies are pretty much made of persons descended from that sort of ancestors?"

"I cannot say that I have found it so; though, when I commanded a frigate, I served several years on the North American station. The larger portion of the Americans, like much the larger portion of the English, are humble labourers, established in a remote colony, where civilization is not far advanced, wants are many, and means few; but, in the way of character, I am not certain that they are not quite on a level with those they left behind them; and, as to the gentry of the colonies, I have seen many men of the best blood of the mother country among them;—younger sons, and their descendants, as a matter of course, but of an honourable and respected ancestry."

"Well, sir, this surprises me; and it is not the general opinion, I am persuaded! Certainly, it is not the fact as respects the gentleman—stranger, I might call him, for stranger he is at Wychecombe—who has not the least right to pretend to belong to us."

"Did you ever know him to lay claim to that honour, sir?"

"Not directly, Sir Gervaise; though I am told he has made many hints to that effect, since he landed here to be cured of his wound. It would have been better had he presented his rights to the landlord, than to present them to the tenants, I think you will allow, as a man of honour, yourself, Sir Gervaise?"

"I can approve of nothing clandestine in matters that require open and fair dealing, Mr. Thomas Wychecombe. But I ought to apologize for thus dwelling on your family affairs, which concern me only as I feel an interest in the wishes and happiness of my new acquaintance, my excellent host."

"Sir Wycherly has property in the funds that is not entailed—quite £1000 a year, beyond the estates—and I know he has left a will," continued Tom; who, with the short-sightedness of a rogue, flattered himself with having made a favourable impression on his companion, and who was desirous of making him useful to himself, in an emergency that he felt satisfied must terminate in the speedy death of his uncle. "Yes, a good £1000 a year, in the fives; money saved from his rents, in a long life. This will probably has some provision in favour of my younger brothers; and perhaps of this namesake of his,"—Tom was well aware that it devised every shilling, real and personal, to himself;—"for a kinder heart does not exist on earth. In fact, this will my uncle put in my possession, as heir at law, feeling it due to my pretensions, I suppose; but I have never presumed to look into it."

Here was another instance of excessive finesse, in which Tom awakened suspicion by his very efforts to allay it. It seemed highly improbable to Sir Gervaise, that a man like the nephew could long possess his uncle's will, and feel no desire to ascertain its contents. The language of the young man was an indirect admission, that he might have examined the will if he would; and the admiral felt disposed to suspect that what he might thus readily have done, he actually had done. The dialogue, however, terminated here; Dutton, just at that moment, entering the room on the errand on which he had been sent by Admiral Bluewater, and Tom joining his old acquaintance, as soon as the latter made his appearance. Sir Gervaise Oakes was too much concerned for the condition of his host, and had too many cares of his own, to think deeply or long on what had just passed between himself and Tom Wychecombe. Had they separated that night, what had been said, and the unfavourable impressions it had made, would have been soon forgotten; but circumstances subsequently conspired to recall the whole to his mind, of which the consequences will be related in the course of our narrative.

Dutton appeared to be a little shocked as he gazed upon the pallid features of Sir Wycherly, and he was not sorry when Tom led him aside, and began to speak confidentially of the future, and of the probable speedy death of his uncle. Had there been one present, gifted with the power of reading the thoughts and motives of men, a deep disgust of human frailties must have come over him, as these two impure spirits betrayed to him their cupidity and cunning. Outwardly, they were friends mourning over a mutual probable loss; while inwardly, Dutton was endeavouring to obtain such a hold of his companion's confidence, as might pave the way to his own future preferment to the high and unhoped-for station of a rich baronet's father-in-law; while Tom thought only of so far mystifying the master, as to make use of him, on an emergency, as a witness to establish his own claims. The manner in which he endeavoured to effect his object, however, must be left to the imagination of the reader, as we have matters of greater moment to record at this particular juncture.

From the time Sir Wycherly was laid on his bed, Mr. Rotherham had been seated at the sick man's side, watching the course of his attack, and ready to interpret any of the patient's feebly and indistinctly expressed wishes. We say indistinctly, because the baronet's speech was slightly affected with that species of paralysis which reduces the faculty to the state that is vulgarly called thick-tongued. Although a three-bottle man, Mr. Rotherham was far from being without his devout feelings, on occasions, discharging all the clerical functions with as much unction as the habits of the country, and the opinions of the day, ordinarily exacted of divines. He had even volunteered to read the prayers for the sick, as soon as he perceived that the patient's recollection had returned; but this kind offer had been declined by Sir Wycherly, under the clearer views of fitness, that the near approach of death is apt to give, and which views left a certain consciousness that the party assembled was not in the best possible condition for that sacred office. Sir Wycherly revived so much, at last, as to look about him with increasing consciousness; and, at length, his eyes passed slowly over the room, scanning each person singly, and with marked deliberation.

"I know you all—now," said the kind-hearted baronet, though always speaking thick, and with a little difficulty; "am sorry to give—much trouble. I have—little time to spare."

"I hope not, Sir Wycherly," put in the vicar, in a consolatory manner; "you have had a sharp attack, but then there is a good constitution to withstand it."

"My time—short—feel it here," rejoined the patient, passing his hand over his forehead.

"Note that, Dutton," whispered Tom Wycherly. "My poor uncle intimates himself that his mind is a little shaken. Under such circumstances, it would be cruel to let him injure himself with business."

"It cannot be done *legally*, Mr. Thomas—I should think Admiral Oakes would interfere to prevent it."

"Rotherham," continued the patient, "I will—settle with—world; then, give—thoughts—to God. Have we—guests—the house?—Men of family—character?"

"Certainly, Sir Wycherly; Admiral Oakes is in the room, even; and Admiral Bluewater, is, I believe, still in the house. You invited both to pass the night with you."

"I remember it—now; my mind—still—confused,"—here Tom Wychecombe again nudged the master—"Sir Gervaise Oakes—an Admiral—ancient baronet—man of high honour. Admiral Bluewater, too—relative—Lord Bluewater; gentleman—universal esteem. You, too, Rotherham; wish my poor brother James—St. James—used to call him—had been living;—you—good neighbour—Rotherham."

"Can I do any thing to prove it, my dear Sir Wycherly? Nothing would make me happier than to know, and to comply with, all your wishes, at a moment so important!"

"Let all quit—room—but yourself—head feels worse—I cannot delay—"

"'Tis cruel to distress my beloved uncle with business, or conversation, in his present state," interposed Tom Wychecombe, with emphasis, and, in a slight degree, with authority.

All not only felt the truth of this, but all felt that the speaker, by his consanguinity, had a clear right to interfere, in the manner he had. Still Sir Gervaise Oakes had great reluctance in yielding to this remonstrance; for, to the distrust he had imbibed of Tom Wychecombe, was added an impression that his host wished to reveal something of interest, in connection with his new favourite, the lieutenant. He felt compelled, notwithstanding, to defer to the acknowledged nephew's better claims, and he refrained from interfering. Fortunately, Sir Wycherly was yet in a state to enforce his own wishes.

"Let all quit—room," he repeated, in a voice that was startling by its unexpected firmness, and equally unexpected distinctness. "All but Sir Gervaise Oakes—Admiral Bluewater—Mr. Rotherham, Gentlemen—favour to remain—rest depart."

Accustomed to obey their master's orders, more especially when given in a tone so decided, the domestics quitted the room, accompanied by Dutton; but Tom Wychecombe saw fit to remain, as if his presence were to be a matter of course.

"Do me—favour—withdraw,—Mr. Wychecombe," resumed the baronet, after fixing his gaze on his nephew for some time, as if expecting him to retire without this request.

"My beloved uncle, it is I—Thomas, your own brother's son—your next of kin—waiting anxiously by your respected bed-side. Do not—do not—confound me with strangers. Such a forgetfulness would break my heart!"

"Forgive me, nephew—but I wish—alone with these gentle——head—getting—confused—"

"You see how it is, Sir Gervaise Oakes—you see how it is, Mr. Rotherham. Ah! there goes the coach that is to take Admiral Bluewater to his boat. My uncle wished for three witnesses to something, and I can remain as one of the three."

"Is it your pleasure, Sir Wycherly, to wish to see us alone?" asked Sir Gervaise, in a manner that showed authority would be exercised to enforce his request, should the uncle still desire the absence of his nephew.

A sign from the sick man indicated the affirmative, and that in a manner too decided to admit of mistake.

"You perceive, Mr. Wychecombe, what are your uncle's wishes," observed Sir Gervaise, very much in the way that a well-bred superior intimates to an inferior the compliance he expects; "I trust his desire will not be disregarded, at a moment like this."

"I am Sir Wycherly Wychecombe's next of kin," said Tom, in a slightly bullying tone; "and no one has the same right as a relative, and, I may say, his heir, to be at his bed-side."

"That depends on the pleasure of Sir Wycherly Wychecombe himself, sir. *He* is master here; and, having done me the honour to invite me under his roof as a guest, and, now, having requested to see me alone, with others he has expressly named—one of whom you are not—I shall conceive it my duty to see his wishes obeyed."

This was said in the firm, quiet way, that the habit of command had imparted to Sir Gervaise's manner; and Tom began to see it might be dangerous to resist. It was important, too, that one of the vice-admiral's character and station should have naught to say against him, in the event of any future controversy; and, making a few professions of respect, and of his desire to please his uncle, Tom quitted the room.

A gleam of satisfaction shot over the sick man's countenance, as his nephew disappeared; and then his eye turned slowly towards the faces of those who remained.

"Bluewater," he said, the thickness of his speech, and the general difficulty of utterance, seeming to increase; "the rear-admiral—I want all—respectable—witnesses in the house."

"My friend has left us, I understand," returned Sir Gervaise, "insisting on his habit of never sleeping out of his ship; but Atwood must soon be back; I hope *he* will answer!"

A sign of assent was given; and, then, there was the pause of a minute, or two, ere the secretary made his appearance. As soon, however, as he had returned, the three collected around the baronet's bed, not without some of the weakness which men are supposed to have inherited from their common mother Eve, in connection with the motive for this singular proceeding of the baronet.

"Sir Gervaise—Rotherham—Mr. Atwood," slowly repeated the patient, his eye passing from the face of one to that of another, as he uttered the name of each; "three witnesses—that will do—Thomas said—must have *three*—three *good* names."

"What can we do to serve you, Sir Wycherly?" inquired the admiral, with real interest. "You have only to name your requests, to have them faithfully attended to."

"Old Sir Michael Wychecombe, Kt.—two wives—Margery and Joan. Two wives—two sons—half-blood—Thomas, James, Charles, and Gregory, *whole*—Sir Reginald Wychecombe, *half*. Understand—hope—gentlemen?"

"This is not being very clear, certainly," whispered Sir Gervaise; "but, perhaps by getting hold of the other end of the rope, we may under-run it, as we sailors say, and come at the meaning—we will let the poor man proceed, therefore. Quite plain, my dear sir, and what have you next to tell us. You left off without saying only *half* about Sir Reginald."

"Half-blood; only *half*—Tom and the rest, whole. Sir Reginald, no *nullius*—young Tom, a *nullius*."

"A *nullius*, Mr. Rotherham! You understand Latin, sir; what can a *nullius*, mean? No such rope in the ship, hey! Atwood?"

"*Nullius*, or *nullius*, as it ought sometimes to be pronounced, is the genitive case, singular, of the pronoun *nullus; nullus, nulla, nullum*; which means, 'no man,' 'no woman,' 'no thing.' *Nullius* means, 'of no man,' 'of no woman,' 'of no thing.'"

The vicar gave this explanation, much in the way a pedagogue would have explained the matter to a class.

"Ay-ay—any school-boy could have told that, which is the first form learning. But what the devil can 'Nom. *nullus, nulla, nullum*; Gen. *nullius, nullius, nullius*,' have to do with Mr. Thomas Wychecombe, the nephew and heir of the present baronet?"

"That is more than I can inform you, Sir Gervaise," answered the vicar, stiffly; "but, for the Latin, I will take upon myself to answer, that it is good."

Sir Gervaise was too-well bred to laugh, but he found it difficult to suppress a smile.

"Well, Sir Wycherly," resumed the vice-admiral, "this is quite plain—Sir Reginald is only *half*, while your nephew Tom, and the rest, are *whole*—Margery and Joan, and all that. Any thing more to tell us, my dear sir?"

"Tom *not* whole—*nullus*, I wish to say. Sir Reginald *half*—no *nullus*."

"This is like being at sea a week, without getting a sight of the sun! I am all adrift, now, gentlemen."

"Sir Wycherly does not attend to his cases," put in Atwood, drily. "At one time, he is in the *genitive*, and then he gets back to the *nominative*, which is leaving us in the *vocative*"

"Come—come—Atwood, none of your gun-room wit, on an occasion so solemn as this. My dear Sir Wycherly, have you any thing more to tell us? I believe we perfectly understand you, now. Tom is not *whole*—you wish to say *nullus*, and not to say *nullius*. Sir Reginald is only *half*, but he is no *nullus*."

"Yes, sir—that is it," returned the old man, smiling. "*Half*, but no *nullus*. Change my mind—seen too much of the other, lately—Tom, my nephew— want to make *him* my heir."

"This is getting clearer, out of all question. You wish to make your nephew, Tom, your heir. But the law does that already, does it not my dear sir? Mr. Baron Wychecombe was the next brother of the baronet; was he not, Mr. Rotherham?"

"So I have always understood, sir; and Mr. Thomas Wychecombe must be the heir at law."

"No—no—*nullus*—*nullus*," repeated Sir Wycherly, with so much eagerness as to make his voice nearly indistinct; "Sir Reginald—Sir Reginald—Sir Reginald."

"And pray, Mr. Rotherham, who may this Sir Reginald be? Some old baronet of the family, I presume."

"Not at all, sir; it is Sir Reginald Wychecombe of Wychecombe-Regis, Herts; a baronet of Queen Anne's time, and a descendant from a cadet of this family, I am told."

"This is getting on soundings—I had taken it into my head this Sir Reginald was some old fellow of the reign of one of the Plantagenets. Well, Sir Wycherly, do you wish us to send an express into Hertfordshire, in quest of Sir Reginald Wychecombe, who is quite likely your executor? Do not give yourself the pain to speak; a sign will answer."

Sir Wycherly seemed struck with the suggestion, which, the reader will readily understand, was far from being his real meaning; and then he smiled, and nodded his head in approbation.

Sir Gervaise, with the promptitude of a man of business, turned to the table where the vicar had written notes to the medical men, and dictated a short letter to his secretary. This letter he signed, and in five minutes Atwood left the room, to order it to be immediately forwarded by express. When this was done, the admiral rubbed his hands, in satisfaction, like a man who felt he had got himself cleverly out of a knotty difficulty.

"I don't see, after all, Mr. Rotherham," he observed to the vicar, as they stood together, in a corner of the room, waiting the return of the secretary; "what he lugged in that school-boy Latin for—*nullus, nulla, nullum*! Can you possibly explain *that*?"

"Not unless it was Sir Wycherly's desire to say, that Sir Reginald, being descended from a younger son, was nobody—as yet, had no woman—and I believe he is not married—and was poor, or had 'no *thing*.'"

"And is Sir Wycherly such a desperate scholar, that he would express himself in this hieroglyphical manner, on what I fear will prove to be his death-bed?"

"Why, Sir Gervaise, Sir Wycherly was educated like all other young gentlemen, but has forgotten most of his classics, in the course of a long life of ease and affluence. Is it not probable, now, that his recollection has returned to him suddenly, in consequence of this affection of the head? I think I have read of some curious instances of these reviving memories, on a death-bed, or after a fit of sickness."

"Ay, that you may have done!" exclaimed Sir Gervaise, smiling; "and poor, good Sir Wycherly, must have begun afresh, at the very place where he left off. But here is Atwood, again."

After a short consultation, the three chosen witnesses returned to the bed-side, the admiral being spokesman.

"The express will be off in ten minutes. Sir Wycherly," he said; "and you may hope to see your relative, in the course of the next two or three days."

"Too late—too late," murmured the patient, who had an inward consciousness of his true situation; "too late—turn the will round—Sir Reginald, Tom;—Tom, Sir Reginald. Turn the will round."

"Turn the will round!—this is very explicit, gentlemen, to those who can understand it. Sir Reginald, Tom;—Tom, Sir Reginald. At all events, it is clear that his mind is dwelling on the disposition of his property, since he speaks of wills. Atwood, make a note of these words, that there need be no mistake. I wonder he has said nothing of our brave young lieutenant, his namesake. There can be no harm, Mr. Rotherham, in just mentioning that fine fellow to him, in a moment like this?"

"I see none, sir. It is *our* duty to remind the sick of *their* duties."

"Do you not wish to see your young namesake, Lieutenant *Wycherly* Wychecombe, Sir Wycherly?" asked the admiral; sufficiently emphasizing the

Christian name. "He must be in the house, and I dare say would be happy to obey your wishes."

"I hope he is well, sir—fine young gentleman—honour to the name, sir."

"Quite true, Sir Wycherly; and an honour to the *nation*, too."

"Didn't know Virginia was a *nation*—so much the better—fine young *Virginian*, sir."

"Of your *family*, no doubt, Sir Wycherly, as well as of your name," added the admiral, who secretly suspected the young sailor of being a son of the baronet, notwithstanding all he had heard to the contrary. "An exceedingly fine young man, and an honour to any house in England!"

"I suppose they *have* houses in Virginia—bad climate; houses necessary. No relative, sir;—probably a *nullus*. Many Wychecombes, *nulluses*. Tom, a *nullus*—this young gentleman, a *nullus*—Wychecombes of Surrey, all *nulluses*—Sir Reginald no *nullus*; but a *half*—Thomas, James, Charles, and Gregory, all *whole*. My brother, Baron Wychecombe, told me—before died."

"*Whole what*, Sir Wycherly?" asked the admiral, a little vexed at the obscurity of the other's language.

"Blood—*whole blood*, sir. Capital law, Sir Gervaise; had it from the baron—first hand."

Now, one of the peculiarities of England is, that, in the division of labour, few know any thing material about the law, except the professional men. Even their knowledge is divided and sub-divided, in a way that makes a very fair division of profit. Thus the conveyancer is not a barrister; the barrister is not an attorney; and the chancery practitioner would be an unsafe adviser for one of the purely law courts. That particular provision of the common law, which Baron Wychecombe had mentioned to his brother, as the rule of the *half-blood*, has been set aside, or modified, by statute, within the last ten years; but few English laymen would be at all likely to know of such a law of descent even when it existed; for while it did violence to every natural sentiment of right, it lay hidden in the secrets of the profession. Were a case stated to a thousand intelligent Englishmen, who had not read law, in which it was laid down that brothers, by different mothers, though equally sons of the founder of the estate, could not take from each other, unless by devise or entail, the probability is that quite nine in ten would deny the existence of any rule so absurd; and this, too, under the influence of feelings that were creditable to their sense of natural justice. Nevertheless, such was one of the important provisions of the "perfection of reason," until the recent reforms in English law; and it has struck us as surprising, that an ingenious writer of fiction, who has recently charmed his readers with a tale, the interest of which turns principally on the vicissitudes of practice, did not bethink him of this peculiar feature of his country's laws; inasmuch as it would have supplied mystery sufficient for a dozen ordinary romances, and improbabilities enough for a hundred. That Sir Gervaise and his companions should be ignorant of the "law of the half-blood," is, consequently, very much a matter of course; and no one ought to be surprised that the worthy baronet's repeated allusions to the "whole," and the "half," were absolutely enigmas, which neither had the knowledge necessary to explain.

"What *can* the poor fellow mean?" demanded the admiral, more concerned than he remembered ever before to have been, on any similar occasion. "One could wish to serve him as much as possible, but all this about '*nullus*,' and 'whole blood,' and 'half,' is so much gibberish to me—can you make any thing of it,—hey! Atwood?"

"Upon my word, Sir Gervaise, it seems a matter for a judge, rather than for man-of-war's men, like ourselves."

"It certainly can have no connection with this rising of the Jacobites? *That* is an affair likely to trouble a loyal subject, in his last moments, Mr. Rotherham!"

"Sir Wycherly's habits and age forbid the idea that he knows more of *that*, sir, than is known to us all. His request, however, to 'turn the will round,' I conceive to be altogether explicit. Several capital treatises have appeared lately on the 'human will,' and I regret to say, my honoured friend and patron has not always been quite as orthodox on that point, as I could wish. I, therefore, consider his words as evidence of a hearty repentance."

Sir Gervaise looked about him, as was his habit when any droll idea crossed his mind; but again suppressing the inclination to smile, he answered with suitable gravity—

"I understand you, sir; you think all these inexplicable terms are connected with Sir Wycherly's religious feelings. You may certainly be right, for it exceeds my knowledge to connect them with any thing else. I wish, notwithstanding, he had not disowned this noble young lieutenant of ours! Is it quite certain the young man is a Virginian?"

"So I have always understood it, sir. He has never been known in this part of England, until he was landed from a frigate in the roads, to be cured of a serious wound. I think none of Sir Wycherly's allusions have the least reference to *him*."

Sir Gervaise Oakes now joined his hands behind his back, and walked several times, quarter-deck fashion, to and fro, in the room. At each turn, his eyes glanced towards the bed, and he ever found the gaze of the sick man anxiously fastened on himself. This satisfied him that religion had nothing to do with his host's manifest desire to make himself understood; and his own trouble was greatly increased. It seemed to him, as if the dying man was making incessant appeals to his aid, without its being in his power to afford it. It was not possible for a generous man, like Sir Gervaise, to submit to such a feeling without an effort; and he soon went to the side of the bed, again, determined to bring the affair to some intelligible issue.

"Do you think, Sir Wycherly, you could write a few lines, if we put pen, ink, and paper before you?" he asked, as a sort of desperate remedy.

"Impossible—can hardly see; have got no strength—stop—will try—if you please."

Sir Gervaise was delighted with this, and he immediately directed his companions to lend their assistance. Atwood and the vicar bolstered the old man up, and the admiral put the writing materials before him, substituting a large quarto bible for a desk. Sir Wycherly, after several abortive attempts, finally got the pen in his hand, and with great difficulty traced six or seven nearly illegible words, running the line diagonally across the paper. By this time his powers failed him altogether, and he sunk back, dropping the pen, and closing his eyes in a partial insensibility. At this critical instant, the surgeon entered, and at once put an end to the interview, by taking charge of the patient, and directing all but one or two necessary attendants, to quit the room.

The three chosen witnesses of what had just past, repaired together to a parlour; Atwood, by a sort of mechanical habit, taking with him the paper on which the baronet had scrawled the words just mentioned. This, by a sort of mechanical use, also, he put into the hands of Sir Gervaise, as soon as they entered the room; much as he would have laid before his superior, an order to sign, or a copy of a letter to the secretary of the Navy Board.

"This is as bad as the '*nullus*!'" exclaimed Sir Gervaise, after endeavouring to decipher the scrawl in vain. "What is this first word, Mr. Rotherham—'Irish,' is it not,—hey! Atwood?"

"I believe it is no move than 'I-n,' stretched over much more paper than is necessary."

"You are right enough, vicar; and the next word is 'the,' though it looks like a *chevaux de frise*—what follows? It looks like 'man-of-war.' Atwood?"

"I beg your pardon, Sir Gervaise; this first letter is what I should call an elongated n—the next is certainly an a—the third looks like the waves of a river—ah! it is an m—and the last is an e—n-a-m-e—that makes 'name,' gentlemen."

"Yes," eagerly added the vicar, "and the two next words are, 'of God.'"

"Then it is religion, after all, that was on the poor man's mind!" exclaimed Sir Gervaise, in a slight degree disappointed, if the truth must be told. "What's this A-m-e-n—'Amen'—why it's a sort of prayer."

"This is the form in which it is usual to commence wills, I believe, Sir Gervaise," observed the secretary, who had written many a one, on board ship, in his day. "'In the name of God, Amen.'"

"By George, you're right, Atwood; and the poor man was trying, all the while, to let us know how he wished to dispose of his property! What could he mean by the *nullus*—it is not possible that the old gentleman has nothing to leave?"

"I'll answer for it, Sir Gervaise, *that* is not the true explanation," the vicar replied. "Sir Wycherly's affairs are in the best order; and, besides the estate, he has a large sum in the funds."

"Well, gentlemen, we can do no more to-night. A medical man is already in the house, and Bluewater will send ashore one or two others from the fleet. In the morning, if Sir Wycherly is in a state to converse, this matter shall be attended to."

The party now separated; a bed being provided for the vicar, and the admiral and his secretary retiring to their respective rooms.

CHAPTER X.

"Bid physicians talk our veins to temper,
And with an argument new-set a pulse;
Then think, my lord, of reasoning into love."

<small>YOUNG.</small>

While the scene just related, took place in the chamber of the sick man, Admiral Bluewater, Mrs. Dutton, and Mildred left the house, in the old family-coach. The rear-admiral had pertinaciously determined to adhere to his practice of sleeping in his ship; and the manner in which he had offered seats to his two fair companions—for Mrs. Dutton still deserved to be thus termed—has already been seen. The motive was simply to remove them from any further brutal exhibitions of Dutton's cupidity, while he continued in his present humour; and, thus influenced, it is not probable that the gallant old sailor would be likely to dwell, more than was absolutely necessary, on the unpleasant scene of which he had been a witness. In fact, no allusion was made to it, during the quarter of an hour the party was driving from the Hall to the station-house. They all spoke, with regret,—Mildred with affectionate tenderness, even,—of poor Sir Wycherly; and several anecdotes, indicative of his goodness of heart, were eagerly related to Bluewater, by the two females, as the carriage moved heavily along. In the time mentioned, the vehicle drew up before the door of the cottage, and all three alighted.

If the morning of that day had been veiled in mist, the sun had set in as cloudless a sky, as is often arched above the island of Great Britain. The night was, what in that region, is termed a clear moonlight. It was certainly not the mimic day that is so often enjoyed in purer atmospheres, but the panorama of the head-land was clothed in a soft, magical sort of semi-distinctness, that rendered objects sufficiently obvious, and exceedingly beautiful. The rounded, shorn swells of the land, hove upward to the eye, verdant and smooth; while the fine oaks of the park formed a shadowy background to the picture, inland. Seaward, the ocean was glittering, like a reversed plane of the firmament, far as eye could reach. If our own hemisphere, or rather this latitude, may boast of purer skies than are enjoyed by the mother country, the latter has a vast superiority in the tint of the water. While the whole American coast is bounded by a dull-looking sheet of sea-green, the deep blue of the wide ocean appears to be carried close home to the shores of Europe. This glorious tint, from which the term of "ultramarine" has been derived, is most remarkable in the Mediterranean, that sea of delights; but it is met with, all along the rock-bound coasts of the Peninsula of Spain and Portugal, extending through the British Channel, until it is in a measure, lost on the shoals of the North Sea; to be revived, however, in the profound depths of the ocean that laves the wild romantic coast of Norway.

"'Tis a glorious night!" exclaimed Bluewater, as he handed Mildred, the last, from the carriage; "and one can hardly wish to enter a cot, let it swing ever so lazily."

"Sleep is out of the question," returned Mildred, sorrowfully. "These are nights in which even the weary are reluctant to lose their consciousness; but who can sleep while there is this uncertainty about dear Sir Wycherly."

"I rejoice to hear you say this, Mildred,"—for so the admiral had unconsciously, and unrepelled, begun to call his sweet companion—"I rejoice to hear you say this, for I am an inveterate star-gazer and moon-ite; and I shall hope to persuade you and Mrs. Dutton to waste yet another hour, with me, in walking on this height. Ah! yonder is Sam Yoke, my coxswain, waiting to report the barge; I can send Sir Gervaise's message to the surgeons, by deputy, and there will be no occasion for my hastening from this lovely spot, and pleasant company."

The orders were soon given to the coxswain. A dozen boats, it would seem, were in waiting for officers ashore, notwithstanding the lateness of the hour; and directions were sent for two of them to pull off, and obtain the medical men. The coach was sent round to receive the latter, and then all was tranquil, again, on the height. Mrs. Dutton entered the house, to attend to some of her domestic concerns, while the rear-admiral took the arm of Mildred, and they walked, together, to the verge of the cliffs.

A fairer moonlight picture seldom offered itself to a seaman's eye, than that which now lay before the sight of Admiral Bluewater and Mildred. Beneath them rode the fleet; sixteen sail of different rigs, eleven of which, however, were two-decked ships of the largest size then known in naval warfare; and all of which were in that perfect order, that an active and intelligent commander knows how to procure, even from the dilatory and indifferent. If Admiral Bluewater was conspicuous in man[oe]uvring a fleet, and in rendering every vessel of a line that extended a league, efficient, and that too, in her right place, Sir Gervaise Oakes had the reputation of being one of the best seamen, in the ordinary sense of the word, in England. No vessel under his command, ever had a lubberly look; and no ship that had any sailing in her, failed to have it brought out of her. The vice-admiral was familiar with that all-important fact—one that members equally of Congress and of Parliament are so apt to forgot, or rather not to know at all—that the efficiency of a whole fleet, as a fleet, is necessarily brought down to the level of its worst ships. Of little avail is it, that four or five vessels of a squadron sail fast, and work well, if the eight or ten that remain, behave badly, and are dull. A separation of the vessels is the inevitable consequence, when the properties of all are thoroughly tried; and the division of a force, is the first step towards its defeat; as its proper concentration, is a leading condition of victory. As the poorer vessels cannot imitate the better, the good are compelled to regulate their movements by the bad; which is at once essentially bringing down the best ships of a fleet to the level of its worst; the proposition with which we commenced.

Sir Gervaise Oakes was so great a favourite, that all he asked was usually conceded to him. One of his conditions was, that his vessels should sail equally well; "If you give me fast ships," he said, "I can overtake the enemy; if dull, the enemy can overtake me; and I leave you to say which course will be most likely to bring on an action. At any rate, give me *consorts*; not one flyer, and one drag; but vessels that can keep within hail of each other, without anchoring." The admiralty professed every desire to oblige the gallant commander; and, as he was resolved never to quit the Plantagenet until she was worn out, it was indispensably necessary to find as many fast vessels as possible, to keep her company. The result was literally a fleet of "horses," as Galleygo used to call it; and it was generally said in the service, that "Oakes had a squadron of flyers, if not a flying-squadron."

Vessels like these just mentioned, are usually symmetrical and graceful to the eye, as well as fast. This fact was apparent to Mildred, accustomed as she was to the sight of ships and she ventured to express as much, after she and her companion had stood quite a minute on the cliff, gazing at the grand spectacle beneath them.

"Your vessels look even handsomer than common, Admiral Bluewater," she said, "though a ship, to me, is always an attractive sight."

"This is because they *are* handsomer than common, my pretty critic. Vice-Admiral Oakes is an officer who will no more tolerate an ugly ship in his fleet, than a peer of the realm will marry any woman but one who is handsome; unless indeed she happen to be surpassingly rich."

"I have heard that men are accustomed to lose their hearts under such an influence," said Mildred, laughing; "but I did not know before, that they were ever frank enough to avow it!"

"The knowledge has been imparted by a prudent mother, I suppose," returned the rear-admiral, in a musing manner; "I wish I stood sufficiently in the parental relation to you, my young friend, to venture to give a little advice, also. Never, before, did I feel so strong a wish to warn a human being of a great danger that I fear is impending over her, could I presume to take the liberty."

"It is not a liberty, but a duty, to warn any one of a danger that is known to ourselves, and not to the person who incurs the risk. At least so it appears to the eyes of a very young girl."

"Yes, if the danger was of falling from these cliffs, or of setting fire to a house, or of any other visible calamity. The case is different, when young ladies, and setting fire to the heart, are concerned."

"Certainly, I can perceive the distinction," answered Mildred, after a short pause; "and can understand that the same person who would not scruple to give the alarm against any physical danger, would hesitate even at hinting at one of a moral character. Nevertheless, if Admiral Bluewater think a simple girl, like me, of sufficient importance to take the trouble to interest himself in her welfare, I should hope he would not shrink from pointing out this danger. It is a terrible word to sleep on; and I confess, besides a little uneasiness, to a good deal of curiosity to know more."

"This is said, Mildred, because you are unaccustomed to the shocks which the tongue of rude man may give your sensitive feelings."

"Unaccustomed!" said Mildred, trembling so that the weakness was apparent to her companion. "Unaccustomed! Alas! Admiral Bluewater, can this be so, after what you have seen and heard!"

"Pardon me, dear child: nothing was farther from my thoughts, than to wish to revive those unpleasant recollections. If I thought I should be forgiven, I might venture, yet, to reveal my secret; for never before—though I cannot tell the reason of so sudden and so extraordinary an interest in one who is almost a stranger—"

"No—no—not a stranger, dear sir. After all that has passed to-day; after you have been admitted, though it were by accident, to one most sacred secret;—after all that was said in the carriage, and the terrible scenes my beloved mother went through in your presence so many years since, you can never be a stranger to *us*, whatever may be your own desire to fancy yourself one."

"Girl, you do not fascinate—you do not charm me, but you *bind* me to you in a way I did not think it in the power of any human being to subjugate my feelings!"

This was said with so much energy, that Mildred dropped the arm she held, and actually recoiled a step, if not in alarm, at least in surprise. But, on looking up into the face of her companion, and perceiving large tears actually glistening on his cheek, and seeing the hair that exposure and mental cares had whitened more than time, all her confidence returned, and she resumed the place she had abandoned, of her own accord, and as naturally as a daughter would have clung to the side of a father.

"I am sure, sir, my gratitude for this interest ought to be quite equal to the honour it does me," Mildred said, earnestly. "And, now, Admiral Bluewater, do not hesitate to speak to me with the frankness that a parent might use. I will listen with the respect and deference of a daughter."

"Then do listen to what I have to say, and make no answer, if you find yourself wounded at the freedom I am taking. It would seem that there is but one subject on which a man, old fellow or young fellow, can speak to a lovely young girl, when he gets her alone, under the light of a fine moon;—and that is love. Nay, start not again, my dear, for, if I am about to speak on so awkward a subject, it is not in my own behalf I hardly know whether you will think it in behalf of any one; as what I have to say, is not an appeal to your affections, but a warning against bestowing them."

"A warning, Admiral Bluewater! Do you really think that can be necessary?"

"Nay, my child, that is best known to yourself. Of one thing I am certain; the young man I have in my eye, affects to admire you, whether he does or not; and when young women are led to believe they are loved, it is a strong appeal to all their generous feelings to answer the passion, if not with equal warmth, at least with something very like it."

"Affects to admire, sir!—And why should any one be at the pains of *affecting* feelings towards me, that they do not actually entertain? I have neither rank, nor money, to bribe any one to be guilty of an hypocrisy so mean, and which, in my ease, would be so motiveless."

"Yes, if it *were* motiveless to win the most beautiful creature in England! But, no matter. We will not stop to analyze motives, when *facts* are what we aim at. I should think there must be some passion in this youth's suit, and that will only make it so much the more dangerous to its object. At all events, I feel a deep conviction that he is altogether unworthy of you. This is a bold expression of opinion on an acquaintance of a day; but there are such reasons for it, that a man of my time of life, if unprejudiced, can scarcely be deceived."

"All this is very singular, sir, and I had almost used your own word of 'alarming,'" replied Mildred, slightly agitated by curiosity, but more amused. "I shall be as frank as yourself, and say that you judge the gentleman harshly. Mr. Rotherham may not have all the qualities that a clergyman ought to possess, but he is far from being a bad man. Good or bad, however, it is not probable that he will carry his transient partiality any farther than he has gone already."

"Mr. Rotherham!—I have neither thought nor spoken of the pious vicar at all!"

Mildred was now sadly confused. Mr. Rotherham had made his proposals for her, only the day before, and he had been mildly, but firmly refused. The recent occurrence was naturally uppermost in her mind; and the conjecture that her rejected suitor, under the influence of wine, might have communicated the state of his wishes, or what he fancied to be the state of his wishes, to her companion, was so very easy, that she had fallen into the error, almost without reflection.

"I beg pardon, sir—I really imagined," the confused girl answered; "but, it was a natural mistake for me to suppose you meant Mr. Rotherham, as he is the only person who has ever spoken to my mother on the subject of any thing like a preference for me."

"I should have less fear of those who spoke to your mother, Mildred, than of those who spoke only to *you*. As I hate ambiguity, however, I will say, at once, that my allusion was to Mr. Wychecombe."

"Mr. Wychecombe, Admiral Bluewater!"—and the veteran felt the arm that leaned on him tremble violently, a sad confirmation of even more than he apprehended, or he would not have been so abrupt. "Surely—surely—the warning you mean, cannot, *ought* not to apply to a gentleman of Mr. Wychecombe's standing and character!"

"Such is the world, Miss Dutton, and we old seamen, in particular, get to know it, whether willingly or not. My sudden interest in you, the recollection of former, but painful scenes, and the events of the day, have made me watchful, and, you will add, bold—but I am resolved to speak, even at the risk of disobliging you for ever—and, in speaking, I must say that I never met with a young man who has made so unfavourable an impression on me, as this same Mr. Wychecombe."

Mildred, unconsciously to herself, withdrew her arm, and she felt astonished at her own levity, in so suddenly becoming sufficiently intimate with a stranger to permit him thus to disparage a confirmed friend.

"I am sorry, sir, that you entertain so indifferent an opinion of one who is, I believe, a general favourite, in this part of the country," she answered, with a coldness that rendered her manner marked.

"I perceive I shall share the fate of all unwelcome counsellors, but can only blame my own presumption. Mildred, we live in momentous times, and God knows what is to happen to myself, in the next few months; but, so strong is the inexplicable interest that I feel in your welfare, that I shall venture still to offend. I like not this Mr. Wychecombe, who is so devout an admirer of yours—real or affected—and, as to the liking of dependants for the heir of a considerable estate, it is so much a matter of course, that I count it nothing."

"The heir of a considerable estate!" repeated Mildred, in a voice to which the natural sweetness returned, quietly resuming the arm, she had so unceremoniously dropped—"Surely, dear sir, you are not speaking of Mr. Thomas Wychecombe, Sir Wycherly's nephew."

"Of whom else should I speak?—Has he not been your shadow the whole day?—so marked in his attentions, as scarce to deem it necessary to conceal his suit?"

"Has it really struck you thus, sir?—I confess I did not so consider it. We are so much at home at the Hall, that we rather expect all of that family to be kind to us. But, whether you are right in your conjecture, or not, Mr. Thomas Wychecombe can never be ought to me—and as proof, Admiral Bluewater, that I take your warning, as it is meant, in kindness and sincerity, I will add, that he is not a very particular favourite."

"I rejoice to hear it! Now there is his namesake, our young lieutenant, as gallant and as noble a fellow as ever lived—would to Heaven be was not so wrapt up in his profession, as to be insensible to any beauties, but those of a ship. Were you my own daughter, Mildred, I could give you to that lad, with as much freedom as I would give him my estate, were he my son."

Mildred smiled—and it was archly, though not without a shade of sorrow, too—but she had sufficient self-command, to keep her feelings to herself, and too much maiden reserve not to shrink from betraying her weakness to one who, after all, was little more than a stranger.

"I dare say, sir," she answered, with an equivocation which was perhaps venial, "that your knowledge of the world has judged both these gentlemen, rightly. Mr. Thomas Wychecombe, notwithstanding all you heard from my poor father, is not likely to think seriously of me; and I will answer for my own feelings as regards *him*. I am, in no manner, a proper person to become Lady Wychecombe; and, I trust, I should have the prudence to decline the honour were it even offered to me. Believe me, sir, my father would have held a different language to-night, had it not been for Sir Wycherly's wine, and the many loyal toasts that were drunk. He *must* be conscious, in his reflecting moments, that a child of his is unsuited to so high a station. Our prospects in life were once better than they are now, Admiral Bluewater; but they have never been such as to raise these high expectations in us."

"An officer's daughter may always claim to be a gentlewoman, my dear; and, as such, you might become the wife of a duke, did he love you. Since I find my warning unnecessary, however, we will change the discourse. Did not something extraordinary occur at this cliff, this morning, and in connection with this very Mr. Thomas Wychecombe? Sir Gervaise was my informant; but he did not relate the matter very clearly."

Mildred explained the mistake, and then gave a vivid description of the danger in which the young lieutenant had been placed, as well as of the manner in which he had extricated himself. She particularly dwelt on the extraordinary presence of mind and resolution, by means of which he had saved his life, when the stone first gave way beneath his foot.

"All this is well, and what I should have expected from so active and energetic a youth," returned the rear-admiral, a little gravely; "but, I confess I would rather it had not happened. Your inconsiderate and reckless young men, who risk their necks idly, in places of this sort, seldom have much in them, after all. Had there been a motive, it would have altered the case."

"Oh! but there *was* a motive, sir; he was far from doing so silly a thing for nothing!"

"And what was the motive, pray?—I can see no sufficient reason why a man of sense should trust his person over a cliff as menacing as this. One may approach it, by moonlight; but in the day, I confess to you I should not fancy standing as near it, as we do at this moment."

Mildred was much embarrassed for an answer. Her own heart told her Wycherly's motive, but that it would never do to avow to her companion, great as was the happiness she felt in avowing it to herself. Gladly would she have changed the discourse; but, as this could not be done, she yielded to her native integrity of character, and told the truth, as far as she told any thing.

"The flowers that grow on the sunny side of these rocks, Admiral Bluewater, are singularly fragrant and beautiful," she said; "and hearing my mother and myself speaking of them, and how much the former delighted in them, though they were so seldom to be had, he just ventured over the cliff—not here, where it is so *very* perpendicular, but yonder, where one *may* cling to it, very well, with a little care—and it was in venturing a little—just a *very* little too far, he told me, himself, sir, to-day, after dinner,—that the stone broke, and the accident occurred, I do not think Mr. Wycherly Wychecombe in the least fool-hardy, and not at all disposed to seek a silly admiration, by a silly exploit."

"He has a most lovely and a most eloquent advocate," returned the admiral, smiling, though the expression of his countenance was melancholy, even to sadness; "and he is acquitted. I think few men of his years would hesitate about risking their necks for flowers so fragrant and beautiful, and so much coveted by *your* mother, Mildred."

"And he a sailor, sir, who thinks so little of standing on giddy places, and laughs at fears of this nature?"

"Quite true; though there are few cliffs on board ship. Ropes are our sources of courage."

"So I should think, by what passed to-day," returned Mildred, laughing. "Mr. Wycherly called out for a rope, and we just threw him one, to help him out of his difficulty. The moment he got his rope, though it was only yonder small signal-halyards, he felt himself as secure as if he stood up here, on the height, with acres of level ground around him. I do not think he was frightened, at any time; but when he got hold of that little rope, he was fairly valiant!"

Mildred endeavoured to laugh at her own history, by way of veiling her interest in the event; but her companion was too old, and too discerning, to be easily deceived. He continued silent, as he led her away from the cliff; and when he entered the cottage, Mildred saw, by the nearer light of the candles, that his countenance was still sad.

Admiral Bluewater remained half an hour longer in the cottage, when he tore himself away, from a society which, for him, possessed a charm that he could not account for, nor yet scarcely estimate. It was past one, when he bid Mrs. Dutton and her daughter adieu; promising, however, to see them again, before the fleet sailed. Late as it was, the mother and Mildred felt no disposition to retire, after the exciting scenes they had gone through; but, feeling a calm on their spirits, succeeding the rude interruption produced by Dutton's brutality, they walked out on the cliff, to enjoy the cool air, and the bland scenery of the head-land, at that witching hour.

"I should feel alarm at this particularity of attention, from most men, my child," observed the prudent mother, as they left the house: "but the years, and especially the character of Admiral Bluewater, are pledges that he meditates nothing foolish, nor wrong."

"His *years* would be sufficient, mother," cried Mildred, laughing—for her laugh came easily, since the opinion she had just before heard of Wycherly's merit—"leaving the character out of the question."

"For you, perhaps, Mildred, but not for himself. Men rarely seem to think themselves too old to win the young of our sex; and what they want in attraction, they generally endeavour to supply by flattery and artifice. But, I acquit our new friend of all that."

"Had he been my own father, dearest mother, his language, and the interest he took in me, could not have been more paternal. I have found it truly delightful to listen to such counsel, from one of his sex; for, in general, they do not treat me in so sincere and fatherly a manner."

Mrs. Dutton's lip quivered, her eye-lids trembled too, and a couple of tears fell on her cheeks.

"It *is* new to you, Mildred, to listen to the language of disinterested affection and wisdom from one of his years and sex. I do not censure your listening with pleasure, but merely tell you to remember the proper reserve of your years and character. Hist! there are the sounds of his barge's oars."

Mildred listened, and the measured but sudden jerk of oars in the rullocks, ascended on the still night-air, as distinctly as they might have been heard in the boat. At the next instant, an eight-oared barge moved swiftly out from under the cliff, and glided steadily on towards a ship, that had one lantern suspended from the end of her gaff, another in her mizzen-top, and the small night-flag of a rear-admiral, fluttering at her mizzen-royal-mast-head. The cutter lay nearest to the landing, and, as the barge approached her, the ladies heard the loud hail of "boat-ahoy!" The answer was also audible; though given in the mild gentleman-like voice of Bluewater, himself. It was simply, "rear-admiral's flag." A death-like stillness succeeded this annunciation of the rank of the officer in the passing boat, interrupted only by the measured jerk of the oars. Once or twice, indeed, the keen hearing of Mildred made her fancy she heard the common dip of the eight oars, and the wash of the water, as they rose from the element, to gain a renewed purchase. As each vessel was approached, however, the hail and the answer were renewed, the quiet of midnight, in every instance, succeeding. At length the barge was seen shooting along on the quarter of the Cæsar, the rear-admiral's own ship, and the last hail was given. This time, there was a slight stir in the vessel; and, soon after the sound of the oars ceased, the lanterns descended from the stations they had held, since nightfall. Two or three other lanterns were still displayed at the gaffs of other vessels, the signs that their captains were not on board; though whether they were ashore, or visiting in the fleet, were facts best known to themselves. The Plantagenet, however, had no light; it being known that Sir Gervaise did not intend to come off that night.

When all this was over, Mrs. Dutton and Mildred sought their pillows, after an exciting day, and, to them, one far more momentous than they were then aware of.

CHAPTER XI.

"When I consider life, 'tis all a cheat;
Yet fool'd with hope, men favour the deceit;
Trust on, and think to-morrow will repay;
To-morrow's falser than the former day."

DRYDEN.

Although Admiral Bluewater devoted the minimum of time to sleep, he was not what the French term *matinal*. There is a period in the morning, on board of a ship of war,—that of washing decks,—which can best be compared to the discomfort of the American purification, yelep'd "a house-cleaning." This occurs daily, about the rising of the sun; and no officer, whose rank raises him above mingling with the duty, ever thinks, except on extraordinary occasions that may require his presence for other purposes, of intruding on its sacred mysteries. It is a rabid hour in a ship, and the wisest course, for all idlers, and all watch-officers, who are not on duty, is to keep themselves under hatches, if their convenience will possibly allow it. He who wears a flag, however, is usually reposing in his cot, at this critical moment; or, if risen at all, he is going through similar daily ablutions of his own person.

Admiral Bluewater was in the act of opening his eyes, when the splash of the first bucket of water was heard on the deck of the Cæsar, and he lay in the species of enjoyment which is so peculiar to naval men, after they have risen to the station of commander; a sort of semi-trance, in which the mind summons all the ancient images, connected with squalls; reefing top-sails in the rain; standing on the quarter of a yard, shouting "haul out to leeward;" peering over the weather hammock-cloths to eye the weather, with the sleet pricking the face like needles;—and, washing decks! These dreamy images of the past, however, are summoned merely to increase the sense of present enjoyment. They are so many well-contrived foils, to give greater brilliancy to the diamonds of a comfortable cot, and the entire consciousness of being no longer exposed to an untimely summons on deck.

Our rear-admiral, nevertheless, was not a vulgar dreamer, on such occasions. He thought little of personal comforts at any time, unless indeed when personal discomforts obtruded themselves on his attention; he knew little, or nothing, of the table, whereas his friend was a knowing cook, and in his days of probation had been a distinguished caterer; but he was addicted to a sort of dreaming of his own, even when the sun stood in the zenith, and he was walking the poop, in the midst of a circle of his officers. Still, he could not refrain from glancing back at the past, that morning, as plash after plash was heard, and recalling the time when *magna pars quorum* FUIT. At this delectable instant, the ruddy face of a "young gentleman" appeared in his state-room door, and, first ascertaining that the eyes of his superior were actually open, the youngster said—

"A note from Sir Gervaise, Admiral Bluewater."

"Very well, sir,"—taking the note.—"How's the wind, Lord Geoffrey?"

"An Irishman's hurricane, sir; right up and down. Our first says, sir, he never knew finer channel weather."

"Our first is a great astrologer. Is the fleet riding flood yet?"

"No, sir; it's slack-water; or, rather, the ebb is just beginning to make."

"Go on deck, my lord, and see if the Dover has hove in any upon her larboard bower, so as to bring her more on our quarter."

"Ay-ay-sir," and this cadet of one of the most illustrious houses of England, skipped up the ladder to ascertain this fact.

In the mean while, Bluewater stretched out an arm, drew a curtain from before his little window, fumbled for some time among his clothes before he got his spectacles, and then opened the note. This early epistle was couched in the following words—

"DEAR BLUE:—

"I write this in a bed big enough to ware a ninety in. I've been athwart ships half the night, without knowing it. Galleygo has just been in to report 'our fleet' all well, and the ships riding flood. It seems there is a good look-out from the top of the house, where part of the roads are visible. Magrath, and the rest of them, have been at poor Sir Wycherly all night. I learn, but he remains down by the head, yet. I am afraid the good old man will never be in trim again. I shall remain here, until something is decided; and as we cannot expect our orders until next day after to-morrow, at the soonest, one might as well be here, as on board. Come ashore and breakfast with us; when we can consult about the propriety of remaining, or of abandoning the wreck. Adieu,

"OAKES.
"REAR-ADMIRAL BLUEWATER

"P.S.—There was a little occurrence last night, connected with Sir Thomas Wycherly's will, that makes me particularly anxious to see you, as early as possible, this morning.

"O."

Sir Gervaise, like a woman, had written his mind in his postscript. The scene of the previous night had forcibly presented itself to his recollection on awakening, and calling for his writing-desk, he had sent off this note, at the dawn of day, with the wish of having as many important witnesses as he could well obtain, at the interview he intended to demand, at the earliest practicable hour.

"What the deuce can Oakes have to do with Sir Wycherly Wychecombe's will?" thought the rear-admiral. "By the way, that puts me in mind of my own; and of my own recent determination. What are my poor £30,000 to a man with the fortune of Lord Bluewater. Having neither a wife nor child, brother nor sister of my own, I'll do what I please with my money. Oakes *won't* have it; besides, he's got enough of his own, and to spare. An estate of £7000 a year, besides heaps of prize-money funded. I dare say, he has a good £12,000 a year, and nothing but a nephew to inherit it all. I'm determined to do as I please with my money. I made every shilling of it, and I'll give it to whom I please."

The whole time, Admiral Bluewater lay with his eyes shut, and with a tongue as motionless as if it couldn't stir. With all his *laissez aller* manner, however, he had the promptitude of a sailor, when his mind was made up to do a thing, though he always performed it in his own peculiar mode. To rise, dress, and prepare to quit his state-room, occupied him but a short time; and he was seated before his own writing-desk, in the after-cabin, within twenty minutes after the thoughts just recorded, had passed through his mind. His first act was to take a folded paper from a private drawer, and glance his eye carelessly over it. This was the will in favour of Lord Bluewater: It was expressed in very concise terms, filling only the first side of a page. This will he copied, *verbatim et literatim*, leaving blanks for the name of the legatee, and appointing Sir Gervaise Oakes his executor, as in the will already executed. When finished in this manner, he set about filling up the blanks. For a passing instant, he felt tempted to insert the name of the Pretender; but, smiling at his own folly, he wrote that of "Mildred Dutton, daughter of Francis Dutton, a master in His Majesty's Navy," in all the places that it was requisite so to do. Then he affixed the seal, and, folding all the upper part of the sheet over, so as to conceal the contents, he rang a little silver bell, which always stood at his elbow. The outer cabin-door was opened by the sentry, who thrust his head in at the opening.

"I want one of the young gentlemen, sentry," said the rear-admiral.

The door closed, and, in another minute, the smiling face of Lord Geoffrey was at the entrance of the after-cabin.

"Who's on deck, my lord," demanded Bluewater, "beside the watch?"

"No one, sir. All the idlers keep as close as foxes, when the decks are getting it; and as for any of our snorers showing their faces before six bells, it's quite out of the question, sir."

"Some one must surely be stirring in the gun-room, by this time! Go and ask the chaplain and the captain of marines to do me the favour to step into the cabin—or the first lieutenant; or the master; or any of the idlers."

The midshipman was gone two or three minutes, when he returned with the purser and the chaplain.

"The first lieutenant is in the forehold, sir; all the marines have got their dead-lights still in, and the master is working-up his log, the gun-room steward says. I hope these will do, sir; they are the greatest idlers in the ship, I believe."

Lord Geoffrey Cleveland was the second son of the third duke in the English empire, and he knew it, as well as any one on board. Admiral Bluewater had no slavish respect for rank; nevertheless, like all men educated under an aristocratic system, he was influenced by the feeling to a degree of which he himself was far from being conscious. This young scion of nobility was not in the least favoured in matters of duty, for this his own high spirit would have resented; but he dined in the cabin twice as often as any other midshipman on board, and had obtained for himself a sort of license for the tongue, that emboldened him to utter what passed for smart things in the cock-pit and gun-room, and which, out of all doubt, were pert things everywhere. Neither the chaplain nor the purser took offence at his liberties on the present occasion; and, as for the rear-admiral, he had not attended to what had been uttered. As soon, however, as he found others in his cabin, he motioned to them to approach his desk, and pointed to the paper, folded down, as mentioned.

"Every prudent man," he said, "and, especially every prudent sailor and soldier, in a time of war, ought to be provided with a will. This is mine, just drawn up, by myself; and that instrument is an old one, which I now destroy in your presence. I acknowledge this to be my hand and seal," writing his name, and touching the seal with a finger as he spoke; "affixed to this my last will and testament. Will you have the kindness to act as witnesses?"

When the chaplain and purser had affixed their names, there still remained a space for a third signature. This, by a sign from his superior, the laughing midshipman filled with his own signature.

"I hope you've recollected, sir," cried the boy, with glee, as he took his seat to obey; "that the Bluewaters and Clevelands are related. I shall be grievously disappointed, when this will is proved, if my name be not found somewhere in it!"

"So shall I, too, my lord," drily returned Bluewater; "for, I fully expect it will appear as a witness; a character that is at once fatal to all claims as a legatee."

"Well, sir, I suppose flag-officers can do pretty much as they please with their money, since they do pretty much as they please with the ships, and all in them. I must lean so much the harder on my two old aunts, as I appear to have laid myself directly athwart-hawse of fortune, in this affair!"

"Gentlemen," said the rear-admiral, with easy courtesy, "I regret it is not in my power to have your company at dinner, to-day, as I am summoned ashore by Sir Gervaise, and it is uncertain when I can get off, again; but to-morrow I shall hope to enjoy that pleasure."

The officers bowed, expressed their acknowledgments, accepted the invitation, bowed once or twice more each, and left the cabin, with the exception of the midshipman.

"Well, sir," exclaimed Bluewater, a little surprised at finding he was not alone, after a minute of profound reverie; "to what request am I indebted still for the pleasure of your presence?"

"Why, sir, it's just forty miles to my father's house in Cornwall, and I know the whole family is there; so I just fancied, that by bending on two extra horses, a chaise might make the Park gates in about five hours; and by getting under way on the return passage, to-morrow about this time, the old Cæsar would never miss a crazy reefer, more or less."

"Very ingeniously put, young gentleman, and quite plausible. When I was of your age, I was four years without once seeing either father or mother."

"Yes, sir, but that was such a long time ago! Boys can't stand it, half as well now, as they did then, as all old people say."

The rear-admiral's lips moved slightly, as if a smile struggled about his mouth; then his face suddenly lost the expression, in one approaching to sadness.

"You know, Geoffrey, I am not commander-in-chief. Sir Gervaise alone can give a furlough."

"Very true, sir; but whatever you ask of Sir Gervaise, he always does; more especially as concerns us of your flag-ship."

"Perhaps that is true. But, my boy, we live in serious times, and we may sail at an hour's notice. Are you ignorant that Prince Charles Edward has landed in Scotland, and that the Jacobites are up and doing? If the French back him, we may have our hands full here, in the channel."

"Then my dear mother must go without a kiss, for the next twelvemonth!" cried the gallant boy, dashing a hand furtively across his eyes, in spite of his resolution. "The throne of old England must be upheld, even though not a mother nor a sister in the island, see a midshipman in years!"

"Nobly said, Lord Geoffrey, and it shall be known at head-quarters. *Your* family is whig; and you do well, at your time of life, to stick to the family politics."

"A small run on the shore, sir, would be a great pleasure, after six months at sea?"

"You must ask Captain Stowel's leave for that. You know I never interfere with the duty of the ship."

"Yes, sir, but there are so many of us, and all have a hankering after *terra firma*. Might I just say, that I have your permission, to ask Captain Stowel, to let me have a run on the cliffs?"

"You may do *that*, my lord, if you wish it; but Stowel knows that he can do as he pleases."

"He would be a queer captain of a man-of-war, if he didn't sir! Thank you, Admiral Bluewater; I will write to my mother, and I know she'll be satisfied with the reason I shall give her, for not coming to see her. Good-morning, sir."

"Good-morning,"—then, when the boy's hand was on the lock of the cabin-door—"my lord?"

"Did you wish to say any thing more, sir?"

"When you write, remember me kindly to the Duchess. We were intimate, when young people; and, I might say, loved each other."

The midshipman promised to do as desired; then the rear-admiral was left alone. He walked the cabin, for half an hour, musing on what he had done in relation to his property, and on what he ought to do, in relation to the Pretender; when he suddenly summoned his coxswain, gave a few directions, and sent an order on deck to have his barge manned. The customary reports went their usual rounds, and reached the cabin in about three minutes more; Lord Geoffrey bringing them down, again.

"The barge is manned, sir," said the lad, standing near the cabin-door, rigged out in the neat, go-ashore-clothes of a midshipman.

"Have you seen Captain Stowel, my lord?" demanded the rear-admiral.

"I have, sir; and he has given me permission to drift along shore, until sunset; to be off with the evening gun of the vice-admiral."

"Then do me the favour to take a seat in my barge, if you are quite ready."

This offer was accepted, and, in a few minutes, all the ceremonies of the deck had been observed, and the rear-admiral was seated in his barge. It was now so late, that etiquette had fair play, and no point was omitted on the occasion. The captain was on deck, in person, as well as gun-room officers enough to represent their body; the guard was paraded, under its officers; the drums rolled; the boatswain piped six side boys over, and Lord Geoffrey skipped down first into the boat, remaining respectfully standing, until his superior was seated. All these punctilios observed, the boat was shoved off from the vessel's side, the eight oars dropped, as one, and the party moved towards the shore. Every cutter, barge, yawl, or launch that was met, and which did not contain an officer of rank itself, tossed its oars, as this barge, with the rear-admiral's flag fluttering in its bow, passed, while the others lay on theirs, the gentlemen saluting with their hats. In this manner the barge passed the fleet, and approached the shore. At the landing, a little natural quay formed by a low flat rock, there was a general movement, as the rear-admiral's flag was seen to draw near; and even the boats of captains were shoved aside, to give the naval *pas*. As soon, however, as the foot of Bluewater touched the rock, the little flag was struck; and, a minute later, a cutter, with only a lieutenant in her, coming in, that officer ordered the barge to make way for *him*, with an air of high and undisputed authority.

Perhaps there was not a man in the British marine, to whom the etiquette of the service gave less concern, than to Bluewater. In this respect, he was the very reverse of his friend; for Sir Gervaise was a punctilious observer, and a rigid enforcer of all the prescribed ceremonials. This was by no means the only professional point on which these two distinguished officers differed. It has already been mentioned, that the rear-admiral was the best tactician in England, while the vice-admiral was merely respectable in that branch of his duty. On the other hand, Sir Gervaise was deemed the best practical seaman afloat, so far as a single ship was concerned, while Bluewater had no particular reputation in that way. Then, as to discipline, the same distinction existed. The commander-in-chief was a little of a *martinet*, exacting compliance with the most minute regulations; while his friend, even when a captain, had thrown the police duty of his ship very much on what is called the executive officer: or the first lieutenant; leaving to that important functionary, the duty of devising, as well as of executing the system by which order and cleanliness were maintained in the vessel. Nevertheless, Bluewater had his merit even in this peculiar feature of the profession. He had made the best captain of the fleet to his friend, that had ever been met with. This office, which, in some measure, corresponds to that of an adjutant-general on shore, was suited to his generalizing and philosophical turn of mind; and he had brought all its duties within the circle and control of clear and simple principles, which rendered them pleasant and easy. Then, too, whenever he commanded in chief, as frequently happened, for a week or two at a time, Sir

Gervaise being absent, it was remarked that the common service of the fleet went on like clock-work; his mind seeming to embrace generals, when it refused to descend to details. In consequence of these personal peculiarities, the captains often observed, that Bluewater ought to have been the senior, and Oakes the junior; and then, their joint commands would have produced perfection; but these criticisms must be set down, in a great measure, to the natural propensity to find fault, and an inherent desire in men, even when things are perfectly well in themselves, to prove their own superiority, by pointing out modes and means by which they might be made much better. Had the service been on land, this opinion might possibly have had more practical truth in it; but, the impetuosity and daring of Sir Gervaise, were not bad substitutes for tactics, in the straight-forward combats of ships. To resume the narrative.

When Bluewater landed, he returned the profound and general salute of all on or near the rock, by a sweeping, but courteous bow, which was nevertheless given in a vacant, slovenly manner; and immediately began to ascend the ravine. He had actually reached the grassy acclivity above, before he was at all aware of any person's being near him. Turning, he perceived that the midshipman was at his heels, respect alone preventing one of the latter's active limbs and years from skipping past his superior on the ascent. The admiral recollected how little there was to amuse one of the boy's habits in a place like Wychecombe, and he good-naturedly determined to take him along with himself.

"You are little likely to find any diversion here, Lord Geoffrey," he said; "if you will accept of the society of a dull old fellow, like myself, you shall see all I see, be it more or less."

"I've shipped for the cruise, sir, and am ready and happy, too, to follow your motions, with or without signals," returned the laughing youngster. "I suppose Wychecombe is about as good as Portsmouth, or Plymouth; and I'm sure these green fields are handsomer than the streets of any dirty town I ever entered."

"Ay, green fields are, indeed, pleasant to the eyes of us sailors, who see nothing but water, for months at a time. Turn to the right, if you please, my lord; I wish to call at yonder signal-station, on my way to the Hall."

The boy, as is not usual with lads of his age, inclined in "the way he was told to go," and in a few minutes both stood on the head-land. As it would not have done for the master to be absent from his staff, during the day, with a fleet in the roads, Dutton was already at his post, cleanly dressed as usual, but trembling again with the effect of the last night's debauch on his nerves. He arose, with great deference of manner, to receive the rear-admiral, and not without many misgivings of conscience; for, while memory furnished a tolerable outline of what had occurred in the interview between himself and his wife and daughter, wine had lost its influence, and no longer helped to sustain his self-command. He was much relieved, however, by the discreet manner in which he was met by Bluewater.

"How is Sir Wycherly?" inquired the admiral saluting the master, as if nothing had happened; "a note from Sir Gervaise, written about day-break, tells me he was not, then, essentially better."

"I wish it were in my power to give you any good news, sir. He must be conscious, notwithstanding; for Dick, his groom, has just ridden over with a note from Mr. Rotherham, to say that the excellent old baronet particularly desires to see my wife and daughter; and that the coach will be here, to take them over in a few minutes. If you are bound to the Hall, this morning, sir, I'm certain the ladies would be delighted to give you a seat."

"Then I will profit by their kindness," returned Bluewater, seating himself on the bench at the foot of the staff; "more especially, if you think they will excuse my adding Lord Geoffrey Cleveland, one of Stowel's midshipmen, to the party. He has entered, to follow my motions, with or without signals."

Dutton uncovered again, and bowed profoundly, at this announcement of the lad's name and rank; the boy himself, taking the salute in an off-hand and indifferent way, like one already wearied with vulgar adulation, while he gazed about him, with some curiosity, at the head-land and flag-staff.

"This a good look-out, sir," observed the midshipman; "and one that is somewhat loftier than our cross-trees. A pair of sharp eyes might see every thing that passes within twenty miles; and, as a proof of it, I shall be the first to sing out, 'sail, ho!'"

"Where-away, my young lord?" said Dutton, fidgeting, as if he had neglected his duty, in the presence of a superior; "I'm sure, your lordship can see nothing but the fleet at anchor, and a few boats passing between the different ships and the landing!"

"Where-away, sure enough, youngster?" added the admiral. "I see some gulls glancing along the surface of the water, a mile or two outside the ships, but nothing like a sail."

The boy caught up Dutton's glass, which lay on the seat, and, in a minute, he had it levelled at the expanse of water. It was some little time, and not without much sighting along the barrel of the instrument, that he got it to suit himself.

"Well, Master Sharp-eyes," said Bluewater, drily, "is it a Frenchman, or a Spaniard?"

"Hold on, a moment, sir, until I can get this awkward glass to bear on it.—Ay—now I have her—she's but a speck, at the best—royals and head of top-gallant-sails—no, sir, by George, it's our own cutter, the Active, with her square-sail set, and the heads of her lower sails just rising. I know her by the way she carries her gaff."

"The Active!—that betokens news," observed Bluewater, thoughtfully—for the march of events, at that moment, must necessarily brink on a crisis in his own career. "Sir Gervaise sent her to look into Cherbourg."

"Yes, sir; we all know that—and, there she comes to tell us, I hope, that Monsieur de Vervillin, has, at last, made up his mind to come out and face us, like a man. Will you look at the sail, sir?"

Bluewater took the glass, and sweeping the horizon, he soon caught a view of his object. A short survey sufficed, for one so experienced, and he handed the glass back to the boy.

"You have quick eyes, sir," he said, as he did so; "that is a cutter, certainly, standing in for the roads, and I believe you may be right in taking her for the Active."

"'Tis a long way to know so small a craft!" observed Dutton, who also took his look at the stranger.

"Very true, sir," answered the boy; "but one ought to tell a friend as far as he can see him. The Active carries a longer and a lower gaff, than any other cutter in the navy, which is the way we all tell her from the Gnat, the cutter we have with us."

"I am glad to find your lordship is so close an observer," returned the complaisant Dutton; "a certain sign, my lord, that your lordship will make a good sailor, in time."

"Geoffrey is a good sailor, already," observed the admiral, who knew that the youngster was never better pleased, than when he dropped the distance of using his title, and spoke to, or of him, as of a connection; which, in truth, he was. "He has now been with me four years; having joined when he was only twelve. Two more years will make an officer of him."

"Yes, sir," said Dutton, bowing first to one, and then to the other. "Yes, sir; his lordship may well look forward to that, with *his* particular merit, *your* esteemed favour, and his *own* great name. Ah! sir, they've caught a sight of the stranger in the fleet, and bunting is at work, already."

In anchoring his ships, Admiral Bluewater had kept them as close together, as the fog rendered safe; for one of the great difficulties of a naval commander is to retain his vessels in compact order, in thick or heavy weather. Orders had been given, however, for a sloop and a frigate to weigh, and stretch out into the offing a league or two, as soon as the fog left them, the preceding day, in order to sweep as wide a reach of the horizon as was convenient. In order to maintain their ground in a light wind, and with a strong tide running, these two cruisers had anchored; one, at the distance of a league from the fleet, and the other, a mile or two farther outside, though more to the eastward. The sloop lay nearest to the stranger, and signals were flying at her main-royal-mast-head, which the frigate was repeating, and transmitting to the flag-ship of the commander-in-chief. Bluewater was so familiar with all the ordinary signals, that it was seldom he had recourse to his book for the explanations; and, in the present instance, he saw at once that it was the Active's number that was shown. Other signals, however, followed, which it surpassed the rear-admiral's knowledge to read, without assistance; from all which he was satisfied that the stranger brought intelligence of importance, and which could only be understood by referring to the private signal-book.

While these facts were in the course of occurrence, the coach arrived to convey Mrs. Dutton and Mildred to the Hall. Bluewater now presented himself to the ladies, and was received as kindly as they had separated from him a few hours before; nor were the latter displeased at hearing he was to be their companion back to the dwelling of Sir Wycherly.

"I fear this summons bodes evil tidings," said Mrs. Dutton; "he would hardly think of desiring to see us, unless something quite serious were on his mind; and the messenger said he was no better."

"We shall learn all, my dear lady, when we reach the Hall," returned Bluewater; "and the sooner we reach it, the sooner our doubts will be removed. Before we enter the carriage, let me make you acquainted with my young friend, Lord Geoffrey Cleveland, whom I have presumed to invite to be of the party."

The handsome young midshipman was well received, though Mrs. Dutton had been too much accustomed, in early life, to see people of condition, to betray the same deference as her husband for the boy's rank. The ladies occupied, as usual, the hind seat of the coach, leaving that in front to their male companions. The arrangement accidentally brought Mildred and the midshipman opposite each other; a circumstance that soon attracted the attention of the admiral, in a way that was a little odd; if not remarkable. There is a charm in youth, that no other period of life possesses; infancy, with its helpless beauty, scarcely seizing upon the imagination and senses with an equal force. Both the young persons in question, possessed this advantage in a high degree; and had there been no other peculiarity, the sight might readily have proved pleasing to one of Bluewater's benevolence and truth of feeling. The boy was turned of sixteen; an age in England when youth does not yet put on the appearance of manhood; and he retained all the evidences of a gay, generous boyhood, rendered a little *piquant*, by the dash of archness, roguery, and fun, that a man-of-war is tolerably certain to impart to a lad of spirit. Nevertheless, his countenance retained an expression of ingenuousness and of sensitive feeling, that was singularly striking in one of his sex, and which, in spite of her beauty of feature, hair, and complexion, formed the strongest attraction in the loveliness of Mildred; that expression, which had so much struck and charmed Bluewater—haunted him, we might add—since the previous day, by appearing so familiar, even while so extraordinary, and for which he had been unable to recollect a counterpart. As she now sat, face to face with Lord Geoffrey, to his great surprise, the rear-admiral found much of the same character of this very expression in the handsome boy, as in the lovely girl. It is true, the look of ingenuousness and of sensitive feeling, was far less marked in young Cleveland, than in Mildred, and there was little general resemblance of feature or countenance between the two; still, the first was to be found in both, and so distinctly, as to be easily traced, when placed in so close contact. Geoffrey Cleveland had the reputation of being like his mother; and, furnished with this clue, the fact suddenly flashed on Bluewater's mind, that the being whom Mildred so nearly and strikingly resembled, was a deceased sister of the Duchess, and a beloved cousin of his own. Miss Hedworth, the young lady in question, had long been dead; but, all who had known her, retained the most pleasing impressions equally of her charms of person and of mind. Between her and Bluewater there had existed a tender friendship, in which, however, no shade of passion had mingled; a circumstance that was in part owing to the difference in their years, Captain Bluewater having been nearly twice his young relative's age; and in part, probably, to the invincible manner in which the latter seemed wedded to his profession, and his ship. Agnes Hedworth, notwithstanding, had been very dear to our sailor, from a variety of causes,— far more so, than her sister, the Duchess, though *she* was a favourite—and the rear-admiral, when his mind glanced rapidly through the chain of association, that traced the accidental resemblance of Mildred to this esteemed object, had a sincere delight in finding he had thus been unconsciously attracted by one whose every look and smile now forcibly reminded him of the countenance of a being whom, in her day, he had thought so near perfection. This delight, however, was blended with sadness, on various accounts; and the short excursion proved to be so melancholy, that no one was sorry when it terminated.

CHAPTER XII.

"Nath. Truly, Master Holofernes, the epithets are sweetly varied, like a scholar at the least. But, sir, I assure ye, it was a buck of the first head.

Hol. Sir Nathaniel, *haud credo.*

Bull. 'Twas not a *haud credo*, 'twas a pricket."

LOVE'S LABOUR LOST

Every appearance of the jolly negligence which had been so characteristic of life at Wychecombe-Hall, had vanished, when the old coach drew up in the court, to permit the party it had brought from the station to alight. As no one was expected but Mrs. Dutton and her daughter, not even a footman appeared to open the door of the carriage; the vulgar-minded usually revenging their own homage to the powerful, by manifesting as many slights as possible to the weak. Galleygo let the new-comers out, and, consequently, he was the first person of whom inquiries were made, as to the state of things in the house.

"Well," said Admiral Bluewater, looking earnestly at the steward; "how is Sir Wycherly, and what is the news?"

"Sir Wycherly is still on the doctor's list, your honour; and I expects his case is set down as a hard 'un. We's as well as can be expected, and altogether in good heart. Sir Jarvy turned out with the sun, thof he didn't turn in 'till the middle-watch was half gone—or *two* bells, as they calls 'em aboard this house—*four* bells, as we should say in the old Planter—and chickens, I hears, has riz, a shillin' a head, since our first boat landed."

"It's a melancholy business, Mrs. Dutton; I fear there can be little hope."

"Yes, it's all *that*, Admiral Blue," continued Galleygo, following the party into the house, no one but himself hearing a word he uttered; "and 'twill be worse, afore it's any better. They tells me potaties has taken a start, too; and, as all the b'ys of all the young gentlemen in the fleet is out, like so many wild locusts of Hegypt, I expects nothing better than as our mess will fare as bad as sogers on a retreat."

In the hall, Tom Wychecombe, and his namesake, the lieutenant, met the party. From the formal despondency of the first, every thing they apprehended was confirmed. The last, however, was more cheerful, and not altogether without hope; as he did not hesitate openly to avow.

"For myself, I confess I think Sir Wycherly much better," he said; "although the opinion is not sanctioned by that of the medical men. His desiring to see these ladies is favourable; and then cheering news for him has been brought back, already, by the messenger sent, only eight hours since, for his kinsman, Sir Reginald Wychecombe. He has sensibly revived since that report was brought in."

"Ah! my dear namesake," rejoined Tom, shaking his head, mournfully; "you cannot know my beloved uncle's constitution and feelings as well as I! Rely on it, the medical men are right; and your hopes deceive you. The sending for Mrs. Dutton and Miss Mildred, both of whom my honoured uncle respects and esteems, looks more like leave-taking than any thing else; and, as to Sir Reginald Wychecombe,—though a relative, beyond a question,—I think there has been some mistake in sending for him; since he is barely an acquaintance of the elder branch of the family, and he is of the half-blood."

"*Half* what, Mr. Thomas Wychecombe?" demanded the vice-admiral so suddenly, behind the speaker, as to cause all to start; Sir Gervaise having hastened to meet the ladies and his friend, as soon as he knew of their arrival. "I ask pardon, sir, for my abrupt inquiry; but, as *I* was the means of sending for Sir Reginald Wychecombe, I feel an interest in knowing his exact relationship to my host?"

Tom started, and even paled, at this sudden question; then the colour rushed into his temples; he became calmer, and replied:

"*Half-blood*, Sir Gervaise," he said, steadily. "This is an affinity that puts a person altogether out of the line of succession; and, of course, removes any necessity, or wish, to see Sir Reginald."

"Half-*blood*—hey! Atwood?" muttered the vice-admiral, turning away towards his secretary, who had followed him down stairs. "This may be the solution, after all! Do you happen to know what half-*blood* means? It cannot signify that Sir Reginald comes from one of those, who have no father—all their ancestry consisting only of a mother?"

"I should think not, Sir Gervaise; in that case, Sir Reiginald would scarcely be considered of so honourable a lineage, as he appears to be. I have not the smallest idea, sir, what half-*blood* means; and, perhaps, it may not be amiss to inquire of the medical gentlemen. Magrath is up stairs; possibly he can tell us."

"I rather think it has something to do with the law. If this out-of-the-way place, now, could furnish even a lubberly attorney, we might learn all about it. Harkee, Atwood; you must stand by to make Sir Wycherly's will, if he says any thing more about it—have you got the heading all written out, as I desired."

"It is quite ready, Sir Gervaise—beginning, as usual, 'In the name of God, Amen.' I have even ventured so far as to describe the testator's style and residence, &c. &c.—'I, Sir Wycherly Wychecombe, Bart., of Wychecombe Hall, Devon, do make and declare this to be my last will and testament, &c. &c.' Nothing is wanting but the devises, as the lawyers call them. I can manage a will, well enough, Sir Gervaise, I believe. One of mine has been in the courts, now, these five years, and they tell me it sticks there, as well as if it had been drawn in the Middle Temple."

"Ay, I know your skill. Still, there can be no harm in just asking Magrath; though I think it must be law, after all! Run up and ask him, Atwood, and bring me the answer in the drawing-room, where I see Bluewater has gone with his convoy; and—harkee—tell the surgeons to let us know the instant the patient says any thing about his temporal affairs. The twenty thousand in the funds are his, to do what he pleases with; let the land be tied up, as it may."

While this "aside," was going on in the hall, Bluewater and the rest of the party had entered a small parlour, that was in constant use, still conversing of the state of Sir Wycherly. As all of them, but the two young men, were ignorant of the nature of the message to Sir Reginald Wychecombe, and of the intelligence in connection with that gentleman, which had just been received, Mrs. Dutton ventured to ask an explanation, which was given by Wycherly, with a readiness that proved *he* felt no apprehensions on the subject.

"Sir Wycherly desired to see his distant relative, Sir Reginald," said the lieutenant; "and the messenger who was sent to request his attendance, fortunately learned from a post-boy, that the Hertfordshire baronet, in common with many other gentlemen, is travelling in the west, just at this moment; and that he slept last night, at a house only twenty miles distant. The express reached him several hours since, and an answer has been received, informing us that we may expect to see him, in an hour or two."

Thus much was related by Wycherly; but, we may add that Sir Reginald Wychecombe was a Catholic, as it was then usual to term the Romanists, and in secret, a Jacobite; and, in common with many of that religious persuasion, he was down in the west, to see if a rising could not be organized in that part of the kingdom, as a diversion to any attempt to repel the young Pretender in the north. As the utmost caution was used by the conspirators, this fact was not even suspected by any who were not in the secret of the whole proceeding. Understanding that his relation was an inefficient old man, Sir Reginald, himself an active and sagacious intriguer, had approached thus near to the old paternal residence of his family, in order to ascertain if his own name and descent might not aid him in obtaining levies among the ancient tenantry of the estate. That day he had actually intended to appear at Wychecombe, disguised, and under an assumed name. He proposed venturing on this step, because circumstances put it in his power, to give what he thought would be received as a sufficient excuse, should his conduct excite comment.

Sir Reginald Wychecombe was a singular, but by no means an unnatural compound of management and integrity. His position as a Papist had disposed him to intrigue, while his position as one proscribed by religious hostility, had disposed him to be a Papist. Thousands are made men of activity, and even of importance, by persecution and proscription, who would pass through life quietly and unnoticed, if the meddling hand of human forethought did not force them into situations that awaken their hostility, and quicken their powers. This gentleman was a firm believer in all the traditions of his church, though his learning extended little beyond his missal; and he put the most implicit reliance on the absurd, because improbable, fiction of the Nag's Head consecration, without having even deemed it necessary to look into a particle of that testimony by which alone such a controversy could be decided. In a word, he was an instance of what religious intolerance has ever done, and will probably for ever continue to do, with so wayward a being as man.

Apart from this weakness, Sir Reginald Wychecombe had both a shrewd and an inquiring mind. His religion he left very much to the priests; but of his temporal affairs he assumed a careful and prudent supervision. He was much richer than the head of the family; but, while he had no meannesses connected with money, he had no objection to be the possessor of the old family estates. Of his own relation to the head of this family, he was perfectly aware, and the circumstance of the half-blood, with all its legal consequences, was no secret to him. Sir Reginald Wychecombe was not a man to be so situated, without having recourse to all proper means, in order, as it has become the fashion of the day to express it, "to define his position." By means of a shrewd attorney, if not of his own religious, at least of his own political opinions, he had ascertained the fact, and this from the mouth of Martha herself, that Baron Wychecombe had never married; and that, consequently, Tom and his brothers were no more heirs at law to the Wychecombe estate, than he was in his own person. He fully understood, too, that there *was* no heir at law; and that the lands must escheat, unless the present owner made a will; and to this last act, his precise information told him that Sir Wycherly had an unconquerable reluctance. Under such circumstances, it is not at all surprising, that when the Hertfordshire baronet was thus unexpectedly summoned to the bed-side of his distant kinsman, he inferred that his own claims were at length to be tardily acknowledged, and that he was about to be put in possession of the estates of his legitimate ancestors. It is still less wonderful, that, believing this, he promptly promised to lose no time in obeying the summons, determining momentarily to forget his political, in order to look a little after his personal interests.

The reader will understand, of course, that all these details were unknown to the inmates of the Hall, beyond the fact of the expected arrival of Sir Reginald Wychecombe, and that of the circumstance of the half-blood; which, in its true bearing, was known alone to Tom. Their thoughts were directed towards the situation of their host, and little was said, or done, that had not his immediate condition for the object. It being understood, however, that the surgeons kept the sick chamber closed against all visiters, a silent and melancholy breakfast was taken by the whole party, in waiting for the moment when they might be admitted. When this cheerless meal was ended, Sir Gervaise desired Bluewater to follow him to his room, whither he led the way in person.

"It is possible, certainly, that Vervillin is out," commenced the vice-admiral, when they were alone; "but we shall know more about it, when the cutter gets in, and reports. You saw nothing but her number, I think you told me?"

"She was at work with private signals, when I left the head-land; of course I was unable to read them without the book."

"That Vervillin is a good fellow," returned Sir Gervaise, rubbing his hands; a way he had when much pleased; "and has stuff in him. He has thirteen two-decked ships, Dick, and that will be one apiece for our captains, and a spare one for each of our flags. I believe there is no three-decker in that squadron?"

"There you've made a small mistake, Sir Gervaise, as the Comte de Vervillin had his flag in the largest three-decker of France; *le Bourbon* 120. The rest of his ships are like our own, though much fuller manned."

"Never mind, Blue—never mind:—we'll put two on the Bourbon, and try to make our frigates of use. Besides, you have a knack at keeping the fleet so compact, that it is nearly a single battery."

"May I venture to ask, then, if it's your intention to go out, should the news by the Active prove to be what you anticipate?"

Sir Gervaise cast a quick, distrustful glance at the other, anxious to read the motive for the question, at the same time that he did not wish to betray his own feelings; then he appeared to meditate on the answer.

"It is not quite agreeable to lie here, chafing our cables, with a French squadron roving the channel," he said; "but I rather think it's my duty to wait for orders from the Admiralty, under present circumstances."

"Do you expect my lords will send you through the Straits of Dover, to blockade the Frith?"

"If they do, Bluewater, I shall hope for your company. I trust, a night's rest has given you different views of what ought to be a seaman's duty, when his country is at open war with her ancient and most powerful enemies."

"It is the prerogative of the *crown* to declare war, Oakes. No one but a *lawful* sovereign can make a *lawful* war."

"Ay, here come your cursed distinctions about *de jure* and *de facto*, again. By the way, Dick, you are something of a scholar—can you tell me what is understood by calling a man a *nullus?*"

Admiral Bluewater, who had taken his usual lolling attitude in the most comfortable chair he could find, while his more mercurial friend kept pacing the room, now raised his head in surprise, following the quick motions of the other, with his eyes, as if he doubted whether he had rightly heard the question.

"It's plain English, is it not?—or plain *Latin*, if you will—what is meant by calling a man a *nullus?*" repeated Sir Gervaise, observing the other's manner.

"The Latin is *plain* enough, certainly," returned Bluewater, smiling; "you surely do not mean *nullus, nulla, nullum?*"

"Exactly that—you've hit it to a gender.—*Nullus, nulla, nullum.* No *man*, no *woman*, no *thing*. Masculine, feminine, neuter."

"I never heard the saying. If ever used, it must be some silly play on sounds, and mean a numskull—or, perhaps, a fling at a fellow's position, by saying he is a 'nobody.' Who the deuce has been calling another a *nullus*, in the presence of the commander-in-chief of the southern squadron?"

"Sir Wycherly Wychecombe—our unfortunate host, here: the poor man who is on his death-bed, on this very floor."

Again Bluewater raised his head, and once more his eye sought the face of his friend. Sir Gervaise had now stopped short, with his hands crossed behind his back, looking intently at the other, in expectation of the answer.

"I thought it might be some difficulty from the fleet—some silly fellow complaining of another still more silly for using such a word. Sir Wycherly!— the poor man's mind must have failed him."

"I rather think not; if it has, there is 'method in his madness,' for he persevered most surprisingly, in the use of the term. His nephew, Tom Wychecombe, the presumptive heir, he insists on it, is a *nullus*; while this Sir

Reginald, who is expected to arrive every instant, he says is only *half*—or half-*blood*, as it has since been explained to us."

"I am afraid this nephew will prove to be any thing but *nullus*, when he succeeds to the estate and title," answered Bluewater, gravely. "A more sinister-looking scoundrel, I never laid eyes on."

"That is just my way of thinking; and not in the least like the family."

"This matter of likenesses is not easily explained, Oakes. We see parents and children without any visible resemblance to each other; and then we find startling likenesses between utter strangers."

"*Bachelor's children* may be in that predicament, certainly; but I should think few others. I never yet studied a child, that I did not find some resemblance to both parents; covert and only transitory, perhaps; but a likeness so distinct as to establish the relationship. What an accursed chance it is, that our noble young lieutenant should have no claim on this old baronet; while this d——d *nullus* is both heir at law, and heir of entail! I never took half as much interest in any other man's estate, as I take in the succession to this of our poor host!"

"There you are mistaken, Oakes; you took more in *mine*; for, when I made a will in your own favour, and gave it to you to read, you tore it in two, and threw it overboard, with your own hand."

"Ay, that was an act of lawful authority. As your superior, I countermanded that will! I hope you've made another, and given your money, as I told you, to your cousin, the Viscount."

"I did, but *that* will has shared the fate of the first. It appearing to me, that we are touching on serious times, and Bluewater being rich already, I destroyed the devise in his favour, and made a new one, this very morning. As you are my executor, as usual, it may be well to let you know it."

"Dick, you have not been mad enough to cut off the head of your own family—your own flesh and blood, as it might be—to leave the few thousands you own, to this mad adventurer in Scotland!"

Bluewater smiled at this evidence of the familiarity of his friend with his own way of thinking and feeling; and, for a single instant, he regretted that he had not put his first intention in force, in order that the conformity of views might have been still more perfect; but, putting a hand in his pocket he drew out the document itself, and leaning forward, gave it carelessly to Sir Gervaise.

"There is the will; and by looking it over, you will know what I've done," he said. "I wish you would keep it; for, if 'misery makes us acquainted with strange bed-fellows,' revolutions reduce us, often, to strange plights, and the paper will be safer with you than with me. Of course, you will keep my secret, until the proper time to reveal it shall arrive."

The vice-admiral, who knew that he had no direct interest in his friend's disposition of his property, took the will, with a good deal of curiosity to ascertain its provisions. So short a testament was soon read; and his eye rested intently on the paper until it had taken in the last word. Then his hand dropped, and he regarded Bluewater with a surprise he neither affected, nor wished to conceal. He did not doubt his friend's sanity, but he greatly questioned his discretion.

"This is a very simple, but a very ingenious arrangement, to disturb the order of society," he said; "and to convert a very modest and unpretending, though lovely girl, into a forward and airs-taking old woman! What is this Mildred Dutton to you, that you should bequeath to her £30,000?"

"She is one of the meekest, most ingenuous, purest, and loveliest, of her meek, ingenuous, pure, and lovely sex, crushed to the earth by the curse of a brutal, drunken father; and, I am resolute to see that this world, for once, afford some compensation for its own miseries."

"Never doubt that, Richard Bluewater; never doubt *that*. So certain is vice, or crime, to bring its own punishment in this life, that one may well question if any other hell is needed. And, depend on it, your meek, modest ingenuousness, in its turn, will not go unrewarded."

"Quite true, so far as the spirit is concerned; but, I mean to provide a little for the comfort of the body. You remember Agnes Hedworth, I take it for granted?"

"Remember her!—out of all question. Had the war left me leisure for making love, she was the only woman I ever knew, who could have brought me to her feet—I mean as a dog, Dick."

"Do you see any resemblance between her and this Mildred Dutton? It is in the expression rather than in the features—but, it is the expression which alone denotes the character."

"By George, you're right, Bluewater; and this relieves me from some embarrassment I've felt about that very expression of which you speak. She *is* like poor Agnes, who became a saint earlier than any of us could have wished. Living or dead, Agnes Hedworth must be an angel! You were fonder of her, than of any other woman, I believe. At one time, I thought you might propose for her hand."

"It was not that sort of affection, and you could not have known her private history, or you would not have fancied this. I was so situated in the way of relatives, that Agnes, though only the child of a cousin-german, was the nearest youthful female relative I had on earth; and I regarded her more as a sister, than as a creature who could ever become my wife. She was sixteen years my junior; and by the time she had become old enough to marry, I was accustomed to think of her only as one destined for another station. The same feeling existed as to her sister, the Duchess, though in a greatly lessened degree."

"Poor, sweet Agnes!—and it is on account of this accidental resemblance, that you have determined to make the daughter of a drunken sailing-master your heiress?"

"Not altogether so; the will was drawn before I was conscious that the likeness existed. Still, it has probably, unknown to myself, greatly disposed me to view her with favour. But, Gervaise, Agnes herself was not fairer in person, or more lovely in mind, than this very Mildred Dutton."

"Well, you have not been accustomed to regard *her* as a sister; and *she* has become marriageable, without there having been any opportunity for your regarding her as so peculiarly sacred, Dick!" returned Sir Gervaise, half suppressing a smile as he threw a quiet glance at his friend.

"You know this to be idle, Oakes. Some one must inherit my money; my brother is long since dead; even poor, poor Agnes is gone; her sister don't need it; Bluewater is an over-rich bachelor, already; *you* won't take it, and what better can I do with it? If you could have seen the cruel manner in which the spirits of both mother and daughter were crushed to the earth last night, by that beast of a husband and father, you would have felt a desire to relieve their misery, even though it had cost you Bowldero, and half your money in the funds."

"Umph! Bowldero has been in my family five centuries, and is likely to remain there, Master Bluewater, five more; unless, indeed, your dashing Pretender should succeed, and take it away by confiscation."

"There, again, was another inducement. Should I leave my cash to a rich person, and should chance put me on the wrong side in this struggle, the king, *de facto*, would get it all; whereas, even a German would not have the heart to rob a poor creature like Mildred of her support."

"The *Scotch* are notorious for bowels, in such matters! Well, have it your own way, Dick. It's of no great moment what you do with your prize-money; though I had supposed it would fall into the hands of this boy, Geoffrey Cleveland, who is no discredit to your blood."

"He will have a hundred thousand pounds, at five-and-twenty, that were left him by old Lady Greenfield, his great-aunt, and that is more than he will know what to do with. But, enough of this. Have you received further tidings from the north, during the night?"

"Not a syllable. This is a retired part of the country, and half Scotland might be capsized in one of its loughs, and we not know of it, for a week, down here in Devonshire. Should I get no intelligence or orders, in the next thirty-six hours, I think of posting up to London, leaving you in command of the fleet."

"That may not be wise. You would scarcely confide so important a trust, in such a crisis, to a man of my political feelings—I will not say *opinions*; since you attribute all to sentiment."

"I would confide my life and honour to you, Richard Bluewater, with the utmost confidence in the security of both, so long as it depended on your own acts or inclinations. We must first see, however, what news the Active brings us; for, if de Vervillin is really out, I shall assume that the duty of an English sailor is to beat a Frenchman, before all other considerations."

"If he *can*," drily observed the other, raising his right leg so high as to place the foot on the top of an old-fashioned chair; an effort that nearly brought his back in a horizontal line.

"I am far from regarding it as a matter of course, Admiral Bluewater; but, it *has* been done sufficiently often, to render it an event of no very violent *possibility*. Ah, here is Magrath to tell us the condition of his patient."

The surgeon of the Plantagenet entering the room, at that moment, the conversation was instantly changed.

"Well, Magrath," said Sir Gervaise, stopping suddenly in his quarter-deck pace; "what news of the poor man?"

"He is reviving, Admiral Oakes," returned the phlegmatic surgeon; "but it is like the gleaming of sunshine that streams through clouds, as the great luminary sets behind the hills—"

"Oh! hang your poetry, doctor; let us have nothing but plain matter-of-fact, this morning."

"Well, then, Sir Gervaise, as commander-in-chief, you'll be obeyed, I think. Sir Wycherly Wychecombe is suffering under an attack of apoplexy—or [Greek: apoplêxis], as the Greeks had it. The diagnosis of the disease is not easily mistaken, though it has its affinities as well as other maladies. The applications for gout, or *arthritis*—sometimes produce apoplexy; though one disease is seated in the head, while the other usually takes refuge in the feet. Ye'll understand this the more readily, gentlemen, when ye reflect that as a thief is chased from one hiding-place, he commonly endeavours to get into another. I much misgive the prudence of the phlebotomy ye practised among ye, on the first summons to the patient."

"What the d——l does the man mean by phlebotomy?" exclaimed Sir Gervaise, who had an aversion to medicine, and knew scarcely any of the commonest terms of practice, though expert in bleeding.

"I'm thinking it's what you and Admiral Bluewater so freely administer to His Majesty's enemies, whenever ye fall in with 'em at sea;—he-he-he—" answered Magrath, chuckling at his own humour; which, as the quantity was small, was all the better in quality.

"Surely he does not mean powder and shot! We give the French shot; Sir Wycherly has not been shot?"

"Varra true, Sir Gervaise, but ye've let him blood, amang ye: a measure that has been somewhat precipitately practised, I've my misgivings!"

"Now, any old woman can tell us better than that, doctor. Blood-letting is the every-day remedy for attacks of this sort."

"I do not dispute the dogmas of elderly persons of the other sex, Sir Gervaise, or your *every-day remedia*. If 'every-day' doctors would save life and alleviate pain, diplomas would be unnecessary; and we might, all of us, practise on the principle of the 'de'el tak' the hindmaist,' as ye did yoursel', Sir Gervaise, when ye cut and slash'd amang the Dons, in boarding El Lirio. I was there, ye'll both remember, gentlemen; and was obleeged to sew up the gashes ye made with your own irreverent and ungodly hands."

This speech referred to one of the most desperate, hand-to-hand struggles, in which the two flag-officers had ever been engaged; and, as it afforded them the means of exhibiting their personal gallantry, when quite young men, both usually looked back upon the exploit with great self-complacency; Sir Gervaise, in particular, his friend having often declared since, that they ought to have been laid on the shelf for life, as a punishment for risking their men in so mad an enterprise, though it did prove to be brilliantly successful.

"That was an affair in which one might engage at twenty-two, Magrath," observed Bluewater; "but which he ought to hesitate about thinking of even, after thirty."

"I'd do it again, this blessed day, if you would give us a chance!" exclaimed Sir Gervaise, striking the back of one hand into the palm of the other, with a sudden energy, that showed how much he was excited by the mere recollection of the scene.

"That w'ud ye!—that w'ud ye!" said Magrath, growing more and more Scotch, as he warmed in the discourse; "ye'd board a mackerel-hoy, rather than not have an engagement. Ye'r a varra capital vice-admiral of the red, Sir Gervaise, but I'm judging ye'd mak' a varra indeeferent loblolly-boy."

"Bluewater, I shall be compelled to change ships with you, in order to get rid of the old stand-by's of the Plantagenets! They stick to me like leeches; and have got to be so familiar, that they criticise all my orders, and don't more than half obey them, in the bargain."

"No one will criticise your nautical commands, Sir Gervaise; though, in the way of the healing airt,—science, it should be called—ye're no mair to be trusted, than one of the young gentlemen. I'm told ye drew ye'r lancet on this poor gentleman, as ye'd draw ye'r sword on an enemy!"

"I did, indeed, sir; though Mr. Rotherham had rendered the application of the instrument unnecessary. Apoplexy is a rushing of the blood to the head; and by diminishing the quantity in the veins of the arms or temples, you lessen the pressure on the brain."

"Just layman's practice, sir—just layman's practice. Will ye tell me now if the patient's face was red or white? Every thing depends on *that*; which is the true diagnosis of the malady."

"Red, I think; was it not, Bluewater? Red, like old port, of which I fancy the poor man had more than his share."

"Weel, in that case, you were not so varra wrong; but, they tell me his countenance was pallid and death-like; in which case ye came near to committing murder. There is one principle that controls the diagnosis of all cases of apoplexy among ye'r true country gentlemen—and that is, that the system is reduced and enfeebled, by habitual devotion to the decanter. In such attacks ye canna' do warse, than to let blood. But, I'll no be hard upon you, Sir Gervaise; and so we'll drop the subject—though, truth to say, I do not admire your poaching on my manor. Sir Wycherly is materially better, and expresses, as well as a man who has not the use of his tongue, *can* express a thing, his besetting desire to make his last will and testament. In ordinary cases of *apoplexia*, it is good practice to oppose this craving; though, as it is my firm opinion that nothing can save the patient's life, I do not set myself against the measure, in this particular case. Thar' was a curious discussion at Edinbro', in my youth, gentlemen, on the question whether the considerations connected with the disposition of the property, or the considerations connected with the patient's health, ought to preponderate in the physician's mind, when it might be reasonably doubted whether the act of making a will, would or would not essentially affect the nervous system, and otherwise derange the functions of the body. A very pretty argument, in excellent Edinbro' Latin, was made on each side of the question. I think, on the whole, the physicos had the best o' it; for they could show a plausible present evil, as opposed to a possible remote good."

"Has Sir Wycherly mentioned my name this morning?" asked the vice-admiral, with interest.

"He has, indeed, Sir Gervaise; and that in a way so manifestly connected with his will, that I'm opining ye'll no be forgotten in the legacies. The name of Bluewater was in his mouth, also."

"In which case no time should be lost; for, never before have I felt half the interest in the disposition of a stranger's estate. Hark! Are not those wheels rattling in the court-yard?"

"Ye'r senses are most pairfect, Sir Gervaise, and that I've always said was one reason why ye'r so great an admiral," returned Magrath. "Mind, only *one*, Sir Gervaise; for many qualities united, are necessary to make a truly great man. I see a middle-aged gentleman alighting, and servants around him, who wear the same liveries as those of this house. Some relative, no doubt, come to look after the legacies, also."

"This must be Sir Reginald Wychecombe; it may not be amiss if we go forward to receive him, Bluewater."

At this suggestion, the rear-admiral drew in his legs, which had not changed their position on account of the presence of the surgeon, arose, and followed Sir Gervaise, as the latter left the room.

CHAPTER XIII.

"Videsne quis venit?""Video, et gaudeo."

NATHANIEL ET HOLOFERNES.

Tom Wychecombe had experienced an uneasiness that it is unnecessary to explain, ever since he learned that his reputed uncle had sent a messenger to bring the "half-blood" to the Hall. From the moment he got a clue to the fact, he took sufficient pains to ascertain what was in the wind; and when Sir Reginald Wychecombe entered the house, the first person he met was this spurious supporter of the honours of his name.

"Sir Reginald Wychecombe, I presume, from the arms and the liveries," said Tom, endeavouring to assume the manner of a host. "It is grateful to find that, though we are separated by quite two centuries, all the usages and the bearings of the family are equally preserved and respected, by both its branches."

"I am Sir Reginald Wychecombe, sir, and endeavour not to forget the honourable ancestry from which I am derived. May I ask what kinsman I have the pleasure now to meet?"

"Mr. Thomas Wychecombe, sir, at your command; the *eldest* son of Sir Wycherly's next brother, the late Mr. Baron Wychecombe. I trust, Sir Reginald, you have not considered us as so far removed in blood, as to have entirely overlooked our births, marriages, and deaths."

"I have *not*, sir," returned the baronet, drily, and with an emphasis that disturbed his listener, though the cold jesuitical smile that accompanied the words, had the effect to calm his vivid apprehensions. "*All* that relates to the house of Wychecombe has interest in my eyes; and I have endeavoured, successfully I trust, to ascertain *all* that relates to its births, *marriages*, and deaths. I greatly regret that the second time I enter this venerable dwelling, should be on an occasion as melancholy as this, on which I am now summoned. How is your respectable—how is Sir Wycherly Wychecombe, I wish to say?"

There was sufficient in this answer, taken in connection with the deliberate, guarded, and yet expressive manner of the speaker to make Tom extremely uncomfortable, though there was also sufficient to leave him in doubts as to his namesake's true meaning. The words emphasized by the latter, were touched lightly, though distinctly; and the cold, artificial smile with which they were uttered, completely baffled the sagacity of a rogue, as common-place as the heir-expectant. Then the sudden change in the construction of the last sentence, and the substitution of the name of the person mentioned, for the degree of affinity in which he was supposed to stand to Tom, might be merely a rigid observance of the best tone of society, or it might be equivocal. All these little distinctions gleamed across the mind of Tom Wychecombe; but that was not the moment to pursue the investigation. Courtesy required that he should make an immediate answer, which he succeeded in doing steadily enough as to general appearances, though his sagacious and practised questioner perceived that his words had not failed of producing the impression he intended; for he had looked to their establishing a species of authority over the young man.

"My honoured and beloved uncle has revived a little, they tell me," said Tom; "but I fear these appearances are delusive. After eighty-four, death has a fearful hold upon us, sir! The worst of it is, that my poor, dear uncle's mind is sensibly affected; and it is quite impossible to get at any of his little wishes, in the way of memorials and messages—"

"How then, sir, came Sir Wycherly to honour *me* with a request to visit him?" demanded the other, with an extremely awkward pertinency.

"I suppose, sir, he has succeeded in muttering your name, and that a natural construction has been put on its use, at such a moment. His will has been made some time, I understand; though I am ignorant of even the name of the executor, as it is closed in an envelope, and sealed with Sir Wycherly's arms. It cannot be, then, on account of a *will*, that he has wished to see you. I rather think, as the next of the family, *out of the direct line of succession*, he may have ventured to name you as the executor of the will in existence, and has thought it proper to notify you of the same."

"Yes, sir," returned Sir Reginald, in his usual cold, wary manner; "though it would have been more in conformity with usage, had the notification taken the form of a request to serve, previously to making the testament. My letter was signed 'Gervaise Oakes,' and, as they tell me a fleet is in the neighbourhood, I have supposed that the celebrated admiral of that name, has done me the honour to write it."

"You are not mistaken, sir; Sir Gervaise Oakes is in the house—ah—here he comes to receive you, accompanied by Rear-Admiral Bluewater, whom the sailors call his mainmast."

The foregoing conversation had taken place in a little parlour that led off from the great hall, whither Tom had conducted his guest, and in which the two admirals now made their appearance. Introductions were scarcely necessary, the uniform and star—for in that age officers usually appeared in their robes—the uniform and star of Sir Gervaise at once proclaiming his rank and name; while, between Sir Reginald and Bluewater there existed a slight personal acquaintance, which had grown out of their covert, but deep, Jacobite sympathies.

"Sir Gervaise Oakes," and "Sir Reginald Wychecombe," passed between the gentlemen, with a hearty shake of the hand from the admiral, which was met by a cold touch of the fingers on the part of the other, that might very well have passed for the great model of the sophisticated manipulation of the modern salute, but which, in fact, was the result of temperament rather than of fashion. As soon as this ceremony was gone through, and a few brief expressions of courtesy were exchanged, the new comer turned to Bluewater, with an air of greater freedom, and continued—

"And you, too, Sir Richard Bluewater! I rejoice to meet an acquaintance in this melancholy scene."

"I am happy to see you, Sir Reginald; though you have conferred on me a title to which I have no proper claim."

"No!—the papers tell us that you have received one of the lately vacant red ribands?"

"I believe some such honour has been in contemplation—"

"Contemplation!—I do assure you, sir, your name is fairly and distinctly gazetted—as, by sending to my carriage, it will be in my power to show you. I am, then, the first to call you Sir Richard."

"Excuse me, Sir Reginald—there is some little misapprehension in this matter; I prefer to remain plain Rear-Admiral Bluewater. In due season, all will be explained."

The parties exchanged looks, which, in times like those in which they lived, were sufficiently intelligible to both; and the conversation was instantly changed. Before Sir Reginald relinquished the hand he held, however, he gave it a cordial squeeze, an intimation that was returned by a warm pressure from Bluewater. The party then began to converse of Sir Wycherly, his actual condition, and his probable motive in desiring to see his distant kinsman. This motive, Sir Gervaise, regardless of the presence of Tom Wychecombe, declared to be a wish to make a will; and, as he believed, the intention of naming Sir Reginald his executor, if not in some still more interesting capacity.

"I understand Sir Wycherly has a considerable sum entirely at his own disposal," continued the vice-admiral; "and I confess I like to see a man remember his friends and servants, generously, in his last moments. The estate is entailed, I hear; and I suppose Mr. Thomas Wychecombe here, will be none the worse for that precaution in his ancestor; let the old gentleman do as he pleases with his savings."

Sir Gervaise was so much accustomed to command, that he did not feel the singularity of his own interference in the affairs of a family of what might be called strangers, though the circumstance struck Sir Reginald, as a little odd. Nevertheless, the last had sufficient penetration to understand the vice-admiral's character at a glance, and the peculiarity made no lasting impression. When the allusion was made to Tom's succession, as a matter of course, however, he cast a cold, but withering look, at the reputed heir, which almost chilled the marrow in the bones of the jealous rogue.

"Might I say a word to you, in your own room, Sir Gervaise?" asked Sir Reginald, in an aside. "These matters ought not to be indecently hurried; and I wish to understand the ground better, before I advance."

This question was overheard by Bluewater; who, begging the gentlemen to remain where they were, withdrew himself, taking Tom Wychecombe with him. As soon as they were alone, Sir Reginald drew from his companion, by questions warily but ingeniously put, a history of all that had occurred within the last twenty-four hours; a knowledge of the really helpless state of Sir Wycherly, and of the manner in which he himself had been summoned, included. When satisfied, he expressed a desire to see the sick man.

"By the way, Sir Reginald," said the vice-admiral, with his hand on the lock of the door, arresting his own movement to put the question; "I see, by your manner of expressing yourself, that the law has not been entirely overlooked in your education. Do you happen to know what 'half-blood' means? it is either a medical or a legal term, and I understand few but nautical."

"You could not apply to any man in England, Sir Gervaise, better qualified to tell you," answered the Hertfordshire baronet, smiling expressively. "I am a barrister of the Middle Temple, having been educated as a younger son, and having since succeeded an elder brother, at the age of twenty-seven; I stand in the unfortunate relation of the 'half-blood' myself, to this very estate, on which we are now conversing."

Sir Reginald then proceeded to explain the law to the other, as we have already pointed it out to the reader; performing the duty succinctly, but quite clearly.

"Bless me!—bless me! Sir Reginald," exclaimed the direct-minded and *just-minded* sailor—"here must be some mistake! A fortieth cousin, or the king, take this estate before yourself, though you are directly descended from all the old Wychecombes of the times of the Plantagenets!"

"Such is the common law, Sir Gervaise. Were I Sir Wycherly's half-brother, or a son by a second wife of our common father, I could not take from *him*, although that common father had earned the estate by his own hands, or services."

"This is damnable, sir—damnable—and you'll pardon me, but I can hardly believe we have such a monstrous principle in the good, honest, well-meaning laws, of good, honest, well-meaning old England!"

Sir Reginald was one of the few lawyers of his time, who did not recognize the virtue of this particular provision of the common law; a circumstance that probably arose from his having so *small* an interest now in the mysteries of the profession, and so *large* an interest in the family estate of Wychecombe, destroyed by its *dictum*. He was, consequently, less surprised, and not at all hurt, at the evident manner in which the sailor repudiated his statement, as doing violence equally to reason, justice, and probability.

"Good, honest, well-meaning old England tolerates many grievous things, notwithstanding, Sir Gervaise," he answered; "among others, it tolerates the law of the half-blood. Much depends on the manner in which men view these things; that which seems gold to one, resembling silver in the eyes of another. Now, I dare say,"—this was said as a feeler, and with a smile that might pass for ironical or confiding, as the listener pleased to take it—"Now, I dare say, the clans would tell us that England tolerates an usurper, while her lawful prince was in banishment; though *you* and *I* might not feel disposed to allow it."

Sir Gervaise started, and cast a quick, suspicious glance at the speaker; but there the latter stood, with as open and guileless an expression on his handsome features, as was ever seen in the countenance of confiding sixteen.

"Your supposititious case is no parallel," returned the vice-admiral, losing every shade of suspicion, at this appearance of careless frankness; "since men often follow their feelings in their allegiance, while the law is supposed to be governed by reason and justice. But, now we are on the subject, will you tell me. Sir Reginald, if you also know what a *nullus* is?"

"I have no farther knowledge of the subject, Sir Gervaise," returned the other, smiling, this time, quite naturally; "than is to be found in the Latin dictionaries and grammars."

"Ay—you mean *nullus, nulla, nullum*. Even we sailors know *that*; as we all go to school before we go to sea. But, Sir Wycherly, in efforts to make himself understood, called you a 'half-blood.'"

"And quite correctly—I admit such to be the fact; and that I have no more *legal* claim, whatever on this estate, than you have yourself. My *moral* right, however, may be somewhat better."

"It is much to your credit, that you so frankly admit it, Sir Reginald; for, hang me, if I think even the judges would dream of raising such an objection to your succeeding, unless reminded of it."

"Therein you do them injustice, Sir Gervaise; as it is their duty to administer the laws, let them be what they may."

"Perhaps you are right, sir. But the reason for my asking what a *nullus* is, was the circumstance that Sir Wycherly, in the course of his efforts to speak, repeatedly called his nephew and heir, Mr. Thomas Wychecombe, by that epithet."

"Did he, indeed?—Was the epithet, as you well term it, *filius nullius?*"

"I rather think it was *nullus*—though I do believe the word *filius* was muttered, once or twice, also."

"Yes, sir, this has been the case; and I am not sorry Sir Wycherly is aware of the fact, as I hear that the young man affects to consider himself in a different point of view. A *filius nullius* is the legal term for a bastard—the 'son of nobody,' as you will at once understand. I am fully aware that such is the unfortunate predicament of Mr. Thomas Wychecombe, whose father, I possess complete evidence to show, was never married to his mother."

"And yet, Sir Reginald, the impudent rascal carries in his pocket even, a certificate, signed by some parish priest in London, to prove the contrary."

The civil baronet seemed surprised at this assertion of his military brother; but Sir Gervaise explaining what had passed between himself and the young man, he could no longer entertain any doubt of the fact.

"Since you have seen the document," resumed Sir Reginald, "it must, indeed, be so; and this misguided boy is prepared to take any desperate step in order to obtain the title and the estate. All that he has said about a will must be fabulous, as no man in his senses would risk his neck to obtain so hollow a distinction as a baronetcy—we are equally members of the class, and may speak frankly, Sir Gervaise—and the will would secure the estate, if there were one. I cannot think, therefore, that there is a will at all."

"If this will were not altogether to the fellow's liking, would not the marriage, beside the hollow honour of which you have spoken, put the whole of the landed property in his possession, under the entail?"

"It would, indeed; and I thank you for the suggestion. If, however, Sir Wycherly is desirous, *now*, of making a *new* will, and has strength and mind sufficient to execute his purpose, the *old* one need give us no concern. This is a most delicate affair for one in my situation to engage in, sir; and I greatly rejoice that I find such honourable and distinguished witnesses, in the house, to clear my reputation, should any thing occur to require such exculpation. On the one side, Sir Gervaise, there is the danger of an ancient estate's falling into the hands of the crown, and this, too, while one of no *stain* of blood, derived from the same honourable ancestors as the last possessor, is in existence; or, on the other, of its becoming the prey of one of base blood, and of but very doubtful character. The circumstance that Sir Wycherly desired my presence, is a great deal; and I trust to you, and to those with you, to vindicate the fairness of my course. If it's your pleasure, sir, we will now go to the sick chamber."

"With all my heart. I think, however, Sir Reginald," said the vice-admiral, as he approached the door; "that even in the event of an escheat, you would find these Brunswick princes sufficiently liberal to restore the property. I could not answer for those wandering Scotchmen; who have so many breechless nobles to enrich; but, I think, with the Hanoverians, you would be safe."

"The last have certainly one recommendation the most," returned the other, smiling courteously, but in a way so equivocal that even Sir Gervaise was momentarily struck by it; "they have fed so well, now, at the crib, that they may not have the same voracity, as those who have been long fasting. It would be, however, more pleasant to take these lands from a Wychecombe— a Wychecombe to a Wychecombe—than to receive them anew from even the Plantagenet who made the first grant."

This terminated the private dialogue, as the colloquists entered the hall, just as the last speaker concluded. Wycherly was conversing, earnestly, with Mrs. Dutton and Mildred, at the far end of the hall, when the baronets appeared; but, catching the eye of the admiral, he said a few words hastily to his companions, and joined the two gentlemen, who were now on their way to the sick man's chamber.

"Here is a namesake, if not a relative, Sir Reginald," observed Sir Gervaise, introducing the lieutenant; "and one, I rejoice to say, of whom all of even your honourable name have reason to be proud."

Sir Reginald's bow was courteous and bland, as the admiral proceeded to complete the introduction; but Wycherly felt that the keen, searching look he bestowed on himself, was disagreeable.

"I am not at all aware, that I have the smallest claim to the honour of being Sir Reginald Wychecombe's relative," he said, with cold reserve. "Indeed, until last evening, I was ignorant of the existence of the Hertfordshire branch of this family; and you will remember, Sir Gervaise, that I am a Virginian."

"A Virginian!" exclaimed his namesake, taken so much by surprise as to lose a little of his self-command, "I did not know, indeed, that any who bear the name had found their way to the colonies."

"And if they had, sir, they would have met with a set of fellows every way fit to be their associates, Sir Reginald. We English are a little clannish—I hate the word, too; it has such a narrow Scotch sound—but we *are* clannish, although generally provided with garments to our nether limbs; and we sometimes look down upon even a son, whom the love of adventure has led into that part of the world. In my view an Englishman is an Englishman, let him come from what part of the empire he may. That is what I call genuine liberality, Sir Reginald."

"Quite true, Sir Gervaise; and a Scotchman is a Scotchman, even though he come from the north of Tweed."

This was quietly said, but the vice-admiral felt the merited rebuke it contained, and he had the good-nature and the good sense to laugh at it, and to admit his own prejudices. This little encounter brought the party to Sir Wycherly's door, where all three remained until it was ascertained that they might enter.

The next quarter of an hour brought about a great change in the situation of all the principal inmates of Wychecombe Hall. The interdict was taken off the rooms of Sir Wycherly, and in them had collected all the gentlemen, Mrs. Dutton and her daughter, with three or four of the upper servants of the establishment. Even Galleygo contrived to thrust his ungainly person in, among the rest, though he had the discretion to keep in the background among his fellows. In a word, both dressing-room and bed-room had their occupants, though the last was principally filled by the medical men, and those whose rank gave them claims to be near the person of the sick.

It was now past a question known that poor Sir Wycherly was on his death-bed. His mind had sensibly improved, nor was his speech any worse; but his physical system generally had received a shock that rendered recovery hopeless. It was the opinion of the physicians that he might possibly survive several days; or, that he might be carried off, in a moment, by a return of the paralytic affection.

The baronet, himself, appeared to be perfectly conscious of his situation; as was apparent by the anxiety he expressed to get his friends together, and more especially the concern he felt to make a due disposition of his worldly affairs. The medical men had long resisted both wishes, until, convinced that the question was reduced to one of a few hours more or less of life, and that denial was likely to produce worse effects than compliance, they finally and unanimously consented.

"It's no a great concession to mortal infirmity to let a dying man have his way," whispered Magrath to the two admirals, as the latter entered the room. "Sir Wycherly is a hopeless case, and we'll just consent to let him make a few codicils, seeing that he so fairvently desires it; and then there may be fewer hopeless deevils left behind him, when he's gathered to his forefathers."

"Here we are, my dear Sir Wycherly," said the vice-admiral, who never lost an occasion to effect his purpose, by any unnecessary delay; "here we all are anxious to comply with your wishes. Your kinsman, Sir Reginald Wychecombe, is also present, and desirous of doing your pleasure."

It was a painful sight to see a man on his death-bed, so anxious to discharge the forms of the world, as the master of the Hall now appeared to be. There had been an unnecessary alienation between the heads of the two branches of the family; not arising from any quarrel, or positive cause of disagreement, but from a silent conviction in both parties, that each was unsuited to the other. They had met a few times, and always parted without regret. The case was now different; the separation was, in one sense at least, to be eternal; and all minor considerations, all caprices of habits or despotism of tastes, faded before the solemn impressions of the moment. Still, Sir Wycherly could not forget that he was master of Wychecombe, and that his namesake was esteemed a man of refinement; and, in his simple way of thinking he would fain have arisen, in order to do him honour. A little gentle violence, even, was necessary to keep the patient quiet.

"Much honoured, sir—greatly pleased," muttered Sir Wycherly, the words coming from him with difficulty. "Same ancestors—same name—Plantagenets—old house, sir—head go, new one come—none better, than—"

"Do not distress yourself to speak, unnecessarily, my dear sir," interrupted Sir Reginald, with more tenderness for the patient than consideration for his own interest, as the next words promised to relate to the succession. "Sir Gervaise Oakes tells me, he understands your wishes, generally, and that he is now prepared to gratify them. First relieve your mind, in matters of business; and, then, I shall be most happy to exchange with you the feelings of kindred."

"Yes, Sir Wycherly," put in Sir Gervaise, on this hint; "I believe I have now found the clue to all you wish to say. The few words written by you, last night, were the commencement of a will, which it is your strong desire to make. Do not speak, but raise your right hand, if I am not mistaken."

The sick man actually stretched his right arm above the bed-clothes, and his dull eyes lighted with an expression of pleasure, that proved how strongly his feelings were enlisted in the result.

"You see, gentlemen!" said Sir Gervaise, with emphasis. "No one can mistake the meaning of this! Come nearer, doctor—Mr. Rotherham—all who have no probable interest in the affair—I wish it to be seen that Sir Wycherly Wychecombe is desirous of making his will."

The vice-admiral now went through the ceremony of repeating his request, and got the same significant answer.

"So I understood it, Sir Wycherly, and I believe now I also understand all about the 'half,' and the 'whole,' and the '*nullus*.' You meant to tell us that your kinsman, Sir Reginald Wychecombe, was of the 'half-blood' as respects yourself, and that Mr. Thomas Wychecombe, your nephew, is what is termed in law—however painful this may be, gentlemen, at such solemn moments the truth must be plainly spoken—that Mr. Thomas Wychecombe is what the law terms a '*filius nullius*.' If we have understood you in this, also, have the goodness to give this company the same sign of assent."

The last words were scarcely spoken, before Sir Wycherly again raised his arm, and nodded his head.

"Here there can be no mistake, and no one rejoices in it more than I do myself; for, the unintelligible words gave me a great deal of vexation. Well, my dear sir, understanding your wishes, my secretary, Mr. Atwood, has drawn the commencement of a will, in the usual form, using your own pious and proper language of—'In the name of God, Amen,' as the commencement; and he stands ready to write down your bequests, as you may see fit to name them. We will take them, first, on a separate piece of paper; then read them to you, for your approbation; and afterwards, transcribe them into the will. I believe, Sir Reginald, that mode would withstand the subtleties of all the gentlemen of all the Inns of Court?"

"It is a very proper and prudent mode for executing a will, sir, under the peculiar circumstances," returned he of Hertfordshire. "But, Sir Gervaise, my situation, here, is a little delicate, as may be that of Mr. Thomas Wychecombe—others of the name and family, if any such there be. Would it not be well to inquire if our presence is actually desired by the intended testator?"

"Is it your wish, Sir Wycherly, that your kinsmen and namesakes remain in the room, or shall they retire until the will is executed? I will call over the names of the company, and when you wish any one, in particular, to stay in the room, you will nod your head."

"All—all stay," muttered Sir Wycherly; "Sir Reginald—Tom—Wycherly—all—"

"This seems explicit enough, gentlemen," resumed the vice-admiral. "You are *all* requested to stay; and, if I might venture an opinion, our poor friend has named those on whom he intends his bequests to fall—and pretty much, too, in the order in which they will come."

"That will appear more unanswerably when Sir Wycherly has expressed his intentions in words," observed Sir Reginald, very desirous that there should not be the smallest appearance of dictation or persuasion offered to his kinsman, at a moment so grave. "Let me entreat that no leading questions be put."

"Sir Gervaise understands leading in battle, much better than in a cross-examination, Sir Reginald," Bluewater observed, in a tone so low, that none heard him but the person to whom the words were addressed. "I think we shall sooner get at Sir Wycherly's wishes, by allowing him to take his own course."

The other bowed, and appeared disposed to acquiesce. In the mean time preparations were making for the construction of the will. Atwood seated himself at a table near the bed, and commenced nibbing his pens; the medical men administered a cordial; Sir Gervaise caused all the witnesses to range themselves around the room, in a way that each might fairly see, and be seen; taking care, however, so to dispose of Wycherly, as to leave no doubt of his handsome person's coming into the sick man's view. The lieutenant's modesty might have rebelled at this arrangement, had he not found himself immediately at the side of Mildred.

CHAPTER XIV.

"Yet, all is o'er!—fear, doubt, suspense, are fled,
Let brighter thoughts be with the virtuous dead!
The final ordeal of the soul is past,
And the pale brow is sealed to Heaven at last."

MRS. HEMANS.

It will be easily supposed that Tom Wychecombe witnessed the proceedings related in the preceding chapter with dismay. The circumstance that he actually possessed a *bona fide* will of his uncle, which left him heir of all the latter owned, real or personal, had made him audacious, and first induced him to take the bold stand of asserting his legitimacy, and of claiming all its consequences. He had fully determined to assume the title on the demise of Sir Wycherly; plausibly enough supposing that, as there was no heir to the baronetcy, the lands once in his quiet possession, no one would take sufficient interest in the matter to dispute his right to the rank. Here, however, was a blow that menaced death to all his hopes. His illegitimacy seemed to be known to others, and there was every prospect of a new will's supplanting the old one, in its more important provisions, at least. He was at a loss to imagine what had made this sudden change in his uncle's intentions; for he did not sufficiently understand himself, to perceive that the few months of close communion which had succeeded the death of his reputed father, had sufficed to enlighten Sir Wycherly on the subject of his own true character, and to awaken a disgust that had remained passive, until suddenly aroused by the necessity of acting; and, least of all, could he understand how surprisingly the moral vision of men is purified and enlarged, as respects both the past and the future, by the near approach of death. Although symptoms of strong dissatisfaction escaped him, he quieted his feelings as much as possible, cautiously waiting for any occurrence that might be used in setting aside the contemplated instrument, hereafter; or, what would be still better, to defeat its execution, now.

As soon as the necessary preparations were made, Atwood, his pen nibbed, ink at hand, and paper spread, was ready to proceed: and a breathless stillness existing in the chamber, Sir Gervaise resumed the subject on which they were convened.

"Atwood will read to you what he has already written, Sir Wycherly," he said; "should the phraseology be agreeable to you, you will have the goodness to make a sign to that effect. Well, if all is ready, you can now commence—hey! Atwood?"

"'In the name of God, Amen,'" commenced the methodical secretary; "'I, Wycherly Wychecombe, Bart., of Wychecombe-Hall, in the county of Devon, being of sound mind, but of a feeble state of health, and having the view of death before my eyes, revoking all other wills, codicils, or testamentary devises, whatsoever, do make and declare this instrument to be my last will and testament: that is to say, Imprimis, I do hereby constitute and appoint —— —— of ——, the executor of this my said will, with all the powers and authority that the law gives, or may hereafter give to said executor. Secondly, I give and bequeath to ——.' This is all that is yet written, Sir Gervaise, blanks being left for the name or names of the executor or executors, as well for the 's' at the end of 'executor,' should the testator see fit to name more than one."

"There, Sir Reginald," said the vice-admiral, not altogether without exultation; "this is the way we prepare these things on board a man-of-war! A flag-officer's secretary needs have himself qualified to do any thing, short of a knowledge of administering to the cure of souls!"

"And the cure of bodies, ye'll be permitting me to add, Sir Gervaise," observed Magrath, taking an enormous pinch of a strong yellow snuff.

"Our secretary would make but a lubberly fist at turning off a delicate turtle-soup out of pig's-head; such as we puts on our table at sea, so often," muttered Galleygo in the ear of Mrs. Larder.

"I see nothing to object to, Sir Gervaise, if the language is agreeable to Sir Wycherly," answered the barrister by profession, though not by practice. "It would be advisable to get his approbation of even the language."

"That we intend to do, of course, sir. Sir Wycherly, do you find the terms of this will to your liking?"

Sir Wycherly smiled, and very clearly gave the sign of assent.

"I thought as much—for, Atwood has made the wills of two admirals, and of three captains, to my knowledge; and my Lord Chief Justice said that one of the last would have done credit to the best conveyancer in England, and that it was a pity the testator had nothing to bequeath. Now, Sir Wycherly, will you have one executor, or more? If *one*, hold up a single finger; and a finger for each additional executor you wish us to insert in these blanks. One, Atwood—you perceive, gentlemen, that Sir Wycherly raises but *one* finger; and so you can give a flourish at the end of the 'r,' as the word will be in the singular;—hey! Atwood?"

The secretary did as directed, and then reported himself ready to proceed.

"It will be necessary for you now to *name* your executor, Sir Wycherly—make as little effort as possible, as we shall understand the name, alone."

Sir Wycherly succeeded in uttering the name of "Sir Reginald Wychecombe," quite audibly.

"This is plain enough," resumed the vice-admiral; "how does the sentence read now, Atwood?"

"'*Imprimis:*—I do hereby constitute and appoint Sir Reginald Wychecombe of Wychecombe-Regis, in the county of Herts, Baronet, the executor of this my said will, &c.'"

"If that clause is to your liking, Sir Wycherly, have the goodness to give the sign agreed on."

The sick man smiled, nodded his head, raised his hand, and looked anxiously at his kinsman.

"I consent to serve, Sir Wycherly, if such is your desire," observed the nominee, who detected the meaning of his kinsman's look.

"And now, sir," continued the vice-admiral; "it is necessary to ask you a few questions, in order that Atwood may know what next to write. Is it your desire to bequeath any real estate?" Sir Wycherly assented. "Do you wish to bequeath *all* your real estate?" The same sign of assent was given. "Do you wish to bequeath *all* to one person?" The sign of assent was given to this also. "This makes plain sailing, and a short run,—hey! Atwood?"

The secretary wrote as fast as possible, and in two or three minutes he read aloud, as follows—

"'Secondly, I make and declare the following bequests or devises—that is to say, I give and bequeath to —— —— of ———, all the real estate of which I may die seised, together with all the houses, tenements, hereditaments, and appurtenances thereunto belonging, and all my rights to the same, whether in law or equity, to be possessed and enjoyed by the said —— —— of —— —— in fee, by —— heirs, executors, administrators, or assigns, for ever.' There are blanks for the name and description, as well as for the sex of the devisee," added the secretary.

"All very proper and legal, I believe, Sir Reginald?—I am glad you think so, sir. Now, Sir Wycherly, we wait for the name of the lucky person you mean thus to favour."

"Sir Reginald Wychecombe," the sick man uttered, painfully; "half-blood—no *nullus*. Sir Michael's heir—*my* heir."

"This is plain English!" cried Sir Gervaise, in the way of a man who is not displeased; "put in the name of 'Sir Reginald Wychecombe of Wychecombe-Regis, Herts,' Atwood—ay—that justs fills the blank handsomely—you want '*his* heirs, executors, &c.' in the other blank."

"I beg your pardon, Sir Gervaise; it should read 'by *himself, his* heirs, &c.'"

"Very true—very true, Atwood. Now read it slowly, and Sir Wycherly will assent, if he approve."

This was done, and Sir Wycherly not only approved, but it was apparent to all present, the abashed and confounded Tom himself not excepted, that he approved, with a feeling akin to delight.

"That gives a black eye to all the land,—hey! Atwood?" said Sir Gervaise; who, by this time, had entered into the business in hand, with all the interest of a regular notary—or, rather, with that of one, on whose shoulders rested the responsibility of success or failure. "We come next to the personals. Do you wish to bequeath your furniture, wines, horses, carriages, and other things of that sort, to any particular person, Sir Wycherly?"

"All—Sir Reginald—Wychecombe—half-blood—old Sir Michael's heir," answered the testator.

"Good—clap that down, Atwood, for it is doing the thing, as I like to see family affairs settled. As soon as you are ready, let us hear how it sounds in writing."

"I furthermore bequeath to the said Sir Reginald Wychecombe of Wychecombe-Regis, as aforesaid, baronet, all my personal property, whatsoever,'" read Atwood, as soon as ready; "'including furniture, wines, pictures, books, horses and carriages, and all other goods and chattels, of which I may die possessed, excepting thereout and therefrom, nevertheless, such sums in money, stocks, bonds, notes, or other securities for debts, or such articles as I may in this instrument especially devise to any other person.' We can now go to especial legacies, Sir Gervaise, and then another clause may make Sir Reginald residuary legatee, if such be Sir Wycherly's pleasure."

"If you approve of that clause, my dear sir, make the usual sign of assent."

Sir Wycherly both raised his hand and nodded his head, evidently quite satisfied.

"Now, my good sir, we come to the pounds—no—guineas? You like that better—well, I confess that it sounds better on the ear, and is more in conformity with the habits of gentlemen. Will you now bequeath guineas? Good—first name the legatee—is that right, Sir Reginald?"

"Quite right, Sir Gervaise; and Sir Wycherly will understand that he now names the first person to whom he wishes to bequeath any thing else."

"Milly," muttered the sick man.

"What? Mills!—the mills go with the lands, Sir Reginald?"

"He means Miss Mildred Dutton," eagerly interposed Wycherly, though with sufficient modesty.

"Yes—right—right," added the testator. "Little Milly—Milly Dutton—good little Milly."

Sir Gervaise hesitated, and looked round at Bluewater, as much as to say "this is bringing coals to Newcastle;" but Atwood took the idea, and wrote the bequest, in the usual form.

"'I give and bequeath to Mildred Dutton,'" he read aloud, "'daughter of Francis Dutton of the Royal Navy, the sum of ——' what sum shall I fill the blank with, Sir Wycherly?"

"Three—three—yes, three."

"Hundreds or thousands, my good sir?" asked Sir Gervaise, a little surprised at the amount of the bequest.

"Guineas—three—thousand—guineas—five per cents."

"That's as plain as logarithms. Give the young lady three thousand guineas in the fives, Atwood."

"'I give and bequeath to Mildred Dutton, daughter of Francis Dutton of the Royal Navy, the sum of three thousand guineas in the five per cent. stocks of this kingdom.' Will that do, Sir Wycherly?"

The old man looked at Mildred and smiled benevolently; for, at that moment, he felt he was placing the pure and lovely girl above the ordinary contingencies of her situation, by rendering her independent.

"Whose name shall we next insert, Sir Wycherly?" resumed the vice-admiral. "There must be many more of these guineas left."

"Gregory—and—James—children of my brother Thomas—Baron Wychecombe—five thousand guineas each," added the testator, making a great effort to express his meaning as clearly as possible.

He was understood; and, after a short consultation with the vice-admiral, Atwood wrote out the devise at length.

"'I give and bequeath to my nephews, Gregory and James Wychecombe, the reputed sons of my late brother, Thomas Wychecombe, one of the Barons of His Majesty's Exchequer, the sum of five thousand guineas, each, in the five per cent. funded debt of this kingdom.'"

"Do you approve of the devise, Sir Wycherly? if so, make the usual sign of assent?"

Sir Wycherly complied, as in all the previous cases of his approval.

"Whose name shall we next insert, in readiness for a legacy, Sir Wycherly?" asked the admiral.

Here was a long pause, the baronet evidently turning over in his mind, what he had done, and what yet remained to do.

"Spread yourselves, my friends, in such a way as to permit the testator to see you all," continued the vice-admiral, motioning with his hand to widen the circle around the bed, which had been contracted a little by curiosity and interest; "stand more this way, *Lieutenant Wycherly Wychecombe*, that the ladies may see and be seen; and you, too, Mr. Thomas Wychecombe, come further in front, where your uncle will observe you."

This speech pretty exactly reflected the workings of the speaker's mind. The idea that Wycherly was a natural child of the baronet's, notwithstanding the Virginian story, was uppermost in his thoughts; and, taking the supposed fact in connection with the young man's merit, he earnestly desired to obtain a legacy for him. As for Tom, he cared little whether his name appeared in the will or not. Justice was now substantially done, and the judge's property being sufficient for his wants, the present situation of the lately reputed heir excited but little sympathy. Nevertheless, Sir Gervaise thought it would be generous, under the circumstances, to remind the testator that such a being as Tom Wychecombe existed.

"Here is your nephew, Mr. Thomas, Sir Wycherly," he said; "is it your wish to let his name appear in your will?"

The sick man smiled coldly; but he moved his head, as much as to imply assent.

"'I give and bequeath to Thomas Wychecombe, the eldest reputed son of my late brother, Thomas, one of the Barons of His Majesty's Exchequer,'" read Atwood, when the clause was duly written; "'the sum of ——, in the five per cent. stocks of this kingdom.'"

"What sum will you have inserted, Sir Wycherly?" asked the vice-admiral.

"Fifty—fifty—*pounds*" said the testator, in a voice clearer and fuller than he had before used that day.

The necessary words were immediately inserted; the clause, as completed, was read again, and the approval was confirmed by a distinctly pronounced "yes." Tom started, but, as all the others maintained their self-command, the business of the moment did not the less proceed.

"Do you wish any more names introduced into your will, Sir Wycherly?" asked the vice-admiral. "You have bequeathed but—a-a-a—how much—

hey! Atwood?—ay, ten and three are thirteen, and fifty *pounds*, make £13,180; and I hear you have £20,000 funded, besides loose cash, beyond a doubt."

"Ann Larder—Samuel Cork—Richard Bitts—David Brush—Phoebe Keys," said Sir Wycherly, slowly, giving time after each pause, for Atwood to write; naming his cook, butler, groom, valet or body-servant, and housekeeper, in the order they have been laid before the reader.

"How much to each, Sir Wycherly?—I see Atwood has made short work, and put them all in the same clause—that will never do, unless the legacies are the same."

"Good—good—right," muttered the testator; "£200—each—£1000—all—money—money."

This settled the point, and the clause was regularly written, read, and approved.

"This raises the money bequests to £14,180, Sir Wycherly—some 6 or £7000 more must remain to be disposed of. Stand a little further this way, if you please, Mr. *Wycherly* Wychecombe, and allow the ladies more room. Whose name shall we insert next, sir?"

Sir Wycherly, thus directed by the eager desire of the admiral to serve the gallant lieutenant, fastened his eyes on the young man, regarding him quite a minute in silent attention.

"Virginian—same name—American—colonies—good lad—*brave* lad—£1000," muttered the sick man between his teeth; and, yet so breathless was the quiet of the chamber, at that moment, every syllable was heard by all present. "Yes—£1000—Wycherly Wychecombe—royal navy—"

Atwood's pen was running rapidly over the paper, and had just reached the name of the contemplated legatee, when his hand was arrested by the voice of the young man himself.

"Stop, Mr. Atwood—do not insert any clause in my favour!" cried Wycherly, his face the colour of crimson, and his chest heaving with the emotions he felt it so difficult to repress. "I decline the legacy—it will be useless to write it, as I will not receive a shilling."

"Young sir," said Sir Gervaise, with a little of the severity of a superior, when he rebukes an interior, in his manner; "you speak hastily. It is not the office of an auditor or of a spectator, to repel the kindness of a man about to pass from the face of the earth, into the more immediate presence of his God!"

"I have every sentiment of respect for Sir Wycherly Wychecombe, sir;—every friendly wish for his speedy recovery, and a long evening to his life;

but, I will accept of the money of no man who holds my country in such obvious distaste, as, it is apparent, the testator holds mine."

"You are an Englishman, I believe, *Lieutenant* Wychecombe; and a servant of King George II.?"

"I am *not* an Englishman, Sir Gervaise Oakes—but an American; a Virginian, entitled to all the rights and privileges of a British subject. I am no more an Englishman, than Dr. Magrath may lay claim to the same character."

"This is putting the case strongly,—hey! Atwood?" answered the vice-admiral, smiling in spite of the occasion. "I am far from saying that you are an Englishman, in all senses, sir; but you are one in the sense that gives you national character and national rights. You are a *subject* of *England*."

"No, Sir Gervaise; your pardon. I am the subject of George II., but in no manner a subject of *England*. I am, in one sense, perhaps, a subject of the British empire; but I am not the less a Virginian, and an American. Not a shilling of any man's money will I ever touch, who expresses his contempt for either."

"You forget yourself, young man, and overlook the future. The hundred or two of prize-money, bought at the expense of your blood, in the late affair at Groix, will not last for ever."

"It is gone, already, sir, every shilling of it having been sent to the widow of the boatswain who was killed at my side. I am no beggar, Sir Gervaise Oakes, though only an American. I am the owner of a plantation, which affords me a respectable independence, already; and I do not serve from necessity, but from choice. Perhaps, if Sir Wycherly knew this, he would consent to omit my name. I honour and respect him; would gladly relieve his distress, either of body or mind; but I cannot consent to accept his money when offered on terms I consider humiliating."

This was said modestly, but with a warmth and sincerity which left no doubt that the speaker was in earnest. Sir Gervaise too much respected the feelings of the young man to urge the matter any further, and he turned towards the bed, in expectation of what the sick man might next say. Sir Wycherly heard and understood all that passed, and it did not fail to produce an impression, even in the state to which he was reduced. Kind-hearted, and indisposed to injure even a fly, all the natural feelings of the old man resumed their ascendency, and he would gladly have given every shilling of his funded property to be able freely to express his compunction at having ever uttered a syllable that could offend sensibilities so noble and generous. But this exceeded his powers, and he was fain to do the best he could, in the painful situation in which he was placed.

"Noble fellow!" he stuttered out; "honour to name—come here—Sir Gervaise—bring here—"

"I believe it is the wish of Sir Wycherly, that you would draw near the bed, Mr. Wychecombe of *Virginia*," said the vice-admiral, pithily, though he extended a hand to, and smiled kindly on, the youth as the latter passed him in compliance.

The sick man now succeeded, with a good deal of difficulty, in drawing a valuable signet-ring from a finger.—This ring bore the Wychecombe arms, engraved on it. It was without the bloody hand, however; for it was far older than the order of baronets, having, as Wycherly well knew, been given by one of the Plantagenet Dukes to an ancestor of the family, during the French wars of Henry VI., and that, too, in commemoration of some signal act of gallantry in the field.

"Wear this—noble fellow—honour to name," said Sir Wycherly. "*Must* be descended—all Wychecombes descended—him—"

"I thank you, Sir Wycherly, for this present, which I prize as it ought to be prized," said Wycherly, every trace of any other feeling than that of gratitude having vanished from his countenance. "I may have no claims to your honours or money; but this ring I need not be ashamed to wear, since it was bestowed on one who was as much *my* ancestor, as he was the ancestor of any Wychecombe in England."

"Legitimate?" cried Tom, a fierce feeling of resentment upsetting his caution and cunning.

"Yes, sir, *legitimate*," answered Wycherly, turning to his interrogator, with the calmness of one conscious of his own truth, and with a glance of the eye that caused Tom to shrink back again into the circle. "I need no *bar*, to enable me to use this seal, which, you may perceive, Sir Gervaise Oakes, is a *fac simile* of the one I ordinarily wear, and which was transmitted to me from my direct ancestors."

The vice-admiral compared the seal on Wycherly's watch-chain with that on the ring, and, the bearings being principally griffins, he was enabled to see that one was the exact counterpart of the other. Sir Reginald advanced a step, and when the admiral had satisfied himself, he also took the two seals and compared them. As all the known branches of the Wychecombes of Wychecombe, bore the same arms, viz., griffins for Wychecombe, with three battering-rams quartered, for Wycherly,—he saw, at once, that the young man habitually carried about his person, this proof of a common origin. Sir Reginald knew very well that arms were often assumed, as well as names, and the greater the obscurity of the individual who took these liberties, the greater was his impunity; but the seal was a very ancient one, and innovations on personal rights were far less frequent a century since, than they are to-day. Then the character and appearance of Wycherly put fraud out of the question, so far as the young lieutenant himself was concerned. Although the elder branch of the family, legitimately speaking, was reduced to the helpless old man who was now stretched upon his death-bed, his own had been extensive; and it well might be that some cadet of the Wychecombes of Wychecombe-Regis, had strayed into the colonies and left descendants. Secretly resolving to look more closely into these facts, he gravely returned the seals, and intimated to Sir Gervaise that the more important business before them had better proceed. On this hint, Atwood resumed the pen, and the vice-admiral his duties.

"There want yet some 6 or £7000 to make up £20,000, Sir Wycherly, which I understand is the sum you have in the funds. Whose name or names will you have next inserted?"

"Rotherham—vicar—poor St. James—gone; yes—Mr.—Rotherham—vicar."

The clause was written, the sum of £1000 was inserted, and the whole was read and approved.

"This still leaves us some £5000 more to deal with, my dear sir?"

A long pause succeeded, during which time Sir Wycherly was deliberating what to do with the rest of his ready money. At length his wandering eye rested on the pale features of Mrs. Dutton; and, while he had a sort of liking, that proceeded from habit, for her husband, he remembered that she had many causes for sorrow. With a feeling that was creditable to his own heart, he uttered her name, and the sum of £2000. The clause was written, accordingly, read and approved.

"We have still £3000 certainly, if not £4000," added Sir Gervaise.

"Milly—dear little—Milly—pretty Milly," stammered out the baronet, affectionately.

"This must go into a codicil, Sir Gervaise," interrupted Atwood; "there being already one legacy in the young lady's favour. Shall it be one, two, three, or four thousand pounds, Sir Wycherly, in favour of Miss Mildred, to whom you have already bequeathed £3000."

The sick man muttered the words "three thousand," after a short pause, adding "codicil."

His wishes were complied with, and the whole was read and approved. After this, Sir Gervaise inquired if the testator wished to make any more devises. Sir Wycherly, who had in effect bequeathed, within a few hundred pounds, all he had to bestow, bethought himself, for a few moments, of the state of his affairs, and then he signified his satisfaction with what had been done.

"As it is possible, Sir Wycherly, that you may have overlooked something," said Sir Gervaise, "and it is better that nothing should escheat to the crown, I will suggest the expediency of your making some one residuary legatee."

The poor old man smiled an assent, and then he succeeded in muttering the name of "Sir Reginald Wychecombe."

This clause, like all the others, was written, read, and approved. The will was now completed, and preparations were made to read it carefully over to the intended testator. In order that this might be done with sufficient care for future objections, the two admirals and Atwood, who were selected for the witnesses, each read the testament himself, in order to say that nothing was laid before the testator but that which was fairly contained in the instrument, and that nothing was omitted. When all was ready, the will was audibly and slowly read to Sir Wycherly, by the secretary, from the beginning to the end. The old man listened with great attention; smiled when Mildred's name was mentioned; and clearly expressed, by signs and words, his entire satisfaction when all was ended. It remained only to place a pen in his hand, and to give him such assistance as would enable him to affix his name twice; once to the body of the instrument; and, when this was duly witnessed, then again to the codicil. By this time, Tom Wychecombe thought that the moment for interposing had arrived. He had been on thorns during the whole proceeding, forming desperate resolutions to sustain the bold fraud of his legitimacy, and thus take all the lands and heirlooms of the estate, under the entail; still he well knew that a subordinate but important question might arise, as between the validity of the two wills, in connection with Sir Wycherly's competency to make the last. It was material, therefore, in his view of the case, to enter a protest.

"Gentlemen," he said, advancing to the foot of the bed; "I call on you all to observe the nature of this whole transaction. My poor, beloved, but misled uncle, no longer ago than last night, was struck with a fit of apoplexy, or something so very near it as to disqualify him to judge in these matters; and here he is urged to make a will—"

"By whom, sir?" demanded Sir Gervaise, with a severity of tone that induced the speaker to fall back a step.

"Why, sir, in my judgment, by all in the room. If not with their tongues, at least with their eyes."

"And why should all in the room do this? Am I a legatee?—is Admiral Bluewater to be a gainer by this will?—*can* witnesses to a will be legatees?"

"I do not wish to dispute the matter with you, Sir Gervaise Oakes; but I solemnly protest against this irregular and most extraordinary manner of making a will. Let all who hear me, remember this, and be ready to testify to it when called on in a court of justice."

Here Sir Wycherly struggled to rise in the bed, in evident excitement, gesticulating strongly to express his disgust, and his wish for his nephew to withdraw. But the physicians endeavoured to pacify him, while Atwood, with the paper spread on a port-folio, and a pen in readiness, coolly proceeded to obtain the necessary signatures. Sir Wycherly's hand trembled so much when it received the pen, that, for the moment, writing was out of the question, and it became necessary to administer a restorative in order to strengthen his nerves.

"Away—out of sight," muttered the excited baronet, leaving no doubt on all present, that the uppermost feeling of the moment was the strong desire to rid himself of the presence of the offensive object. "Sir Reginald—little Milly—poor servants—brothers—all the rest, stay."

"Just be calming the mind, Sir Wycherly Wychecombe," put in Magrath, "and ye'll be solacing the body by the same effort. When the mind is in a state of exaltation, the nervous system is apt to feel the influence of sympathy. By bringing the two in harmonious co-operation, the testamentary devises will have none the less of validity, either in reality or in appearances."

Sir Wycherly understood the surgeon, and he struggled for self-command. He raised the pen, and succeeded in getting its point on the proper place. Then his dim eye lighted, and shot a reproachful glance at Tom; he smiled in a ghastly manner, looked towards the paper, passed a hand across his brow, closed his eyes, and fell back on the pillow, utterly unconscious of all that belonged to life, its interests, its duties, or its feelings. In ten minutes, he ceased to breathe.

Thus died Sir Wycherly Wychecombe, after a long life, in which general qualities of a very negative nature, had been somewhat relieved, by kindness of feeling, a passive if not an active benevolence, and such a discharge of his responsible duties as is apt to flow from an absence of any qualities that are positively bad; as well as of many of material account, that are affirmatively good.

CHAPTER XV.

"Come ye, who still the cumbrous load of life
Push hard up hill; but at the farthest steep
You trust to gain, and put on end to strife,
Down thunders back the stone with mighty sweep,
And hurls your labours to the valley deep;—"

THOMSON.

The sudden, and, in some measure, unlooked-for event, related in the close of the last chapter, produced a great change in the condition of things at Wychecombe Hall. The first step was to make sure that the baronet was actually dead; a fact that Sir Gervaise Oakes, in particular, was very unwilling to believe, in the actual state of his feelings. Men often fainted, and apoplexy required *three* blows to kill; the sick man might still revive, and at least be able to execute his so clearly expressed intentions.

"Ye'll never have act of any sort, testamentary or matrimonial, legal or illegal, in this life, from the late Sir Wycherly Wychecombe of Wychecombe Hall, Devonshire," coolly observed Magrath, as he collected the different medicines and instruments he had himself brought forth for the occasion. "He's far beyond the jurisdiction of My Lord High Chancellor of the college of Physicians and Surgeons; and therefore, ye'll be acting prudently to consider him as deceased; or, in the light in which the human body is placed by the cessation of all the animal functions."

This decided the matter, and the necessary orders were given; all but the proper attendants quitting the chamber of death. It would be far from true to say that no one lamented Sir Wycherly Wychecombe. Both Mrs. Dutton and Mildred grieved for his sudden end, and wept sincerely for his loss; though totally without a thought of its consequences to themselves. The daughter did not even once think how near she had been to the possession of £6000, and how unfortunately the cup of comparative affluence had been dashed from her lips; though truth compels us to avow that the mother did once recall this circumstance, with a feeling akin to regret. A similar recollection had its influence on the manifestations of sorrow that flowed from others. The domestics, in particular, were too much astounded to indulge in any very abstracted grief, and Sir Gervaise and Atwood were both extremely vexed. In short, the feelings, usual to such occasions were but little indulged in, though there was a strict observance of decorum.

Sir Reginald Wychecombe noted these circumstances attentively, and he took his measures accordingly. Seizing a favourable moment to consult with the two admirals, his decision was soon made; and, within an hour after his kinsman's death, all the guests and most of the upper servants were assembled in the room, which it was the usage of the house to call the library; though the books were few, and seldom read. Previously, there had been a consultation between Sir Reginald and the two admirals, to which Atwood had been admitted, *ex officio*. As every thing, therefore, had been arranged in advance, there was no time lost unnecessarily, when the company was collected; the Hertfordshire baronet coming to the point at once, and that in the clearest manner.

"Gentlemen, and you, good people, domestics of the late Sir Wycherly Wychecombe," he commenced; "you are all acquainted with the unfortunate state of this household. By the recent death of its master, it is left without a head; and the deceased departing this life a bachelor, there is no child to assume his place, as the natural and legal successor. In one sense, I might be deemed the next of kin; though, by a *dictum* of the common law I have no claim to the succession. Nevertheless, you all know it was the intention of our late friend to constitute me his executor, and I conceive it proper that search should now be made for a will, which, by being duly executed, must dispose of all in this house, and let us know who is entitled to command at this solemn and important moment. It strikes me, Sir Gervaise Oakes, that the circumstances are so peculiar as to call for prompt proceedings."

"I fully agree with you, Sir Reginald," returned the vice-admiral; "but before we proceed any further, I would suggest the propriety of having as many of those present as possible, who have an interest in the result. Mr. Thomas Wychecombe, the reputed nephew of the deceased, I do not see among us."

On examination, this was found to be true, and the man of Tom Wychecombe, who had been ordered by his master to be present as a spy, was immediately sent to the latter, with a request that he would attend. After a delay of two or three minutes, the fellow returned with the answer.

"Sir Thomas Wychecombe's compliments, gentlemen," he said, "and he desires to know the object of your request. He is in his room, indulging in natural grief for his recent loss; and he prefers to be left alone with his sorrows, just at this moment, if it be agreeable to you."

This was taking high ground in the commencement; and, as the man had his cue, and delivered his message with great distinctness and steadiness, the effect on the dependants of the household was very evident. Sir Reginald's face flushed, while Sir Gervaise bit his lip; Bluewater played with the hilt of his sword, very indifferent to all that was passing; while Atwood and the surgeons shrugged their shoulders and smiled. The first of these persons well knew that Tom had no shadow of a claim to the title he had been in so much haste to assume, however, and he hoped that the feebleness of his rights in all particulars, was represented by the mixed feebleness and impudence connected with this message. Determined not to be bullied from his present purpose, therefore, he turned to the servant and sent him back with a second message, that did not fail of its object. The man was directed to inform his master, that Sir Reginald Wychecombe was in possession of facts that, in his opinion, justified the course he was taking, and if "Mr. Thomas Wychecombe" did not choose to appear, in order to look after his own interests, he should proceed without him. This brought Tom into the room, his face pale with uncertainty, rather than with grief, and his mind agitated with such apprehensions as are apt to beset even the most wicked, when they take their first important step in evil. He bowed, however, to the company with an air that he intended to represent the manner of a well-bred man acknowledging his duties to respected guests.

"If I appear remiss in any of the duties of a host, gentlemen," he said, "you will overlook it, I trust, in consideration of my present feelings. Sir Wycherly was my father's elder brother, and was very dear, as he was very *near* to me. By this melancholy death, Sir Reginald, I am suddenly and unexpectedly elevated to be the head of our ancient and honourable family; but I know my own personal unworthiness to occupy that distinguished place, and feel how much better it would be filled by yourself. Although the law has placed a wide and impassable barrier between all of your branch of the family and ourselves, I shall ever be ready to acknowledge the affinity, and to confess that it does us quite as much honour as it bestows."

Sir Reginald, by a great effort, commanded himself so far as to return the bow, and apparently to receive the condescending admissions of the speech, with a proper degree of respect.

"Sir, I thank you," he answered, with formal courtesy; "no affinity that can be properly and legally established, will ever be disavowed by me. Under present circumstances, however, summoned as I have been to the side of his death-bed, by the late Sir Wycherly, himself, and named by him, as one might say, with his dying breath, as his executor, I feel it a duty to inquire into the rights of all parties, and, if possible, to ascertain who is the successor, and consequently who has the best claim to command here."

"You surely do not attach any validity, Sir Reginald, to the pretended will that was so singularly drawn up in my dear uncle's presence, an hour before he died! Had that most extraordinary instrument been duly signed and sealed, I cannot think that the Doctor's Commons would sustain it; but *unsigned* and *unsealed*, it is no better than so much waste paper."

"As respects the real estate, sir, though so great a loser by the delay of five minutes, I am willing to admit that you are right. With regard to the personals, a question in equity—one of clearly-expressed intention—might possibly arise; though even of that I am by no means certain."

"No, sir; no—" cried Tom, a glow of triumph colouring his cheek, in spite of every effort to appear calm; "no English court would ever disturb the natural succession to the personals! I am the last man to wish to disturb some of these legacies—particularly that to Mr. Rotherham, and those to the poor, faithful domestics,"—Tom saw the prudence of conciliating allies, at such a critical moment, and his declaration had an instant and strong effect, as was evident by the countenances of many of the listeners;—"and I may say, that to Miss Mildred Dutton; all of which will be duly paid, precisely as if my beloved uncle had been in his right mind, and had actually made the bequests; for this mixture of reason and justice, with wild and extraordinary conceits, is by no means uncommon among men of great age, and in their last moments. However, Sir Reginald, I beg you will proceed, and act as in your judgment the extraordinary circumstances of what may be called a very peculiar case, require."

"I conceive it to be our duty, sir, to search for a will. If Sir Wycherly has actually died intestate, it will be time enough to inquire into the question of the succession at common law. I have here the keys of his private secretary; and Mr. Furlong, the land-steward, who has just arrived, and whom you see in the room, tells me Sir Wycherly was accustomed to keep all his valuable papers in this piece of furniture. I shall now proceed to open it."

"Do so, Sir Reginald; no one can have a stronger desire than myself to ascertain my beloved uncle's pleasure. Those to whom he *seemed* to wish to give, even, shall not be losers for the want of his name."

Tom was greatly raised in the opinions of half in the room, by this artful declaration, which was effectually securing just so many friends, in the event of any occurrence that might render such support necessary. In the mean time, Sir Reginald, assisted by the steward, opened the secretary, and found the deposite of papers. The leases were all in order; the title-deeds were properly arranged; the books and accounts appeared to be exactly kept: ordinary bills and receipts were filed with method; two or three bags of guineas proved that ready cash was not wanting; and, in short, every thing showed that the deceased had left his affairs in perfect order, and in a very intelligible condition. Paper after paper, however, was opened, and nothing like a will, rough draft or copied, was to be found. Disappointment was strongly painted on the faces of all the gentlemen present; for, they had ignorantly imbibed the opinion, that the production of a will would, in some unknown manner, defeat the hopes of the *soi-disant* Sir Thomas Wychecombe. Nor was Tom, himself, altogether without concern; for, since the recent change in his uncle's feelings towards himself, he had a secret apprehension that some paper might be found, to defeat all his hopes. Triumph, however, gradually assumed the place of fear, in the expression of his countenance; and when Mr. Furlong, a perfectly honest man, declared that, from the late baronet's habits, as well as from the result of this search, he did not believe that any such instrument existed, his feelings overflowed in language.

"Not so fast, Master Furlong—not so fast," he cried; "here is something that possibly even your legal acumen may be willing to term a will. You perceive, gentlemen, I have it in my possession on good authority, as it is addressed to me by name, and that, too, in Sir Wycherly's own hand-writing; the envelope is sealed with his private seal. You will pronounce this to be my dear uncle's hand. Furlong,"—showing the superscription of the letter—"and this to be his seal?"

"Both are genuine, gentlemen," returned the steward, with a sigh. "Thus far, Mr. Thomas is in the right."

"*Mr.* Thomas, sirrah!—and why not *Sir* Thomas? Are baronets addressed as other men, in England? But, no matter! There is a time for all things. Sir Gervaise Oakes, as you are perfectly indifferent in this affair, I ask of you the favour to break the seal, and to inquire into the contents of the paper?"

The vice-admiral was not slow in complying; for, by this time, he began to feel an intense interest in the result. The reader will readily understand that Tom had handed to Sir Gervaise the will drawn up by his father, and which, after inserting his reputed nephew's name, Sir Wycherly had duly executed, and delivered to the person most interested. The envelope, address, and outer seal, Tom had obtained the very day the will was signed, after assuring himself of the contents of the latter, by six or eight careful perusals. The vice-admiral read the instrument from beginning to end, before he put it into the hands of Sir Reginald to examine. The latter fully expected to meet with a clumsy forgery; but the instant his eyes fell on the phraseology, he perceived that the will had been drawn by one expert in the law. A second look satisfied him that the hand was that of Mr. Baron Wychecombe. It has already been said, that in this instrument, Sir Wycherly bequeathed all he had on earth, to "his nephew, Thomas Wychecombe, son, &c., &c.," making his heir, also, his executor.

"This will appears to me to have been drawn up by a very skilful lawyer; the late Baron Wychecombe," observed the baronet.

"It was, Sir Reginald," answered Tom, endeavouring to appear unconcerned. "He did it to oblige my respected uncle, leaving blanks for the name of the devisee, not liking to make a will so very decidedly in favour of his own son. The writing in the blanks is by Sir Wycherly himself, leaving no doubts of *his* intentions."

"I do not see but you may claim to be the heir of Wychecombe, sir, as well as of the personals; though your claims to the baronetcy shall certainly be contested and defeated."

"And why defeated?" demanded Wycherly, stepping forward for the first time, and speaking with a curiosity he found it difficult to control. "Is not Mr. Thomas—*Sir* Thomas, I ought rather to say,—the eldest son of the late Sir Wycherly's next brother; and, as a matter of course, heir to the title, as well as to the estate?"

"Not he, as I can answer from a careful examination of proofs. Mr. Baron Wychecombe was never married, and thus *could have* no heir at law."

"Is this possible!—How have we all been deceived then, in America!"

"Why do you say this, young gentleman? Can *you* have any legal claims here?"

"I am Wycherly, the *only* son of Wycherly, who was the eldest son of Gregory, the younger brother of the late baronet; and if what you say be true, the next in succession to the baronetcy, at least."

"This is—" Tom's words stuck in his throat; for the quiet, stern eye of the young sailor met his look and warned him to be prudent.—"This is a *mistake*," he resumed. "My uncle Gregory was lost at sea, and died a bachelor. He can have left no lawful issue."

"I must say, young gentleman," added Sir Reginald, gravely, "that such has always been the history of his fate. I have had too near an interest in this family, to neglect its annals."

"I know, sir, that such has been the opinion here for more than half a century; but it was founded in error. The facts are simply these. My grandfather, a warm-hearted but impetuous young man, struck an older lieutenant, when ashore and on duty, in one of the West India Islands. The penalty was death; but, neither the party injured nor the commander of the vessel, wished to push matters to extremity, and the offender was advised to absent himself from the ship, at the moment of sailing. The injured party was induced to take this course, as in a previous quarrel, my grandfather had received his fire, without returning it; frankly admitting his fault. The ship did sail without Mr. Gregory Wychecombe, and was lost, every soul on board perishing. My grandfather passed into Virginia, where he remained a twelvemonth, suppressing his story, lest its narration might lead to military punishment. Love next sealed his future fate. He married a woman of fortune, and though his history was well known in his own retired circle, it never spread beyond it. No one supposed him near the succession, and there was no motive for stating the fact, on account of his interests. Once he wrote to Sir Wycherly, but he suppressed the letter, as likely to give more pain than pleasure. That letter I now have, and in his own hand-writing. I have also his commission, and all the other proofs of identity that such a person would be apt to possess. They are as complete as any court in Christendom would be likely to require, for he never felt a necessity for changing his name. He has been dead but two years, and previously to dying he saw that every document necessary to establish my claim, should a moment for enforcing it ever arrive, was put in such a legal form as to admit of no cavilling. He outlived my own father, but none of us thought there was any motive for presenting ourselves, as all believed that the sons of Baron Wychecombe were legitimate. I can only say, sir, that I have complete legal evidence that I am heir at law of Gregory, the younger brother of the late Sir Wycherly Wychecombe. Whether the fact will give me any rights here, you best can say."

"It will make you heir of entail to this estate, master of this house, and of most of what it contains, and the present baronet. You have only to prove what you say, to defeat every provision of this will, with the exception of that which refers to the personal estate."

"Bravo!" cried Sir Gervaise, fairly rubbing his hands with delight. "Bravo, Dick; if we were aboard the Plantagenet, by the Lord, I'd turn the hands up, and have three cheers. So then, my brave young seaman, you turn out to be Sir Wycherly Wychecombe, after all!"

"Yes, that's the way we always does, on board ship," observed Galleygo, to the group of domestics; "whenever any thing of a hallooing character turns up. Sometimes we makes a signal to Admiral Blue and the rest on 'em, to 'stand by to cheer,' and all of us sets to, to cheer as if our stomachs was lull of hurrahs, and we wanted to get rid on 'em. If Sir Jarvy would just pass the word now, you'd have a taste of that 'ere custom, that would do your ears good for a twelvemonth. It's a cheering matter when the one of the trade falls heir to an estate."

"And would this be a proper mode of settling a question of a right of property, Sir Gervaise Oakes?" asked Tom, with more of right and reason than he commonly had of his side; "and that, too, with my uncle lying dead beneath this roof?"

"I acknowledge the justice of the reproof, young sir, and will say no more in the matter—at least, nothing as indiscreet as my last speech. Sir Reginald, you have the affair in hand, and I recommend it to your serious attention."

"Fear nothing, Sir Gervaise," answered he of Hertfordshire. "Justice shall be done in the premises, if justice rule in England. Your story, young gentleman, is probable, and naturally told, and I see a family likeness between you and the Wychecombes, generally; a likeness that is certainly not to be traced in the person of the other claimant. Did the point depend on the legitimacy of

Mr. Thomas Wychecombe, it might be easily determined, as I have his own mother's declaration to the fact of his illegitimacy, as well as of one other material circumstance that may possibly unsettle even the late Baron Wychecombe's will. But this testamentary devise of Sir Wycherly appears to be perfect, and nothing but the entail can defeat it. You speak of your proofs; where are they? It is all-important to know which party is entitled to possession."

"Here they are, sir," answered Wycherly, removing a belt from his body, and producing his papers; "not in the originals, certainly; for most of *them* are matters of official record, in Virginia; but in, what the lawyers call 'exemplified copies,' and which I am told are in a fit state to be read as evidence in any court in England, that can take cognizance of the matter."

Sir Reginald took the papers, and began to read them, one by one, and with deep attention. The evidence of the identity of the grandfather was full, and of the clearest nature. He had been recognised as an old schoolfellow, by one of the governors of the colony, and it was at this gentleman's suggestion that he had taken so much pains to perpetuate the evidence of his identity. Both the marriages, one with Jane Beverly, and the other with Rebecca Randolph, were fully substantiated, as were the two births. The personal identity of the young man, and this too as the only son of Wycherly, the *eldest* son of Gregory, was well certified to, and in a way that could leave no doubt as to the person meant. In a word, the proofs were such as a careful and experienced lawyer would have prepared, in a case that admitted of no doubt, and which was liable to be contested in a court of law. Sir Reginald was quite half an hour in looking over the papers; and during this time, every eye in the room was on him, watching the expression of his countenance with the utmost solicitude. At length, he finished his task, when he again turned to Wycherly.

"These papers have been prepared with great method, and an acute knowledge of what might be required," he said. "Why have they been so long suppressed, and why did you permit Sir Wycherly to die in ignorance of your near affinity to him, and of your claims?"

"Of my claims I was ignorant myself, believing not only Mr. Thomas Wychecombe, but his two brothers, to stand before me. This was the opinion of my grandfather, even when he caused these proofs to be perpetuated. They were given to me, that I might claim affinity to the family on my arrival in England; and it was the injunction of my grandfather that they should be worn on my person, until the moment arrived when I could use them."

"This explains your not preferring the claim—why not prefer the relationship?"

"What for, sir? I found America and Americans looked down on, in England—colonists spoken of as a race of inferior beings—of diminished stature, feebler intellects, and a waning spirit, as compared to those from whom they had so recently sprung; and I was too proud to confess an affinity where I saw it was not desired. When wounded, and expecting to die, I was landed here, at my own request, with an intention to state the facts; but, falling under the care of ministering angels,"—here Wycherly glanced his eye at Mildred and her mother—"I less felt the want of relatives. Sir Wycherly I honoured; but he too manifestly regarded us Americans as inferiors, to leave any wish to tell him I was his great-nephew."

"I fear we are not altogether free from this reproach, Sir Gervaise," observed Sir Reginald, thoughtfully. "We do appear to think there is something in the air of this part of the island, that renders us better than common. Nay, if a claim comes from *over water*, let it be what it may, it strikes us as a foreign and inadmissible claim. The fate from which even princes are not exempt, humbler men must certainly submit to!"

"I can understand the feeling, and I think it honourable to the young man. Admiral Bluewater, you and I have had occasion often to rebuke this very spirit in our young officers; and you will agree with me when I say that this gentleman has acted naturally, in acting as he has."

"I must corroborate what you say, Sir Gervaise," answered Bluewater; "and, as one who has seen much of the colonies, and who is getting to be an old man, I venture to predict that this very feeling, sooner or later, will draw down upon England its own consequences, in the shape of condign punishment."

"I don't go as far as that, Dick—I don't go as far as that. But it is unwise and unsound, and we, who know both hemispheres, ought to set our faces against it. We have already some gallant fellows from that quarter of the world among us, and I hope to live to see more."

This, let it be remembered, was said before the Hallowells, and Coffins, and Brentons of our own times, were enrolled in a service that has since become foreign to that of the land of their birth; but it was prophetic of their appearance, and of that of many other high names from the colonies, in the lists of the British marine. Wycherly smiled proudly, but he made no answer. All this time, Sir Reginald had been musing on what had passed.

"It would seem, gentlemen," the latter now observed, "that, contrary to our belief, there is an heir to the baronetcy, as well as to the estate of Wychecombe; and all our regrets that the late incumbent did not live to execute the will we had drawn at his request, have become useless. Sir Wycherly Wychecombe, I congratulate you, on thus succeeding to the honours and estates of your family; and, as a member of the last, I may be permitted to congratulate all of the name in being so worthily represented. For one of that family I cheerfully recognise you as its head and chief."

Wycherly bowed his acknowledgments, receiving also the compliments of most of the others present. Tom Wychecombe, however, formed an exception, and instead of manifesting any disposition to submit to this summary disposal of his claims, he was brooding over the means of maintaining them. Detecting by the countenances of the upper servants that they were effectually bribed by his promise to pay the late baronet's legacies, he felt tolerably confident of support from that quarter. He well knew that possession was nine points of the law, and his thoughts naturally turned towards the means necessary to securing this great advantage. As yet, the two claimants were on a par, in this respect; for while the executed will might seem to give him a superior claim, no authority that was derived from an insufficient source would be deemed available in law; and Sir Wycherly had clearly no right to devise Wychecombe, so long as there existed an heir of entail. Both parties, too, were merely guests in the house; so that neither had any possession that would require a legal process to eject him. Tom had been entered at the Temple, and had some knowledge of the law of the land; more especially as related to real estate; and he was aware that there existed some quaint ceremony of taking possession, as it existed under the feudal system; but he was ignorant of the precise forms, and had some reasonable doubts how far they would benefit him, under the peculiar circumstances of this case. On the whole, therefore, he was disposed to try the effect of intimidation, by means of the advantages he clearly possessed, and of such little reason as the facts connected with his claim, allowed him to offer.

"Sir Reginald Wychecombe," he said gravely, and with as much indifference as he could assume; "you have betrayed a facility of belief in this American history, that has surprised me in one with so high a reputation for prudence and caution. This sudden revival of the dead may answer for the credulous lovers of marvels, but it would hardly do for a jury of twelve sober-minded and sworn men. Admitting the whole of this gentleman's statement to be true, however, you will not deny the late Sir Wycherly's right to make a will, if he only devised his old shoes; and, having this right, that of naming his executor necessarily accompanied it. Now, sir, I am clearly that executor, and as such I demand leave to exercise my functions in this house, as its temporary master at least."

"Not so fast—not so fast, young sir. Wills must be proved and executors qualified, before either has any validity. Then, again, Sir Wycherly could only give authority over that which was his own. The instant he ceased to breathe, his brother Gregory's grandson became the life-tenant of this estate, the house included; and I advise him to assert that right, trusting to the validity of his claim, for his justification in law, should it become necessary. In these matters he who is right is safe; while he who is wrong must take the consequences of his own acts. Mr. Furlong, your steward-ship ceased with the life of your principal; if you have any keys or papers to deliver, I advise your placing them in the hands of this gentleman, whom, beyond all cavil, I take to be the rightful Sir Wycherly Wychecombe."

Furlong was a cautious, clear-headed, honest man, and with every desire to see Tom defeated, he was tenacious of doing his duty. He led Sir Reginald aside, therefore, and examined him, at some length, touching the nature of the proofs that had been offered; until, quite satisfied that there could be no mistake, he declared his willingness to comply with the request.

"Certainly, I hold the keys of the late Sir Wycherly's papers,—those that have just been seen in the search for the will," he said, "and have every wish to place them in the hands of their proper owner. Here they are, Sir Wycherly; though I would advise you to remove the bags of gold that are in the secretary, to some other place; as *those* your uncle had a right to bequeath to whom he saw fit. Every thing else in the secretary goes with the estate; as do the plate, furniture, and other heir-looms of the Hall."

"I thank you, Mr. Furlong, and I will first use these keys to follow your advice," answered the new baronet; "then I will return them to you with a request that you will still retain the charge of all your former duties."

This was no sooner said than done; Wycherly placing the bags of gold on the floor, until some other place of security could be provided.

"All that I legally can, Sir Wycherly, will I cheerfully do, in order to aid you in the assertion of your right; though I do not see how I can transfer more than I hold. *Qui facit per alium, facit per se*, is good law, Sir Reginald; but the principal must have power to act, before the deputy can exercise authority. It appears to me that this is a case, in which each party stands on his own rights, at his own peril. The possession of the farms is safe enough, for the time being, with the tenants; but as to the Hall and Park, there would seem to be no one in the legal occupancy. This makes a case in which title is immediately available."

"Such is the law, Mr. Furlong, and I advise Sir Wycherly to take possession of the key of the outer door at once, as master of the tenement."

No sooner was this opinion given, than Wycherly left the room, followed by all present to the hall. Here he proceeded alone to the vestibule, locked the great door of the building, and put the key in his pocket. This act was steadily performed, and in a way to counteract, in a great degree, the effect on the domestics, of Tom's promises concerning the legacies. At the same moment, Furlong whispered something in the ear of Sir Reginald.

"Now you are quietly in possession, Sir Wycherly," said the latter, smiling; "there is no necessity of keeping us all prisoners in order to maintain your claims. David, the usual porter, Mr. Furlong tells me, is a faithful servant, and if he will accept of the key as *your* agent it may be returned to him with perfect legal safety."

As David cheerfully assented to this proposition, the key was put into his hands again, and the new Sir Wycherly was generally thought to be in possession. Nor did Tom dare to raise the contemplated question of his own legitimacy before Sir Reginald, who, he had discovered, possessed a clue to the facts; and he consequently suppressed, for the moment at least, the certificate of marriage he had so recently forged. Bowing round to the whole company, therefore, with a sort of sarcastic compliance, he stalked off to his own room with the air of an injured man. This left our young hero in possession of the field; but, as the condition of the house was not one suitable to an unreasonable display of triumph, the party soon separated; some to consult concerning the future, some to discourse of the past, and all to wonder, more or less, at the present.

CHAPTER XVI.

"Let winds be shrill, let waves roll high,
I fear not wove nor wind;
Yet marvel not, Sir Childe, that I
Am sorrowful of mind."

CHILDE HAROLD.

"Well, Sir Jarvy," said Galleygo, following on the heels of the two admirals, as the latter entered the dressing-room of the officer addressed; "it has turned out just as I thought; and the County of Fairvillain has come out of his hole, like a porpoise coming up to breathe, the moment our backs is turned! As soon as we gives the order to square-away for England, and I see the old Planter's cabin windows turned upon Franco, I foreesed them consequences. Well, gentlemen, here's been a heap of prize-money made in this house without much fighting. We shall have to give the young lieutenant a leave, for a few months, in order that he may take his swing ashore, here, among his brother squires!"

"Pray, sir, what may be your pleasure?" demanded Sir Gervaise; "and what the devil has brought you at my heels?"

"Why, big ships always tows small craft, your honour," returned Galleygo, simpering. "Howsever, I never comes without an errand, as every body knows. You see, Sir Jarvy,—you see, Admiral Blue, that our signal-officer is ashore, with a report for us; and meeting me in the hall, he made it to me first like, that I might bring it up to you a'terwards. His news is that the French county is gone to sea, as I has just told you, gentlemen."

"Can it be possible that Bunting has brought any such tidings here! Harkee, Galleygo; desire Mr. Bunting to walk up; and then see that you behave yourself as is decent in a house of mourning."

"Ay-ay-sir. No fears of I, gentlemen. I can put on as grievous a look as the best on 'em, and if they wishes to see sorrow becomingly, and ship-shape, let them study my conduct and countenance. We has all seen dead men afore now, gentlemen, as we all knows. When we fou't Mounsheer Graveland, (Gravelin,) we had forty-seven slain, besides the hurt that lived to tell their own pain; and when we had the—"

"Go to the devil, Master Galleygo, and desire Mr. Bunting to walk up stairs," cried Sir Gervaise, impatiently.

"Ay-ay-sir. Which will your honour have done first?"

"Let me see the signal-officer, *first*," answered the vice-admiral, laughing; "then be certain of executing the other order."

"Well," muttered Galleygo, as he descended the stairs; "if I was to do as he says, now, what would we do with the fleet? Ships wants orders to fight; and flags wants food to give orders; and food wants stewards to be put upon the table; and stewards wants no devils to help 'em do their duty. No—no—Sir Jarvy; I'll not pay that visit, till we all goes in company, as is suitable for them that has sailed so long together."

"This will be great news, Dick, if de Vervillin has really come out!" cried Sir Gervaise, rubbing his hands with delight. "Hang me, if I wait for orders from London; but we'll sail with the first wind and tide. Let them settle the quarrel at home, as they best can; it is *our* business to catch the Frenchman. How many ships do you really suppose the count to have?"

"Twelve of two decks, besides one three-decker, and beating us in frigates. Two or three, however, are short vessels, and cannot be quite as heavy as our own. I see no reason why we should not engage him."

"I rejoice to hear you say so! How much more honourable is it to seek the enemy, than to be intriguing about a court! I hope you intend to let me announce that red riband in general orders to-morrow, Dick?"

"Never, with my consent, Sir Gervaise, so long as the house of Hanover confers the boon. But what an extraordinary scene we have just had below! This young lieutenant is a noble fellow, and I hope, with all my heart, he will be enabled to make good his claim."

"Of that Sir Reginald assures me there can be no manner of doubt. His papers are in perfect order, and his story simple and probable. Do you not remember hearing, when we were midshipmen in the West Indies, of a lieutenant of the Sappho's striking a senior officer, ashore; and of his having been probably saved from the sentence of death, by the loss of the ship?"

"As well as if it were yesterday, now you name the vessel. And this you suppose to have been the late Sir Wycherly's brother. Did he belong to the Sappho?"

"So they tell me, below; and it leaves no doubt on my mind, of the truth of the whole story."

"It is a proof, too, how easy it is for one to return to England, and maintain his rights, after an absence of more than half a century. He in Scotland has a claim quite as strong as that of this youth!"

"Dick Bluewater, you seem determined to pull a house down about your own ears! What have you or I to do with these Scotch adventurers, when a gallant enemy invites us to come out and meet him! But, mum—here is Bunting."

At this instant the signal-lieutenant of the Plantagenet was shown into the room, by Galleygo, in person.

"Well, Bunting; what tidings from the fleet?" demanded Sir Gervaise. "Do the ships still ride to the flood?"

"It is slack-water, Sir Gervaise, and the vessels are looking all ways at once. Most of us are clearing hawse, for there are more round turns in our cables, than I remember ever to have seen in so short a time."

"That comes of there being no wind, and the uselessness of the stay-sails and spankers. What has brought you ashore? Galleygo tells us something of a cutter's coming in, with information that the French are out; but *his* news is usually *galley*-news."

"Not always, Sir Gervaise," returned the lieutenant, casting a side-look at the steward, who often comforted him with ship's delicacies in the admiral's cabin; "this time, he is right, at least. The Active is coming in slowly, and has been signalling us all the morning. We make her out to say that Monsieur Vervillin is at sea with his whole force."

"Yes," muttered Galleygo to the rear-admiral, in a sort of aside; "the County of Fairvillain has come out of his hole, just as I told Sir Jarvy. Fair-weather-villains they all is, and no bones broken."

"Silence—and you think, Bunting, you read the signals clearly?"

"No doubt of it, Sir Gervaise. Captain Greenly is of the same opinion, and has sent me ashore with the news. He desired me to tell you that the ebb would make in half an hour, and that we can then fetch past the rocks to the westward, light as the wind is."

"Ay, that is Greenly, I can swear!—He'll not sit down until we are all aweigh, and standing out. Does the cutter tell us which way the count was looking?"

"To the westward, sir; on an easy bowline, and under short canvass."

"The gentleman is in no hurry, it would seem. Has he a convoy?"

"Not a sail, sir. Nineteen sail, all cruisers, and only twelve of the line. He has one two-decker, and two frigates more than we can muster; just a Frenchman's odds, sir."

"The count has certainly with him, the seven new ships that were built last season," quietly observed Bluewater, leaning back in his easy-chair, until his body inclined at an angle of forty-five degrees, and stretching a leg on an empty stand, in his usual self-indulgent manner. "They are a little heavier than their old vessels, and will give us harder work."

"The tougher the job, the more creditable the workmanship. The tide is turning, you say, Bunting?"

"It is, Sir Gervaise; and we shall all tend ebb, in twenty minutes. The frigates outside are riding down channel already. The Chloe seems to think that we shall be moving soon, as she has crossed top-gallant and royal-yards. Even Captain Greenly was thinking of stretching along the messenger."

"Ah! you're a set of uneasy fellows, all round!—You tire of your native land in twenty-four hours, I find. Well, Mr. Bunting; you can go off, and say that all is very well. This house is in a sad state of confusion, as, I presume, you know. Mention this to Captain Greenly."

"Ay-ay-sir; is it your pleasure I should tell him any thing else, Sir Gervaise Oakes?"

"Why—yes—Bunting," answered the vice-admiral, smiling; "you may as well give him a hint to get all his fresh grub off, as fast as he can—and—yes; to let no more men quit the ship on liberty."

"Any thing more, Sir Gervaise?" added the pertinacious officer.

"On the whole, you may as well run up a signal to be ready to unmoor. The ships can very well ride at single anchors, when the tide has once fairly made. What say you, Bluewater?"

"A signal to unmoor, at once, would expedite matters. You know very well, you intend to go to sea, and why not do the thing off-hand?"

"I dare say, now, Bunting, you too would like to give the commander-in-chief a nudge of some sort or other."

"If I could presume so far, Sir Gervaise. I can only say, sir, that the sooner we are off, the sooner we shall flog the French."

"And Master Galleygo, what are your sentiments, on this occasion? It is a full council, and all ought to speak, freely."

"You knows, Sir Jarvy, that I never speaks in these matters, unless spoken to. Admiral Blue and your honour are quite enough to take care of the fleet in most circumstances, though there is some knowledge in the tops, as well as in the cabin. My ideas is, gentlemen, that, by casting to starboard on this ebb tide, we shall all have our heads off-shore, and we shall fetch into the offing as easily as a country wench turns in a jig. What we shall do with the fleet, when we gets out, will be shown in our ultra movements."

By "ultra," David meant "ulterior," a word he had caught up from hearing despatches read, which he understood no better than those who wrote them at the admiralty.

"Thanks to you all, my friends!" cried Sir Gervaise, who was so delighted at the prospect of a general engagement, that he felt a boyish pleasure in this fooling; "and now to business, seriously. Mr. Bunting, I would have the signal for sailing shown. Let each ship fire a recall-gun for her boats. Half an hour later, show the bunting to unmoor; and send my boat ashore as soon as you begin to heave on the capstan. So, good-morning, my fine fellow, and show your activity."

"Mr. Bunting, as you pass the Cæsar, do me the favour to ask for my boat, also," said Bluewater, lazily, but half-raising his body to look after the retiring lieutenant. "If we are to move, I suppose I shall have to go with the rest of them. Of course we shall repeat all your signals."

Sir Gervaise waited until Bunting was out of the room, when he turned to the steward, and said with some dryness of manner—

"Mr. Galleygo, you have my permission to go on board, bag and baggage."

"Yes, Sir Jarvy, I understands. We are about to get the ships under way, and good men ought to be in their places. Good-by, Admiral Blue. We shall meet before the face of the French, and then I expects every man on us will set an example to himself of courage and devotion."

"That fellow grows worse and worse, each day, and I shall have to send him forward, in order to check his impertinence," said Sir Gervaise, half-vexed and half-laughing. "I wonder you stand his saucy familiarity as well as you appear to do—with his Admiral Blues!"

"I shall take offence as soon as I find Sir Jarvy really out of humour with him. The man is brave, honest, and attached; and these are virtues that would atone for a hundred faults."

"Let the fellow go to the devil!—Do you not think I had better go out, without waiting for despatches from town?"

"It is hard to say. Your orders may send us all down into Scotland, to face Charles Stuart. Perhaps, too, they may make you a duke, and me a baron, in order to secure our fidelity!"

"The blackguards!—well, say no more of that, just now. If M. de Vervillin is steering to the westward, he can hardly be aiming at Edinburgh, and the movements in the north."

"That is by no means so certain. Your really politic fellows usually look one way and row another."

"It is my opinion, that his object is to effect a diversion, and my wish is to give it to him, to his heart's content. So long as this force is kept near the chops of the channel, it can do no harm in the north, and, in-so-much, must leave the road to Germany open."

"For one, I think it a pity—not to say a disgrace—that England cannot settle her own quarrels without calling in the aid of either Frenchman or Dutchman."

"We must take the world as it is, Dick, and act like two straight-forward seamen, without stopping to talk politics. I take it for granted, notwithstanding your Stuart fervour, that you are willing enough to help me thresh Monsieur de Vervillin."

"Beyond a question. Nothing but the conviction that he was directly employed in serving my natural and legitimate prince, could induce me to show him any favour. Still, Oakes, it is possible he may have succours for the Scotch on board, and be bound to the north by the way of the Irish channel!"

"Ay, pretty succours, truly, for an Englishman to stomach! *Mousquetaires*, and *régiments de Croy*, or *de Dillon*, or some d——d French name or other; and, perhaps, beautiful muskets from the *Bois de Vincennes*; or some other infernal nest of Gallic inventions to put down the just ascendency of old England! No—no—Dick Bluewater, your excellent, loyal, true-hearted English mother, never bore you to be a dupe of Bourbon perfidy and trick. I dare say she sickened at the very name of Louis!"

"I'll not answer for that, Sir Jarvy," returned the rear-admiral, with a vacant smile; "for she passed some time at the court of *le Grand Monarque*. But all this is idle; we know each other's opinions, and, by this time, ought to know each other's characters. Have you digested any plan for your future operations; and what part am I to play in it?"

Sir Gervaise paced the room, with hands folded behind his back, in an air of deep contemplation, for quite five minutes, before he answered. All this time, Bluewater remained watching his countenance and movements, in anticipation of what was to come. At length, the vice-admiral appeared to have made up his mind, and he delivered himself of his decision, as follows.

"I have reflected on them, Dick," he said, "even while my thoughts have seemed to be occupied with the concerns of others. If de Vervillin is out, he must still be to the eastward of us; for, running as the tides do on the French coast, he can hardly have made much westing with this light south-west wind. We are yet uncertain of his destination, and it is all-important that we get immediate sight of him, and keep him in view, until he can be brought to action. Now, my plan is this. I will send out the ships in succession, with orders to keep on an easy bowline, until each reaches the chops of the channel, when she is to go about and stand in towards the English coast. Each succeeding vessel, however, will weigh as soon as her leader is hull down, and keep within signal distance, in order to send intelligence through the whole line. Nothing will be easier than to keep in sight of each other, in such fine weather; and by these means we shall spread a wide clew,—quite a hundred miles,—and command the whole of the channel. As soon as Monsieur de Vervillin is made, the fleet can close, when we will be governed by circumstances Should we see nothing of the French, by the time we make their coast, we may be certain they have gone up channel; and then, a signal from the van can reverse the order of sailing, and we will chase to the eastward, closing to a line abreast as fast as possible."

"All this is very well, certainly; and by means of the frigates and smaller cruisers we can easily sweep a hundred and fifty miles of ocean;—nevertheless, the fleet will be much scattered."

"You do not think there will be any danger of the French's engaging the van, before the rear can close to aid it?" asked Sir Gervaise, with interest, for he had the profoundest respect for his friend's professional opinions. "I intended to lead out in the Plantagenet, myself, and to have five or six of the fastest ships next to me, with a view that we might keep off, until you could bring up the rear. If they chase, you know we can retire."

"Beyond a doubt, if Sir Gervaise Oakes can make up his mind to *retire*, before any Frenchman who was ever born," returned Bluewater, laughing. "All this sounds well; but, in the event of a meeting, I should expect to find you, with the whole van dismasted, fighting your hulks like bull-dogs, and keeping the Count at bay, leaving the glory of covering your retreat to me."

"No—no—Dick: I'll give you my honour I'll do nothing so boyish and silly. I'm a different man at fifty-five, from what I was at twenty-five. You may be certain that I will run, until I think myself strong enough to fight."

"Will you allow me to make a suggestion, Admiral Oakes; and this with all the frankness that ought to characterize our ancient friendship?"

Sir Gervaise stopped short in his walk, looked Bluewater steadily in the face, and nodded his head.

"I understand by the expression of your countenance," continued the other, "that I am expected to speak. I had no more to say, than to make the simple suggestion that your plan would be most likely to be executed, were I to lead the van, and were *you* to bring up the rear."

"The devil you do!—This comes as near mutiny—or *scandalum magnatum*—as one can wish! And why do you suppose that the plan of the commander-in-chief will be least in danger of failing, if Admiral Bluewater lead on this occasion, instead of Admiral Oakes?"

"Merely because I think Admiral Oakes, when an enemy is pressing him, is more apt to take counsel of his heart than of his head; while Admiral Bluewater is *not*. You do not know yourself, Sir Jarvy, if you think it so easy a matter to run away."

"I've spoiled you, Dick, by praising your foolish man[oe]uvring so much before your face, and that's the whole truth of the matter. No—my mind is made up; and, I believe you know me well enough to feel sure, when that is the case, even a council of war could not move it. *I* lead out, in the *first* two-decked ship that lifts her anchor, and *you* follow in the *last*. You understand my plan, and will see it executed, as you see every thing executed, in face of the enemy."

Admiral Bluewater smiled, and not altogether without irony in his manner; though he managed, at the same time, to get the leg that had been lowest for the last five minutes, raised by an ingenuity peculiar to himself, several inches above its fellow.

"Nature never made you for a conspirator, Oakes," he said, as soon as this change was effected to his mind; "for you carry a top-light in your breast that even the blind can see!"

"What crotchet is uppermost in your mind, now, Dick? Ar'n't the orders plain enough to suit you?"

"I confess it;—as well as the motive for giving them just in this form."

"Let's have it, at once. I prefer a full broadside to your minute-guns. What is my motive?"

"Simply that you, Sir Jarvy, say to a certain Sir Gervaise Oakes, Bart., Vice-Admiral of the Red, and Member for Bowldero, in your own mind, 'now, if I can just leave that fellow, Dick Bluewater, behind me, with four or five ships, he'll never desert *me*, when in front of the enemy, whatever he might do with *King George*; and so I'll make sure of him by placing the question in such a light that it shall be one of friendship, rather than one of loyalty.'"

Sir Gervaise coloured to the temples, for the other had penetrated into his most secret thoughts; and, yet, spite of his momentary vexation, he faced his accuser, and both laughed in the heartfelt manner that the circumstance would be likely to excite.

"Harkee, Dick," said the vice-admiral, as soon as he could command sufficient gravity to speak; "they made a mistake when they sent you to sea; you ought to have been apprenticed to a conjuror. I care not what you think about it; my orders are given, and they must be obeyed. Have you a clear perception of the plan?"

"One quite as clear, I tell you, as I have of the motive."

"Enough of this, Bluewater; we have serious duties before us."

Sir Gervaise now entered more at length into his scheme; explaining to his friend all his wishes and hopes, and letting him know, with official minuteness, what was expected at his hands. The rear-admiral listened with his accustomed respect, whenever any thing grave was in discussion between them; and, had any one entered while they were thus engaged, he would have seen in the manner of one, nothing but the dignified frankness of a friendly superior, and in the other the deference which the naval inferior usually pays to rank. As he concluded Sir Gervaise rang his bell, and desired the presence of Sir Wycherly Wychecombe.

"I could have wished to remain and see this battle for the succession fairly fought," he said; "but a battle of a different sort calls us in another quarter. Show him in," he added, as his man intimated that the young baronet was in waiting.

"What between the duties of our professional stations, and those of the guest to the host," said the vice-admiral, rising and bowing to the young man; "it is not easy to settle the question of etiquette between us, Sir Wycherly; and I have, from habit, thought more of the admiral and the lieutenant, than of the lord of the manor and his obliged guests. If I have erred, you will excuse me."

"My new situation is so very novel, that I still remain all sailor, Sir Gervaise," answered the other, smiling; "as such I hope *you* will ever consider me. Can I be of any service, here?"

"One of our cutters has just come in with news that will take the fleet to sea, again, this morning; or, as soon as the tide begins to run a strong ebb. The French are out, and we must go and look for them. It was my intention and my hope, to be able to take you to sea with me in the Plantagenet. The date of your commission would not put you very high among her lieutenants; but, Bunting deserves a first lieutenancy, and I meant to give it to him this afternoon, in which case there would be a vacancy in the situation of my own signal-officer, a duty you could well perform. As it is, you ought not to quit this house, and I must take my leave of you with regret it is so."

"Admiral Oakes, what is there that ought to keep one of my station ashore, on the eve of a general battle? I sincerely hope and trust you will alter the last determination, and return to the first."

"You forget your own important interests—remember that possession is nine points of the law."

"We had heard the news below, and Sir Reginald, Mr. Furlong, and myself, were discussing the matter when I received your summons. These gentlemen tell me, that possession can be held by deputy, as well as in person. I am satisfied we can dispose of this objection."

"Your grandfather's brother, and the late head of your family, lies dead in this house; it is proper his successor should be present at his funeral obsequies."

"We thought of that, also. Sir Reginald has kindly offered to appear in my place; and, then, there is the chance that the meeting with Monsieur de Vervillin will take place within the next eight-and-forty hours; whereas my uncle cannot be interred certainly for a week or ten days."

"I see you have well calculated all the chances, young sir," said Sir Gervaise, smiling. "Bluewater, how does this matter strike you?"

"Leave it in my hands, and I will see to it. You will sail near or quite twenty-four hours before me, and there will be time for more reflection. Sir Wycherly can remain with me in the Cæsar, in the action; or he can be thrown aboard the Plantagenet, when we meet."

After a little reflection, Sir Gervaise, who liked to give every one a fair chance, consented to the arrangement, and it was decided that Wycherly should come out in the Cæsar, if nothing occurred to render the step improper.

This arrangement completed, the vice-admiral declared he was ready to quit the Hall. Galleygo and the other servants had already made the dispositions necessary for embarking, and it only remained to take leave of the inmates of the dwelling. The parting between the baronets was friendly; for the common interest they felt in the success of Wycherly, had, in a degree, rendered them intimates, and much disposed Sir Reginald to overlook the sailor's well-known Whiggery. Dutton and the ladies took their departure at the same time, and what passed between them and Sir Gervaise on this occasion, took place on the road to the head-land, whither all parties proceeded on foot.

A person so important as Sir Gervaise Oakes did not leave the roof that had sheltered him, to embark on board his own ship, without a due escort to the shore. Bluewater accompanied him, in order to discuss any little point of duty that might occur to the mind of either, at the last moment; and Wycherly was of the group, partly from professional feeling, and more from a desire to be near Mildred. Then there were Atwood, and the surgeons, Mr. Rotherham, and two or three of the cabin attendants. Lord Geoffrey, too, strolled along with the rest, though it was understood that his own ship would not sail that day.

Just as the party issued from the gate of the park into the street of the hamlet, a heavy gun was fired from the fleet. It was soon succeeded by others, and whiffs and cornets were seen flying from the mast-heads that rose above the openings in the cliffs, the signals of recall for all boats. This set every one in motion, and, never within the memory of man, had Wychecombe presented such a scene of confusion and activity. Half-intoxicated seamen were driven down to the boats, by youngsters with the cloth diamond in their collars, like swine, who were reluctant to go, and yet afraid to stay. Quarters of beeves were trundled along in carts or barrows, and were soon seen swinging at different main-stays; while the gathering of eggs, butter, poultry, mutton, lamb, and veal, menaced the surrounding country with a scarcity. Through this throng of the living and the dead, our party held its way, jostled by the eager countrymen, and respectfully avoided by all who belonged to the fleet, until it reached the point where the roads to the cliffs and the landing separated, when the vice-admiral turned to the only midshipman present, and courteously lifting his hat, as if reluctant to impose such a duty on a "young gentleman" on liberty, he said—

"Do me the favour, Lord Geoffrey, to step down to the landing and ascertain if my barge is there. The officer of the boat will find me at the signal-station."

The boy cheerfully complied; and this son of an English duke, who, by the death of an elder brother, became in time a duke himself, went on a service that among gentlemen of the land would be deemed nearly menial, with as much alacrity as if he felt honoured by the request. It was by a training like this, that England came, in time, to possess a marine that has achieved so many memorable deeds; since it taught those who were destined to command, the high and useful lesson how to obey.

While the midshipman was gone to look for the boat, the two admirals walked the cliff, side by side, discussing their future movements; and when all was ready, Sir Gervaise descended to the shore, using the very path by which he had ascended the previous day; and, pushing through the throng that crowded the landing, almost too much engaged to heed even his approach, he entered his barge. In another minute, the measured strokes of the oars urged him swiftly towards the Plantagenet.

CHAPTER XVII.

"'Twas not without some reason, for the wind
Increased at night, until it blew a gale;
And though 'twas not much to a naval mind,
Some landsmen would have look'd a little pale,
For sailors are, in fact, a different kind;
At sunset they began to take in sail,
For the sky show'd it would come on to blow,
And carry away, perhaps, a mast or so."

BYRON.

As it was just past the turn of the day, Bluewater determined to linger on the cliffs for several hours, or until it was time to think of his dinner. Abstracted as his thoughts were habitually, his mind found occupation and pleasure in witnessing the evolutions that succeeded among the ships; some of which evolutions it may be well now briefly to relate.

Sir Gervaise Oakes' foot had not been on the deck of the Plantagenet five minutes, before a signal for all commanders was flying at that vessel's mast-head. In ten minutes more every captain of the fleet, with the exception of those belonging to the vessels in the offing, were in the flag-ship's cabin, listening to the intentions and instructions of the vice-admiral.

"My plan of sailing, gentlemen, is easily comprehended," continued the commander-in-chief, after he had explained his general intentions to chase and engage; "and everyone of you will implicitly follow it. We have the tide strong at ebb, and a good six-knot breeze is coming up at south-west. I shall weigh, with my yards square, and keep them so, until the ship has drawn out of the fleet, and then I shall luff up on a taut bowline and on the starboard tack, bringing the ebb well under my lee-bow. This will hawse the ship over towards Morlaix, and bringing us quite as far to windward as is desirable. While the ebb lasts, and this breeze stands, we shall have plain sailing; the difficulty will come on the flood, or with a shift of wind. The ships that come out last must be careful to keep their seconds, ahead and astern, in plain sight, and regulate their movements, as much as they can, by the leading vessels. The object is to spread as wide a clew as possible, while we hold the ships within signal-distance of each other. Towards sunset I shall shorten sail, and the line will close up within a league from vessel to vessel, and I have told Bluewater to use his discretion about coming out with the last ships, though I have requested him to hold on as long as he shall deem it prudent, in the hope of receiving another express from the Admiralty. When the flood makes, I do not intend to go about, but shall continue on the starboard tack, and I wish you all to do the same. This will bring the leading vessels considerably to windward of those astern, and may possibly throw the fleet into a bow and quarter line. Being in the van, it will fall to my duty to look to this, and to watch for the consequences. But I ask of you to keep an eye on the weather, and to hold your ships within plain signal-distance of each other. If it come on thick, or to blow very hard, we must close, from van to rear, and try our luck, in a search in compact order. Let the man who first sees the enemy make himself heard at once, and send the news, with the bearings of the French, both ahead and astern, as fast as possible. In that case you will all close on the point from which the intelligence comes; and, mark me, no cruising to get to windward, in your own fashions, as if you sailed with roving commissions. You know I'll not stand *that*. And now, gentlemen, it is probable that we shall all never meet again. God bless you! Come and shake hands with me, one by one, and then to your boats, for the first lieutenant has just sent Greenly word that we are up and down. Let him trip, Greenly, and be off as soon as we can."

The leave-taking, a scene in which joyousness and sadness were strangely mingled, succeeded, and then the captains disappeared. From that moment every mind was bent on sailing.

Although Bluewater did not witness the scene in the Plantagenet's cabin, he pictured it, in his mind's eye, and remained on the cliffs to watch the succeeding movements. As Wycherly had disappeared in the house, and Dutton clung to his flag-staff, the rear-admiral had no one but Lord Geoffrey for a companion. The latter, perceiving that his relation did not seem disposed to converse, had the tact to be silent himself; a task that was less difficult than common, on account of the interest he felt in the spectacle.

The boats of the different captains were still shoving off from the starboard side of the Plantagenet, whither etiquette had brought them together, in a little crowd, when her three top-sails fell, and their sheets steadily drew the clews towards the ends of the lower yards. Even while this was in process, the yards began to ascend, and rose with that steady but graduated movement which marks the operation in a man-of-war. All three were fairly mast-headed in two minutes. As the wind struck the canvass obliquely, the sails filled as they opened their folds, and, by the time their surfaces were flattened by distension, the Plantagenet steadily moved from her late berth, advancing slowly against a strong tide, out of the group of ships, among which she had been anchored. This was a beautiful evolution, resembling that of a sea-fowl, which lazily rises on its element, spreads its wings, emerges from the water, and glides away to some distant and unseen point.

The movement of the flag-ship was stately, measured, and grand. For five minutes she held her way nearly due east, with the wind on her starboard quarter, meeting the tide in a direct line; until, having drawn sufficiently ahead of the fleet, she let fall her courses, sheeted home top-gallant-sails and royals, set her spanker, jibs, and stay-sails, and braced up sharp on a wind, with her head at south-southeast. This brought the tide well under her lee fore-chains, and set her rapidly off the land, and to windward. As she trimmed her sails, and steadied her bowlines, she fired a gun, made the numbers of the vessels in the offing to weigh, and to pass within hail. All this did Bluewater note, with the attention of an *amateur*, as well as with the critical analysis of a *connoisseur*.

"Very handsomely done, Master Geoffrey—very handsomely done, it must be allowed! never did a bird quit a flock with less fuss, or more beautifully, than the Plantagenet has drawn out of the fleet. It must be admitted that Greenly knows how to handle his ship."

"I fancy Captain Stowel would have done quite as well with the Cæsar, sir," answered the boy, with a proper esprit-de-*ship*. "Don't you remember, Admiral Bluewater, the time when we got under way off l'Orient, with the wind blowing a gale directly on shore? Even Sir Gervaise said, afterwards, that we lost less ground than any ship in the fleet, and yet the Plantagenet is the most weatherly two-decker in the navy; as every body says."

"Every body!—She is certainly a weatherly vessel, but not more so than several others. Whom did you ever hear give that character to this particular ship?"

"Why, sir, her reefers are always bragging as much as *that*; and a great deal *more*, too."

"Her reefers!—Young gentlemen are particularly struck with the charms of their first loves, both ashore and afloat, my boy. Did you ever hear an *old seaman* say that much for the Plantagenet?"

"I think I have, sir," returned Lord Geoffrey, blushing. "Galleygo, Sir Gervaise's steward, is commonly repeating some such stuff or other. They are furious braggarts, the Plantagenet's, all round, sir."

"That comes honestly," answered Bluewater, smiling, "her namesakes and predecessors of old, having some such characteristic, too. Look at that ship's yards, boy, and learn how to trim a vessel's sails on a wind. The pencil of a painter could not draw lines more accurate!"

"Captain Stowel tells us, sir, that the yards ought not to be braced in exactly alike; but that we ought to check the weather-braces, a little, as we go aloft, so that the top-sail yard should point a little less forward than the lower yard, and the topgallant than the top-sail."

"You are quite right in taking Stowel's opinion in all such matters, Geoffrey: but has not Captain Greenly done the same thing in the Plantagenet? When I speak of symmetry, I mean the symmetry of a seaman."

The boy was silenced, though exceedingly reluctant to admit that any ship could equal his own. In the mean time, there was every appearance of a change in the weather. Just about the time the Plantagenet braced up, the wind freshened, and in ten minutes it blew a stiff breeze. Some time before the admiral spoke the vessels outside, he was compelled to take in all his light canvass; and when he filled, again, after giving his orders to the frigate and sloop, the topgallant sheets were let fly, a single reef was taken in the top-sails, and the lighter sails were set over them. This change in the weather, more especially as the night threatened to be clouded, if not absolutely dark, would necessarily bring about a corresponding change in the plan of sailing, reducing the intervals between the departures of the vessels, quite one-half. To such vicissitudes are all maritime operations liable, and it is fortunate when there is sufficient capacity in the leaders to remedy them.

In less than an hour, the Plantagenet's hull began to sink, to those on a level with it, when the Carnatic tripped her anchor, opened her canvass, shot out of the fleet, hauled by the wind, and followed in the admiral's wake. So accurate was the course she steered, that, half an hour after she had braced up, a hawse-bucket, which had been dropped from the Plantagenet in hauling water, was picked up. We may add, here, though it will be a little anticipating events, that the Thunderer followed the Carnatic; the Blenheim the Thunderer; the Achilles the Blenheim; the Warspite the Achilles; the Dover the Warspite; the York the Dover; the Elizabeth the York; the Dublin the Elizabeth; and the Cæsar the Dublin. But hours passed before all these ships were in motion, and hours in which we shall have some occurrences to relate that took place on shore. Still it will aid the reader in better understanding the future incidents of our tale, if we describe, at once, some of the circumstances under which all these ships got in motion.

By the time the Plantagenet's top-sails were beginning to dip from the cliffs, the Carnatic, the Thunderer, the Blenheim, the Achilles, and the Warspite were all stretching out in line, with intervals of quite two leagues between them, under as much canvass as they could now bear. The admiral had shortened sail the most, and was evidently allowing the Carnatic to close, most probably on account of the threatening look of the sky, to windward; while he was suffering the frigate and sloop, the Chloe and Driver, to pass ahead of him, the one on his weather, and the other on his lee bow. When the Dover weighed, the admiral's upper sail was not visible from her tops, though the Warspite's hull had not yet disappeared from her deck. She left the fleet, or the portions of it that still remained at anchor, with her fore-course set, and hauled by the wind, under double-reefed top-sails, a single reef in her main-sail, and with her main-topgallant sail set over its proper sail. With this reduced canvass, she started away on the track of her consorts, the brine foaming under her bows, and with a heel that denoted the heavy pressure that bore on her sails. By this time, the York was aweigh, the tide had turned, and it became necessary to fill on the other tack in order to clear the land to the eastward. This altered the formation, but we will now revert to the events as they transpired on the shore, with a view to relate them more in their regular order.

It is scarcely necessary to say that Bluewater must have remained on, or about the cliffs several hours, in order to witness the departure of so many of the vessels. Instead of returning to the Hall at the dinner hour, agreeably to promise, he profited by the appearance of Wycherly, who left the cottage with a flushed, agitated manner, just as he was thinking of the necessity of sending a message to Sir Reginald, and begged the young man to be the bearer of his excuses. He thought that the change in the weather rendered it necessary for him to remain in sight of the sea. Dutton overheard this message, and, after a private conference with his wife, he ventured to invite his superior to appease his appetite under his own humble roof. To this Bluewater cheerfully assented; and when the summons came to the table, to his great joy he found that his only companion was to be Mildred, who, like himself, for some reason known only to her own bosom, had let the ordinary dining hour pass without appearing at table, but whom her mother had now directed to take some sustenance.

"The late events at the Hall have agitated the poor child, sir," said Mrs. Dutton, in the way of apology, "and she has not tasted food since morning. I have told her you would excuse the intrusion, and receive her carving and attentions as an excuse for her company."

Bluewater looked at the pallid countenance of the girl, and never before had he found the resemblance to Agnes Hedworth so strong, as that moment. The last year or two of his own sweet friend's life had been far from happy, and the languid look and tearful eyes of Mildred revived the recollection of the dead with painful distinctness.

"Good God!" he murmured to himself; "that two such beings should exist only to suffer! my good Mrs. Dutton, make no excuses; but believe me when I say that you could not have found in England another that would have proved as welcome as my present little messmate."

Mildred struggled for a smile; and she did succeed in looking extremely grateful. Beyond this, however, it exceeded her powers to go. Mrs. Dutton was gratified, and soon left the two to partake of their neat, but simple meal, by themselves; household duties requiring her presence elsewhere.

"Let me persuade you to take a glass of this really excellent port, my child," said Bluewater. "If you had cruised as long as I have done, on the coast of Portugal, you would know how to value a liquor as pure as this. I don't know of an admiral that has as good!"

"It is probably *our* last, sir," answered Mildred, shaking a tear from each of her long dark lashes, by an involuntarily trembling motion, as she spoke. "It was a present from dear, old, Sir Wycherly, who never left my mother wholly unsupplied with such plain delicacies, as he fancied poverty placed beyond our reach. The wine we can easily forget; not so easily the donor."

Bluewater felt as if he could draw a cheque for one-half the fortune he had devised to his companion; and, yet, by a caprice of feeling that is not uncommon to persons of the liveliest susceptibility, he answered in a way to smother his own emotion.

"There will not soon be another *old* Sir Wycherly to make his neighbours comfortable; but there is a *young* one, who is not likely to forget his uncle's good example. I hope you all here, rejoice at the sudden rise in fortune, that has so unexpectedly been placed within the reach of our favourite lieutenant?"

A look of anguish passed over Mildred's face, and her companion noted it; though surprise and pity—not to say resentment—prevented his betraying his discovery.

"We *endeavour* to be glad, sir," answered Mildred, smiling in so suffering a manner, as to awaken all her companion's sympathies; "but it is not easy for us to rejoice at any thing which is gained by the loss of our former valued friend."

"I am aware that a young follow, like the present Sir Wycherly, can be no substitute for an old fellow like the last Sir Wycherly, my dear; but as one is a sailor, and the other was only a landsman, my professional prejudices may not consider the disparity as great as it may possibly appear to be to your less partial judgment."

Bluewater thought the glance he received was imploring, and he instantly regretted that he had taken such means to divert his companion's sadness. Some consciousness of this regret probably passed through Mildred's mind, for she rallied her spirits, and made a partially successful effort to be a more agreeable companion.

"My father thinks, sir," she said, "that our late pleasant weather is about to desert us, and that it is likely to blow heavily before six-and-thirty hours are over."

"I am afraid Mr. Dutton will prove to be too accurate an almanac. The weather has a breeding look, and I expect a dirty night. Good or bad, we seamen must face it, and that, too, in the narrow seas, where gales of wind are no gales of Araby."

"Ah, sir, it is a terrible life to lead! By living on this cliff, I have learned to pity sailors."

"Perhaps, my child, you pity us when we are the most happy. Nine seamen in ten prefer a respectable gale to a flat calm. There are moments when the ocean is terrific; but, on the whole, it is capricious, rather than malignant. The night that is before us promises to be just such a one as Sir Gervaise Oakes delights in. He is never happier than when he hears a gale howling through the cordage of his ship."

"I have heard him spoken of as a very daring and self-relying commander. But *you* cannot entertain such feelings, Admiral Bluewater; for to me you seem better fitted for a fireside, well filled with friends and relatives, than for the conflicts and hardships of the sea."

Mildred had no difficulty now in forcing a smile, for the sweet one she bestowed on the veteran almost tempted him to rise and fold her in his arms, as a parent would wrap a beloved daughter to his heart. Discretion, however, prevented a betrayal of feelings that might have been misinterpreted, and he answered in his original vein.

"I fear I am a wolf in sheep's clothing," he said; "while Oakes admits the happiness he feels in seeing his ship ploughing through a raging sea, in a dark night, he maintains that my rapture is sought in a hurricane. I do not plead guilty to the accusation, but I will allow there is a sort of fierce delight in participating, as it might be, in a wild strife of the elements. To me, my very nature seems changed at such moments, and I forget all that is mild and gentle. That comes of having lived so much estranged from your sex, my dear; desolate bachelor, as I am."

"Do you think sailors ought to marry?" asked Mildred, with a steadiness that surprised herself; for, while she put the question, consciousness brought the blood to her temples.

"I should be sorry to condemn a whole profession, and that one I so well love, to the hopeless misery of single life. There are miseries peculiar to the wedded lives of both soldiers and sailors; but are there not miseries peculiar to those who never separate? I have heard seamen say—men, too, who loved their wives and families—that they believed the extreme pleasure of meetings after long separations, the delights of hope, and the zest of excited feelings, have rendered their years of active service more replete with agreeable sensations, than the stagnant periods of peace. Never having been married myself, I can only speak on report."

"Ah! this may be so with *men*; but—surely—surely—*women* never can feel thus!"

"I suppose, a sailor's daughter yourself, you know Jack's account of his wife's domestic creed! 'A good fire, a clean hearth, the children abed, and the husband at sea,' is supposed to be the climax of felicity."

"This may do for the sailor's jokes, Admiral Bluewater," answered Mildred, smiling; "but it will hardly ease a breaking heart. I fear from all I have heard this afternoon, and from the sudden sailing of the ships, that a great battle is at hand?"

"And why should you, a British officer's daughter, dread that? Have you so little faith in us, as to suppose a battle will necessarily bring defeat! I have seen much of my own profession, Miss Dutton, and trust I am in some small degree above the rhodomontade of the braggarts; but it is *not* usual for us to meet the enemy, and to give those on shore reason to be ashamed of the English flag. It has never yet been my luck to meet a Frenchman who did not manifest a manly desire to do his country credit; and I have always felt that we must fight hard for him before we could get him; nor has the result ever disappointed me. Still, fortune, or skill, or *right*, is commonly of our side, and has given us the advantage in the end."

"And to which, sir, do you ascribe a success at sea, so very uniform?"

"As a Protestant, I ought to say to our *religion*; but, this my own knowledge of Protestant *vices* rejects. Then to say *fortune* would be an exceeding self-abasement—one, that between us, is not needed; and I believe I must impute it to skill. As plain seamen, I do believe we are more expert than most of our neighbours; though I am far from being positive we have any great advantage over them in tactics. If any, the Dutch are our equals."

"Notwithstanding, you are quite certain of success. It must be a great encouragement to enter into the fight with a strong confidence in victory! I suppose—that is, it seems to me—it is a matter of course, sir,—that our new Sir Wycherly will not be able to join in the battle, this time?"

Mildred spoke timidly, and she endeavoured to seem unconcerned; but Bluewater read her whole heart, and pitied the pain which she had inflicted on herself, in asking the question. It struck him, too, that a girl of his companion's delicacy and sensibility would not thus advert to the young man's movements at all, if the latter had done aught justly to awaken censure; and this conviction greatly relieved his mind as to the effect of sudden elevation on the handsome lieutenant. As it was necessary to answer, however, lest Mildred might detect his consciousness of her feelings, not a moment was lost before making a reply.

"It is not an easy matter to prevent a young, dashing sailor, like this Sir Wycherly Wychecombe, from doing his part in a general engagement, and that, too, of the character of the one to which we are looking forward," he said. "Oakes has left the matter in my hands; I suppose I shall have to grant the young man's request."

"He has then requested to be received in your ship?" asked Mildred, her hand shaking as she used the spoon it held.

"That of course. No one who wears the uniform could or would do less. It seems a ticklish moment for him to quit Wychecombe, too; where I fancy he will have a battle of his own to fight ere long; but professional feeling will overshadow all others, in young men. Among us seamen, it is said to be even stronger than love."

Mildred made no answer; but her pale cheek and quivering lips, evidences of feeling that her artlessness did not enable her to conceal, caused Bluewater again to regret the remark. With a view to restore the poor girl to her self-command, he changed the subject of conversation, which did not again advert to Wycherly. The remainder of the meal was consequently eaten in peace, the admiral manifesting to the last, however, the sudden and generous interest he had taken in the character and welfare of his companion. When they rose from table, Mildred joined her mother, and Bluewater walked out upon the cliffs again.

It was now evening, and the waste of water that lay stretched before the eye, though the softness of summer was shed upon it, had the wild and dreary aspect that the winds and waves lend to a view, as the light of day is about to abandon the ocean to the gloom of night. All this had no effect on Bluewater, however, who knew that two-decked ships, strongly manned, with their heavy canvass reduced, would make light work of worrying through hours of darkness that menaced no more than these. Still the wind had freshened, and when he stood on the verge of the cliff sustained by the breeze, which pressed him back from the precipice, rendering his head more steady, and his footing sure, the Elizabeth was casting, under close-reefed top-sails, and two reefs in her courses, with a heavy stay-sail or two, to ease her helm. He saw that the ponderous machine would stagger under even this short canvass, and that her captain had made his dispositions for a windy night. The lights that the Dover and the York carried in their tops were just beginning to be visible in the gathering gloom, the last about a league and a half down channel, the ship standing in that direction to get to windward, and the former, more to the southward, the vessel having already tacked to follow the admiral. A chain of lights connected the whole of the long line, and placed the means of communication in the power of the captains. At this moment, the Plantagenet was full fifty miles at sea, ploughing through a heavy south-west swell, which the wind was driving into the chops of the channel, from the direction of the Bay of Biscay, and the broad Atlantic.

Bluewater buttoned his coat, and he felt his frame invigorated by a gale that came over his person, loaded by the peculiar flavour of the sea. But two of the heavy ships remained at their anchors, the Dublin and the Cæsar; and his experienced eye could see that Stowel had every thing on board the latter ready to trip and be off, as soon as he, himself, should give the order. At this moment the midshipman, who had been absent for hours, returned, and stood again at his side.

"Our turn will soon come, sir," said the gallant boy, "and, for one, I shall not be sorry to be in motion. Those chaps on board the Plantagenet will swagger like so many Dons, if they should happen to get a broadside at Monsieur de Vervillin, while we are lying here, under the shore, like a gentleman's yacht hauled into a bay, that the ladies might eat without disturbing their stomachs."

"Little fear of that, Geoffrey. The Active is too light of foot, especially in the weather we have had, to suffer heavy ships to be so close on her heels. She must have had some fifteen or twenty miles the start, and the French have been compelled to double Cape la Hogue and Alderney, before they could even look this way. If coming down channel at all, they are fully fifty miles to the eastward; and should our van stretch far enough by morning to head them off, it will bring us handsomely to windward. Sir Gervaise never set a better trap, than he has done this very day. The Elizabeth has her hands full, boy, and the wind seems to be getting scant for her. If it knock her off much more, it will bring the flood on her weather-bow, and compel her to tack. This will throw the rear of our line into confusion!"

"What should we do, sir, in such a case? It would never answer to leave poor Sir Jarvy out there, by himself!"

"We would try not to do *that*!" returned Bluewater, smiling at the affectionate solicitude of the lad, a solicitude that caused him slightly to forget his habitual respect for the commander-in-chief, and to adopt the *sobriquet* of the fleet. "In such a case, it would become my duty to collect as many ships as I could, and to make the best of our way towards the place where we might hope to fall in with the others, in the morning. There is little danger of losing each other, for any length of time, in these narrow waters, and I have few apprehensions of the French being far enough west, to fall in with our leading vessels before morning. If they *should*, indeed, Geoffrey—"

"Ay, sir, if they *should*, I know well enough what would come to pass!"

"What, boy?—On the supposition that Monsieur de Vervillin *did* meet with Sir Gervaise by day-break, what, in your experienced eyes, seem most likely to be the consequences?"

"Why, sir, Sir Jarvy, would go at 'em, like a dolphin at a flying-fish; and if he *should* really happen to catch one or two of 'em, there'll be no sailing in company with the Plantagenet's, for us Cæsar's!—When we had the last 'bout with Monsieur de Gravelin, they were as saucy as peacocks, because we didn't close until their fore-yard and mizzen-top-gallant-mast were gone, although the shift of wind brought us dead to leeward, and, after all, we had eleven men the most hurt in the fight. You don't know them Plantagenet's, sir; for they never *dare* say any thing before *you*!"

"Not to the discredit of my young Cæsars, I'll answer for it. Yet, you'll remember Sir Gervaise gave us full credit, in his despatches."

"Yes, sir, all very true. Sir Gervaise knows better; and then *he* understands what the Cæsar *is*; and what she *can* do, and *has* done. But it's a very different matter with his youngsters, who fancy because they carry a red flag at the fore, they are so many Blakes and Howards, themselves. There's Jack Oldcastle, now; he's always talking of our reefers as if there was no sea-blood in our veins, and that just because his own father happened to be a captain— a *commodore*, he says, because he happened once to have three frigates under his orders."

"Well, that would make a commodore, for the time being. But, surely he does not claim privilege for the Oldcastle blood, over that of the Clevelands!"

"No, sir, it isn't that sort of thing, at all," returned the fine boy, blushing a little, in spite of his contempt for any such womanly weakness; "you know we never talk of that nonsense in our squadron. With us it's all service, and that sort of thing. Jack Oldcastle says the Clevelands are all civilians, as he calls 'em; or *soldiers*, which isn't much better, as you know, sir. Now, I tell him that there is an old picture of one of 'em, with an anchor-button, and that was long before Queen Anne's time—Queen Elizabeth's, perhaps,—and then you know, sir, I fetch him up with a yarn about the Hedworths; for I am just as much Hedworth as Cleveland."

"And what does the impudent dog say to that, Geoffrey?"

"Why, sir, he says the name should be spelt Head*work*, and that they were all *lawyers*. But I gave him as good as he sent for that saucy speech, I'm certain!"

"And what did you give him, in return for such a compliment? Did you tell him the Oldcastles were just so much stone, and wood, and old iron; and that, too, in a tumbledown condition?"

"No, sir, not I," answered the boy, laughing; "I didn't think of any answer half so clever; and so I just gave him a dig in the nose, and that, laid on with right good will."

"And how did he receive that argument? Was it conclusive;—or did the debate continue?"

"Oh, of course, sir, we fought it out. 'Twas on board the Dover, and the first lieutenant saw fair play. Jack carried too many guns for me, sir, for he's more than a year older; but I hulled him so often that he owned it was harder work than being mast-headed. After that the Dover's chaps took my part, and they said the Hedworths had no Head*work* at all, but they were regular sailors; admirals, and captains, and youngsters, you know, sir, like all the rest of us. I told 'em my grandfather Hedworth was an admiral, and a good one, too."

"In that you made a small mistake. Your mother's father was only a *general*; but *his* father was a full admiral of the red,—for he lived before that grade was abolished—and as good an officer as ever trod a plank. He was my mother's brother, and both Sir Gervaise and myself served long under his orders. He was a sailor of whom you well might boast."

"I don't think any of the Plantagenets will chase in that quarter again, sir; for we've had an overhauling among our chaps, and we find we can muster four admirals, two commodores, and thirteen captains in our two messes; that is, counting all sorts of relatives, you know, sir."

"Well, my dear boy, I hope you may live to reckon all that and more too, in your own persons, at some future day. Yonder is Sir Reginald Wychecombe, coming this way, to my surprise; perhaps he wishes to see me alone. Go down to the landing and ascertain if my barge is ashore, and let me know it, as soon as is convenient. Remember, Geoffrey, you will go off with me; and hunt up Sir Wycherly Wychecombe, who will lose his passage, unless ready the instant he is wanted."

The boy touched his cap, and went bounding down the hill to execute the order.

CHAPTER XVIII.

"So glozed the Tempter, and his poison tuned;
Into the heart of Eve his words made way,
Though at the voice much marvelling."

MILTON.

It was, probably, a species of presentiment, that induced Bluewater to send away the midshipman, when he saw the adherent of the dethroned house approaching. Enough had passed between the parties to satisfy each of the secret bias of the other; and, by that sort of free-masonry which generally accompanies strong feelings of partisanship, the admiral felt persuaded that the approaching interview was about to relate to the political troubles of the day.

The season and the hour, and the spot, too, were all poetically favourable to an interview between conspirators. It was now nearly dark; the head-land was deserted, Dutton having retired, first to his bottle, and then to his bed; the wind blew heavily athwart the bleak eminence, or was heard scuffling in the caverns of the cliffs, while the portentous clouds that drove through the air, now veiled entirely, and now partially and dimly revealed the light of the moon, in a way to render the scene both exciting and wild. No wonder, then, that Bluewater, his visiter drawing near, felt a stronger disposition than had ever yet come over him to listen to the tale of the tempter, as, under all the circumstances, it would scarcely exceed the bounds of justice to call Sir Reginald.

"In seeking you at such a spot, and in the midst of this wild landscape," said the latter, "I might have been assured I should be certain of finding one who really loved the sea and your noble profession. The Hall is a melancholy house, just at this moment; and when I inquired for you, no one could say whither you had strolled. In following what I thought a seaman's instinct, it appears that I did well.—Do my eyes fail me, or are there no more than three vessels at anchor yonder?"

"Your eyes are still good, Sir Reginald; Admiral Oakes sailed several hours since, and he has been followed by all the fleet, with the exception of the two line-of-battle ships, and the frigate you see; leaving me to be the last to quit the anchorage."

"Is it a secret of state, or are you permitted to say whither so strong a force has so suddenly sailed?" demanded the baronet, glancing his dark eye so expressively towards the other as to give him, in the growing obscurity, the appearance of an inquisitor. "I had been told the fleet would wait for orders from London?"

"Such was the first intention of the commander-in-chief; but intelligence of the sailing of the Comte de Vervillin has induced Sir Gervaise to change his mind. An English admiral seldom errs when he seeks and beats an active and dangerous enemy."

"Is this always true, Admiral Bluewater?" returned Sir Reginald, dropping in at the side of the other, and joining in his walk, as he paced, to and fro, a short path that Dutton called his own quarter-deck; "or is it merely an unmeaning generality that sometimes causes men to become the dupes of their own imaginations. Are those *always* our enemies who may seem to be so? or, are we so infallible that every feeling or prejudice may be safely set down as an impulse to which we ought to submit, without questioning its authority?"

"Do you esteem it a prejudice to view France as the natural enemy of England, Sir Reginald?"

"By heaven, I do, sir! I can conceive that England may be much more her own enemy than France has ever proved to be. Then, conceding that ages of warfare have contributed to awaken some such feeling as this you hint at, is there not a question of right and wrong that lies behind all? Reflect how often England has invaded the French soil, and what serious injuries she has committed on the territory of the latter, while France has so little wronged us, in the same way; how, even her throne has been occupied by our princes, and her provinces possessed by our armies."

"I think you hardly allow for all the equity of the different cases. Parts of what is now France, were the just inheritance of those who have sat on the English throne, and the quarrels were no more than the usual difficulties of neighbourhood. When our claims were just in themselves, you surely could not have wished to see them abandoned."

"Far from it; but when claims were disputed, is it not natural for the loser to view them as a hardship? I believe we should have had a much better neighbourhood, as you call it, with France, had not the modern difficulties connected with religious changes, occurred."

"I presume you know. Sir Reginald, that I, and all my family are Protestants."

"I do, Admiral Bluewater; and I rejoice to find that a difference of opinion on this great interest, does not necessarily produce one on all others. From several little allusions that have passed between us to-day, I am encouraged to believe that we think alike on certain temporal matters, however wide the chasm between us on spiritual things."

"I confess I have fallen into the same conclusion; and I should be sorry to be undeceived if wrong."

"What occasion, then, for farther ambiguity? Surely two honourable men may safely trust each other with their common sentiments, when the times call for decision and frankness! I am a Jacobite, Admiral Bluewater; if I risk life or fortune by making the avowal, I place both, without reserve at your mercy."

"They could not be in safer hands, sir; and I know no better mode of giving you every possible assurance that the confidence will not be abused, than by telling you in return, that I would cheerfully lay down my life could the sacrifice restore the deposed family to the throne."

"This is noble, and manly, and frank, as I had hoped from a sailor!" exclaimed Sir Reginald, more delighted than he well knew how to express at the moment. "This simple assurance from your lips, carries more weight than all the oaths and pledges of vulgar conspiracy. We understand each other, and I should be truly sorry to inspire less confidence than I feel."

"What better proof can I give you of the reliance placed on your faith, than the declaration you have heard, Sir Reginald? My head would answer for your treachery in a week; but I have never felt it more securely on my shoulders than at this moment."

The baronet grasped the other's hand, and each gave and received a pressure that was full of meaning. Then both walked on, thoughtful and relieved, for quite a minute, in profound silence.

"This sudden appearance of the prince in Scotland has taken us all a little by surprise," Sir Reginald resumed, after the pause; "though a few of us knew that his intentions led him this way. Perhaps he has done well to come unattended by a foreign force, and to throw himself, as it might be singly, into the arms of his subjects; trusting every thing to their generosity, loyalty, and courage. Some blame him; but I do not. He will awaken interest, now, in every generous heart in the nation,"—this was artfully adapted to the character of the listener;—"whereas some might feel disposed to be lukewarm under a less manly appeal to their affections and loyalty. In Scotland, we learn from all directions that His Royal Highness is doing wonders, while the friends of his house are full of activity in England, though compelled, for a time, to be watchful and prudent."

"I rejoice, from the bottom of my heart, to hear this!" said Bluewater, drawing a long breath, like one whose mind was unexpectedly relieved from a heavy load. "From the bottom of my heart, do I rejoice! I had my apprehensions that the sudden appearance of the prince might find his well-wishers unprepared and timid."

"As far from that as possible, my dear sir; though much still depends on the promptitude and resolution of the master spirits of the party. We are strong enough to control the nation, if we can bring those forward who have the strength to lead and control ourselves. All we now want are some hundred or two of prominent men to step out of their diffidence, and show us the way to honourable achievement and certain success."

"Can such men be wanting, at a moment like this?"

"I think we are secure of most of the high nobility, though their great risks render them all a little wary in the outset. It is among the professional men— the gallant soldiers, and the bold, ardent seamen of the fleet, that we must look for the first demonstrations of loyalty and true patriotism. To be honest with you, sir, I tire of being ruled by a German."

"Do you know of any intention to rally a force in this part of England, Sir Reginald? If so, say but the word—point out the spot where the standard is to be raised, and I will rally under it, the instant circumstances will permit!"

"This is just what I expected, Mr. Bluewater," answered the baronet, more gratified than he thought it prudent to express; "though it is not exactly the *form* in which you can best serve us at this precise moment. Cut off from the north, as we are in this part of the island, by all the resources of the actual government, it would be the height of imprudence in us to show our hands, until all the cards are ready to be played. Active and confidential agents are at work in the army; London has its proper share of business men, while others are in the counties, doing their best to put things in a shape for the consummation we so anxiously look for. I have been with several of our friends in this vicinity, to bring matters into a combined state; and it was my intention to visit this very estate, to see what my own name might do with the tenantry, had not the late Sir Wycherly summoned me as he did, to attend his death-bed. Have you any clue to the feelings of this new and young head of my family, the sea-lieutenant and present baronet?"

"Not a very plain one, sir, though I doubt if they be favourable to the House of Stuart."

"I feared as much; this very evening I have had an anonymous communication that I think must come from his competitor, pretty plainly intimating that, by asserting *his* rights, as they are called, the whole Wychecombe tenantry and interest could be united, in the present struggle, on whichever side I might desire to see them."

"This is a bold and decided stroke, truly! May I inquire as to your answer, Sir Reginald?"

"I shall give none. Under all circumstances I will ever refuse to place a bastard in the seat of a legitimate descendant of my family. We contend for legal and natural rights, my dear admiral, and the means employed should not be unworthy of the end. Besides, I know the scoundrel to be unworthy of trust, and shall not have the weakness to put myself in his power. I could wish the other boy to be of another mind; but, by getting him off to sea, whither he tells me he is bound, we shall at least send him out of harm's way."

In all this Sir Reginald was perfectly sincere; for, while he did not always hesitate about the employment of means, in matters of politics, he was rigidly honest in every thing that related to private properly; a species of moral contradiction that is sometimes found among men who aim at the management of human affairs; since those often yield to a besetting weakness who are nearly irreproachable in other matters. Bluewater was glad to hear this declaration; his own simplicity of character inducing him to fancy it was an indication to the general probity of his companion.

"Yes," observed the latter, "in all eases, we must maintain the laws of the land, in an affair of private right. This young man is not capable, perhaps, of forming a just estimate of his political duties, in a crisis like this, and it may be well, truly, to get him off to sea, lest by taking the losing side, he endangers his estate before he is fairly possessed of it. And having now disposed of Sir Wycherly, what can I do most to aid the righteous and glorious cause?"

"This is coming to the point manfully, Sir Richard—I beg pardon for thus styling you, but I happen to know that your name has been before the prince, for some time, as one of those who are to receive the riband from a sovereign really *authorized* to bestow it; if I have spoken a little prematurely, I again entreat your pardon;—but, this is at once coming manfully to the point! Serve us you can, of course, and that most effectually, and in an all-important manner. I now greatly regret that my father had not put me in the army, in my youth, that I might serve my prince as I could wish, in this perilous trial. But we have many friends accustomed to arms, and among them your own honourable name will appear conspicuous as to the past, and encouraging as to the future."

"I have carried arms from boyhood, it is true, Sir Reginald, but it is in a service that will scarcely much avail us in this warfare. Prince Edward has no ships, nor do I know he will need any."

"True, my dear sir, but King George has! As for the necessity, permit me to say you are mistaken; it will soon be all-important to keep open the communication with the continent. No doubt, Monsieur de Vervillin is out, with some such object, already."

Bluewater started, and he recoiled from the firm grasp which the other took of his arm, in the earnestness of discourse, with some such instinctive aversion as a man recoils from the touch of the reptile. The thought of a treachery like that implied in the remark of his companion had never occurred to him, and his honest mind turned with a strong disrelish, from even the implied proposition of the other. Still, he was not quite certain how far Sir Reginald wished to urge him, and he felt it just to ascertain his real views before he answered them. Plausible as this appeared, it was a dangerous delay for one so simple-minded, when brought in contact with a person so practised as the baronet; Sir Reginald having the tact to perceive that his new friend's feelings had already taken the alarm, and at once determined to be more wary.

"What am I to understand by this, Sir Reginald Wychecombe?" demanded the rear-admiral. "In what manner can I possibly be connected with the naval resources of the House of Hanover, when it is my intention to throw off its service? King George's fleets will hardly aid the Stuarts; and they will, at least, obey the orders of their own officers."

"Not the least doubt in the world of this, Admiral Bluewater! What a glorious privilege it was for Monk to have it in his power to put his liege sovereign in his rightful seat, and thus to save the empire, by a *coup de main*, from the pains and grievances of a civil contest! Of all the glorious names in English history, I esteem that of George Monk as the one most to be envied! It is a great thing to be a prince—one born to be set apart as God's substitute on earth, in all that relates to human justice and human power;—yet it is greater, in my eyes, to be the subject to *restore* the order of these almost divine successions, when once deranged by lawless and presuming men."

"This is true enough, sir; though I would rather have joined Charles on the beach at Dover, armed only with an untainted sword, than followed by an army at my heels!"

"What, when that army followed *cheerfully*, and was equally eager with yourself to serve their sovereign!"

"That, indeed, might somewhat qualify the feeling. But soldiers and sailors are usually influenced by the opinions of those who have been placed over them by the higher authorities."

"No doubt they are; and that is as it should be. We are encouraged to believe that some ten or fifteen captains are already well-disposed towards us, and will cheerfully take their respective ships to the points our wants require, the moment they feel assured of being properly led, when collected. By a little timely concert, we can command the North Sea, and keep open important communications with the continent. It is known the ministry intend to employ as many German troops as they can assemble, and a naval force will be all-important in keeping these mustachoed foreigners at a distance The quarrel is purely English, sir, and ought to be decided by Englishmen only."

"In that, indeed, I fully concur, Sir Reginald," answered Bluewater, breathing more freely. "I would cruise a whole winter in the North Sea to keep the Dutchmen at home, and let Englishmen decide who is to be England's king. To me, foreign interference, in such a matter, is the next evil to positive disloyalty to my rightful prince."

"These are exactly my sentiments, dear sir, and I hope to see you act on them. By the way, how happens it you are left alone, and in what manner do you admirals divide your authority when serving in company?"

"I do not know I comprehend your question, Sir Reginald. I am left here to sail the last with the Cæsar; Sir Gervaise leading out in the Plantagenet, with a view to draw a line across the channel that shall effectually prevent de Vervillin from getting to the westward."

"To the *westward*!" repeated the other, smiling ironically, though the darkness prevented the admiral from seeing the expression of his features. "Does Admiral Oakes then think that the French ships are steering in *that* direction?"

"Such is our information; have you any reason to suppose that the enemy intend differently?"

The baronet paused, and he appeared to ruminate. Enough had already passed to satisfy him he had not an ordinary mind in that of his companion to deal with, and he was slightly at a loss how to answer. To bring the other within his lures, he was fully resolved; and the spirits that aid the designing just at that moment suggested the plan which, of all others, was most likely to be successful. Bluewater had betrayed his aversion to the interference of foreign troops in the quarrel, and on this subject he intended to strike a chord which he rightly fancied would thrill on the rear-admiral's feelings.

"We have our information, certainly," answered Sir Reginald, like one who was reluctant to tell all he knew; "though good faith requires it should not actually be exposed. Nevertheless, any one can reason on the probabilities. The Duke of Cumberland will collect his German auxiliaries, and they must get into England the best way that they can. Would an intelligent enemy with a well-appointed fleet suffer this junction, if he could prevent it? We know he would not; and when we remember the precise time of the sailing of the Comte, his probable ignorance of the presence of this squadron of yours, in the channel, and all the other circumstances of the case, who can suppose otherwise than to believe his aim is to intercept the German regiments."

"This does seem plausible; and yet the Active's signals told us that the French were steering west; and that, too, with a light westerly wind."

"Do not fleets, like armies, frequently make false demonstrations? Might not Monsieur de Vervillin, so long as his vessels were in sight from the shore, have turned toward the west, with an intention, as soon as covered by the darkness, to incline to the east, again, and sail up channel, under English ensigns, perhaps? Is it not possible for him to pass the Straits of Dover, even, as an English squadron—your own, for instance—and thus deceive the Hanoverian cruisers until ready to seize or destroy any transports that may be sent?"

"Hardly, Sir Reginald," said Bluewater, smiling. "A French ship can no more be mistaken for an English ship, than a Frenchman can pass for a Briton. We sailors are not as easily deceived as that would show. It is true, however, that a fleet might well stand in one direction, until far enough off the land or covered by night, when it might change its course suddenly, in an opposite direction; and it *is possible* the Comte de Vervillin has adopted some such stratagem. If he actually knew of the intention to throw German troops into the island, it is even quite *probable*. In that case, for one, I could actually wish him success!"

"Well, my dear sir, and what is to prevent it?" asked Sir Reginald, with a triumph that was not feigned. "Nothing, you will say, unless he fall in with Sir Gervaise Oakes. But you have not answered my inquiry, as to the manner in which flag-officers divide their commands, at sea?"

"As soldiers divide their commands ashore. The superior orders, and the inferior obeys."

"Ay, this is true; but it does not meet my question. Here are eleven large ships, and two admirals; now what portion of these ships are under your particular orders, and what portion under those of Sir Gervaise Oakes?"

"The vice-admiral has assigned to himself a division of six of the ships, and left me the other five. Each of us has his frigates and smaller vessels. But an order that the commander-in-chief may choose to give any captain must be obeyed by him, as the inferior submits, as a rule, to the last order."

"And *you*," resumed Sir Reginald, with quickness; "how are *you* situated, as respects these captains?"

"Should I give a direct order to any captain in the fleet, it would certainly be his duty to obey it; though circumstances might occur which would render it obligatory on him to let me know that he had different instructions from our common superior. But, why these questions, Sir Reginald?"

"Your patience, my dear admiral;—and what ships have you specifically under your care?"

"The Cæsar, my own; the Dublin, the Elizabeth, the York, and the Dover. To these must be added the Druid frigate, the sloop of war, and the Gnat. My division numbers eight in all."

"What a magnificent force to possess at a moment as critical as this!—But where are all these vessels? I see but four and a cutter, and only two of these seem to be large."

"The light you perceive there, along the land to the westward, is on board the Elizabeth; and that broad off here, in the channel, is on board the York. The Dover's lantern has disappeared further to the southward. Ah! there the Dublin casts, and is off after the others!"

"And you intend to follow, Admiral Bluewater?"

"Within an hour, or I shall lose the division. As it is, I have been deliberating on the propriety of calling back the sternmost ships, and collecting them in close squadron; for this increase and hauling of the wind render it probable they will lose the vice-admiral, and that day-light will find the line scattered and in confusion. One mind must control the movements of ships, as well as of battalions, Sir Reginald, if they are to act in concert."

"With what view would you collect the vessels you have mentioned, and in the manner you have named, if you do not deem my inquiry indiscreet?" demanded the baronet, with quickness.

"Simply that they might be kept together, and brought in subjection to my own particular signals. This is the duty that more especially falls to my share, as head of the division."

"Have you the means to effect this, here, on this hill, and by yourself, sir?"

"It would be a great oversight to neglect so important a provision. My signal-officer is lying under yonder cover, wrapped in his cloak, and two quarter-masters are in readiness to make the very signal in question; for its necessity has been foreseen, and really would seem to be approaching. If done at all, it must be done quickly, too. The light of the York grows dim in the distance. It *shall* be done, sir; prudence requires it, and you shall see the manner in which we hold our distant ships in command."

Bluewater could not have announced more agreeable intelligence to his companion. Sir Reginald was afraid to propose the open treason he meditated; but he fancied, if the rear-admiral could fairly withdraw his own division from the fleet, it would at once weaken the vice-admiral so much, as to render an engagement with the French impossible, and might lead to such a separation of the commands as to render the final defection of the division inshore easier of accomplishment. It is true, Bluewater, himself, was actuated by motives directly contrary to these wishes; but, as the parties travelled the same road to a certain point, the intriguing baronet had his expectations of being able to persuade his new friend to continue on in his own route.

Promptitude is a military virtue, and, among seamen, it is a maxim to do every thing that is required to be done, with activity and vigour. These laws were not neglected on the present occasion. No sooner had the rear-admiral determined on his course, than he summoned his agents to put it in execution. Lord Geoffrey had returned to the heights and was within call, and he carried the orders to the lieutenant and the quarter-masters. The lanterns only required lighting, and then they were run aloft on Dutton's staff, as regularly as the same duty could have been performed on the poop of the Cæsar. Three rockets were thrown up, immediately after, and the gun kept on the cliffs for that purpose was fired, to draw attention to the signal. It might have been a minute ere the heavy ordnance of the Cæsar repeated the summons, and the same signal was shown at her mast-head. The Dublin was still so near that no time was lost, but according to orders, she too repeated the signal; for in the line that night, it was understood that an order of this nature was to be sent from ship to ship.

"Now for the Elizabeth!" cried Bluewater; "she cannot fail to have heard our guns, and to see our signals."

"The York is ahead of her, sir!" exclaimed the boy; "see; she has the signal up already!"

All this passed in a very few minutes, the last ships having sailed in the expectation of receiving some such recall. The York preceded the ship next to her in the line, in consequence of having gone about, and being actually nearer to the rear-admiral than her second astern. It was but a minute, before the gun and the lanterns of the Elizabeth, however, announced her knowledge of the order, also.

The two ships last named were no longer visible from the cliffs, though their positions were known by their lights; but no sign whatever indicated the part of the ocean on which the Dover was struggling along through the billows. After a pause of several minutes, Bluewater spoke.

"I fear we shall collect no more," he said; "one of my ships must take her chance to find the commander-in-chief, alone. Ha!—that means something!"

At this instant a faint, distant flash was seen, for a single moment, in the gloom, and then all heads were bent forward to listen, in breathless attention. A little time had elapsed, when the dull, smothered report of a gun proclaimed that even the Dover had caught the rapidly transmitted order.

"What means that, sir?" eagerly demanded Sir Reginald, who had attended to every thing with intense expectation.

"It means, sir, that all of the division are still under my command. No other ship would note the order. *Their* directions, unless specifically pointed out by their numbers, must come from the vice-admiral. Is my barge ashore, Lord Geoffrey Cleveland?"

"It is, sir, as well as the cutter for Mr. Cornet and the quarter-masters."

"It is well. Gentlemen, we will go on board; the Cæsar must weigh and join the other vessels in the offing. I will follow you to the landing, but you will shove off, at once, and desire Captain Stowel to weigh and cast to-port. We will fill on the starboard tack, and haul directly off the land."

The whole party immediately left the station, hurrying down to the boats, leaving Bluewater and Sir Reginald to follow more leisurely. It was a critical moment for the baronet, who had so nearly effected his purpose, that his disappointment would have been double did he fail of his object altogether. He determined, therefore, not to quit the admiral while there was the slightest hope of success. The two consequently descended together to the shore, walking, for the first minute or two, in profound silence.

"A great game is in your hands, Admiral Bluewater," resumed the baronet; "rightly played, it may secure the triumph of the good cause. I think I may say I *know* de Vervillin's object, and that his success will reseat the Stuarts on the thrones of their ancestors! One who loves them should ponder well before he does aught to mar so glorious a result."

This speech was as bold as it was artful. In point of fact, Sir Reginald Wychecombe knew no more of the Comte de Vervillin's intended movements than his companion; but he did not hesitate to assert what he now did, in order to obtain a great political advantage, in a moment of so much importance. To commit Bluewater and his captains openly on the side of the Stuarts would be a great achievement in itself; to frustrate the plans of Sir Gervaise might safely be accounted another; and, then, there were all the chances that the Frenchman was not at sea for nothing, and that his operations might indeed succour the movements of the prince. The baronet, upright as he was in other matters, had no scruples of conscience on this occasion; having long since brought himself over to the belief that it was justifiable to attain ends as great as those he had in view, by the sacrifice of any of the minor moral considerations.

The effect on Bluewater was not trifling. The devil had placed the bait before his eyes in a most tempting form; for he felt that he had only to hold his division in reserve to render an engagement morally improbable. Abandon his friend to a superior force he could and would not; but, it is our painful duty to avow that his mind had glimpses of the possibility of doing the adventurer in Scotland a great good, without doing the vice-admiral and the van of the fleet any very essential harm. Let us be understood, however. The rear-admiral did not even contemplate treason, or serious defection of any sort; but through one of those avenues of frailty by which men are environed, he had a glance at results that the master-spirit of evil momentarily placed before his mental vision as both great and glorious.

"I wish we were really certain of de Vervillin's object," he said; the only concession he made to this novel feeling, in words. "It might, indeed, throw a great light on the course we ought to take ourselves. I do detest this German alliance, and would abandon the service ere I would convoy or transport a ragamuffin of them all to England."

Here Sir Reginald proved how truly expert he was in the arts of management. A train of thought and feeling had been lighted in the mind of his companion, which he felt might lead to all he wished, while he was apprehensive that further persuasion would awaken opposition, and renew old sentiments. He wisely determined, therefore, to leave things as they were, trusting to the strong and declared bias of the admiral in favour of the revolution, to work out its own consequences, with a visible and all-important advantage so prominently placed before his eyes.

"I know nothing of ships," he answered, modestly; "but I do *know* that the Comte has our succour in view. It would ill become me to advise one of your experience how to lead a force like this, which is subject to your orders; but a friend of the good cause, who is now in the west, and who was lately in the presence itself, tells me that the prince manifested extreme satisfaction when he learned how much it might be in your power to serve him."

"Do you then think my name has reached the royal ear, and that the prince has any knowledge of my real feelings?"

"Nothing but your extreme modesty could cause you to doubt the first, sir; as to the last, ask yourself how came I to approach you to-night, with my heart in my hand, as it might be, making you master of my life as well as of my secret. Love and hatred are emotions that soon betray themselves."

It is matter of historical truth that men of the highest principles and strongest minds have yielded to the flattery of rank. Bluewater's political feelings had rendered him indifferent to the blandishments of the court at London, while his imagination, that chivalrous deference to antiquity and poetical right, which lay at the root of his Jacobitism, and his brooding sympathies, disposed him but too well to become the dupe of language like this. Had he been more a man of facts, one less under the influence of his own imagination; had it been his good fortune to live even in contact with those he now so devoutly worshipped, in a political sense at least, their influence over a mind as just and clear-sighted as his own, would soon have ceased; but, passing his time at sea, they had the most powerful auxiliary possible, in the high faculty he possessed of fancying things as he wished them to be. No wonder, then, that he heard this false assertion of Sir Reginald with a glow of pleasure; with even a thrill at the heart to which he had long been a stranger. For a time, his better feelings were smothered in this new and treacherous sensation.

The gentlemen, by this time, were at the landing, and it became necessary to separate. The barge of the rear-admiral was with difficulty kept from leaping on the rock, by means of oars and boat-hooks, and each instant rendered the embarkation more and more difficult. The moments were precious on more accounts than one, and the leave-taking was short. Sir Reginald said but little, though he intended the pressure of the hand he gave his companion to express every thing.

"God be with you," he added; "and as you prove true, may you prove successful! Remember, 'a lawful prince, and the claims of birth-right.' God be with you!"

"Adieu, Sir Reginald; when we next meet, the future will probably be more apparent to us all.—But who comes hither, rushing like a madman towards the boat?"

A form came leaping through the darkness; nor was it known, until it stood within two feet of Bluewater, it was that of Wycherly. He had heard the guns and seen the signals. Guessing at the reasons, he dashed from the park, which he was pacing to cool his agitation, and which now owned him for a master, and ran the whole distance to the shore, in order not to be left. His arrival was most opportune; for, in another minute, the barge left the rock.

———————————————————————————

CHAPTER XIX.

"O'er the glad waters of the dark-blue sea.
Our thoughts as boundless, and our souls as free.
Far as the breeze can bear, the billows foam,
Survey our empire and behold our home."

THE CORSAIR.

One is never fully aware of the extent of the movement that agitates the bosom of the ocean until fairly subject to its action himself, when indeed we all feel its power and reason closely on its dangers. The first pitch of his boat told Bluewater that the night threatened to be serious. As the lusty oarsmen bent to their stroke, the barge rose on a swell, dividing the foam that glanced past it like a marine Aurora Borealis, and then plunged into the trough as if descending to the bottom. It required several united and vigorous efforts to force the little craft from its dangerous vicinity to the rocks, and to get it in perfect command. This once done, however, the well-practised crew urged the barge slowly but steadily ahead.

"A dirty night!—a dirty night!" muttered Bluewater, unconsciously to himself; "we should have had a wild berth, had we rode out this blow, at anchor. Oakes will have a heavy time of it out yonder in the very chops of the channel, with a westerly swell heaving in against this ebb."

"Yes, sir," answered Wycherly; "the vice-admiral will be looking out for us all, anxiously enough, in the morning."

Not another syllable did Bluewater utter until his boat had touched the side of the Cæsar. He reflected deeply on his situation, and those who know his feelings will easily understand that his reflections were not altogether free from pain. Such as they were, he kept them to himself, however, and in a man-of-war's boat, when a flag-officer chooses to be silent, it is a matter of course for his inferiors to imitate his example.

The barge was about a quarter of a mile from the landing, when the heavy flap of the Cæsar's main-top-sail was heard, as, close-reefed, it struggled for freedom, while her crew drew its sheets down to the blocks on the lower yard-arms. A minute later, the Gnat, under the head of her fore-and-aft-main-sail, was seen standing slowly off from the land, looking in the darkness like some half-equipped shadow of herself. The sloop of war, too, was seen bending low to the force of the wind, with her mere apology of a top-sail thrown aback, in waiting for the flag-ship to cast.

The surface of the waters was a sheet of glancing foam, while the air was filled with the blended sounds of the wash of the element, and the roar of the winds. Still there was nothing chilling or repulsive in the temperature of the air, which was charged with the freshness of the sea, and was bracing and animating, bringing with it the flavour that a seaman loves. After fully fifteen minutes' severe tugging at the oars, the barge drew near enough to permit the black mass of the Cæsar to be seen. For some time, Lord Geoffrey, who had seated himself at the tiller,—yoke-lines were not used a century since,—steered by the top-light of the rear-admiral; but now the maze of hamper was seen waving slowly to and fro in the lurid heavens, and the huge hull became visible, heaving and setting, as if the ocean groaned with the labour of lifting such a pile of wood and iron. A light gleamed from the cabin-windows, and ever and anon, one glanced athwart an open gun-room port. In all other respects, the ship presented but one hue of blackness. Nor was it an easy undertaking, even after the barge was under the lee of the ship, for those in it, to quit its uneasy support and get a firm footing on the cleets that lined the vessel's side like a ladder. This was done, however, and all ascended to the deck but two of the crew, who remained to hook-on the yard and stay-tackles. This effected, the shrill whistle gave the word, and that large boat, built to carry at need some twenty souls, was raised from the raging water, as it were by some gigantic effort of the ship herself, and safely deposited in her bosom.

"We are none too soon, sir," said Stowel, the moment he had received the rear-admiral with the customary etiquette of the hour. "It's a cap-full of wind already, and it promises to blow harder before morning. We are catted and fished, sir, and the forecastle-men are passing the shank-painter at this moment."

"Fill, sir, and stretch off, on an easy bowline," was the answer; "when a league in the offing, let me know it. Mr. Cornet, I have need of you, in my cabin."

As this was said, Bluewater went below, followed by his signal-officer. At the same instant the first lieutenant called out to man the main-braces, and to fill the top-sail. As soon as this command was obeyed, the Cæsar started ahead. Her movement was slow, but it had a majesty in it, that set at naught the turbulence of the elements.

Bluewater had paced to and fro in his cabin no less than six times, with his head drooping, in a thoughtful attitude, ere his attention was called to any external object.

"Do you wish my presence, Admiral Bluewater?" the signal-officer at length inquired.

"I ask your pardon, Mr. Cornet; I was really unconscious that you were in the cabin. Let me see—ay—our last signal was, 'division come within hail of rear-admiral.' They must get close to us, to be able to do *that* to-night, Cornet! The winds and waves have begun their song in earnest."

"And yet, sir, I'll venture a month's pay that Captain Drinkwater brings the Dover so near us, as to put the officer of the watch and the quarter-master at the wheel in a fever. We once made that signal, in a gale of wind, and he passed his jib-boom-end over our taffrail."

"He is certainly a most literal gentleman, that Captain Drinkwater, but he knows how to take care of his ship. Look for the number of 'follow the rear-admiral's motions.' 'Tis 211, I think."

"No, sir; but 212. Blue, red, and white, with the flags. With the lanterns, 'tis one of the simplest signals we have."

"We will make it, at once. When that is done, show 'the rear-admiral; keep in his wake, in the general order of sailing.' That I am sure is 204."

"Yes, sir; you are quite right. Shall I show the second signal as soon as all the vessels have answered the first, sir?"

"That is my intention, Cornet. When all have answered, let me know it."

Mr. Cornet now left the cabin, and Bluewater took a seat in an arm-chair, in deep meditation. For quite half an hour the former was busy on the poop, with his two quarter-masters, going through the slow and far from easy duty of making night-signals, as they were then practised at sea. It was some time before the most distant vessel, the Dover, gave any evidence of comprehending the first order, and then the same tardy operation had to be gone through with for the second. At length the sentinel threw open the cabin-door, and Cornet re-appeared. During the whole of his absence on deck, Bluewater had not stirred; scarce seemed to breathe. His thoughts were away from his ships, and for the first time, in the ten years he had worn a flag, he had forgotten the order he had given.

"The signals are made and answered, sir," said Cornet, as soon as he had advanced to the edge of the table, on which the rear-admiral's elbow was leaning. "The Dublin is already in our wake, and the Elizabeth is bearing down fast on our weather-quarter; she will bring herself into her station in ten minutes."

"What news of the York and Dover, Cornet?" asked Bluewater, rousing himself from a fit of deep abstraction.

"The York's light nears us, quite evidently; though that of the Dover is still a fixed star, sir," answered the lieutenant, chuckling a little at his own humour; "it seems no larger than it did when we first made it."

"It is something to have made it at all. I was not aware it could be seen from deck?"

"Nor can it, sir; but, by going up half-a-dozen ratlins we get a look at it. Captain Drinkwater bowses up his lights to the gaff-end, and I can see him always ten minutes sooner than any other ship in the fleet, under the same circumstances."

"Drinkwater is a careful officer; do the bearings of his light alter enough to tell the course he is steering?"

"I think they do, sir, though our standing out athwart his line of sailing would make the change slow, of course. Every foot we get to the southward, you know, sir, would throw his bearings farther west; while every foot he comes east, would counteract that change and throw his bearings further south."

"That's very clear; but, as he must go three fathoms to our one, running off with square yards before such a breeze, I think we should be constantly altering his bearings to the southward."

"No doubt of it, in the world, sir; and that is just what we *are* doing. I think I can see a difference of half a point, already; but, when we get his light fairly in view from the poop, we shall be able to tell with perfect accuracy."

"All very well, Cornet. Do me the favour to desire Captain Stowel to step into the cabin and keep a bright look-out for the ships of the division. Stay, for a single instant; what particularly sharp-eyed youngster happens to belong to the watch on deck?"

"I know none keener in that way than Lord Geoffrey Cleveland, sir; he can see all the roguery that is going on in the whole fleet, at any rate, and ought to see other things."

"He will do perfectly well; send the young gentleman to me, sir; but, first inform the officer of the watch that I have need of him."

Bluewater was unusually fastidious in exercising his authority over those who had temporary superiors on the assigned duty of the ship; and he never sent an order to any of the watch, without causing it to pass through the officer of that watch. He waited but a minute before the boy appeared.

"Have you a good gripe to-night, boy?" asked the rear-admiral, smiling; "or will it be both hands for yourself and none for the king? I want you on the fore-top-gallant-yard, for eight or ten minutes."

"Well, sir, it's a plain road there, and one I've often travelled," returned the lad, cheerfully.

"That I well know; you are certainly no skulk when duty is to be done. Go aloft then, and ascertain if the lights of any of Sir Gervaise's squadron are to be seen. You will remember that the Dover bears somewhere about south-west from us, and that she is still a long way to seaward. I should think all of Sir Gervaise's ships must be quite as far to windward as that point would bring them, but much further off. By looking sharp a point or half a point to windward of the Dover, you may possibly see the light of the Warspite, and then we shall get a correct idea of the bearings of all the rest of the division—"

"Ay-ay-sir," interrupted the boy; "I think I understand exactly what you wish to know, Admiral Bluewater."

"That is a natural gift at sixteen, my lord," returned the admiral, smiling; "but it may be improved a little, perhaps, by the experience of fifty. Now, it is possible Sir Gervaise may have gone about, as soon as the flood made; in which case he ought to bear nearly west of us, and you will also look in that direction. On the other hand, Sir Gervaise may have stretched so far over towards the French coast before night shut in, as to feel satisfied Monsieur de Vervillin is still to the eastward of him; in which case he would keep off a little, and may, at this moment, be nearly ahead of us. So that, under all the circumstances, you will sweep the horizon, from the weather-beam to the lee-bow, ranging forward. Am I understood, now, my lord?"

"Yes, sir, I think you are," answered the boy, blushing at his own impetuosity. "You will excuse my indiscretion, Admiral Bluewater; but I *thought* I understood all you desired, when I spoke so hastily."

"No doubt you did, Geoffrey, but you perceive you did not. Nature has made you quick of apprehension, but not quick enough to *foresee* all an old man's gossip. Come nearer, now, and let us shake hands. So go aloft, and hold on well, for it is a windy night, and I do not desire to lose you overboard."

The boy did as told, squeezed Bluewater's hand, and dashed out of the cabin to conceal his tears. As for the rear-admiral, he immediately relapsed into his fit of forgetfulness, waiting for the arrival of Stowel.

A summons to a captain does not as immediately produce a visit, on board a vessel of war, as a summons to a midshipman. Captain Stowel was busy in looking at the manner in which his boats were stowed, when Cornet told him of the rear-admiral's request; and then he had to give some orders to the first lieutenant concerning the fresh meat that had been got off, and one or two other similar little things, before he was at leisure to comply.

"See me, do you say, Mr. Cornet; in his own cabin, as soon as it is convenient?" he at length remarked, when all these several offices had been duly performed.

The signal-officer repeated the request, word for word as he had heard it, when he turned to take another look at the light of the Dover. As for Stowel, he cared no more for the Dover, windy and dark as the night promised to be, than the burgher is apt to care for his neighbour's house when the whole street is threatened with destruction. To him the Cæsar was the great centre of attraction, and Cornet paid him off in kind; for, of all the vessels in the fleet, the Cæsar was precisely the one to which he gave the least attention; and this for the simple reason that she was the only ship to which he never gave, or from which he never received, a signal.

"Well, Mr. Bluff," said Stowel to the first lieutenant; "one of us will have to be on deck most of the night, and I'll take a slant below, for half an hour first, and see what the admiral wishes."

Thus saying, the captain left the deck, in order to ascertain his superior's pleasure. Captain Stowel was several years the senior of Bluewater, having actually been a lieutenant in one of the frigates in which the rear-admiral had served as a midshipman; a circumstance to which he occasionally alluded in their present intercourse. The change in the relative positions was the result of the family influence of the junior, who had passed his senior in the grade of master and commander; a rank that then brought many an honest man up for life, in the English marine. At the age of five-and-forty, that at which Bluewater first hoisted his flag, Stowell was posted; and soon after he was invited by his old shipmate, who had once had him under him as his first lieutenant in a sloop of war, to take the command of his flag-ship. From that day down to the present moment, the two officers had sailed together, whenever they sailed at all, perfectly good friends; though the captain never appeared entirely to forget the time when they were in the aforesaid frigate; one a gun-room officer, and the other only a "youngster."

Stowel must now have been about sixty-five; a square, hard-featured, red-faced seaman, who knew all about his ship, from her truck to her limber-rope, but who troubled himself very little about any thing else. He had married a widow when he was posted, but was childless, and had long since permitted his affections to wander back into their former channels; from the domestic hearth to his ship. He seldom spoke of matrimony, but the little he saw fit to say on the subject was comprehensive and to the point. A perfectly sober man, he consumed large quantities of both wine and brandy, as well as of tobacco, and never seemed to be the worse for either. Loyal he was by political faith, and he looked upon a revolution, let its object be what it might, as he would have regarded a mutiny in the Cæsar. He was exceedingly pertinacious of his rights as "captain of his own ship," both ashore and afloat; a disposition that produced less trouble with the mild and gentlemanly rear-admiral, than with Mrs. Stowel. If we add that this plain sailor never looked into a book, his proper scientific works excepted, we shall have said all of him that his connection with our tale demands.

"Good-evening, Admiral Bluewater," said this true tar, saluting the rear-admiral, as one neighbour would greet another, on dropping in of an evening, for they occupied different cabins. "Mr. Cornet told me you would like to say a word to me, before I turned in; if, indeed, turn in at all, I do this blessed night."

"Take a seat, Stowel, and a glass of this sherry, in the bargain," Bluewater answered, kindly, showing how well he understood his man, by the manner in which he shoved both bottle and glass within reach of his hand. "How goes the night?—and is this wind likely to stand?"

"I'm of opinion, sir—we'll drink His Majesty, if you've no objection, Admiral Bluewater,—I'm of opinion, we shall stretch the threads of that new main-top-sail, before we've done with the breeze, sir. I believe I've not told you, yet, that I've had the new sail bent, since we last spoke together on the subject. It's a good fit, sir; and, close-reefed, the sails stands like the side of a house."

"I'm glad to hear it, Stowel; though I think all your canvass usually appears to be in its place."

"Why you know, Admiral Bluewater, that I've been long enough at it, to understand something about the matter. It is now more than forty years since we were in the Calypso together, and ever since that time I've borne the commission of an officer. You were then a youngster, and thought more of your joke, than of bending sails, or of seeing how they would stand."

"There wasn't much of me, certainly, forty years ago, Stowel; but I well remember the knack you had of making every robin, sheet, bowline, and thread do its duty, then, as you do to-day. By the way, can you tell me any thing of the Dover, this evening?"

"Not I, sir; she came out with the rest of us I suppose, and must be somewhere in the fleet; though I dare say the log will have it all, if she has been anywhere near us, lately. I am sorry we did not go into one of the watering-ports, instead of this open roadstead, for we must be at least twenty-seven hundred gallons short of what we ought to have, by my calculation; and then we want a new set of light spars, pretty much all round; and the lower hold hasn't as many barrels of provisions in it, by thirty-odd, as I could wish to see there."

"I leave these things to you, entirely, Stowel; you will report in time to keep the ship efficient."

"No fear of the Cæsar, sir; for, between Mr. Bluff, the master, and myself, we know pretty much all about *her*, though I dare say there are men in the fleet who can tell you more about the Dublin, or the Dover, or the York. We will drink the queen, and all the royal family, if you please, sir."

As usual, Bluewater merely bowed, for his companion required no further acquiescence in his toasts. Just at that moment, too, it would have needed a general order, at least, to induce him to drink any of the family of the reigning house.

"Oakes must be well off, mid-channel, by this time, Captain Stowel?"

"I should think he might be, sir; though I can't say I took particular notice of the time he sailed. I dare say it's all in the log. The Plantagenet is a fast ship, sir, and Captain Greenly understands her trim, and what she can do on all tacks; and, yet, I do think His Majesty has one ship in this fleet that can find a Frenchman quite as soon, and deal with him, when found, quite as much to the purpose."

"Of course you mean the Cæsar;—well, I'm quite of your way of thinking, though Sir Gervaise manages never to be in a slow ship. I suppose you know, Stowel, that Monsieur de Vervillin is out, and that we may expect to see or hear something of him, to-morrow."

"Yes, sir, there is some such conversation in the ship, I know; but the quantity of galley-news is so great in this squadron, that I never attend much to what is said. One of the officers brought off a rumour, I believe, that there was a sort of a row in Scotland. By the way, sir, there is a supernumerary lieutenant on board, and as he has joined entirely without orders, I'm at a loss how to berth or to provision him. We can treat the gentleman hospitably to-night; but in the morning I shall be obliged to get him regularly on paper."

"You mean Sir Wycherly Wychecombe; he shall come into my mess, rather than give you any trouble."

"I shall not presume to meddle with any gentleman you may please to invite into your cabin, sir," answered Stowel, with a stiff bow, in the way of apology. "That's what I always tell Mrs. Stowel, sir;—that my *cabin* is my *own*, and even a wife has no right to shake a broom in it."

"Which is a great advantage to us seamen; for it gives us a citadel to retreat to, when the outworks are pressed. You appear to take but little interest in this civil war, Stowel!"

"Then it's true, is it, sir? I didn't know but it might turn out to be galley-news. Pray what is the rumpus all about, Admiral Bluewater? for, I never could get that story fidded properly, so as to set up the rigging, and have the spar well stayed in its place."

"It is merely a war to decide who shall be king of England; nothing else, I do assure you, sir."

"They're an uneasy set ashore, sir, if the truth must be said of them! We've got one king, already; and on what principle does any man wish for more? Now, there was Captain Blakely, from the Elizabeth, on board of me this afternoon; and we talked the matter over a little, and both of us concluded that they got these things up much as a matter of profit among the army contractors, and the dealers in warlike stores."

Bluewater listened with intense interest, for here was proof how completely two of his captains, at least, would be at his own command, and how little they would be likely, for a time, at least, to dispute any of his orders. He thought of Sir Reginald, and of the rapture with which *he* would have received this trait of nautical character.

"There are people who set their hearts on the result, notwithstanding," carelessly observed the rear-admiral; "and some who see their fortunes marred or promoted, by the success or downfall of the parties. They think de Vervillin is out on some errand connected with this rising in the north."

"Well, I don't see what *he* has got to do with the matter at all; for, I don't suppose that King Louis is such a fool as to expect to be king of England as well as king of France!"

"The dignity would be too much for one pair of shoulders to bear. As well might one admiral wish to command all the divisions of his own fleet, though they were fifty leagues asunder."

"Or one captain two ships; or what is more to the purpose, sir, one ship to keep two captains. We'll drink to discipline, if you've no objection, sir. 'Tis the soul of order and quiet, ashore or afloat. For my part, I want no *co-equal*— I believe that's the cant word they use on such occasions—but I want no co-equal, in the Cæsar, and I am unwilling to have one in the house at Greenwich; though Mrs. Stowel thinks differently. Here's my ship; she's in her place in the line; it's my business to see she is fit for any service that a first-class two-decker can undertake, and that duty I endeavour to perform; and I make no doubt it is all the better performed because there's no wife or co-equal aboard here. *Where* the ship is to *go*, and *what* she is to *do*, are other matters, which I take from general orders, special orders, or signals. Let them act up to this principle in London, and we should hear no more of disturbances, north or south."

"Certainly, Stowel, your doctrine would make a quiet nation, as well as a quiet ship. I hope you do me the justice to think there is no co-equal in my commands!"

"That there is not, sir—and I have the honour to drink your health—that there is not. When we were in the Calypso together, I had the advantage; and I must say that I never had a youngster under me who ever did his duty more cheerfully. Since that day we've shifted places; end for end, as one might say; and I endeavour to pay you, in your own coin. There is no man whose orders I obey more willingly or more to my own advantage; always excepting those of Admiral Oakes, who, being commander-in-chief, overlays us all with his anchor. We must dowse our peaks to his signals, though we *can* maintain, without mutinying, that the Cæsar is as good a boat on or off a wind, as the Plantagenet, the best day Sir Jarvy ever saw."

"There is no manner of doubt of that. You have all the notions of a true sailor, I find, Stowel; obey orders before all other things. I am curious to know how our captains, generally, stand affected to this claim which the Pretender has set up to the throne."

"Can't tell you, on my soul, sir; though I fancy few of them give themselves any great anxiety in the matter. When the wind is fair we can run off large, and when it is foul we must haul upon a bowline, let who will reign. I was a youngster under Queen Anne, and she was a Stuart, I believe; and I have served under the German family ever since; and to be frank with you, Admiral Bluewater, I see but little difference in the duty, the pay, or the rations. My maxim is to obey orders, and then I know the blame will fall on them that give them, if any thing goes wrong."

"We have many Scotchmen in the fleet, Stowel," observed the rear-admiral, in a musing manner, like one who rather thought aloud than spoke. "Several of the captains are from the north of Tweed."

"Ay, sir, one is pretty certain of meeting gentlemen from that part of the island, in almost all situations in life. I never have understood that Scotland had much of a navy in ancient times, and yet the moment old England has to pay for it, the lairds are willing enough to send their children to sea."

"Nevertheless it must be owned that they make gallant and useful officers, Stowel."

"No doubt they do, sir; but gallant and useful men are not scarce anywhere. You and I are too old and too experienced, Admiral Bluewater, to put any faith in the notion that courage belongs to any particular part of the world, or usefulness either. I never fought a Frenchman yet that I thought a coward; and, in my judgment, there are brave men enough in England, to command all her ships, and to fight them too."

"Let this be so, Stowel, still we must take things as they come. What do you think of the night?"

"Dirty enough before morning, I should think, sir, though it is a little out of rule, that it does not rain with this wind, already. The next time we come-to, Admiral Bluewater, I intend to anchor with a shorter scope of cable than we have been doing lately; for, I begin to think there is no use in wetting so many yarns in the summer months. They tell me the York brings up always on forty fathoms."

"That's a short range, I should think, for a heavy ship. But here is a visiter."

The sentinel opened the cabin-door, and Lord Geoffrey, with his cap fastened to his head by a pocket-handkerchief, and his face red with exposure to the wind, entered the cabin.

"Well," said Bluewater, quietly; "what is the report from aloft?"

"The Dover is running down athwart our forefoot, and nearing us fast, sir," returned the midshipman. "The York is close on our weather-beam, edging in to her station; but I can make out nothing ahead of us, though I was on the yard twenty minutes."

"Did you look well on the weather-beam, and thence forward to the lee-bow?"

"I did, sir; if any light is in view, better eyes than mine must find it."

Stowel looked from one to the other, as this short conversation was held; but, as soon as there was a pause, he put in a word in behalf of the ship.

"You've been up forward, my lord?" he said.

"Yes, I have, Captain Stowel."

"And did you think of seeing how the heel of the top-gallant-mast stood it, in this sea? Bluff tells me 'tis too loose to be fit for very heavy weather."

"I did not, sir. I was sent aloft to look out for the ships of the commander-in-chief's division, and didn't think of the heel of the top-gallant-mast's being too loose, at all."

"Ay, that's the way with all the youngsters, now-a-days. In my time, or even in *yours*, Admiral Bluewater, we never put our feet on a ratlin, but hands and eyes were at work, until we reached the halting place, even though it should be the truck. That is the manner to know what a ship is made of!"

"I kept my hands and eyes at work, too, Captain Stowel; but it was to hold on well, and to look out well."

"That will never do—that will never do, if you wish to make yourself a sailor. Begin with your own ship first; learn all about *her*, then, when you get to be an admiral, as your father's son, my lord, will be certain to become, it will be time enough to be inquiring about the rest of the fleet."

"You forget, Captain Stowel—"

"That will do, Lord Geoffrey," Bluewater soothingly interposed, for he knew that the Captain preached no more than he literally practised; "if *I* am satisfied with your report, no one else has a right to complain. Desire Sir Wycherly Wychecombe to meet me on deck, where we will now go, Stowel, and take a look at the weather for ourselves."

"With all my heart, Admiral Bluewater, though I'll just drink the First Lord's health before we quit this excellent liquor. That youngster has stuff in him, in spite of his nobility, and by fetching him up, with round turns, occasionally, I hope to make a man of him, yet."

"If he do not grow into that character, physically and morally, within the next few years, sir, he will be the first person of his family who has ever failed of it."

As Bluewater said this, he and the captain left his cabin, and ascended to the quarter-deck. Here Stowel stopped to hold a consultation with his first lieutenant, while the admiral went up the poop-ladder, and joined Cornet. The last had nothing new to communicate, and as he was permitted to go below, he was desired to send Wycherly up to the poop, where the young man would be expected by the rear-admiral.

Some little time elapsed before the Virginian could be found; no sooner was this effected, however, than he joined Bluewater. They had a private conversation of fully half an hour, pacing the poop the whole time, and then Cornet was summoned back, again, to his usual station. The latter immediately received an order to acquaint Captain Stowel the rear-admiral desired that the Cæsar might be hove-to, and to make a signal for the Druid 36, to come under the flag-ship's lee, and back her main-top-sail. No sooner did this order reach the quarter-deck than the watch was sent to the braces, and the main-yard was rounded in, until the portion of sail that was still set lay against the mast. This deadened the way of the huge body, which rose and fell heavily in the seas, as they washed under her, scarcely large enough to lift the burthen it imposed upon them. Just at this instant, the signal was made.

The sudden check to the movement of the Cæsar brought the Dublin booming up in the darkness, when putting her helm up, that ship surged slowly past to leeward, resembling a black mountain moving by in the gloom. She was hailed and directed to heave-to, also, as soon as far enough ahead. The Elizabeth followed, clearing the flag-ship by merely twenty fathoms, and receiving a similar order. The Druid had been on the admiral's weather-quarter, but she now came gliding down, with the wind abeam, taking room to back her top-sail under the Cæsar's lee-bow. By this time a cutter was in the water, rising six or eight feet up the black side of the ship, and sinking as low apparently beneath her bottom. Next, Wycherly reported himself ready to proceed.

"You will not forget, sir," said Bluewater, "any part of my commission; but inform the commander-in-chief of the *whole*. It may be important that we understand each other fully. You will also hand him this letter which I have hastily written while the boat was getting ready."

"I think I understand your wishes, sir;—at least, I *hope* so;—and I will endeavour to execute them."

"God bless you, Sir Wycherly Wychecombe," added Bluewater, with emotion. "We may never meet again; we sailors carry uncertain lives; and we may be said to carry them in our hands."

Wycherly took his leave of the admiral, and he ran down the poop-ladder to descend into the boat. Twice he paused on the quarter-deck, however, in the manner of one who felt disposed to return and ask some explanation; but each time he moved on, decided to proceed.

It needed all the agility of our young sailor to get safely into the boat. This done, the oars fell and the cutter was driven swiftly away to leeward. In a few minutes, it shot beneath the lee of the frigate, and discharged its freight. Wycherly could not have been three minutes on the deck of the Druid, ere her yards were braced up, and her top-sail filled with a heavy flap. This caused her to draw slowly ahead. Five minutes later, however, a white cloud was seen dimly fluttering over her hull, and the reefed main-sail was distended to the wind. The effect was so instantaneous that the frigate seemed to glide away from the flag-ship, and in a quarter of an hour, under her three top-sails double-reefed, and her courses, she was a mile distant on her weather-bow. Those who watched her movements without understanding them, observed that she lowered her light, and appeared to detach herself from the rest of the division.

It was some time before the Cæsar's boat was enabled to pull up against the tide, wind, and sea. When this hard task was successfully accomplished, the ship filled, passed the Dublin and Elizabeth, and resumed her place in the line.

Bluewater paced the poop an hour longer, having dismissed his signal-officer and the quarter-masters to their hammocks. Even Stowel had turned in, nor did Mr. Bluff deem it necessary to remain on deck any longer. At the end of the hour, the rear-admiral bethought him of retiring too. Before he quitted the poop, however, he stood at the weather-ladder, holding on to the mizzen-rigging, and gazing at the scene.

The wind had increased, as had the sea, but it was not yet a gale. The York had long before hauled up in her station, a cable's length ahead of the Cæsar, and was standing on, under the same canvass as the flag-ship, looking stately and black. The Dover was just shooting into her berth, under the standing sailing-orders, at the same distance ahead of the York; visible, but much less distinct and imposing. The sloop and the cutter were running along, under the lee of the heavy snips, a quarter of a mile distant, each vessel keeping her relative position, by close attention to her canvass. Further than this, nothing was in sight. The sea had that wild mixture of brightness and gloom, which belongs to the element when much agitated in a dark night, while the heavens were murky and threatening.

Within the ship, all was still. Here and there a lantern threw its wavering light around, but the shadows of the masts and guns, and other objects, rendered this relief to the night trifling. The lieutenant of the watch paced the weather side of the quarter-deck, silent but attentive. Occasionally he hailed the look-outs, and admonished them to be vigilant, also, and at each turn he glanced upward to see how the top-sail stood. Four or five old and thoughtful seamen walked the waist and forecastle, but most of the watch were stowed between the guns, or in the best places they could find, under the lee of the bulwarks, catching cat's naps. This was an indulgence denied the young gentlemen, of whom one was on the forecastle, leaning against the mast, dreaming of home, one in the waist, supporting the nettings, and one walking the lee-side of the quarter-deck, his eyes shut, his thoughts confused, and his footing uncertain. As Bluewater stepped on the quarter-deck-ladder, to descend to his own cabin, the youngster hit his foot against an eye-bolt, and fetched way plump up against his superior. Bluewater caught the lad in his arms, and saved him from a fall, setting him fairly on his feet before he let him go.

"'Tis seven bells, Geoffrey," said the admiral, in an under tone. "Hold on for half an hour longer, and then go dream of your dear mother."

Before the boy could recover himself to thank his superior, the latter had disappeared.

CHAPTER XX.

"Yet notwithstanding, being incensed, he's flint;
As humorous as winter, and as sudden
As flaws congealed in the spring of day.
His temper, therefore, must be well observed."

SHAKESPEARE.

The reader will remember that the wind had not become fresh when Sir Gervaise Oakes got into his barge, with the intention of carrying his fleet to sea. A retrospective glance at the state of the weather, will become necessary to the reader, therefore, in carrying his mind back to that precise period whither it has now become our duty to transport him in imagination.

The vice-admiral governed a fleet on principles very different from those of Bluewater. While the last left so much to the commanders of the different vessels, his friend looked into every thing himself. The details of the service he knew were indispensable to success on a larger scale, and his active mind descended into all these minutiæ, to a degree sometimes, that annoyed his captains. On the whole, however, he was sufficiently observant of that formidable barrier to excessive familiarity, and that great promoter of heart-burnings in a squadron, naval etiquette, to prevent any thing like serious misunderstandings, and the best feelings prevailed between him and the several magnates under his orders. Perhaps the circumstance that he was a *fighting* admiral contributed to this internal tranquillity; for, it has been often remarked, that armies and fleets will both tolerate more in leaders that give them plenty to do with the enemy, than in commanders who leave them inactive and less exposed. The constant encounters with the foe would seem to let out all the superfluous quarrelsome tendencies. Nelson, to a certain extent, was an example of this influence in the English marine, Suffren[1] in that of France, and Preble, to a much greater degree than in either of the other cases, in our own. At all events, while most of his captains sensibly felt themselves less of commanders, while Sir Gervaise was on board or around their ships, than when he was in the cabin of the Plantagenet, the peace was rarely broken between them, and he was generally beloved as well as obeyed. Bluewater was a more invariable favourite, perhaps, though scarcely as much respected; and certainly not half as much feared.

On the present occasion, the vice-admiral did not pull through the fleet, without discovering the peculiar propensity to which we have alluded. In passing one of the ships, he made a sign to his coxswain to cause the boat's crew to lay on their oars, when he hailed the vessel, and the following dialogue occurred.

"Carnatic, ahoy!" cried the admiral.

"Sir," exclaimed the officer of the deck, jumping on a quarter-deck gun, and raising his hat.

"Is Captain Parker on board, sir?"

"He is, Sir Gervaise; will you see him, sir?"

A nod of the head sufficed to bring the said Captain Parker on deck, and to the gangway, where he could converse with his superior, without inconvenience to either.

"How do you do, *Captain* Parker?"—a certain sign Sir Gervaise meant to rap the other over the knuckles, else would it have been *Parker*."—How do you do, *Captain* Parker? I am sorry to see you have got your ship too much down by the head, sir. She'll steer off the wind, like a colt when he first feels the bridle; now with his head on one side, and now on the other. You know I like a compact line, and straight wakes, sir."

"I am well aware of that, Sir Gervaise," returned Parker, a gray-headed, meek old man, who had fought his way up from the forecastle to his present honourable station, and, who, though brave as a lion before the enemy, had a particular dread of all his commanders; "but we have been obliged to use more water aft than we could wish, on account of the tiers. We shall coil away the cables anew, and come at some of the leaguers forward, and bring all right again, in a week, I hope, sir."

"A week?—the d——l, sir; that will never do, when I expect to see de Vervillin *to-morrow*. Fill all your empty casks aft with salt-water, immediately; and if that wont do, shift some of your shot forward. I know that craft of yours, well; she is as tender as a fellow with corns, and the shoe musn't pinch anywhere."

"Very well, Sir Gervaise; the ship shall be brought in trim, as soon as possible."

"Ay, ay, sir, that is what I expect from every vessel, at *all* times; and more especially when we are ready to meet an enemy. And, I say, *Parker*,"—making a sign to his boat's crew to stop rowing again—"I say, *Parker*, I know you love brawn;—I'll send you some that Galleygo tells me he has picked up, along-shore here, as soon as I get aboard. The fellow has been robbing all the hen-roosts in Devonshire, by his own account of the matter."

Sir Gervaise waved his hand, *Parker* smiled and bowed his thanks, and the two parted with feelings of perfect kindness, notwithstanding the little skirmish with which the interview had commenced.

"Mr. Williamson," said Captain Parker to his first lieutenant, on quitting the gangway, "you hear what the commander-in-chief says; and he must be obeyed. I *don't* think the Carnatic would have sheered out of the line, even if she is a little by the head; but have the empty casks filled, and bring her down six inches more by the stern."

"That's a good fellow, that old Parker," said Sir Gervaise to his purser, whom he was carrying off good-naturedly to the ship, lest he might lose his passage; "and I wonder how he let his ship get her nose under water, in that fashion. I like to have him for a second astern; for I feel sure he'd follow if I stood into Cherbourg, bows on! Yes; a good fellow is Parker; and, Locker,"—to his own man, who was also in the boat;—"mind you send him *two* of the best pieces of that brawn—hey!—hey!—hey!—what the d——l has Lord Morganic"—a descendant from royalty by the left hand,—"been doing now! That ship is kept like a tailor's jay figure, just to stuff jackets and gim-cracks on her—Achilles, there!"

A quarter-master ran to the edge of the poop, and then turning, he spoke to his captain, who was walking the deck, and informed him that the commander-in-chief hailed the ship. The Earl of Morganic, a young man of four-and-twenty, who had succeeded to the title a few years before by the death of an elder brother,—the usual process by which an *old* peer is brought into the British navy, the work being too discouraging for those who have fortune before their eyes from the start,—now advanced to the quarter of the ship, bowed with respectful ease, and spoke with a self-possession that not one of the old commanders of the fleet would have dared to use. In general, this nobleman's intercourse with his superiors in naval rank, betrayed the consciousness of his own superiority in civil rank; but Sir Gervaise being of an old family, and quite as rich as he was himself, the vice-admiral commanded more of his homage than was customary. His ship was full of "nobs," as they term it in the British navy, or the sons and relatives of nobles; and it was by no means an uncommon thing for her messes to have their jokes at the expense of even flag-officers, who were believed to be a little ignorant of the peculiar sensibilities that are rightly enough imagined to characterize social station.

"Good-morning, Sir Gervaise," called out this noble captain; "I'm glad to see you looking so well, after our long cruise in the Bay; I intended to have the honour to inquire after your health in person, this morning, but they told me you slept out of your ship. We shall have to hold a court on you, sir, if you fall much into that habit!"

All within hearing smiled, even to the rough old tars, who were astraddle of the yards; and even Sir Gervaise's lip curled a little, though he was not exactly in a joking humour.

"Come, come, Morganic, do you let my habits alone, and look out for your own fore-top-mast. Why, in the name of seamanship, is that spar stayed forward in such a fashion, looking like a xebec's foremast?"

"Do you dislike it, Sir Gervaise?—Now to our fancies aboard here, it gives the Achilles a knowing look, and we hope to set a fashion. By carrying the head-sails well forward, we help the ship round in a sea, you know, sir."

"Indeed, I know no such thing, my lord. What you gain after being taken aback, you lose in coming to the wind. If I had a pair of scales suitable to such a purpose, I would have all that hamper you have stayed away yonder over your bows, on the end of such a long lever, weighed, in order that you might learn what a beautiful contrivance you've invented, among you, to make a ship pitch in a head sea. Why, d——e, if I think you'd lie-to, at all, with so much stuff aloft to knock you off to leeward. Come up, every thing, forward; come up every thing, my lord, and bring the mast as near perpendicular as possible. It's a hard matter, I find, to make one of your new-fashioned captains keep things in their places."

"Well, now, Sir Gervaise, I think the Achilles makes as good an appearance as most of the other ships; and as to travelling or working, I do not know that she is either dull or clumsy!"

"She's pretty well, Morganic, considering how many Bond-street ideas you have got among you; but she'll never do in a head sea, with that fore-top-mast threatening your knight-heads. So get the mast up-and-down, again, as soon as convenient, and come and dine with me, without further invitation, the first fine day we have at sea. I'm going to send Parker some brawn; but, I'll feed *you* on some of Galleygo's turtle-soup, made out of pig's heads."

"Thank'ee, Sir Gervaise; we'll endeavour to straighten the slick, since you *will* have it so; though, I confess I get tired of seeing every thing to-day, just as we had it yesterday."

"Yes—yes—that's the way with most of these St. James cruisers," continued the vice-admiral, as he rowed away. "They want a fashionable tailor to rig a man-of-war, as they are rigged themselves. There's my old friend and neighbour, Lord Scupperton—he's taken a fancy to yachting, lately, and when his new brig was put into the water, Lady Scupperton made him send for an upholsterer from town to fit out the cabin; and when the blackguard had surveyed the unfortunate craft, as if it were a country box, what does he do but give an opinion, that 'this here edifice, my lord, in my judgment, should be furnished in cottage style,'—the vagabond!"

This story, which was not particularly original, for Sir Gervaise himself had told it at least a dozen times before, put the admiral in a good humour, and he found no more fault with his captains, until he reached the Plantagenet.

"Daly," said the Earl of Morganic to his first lieutenant, an experienced old Irishman of fifty, who still sung a good song and told a good story, and what was a little extraordinary for either of these accomplishments, knew how to take good care of a ship;—"Daly, I suppose we must humour the old gentleman, or he'll be quarantining me, and that I shouldn't particularly like on the eve of a general action; so we'll ease off forward, and set up the strings aft, again. Hang me if I think he could find it out if we didn't, so long as we kept dead in his wake!"

"That wouldn't be a very safe desait for Sir Jarvy, my lord, for he's a wonderful eye for a rope! Were it Admiral Blue, now, I'd engage to cruise in his company for a week, with my mizzen-mast stowed in the hold, and there should be no bother about the novelty, at all; quite likely he'd be hailing us, and ask 'what brig's that?' But none of these tricks will answer with t'other, who misses the whipping off the end of a gasket, as soon as any first luff of us all. And so I'll just go about the business in earnest; get the carpenter up with his plumb-bob, and set every thing as straight up-and-down as the back of a grenadier."

Lord Morganic laughed, as was usual with him when his lieutenant saw fit to be humorous; and then his caprice in changing the staying of his masts, as well as the order which countermanded it, was forgotten.

The arrival of Sir Gervaise on board his own ship was always an event in the fleet, even though his absence had lasted no longer than twenty-four hours. The effect was like that which is produced on a team of high-mettled cattle, when they feel that the reins are in the hands of an experienced and spirited coachman.

"Good-morning, Greenly, good-morning to you all, gentlemen," said the vice-admiral, bowing to the quarter-deck in gross, in return for the 'present-arms,' and rattling of drums, and lowering of hats that greeted his arrival; "a fine day, and it is likely we shall have a fresh breeze. Captain Greenly, your sprit-sail-yard wants squaring by the lifts; and, Bunting, make the Thunderer's signal to get her fore-yard in its place, as soon as possible. She's had it down long enough to make a new one, instead of merely fishing it. Are your boats all aboard, Greenly?"

"All but your own barge, Sir Gervaise, and that is hooked on."

"In with it, sir; then trip, and we'll be off. Monsieur de Vervillin has got some mischief in his head, gentlemen, and we must go and take it out of him."

These orders were promptly obeyed; but, as the manner in which the Plantagenet passed out of the fleet, and led the other ships to sea, has been already related, it is unnecessary to repeat it. There was the usual bustle, the customary orderly confusion, the winding of calls, the creaking of blocks, and the swinging of yards, ere the vessels were in motion. As the breeze freshened, sail was reduced, as already related, until, by the time the leading ship was ten leagues at sea, all were under short canvass, and the appearance of a windy, if not a dirty night, had set in. Of course, all means of communication between the Plantagenet and the vessels still at anchor, had ceased, except by sending signals down the line; but, to those Sir Gervaise had no recourse, since he was satisfied Bluewater understood his plans, and he then entertained no manner of doubt of his friend's willingness to aid them.

Little heed was taken of any thing astern, by those on board the Plantagenet. Every one saw, it is true, that ship followed ship in due succession, as long as the movements of those inshore could be perceived at all; but the great interest centred on the horizon to the southward and eastward. In that quarter of the channel the French were expected to appear, for the cause of this sudden departure was a secret from no one in the fleet. A dozen of the best look-outs in the ship were kept aloft the whole afternoon, and Captain Greenly, himself, sat in the forward-cross-trees, with a glass, for more than an hour, just as the sun was setting, in order to sweep the horizon. Two or three sail were made, it is true, but they all proved to be English coasters; Guernsey or Jerseymen, standing for ports in the west of England, most probably laden with prohibited articles from the country of the enemy. Whatever may be the dislike of an Englishman for a Frenchman, he has no dislike to the labour of his hands; and there probably has not been a period since civilization has introduced the art of smuggling among its other arts, when French brandies, and laces, and silks, were not exchanged against English tobacco and guineas, and that in a contraband way, let it be in peace or let it be in war. One of the characteristics of Sir Gervaise Oakes was to despise all petty means of annoyance; usually he disdained even to turn aside to chase a smuggler. Fishermen he never molested at all; and, on the whole, he carried on a marine warfare, a century since, in a way that some of his successors might have imitated to advantage in our own times. Like that high-spirited Irishman, Caldwell,[2] who conducted a blockade in the Chesapeake, at the commencement of the revolution, with so much liberality, that his enemies actually sent him an invitation to a public dinner, Sir Gervaise knew how to distinguish between the combatant and the non-combatant, and heartily disdained all the money-making parts of his profession, though large sums had fallen into his hands, in this way, as pure God-sends. No notice was taken, therefore, of any thing that had not a warlike look; the noble old ship standing steadily on towards the French coast, as the mastiff passes the cur, on his way to encounter another animal, of a mould and courage more worthy of his powers.

"Make nothing of 'em, hey! Greenly," said Sir Gervaise, as the captain came down from his perch, in consequence of the gathering obscurity of evening, followed by half-a-dozen lieutenants and midshipmen, who had been aloft as volunteers. "Well, we know they cannot yet be to the westward of us, and by standing on shall be certain of heading them off, before this time six months. How beautifully all the ships behave, following each other as accurately as if Bluewater himself were aboard each vessel to conn her!"

"Yes, sir, they do keep the line uncommonly well, considering that the tides run in streaks in the channel. I *do* think if we were to drop a hammock overboard, that the Carnatic would pick it up, although she must be quite four leagues astern of us."

"Let old Parker alone for that! I'll warrant you, *he* is never out of the way. Were it Lord Morganic, now, in the Achilles, I should expect him to be away off here on our weather-quarter, just to show us how his ship can eat us out of the wind when he *tries*: or away down yonder, under our lee, that we might understand how she falls off, when he *don't* try."

"My lord is a gallant officer, and no bad seaman, for his years, notwithstanding, Sir Gervaise," observed Greenly, who generally took the part of the absent, whenever his superior felt disposed to berate them.

"I deny neither, Greenly, most particularly the first. I know very well, were I to signal Morganic, to run into Brest, he'd do it; but whether he would go in, ring-tail-boom, or jib-boom first, I couldn't tell till I saw it. Now you are a youngish man yourself. Greenly—"

"Every day of eight-and-thirty, Sir Gervaise, and a few months to spare; and I care not if the ladies know it."

"Poh!—They like us old fellows, half the time, as well as they do the boys. But you are of an age not to feel time in your bones, and can see the folly of some of our old-fashioned notions, perhaps; though you are not quite as likely to understand the fooleries that have come in, in your own day. Nothing is more absurd than to be experimenting on the settled principles of ships. They are machines, Greenly, and have their laws, just the same as the planets in the heavens. The idea comes from a fish,—head, run, and helm; and all we have to do is to study the fishes in order to get the sort of craft we want. If there is occasion for bulk, take the whale, and you get a round bottom, full fore-body, and a clean run. When you want speed, models are plenty—take the dolphin, for instance,—and there you find an entrance like a wedge, a lean fore-body, and a run as clean as this ship's decks. But some of our young captains would spoil a dolphin's sailing, if they could breathe under water, so as to get at the poor devils. Look at their fancies! The First Lord shall give one of his cousins a frigate, now, that is moulded after nature itself, as one might say; with a bottom that would put a trout to shame. Well, one of the first things the lad does, when he gets on board her, is to lengthen his gaff, perhaps, put a cloth or two in his mizzen, and call it a spanker, settle away the peak till it sticks out over his taffrail like a sign-post, and then away he goes upon a wind, with his helm hard-up, bragging what a weatherly craft he has, and how hard it is to make her even *look* to leeward."

"I have known such sailors, I must confess, Sir Gervaise; but time cures them of that folly."

"That is to be hoped; for what would a man think of a fish to which nature had fitted a tail athwart-ships, and which was obliged to carry a fin, like a lee-board, under its lee-jaw, to prevent falling off dead before the wind!"

Here Sir Gervaise laughed heartily at the picture of the awkward creature to which his own imagination had given birth; Greenly joining in the merriment, partly from the oddity of the conceit, and partly from the docility with which commander-in-chief's jokes are usually received. The feeling of momentary indignation which had aroused Sir Gervaise to such an expression of his disgust at modern inventions, was appeased by this little success; and, inviting his captain to sup with him,—a substitute for a dinner,—he led the way below in high good-humour, Galleygo having just announced that the table was ready.

The *convives* on this occasion were merely the admiral himself, Greenly, and Atwood. The fare was substantial, rather than scientific; but the service was rich; Sir Gervaise uniformly eating off of plate. In addition to Galleygo, no less than five domestics attended to the wants of the party. As a ship of the Plantagenet's size was reasonably steady at all times, a gale of wind excepted, when the lamps and candles were lighted, and the group was arranged, aided by the admixture of rich furniture with frowning artillery and the other appliances of war, the great cabin of the Plantagenet was not without a certain air of rude magnificence. Sir Gervaise kept no less than three servants in livery, as a part of his personal establishment, tolerating Galleygo, and one or two more of the same stamp, as a homage due to Neptune.

The situation not being novel to either of the party, and the day's work having been severe, the first twenty minutes were pretty studiously devoted to the duty of "restoration," as it is termed by the great masters of the science of the table. By the end of that time, however, the glass began to circulate, though moderately, and with it tongues to loosen.

"Your health, Captain Greenly—Atwood, I remember you," said the vice-admiral, nodding his head familiarly to his two guests, on the eve of tossing off a glass of sherry. "These Spanish wines go directly to the heart, and I only wonder why a people who can make them, don't make better sailors."

"In the days of Columbus, the Spaniards had something to boast of in that way, too, Sir Gervaise," Atwood remarked.

"Ay, but that was a long time ago, and they have got bravely over it. I account for the deficiencies of both the French and Spanish marines something in this way, Greenly. Columbus, and the discovery of America, brought ships and sailors into fashion. But a ship without an officer fit to command her, is like a body without a soul. Fashion, however, brought your young nobles into their services, and men were given vessels because their fathers were dukes and counts, and not because they knew any thing about them."

"Is our own service entirely free from this sort of favouritism?" quietly demanded the captain.

"Far from it, Greenly; else would not Morganic have been made a captain at twenty, and old Parker, for instance, one only at fifty. But, somehow, our classes slide into each other, in a way that neutralizes, in a great degree, the effect of birth. Is it not so, Atwood?"

"*Some* of our classes, Sir Gervaise, manage to *slide* into all the best places, if the truth must be said."

"Well, that is pretty bold for a Scotchman!" rejoined the vice-admiral, good-humouredly. "Ever since the accession of the house of Stuart, we've built a bridge across the Tweed that lets people pass in only one direction. I make no doubt this Pretender's son will bring down half Scotland at his heels, to fill all the berths they may fancy suitable to their merits. It's an easy way of paying bounty—promises."

"This affair in the north, they tell me, seems a little serious," said Greenly. "I believe this is Mr. Atwood's opinion?"

"You'll find it serious enough, if Sir Gervaise's notion about the bounty be true," answered the immovable secretary. "Scotia is a small country, but it's well filled with 'braw sperits,' if there's an opening for them to prove it."

"Well, well, this war between England and Scotland is out of place, while we have the French and Spaniards on our hands. Most extraordinary scenes have we had ashore, yonder, Greenly, with an old Devonshire baronet, who slipped and is off for the other world, while we were in his house."

"Magrath has told me something of it, sir; and, he tells me the *fill-us-null-us*—hang me if I can make out his gibberish, five minutes after it was told to me."

"*Filius nullius*, you mean; nobody's baby—the son of nobody—have you forgotten your Latin, man?"

"Faith, Sir Gervaise, I never had any to forget. My father was a captain of a man-of-war before me, and he kept me afloat from the time I was five, down to the day of his death; Latin was no part of my spoon-meat."

"Ay—ay—my good fellow, I knew your father, and was in the third ship from him, in the action in which he fell," returned the vice-admiral, kindly. "Bluewater was just ahead of him, and we all loved him, as we did an elder brother. You were not promoted, then."

"No, sir, I was only a midshipman, and didn't happen to be in his own ship that day," answered Greenly, sensibly touched with this tribute to his parent's merit; "but I was old enough to remember how nobly you all behaved on the occasion. Well,"—slily brushing his eye with his hand,—"Latin may do a schoolmaster good, but it is of little use on board ship. I never had but one scholar among all my cronies and intimates."

"And who was he, Greenly? You shouldn't despise knowledge, because you don't understand it. I dare say your intimate was none the worse for a little Latin—enough to go through *nullus, nulla, nullum*, for instance. Who was this intimate, Greenly?"

"John Bluewater—handsome Jack, as he was called; the younger brother of the admiral. They sent him to sea, to keep him out of harm's way in some love affair; and you may remember that while he was with the admiral, or *Captain* Bluewater, as he was then, I was one of the lieutenants. Although poor Jack was a soldier and in the guards, and he was four or five years my senior, he took a fancy to me, and we became intimate. *He* understood Latin, better than he did his own interests."

"In what did he fail?—Bluewater was never very communicative to me about that brother."

"There was a private marriage, and cross guardians, and the usual difficulties. In the midst of it all, poor John fell in battle, as you know, and his widow followed him to the grave, within a month or two. 'Twas a sad story all round, and I try to think of it as little as possible."

"A private marriage!" repeated Sir Gervaise, slowly. "Are you quite sure of *that*? I don't think Bluewater is aware of that circumstance; at least, I never heard him allude to it. Could there have been any issue?"

"No one can know it better than myself, as I helped to get the lady off, and was present at the ceremony. That much I *know*. Of issue, I should think there was none; though the colonel lived a year after the marriage. How far the admiral is familiar with all these circumstances I cannot say, as one would not like to introduce the particulars of a private marriage of a deceased brother, to his commanding officer."

"I am glad there was no issue, Greenly—particular circumstances make me glad of that. But we will change the discourse, as these family disasters make one melancholy; and a melancholy dinner is like ingratitude to Him who bestows it."

The conversation now grew general, and in due season, in common with the feast, it ended. After sitting the usual time, the guests retired. Sir Gervaise then went on deck, and paced the poop for an hour, looking anxiously ahead, in quest of the French signal; and, failing of discovering them, he was fain to seek his berth out of sheer fatigue. Before he did this, however, the necessary orders were given; and that to call him, should any thing out of the common track occur, was repeated no less than four times.

CHAPTER XXI.

"Roll on, thou deep and dark-blue ocean—roll
Ten thousand fleets sweep over thee in vain;
Man marks the earth with ruin—his control
Stops with the shore;—upon the watery plain
The wrecks are all thy deed."

CHILDE HAROLD.

It was broad day-light, when Sir Gervaise Oakes next appeared on deck. As the scene then offered to his view, as well as the impression it made on his mind, will sufficiently explain to the reader the state of affairs, some six hours later than the time last included in our account, we refer him to those for his own impressions. The wind now blew a real gale, though the season of the year rendered it less unpleasant to the feelings than is usual with wintry tempests. The air was even bland, and still charged with the moisture of the ocean; though it came sweeping athwart sheets of foam, with a fury, at moments, which threatened to carry the entire summits of waves miles from their beds, in spray. Even the aquatic birds seemed to be terrified, in the instants of the greatest power of the winds, actually wheeling suddenly on their wings, and plunging into the element beneath to seek protection from the maddened efforts of that to which they more properly belonged.

Still, Sir Gervaise saw that his ships bore up nobly against the fierce strife. Each vessel showed the same canvass; viz.—a reefed fore-sail; a small triangular piece of strong, heavy cloth, fitted between the end of the bowsprit and the head of the fore-top-mast; a similar sail over the quarter-deck, between the mizzen and main masts, and a close-reefed main-top-sail Several times that morning, Captain Greenly had thought he should be compelled to substitute a lower surface to the wind than that of the sail last mentioned. As it was an important auxiliary, however, in steadying the ship, and in keeping her under the command of her helm, on each occasion the order had been delayed, until he now began to question whether the canvass could be reduced, without too great a risk to the men whom it would be necessary to send aloft. He had decided to let it stand or blow away, as fortune might decide. Similar reasoning left nearly all the other vessels under precisely the same canvass.

The ships of the vice-admiral's division had closed in the night, agreeably to an order given before quitting the anchorage, which directed them to come within the usual sailing distance, in the event of the weather's menacing a separation. This command had been obeyed by the ships astern carrying sail hard, long after the leading vessels had been eased by reducing their canvass.

The order of sailing was the Plantagenet in the van, and the Carnatic, Achilles, Thunderer, Blenheim, and Warspite following, in the order named; some changes having been made in the night, in order to bring the ships of the division into their fighting-stations, in a line ahead, the vice-admiral leading. The superiority of the Plantagenet was a little apparent, notwithstanding; the Carnatic alone, and that only by means of the most careful watching, being able to keep literally in the commander-in-chief's wake; all the other vessels gradually but almost imperceptibly setting to leeward of it. These several circumstances struck Sir Gervaise, the moment his foot touched the poop, where he found Greenly keeping an anxious look-out on the state of the weather and the condition of his own ship; leaning at the same time, against the spanker-boom to steady himself in the gusts of the gale. The vice-admiral braced his own well-knit and compact frame, by spreading his legs; then he turned his handsome but weather-beaten face towards the line, scanning each ship in succession, as she lay over to the wind, and came wallowing on, shoving aside vast mounds of water with her bows, her masts describing short arcs in the air, and her hull rolling to windward, and lurching, as if boring her way through the ocean. Galleygo, who never regarded himself as a steward in a gale of wind, was the only other person on the poop, whither he went at pleasure by a sort of imprescriptibly right.

"Well done, old Planter!" cried Sir Gervaise, heartily, as soon as his eye had taken in the leading peculiarities of the view. "You see, Greenly, she has every body but old Parker to leeward, and she would have him there, too, but he would carry every stick he has, out of the Carnatic, rather than not keep his berth. Look at Master Morganic; he has his main course close-reefed on the Achilles, to luff into his station, and I'll warrant you will get a good six months' wear out of that ship in this one gale; loosening her knees, and jerking her spars like so many whip-handles; and all for love of the new fashion of rigging an English two-decker like an Algerian xebec! Well, let him tug his way up to windward, Bond-street fashion, if he likes the fun. What has become of the Chloe, Greenly?"

"Here she is, sir, quite a league on our lee-bow, looking out, according to orders."

"Ay, that is her work, and she'll do it effectually.—But I don't see the Driver!"

"She's dead ahead sir," answered Greenly, smiling; "*her* orders being rather more difficult of execution. Her station would be off yonder to windward, half a league ahead of us; but it's no easy matter to get into that position, Sir Gervaise, when the Plantagenet is really in earnest."

Sir Gervaise laughed, and rubbed his hands, then he turned to look for the Active, the only other vessel of his division. This little cutter was dancing over the seas, half the time under water, notwithstanding, under the head of her main-sail, broad off, on the admiral's weather-beam; finding no difficulty in maintaining her station there, in the absence of all top-hamper, and favoured by the lowness of her hull. After this he glanced upward at the sails and spars of the Plantagenet, which he studied closely.

"No signs of *de Vervillin*, hey! Greenly?" the admiral asked, when his survey of the whole fleet had ended. "I was in hopes we might see something of *him*, when the light returned this morning."

"Perhaps it is quite as well as it is, Sir Gervaise," returned the captain. "We could do little besides look at each other, in this gale, and Admiral Bluewater ought to join before I should like even to do *that*."

"Think you so, Master Greenly!—There you are mistaken, then; for I'd lie by him, were I alone in this ship, that I might know where he was to be found as soon as the weather would permit us to have something to say to him."

These words were scarcely uttered, when the look-out in the forward cross-trees, shouted at the top of his voice, "sail-ho!" At the next instant the Chloe fired a gun, the report of which was just heard amid the roaring of the gale, though the smoke was distinctly seen floating above the mists of the ocean; she also set a signal at her naked mizzen-top-gallant-mast-head.

"Run below, young gentleman," said the vice-admiral, advancing to the break of the poop and speaking to a midshipman on the quarter-deck; "and desire Mr. Bunting to make his appearance. The Chloe signals us—tell him not to look for his knee-buckles."

A century since, the last injunction, though still so much in use on ship-board, was far more literal than it is to-day, nearly all classes of men possessing the articles in question, though not invariably wearing them when at sea. The midshipman dove below, however, as soon as the words were out of his superior's mouth; and, in a very few minutes, Bunting appeared, having actually stopped on the main-deck ladder to assume his coat, lest he might too unceremoniously invade the sacred precincts of the quarter-deck, in his shirt-sleeves.

"There it is, Bunting," said Sir Gervaise, handing the lieutenant the glass; "two hundred and twenty-seven—'a large sail ahead,' if I remember right."

"No, Sir Gervaise, '*sails* ahead;' the number of them to follow. Hoist the answering flag, quarter-master."

"So much the better! So much the better, Bunting! The number to follow? Well, *we'll* follow the number, let it be greater or smaller. Come, sirrah, bear a hand up with your answering flag."

The usual signal that the message was understood was now run up between the masts, and instantly hauled down again, the flags seen in the Chloe descending at the same moment.

"Now for the number of the sails, ahead," said Sir Gervaise, as he, Greenly, and Bunting, each levelled a glass at the frigate, on board which the next signal was momentarily expected. "Eleven, by George!"

"No, Sir Gervaise," exclaimed Greenly, "I know better than *that*. Red above, and blue beneath, with the distinguishing pennant *beneath*, make *fourteen*, in our books, now!"

"Well, sir, if they are *forty*, we'll go nearer and see of what sort of stuff they are made. Show your answering flag, Bunting, that we may know what else the Chloe has to tell us."

This was done, the frigate hauling down her signals in haste, and showing a new set as soon as possible.

"What now, Bunting?—what now, Greenly?" demanded Sir Gervaise, a sea having struck the side of the ship and thrown so much spray into his face as to reduce him to the necessity of using his pocket-handkerchief, at the very moment he was anxious to be looking through his glass. "What do you make of *that*, gentlemen?"

"I make out the number to be 382," answered Greenly; "but what it means, I know not."

"'Strange sails, *enemies*,'" read Bunting from the book. "Show the answer, quarter-master."

"We hardly wanted a signal for *that*, Greenly, since there can be no friendly force, here away; and fourteen sail, on this coast, always means mischief. What says the Chloe next?"

"'Strange sails on the larboard tack, heading as follows.'"

"By George, crossing our course!—We shall soon see them from deck. Do the ships astern notice the signals?"

"Every one of them, Sir Gervaise," answered the captain; "the Thunderer has just lowered her answering flag, and the Active is repeating. I have never seen quarter-masters so nimble!"

"So much the better—so much the better—down he comes; stand by for another."

After the necessary pause, the signal to denote the point of the compass was shown from the Chloe.

"Heading how, Bunting?" the vice-admiral eagerly inquired. "Heading how, sir?"

"North-west-and-by-north," or as Bunting pronounced it "nor-west-and-by-loathe, I believe, sir,—no, I am mistaken, Sir Gervaise; it is nor-nor-west."

"Jammed up like ourselves, hard on a wind! This gale comes directly from the broad Atlantic, and one party is crossing over to the north and the other to the south shore. We *must* meet, unless one of us run away—hey! Greenly?"

"True enough, Sir Gervaise; though fourteen sail is rather an awkward odds for seven."

"You forget the Driver and Active, sir; we've *nine*; nine hearty, substantial British cruisers."

"To wit: six ships of the line, one frigate, a *sloop*, and a *cutter*," laying heavy emphasis on the two last vessels.

"What does the Chloe say now, Bunting? That we're enough for the French, although they *are* two to one?"

"Not exactly that, I believe, Sir Gervaise. 'Five more sail ahead.' They increase fast, sir."

"Ay, at that rate, they may indeed grow too strong for us," answered Sir Gervaise, with more coolness of manner; "nineteen to nine are rather heavy odds. I wish we had Bluewater here!"

"That is what I was about to suggest, Sir Gervaise," observed the captain. "If we had the other division, as some of the Frenchmen are probably frigates and corvettes, we might do better. Admiral Bluewater cannot be far from us; somewhere down here, towards north-east—or nor-nor-east. By warring round, I think we should make his division in the course of a couple of hours."

"What, and leave to Monsieur de Vervillin the advantage of swearing he frightened us away! No—no—Greenly; we will first *pass* him fairly and manfully, and that, too, within reach of shot; and then it will be time enough to go round and look after our friends."

"Will not that be putting the French exactly between our two divisions, Sir Gervaise, and give him the advantage of dividing our force. If he stand far, on a nor-nor-west course, I think he will infallibly get between us and Admiral Bluewater."

"And what will he gain by that, Greenly?—What, according to your notions of matters and things, will be the great advantage of having an English fleet on each side of him?"

"Not much, certainly, Sir Gervaise," answered Greenly, laughing; "if these fleets were at all equal to his own. But as they will be much inferior to him, the Comte may manage to close with one division, while the other is so far off as to be unable to assist; and one hour of a hot fire may dispose of the victory."

"All this is apparent enough, Greenly; yet I could hardly brook letting the enemy go scathe less. So long as it blows as it does now, there will not be much fighting, and there can be no harm in taking a near look at M. de Vervillin. In half an hour, or an hour at most, we must get a sight of him from off deck, even with this slow headway of the two fleets. Let them heave the log, and ascertain how fast we go, sir."

"Should we engage the French in such weather, Sir Gervaise," answered Greenly, after giving the order just mentioned; "it would be giving them the very advantage they like. They usually fire at the spars, and one shot would do more mischief, with such a strain on the masts, than half-a-dozen in a moderate blow."

"That will do, Greenly—that will do," said the vice-admiral, impatiently; "if I didn't so well know you, and hadn't seen you so often engaged, I should think you were afraid of these nineteen sail. You have lectured long enough to render me prudent, and we'll say no more."

Here Sir Gervaise turned on his heel, and began to pace the poop, for he was slightly vexed, though not angered. Such little dialogues often occurred between him and his captain, the latter knowing that his commander's greatest professional failing was excess of daring, while he felt that his own reputation was too well established to be afraid to inculcate prudence. Next to the honour of the flag, and his own perhaps, Greenly felt the greatest interest in that of Sir Gervaise Oakes, under whom he had served as midshipman, lieutenant, and captain; and this his superior knew, a circumstance that would have excused far greater liberties. After moving swiftly to and fro several times, the vice-admiral began to cool, and he forgot this passing ebullition of quick feelings. Greenly, on the other hand, satisfied that the just mind of the commander-in-chief would not fail to appreciate facts that had been so plainly presented to it, was content to change the subject. They conversed together, in a most friendly manner, Sir Gervaise being even unusually frank and communicative, in order to prove he was not displeased, the matter in discussion being the state of the ship and the situation of the crew.

"You are always ready for battle, Greenly," the vice-admiral said, smilingly, in conclusion; "when there is a necessity; and always just as ready to point out the inexpediency of engaging, where you fancy nothing is to be gained by it. You would not have me run away from a shadow, however; or a signal;

- 255 -

and that is much the same thing: so we will stand on, until we make the Frenchmen fairly from off-deck, when it will be time enough to determine what shall come next."

"Sail-ho!" shouted one of the look-outs from aloft, a cry that immediately drew all eyes towards the mizzen-top-mast-cross-trees, whence the sound proceeded.

The wind blew too fresh to render conversation, even by means of a trumpet, easy, and the man was ordered down to give an account of what he had seen. Of course he first touched the poop-deck, where he was met by the admiral and captain, the officer of the watch, to whom he properly belonged, giving him up to the examination of his two superiors, without a grimace.

"Where-away is the sail you've seen, sir?" demanded Sir Gervaise a little sharply, for he suspected it was no more than one of the ships ahead, already signaled. "Down yonder to the southward and eastward—hey! sirrah?"

"No, Sir Jarvy," answered the top-man, hitching his trowsers with one hand, and smoothing the hair on his forehead with the other; "but out here, to the forward and westward, on our weather-quarter. It's none o' them French chaps as is with the County of Fairvillian,"—for so all the common men of the fleet believed their gallant enemy to be rightly named,—"but is a square-rigged craft by herself, jammed up on a wind, pretty much like all on us."

"That alters the matter, Greenly! How do you know she is square-rigged, my man?"

"Why, Sir Jarvy, your honour, she's under her fore and main-taw-sails, close-reefed, with a bit of the main-sail set, as well as I can make it out, sir."

"The devil she is! It must be some fellow in a great hurry, to carry that canvass in this blow! Can it be possible, Greenly, that the leading vessel of Bluewater is heaving in sight?"

"I rather think not, Sir Gervaise; it would be too far to windward for any of his two-deckers. It may turn out to be a look-out ship of the French, got round on the other tack to keep her station, and carrying sail hard, because she dislikes our appearance."

"In that case she must claw well to windward to escape us! What's your name, my lad—Tom Davis, if I'm not mistaken?"

"No, Sir Jarvy, it's Jack Brown; which is much the same, your honour. We's no ways partic'lar about names."

"Well, Jack, does it blow hard aloft? So as to give you any trouble in holding on?"

"Nothing to speak on, Sir Jarvy. A'ter cruising a winter and spring in the Bay of Biscay, I looks on this as no more nor a puff. Half a hand will keep a fellow in his berth, aloft."

"Galleygo—take Jack Brown below to my cabin, and give him a fresh nip in his jigger—he'll hold on all the better for it."

This was Sir Gervaise's mode of atoning for the error in doing the man injustice, by supposing he was mistaken about the new sail, and Jack Brown went aloft devoted to the commander-in-chief. It costs the great and powerful so little to become popular, that one is sometimes surprised to find that any are otherwise; but, when we remember that it is also their duty to be just, astonishment ceases; justice being precisely the quality to which a large portion of the human race are most averse.

Half an hour passed, and no further reports were received from aloft. In a few minutes, however, the Warspite signalled the admiral, to report the stranger on her weather-quarter, and, not long after, the Active did the same. Still neither told his character; and the course being substantially the same, the unknown ship approached but slowly, notwithstanding the unusual quantity of sail she had set. At the end of the period mentioned, the vessels in the south-eastern board began to be visible from the deck. The ocean was so white with foam, that it was not easy to distinguish a ship, under short canvass, at any great distance; but, by the aid of glasses, both Sir Gervaise and Greenly satisfied themselves that the number of the enemy at the southward amounted to just twenty; one more having hove in sight, and been signalled by the Chloe, since her first report. Several of these vessels, however, were small; and, the vice-admiral, after a long and anxious survey, lowered his glass and turned to his captain in order to compare opinions.

"Well, Greenly," he asked, "what do you make of them, now?—According to my reckoning, there are thirteen of the line, two frigates, four corvettes, and a lugger; or twenty sail in all."

"There can be no doubt of the twenty sail, Sir Gervaise, though the vessels astern are still too distant to speak of their size. I rather think it will turn out *fourteen* of the line and only three frigates."

"That is rather too much for us, certainly, without Bluewater. His five ships, now, and this westerly position, would make a cheering prospect for us. We might stick by Mr. de Vervillin until it moderated, and then pay our respects to him. What do you say to *that*, Greenly?"

"That it is of no great moment, Sir Gervaise, so long as the other division is *not* with us. But yonder are signals flying on board the Active, the Warspite, and the Blenheim."

"Ay, they've something to tell us of the chap astern and to windward. Come, Bunting, give us the news."

"'Stranger in the north-west shows the Druid's number;'" the signal-officer read mechanically from the book.

"The deuce he does! Then Bluewater cannot be far off. Let Dick alone for keeping in his proper place; he has an instinct for a line of battle, and I never knew him fail to be in the very spot I could wish to have him, looking as much at home, as if his ships had all been built there! The Druid's number! The Cæsar and the rest of them are in a line ahead, further north, heading up well to windward even of our own wake. This puts the Comte fairly under our lee."

But Greenly was far from being of a temperament as sanguine as that of the vice-admiral's. He did not like the circumstance of the Druid's being alone visible, and she, too, under what in so heavy a gale, might be deemed a press of canvass. There was no apparent reason for the division's carrying sail so hard, while the frigate would he obliged to do it, did she wish to overtake vessels like the Plantagenet and her consorts. He suggested, therefore, the probability that the ship was alone, and that her object might be to speak them.

"There is something in what you say, Greenly," answered Sir Gervaise, after a minute's reflection; "and we must look into it. If Denham doesn't give us any thing new from the Count to change our plans, it may be well to learn what the Druid is after."

Denham was the commander of the Chloe, which ship, a neat six-and-thirty, was pitching into the heavy seas that now came rolling in heavily from the broad Atlantic, the water streaming from her hawse-holes, as she rose from each plunge, like the spouts of a whale. This vessel, it has been stated, was fully a league ahead and to leeward of the Plantagenet, and consequently so much nearer to the French, who were approaching from that precise quarter of the ocean, in a long single line, like that of the English; a little relieved, however, by the look-out vessels, all of which, in their case, were sailing along on the weather-beam of their friends. The distance was still so great, as to render glasses necessary in getting any very accurate notions of the force and the point of sailing of Monsieur de Vervillin's fleet, the ships astern being yet so remote as to require long practice to speak with any certainty of their characters. In nothing, notwithstanding, was the superior practical seamanship of the English more apparent, than in the manner in which these respective lines were formed. That of Sir Gervaise Oakes was compact, each ship being as near as might be a cable's length distant from her seconds, ahead and astern. This was a point on which the vice-admiral prided himself; and by compelling his captains rigidly to respect their line of sailing, and by keeping the same ships and officers, as much as possible, under his orders, each captain of the fleet had got to know his own vessel's rate of speed, and all the other qualities that were necessary to maintain her precise position. All the ships being weatherly, though some, in a slight degree, were more so than others, it was easy to keep the line in weather like the present, the wind not blowing sufficiently hard to render a few cloths more or less of canvass of any very great moment. If there was a vessel sensibly out of her place, in the entire line, it was the Achilles; Lord Morganic not having had time to get all his forward spars as far aft as they should have been; a circumstance that had knocked him off a little more than had happened to the other vessels. Nevertheless, had an air-line been drawn at this moment, from the mizzen-top of the Plantagenet to that of the Warspite, it would have been found to pass through the spars of quite half the intermediate vessels, and no one of them all would have been a pistol-shot out of the way. As there were six intervals between the vessels, and each interval as near as could be guessed at was a cable's length, the extent of the whole line a little exceeded three-quarters of a mile.

On the other hand, the French, though they preserved a very respectable degree of order, were much less compact, and by no means as methodical in their manner of sailing. Some of their ships were a quarter of a mile to leeward of the line, and the intervals were irregular and ill-observed. These circumstances arose from several causes, neither of which proceeded from any fault in the commander-in-chief, who was both an experienced seaman and a skilful tactician. But his captains were new to each other, and some of them were recently appointed to their ships; it being just as much a matter of course that a seaman should ascertain the qualities of his vessel, by familiarity, as that a man should learn the character of his wife, in the intimacy of wedlock.

At the precise moment of which we are now writing, the Chloe might have been about a league from the leading vessel of the enemy, and her position to leeward of her own fleet threatened to bring her, half an hour later, within range of the Frenchmen's guns. This fact was apparent to all in the squadron; still the frigate stood on, having been placed in that station, and the whole being under the immediate supervision of the commander-in-chief.

"Denham will have a warm berth of it, sir, should he stand on much longer," said Greenly, when ten minutes more had passed, during which the ships had gradually drawn nearer.

"I was hoping he might get between the most weatherly French frigate and her line," answered Sir Gervaise; "when I think, by edging rapidly away, we could take her alive, with the Plantagenet."

"In which case we might as well clear for action; such a man[oe]uvre being certain to bring on a general engagement."

"No—no—I'm not quite mad enough for that, Master Telemachus; but, we can wait a little longer for the chances. How many flags can you make out among the enemy, Bunting?"

"I see but two, Sir Gervaise; one at the fore, and the other at the mizzen, like our own. I can make out, now, only twelve ships of the line, too; neither of which is a three-decker."

"So much for rumour; as flagrant a liar as ever wagged a tongue! Twelve ships on two decks, and eight frigates, sloops and luggers. There can be no great mistake in this."

"I think not, Sir Gervaise; their commander-in-chief is in the fourth ship from the head of the line. His flag is just discernible, by means of our best glass. Ay, there goes a signal, this instant, at the end of his gaff!"

"If one could only read French now, Greenly," said the vice-admiral, smiling; "we might get into some of Mr. de Vervillin's secrets. Perhaps it's an order to go to quarters or to clear; look out sharp, Bunting, for any signs of such a movement. What do you make of it?"

"It's to the frigates, Sir Gervaise; all of which answer, while the other vessels do not."

"We want no French to read that signal, sir," put in Greenly; "the frigates themselves telling us what it means. Monsieur de Vervillin has no idea of letting the Plantagenet take any thing he has, *alive.*"

This was true enough. Just as the captain spoke, the object of the order was made sufficiently apparent, by all the light vessels to windward of the French fleet, bearing up together, until they brought the wind abaft their beams, when away they glided to leeward, like floating objects that have suddenly struck a swift current. Before this change in their course, these frigates and corvettes had been struggling along, the seas meeting them on their weather-bows, at the rate of about two knots or rather less; whereas, their speed was now quadrupled, and in a few minutes, the whole of them had sailed through the different intervals in their main line, and had formed as before, nearly half a league to leeward of it. Here, in the event of an action, their principal duties would have been to succour crippled ships that might be forced out of their allotted stations during the combat. All this Sir Gervaise viewed with disgust. He had hoped that his enemy might have presumed on the state of the elements, and suffered his light vessels to maintain their original positions.

"It would be a great triumph to us, Greenly," he said, "if Denham could pass without shifting his berth. There would be something manly and seamanlike in an inferior fleet's passing a superior, in such a style."

"Yes, sir, though it *might* cost us a fine frigate. The count can have no difficulty in fighting his weather main-deck guns, and a discharge from two or three of his leading vessels might cut away some spar that Denham would miss sadly, just at such a moment."

Sir Gervaise placed his hands behind his back, paced the deck a minute, and then said decidedly—

"Bunting, make the Chloe's signal to ware—tacking in this sea, and under that short canvass, is out of the question."

Bunting had anticipated this order, and had even ventured clandestinely to direct the quarter-masters to bend on the necessary flags; and Sir Gervaise had scarcely got the words out of his mouth, before the signal was abroad. The Chloe was equally on the alert; for she too each moment expected the command, and ere her answering flag was seen, her helm was up, the mizen-stay-sail down, and her head falling off rapidly towards the enemy. This movement seemed to be expected all round—and it certainly had been delayed to the very last moment—for the leading French ship fell off three or four points, and as the frigate was exactly end-on to her, let fly the contents of all the guns on her forecastle, as well as of those on her main-deck, as far aft as they could be brought to bear. One of the top-sail-sheets of the frigate was shot away by this rapid and unexpected fire, and some little damage was done to the standing rigging; but luckily, none of immediate moment. Captain Denham was active, and the instant he found his top-sail flapping, he ordered it clewed up, and the main-sail loosed. The latter was set, close-reefed, as the ship came to the wind on the larboard tack, and by the time every thing was braced up and hauled aft, on that tack, the main-top-sail was ready to be sheeted home, anew. During the few minutes that these evolutions required, Sir Gervaise kept his eye riveted on the vessel; and when he saw her fairly round, and trimmed by the wind, again, with the main-sail dragging her ahead, to own the truth, he felt mentally relieved.

"Not a minute too soon, Sir Gervaise," observed the cautious Greenly, smiling. "I should not be surprised if Denham hears more from that fellow at the head of the French line. His weather chase-guns are exactly in a range with the frigate, and the two upper ones might be worked, well enough."

"I think not, Greenly. The forecastle gun, possibly; scarcely any thing below it."

Sir Gervaise proved to be partly right and partly wrong. The Frenchman *did* attempt a fire with his main-deck gun; but, at the first plunge of the ship, a sea slapped up against her weather-bow, and sent a column of water through the port, that drove half its crew into the lee-scuppers. In the midst of this waterspout, the gun exploded, the loggerhead having been applied an instant before, giving a sort of chaotic wildness to the scene in-board. This satisfied the party below; though that on the forecastle fared better. The last fired their gun several times, and always without success. This failure proceeded from a cause that is seldom sufficiently estimated by nautical gunners; the shot having swerved from the line of sight, by the force of the wind against which it flew, two or three hundred feet, by the time it had gone the mile that lay between the vessels. Sir Gervaise anxiously watched the effect of the fire, and perceiving that all the shot fell to leeward of the Chloe, he was no longer uneasy about that vessel, and he began to turn his attention to other and more important concerns.

As we are now approaching a moment when it is necessary that the reader should receive some tolerably distinct impression of the relative positions of the two entire fleets, we shall close the present chapter, here; reserving the duty of explanation for the commencement of a new one.

CHAPTER XXII.

——"All were glad,
And laughed, and shouted, as she darted on,
And plunged amid the foam, and tossed it high,
Over the deck, as when a strong, curbed steed
Flings the froth from him in his eager race."

PERCIVAL

The long twilight of a high latitude had now ended, and the sun, though concealed behind clouds, had risen. The additional light contributed to lessen the gloomy look of the ocean, though the fury of the winds and waves still lent to it a dark and menacing aspect. To windward there were no signs of an abatement of the gale, while the heavens continued to abstain from letting down their floods, on the raging waters beneath. By this lime, the fleet was materially to the southward of Cape la Hogue, though far to the westward, where the channel received the winds and waves from the whole rake of the Atlantic, and the seas were setting in, in the long, regular swells of the ocean, a little disturbed by the influence of the tides. Ships as heavy as the two-deckers moved along with groaning efforts, their bulk-heads and timbers "complaining," to use the language of the sea, as the huge masses, loaded with their iron artillery, rose and sunk on the coming and receding billows. But their movements were stately and full of majesty; whereas, the cutter, sloop, and even the frigates, seemed to be tossed like foam, very much at the mercy of the elements. The Chloe was passing the admiral, on the opposite tack, quite a mile to leeward, and yet, as she mounted to the summit of a wave, her cut-water was often visible nearly to the keel. These are the trials of a vessel's strength; for, were a ship always water-borne equally on all her lines, there would not be the necessity which now exists to make her the well-knit mass of wood and iron she is.

The progress of the two fleets was very much the same, both squadrons struggling along through the billows, at the rate of about a marine league in the hour. As no lofty sail was carried, and the vessels were first made in the haze of a clouded morning, the ships had not become visible to each other until nearer than common; and, by the time at which we have now arrived in our tale, the leading vessels were separated by a space that did not exceed two miles, estimating the distance only on their respective lines of sailing; though there would be about the same space between them, when abreast, the English being so much to windward of their enemies. Any one in the least familiar with nautical man[oe]uvres will understand that these circumstances would bring the van of the French and the rear of their foes much nearer together in passing, both fleets being close-hauled.

Sir Gervaise Oakes, as a matter of course, watched the progress of the two lines with close and intelligent attention. Mons. de Vervillin did the same from the poop of le Foudroyant, a noble eighty-gun ship in which his flag of *vice-admiral* was flying, as it might be, in defiance. By the side of the former stood Greenly, Bunting, and Bury, the Plantagenet's first lieutenant; by the side of the latter his capitaine de vaisseau, a man as little like the caricatures of such officers, as a hostile feeling has laid before the readers of English literature, as Washington was like the man held up to odium in the London journals, at the commencement of the great American war. M. de Vervillin himself was a man of respectable birth, of a scientific education, and of great familiarity with ships, so far as a knowledge of their general powers and principles was concerned; but here his professional excellence ceased, all that infinity of detail which composes the distinctive merit of the practical seaman being, in a great degree, unknown to him, rendering it necessary for him to *think* in moments of emergency; periods when the really prime mariner seems more to act by a sort of *instinct* than by any very intelligible process of ratiocination. With his fleet drawn out before him, however, and with no unusual demands on his resources, this gallant officer was an exceedingly formidable foe to contend with in squadron.

Sir Gervaise Oakes lost all his constitutional and feverish impatience while the fleets drew nigher and nigher. As is not unusual with brave men, who are naturally excitable, as the crisis approached he grew calmer, and obtained a more perfect command over himself; seeing all things in their true colours, and feeling more and more equal to control them. He continued to walk the poop, but it was with a slower step; and, though his hands were still closed behind his back, the fingers were passive, while his countenance became grave and his eye thoughtful. Greenly knew that his interference would now be hazardous; for whenever the vice-admiral assumed that air, he literally became commander-in-chief; and any attempt to control or influence him, unless sustained by the communication of new facts, could only draw down resentment on his own head. Bunting, too, was aware that the "admiral was aboard," as the officers, among themselves, used to describe this state of their superior's mind, and was prepared to discharge his own duty in the most silent and rapid manner in his power. All the others present felt more or less of this same influence of an established character.

"*Mr.* Bunting," said Sir Gervaise, when the distance between the Plantagenet and *le Téméraire* the leading French vessel, might have been about a league, allowing for the difference in the respective lines of sailing—"*Mr.* Bunting, bend on the signal for the ships to go to quarters. We may as well be ready for any turn of the dice."

No one dared to comment on this order: it was obeyed in readiness and silence.

"Signal ready, Sir Gervaise," said Bunting, the instant the last flag was in its place.

"Run it up at once, sir, and have a bright look-out for the answers. Captain Greenly, go to quarters, and see all clear on the main-deck, to use the batteries if wanted. The people can stand fast below, as I think it might be dangerous to open the ports."

Captain Greenly passed off the poop to the quarter-deck, and in a minute the drum and fife struck up the air which is known all over the civilized world as the call to arms. In most services this summons is made by the drum alone, which emits sounds to which the fancy has attached peculiar words; those of the soldiers of France being "*prend ton sac—prend ton sac—prend ton sac*," no bad representatives of the meaning; but in English and American ships, this appeal is usually made in company with the notes of the "ear-piercing fife," which gives it a melody that might otherwise be wanting.

"Signal answered throughout the fleet, Sir Gervaise," said Bunting.

No answer was given to this report beyond a quiet inclination of the head. After a moment's pause, however, the vice-admiral turned to his signal officer and said—

"I should think, Bunting, no captain can need an order to tell him *not* to open his lee-lower-deck ports in such a sea as this?"

"I rather fancy not, Sir Gervaise," answered Bunting, looking drolly at the boiling element that gushed up each minute from beneath the bottom of the ship, in a way to appear as high as the hammock-cloths. "The people at the *main*-deck guns would have rather a wet time of it."

"Bend on the signal, sir, for the ships astern to keep in the vice-admiral's wake. Young gentleman," to the midshipman who always acted as his aid in battle, "tell Captain Greenly I desire to see him as soon as he has received all the reports."

Down to the moment when the first tap of the drum was heard, the Plantagenet had presented a scene of singular quiet and unconcern, considering the circumstances in which she was placed. A landsman would scarcely credit that men could be so near their enemies, and display so much indifference to their vicinity; but this was the result of long habit, and a certain marine instinct that tells the sailor when any thing serious is in the wind, and when not. The difference in the force of the two fleets, the heavy gale, and the weatherly position of the English, all conspired to assure the crew that nothing decisive could yet occur. Here and there an officer or an old seaman might be seen glancing through a port, to ascertain the force and position of the French; but, on the whole, their fleet excited little more attention than if lying at anchor in Cherbourg. The breakfast hour was approaching, and that important event monopolized the principal interest of the moment. The officers' boys, in particular, began to make their appearance around the galley, provided, as usual, with their pots and dishes, and, now and then, one cast a careless glance through the nearest opening to see how the strangers looked; but as to warfare there was much more the appearance of it between the protectors of the rights of the different messes, than between the two great belligerent navies themselves.

Nor was the state of things materially different in the gun-room, or cock-pit, or on the orlops. Most of the people of a two-decked ship are berthed on the lower gun deck, and the order to "clear ship" is more necessary to a vessel of that construction, before going to quarters seriously, than to smaller craft; though it is usual in all. So long as the bags, mess-chests, and other similar appliances were left in their ordinary positions, Jack saw little reason to derange himself; and as reports were brought below, from time to time, respecting the approach of the enemy, and more especially of his being well to leeward, few of those whose duty did not call them on deck troubled themselves about the matter at all. This habit of considering his fortune as attached to that of his ship, and of regarding himself as a point on her mass, as we all look on ourselves as particles of the orb we accompany in its revolutions, is sufficiently general among mariners; but it was particularly so as respects the sailors of a fleet, who were kept so much at sea, and who had been so often, with all sorts of results, in the presence of the enemy. The scene that was passing in the gun-room at the precise moment at which our tale has arrived, was so characteristic, in particular, as to merit a brief description.

All the idlers by this time were out of their berths and cotts; the signs of those who "slept in the country," as it is termed, or who were obliged, for want of state-rooms, to sling in the common apartment, having disappeared. Magrath was reading a treatise on medicine, in good Leyden Latin, by a lamp. The purser was endeavouring to decipher his steward's hieroglyphics, favoured by the same light, and the captain of marines was examining the lock of an aged musket. The third and fourth lieutenants were helping each other to untangle one of their Bay-of-Biscay reckonings, which had set both plane and spherical trigonometry at defiance, by a lamp of their own; and the chaplain was hurrying the steward and the boys along with the breakfast— his usual occupation at that "witching time" in the morning.

While things were in this state, the first lieutenant, Mr. Bury, appeared in the gun-room. His arrival caused one or two of the mess to glance upward at him, though no one spoke but the junior lieutenant, who, being an honourable, was at his ease with every one on board, short of the captain.

"What's the news from deck, Bury?" asked this officer, a youth of twenty, his senior being a man ten years older. "Is Mr. de Vervillin thinking of running away yet?"

"Not he, sir; there's too much of the game-cock about him for *that*."

"I'll warrant you he can *crow*! But what *is* the news, Bury?"

"The news is that the old Planter is as wet as a wash-tub, forward, and I must have a dry jacket—do you hear, there, Tom? Soundings," turning to the master, who just then came in from forward, "have you taken a look out of doors this morning?"

"You know I seldom forget that, Mr. Bury. A pretty pickle the ship would soon be in, if *I* forgot to look about me!"

"He swallowed the deep-sea, down in the bay," cried the honourable, laughing, "and goes every morning at day-light to look for it out at the bridle-ports."

"Well, then, Soundings, what do you think of the third ship in the French line?" continued Bury, disregarding the levity of the youth: "did you ever see such top-masts, as she carries, before?"

"I scarce ever saw a Frenchman without them, Mr. Bury. You'd have just such sticks in this fleet, if Sir Jarvy would stand them."

"Ay, but Sir Jarvy *won't* stand them. The captain who sent such a stick up in his ship, would have to throw it overboard before night. I never saw such a pole in the air in my life!"

"What's the matter with the mast, Mr. Bury?" put in Magrath, who kept up what he called constant scientific skirmishes with the *elder* sea-officers; the *junior* being too inexperienced in his view to be worthy of a contest. "I'll engage the spar is moulded and fashioned agreeably to the most approved pheelosphical principles; for in *that* the French certainly excel us."

"Who ever heard of *moulding* a spar?" interrupted Soundings, laughing loudly, "we *mould* a ship's frame, Doctor, but we *lengthen* and *shorten*, and *scrape* and *fid* her masts."

"I'm answered as usual, gentlemen, and voted down, I suppose by acclamation, as they call it in other learned bodies. I would advise no creature that has a reason to go to sea; an instinct being all that is needed to make a Lord High Admiral of twenty tails."

"I should like Sir Jarvy to hear *that*, my man of books," cried the fourth, who had satisfied himself that a book was not his own forte—"I fancy your instinct, doctor, will prevent you from whispering this in the vice-admiral's ear!"

Although Magrath had a profound respect for the commander-in-chief, he was averse to giving in, in a gun-room discussion. His answer, therefore, partook of the feeling of the moment.

"Sir Gervaise," (he pronounced this word Jairvis,) "Sir Gervaise Oakes, *honourable* sir," he said, with a sneer, "may be a good seaman, but he's no linguist. Now, there he was, ashore among the dead and dying, just as ignorant of the meaning of *filius nullius*, which is boy's Latin, as if he had never seen a horn-book! Nevertheless, gentlemen, it is science, and not even the classics, that makes the man; as for a creature's getting the sciences by instinct, I shall contend it is against the possibilities, whereas the attainment of what you call seamanship, is among even the lesser probabilities."

"This is the most marine-ish talk I ever heard from your mouth, doctor," interrupted Soundings. "How the devil can a man tell how to ware ship by instinct, as you call it, if one may ask the question?"

"Simply, Soundings, because the process of ratiocination is dispensed with. Do you have to *think* in waring ship, now?—I'll put it to your own honour, for the answer."

"Think!—I should be a poor creature for a master, indeed, if much thinking were wanting in so simple a matter as tacking or veering. No—no—your real sea-dog has no occasion for much *thinking*, when he has his work before him."

"That'll just be it, gentlemen!—that'll be just what I'm telling ye," cried the doctor, exulting in the success of his artifice. "Not only will Mr. Soundings not *think*, when he has his ordinary duties to perform, but he holds the process itself in merited contempt, ye'll obsairve; and so my theory is established, by evidence of a pairty concerned; which is more than a postulate logically requires."

Here Magrath dropped his book, and laughed with that sort of hissing sound that seems peculiar to the genus of which he formed a part. He was still indulging in his triumph, when the first tap of the drum was heard. All listened; every ear pricking like that of a deer that hears the hound, when there followed—"r-r-r-ap tap—r-r-r-ap tap—r-r-r-ap tapa-tap-tap—rap-a-tap—a-rap-a-tap a-rap-a-tap—a-tap-tap."

"Instinct or reason, Sir Jarvy is going to quarters!" exclaimed the honourable. "I'd no notion we were near enough to the Monsieurs, for *that*!"

"Now," said Magrath, with a grinning sneer, as he rose to descend to the cock-pit, "there'll may be arise an occasion for a little learning, when I'll promise ye all the science that can be mustered in my unworthy knowledge. Soundings, I may have to heave the lead in the depths of your physical formation, in which case I'll just endeevour to avoid the breakers of ignorance."

"Go to the devil, or to the cock-pit, whichever you please, sir," answered the master; "I've served in six general actions, already, and have never been obliged to one of your kidney for so much as a bit of court-plaster or lint. With me, oakum answers for one, and canvass for the other."

While this was saying, all hands were in motion. The sea and marine officers looking for their side-arms, the surgeon carefully collecting his books, and the chaplain seizing a dish of cold beef, that was hurriedly set upon a table, carrying it down with him to his quarters, by way of taking it out of harm's way. In a minute, the gun-room was cleared of all who usually dwelt there, and their places were supplied by the seamen who manned the three or four thirty-two's that were mounted in the apartment, together with their opposites. As the sea-officers, in particular, appeared among the men, their faces assumed an air of authority, and their voices were heard calling out the order to "tumble up," as they hastened themselves to their several stations.

All this time, Sir Gervaise Oakes paced the poop. Bunting and the quarter-master were in readiness to hoist the new signal, and Greenly merely waited for the reports, to join the commander-in-chief. In about five minutes after the drum had given its first tap, these were completed, and the captain ascended to the poop.

"By standing on, on our present course, Captain Greenly," observed Sir Gervaise, anxious to justify to himself the evolution he contemplated, "the rear of our line and the van of the French will be brought within fair range of shot from each other, and, by an accident, we might lose a ship; since any vessel that was crippled, would necessarily sag directly down upon the enemy. Now, I propose to keep away in the Plantagenet, and just brush past the leading French ships, at about the distance the Warspite will *have* to pass, and so alter the face of matters a little. What do you think would be the consequence of such a man[oe]uvre?"

"That the van of our line and the van of the French will be brought as near together, as you have just said must happen to the rear, Sir Gervaise, in any case."

"It does not require a mathematician to tell that much, sir. You will keep away, as soon as Bunting shows the signal, and bring the wind abeam. Never mind the braces; let *them* stand fast; as soon as we have passed the French admiral, I shall luff, again. This will cause us to lose a little of our weatherly position, but about that I am very indifferent. Give the order, sir—Bunting, run up the signal."

These commands were silently obeyed, and presently the Plantagenet was running directly in the troughs of the seas, with quite double her former velocity. The other ships answered promptly, each keeping away as her second ahead came down to the proper line of sailing, and all complying to the letter with an order that was very easy of execution. The effect, besides giving every prospect of a distant engagement, was to straighten the line to nearly mathematical precision.

"Is it your wish, Sir Gervaise, that we should endeavour to open our lee lower ports?" asked Greenly. "Unless we attempt something of the sort, we shall have nothing heavier than the eighteens to depend on, should Monsieur de Vervillin see fit to begin."

"And will *he* be any better off?—It would be next to madness to think of fighting the lower-deck guns, in such weather, and we will keep all fast. Should the French commence the sport, we shall have the advantage of being to windward; and the loss of a few weather shrouds might bring down the best mast in their fleet."

Greenly made no answer, though he perfectly understood that the loss of a mast would almost certainly ensure the loss of the ship, did one of his own heavier spars go. But this was Sir Gervaise's greatest weakness as a commander, and he knew it would be useless to attempt persuading him to suffer a single ship under his order to pass the enemy nearer than he went himself in the Plantagenet. This was what he called covering his ships; though it amounted to no more than putting all of them in the jeopardy that happened to be unavoidable, as regarded one or two.

The Comte de Vervillin seemed at a loss to understand this sudden and extraordinary movement in the van of his enemy. His signals followed, and his crews went to their guns; but it was not an easy matter for ships that persevered in hugging the wind to make any material alterations in their relative positions, in such a gale. The rate of sailing of the English, however, now menaced a speedy collision, if collision were intended, and it was time to be stirring, in order to be ready for it.

On the other hand, all was quiet, and, seemingly, death-like, in the English ships. Their people were at their quarters, already, and this is a moment of profound stillness in a vessel of war. The lower ports being down, the portions of the crews stationed on those decks were buried, as it might be, in obscurity, while even those above were still partly concealed by the half-ports. There was virtually nothing for the sail-trimmers to do, and every thing was apparently left to the evolutions of the vast machines themselves, in which they floated. Sir Gervaise, Greenly, and the usual attendants still remained on the poop, their eyes scarcely turning for an instant from the fleet of the enemy.

By this time the Plantagenct and *le Téméraire* were little more than a mile apart, each minute lessening this distance. The latter ship was struggling along, her bows plunging into the seas to the hawse-holes, while the former had a swift, easy motion through the troughs, and along the summits of the waves, her flattened sails aiding in steadying her in the heavy lurches that unavoidably accompanied such a movement. Still, a sea would occasionally break against her weather side, sending its crest upward in a brilliant *jet-d'eau*, and leaving tons of water on the decks. Sir Gervaise's manner had now lost every glimmering of excitement. When he spoke, it was in a gentle, pleasant tone, such as a gentleman might use in the society of women. The truth was, all his energy had concentrated in the determination to do a daring deed; and, as is not unusual with the most resolute men, the nearer he approached to the consummation of his purpose, the more he seemed to reject all the spurious aids of manner.

"The French do not open their lower ports, Greenly," observed the vice-admiral, dropping the glass after one of his long looks at the enemy, "although they have the advantage of being to leeward. I take that to be a sign they intend nothing very serious."

"We shall know better five minutes hence, Sir Gervaise. This ship slides along like a London coach."

"His line is lubberly, after all, Greenly! Look at those two ships astern—they are near half a mile to windward of the rest of the fleet, and at least half a mile astern. Hey! Greenly?"

The captain turned towards the rear of the French, and examined the positions of the two ships mentioned with sufficient deliberation; but Sir Gervaise dropped his head in a musing manner, and began to pace the poop again. Once or twice he stopped to look at the rear of the French line, then distant from him quite a league, and as often did he resume his walk.

"Bunting," said the vice-admiral, mildly, "come this way, a moment. Our last signal was to keep in the commander-in-chief's wake, and to follow his motions?"

"It was, Sir Gervaise. The old order to follow motions, 'with or without signals,' as one might say."

"Bend on the signals to close up in line, as near as safe, and to carry sail by the flag-ship."

"Ay, ay, Sir Gervaise—we'll have 'em both up in five minutes, sir."

The commander-in-chief now even seemed pleased. His physical excitement returned a little, and a smile struggled round his lip. His eye glanced at Greenly, to see if he were suspected, and then all his calmness of exterior returned. In the mean time the signals were made and answered. The latter circumstance was reported to Sir Gervaise, who cast his eyes down the line astern, and saw that the different ships were already bracing in, and easing off their sheets, in order to diminish the spaces between the different vessels. As soon as it was apparent that the Carnatic was drawing ahead, Captain Greenly was told to lay his main and fore-yards nearly square, to light up all his stay-sail sheets, and to keep away sufficiently to make every thing draw. Although these orders occasioned surprise, they were implicitly obeyed.

The moment of meeting had now come. In consequence of having kept away so much, the Plantagenet could not be quite three-fourths of a mile on the weather-bow of *le Téméraire*, coming up rapidly, and threatening a semi-transverse fire. In order to prevent this, the French ship edged off a little, giving herself an easier and more rapid movement through the water, and bringing her own broadside more fairly to the shock. This evolution was followed by the two next ships, a little prematurely, perhaps; but the admiral in *le Foudroyant*, disdaining to edge off from her enemy, kept her luff. The ships astern were governed by the course of their superior. This change produced a little disorder in the van of the French, menacing still greater, unless one party or the other receded from the course taken. But time pressed, and the two fleets were closing so fast as to induce other thoughts.

"There's lubberly work for you, Greenly!" said Sir Gervaise, smiling. "A commander-in-chief heading up with the bowlines dragged, and his second and third ahead—not to say fourth—running off with the wind abeam! Now, if we can knock the Comte off a couple of points, in passing, all his fellows astern will follow, and the Warspite and Blenheim and Thunderer will slip by like girls in a country-dance! Send Bury down to the main-deck, with orders to be ready with those eighteens."

Greenly obeyed, of course, and he began to think better of audacity in naval warfare, than he had done before, that day. This was the usual course of things with these two officers; one arguing and deciding according to the dictates of a cool judgment, and the other following his impulses quite as much as any thing else, until facts supervened to prove that human things are as much controlled by adventitious agencies, the results of remote and unseen causes, as by any well-digested plans laid at the moment. In their cooler hours, when they came to reason on the past, the vice-admiral generally consummated his triumphs, by reminding his captain that if he had not been in the way of luck, he never could have profited by it; no bad creed for a naval officer, who is otherwise prudent and vigilant.

The quarter-masters of the fleet were just striking six bells, or proclaiming that it was seven o'clock in the morning watch, as the Plantagenet and *le Téméraire* came abeam of each other. Both ships lurched heavily in the troughs of the seas, and both rolled to windward in stately majesty, and yet both slid through the brine with a momentum that resembled the imperceptible motion of a planet. The water rolled back from their black sides and shining hammock-cloths, and all the other dark panoply that distinguishes a ship-of-war glistened with the spray; but no sign of hostility proceeded from either. The French admiral made no signal to engage, and Sir Gervaise had reasons of his own for wishing to pass the enemy's van, if possible, unnoticed. Minute passed after minute, in breathless silence, on board the Plantagenet and the Carnatic, the latter vessel being now but half a cable's-length astern of the admiral. Every eye that had any outlet for such a purpose, was riveted on the main-deck ports of *le Téméraire* in expectation of seeing the fire issue from her guns. Each instant, however, lessened the chances, as regarded that particular vessel, which was soon out of the line of fire from the Plantagenet, when the same scene was to follow with the same result, in connection with *le Conquereur*, the second ship of the French line. Sir Gervaise smiled as he passed the three first ships, seemingly unnoticed; but as he drew nearer to the admiral, he felt confident this impunity must cease.

"What they *mean* by it all, Greenly," he observed to his companion, "is more than I can say; but we will go nearer, and try to find out. Keep her away a little more, sir; keep her away half a point." Greenly was not disposed to remonstrate now, for his prudent temperament was yielding to the excitement of the moment just reversing the traits of Sir Gervaise's character; the one losing his extreme discretion in feeling, as the other gained by the pressure of circumstances. The helm was eased a little, and the ship sheered nearer to *le Foudroyant*.

As is usual in all services, the French commander-in-chief was in one of the best vessels of his fleet. Not only was the Foudroyant a heavy ship, carrying French forty-twos below, a circumstance that made her rate as an eighty, but, like the Plantagenet, she was one of the fastest and most weatherly vessels of her class known. By "hugging the wind," this noble vessel had got, by this time, materially to windward of her second and third ahead, and had increased her distance essentially from her supports astern. In a word, she was far from being in a position to be sustained as she ought to be, unless she edged off herself, a movement that no one on board her seemed to contemplate.

"He's a noble fellow, Greenly, that Comte de Vervillin!" murmured Sir Gervaise, in a tone of admiration, "and so have I always found him, and so have I always *reported* him, too! The fools about the Gazettes, and the knaves about the offices, may splutter as they will; Mr. de Vervillin would give them plenty of occupation were they *here*. I question if he mean to keep off in the least, but insists on holding every inch he can gain!"

The next moment, however, satisfied Sir Gervaise that he was mistaken in his last conjecture, the bows of the Foudroyant gradually falling off, until the line of her larboard guns bore, when she made a general discharge of the whole of them, with the exception of those on the lower deck. The Plantagenets waited until the ship rose on a sea, and then they returned the compliment in the same manner. The Carnatic's side showed a sheet of flame immediately after; and the Achilles, Lord Morganic, luffing briskly to the wind, so as to bring her guns to bear, followed up the game, like flashes of lightning. All three of these ships had directed their fire at le Foudroyant, and the smoke had not yet driven from among her spars, when Sir Gervaise perceived that all three of her top-masts were hanging to leeward. At this sight, Greenly fairly sprang from the deck, and gave three cheers The men below caught up the cry, even to those who were, in a manner, buried on the lower deck, and presently, spite of the gale, the Carnatic's were heard following their example astern. At this instant the whole French and English lines opened their fire, from van to rear, as far as their guns would bear, or the shot tell.

"Now, sir, now is our time to close with de Vervillin!" exclaimed Greenly, the instant he perceived the manner in which his ship was crippled. "In our close order we might hope to make a thorough wreck of him."

"Not so, Greenly," returned Sir Gervaise calmly. "You see he edges away already, and will be down among his other ships in five minutes; we should have a general action with twice our force. What is done, is *well* done, and we will let it stand. It is *something* to have dismasted the enemy's commander-in-chief; do you look to it that the enemy don't do the same with ours. I heard shot rattling aloft, and every thing now bears a hard strain."

Greenly went to look after his duty, while Sir Gervaise continued to pace the poop. The whole of le Foudroyant's fire had been directed at the Plantagenet, but so rough was the ocean that not a shot touched the hull. A little injury had been done aloft, but nothing that the ready skill of the seamen was not able to repair even in that rough weather. The fact is, most of the shot had touched the waves, and had flown off from their varying surfaces at every angle that offered. One of the secrets that Sir Gervaise had taught his captains was to avoid hitting the surface of the sea, if possible, unless that surface was reasonably smooth, and the object intended to be injured was near at hand. Then the French admiral received the *first* fire—always the most destructive—of three fresh vessels; and his injuries were in proportion.

The scene was now animated, and not without a wild magnificence. The gale continued as heavy as ever, and with the raging of the ocean and the howling of the winds, mingled the roar of artillery, and the smoky canopy of battle. Still the destruction on neither side bore any proportion to the grandeur of the accompaniments; the distance and the unsteadiness of the ships preventing much accuracy of aim. In that day, a large two-decked ship never carried heavier metal than an eighteen above her lower batteries; and this gun, efficient as it is on most occasions, does not bring with it the fearful destruction that attends a more modern broadside. There was a good deal of noise, notwithstanding, and some blood shed in passing; but, on the whole, when the Warspite, the last of the English ships, ceased her fire, on account of the distance of the enemy abreast of her, it would have been difficult to tell that any vessel but le Foudroyant, had been doing more than saluting. At this instant Greenly re-appeared on the poop, his own ship having ceased to fire for several minutes.

"Well, Greenly, the main-deck guns are at least scaled," said Sir Gervaise, smiling; "and *that* is not to be done over again for some time. You keep every thing ready in the batteries, I trust?"

"We are all ready, Sir Gervaise, but there is nothing to be done. It would be useless to waste our ammunition at ships quite two miles under our lee."

"Very true—very true, sir. But *all* the Frenchmen are not quite so far to leeward, Greenly, as you may see by looking ahead. Yonder two, at least, are not absolutely out of harm's way!"

Greenly turned, gazed an instant in the direction in which the commander-in-chief pointed, and then the truth of what Sir Gervaise had really in view in keeping away, flashed on his mind, as it might be, at a glance. Without saying a word, he immediately quitted the poop, and descending even to the lower deck, passed through the whole of his batteries, giving his orders, and examining their condition.

CHAPTER XXIII.

"By Heaven! it is a splendid sight to see,
(For one who hath no friend, nor brother there,)
Their rival scarfs of mixed embroidery—
Their various arms that glitter in the air!"

<small>CHILDE HAROLD.</small>

The little conflict between the English ships and the head of the French line, the evolutions that had grown out of it, the crippling of le Foudroyant, and the continuance of the gale, contributed to produce material changes in the relative positions of the two fleets. All the English vessels kept their stations with beautiful accuracy, still running to the southward in a close line ahead, having the wind a trifle abaft the beam, with their yards braced in. Under the circumstances, it needed but some seven or eight minutes for these ships to glide a mile through the troubled ocean, and this was about the period the most exposed of them all had been under the random and slow fire that the state of the weather permitted. The trifling damages sustained were already repaired, or in a way soon to be so. On the other hand, considerable disorder prevailed among the French. Their line had never been perfect, extending quite a league; a few of the leading vessels, or those near the commander-in-chief, sustaining each other as well as could be desired, while long intervals existed between the ships astern. Among the latter, too, as has been stated, some were much farther to windward than the others; an irregularity that proceeded from a desire of the Comte to luff up as near as possible to the enemy—a desire, which, practised on, necessarily threw the least weatherly vessels to leeward. Thus the two ships in the extreme rear, as has been hinted at already, being jammed up unusually hard upon the wind, had weathered materially on their consorts, while their way through the water had been proportionably less. It was these combined circumstances which brought them so far astern and to windward.

At the time Sir Gervaise pointed out their positions to Greenly, the two vessels just mentioned were quite half a mile to the westward of their nearest consort, and more than that distance to the southward. When it is remembered that the wind was nearly due west, and that all the French vessels, these two excepted, were steering north, the relative positions of the latter will be understood. Le Foudroyant, too, had kept away, after the loss of her top-masts, until fairly in the wake of the ships ahead of her, in her own line, and, as the vessels had been running off with the wind abeam, for several minutes, this man[oe]uvre threw the French still farther to leeward. To make the matter worse, just as the Warspite drew out of the range of shot from the

French, M. de Vervillin showed a signal at the end of his gaff, for his whole fleet to ware in succession; an order, which, while it certainly had a gallant semblance, as it was bringing his vessels round on the same tack as his enemy, and looked like a defiance, was singularly adapted to restoring to the latter all the advantage of the wind they had lost by keeping away. As it was necessary to take room to execute this evolution, in order to clear the ships that were now crowded in the van, when le Téméraire came to the wind again on the starboard tack, she was fully half a mile to leeward of the admiral, who had just put his helm up. As a matter of course, in order to form anew, with the heads of the ships to the southward, each vessel had to get into her leader's wake, which would be virtually throwing the whole French line, again, two miles to leeward of the English. Nevertheless, the stragglers in the rear of the French continued to hug the wind, with a pertinacity that denoted a resolution to have a brush with their enemies in passing. The vessels were le Scipion and la Victoire, each of seventy-four guns. The first of these ships was commanded by a young man of very little professional experience, but of high court influence; while the second had a captain who, like old Parker, had worked his way up to his present station, through great difficulties, and by dint of hard knocks, and harder work. Unfortunately the first ranked, and the humble *capitaine de frégate*, placed by accident in command of a ship of the line, did not dare to desert a *capitaine de vaisseau*, who had a *duc* for an elder brother, and called himself *comte*. There was perhaps a redeeming gallantry in the spirit which determined the Comte de Chélincourt to incur the risk of passing so near six vessels with only two, that might throw a veil over the indiscretion; more especially as his own fleet was near enough to support him in the event of any disaster, and it was certainly possible that the loss of a material spar on board either of his foes, might induce the capture of the vessel. At all events, thus reasoned M. de Chélincourt; who continued boldly on, with his larboard tacks aboard, always hugging the wind, even after the Téméraire was round; and M. Comptant chose to follow him in la Victoire. The Plantagenet, by this time, being not a mile distant from the Scipio, coming on with steady velocity, these intentions and circumstances created every human probability that she would soon be passing her weather beam, within a quarter of a mile, and, consequently, that a cannonade, far more serious than what had yet occurred, must follow. The few intervening minutes gave Sir Gervaise time to throw a glance around him, and to come to his final decision.

The English fleet was never in better line than at that precise moment. The ships were as close to each other as comported with safety, and every thing stood and drew as in the trade winds. The leading French vessels were waring and increasing their distance to leeward, and it would require an hour for them to get up near enough to be at all dangerous in such weather, while all the rest were following, regardless of the two that continued their luff. The

Chloe had already got round, and, hugging the wind, was actually coming up to windward of her own line, though under a press of canvass that nearly buried her. The Active and Driver were in their stations, as usual; one on the weather beam, and the other on the weather bow; while the Druid had got so near as to show her hull, closing fast, with square yards.

"That is either a very bold, or a very obstinate fellow; he, who commands the two ships ahead of us," observed Greenly, as he stood at the vice-admiral's side, and just as the latter terminated his survey. "What object can he possibly have in braving three times his force in a gale like this?"

"If it were an Englishman, Greenly, we should call him a hero! By taking a mast out of one of us, he might cause the loss of the ship, or compel us to engage double *our* force. Do not blame him, but help me, rather, to disappoint him. Now, listen, and see all done immediately."

Sir Gervaise then explained to the captain what his intentions really were, first ordering, himself, (a very unusual course for one of his habits,) the first lieutenant, to keep the ship off as much as practicable, without seeming to wish to do so; but, as the orders will be explained incidentally, in the course of the narrative, it is not necessary to give them here. Greenly then went below, leaving Sir Gervaise, Bunting, and their auxiliaries, in possession of the poop. A private signal had been bent on some little time, and it was now hoisted. In about five minutes it was read, understood, and answered by all the ships of the fleet. Sir Gervaise rubbed his hands like a man who was delighted, and he beckoned to Bury, who had the trumpet on the quarter-deck, to join him on the poop.

"Did Captain Greenly let you into our plot, Bury," asked the vice-admiral, in high good-humour, as soon as obeyed, "I saw he spoke to you in going below?"

"He only told me, Sir Gervaise, to edge down upon the Frenchmen as close as I could, and this we are doing, I think, as fast as mounsheer"—Bury was an Anglo-Gallican—"will at all like."

"Ah! there old Parker sheers bravely to leeward! Trust to him to be in the right place. The Carnatic went fifty fathoms out of the line at that one twist. The Thunderer and Warspite too! Never was a signal more beautifully obeyed. If the Frenchmen don't take the alarm, now, every thing will be to our minds."

By this time, Bury began to understand the man[oe]uvre. Each alternate ship of the English was sheering fast to leeward, forming a weather and a lee line, with increased intervals between the vessels, while all of them were edging rapidly away, so as greatly to near the enemy. It was apparent now, indeed, that the Plantagenet herself must pass within a hundred fathoms of the

Scipio, and that in less than two minutes. The delay in issuing the orders for this evolution was in favour of its success, inasmuch as it did not give the enemy time for deliberation. The Comte de Chélincourt, in fact, did not detect it; or, at least, did not foresee the consequences; though both were quite apparent to the more experienced *capitaine de frégate* astern. It was too late, or the latter would have signalled his superior to put him on his guard; but, as things were, there remained no alternative, apparently, but to run the gauntlet, and trust all to the chances of battle.

In a moment like that we are describing, events occur much more rapidly than they can be related. The Plantagenet was now within pistol-shot of le Scipion, and on her weather bow. At that precise instant, when the bow-guns, on both sides, began to play, the Carnatic, then nearly in a line with the enemy, made a rank sheer to leeward, and drove on, opening in the very act with her weather-bow guns. The Thunderer and Warspite imitated this man[oe]uvre, leaving the Frenchman the cheerless prospect of being attacked on both sides. It is not to be concealed that M. de Chélincourt was considerably disturbed by this sudden change in his situation. That which, an instant before, had the prospect of being a chivalrous, but extremely hazardous, passage in front of a formidable enemy, now began to assume the appearance of something very like destruction. It was too late, however, to remedy the evil, and the young Comte, as brave a man as existed, determined to face it manfully. He had scarcely time to utter a few cheering sentiments, in a dramatic manner, to those on the quarter-deck, when the English flag-ship came sweeping past in a cloud of smoke, and a blaze of fire. His own broadside was nobly returned, or as much of it as the weather permitted, but the smoke of both discharges was still driving between his masts, when the dark hamper of the Carnatic glided into the drifting canopy, which was made to whirl back on the devoted Frenchman in another torrent of flame. Three times was this fearful assault renewed on the Scipio, at intervals of about a minute, the iron hurricane first coming from to windward, and then seeming to be driven back from to leeward, as by its own rebound, leaving no breathing time to meet it. The effect was completely to silence her own fire; for what between the power of the raging elements, and the destruction of the shot, a species of wild and blood-fraught confusion took the place of system and order. Her decks were covered with killed and wounded, among the latter of whom was the Comte de Chélincourt, while orders were given and countermanded in a way to render them useless, if not incoherent. From the time when the Plantagenet fired her first gun, to that when the Warspite fired her last, was just five minutes by the watch. It seemed an hour to the French, and but a moment to their enemies. One hundred and eighty-two men and boys were included in the casualties of those teeming moments on board the Scipio alone; and when that ship issued slowly from the scene of havoc, more by the velocity of her assailants in passing than by her own, the foremast was all that stood, the remainder of her spars dragging under her lee. To cut the last adrift, and to run off nearly before the wind, in order to save the spars forward, and to get within the cover of her own fleet, was all that could now be done. It may as well be said here, that these two objects were effected.

The Plantagenet had received damage from the fire of her opponent. Some ten or fifteen men were killed and wounded; her main-top-sail was split by a shot, from clew to earing; one of the quarter-masters was carried from the poop, literally dragged overboard by the sinews that connected head and body; and several of the spars, with a good deal of rigging, required to be looked to, on account of injuries. But no one thought of these things, except as they were connected with present and pressing duties. Sir Gervaise got a sight of la Victoire, some hundred and twenty fathoms ahead, just as the roar of the Carnatic's guns was rushing upon his ears. The French commander saw and understood the extreme jeopardy of his consort, and he had already put his helm hard up.

"Starboard—starboard hard, Bury!" shouted Sir Gervaise from the poop. "Damn him, run him aboard, if he dare hold on long enough to meet us."

The lieutenant signed with his hand that the order was understood, and the helm being put up, the ship went whirling off to leeward on the summit of a hill of foam. A cheer was heard struggling in the tempest, and glancing over his left shoulder, Sir Gervaise perceived the Carnatic shooting out of the smoke, and imitating his own movement, by making another and still ranker sheer to leeward. At the same moment she set her main-sail close-reefed, as if determined to outstrip her antagonist, and maintain her station. None but a prime seaman could have done such a thing so steadily and so well, in the midst of the wild haste and confusion of such a scene. Sir Gervaise, now not a hundred yards from the Carnatic, waved high his hat in exultation and praise; and old Parker, alone on his own poop, bared his grey hairs in acknowledgment of the compliment. All this time the two ships drove madly ahead, while the crash and roar of the battle was heard astern.

The remaining French ship was well and nimbly handled. As she came round she unavoidably sheered towards her enemies, and Sir Gervaise found it necessary to countermand his last order, and to come swiftly up to the wind, both to avoid her raking broadside, and to prevent running into his own consort. But the Carnatic, having a little more room, first kept off, and then came to the wind again, as soon as the Frenchman had fired, in a way to compel him to haul up on the other tack, or to fall fairly aboard. Almost at the same instant, the Plantagenet closed on his weather quarter and raked. Parker had got abeam, and pressing nearer, he compelled la Victoire to haul her bowlines, bringing her completely between two fires. Spar went after spar, and being left with nothing standing but the lower masts, the Plantagenet and Carnatic could not prevent themselves from passing their victim, though each shortened sail; the first being already without a top-sail. Their places, however, were immediately supplied by the Achilles and the Thunderer, both ships having hauled down their stay-sails to lessen their way. As the Blenheim and Warspite were quite near astern, and an eighteen-pound shot had closed the earthly career of the poor *capitaine de frégate*, his successor in command deemed it prudent to lower his ensign; after a resistance that in its duration was unequal to the promise of its commencement. Still the ship had suffered materially, and had fifty of her crew among the casualties. His submission terminated the combat.

Sir Gervaise Oakes had now leisure and opportunity to look about him. Most of the French ships had got round; but, besides being quite as far astern, when they should get up abeam, supposing himself to remain where he was, they would be at very long gun-shot dead to leeward. To remain where he was, however, formed no part of his plan, for he was fully resolved to maintain all his advantages. The great difficulty was to take possession of his prize, the sea running so high as to render it questionable if a boat would live. Lord Morganic, however, was just of an age and a temperament to bring that question to a speedy issue. Being on the weather-beam of la Victoire, as her flag came down, he ordered his own first lieutenant into the larger cutter, and putting half-a-dozen marines, with the proper crew, into the boat, it was soon seen dangling in the air over the cauldron of the ocean; the oars on-end. To lower, let go, and unhook, were the acts of an instant; the oars fell, and the boat was swept away to leeward. A commander's commission depended on his success, and Daly made desperate efforts to obtain it. The prize offered a lee, and the French, with a national benevolence, courtesy, and magnanimity, that would scarcely have been imitated had matters been reversed, threw ropes to their conquerors, to help to rescue them from a very awkward dilemma. The men did succeed in getting into the prize; but the boat, in the end, was stove and lost.

The appearance of the red flag of England, the symbol of his own professional rank, and worn by most under his own orders, over the white ensign of France, was the sign to Sir Gervaise that the prize-officer was in possession. He immediately made the signal for the fleet to follow the motions of the commander-in-chief. By this time, his own main-sail, close-reefed, had taken the place of the torn top-sail, and the Plantagenet led off to the southward again, as if nothing unusual had occurred. Daly had a quarter of an hour of extreme exertion on board the prize, before he could get her fairly in motion as he desired; but, by dint of using the axe freely, he cut the wreck adrift, and soon had la Victoire liberated from that incumbrance. The fore-sail and fore and mizzen stay-sails were on the ship, and the main-sail, close-reefed also, was about to be set, to drag her-from the *mêlée* of her foes, when her ensign came down. By getting the tack of the latter aboard, and the sheet aft, he would have all the canvass set the gale would allow, and to this all-essential point he directed his wits. To ride down the main-tack of a two-decked ship, in a gale of wind, or what fell little short of a real gale, was not to be undertaken with twenty men, the extent of Daly's command; and he had recourse to the assistance of his enemies. A good natured, facetious Irishman, himself, with a smattering of French, he soon got forty or fifty of the prisoners in a sufficient humour to lend their aid, and the sail was set, though not without great risk of its splitting. From this moment, la Victoire was better off, as respected the gale and keeping a weatherly position, than any of the English ships; inasmuch as she could carry all the canvass the wind permitted, while she was relieved from the drift inseparable from hamper aloft. The effect, indeed, was visible in the first hour, to Daly's great delight and exultation. At the end of that period, he found himself quite a cable's-length to windward of the line. But in relating this last particular, events have been a little anticipated.

Greenly, who had gone below to attend to the batteries, which were not worked without great difficulty in so heavy a sea, and to be in readiness to open the lower ports should occasion offer, re-appeared on deck just as the commander-in-chief showed the signal for the ships to follow his own motions. The line was soon formed, as mentioned, and ere long it became apparent that the prize could easily keep in her station. As most of the day was still before him, Sir Gervaise had little doubt of being able to secure the latter, ere night should come to render it indispensable.

The vice-admiral and his captain shook hands cordially on the poop, and the former pointed out to the latter, with honest exultation, the result of his own bold man[oe]uvres.

"We've clipped the wings of two of them," added Sir Gervaise, "and have fairly bagged a third, my good friend; and, God willing, when Bluewater joins, there will not be much difficulty with the remainder. I cannot see that any of our vessels have suffered much, and I set them all down as sound. There's been time for a signal of inability, that curse to an admiral's evolutions, but no one seems disposed to make it. If we really escape that nuisance, it will be the first instance in my life!"

"Half-a-dozen yards may be crippled, and no one the worse for it, in this heavy weather. Were we under a press of canvass, it would be a different matter; but, now, so long as the main sticks stand, we shall probably do well enough. I can find no injury in my own ship that may not be remedied at sea."

"And she has had the worst of it. 'Twas a decided thing, Greenly, to engage such an odds in a gale; but we owe our success, most probably, to the audacity of the attack. Had the enemy believed it possible, it is probable he would have frustrated it. Well, Master Galleygo, I'm glad to see you unhurt! What is your pleasure?"

"Why, Sir Jarvy, I've two opportunities, as a body might say, on the poop, just now. One is to shake hands, as we always does a'ter a brush, you knows, sir, and to look a'ter each other's health; and the other is to report a misfortin that will bear hard on this day's dinner. You see, Sir Jarvy, I had the dead poultry slung in a net, over the live stock, to be out of harm's way; well, sir, a shot cut the lanyard, and let all the chickens down by the run, in among the gun-room grunters; and as they never half feeds them hanimals, there isn't as much left of the birds as would make a meal for a sick young gentleman. To my notion, no one ought to *have* live stock but the commanders-in-chief."

"To the devil with you and the stock! Give me a shake of the hand, and back into your top—how came you, sir, to quit your quarters without leave?"

"I didn't, Sir Jarvy. Seeing how things was a going on, among the pigs, for our top hoverlooks the awful scene, I axed the young gentleman to let me come down to condole with your honour; and as they always lets me do as I axes, in such matters, why down I come. We has had one rattler in at our top, howsever, that came nigh lo clear us all out on it!"

"Is any spar injured?" asked Sir Gervaise, quickly. "This must be looked to— hey! Greenly?"

"Not to signify, your honour; not to signify. One of them French eighteens aboard the prize just cocked its nose up, as the ship lurched, and let fly a round 'un and a grist of grape, right into our faces. I see'd it coming and sung out 'scaldings;' and 'twas well I did. We all ducked in time, and the round 'un cleared every thing, but a handful of the marbles are planted in the head of the mast, making the spar look like a plum-pudding, or a fellow with the small-pox."

"Enough of this. You are excused from returning to the top;—and, Greenly, beat the retreat. Bunting, show the signal for the retreat from quarters. Let the ships pipe to breakfast, if they will."

This order affords a fair picture of the strange admixture of feelings and employments that characterize the ordinary life of a ship. At one moment, its inmates find themselves engaged in scenes of wild magnificence and fierce confusion, while at the next they revert to the most familiar duties of humanity. The crews of the whole fleet now retired from the guns, and immediately after they were seated around their kids, indulging ravenously in the food for which the exercise of the morning had given keen appetites. Still there was something of the sternness of battle in the merriment of this meal, and the few jokes that passed were seasoned with a bitterness that is not usual among the light-hearted followers of the sea. Here and there, a messmate was missed, and the vacancy produced some quaint and even pathetic allusion to his habits, or to the manner in which he met his death; seamen usually treating the ravages of this great enemy of the race, after the blow has been struck, with as much solemnity and even tenderness, as they regard his approaches with levity. It is when spared themselves, that they most regard the destruction of battle. A man's standing in a ship, too, carries great weight with it, at such times; the loss of the quarter-master, in particular, being much regretted in the Plantagenet. This man messed with a portion of the petty officers, a set of men altogether more thoughtful and grave than the body of the crew; and who met, when they assembled around their mess-chest that morning, with a sobriety and even sternness of mien, that showed how much in the management of the vessel had depended on their individual exertions. Several minutes elapsed in the particular mess of the dead man, before a word was spoken; all eating with appetites that were of proof, but no one breaking the silence. At length an old quarter-gunner, named Tom Sponge, who generally led the discourse, said in a sort of half-inquiring, half-regretting, way—

"I suppose there's no great use in asking why Jack Glass's spoon is idle this morning. They says, them forecastle chaps, that they see'd his body streaming out over the starboard quarter, as if it had been the fly of one of his own ensigns. How was it, Ned? you was thereaway, and ought to know all about it."

"To be sure I does," said Ned, who was Bunting's remaining assistant. "I was there, as you says, and see'd as much of it as a man can see of what passes between a poor fellow and a shot, when they comes together, and that not in a very loving manner. It happened just as we come upon the weather beam of that first chap—him as we winged so handsomely among us. Well, Sir Jarvy had clapped a stopper on the signals, seeing as we had got fairly into the smoke, and Jack and I was looking about us for the muskets, not knowing but a chance might turn up to chuck a little lead into some of the parly-woos; and so says Jack, says he, 'Ned, you's got my musket;—(as I *had*, sure enough)—and says he, 'Ned, you's got my musket; but no matter arter all, as they're much of a muchness.' So when he'd said this, he lets fly; but whether he hit any body, is more than I can say. If he *did*, 'twas likely a Frenchman, as he shot that-a-way. 'Now,' says Jack, says he, 'Ned, as this is your musket, you can load it, and hand over mine, and I'll sheet home another of the b——s.' Well, at that moment the Frenchman lifted for'ard, on a heavy swell, and let drive at us, with all his forecastle guns, fired as it might be with one priming—"

"That was bad gunnery," growled Tom Sponge, "it racks a ship woundily."

"Yes, they'se no judgment in ships, in general. Well, them French twelves are spiteful guns; and a *little* afore they fired, it seemed to me I heard something give Jack a rap on the check, that sounded as if a fellow's ear was boxed with a clap of thunder. I looked up, and there was Jack streaming out like the fly of the ensign, head foremost, with the body towing after it by strings in the neck."

"I thought when a fellow's head was shot off," put in another quarter-master named Ben Barrel, "that the body was left in the ship while only the truck went!"

"That comes of not seeing them things, Ben," rejoined the eye-witness. "A fellow's head is staid in its berth just like a ship's mast. There's for'ard and back-stays, and shrouds, all's one as aboard here; the only difference is that the lanyards are a little looser, so as to give a man more play for his head, than it might be safe to give to a mast. When a fellow makes a bow, why he only comes up a little aft, and bowses on the fore-stay, and now and then you falls in with a chap that is stayed altogether too far for'ard, or who's got a list perhaps from having the shrouds set up too taut to port or to starboard."

"That sounds reasonable," put in the quarter-gunner, gravely; "I've seen such droggers myself."

"If you'd been on the poop an hour or too ago, you'd ha' seen more on it! Now, there's all our marines, their back-stays have had a fresh pull since they were launched, and, as for their captain, I'll warrant you, *he* had a luff upon luff!"

"I've heard the carpenter overhauling them matters," remarked Sam Wad, another quarter-gunner, "and he chalked it all out by the square and compass. It seems reasonable, too."

"If you'd seen Jack's head dragging his body overboard, just like the Frenchman dragging his wreck under his lee, you'd ha' *thought* it reasonable. What's a fellow's shoulders for, but to give a spread to his shrouds, which lead down the neck and are set up under the arms somewhere. They says a great deal about the heart, and I reckons it's likely every thing is key'd there."

"Harkee, Ned," observed a quarter-master, who knew little more than the mess generally, "if what you say is true, why don't these shrouds lead straight from the head to the shoulders, instead of being all tucked up under a skin in the neck? Answer me that, now."

"Who the devil ever saw a ship's shrouds that wasn't cat-harpened in!" exclaimed Ned, with some heat. "A pretty hand a wife would make of it, in pulling her arms around a fellow's neck if the rigging spread in the way you mean! Them things is all settled according to reason when a chap's keel's laid."

This last argument seemed to dispose of the matter, the discourse gradually turning on, and confining itself to the merits of the deceased.

Sir Gervaise had directed Galleygo to prepare his breakfast as soon as the people were piped to their own; but he was still detained on deck in consequence of a movement in one of his vessels, to which it has now become necessary more particularly to recur.

The appearance of the Druid to the northward, early in the morning, will doubtless be remembered by the reader. When near enough to have it made out, this frigate had shown her number; after which she rested satisfied with carrying sail much harder than any vessel in sight. When the fleets engaged, she made an effort to set the fore-top-sail, close-reefed, but several of the critics in the other ships, who occasionally noticed her movements, fancied that some accident must have befallen her, as the canvass was soon taken in, and she appeared disposed to remain content with the sail carried when first seen. As this ship was materially to windward of the line, and she was running the whole time a little free, her velocity was much greater than that of the other vessels, and by this time she had got so near that Sir Gervaise observed she was fairly abeam of the Plantagenet, and a little to leeward of the Active. Of course her hull, even to the bottom, as she rose on a sea, was plainly visible, and such of her people as were in the tops and rigging could be easily distinguished by the naked eye.

"The Druid must have some communication for us from the other division of the fleet," observed the vice-admiral to his signal-officer, as they stood watching the movements of the frigate; "it is a little extraordinary Blewet does not signal! Look at the book, and find me a question to put that will ask his errand?"

Bunting was in the act of turning over the leaves of his little vocabulary of questions and answers, when three or four dark balls, that Sir Gervaise, by the aid of the glass, saw suspended between the frigate's masts, opened into flags, effectually proving that Blewet was not absolutely asleep.

"Four hundred and sixteen, ordinary communication," observed the vice-admiral, with his eye still at the glass. "Look up that, Bunting, and let us know what it means."

"The commander-in-chief—wish to speak him!" read Bunting, in the customary formal manner in which he announced the purport of a signal.

"Very well—answer; then make the Druid's number to come within hail! The fellow has got cloth enough spread to travel two feet to our one; let him edge away and come under our lee. Speaking will be rather close work to-day."

"I doubt if a ship *can* come near enough to make herself heard," returned the other, "though the second lieutenant of that ship never uses a trumpet in the heaviest weather, they tell me, sir. Our gents say his father was a town-crier, and that he has inherited the family estate."

"Ay, our gents are a set of saucy fellows, as is usually the case when there isn't work enough aboard."

"You should make a little allowance, Sir Gervaise, for being in the ship of a successful commander-in-chief. That makes us all carry weather-helms among the other messes."

"Up with your signal, sir; up with your signal. I shall be obliged to order Greenly to put you upon watch-and-watch for a month, in order to bring you down to the old level of manners."

"Signal answered, already, Sir Gervaise. By the way, sir, I'll thank you to request Captain Greenly to give me another quarter-master. It's nimble work for us when there is any thing serious to do."

"You shall have him, Bunting," returned the vice-admiral, a shade passing over his face for the moment. "I had missed poor Jack Glass, and from seeing a spot of blood on the poop, guessed his fate. I fancied, indeed, I heard a shot strike something behind me."

"It struck the poor fellow's head, sir, and made a noise as if a butcher were felling an ox."

"Well—well—let us try to forget it, until something can be done for his son, who is one of the side boys. Ah! there's Blewet keeping away in earnest. How the deuce he is to speak us, however, is more than I can tell."

Sir Gervaise now sent a message to his captain to say that he desired his presence. Greenly soon appeared, and was made acquainted with the intention of the Druid, as well as with the purport of the last signals. By this time, the rent main-top-sail was mended, and the captain suggested it should be set again, close-reefed, as before, and that the main-sail should be taken in. This would lessen the Plantagenet's way, which ship was sensibly drawing ahead of her consorts. Sir Gervaise assenting, the change was made, and the effects were soon apparent, not only in the movement of the ship, but in her greater ease and steadiness of motion.

It was not long before the Druid was within a hundred fathoms of the flag-ship, on her weather-quarter, shoving the brine before her in a way to denote a fearful momentum. It was evidently the intention of Captain Blewet to cross the Plantagenet's stern, and to luff up under her lee quarter; the safest point at which he could approach, in so heavy a swell, provided it were done with discretion. Captain Blewet had a reputation for handling his frigate like a boat, and the occasion was one which would be likely to awaken all his desire to sustain the character he had already earned. Still no one could imagine how he was to come near enough to make a communication of any length. The stentorian lungs of the second lieutenant, however, might effect it; and, as the news of the expected hail passed through the ship, many who had remained below, in apathy, while the enemy was close under their lee, came on deck, curious to witness what was about to pass.

"Hey! Atwood?" exclaimed Sir Gervaise, for the little excitement had brought the secretary up from the commander-in-chief's cabin;—"what is Blewet at! The fellow cannot mean to set a studding-sail!"

"He is running out a boom, nevertheless, Sir Gervaise, or my thirty years' experience of nautical things have been thrown away."

"He is truly rigging out his weather fore-topmast-studding-sail-boom, sir!" added Greenly, in a tone of wonder.

"It *is* out," rejoined the vice-admiral, as one would give emphasis to the report of a calamity. "Hey!—what? Isn't that a man they're running up to the end of it, Bunting? Level your glass, and let us know at once."

"A glass is not necessary to make out that much, Sir Gervaise. It is a man, beyond a doubt, and there he hangs at the boom-end, as if sentenced by a general court-martial."

Sir Gervaise now suppressed every expression of surprise, and his reserve was imitated, quite as a matter of course, by the twenty officers, who, by this time, had assembled on the poop. The Druid, keeping away, approached rapidly, and had soon crossed the flag-ship's wake. Here she came by the wind, and favoured by the momentum with which she had come down, and the addition of the main-sail, drew heavily but steadily up on her lee-quarter. Both vessels being close-hauled, it was not difficult steering; and by watching the helms closely, it would have been possible, perhaps, notwithstanding the heavy sea, to have brought the two hulls within ten yards of each other, and no harm should come of it. This was nearer, however, than it was necessary to approach; the studding-sail-boom, with the man suspended on the end of it, projecting twice that distance, beyond the vessel's bows. Still it was nice work; and while yet some thirty or forty feet from the perpendicular, the man on the boom-end made a sign for attention, swung a coil of line he hold, and when he saw hands raised to catch it, he made a cast. A lieutenant caught the rope, and instantly hauled in the slack. As the object was now understood, a dozen others laid hold of the line, and, at a common signal, when those on board the Plantagenet hauled in strongly, the people of the Druid lowered away. By this simple, but united movement, the man descended obliquely, leaping out of the bowline in which he had sat, and casting the whip adrift. Shaking himself to gain his footing, he raised his cap and bowed to Sir Gervaise, who now saw Wycherly Wychecombe on his poop.

CHAPTER XXIV.

"Yet weep not thou—the struggle is not o'er,
O victors of Philippi! many a field
Hath yielded palms to us:—one effort more,
By one stern conflict must our fate be sealed."

MRS. HEMANS.

As soon as the people of the Plantagenet, who had so far trespassed on discipline, when they perceived a man hanging at the end of the studding-sail-boom, as to appear in the rigging, on the booms, and on the guns, to watch the result, saw the stranger safely landed on the poop, they lifted their hats and caps, and, as one voice, greeted him with three cheers. The officers smiled at this outbreak of feeling, and the violation of usage was forgotten; the rigid discipline of a man-of-war even, giving way occasionally to the sudden impulses of natural feeling.

As the Druid approached the flag-ship, Captain Blewet had appeared in her weather mizzen-rigging, conning his vessel in person; and the order to luff, or keep off, had been given by his own voice, or by a gesture of his own hand. As soon as he saw Wycherly's feet on the poop of the Plantagenet, and his active form freed from the double-bowline, in which it had been seated, the captain made a wide sweep of the arm, to denote his desire to edge away; the helm of the frigate was borne up hard, and, as the two-decker surged ahead on the bosom of a sea, the Druid's bows were knocked off to leeward, leaving a space of about a hundred feet, or more, between the two ships, as it might be, in an instant. The same causes continuing to operate, the Plantagenet drove still farther ahead, while the frigate soon came to the wind again, a cable's-length to leeward, and abreast of the space between the admiral and his second, astern. Here, Captain Blewet seemed disposed to wait for further orders.

Sir Gervaise Oakes was not accustomed to betray any surprise he might feel at little events that occurred on duty. He returned the bow of Wycherly, coolly, and then, without question or play of feature, turned his eyes on the further movements of the Druid. Satisfied that all was right with the frigate, he directed the messenger to follow him, and went below himself, leaving Wycherly to obey as fast as the many inquiries he had to answer as he descended the ladders would allow. Atwood, an interested observer of what had passed, noted that Captain Greenly, of all present, was the only person who seemed indifferent to the nature of the communication the stranger might bring, though perhaps the only one entitled by rank to put an interrogatory.

"You have come aboard of us in a novel and extraordinary mode, Sir Wycherly Wychecombe!" observed the vice-admiral, a little severely, as soon as he found himself in his own cabin, alone with the lieutenant.

"It was the plan of Captain Blewet, sir, and was really the only one that seemed likely to succeed, for a boat could scarcely live. I trust the success of the experiment, and the nature of the communications I may bring, will be thought sufficient excuses for the want of ceremony."

"It is the first time, since the days of the Conqueror, I fancy, that an English vice-admiral's ship has been boarded so cavalierly; but, as you say, the circumstances may justify the innovation. What is your errand, sir?"

"This letter, I presume, Sir Gervaise, will explain itself. I have little to say in addition, except to report that the Druid has sprung her foremast in carrying sail to close with you, and that we have not lost a moment since Admiral Bluewater ordered us to part company with himself."

"You sailed on board the Cæsar, then?" asked Sir Gervaise, a great deal mollified by the zeal for service in a youth, situated ashore, as he knew Wycherly to be. "You left her, with this letter?"

"I did, Sir Gervaise, at Admiral Bluewater's command."

"Did you go aboard the Druid boom-fashion, or was that peculiar style reserved for the commander-in-chief?"

"I left the Cæsar in a boat, Sir Gervaise; and though we were much nearer in with the coast, where the wind has not the rake it has here, and the strength of the gale had not then come, we were nearly swamped."

"If a true Virginian, you would not have drowned, Wychecombe," answered the vice-admiral, in better humour. "You Americans swim like cork. Excuse me, while I read what Admiral Bluewater has to say."

Sir Gervaise had received Wycherly in the great cabin, standing at the table which was lashed in its centre. He would have been puzzled himself, perhaps, to have given the real reason why he motioned to the young man to take a chair, while he went into what he called his "drawing-room;" or the beautiful little apartment between the two state-rooms, aft, which was fitted with an elegance that might have been admired in a more permanent dwelling, and whither he always withdrew when disposed to reflection. It was probably connected, however, with a latent apprehension of the rear-admiral's political bias, for, when by himself, he paused fully a minute before he opened the letter. Condemning this hesitation as unmanly, he broke the seal, however, and read the contents of a letter, which was couched in the following terms:

"My dear Oakes:—Since we parted, my mind has undergone some violent misgivings as to the course duty requires of me, in this great crisis. One hand—one heart—one voice even, may decide the fate of England! In such circumstances, all should listen to the voice of conscience, and endeavour to foresee the consequences of their own acts. Confidential agents are in the west of England, and one of them I have seen. By his communications I find more depends on myself than I could have imagined, and more on the movements of M. de Vervillin. Do not be too sanguine—take time for your own decisions, and grant *me* time; for I feel like a wretch whose fate must soon be sealed. On no account engage, because you think this division near enough to sustain you, but at least keep off until you hear from me more positively, or we can meet. I find it equally hard to strike a blow against my rightful prince, or to desert my friend. For God's sake act prudently, and depend on seeing me in the course of the next twenty-four hours. I shall keep well to the eastward, in the hope of falling in with you, as I feel satisfied de Vervillin has nothing to do very far west. I may send some verbal message by the bearer, for my thoughts come sluggishly, and with great reluctance.

"Ever *yours*,"RICHARD BLUEWATER."

Sir Gervaise Oakes read this letter twice with great deliberation; then he crushed it in his hand, as one would strangle a deadly serpent. Not satisfied with this manifestation of distaste, he tore the letter into pieces so small as to render it impossible to imagine its contents, opened a cabin-window, and threw the fragments into the ocean. When he fancied that every sign of his friend's weakness had thus been destroyed, he began to pace the cabin in his usual manner. Wycherly heard his step, and wondered at the delay; but his duty compelled him to pass an uncomfortable half-hour in silence, ere the door opened, and Sir Gervaise appeared. The latter had suppressed the signs of distress, though the lieutenant could perceive he was unusually anxious.

"Did the rear-admiral send any message, Sir Wycherly?" inquired Sir Gervaise; "in his letter he would seem to refer me to some verbal explanations from yourself."

"I am ashamed to say, sir, none that I can render very intelligible. Admiral Bluewater, certainly, did make a few communications that I was to repeat, but when we had parted, by some extraordinary dullness of my own I fear, I find it is out of my power to give them any very great distinctness or connection."

"Perhaps the fault is less your own, sir, than his. Bluewater is addicted to fits of absence of mind, and then he has no reason to complain that others do not understand him, for he does not always understand himself."

Sir Gervaise said this with a little glee, delighted at finding his friend had not committed himself to his messenger. The latter, however, was less disposed to excuse himself by such a process, inasmuch as he felt certain that the rear-admiral's feelings were in the matter he communicated, let the manner have been what it might.

"I do not think we can attribute any thing to Admiral Bluewater's absence of mind, on this occasion, sir," answered Wycherly, with generous frankness. "His feelings appeared to be strongly enlisted in what he said. It might have been owing to the strength of these feelings that he was a little obscure, but it could not have been owing to indifference."

"I shall best understand the matter, then, by hearing what he did say, sir."

Wycherly paused, and endeavoured to recall what had passed, in a way to make it intelligible.

"I was frequently told to caution you not to engage the French, sir, until the other division had closed, and was ready to assist. But, really, whether this was owing to some secret information that the rear-admiral had obtained, or to a natural desire to have a share in the battle, is more than I can say."

"Each may have had its influence. Was any allusion made to secret intelligence, that you name it?"

"I never felt more cause to be ashamed of my own dullness, than at this present moment, Sir Gervaise Oakes," exclaimed Wycherly, who almost writhed under the awkwardness of his situation; for he really began to suspect that his own personal grounds of unhappiness had induced him to forget some material part of his message;—"recent events ashore, had perhaps disqualified me for this duty."

"It is natural it should be so, my young friend; and as I am acquainted with them all, you can rest satisfied with my indulgence."

"All! no—Sir Gervaise, you know not half—but, I forget myself, sir, and beg your pardon."

"I have no wish to pry into your secrets, Sir Wycherly Wychecombe, and we will drop the subject. You may say, however, if the rear-admiral was in good spirits—as an English seaman is apt to be, with the prospect of a great battle before him."

"I thought not, Sir Gervaise. Admiral Bluewater to me seemed sad, if I may presume to mention it—almost to tears, I thought, sir, one or twice."

"Poor Dick!" mentally ejaculated the vice-admiral; "he never could have made up his mind to desert *me* without great anguish of soul. Was there any thing said," speaking aloud, "about the fleet of M. de Vervillin?"

"Certainly a good deal, sir; and yet am I ashamed to say, I scarce know what! Admiral Bluewater appeared to think the Comte de Vervillin had no intention to strike a blow at any of our colonies, and with this he seemed to connect the idea that there would be less necessity for our engaging him. At all events, I cannot be mistaken in his wish that you would keep off, sir, until he could close."

"Ay, and you see how instinctively I have answered to his wishes!" said Sir Gervaise, smiling a little bitterly. "Nevertheless, had the rear of the fleet been up this morning, Sir Wycherly, it might have been a glorious day for England!"

"It *has* been a glorious day, as it is, sir. We, in the Druid, saw it all; and there was not one among us that did not exult in the name of Englishman!"

"What, even to the Virginian, Wychecombe!" rejoined Sir Gervaise, greatly gratified with the natural commendation conveyed in the manner and words of the other, and looking in a smiling, friendly manner, at the young man. "I was afraid the hits you got in Devonshire might have induced you to separate your nationality from that of old England."

"Even to the Virginian, Sir Gervaise. You have been in the colonies, sir, and must know we do not merit all that we sometimes receive, on this side of the Atlantic. The king has no subjects more loyal than those of America."

"I am fully aware of it, my noble lad, and have told the king as much, with my own mouth. But think no more of this. If your old uncle did give you an occasional specimen of true John Bullism, he has left you an honourable title and a valuable estate. I shall see that Greenly finds a berth for you, and you will consent to mess with me, I hope. I trust some time to see you at Bowldero. At present we will go on deck; and if any thing that Admiral Bluewater has said *should* recur to your mind more distinctly, you will not forget to let me know it."

Wycherly now bowed and left the cabin, while Sir Gervaise sat down and wrote a note to Greenly to request that he would look a little after the comfort of the young man. The latter then went on deck, in person. Although he endeavoured to shake off the painful doubts that beset him, and to appear as cheerful as became an officer who had just performed a brilliant exploit, the vice-admiral found it difficult to conceal the shock he had received from Bluewater's communication. Certain as he felt of striking a decisive blow at the enemy, could he be reinforced with the five ships of the rear division, he would cheerfully forego the triumph of such additional success, to be certain his friend did not intend to carry his disaffection to overt acts. He found it hard to believe that a man like Bluewater could really contemplate carrying off with him the ships he commanded; yet he knew the authority his friend wielded over his captains, and the possibility of such a step would painfully obtrude itself on his mind, at moments. "When a man can persuade himself into all the nonsense connected with the *jus divinum*," thought Sir Gervaise, "it is doing no great violence to common sense to persuade himself into all its usually admitted consequences." Then, again, would interpose his recollections of Bluewater's integrity and simplicity of character, to reassure him, and give him more cheering hopes for the result. Finding himself thus vacillating between hope and dread, the commander-in-chief determined to drive the matter temporarily from his mind, by bestowing his attention on the part of the fleet he had with him. Just as this wise resolution was formed, both Greenly and Wycherly appeared on the poop.

"I am glad to see you with a hungry look, Greenly," cried Sir Gervaise, cheerfully; "here has Galleygo just been to report his breakfast, and, as I know your cabin has not been put in order since the people left the guns, I hope for the pleasure of your company. Sir Wycherly, my gallant young Virginian, here, will take the third chair, I trust, and then our party will be complete."

The two gentlemen assenting, the vice-admiral was about to lead the way below, when suddenly arresting his footsteps, on the poop-ladder, he said—

"Did you not tell me, Wychecombe, that the Druid had sprung her foremast?"

"Badly, I believe, Sir Gervaise, in the hounds. Captain Blewet carried on his ship fearfully, all night."

"Ay, he's a fearful fellow with spars, that Tom Blewet. I never felt certain of finding all the sticks in their places, on turning out of a morning, when he was with you as a lieutenant, Greenly. How many jib-booms and top-gallant yards did he cost us, in that cruise off the Cape of Good Hope? By George, it must have been a dozen, at least!"

"Not quite as bad as that, Sir Gervaise, though he did expend two jib-booms and three top-gallant yards, for me. Captain Blewet has a fast ship, and he wishes people to know it."

"And he has sprung his foremast and he shall see *I* know it! Harkee, Bunting, make the Druid's number to lie by the prize; and when that's answered, tell him to take charge of the Frenchman, and to wait for further orders. I'll send him to Plymouth to get a new foremast, and to see the stranger in. By the way, does any body know the name of the Frenchman—hey! Greenly?"

"I cannot tell you, Sir Gervaise, though some of our gentlemen think it is the ship that was the admiral's second ahead, in our brush off Cape Finisterre. I am not of the same opinion, however; for that vessel had a billet-head, and this has a woman figure-head, that looks a little like a Minerva. The French have a *la Minerve*, I think."

"Not now, Greenly, if this be she, for she is *ours*." Here Sir Gervaise laughed heartily at his own humour, and all near him joined in, as a matter of course. "But la Minerve has been a frigate time out of mind. The Goddess of Wisdom has never been fool enough to get into a line of battle when she has had it in her power to prevent it."

"*We* thought the figure-head of the prize a Venus, as we passed her in the Druid," Wycherly modestly observed.

"There is a way of knowing, and it shall be tried. When you've done with the Druid, Bunting, make the prize's signal to repeat her name by telegraph. You know how to make a prize's number, I suppose, when she has none."

"I confess I do not, Sir Gervaise," answered Bunting, who had shown by his manner that he was at a loss. "Having no number in our books, one would be at a stand how to get at her, sir."

"How would *you* do it, young man?" asked Sir Gervaise, who all this time was hanging on to the man-rope of the poop-ladder. "Let us see how well you've been taught, sir."

"I believe it may be done in different modes, Sir Gervaise," Wycherly answered, without any appearance of triumph at his superior readiness, "but the simplest I know is to hoist the French flag under the English, by way of saying for whom the signal is intended."

"Do it, Bunting," continued Sir Gervaise, nodding his head as he descended the ladder, "and I warrant you, Daly will answer. What sort of work he will make with the Frenchman's flags, is another matter. I doubt, too, if he had the wit to carry one of our books with him, in which case he will be at a loss to read our signal. Try him, however, Bunting; an Irishman always has *something* to say, though it be a bull."

This order given, Sir Gervaise descended to his cabin. In half an hour the party was seated at table, as quietly as if nothing unusual had occurred that day.

"The worst of these little brushes which lead to nothing, is that they leave as strong a smell of gunpowder in your cabin, Greenly, as if a whole fleet had been destroyed," observed the vice-admiral good-humouredly, as he began to help his guests. "I hope the odour we have here will not disturb your appetites, gentlemen."

"You do this day's success injustice, Sir Gervaise, in calling it only a brush," answered the captain, who, to say the truth, had fallen to as heartily upon the delicacies of Galleygo, as if he had not eaten in twenty-four hours. "At any rate, it has brushed the spars out of two of king Louis's ships, and one of them into our hands; ay, and in a certain sense into our pockets."

"Quite true, Greenly—quite true; but what would it have been if—"

The sudden manner in which the commander-in-chief ceased speaking, induced his companions to think that he had met with some accident in eating or drinking; both looked earnestly at him, as if to offer assistance. He *was* pale in the face, but he smiled, and otherwise appeared at his ease.

"It is over, gentlemen," said Sir Gervaise, gently—"we'll think no more of it."

"I sincerely hope you've not been hit, sir?" said Greenly. "I've known men hit, who did not discover that they were hurt until some sudden weakness has betrayed it."

"I believe the French have let me off this time, my good friend—yes, I think Magrath will be plugging no shot-holes in my hull for this affair. Sir Wycherly, those eggs are from your own estate, Galleygo having laid the manor under contribution for all sorts of good things. Try them, Greenly, as coming from our friend's property."

"Sir Wycherly is a lucky fellow in *having* an estate," said the captain. "Few officers of his rank can boast of such an advantage; though, now and then, an old one is better off."

"That is true enough—hey! Greenly? The army fetches up most of the fortunes; for your rich fellows like good county quarters and county balls. I was a younger brother when they sent *me* to sea, but I became a baronet, and a pretty warm one too, while yet a reefer. Poor Josselin died when I was only sixteen, and at seventeen they made me an officer."

"Ay, and we like you all the better, Sir Gervaise, for not giving us up when the money came. Now Lord Morganic was a captain when *he* succeeded, and we think much less of that."

"Morganic remains in service, to teach us how to stay top-masts and paint figure-heads;" observed Sir Gervaise, a little drily. "And yet the fellow handled his ship well to-day; making much better weather of it than I feared he would be able to do."

"I hear we are likely to get another duke in the navy, sir; it's not often we catch one of that high rank."

Sir Gervaise cared much less for things of this sort than Bluewater, but he naturally cast a glance at the speaker, as this was said, as much as to ask whom he meant.

"They tell me, sir, that Lord Montresor, the elder brother of the boy in the Cæsar, is in a bad way, and Lord Geoffrey stands next to the succession. I think there is too much stuff in *him* to quit us now he is almost fit to get his commission."

"True, Bluewater has that boy of high hopes and promise with him, too;" answered Sir Gervaise in a musing manner, unconscious of what he said. "God send he may not forget *that*, among other things!"

"I don't think rank makes any difference with Admiral Bluewater, or Captain Stowel. The nobles are worked up in their ship, as well as the humblest reefer of them all. Here is Bunting, sir, to tell us something."'

Sir Gervaise started from a fit of abstraction, and, turning, he saw his signal-officer ready to report.

"The Druid has answered properly, Sir Gervaise, and has already hauled up so close that I think she will luff through the line, though it may be astern of the Carnatic."

"And the prize, Bunting? Have you signalled the prize, as I told you to do?"

"Yes, sir; and she has answered so properly that I make no question the prize-officer took a book with him. The telegraphic signal was answered like the other."

"Well, what does he say? Have you found out the name of the Frenchman?"

"That's the difficulty, sir; *we* are understood, but Mr. Daly has shown something aboard the prize that the quarter-master swears is a paddy."

"A paddy!—What, he hasn't had himself run up at a yard-arm, or stun'sail-boom end, has he—hey! Wychecombe? Daly's an Irishman, and has only to show *himself* to show a paddy."

"But this is a sort of an image of some kind or other, Sir Gervaise, and yet it isn't Mr. Daly. I rather think he hasn't the flags necessary for our words, and has rigged out a sort of a woman, to let us know his ship's name; for she *has* a woman figure-head, you know, sir."

"The devil he has! Well, that will form an era in signals. Galleygo, look out at the cabin window and let me know if you can see the prize from them—well, sir, what's the news?"

"I sees her, Sir Jarvy," answered the steward, "and I sees her where no French ship as sails in company with British vessels has a right to be. If she's a fathom, your honour, she's fifty to windward of our line! Quite out of her place, as a body might say, and onreasonable."

"That's owing to our having felled the forests of her masts, Mr. Galleygo; every spar that is left helping to put her where she is. That prize must be a weatherly ship, though, hey! Greenly? She and her consort were well to windward of their own line, or we could never have got 'em as we did. These Frenchmen *do* turn off a weatherly vessel now and then, that we must all admit."

"Yes, Sir Jarvy," put in Galleygo, who never let the conversation flag when he was invited to take a part in it; "yes, Sir Jarvy, and when they've turned 'em off the stocks they turns 'em over to us, commonly, to sail 'em. Building a craft is one piece of knowledge, and sailing her *well* is another."

"Enough of your philosophy, sirrah; look and ascertain if there is any thing unusual to be seen hanging in the rigging of the prize. Unless you show more readiness, I'll send one of the Bowlderos to help you."

These Bowlderos were the servants that Sir Gervaise brought with him from his house, having been born on his estate, and educated as domestics in his own, or his father's family; and though long accustomed to a man-of-war, as their ambition never rose above their ordinary service, the steward held them exceedingly cheap. A severer punishment could not be offered him, than to threaten to direct one of these common menials to do any duty that, in the least, pertained to the profession. The present menace had the desired effect, Galleygo losing no time in critically examining the prize's rigging.

"I calls nothing extr'ornary in a Frenchman's rigging, Sir Jarvy," answered the steward, as soon as he felt sure of his fact; "their dock-men have idees of their own, as to such things. Now there is sum'mat hanging at the lee fore-yard-arm of that chap, that looks as if it might be a top-gallant-stun'sail made up to be sent aloft and set, but which stopped when it got as high as it is, on finding out that there's no hamper over-head to spread it to."

"That's it, sir," put in Bunting. "Mr. Daly has run his woman up to the fore-yard-arm, like a pirate."

"Woman!" repeated Galleygo—"do you call that 'ere thing-um-mee a woman, Mr. Buntin'? I calls it a bundle of flags, made up to set, if there was any thing to set 'em to."

"It's nothing but an Irish woman, Master Galleygo, as you'll see for yourself, if you'll level this glass at it."

"I'll do that office myself," cried Sir Gervaise. "Have you any curiosity, gentlemen, to read Mr. Daly's signal? Galleygo, open that weather window, and clear away the books and writing-desk, that we may have a look."

The orders were immediately obeyed, and the vice-admiral was soon seated examining the odd figure that was certainly hanging at the lee fore-yard-arm of the prize; a perfect nondescript as regarded all nautical experience.

"Hang me, if I can make any thing of it. Greenly," said Sir Gervaise, after a long look. "Do *you* take this seat, and try your hand at an observation. It resembles a sort of a woman, sure enough."

"Yes, sir," observed Bunting, with the earnestness of a man who felt his reputation involved in the issue, "I was certain that Mr. Daly has run up the figure to let us know the name of the prize, and that for want of a telegraph-book to signal the letters; and so I made sure of what I was about, before I took the liberty to come below and report."

"And pray what do you make of it, Bunting? The figure-head might tell us better, but that seems to be imperfect."

"The figure-head has lost all its bust, and one arm, by a shot," said Greenly, turning the glass to the object named; "and I can tell Mr. Daly that a part of the gammoning of his bowsprit is gone, too! That ship requires looking to, Sir Gervaise; she'll have no foremast to-morrow morning, if this wind stand! Another shot has raked the lower side of her fore-top, and carried away half the frame. Yes, and there's been a fellow at work, too—"

"Never mind the shot—never mind the shot, Greenly," interrupted the vice-admiral. "A poor devil like him, couldn't have six of us at him, at once, and expect to go 'shot free.' Tell us something of the woman."

"Well, Sir Gervaise, no doubt Daly has hoisted her as a symbol. Ay, no doubt the ship is the Minerva, after all, for there's something on the head like a helmet."

"It never can be the Minerva," said the vice-admiral, positively, "for *she*, I feel certain, is a frigate. Hand me the little book with a red cover, Bunting; that near your hand; it has a list of the enemy's navy. Here it is, '*la Minerve*, 32, *le capitaine de frégate, Mondon*. Built in 1733, old and dull.' That settles the Minerva, for this list is the last sent us by the admiralty."

"Then it must be the Pallas," rejoined Greenly, "for she wears a helmet, too, and I am certain there is not only a cap to resemble a helmet, but a Guernsey frock on the body to represent armour. Both Minerva and Pallas, if I remember right, wore armour."

"This is coming nearer to the point,—hey! Greenly!" the vice-admiral innocently chimed in; "let us look and see if the Pallas is a two-decker or not. By George, there's no such name on the list. That's odd, now, that the French should have one of these goddesses and not the other!"

"They never has any thing right, Sir Jarvy," Galleygo thrust in, by way of commentary on the vice-admiral's and the captain's classical lore; "and it's surprising to me that they should have any goddess at all, seeing that they has so little respect for religion, in general."

Wycherly fidgeted, but respect for his superiors kept him silent. As for Bunting, 'twas all the same to him, his father having been a purser in the navy, and he himself educated altogether on board ship, and this, too, a century since.

"It might not be amiss, Sir Gervaise," observed the captain, "to work this rule backwards, and just look over the list until we find a two-decked ship that *ought* to have a woman figure-head, which will greatly simplify the matter. I've known difficult problems solved in that mode."

The idea struck Sir Gervaise as a good one, and he set about the execution of the project in good earnest. Just as he came to *l'Hécate*, 64, an exclamation from Greenly caught his attention, and he inquired its cause.

"Look for yourself, Sir Gervaise; unless my eyes are good for nothing, Daly is running a kedge up alongside of his woman."

"What, a kedge?—Ay, that is intended for an anchor, and it means Hope. Every body knows that Hope carries an anchor,—hey! Wychecombe? Upon my word, Daly shows ingenuity. Look for the Hope, in that list, Bunting,—you will find the English names printed first, in the end of the book."

"'The Hope, or *l' Esperance*,'" read the signal-officer; "'36, *lee capitang dee frigate dee Courtraii.*'"

"A single-decked ship after all! This affair is as bad as the d——d *nullus*, ashore, there. I'll not be beaten in learning, however, by any Frenchman who ever floated. Go below, Locker, and desire Doctor Magrath to step up here, if he is not occupied with the wounded. He knows more Latin than any man in the ship."

"Yes, Sir Jarvy, but this is French, you knows, your honour, and is'nt as Latin, at all. I expects she'll turn out to have some name as no modest person wishes to use, and we shall have to halter it."

"Ay, he's catted his anchor, sure enough; if the figure be not Hope, it must be Faith, or Charity."

"No fear of them, Sir Jarvy; the French has no faith, nor no charity, no, nor no bowels, as any poor fellow knows as has ever been wrecked on their coast, as once happened to me, when a b'y. I looks upon 'em as no better than so many heatheners, and perhaps that's the name of the ship. I've seed heatheners, a hundred times, Sir Jarvy, in that sort of toggery."

"What, man, did you ever see a heathen with an anchor?—one that will weigh three hundred, if it will weigh a pound?"

"Perhaps not, your honour, with a downright hanchor, but with sum'mat like a killog. But, that's no hanchor, a'ter all, but only a kedge, catted hanchor-fashion, sir."

"Here comes Magrath, to help us out of the difficulty; and we'll propound the matter to him."

The vice-admiral now explained the whole affair to the surgeon, frankly admitting that the classics of the cabin were at fault, and throwing himself on the gun-room for assistance. Magrath was not a little amused, as he listened, for this was one of his triumphs, and he chuckled not a little at the dilemma of his superiors.

"Well, Sir Jairvis," he answered, "ye might do warse than call a council o' war on the matter; but if it's the name ye'll be wanting, I can help ye to that, without the aids of symbols, and signs, and hyeroglyphics of any sort. As we crossed the vessel's wake, a couple of hours since, I read it on her stern, in letters of gold. It's *la Victoire*, or the Victory; a most unfortunate cognomen for an unlucky ship. She's a French victory, however, ye'll remember, gentlemen!"

"That must be a mistake, Magrath; for Daly has shown an anchor, yonder; and Victory carries no anchor."

"It's hard to say, veece-admiral, one man's victory being another man's defeat. As for Mr. Daly's image, it's just an *Irish* goddess; and allowances must be made for the country."

Sir Gervaise laughed, invited the gentlemen to help demolish the breakfast, and sent orders on deck to hoist the answering flag. At a later day, Daly, when called on for an explanation, asserted that the armour and helmet belonged to Victory, as a matter of course; though he admitted that he had at first forgotten the anchor; "but, when I *did* run it up, they read it aboard the ould Planter, as if it had been just so much primmer."

CHAPTER XXV.

"There's beauty in the deep:—
The wave is bluer than the sky;
And, though the light shines bright on high,
More softly do the sea-gems glow,
That sparkle in the depths below;
The rainbow's tints are only made
When on the waters they are laid.
And sun and moon most sweetly shine
Upon the ocean's level brine.
There's beauty in the deep."

BRAINARD.

As Daly was the recognised jester of the fleet, his extraordinary attempt to announce his vessel's name was received as a characteristic joke, and it served to laugh at until something better offered. Under the actual circumstances of the two squadrons, however, it was soon temporarily forgotten in graver things, for few believed the collision that had already taken place was to satisfy a man of the known temperament of the commander-in-chief. As the junction of the rear division was the only thing wanting to bring on a general engagement, as soon as the weather should moderate a little, every ship had careful look-outs aloft, sweeping the horizon constantly with glasses, more particularly towards the east and north-east. The gale broke about noon, though the wind still continued fresh from the same quarter as before. The sea began to go down, however, and at eight bells material changes had occurred in the situations of both fleets. Some of these it may be necessary to mention.

The ship of the French admiral, *le Foudroyant*, and *le Scipion*, had been received, as it might be, in the arms of their own fleet in the manner already mentioned; and from this moment, the movement of the whole force was, in a measure, regulated by that of these two crippled vessels. The former ship, by means of her lower sails, might have continued to keep her station in the line, so long as the gale lasted; but the latter unavoidably fell off, compelling her consorts to keep near, or to abandon her to her fate. M. de Vervillin preferred the latter course. The consequences were, that, by the time the sun was in the zenith, his line, a good deal extended, still, and far from regular, was quite three leagues to leeward of that of the English. Nor was this all: at that important turn in the day, Sir Gervaise Oakes was enabled to make sail on all his ships, setting the fore and mizzen-top-sails close-reefed; while *la Victoire*, a fast vessel, was enabled to keep in company by carrying whole courses. The French could not imitate this, inasmuch as one of their crippled vessels had nothing standing but a foremast. Sir Gervaise had ascertained, before the distance became too great for such observations, that the enemy was getting ready to send up new top-masts, and the other necessary spars on board the admiral, as well as jury lower-masts in *le Scipion*; though the sea would not yet permit any very positive demonstrations to be made towards such an improvement. He laid his own plans for the approaching night accordingly; determining not to worry his people, or notify the enemy of his intentions, by attempting any similar improvement in the immediate condition of his prize.

About noon, each ship's number was made in succession, and the question was put if she had sustained any material injury in the late conflict. The answers were satisfactory in general, though one or two of the vessels made such replies as induced the commander-in-chief to resort to a still more direct mode of ascertaining the real condition of his fleet. In order to effect this important object, Sir Gervaise waited two hours longer, for the double purpose of letting all the messes get through with their dinners, and to permit the wind to abate and the sea to fall, as both were now fast doing. At the expiration of that time, however, he appeared on the poop, summoning Bunting to his customary duty.

At 2 P.M. it blew a whole top-sail breeze, as it is called; but the sea being still high, and the ships close-hauled, the vice-admiral did not see fit to order any more sail. Perhaps he was also influenced by a desire not to increase his distance from the enemy, it being a part of his plan to keep M. de Vervillin in plain sight so long as the day continued, in order that he might have a tolerable idea of the position of his fleet, during the hours of darkness. His present intention was to cause his vessels to pass before him in review, as a general orders his battalions to march past a station occupied by himself and staff, with a view to judge by his own eye of their steadiness and appearance. Vice-Admiral Oakes was the only officer in the British navy who ever resorted to this practice; but he did many things of which other men never dreamed, and, among the rest, he did not hesitate to attack double his force, when an occasion offered, as has just been seen. The officers of the fleet called these characteristic reviews "Sir Jarvy's field-days," finding a malicious pleasure in comparing any thing out of the common nautical track, to some usage of the soldiers.

Bunting got his orders, notwithstanding the jokes of the fleet; and the necessary signals were made and the answers given. Captain Greenly then received his verbal instructions, when the commander-in-chief went below, to prepare himself for the approaching scene. When Sir Gervaise re-appeared on the poop, he was in full uniform, wearing the star of the Bath, as was usual with him on all solemn official occasions. Atwood and Bunting were at his side, while the Bowlderos, in their rich shore-liveries, formed a group at hand. Captain Greenly and his first lieutenant joined the party as soon as their duty with the ship was over. On the opposite side of the poop, the whole of the marines off guard were drawn up in triple lines, with their officers at their head. The ship herself had hauled up her main-sail, hauled down all her stay-sails, and lay with her main-top-sail braced sharp aback, with orders to the quarter-master to keep her little off the wind; the object being to leave a little way through the water, in order to prolong the expected interviews. With these preparations the commander-in-chief awaited the successive approach of his ships, the sun, for the first time in twenty-four hours, making his appearance in a flood of brilliant summer-light, as if purposely to grace the ceremony.

The first ship that drew near the Plantagenet was the Carnatic, as a matter of course, she being the next in the line. This vessel, remarkable, as the commander-in-chief had observed, for never being out of the way, was not long in closing, though as she luffed up on the admiral's weather-quarter, to pass to windward, she let go all her top-sail bowlines, so as to deaden her way, making a sort of half-board. This simple evolution, as she righted her helm, brought her about fifty yards to windward of the Plantagenet, past which ship she surged slowly but steadily, the weather now permitting a conversation to be held at that distance, and by means of trumpets, with little or no effort of the voice.

Most of the officers of the Carnatic were on her poop, as she came sweeping up heavily, casting her shadow on the Plantagenet's decks. Captain Parker himself was standing near the ridge-ropes, his head uncovered, and the grey hairs floating in the breeze. The countenance of this simple-minded veteran was a little anxious, for, had he feared the enemy a tenth part as much as he stood in awe of his commanding officer, he would have been totally unfit for his station. Now he glanced upward at his sails, to see that all was right; then, as he drew nearer, fathom by fathom as it might be, he anxiously endeavoured to read the expression of the vice-admiral's face.

"How do you do, Captain Parker?" commenced Sir Gervaise, with true trumpet formality, making the customary salutation.

"How is Sir Gervaise Oakes to-day? I hope untouched in the late affair with the enemy?"

"Quite well, I thank you, sir. Has the Carnatic received any serious injury in the battle?"

"None to mention, Sir Gervaise. A rough scrape of the foremast; but not enough to alarm us, now the weather has moderated; a little rigging cut, and a couple of raps in the hull."

"Have your people suffered, sir?"

"Two killed and seven wounded, Sir Gervaise. Good lads, most of 'em; but enough like 'em remain."

"I understand, then, Captain Parker, that you report the Carnatic fit for any service?"

"As much so as my poor abilities enable me to make her, Sir Gervaise Oakes," answered the other, a little alarmed at the formality and precision of the question. "Meet her with the helm—meet her with the helm."

All this passed while the Carnatic was making her half-board, and, the helm being righted, she now slowly and majestically fell off with her broadside to the admiral, gathering way as her canvass began to draw again. At this instant, when the yard-arms of the two ships were about a hundred feet asunder, and just as the Carnatic drew up fairly abeam, Sir Gervaise Oakes raised his hat, stepped quickly to the side of the poop, waved his hand for silence, and spoke with a distinctness that rendered his words audible to all in both vessels.

"Captain Parker," he said, "I wish, publicly, to thank you for your noble conduct this day. I have always said a surer support could never follow a commander-in-chief into battle; you have more than proved my opinion to be true. I wish, publicly, to thank you, sir."

"Sir Gervaise—I cannot express—God bless you, Sir Gervaise!"

"I have but one fault to find with you, sir, and that is easily pardoned."

"I'm sure I hope so, sir."

"You handled your ship so rapidly and so surely, that *we* had hardly time to get out of the way of your guns!"

Old Parker could not now have answered had his life depended on it; but he bowed, and dashed a hand across his eyes. There was but a moment to say any more.

"If His Majesty's sword be not laid on *your* shoulder for this day's work, sir, it shall be no fault of mine," added Sir Gervaise, waving his hat in adieu.

While this dialogue lasted, so profound was the stillness in the two ships, that the wash of the water under the bows of the Carnatic, was the only sound to interfere with Sir Gervaise's clarion voice; but the instant he ceased to speak, the crews of both vessels rose as one man, and cheered. The officers joined heartily, and to complete the compliment, the commander-in-chief ordered his own marines to present arms to the passing vessel. Then it was that, every sail drawing, again the Carnatic took a sudden start, and shot nearly her length ahead, on the summit of a sea. In half a minute more, she was ahead of the Plantagenet's flying-jib-boom-end, steering a little free, so as not to throw the admiral to leeward.

The Carnatic was scarcely out of the way, before the Achilles was ready to take her place. This ship, having more room, had easily luffed to windward of the Plantagenet, simply letting go her bowlines, as her bows doubled on the admiral's stern, in order to check her way.

"How do you do to-day, Sir Gervaise?" called out Lord Morganic, without waiting for the commander-in-chief's hail—"allow me to congratulate you, sir, on the exploits of this glorious day!"

"I thank you, my lord, and wish to say I am satisfied with the behaviour of your ship. You've *all* done well, and I desire to thank you *all*. Is the Achilles injured?"

"Nothing to speak of, sir. A little rigging gone, and here and there a stick."

"Have you lost any men, my lord? I desire particularly to know the condition of each ship."

"Some eight or ten poor fellows, I believe, Sir Gervaise; but we are ready to engage this instant."

"It is well, my lord; steady your bowlines, and make room for the Thunderer."

Morganic gave the order, but as his ship drew ahead he called out in a pertinacious way,—"I hope, Sir Gervaise, you don't mean to give that other lame duck up. I've got my first lieutenant on board one of 'em, and confess to a desire to put the second on board another."

"Ay—ay—Morganic, *we* knock down the birds, and *you* bag 'em. I'll give you more sport in the same way, before I've done with ye."

This little concession, even Sir Gervaise Oakes, a man not accustomed to trifle in matters of duty, saw fit to make to the other's rank; and the Achilles withdrew from before the flag-ship, as the curtain is drawn from before the scene.

"I do believe, Greenleaf," observed Lord Morganic to his surgeon, one of his indulged favourites; "that Sir Jarvy is a little jealous of us, because Daly got into the prize before he could send one of his own boats aboard of her. 'Twill tell well in the gazette, too, will it not?—'The French ship was taken possession of, and brought off, by the Achilles, Captain the Earl of Morganic!' I hope the old fellow will have the decency to give us our due. I rather think it *was* our last broadside that brought the colours down?"

A suitable answer was returned, but as the ship is drawing ahead, we cannot follow her to relate it. The vessel that approached the third, was the

Thunderer, Captain Foley. This was one of the ships that had received the fire of the three leading French vessels, after they had brought the wind abeam, and being the leading vessel of the English rear, she had suffered more than any other of the British squadron. The fact was apparent, as she approached, by the manner in which her rigging was knotted, and the attention that had been paid to her spars. Even as she closed, the men were on the yard bending a new main-course, the old one having been hit on the bolt-rope, and torn nearly from the spar. There were also several plugs on her lee-side to mark the spots where the French guns had told.

The usual greetings passed between the vice-admiral and his captain, and the former put his questions.

"We have not been quite exchanging salutes, Sir Gervaise," answered Captain Foley; "but the ship is ready for service again. Should the wind moderate a little, I think everything would stand to carry sail *hard*."

"I'm glad to hear it, sir—*rejoiced* to hear it, sir. I feared more for you, than for any other vessel. I hope you've not suffered materially in your crew?"

"Nine killed. Sir Gervaise; and the surgeon tells me sixteen wounded."

"That proves you've not been in port, Foley! Well, I dare say, could the truth be known, it would be found that M. de Vervillin's vessels bear your marks, in revenge. Adieu—adieu—God bless you."

The Thunderer glided ahead, making room for the Blenheim, Captain Sterling. This was one of your serviceable ships, without any show or style about her; but a vessel that was always ready to give and take. Her commander was a regular sea-dog, a little addicted to hard and outlandish oaths, a great consumer of tobacco and brandy; but who had the discrimination never to swear in the presence of the commander-in-chief, although he had been known to do so in a church; or to drink more than he could well carry, when he was in presence of an enemy or a gale of wind. He was too firm a man, and too good a seaman, to use the bottle as a refuge; it was the companion of his ease and pleasure, and to confess the truth, he then treated it with an affectionate benevolence, that rendered it exceedingly difficult for others not to entertain some of his own partiality for it. In a word, Captain Sterling was a sailor of the "old school;" for there was an "old school" in manners, habits, opinions, philosophy, morals, and reason, a century since, precisely as there *is* to-day, and probably *will* be, a century hence.

The Blenheim made a good report, not having sustained any serious injury whatever; nor had she a man hurt. The captain reported his ship as fit for service as she was the hour she lifted her anchor.

"So much the better, Sterling—so much the better. You shall take the edge off the next affair, by way of giving you another chance. I rely on the Blenheim, and on her captain."

"I thank you, sir," returned Sterling, as his ship moved on; "by the way, Sir Gervaise, would it not be fair-play to rummage the prize's lockers before she gets into the hands of the custom-house? Out here on the high seas, there can be no smuggling in *that*: there must be good claret aboard her."

"There would be 'plunder of a prize,' Sterling," said the vice-admiral, laughing, for he knew that the question was put more as a joke than a serious proposition; "and that is death, without benefit of clergy. Move on; here is Goodfellow close upon your heels."

The last ship in the English line was the Warspite, Captain Goodfellow, an officer remarkable in the service at that day, for a "religious turn," as it was called. As is usually the case with men of this stamp, Captain Goodfellow was quiet, thoughtful, and attentive to his duty. There was less of the real tar in him, perhaps, than in some of his companions; but his ship was in good order, always did her duty, and was remarkably attentive to signals; a circumstance that rendered her commander a marked favourite with the vice-admiral. After the usual questions were put and answered, Sir Gervaise informed Goodfellow that he intended to change the order of sailing so as to bring him near the van.

"We will give old Parker a breathing spell, Goodfellow," added the commander-in-chief, "and you will be my second astern. I must go ahead of you all, or you'll be running down on the Frenchman without orders; pretending you can't see the signals, in the smoke."

The Warspite drove ahead, and the Plantagenet was now left to receive the prize and the Druid; the Chloe, Driver, and Active, not being included in the signal. Daly had been gradually eating the other ships out of the wind, as has been mentioned already, and when the order was given to pass within hail, he grumbled not a little at the necessity of losing so much of his vantage-ground. Nevertheless, it would not do to joke with the commander-in-chief in a matter of this sort, and he was fain to haul up his courses, and wait for the moment when he might close. By the time the Warspite was out of the way, his ship had drifted down so near the admiral, that he had nothing to do but to haul aboard his tacks again, and pass as near as was at all desirable. When quite near, he hauled up his main-sail, by order of the vice-admiral.

"Are you much in want of any thing, Mr. Daly?" demanded Sir Gervaise, as soon as the lieutenant appeared forward to meet his hail. "The sea is going down so fast, that we might now send you some boats."

"Many thanks, Sir Gervaise; I want to get rid of a hundred or two Frenchmen, and to have a hundred Englishmen in their places. We are but twenty-one of the king's subjects here, all told."

"Captain Blewet is ordered to keep company with you, sir; and as soon as it is dark, I intend to send you into Plymouth under the frigate's convoy. Is she a nice ship, hey! Daly?"

"Why, Sir Gervaise, she's like a piece of broken crockery, just now, and one can't tell all her merits. She's not a bad goer, and weatherly, I think, all will call her. But she's thundering French, inside."

"We'll make her English in due time, sir. How are the leaks? do the pumps work freely?"

"Deuce the l'ake has she, Sir Gervaise, and the pumps suck like a nine months' babby. And if they didn't we're scarce the boys to find out the contrary, being but nineteen working hands."

"Very well, Daly; you can haul aboard your main-tack, now; remember, you're to go into Plymouth, as soon as it is dark. If you see any thing of Admiral Bluewater, tell him I rely on his support, and only wait for his appearance to finish Monsieur de Vervillin's job."

"I'll do all that, with hearty good will, sir. Pray, Sir Gervaise," added Daly, grinning, on the poop of the prize, whither he had got by this time, having walked aft as his ship went ahead, "how do you like French signals? For want of a better, we were driven to the classics!"

"Ay, you'd be bothered to explain all your own flags, I fancy. The name of the ship is the Victory, I am told; why did you put her in armour, and whip a kedge up against the poor woman?"

"It's according to the books, Sir Gervaise. Every word of it out of Cicero, and Cordairy, and Cornelius Nepos, and those sort of fellows. Oh! I went to school, sir, before I went to sea, as you say yourself, sometimes, Sir Gervaise; and literature is the same in Ireland, as it is all over the world. Victory needs armour, sir, in order to be victorious, and the anchor is to show that she doesn't belong to 'the cut and run' family. I am as sure that all was right, as I ever was of my moods and tenses."

"Very well, Daly," answered Sir Gervaise, laughing—"My lords shall know your merits in that way, and it may get you named a professor—keep your luff, or you'll be down on our sprit-sail-yard;—remember and follow the Druid."

Here the gentlemen waved their hands in adieu as usual, and la Victoire, clipped as she was of her wings, drew slowly past. The Druid succeeded, and

Sir Gervaise simply gave Blewet his orders to see the prize into port, and to look after his own foremast. This ended the field day; the frigate luffing up to windward of the line again, leaving the Plantagenet in its rear. A few minutes later, the latter ship filled and stood after her consorts.

The vice-admiral having now ascertained, in the most direct manner, the actual condition of his fleet, had *data* on which to form his plans for the future. But for the letter from Bluewater, he would have been perfectly happy; the success of the day having infused a spirit into the different vessels, that, of itself, was a pledge of more important results. Still he determined to act as if that letter had never been written, finding it impossible to believe that one who had so long been true, could really fail him in the hour of need. "I know his heart better than he knows it himself," he caught himself mentally exclaiming, "and before either of us is a day older, this will I prove to him, to his confusion and my triumph." He had several short and broken conversations with Wycherly in the course of the afternoon, with a view to ascertain, if possible, the real frame of mind in which his friend had written, but without success, the young man frankly admitting that, owing to a confusion of thought that he modestly attributed to himself, but which Sir Gervaise well knew ought in justice to be imputed to Bluewater, he had not been able to bring away with him any very clear notions of the rear-admiral's intentions.

In the mean while, the elements were beginning to exhibit another of their changeful humours. A gale in summer is seldom of long duration, and twenty-four hours would seem to be the period which nature had assigned to this. The weather had moderated materially by the time the review had taken place, and five hours later, not only had the sea subsided to a very reasonable swell, but the wind had hauled several points; coming out a fresh top-gallant breeze at north-west. The French fleet wore soon after, standing about north-east-by-north, on an easy bowline. They had been active in repairing damages, and the admiral was all a-tanto again, with every thing set that the other ships carried. The plight of le Scipion was not so easily remedied, though even she had two jury-masts rigged, assistance having been sent from the other vessels as soon as boats could safely pass. As the sun hung in the western sky, wanting about an hour of disappearing from one of the long summer days of that high latitude, this ship set a mizzen-top-sail in the place of a main, and a fore-top-gallant-sail in lieu of a mizzen-top-sail. Thus equipped, she was enabled to keep company with her consorts, all of which were under easy canvass, waiting for the night to cover their movements.

Sir Gervaise Oakes had made the signal for his fleet to tack in succession, from the rear to the van, about an hour before le Scipion obtained this additional sail. The order was executed with great readiness, and, as the ships had been looking up as high as west-south-west before, when they got round, and headed north-north-east, their line of sailing was still quite a league to windward of that of the enemy. As each vessel filled on the larboard tack, she shortened sail to allow the ships astern to keep away, and close to her station. It is scarcely necessary to say, that this change again brought the Plantagenet to the head of the line, with the Warspite, however, instead of the Carnatic, for her second astern; the latter vessel being quite in the rear.

It was a glorious afternoon, and there was every promise of as fine a night. Still, as there were but about six hours of positive darkness at that season of the year, and the moon would rise at midnight, the vice-admiral knew he had no time to lose, if he would effect any thing under the cover of obscurity. Reefs were no longer used, though all the ships were under short canvass, in order to accommodate their movements to those of the prize. The latter, however, was now in tow of the Druid, and, as this frigate carried her top-gallant-sails, aided by her own courses, la Victoire was enabled not only to keep up with the fleet, then under whole top-sails, but to maintain her weatherly position. Such was the state of things just as the sun dipped, the enemy being on the lee bow, distant one and a half leagues, when the Plantagenet showed a signal for the whole fleet to heave to, with the main-top-sails to the masts. This command was scarcely executed, when the officers on deck were surprised to hear a boatswain's mate piping away the crew of the vice-admiral's barge, or that of the boat which was appropriated to the particular service of the commander-in-chief.

"Did I hear aright, Sir Gervaise?" inquired Greenly, with curiosity and interest; "is it your wish to have your barge manned, sir?"

"You heard perfectly right, Greenly; and, if disposed for a row this fine evening, I shall ask the favour of your company. Sir Wycherly Wychecombe, as you are an idler here, I have a flag-officer's right to press yon into my service. By the way, Greenly, I have made out and signed an order to this gentleman to report himself to you, as attached to my family, as the soldiers call it; as soon as Atwood has copied it, it will be handed to him, when I beg you will consider him as my first aid."

To this no one could object, and Wycherly made a bow of acknowledgment. At that instant the barge was seen swinging off over the ship's waist, and, at the next, the yard tackles were heard overhauling themselves. The splash of the boat in the water followed. The crew was in her, with oars on end, and poised boat-hooks, in another minute. The guard presented, the boatswain piped over, the drum rolled, and Wycherly jumped to the gangway and was out of sight quick as thought. Greenly and Sir Gervaise followed, when the boat shoved off.

Although the seas had greatly subsided, and their combs were no longer dangerous, the Atlantic was far from being as quiet as a lake in a summer eventide. At the very first dash of the oars the barge rose on a long, heavy swell that buoyed her up like a bubble, and as the water glided from under her again, it seemed as if she was about to sink into some cavern of the ocean. Few things give more vivid impressions of helplessness than boats thus tossed by the waters when not in their raging humours; for one is apt to expect better treatment than thus to be made the plaything of the element. All, however, who have ever floated on even the most quiet ocean, must have experienced more or less of this helpless dependence, the stoutest boat, impelled by the lustiest crews, appearing half the time like a feather floating in capricious currents of the air.

The occupants of the barge, however, were too familiar with their situation to think much of these matters; and, as soon as Sir Gervaise assented to Wycherly's offer to take the tiller, he glanced upward, with a critical eye, in order to scan the Plantagenet's appearance.

"That fellow, Morganic, has got a better excuse for his xebec-rig than I had supposed, Greenly," he said, after a minute of observation. "Your fore-top-mast is at least six inches too far forward, and I beg you will have it stayed aft to-morrow morning, if the weather permit. None of your Mediterranean craft for me, in the narrow seas."

"Very well, Sir Gervaise; the spar shall be righted in the morning watch," quietly returned the captain.

"Now, there's Goodfellow, half-parson as he is; the man contrives to keep his sticks more upright than any captain in the fleet. You never see a spar half an inch out of its place, on board the Warspite."

"That is because her captain trims every thing by his own life, sir," rejoined Greenly, smiling. "Were we half as good as he is, in other matters, we might be better than we are in seamanship."

"I do not think religion hurts a sailor, Greenly—no, not in the least. That is to say, when he don't wedge his masts too tight, but leaves play enough for all weathers. There is no cant in Goodfellow."

"Not the least of it, sir, and that it is which makes him so great a favourite. The chaplain of the Warspite is of some use; but one might as well have a bowsprit rigged out of a cabin-window, as have our chap."

"Why, we never bury a man, Greenly, without putting him into the water as a Christian should be," returned Sir Gervaise, with the simplicity of a true believer of the decency school. "I hate to see a seaman tossed in the ocean like a bag of old clothes."

"We get along with that part of the duty pretty well; but *before* a man is dead, the parson is of opinion that he belongs altogether to the doctor."

"I'd bet a hundred guineas, Magrath has had some influence over him, in this matter—give the Blenheim a wider berth, Sir Wycherly, I wish to see how she looks aloft,"—he's a d——d fellow, that Magrath,"—no one swore in Sir Gervaise's boat but himself, when the vice-admiral's flag was flying in her bows;—"and he's just the sort of man to put such a notion into the chaplain's head."

"Why, there, I believe you're more than half right, Sir Gervaise; I overheard a conversation between them one dark night, when they were propping the mizzen-mast under the break of the poop, and the surgeon *did* maintain a theory very like that you mention, sir."

"Ah!—he did, did he? It's just like the Scotch rogue, who wanted to persuade me that your poor uncle, Sir Wycherly, ought not to have been blooded, in as clear a case of apoplexy as ever was met with."

"Well, I didn't think he could have carried his impudence as far as that," observed Greenly, whose medical knowledge was about on a par with that of Sir Gervaise. "I didn't think even a doctor would dare to hold such a doctrine! As for the chaplain, to him he laid down the principle that religion and medicine never worked well together. He said religion was an 'alterative,' and would neutralize a salt as quick as fire."

"He's a great vagabond, that Magrath, when he gets hold of a young hand, sir; and I wish with all my heart the Pretender had him, with two or three pounds of his favourite medicines with him—I think, between the two, England might reap some advantage, Greenly.—Now, to my notion, Wychecombe, the Blenheim would make better weather, if her masts were shortened at least two feet."

"Perhaps she might, Sir Gervaise; but would she be as certain a ship, in coming into action in light winds and at critical moments?"

"Umph! It's time for us old fellows to look about us, Greenly, when the boys begin to reason on a line of battle! Don't blush, Wychecombe; don't blush. Your remark was sensible, and shows reflection. No country can ever have a powerful marine, or, one likely to produce much influence in her wars, that does not pay rigid attention to the tactics of fleets. Your frigate actions and sailing of single ships, are well enough as drill; but the great practice must be in squadron. Ten heavy ships, in good *fleet* discipline, and kept at sea, will do more than a hundred single cruisers, in establishing and maintaining discipline; and it is only by using vessels *together*, that we find out what both ships and men can do. Now, we owe the success of this day, to our practice of sailing in close order, and in knowing how to keep our stations; else would six ships never have been able to carry away the palm of victory from twelve—palm!—Ay, that's the very word. Greenly, I was trying to think of this morning. Daly's paddy should have had a palm-branch in its hand, as an emblem of victory."

CHAPTER XXVI.

"He that has sailed upon the dark-blue sea,
Has viewed at times, I ween, a full fair sight;
When the fresh breeze is fair as breeze may be,
The white sail set, the gallant frigate tight;
Mast, spires and strand, retiring to the sight,
The glorious main expanding o'er the bow,
The convoy spread like wild swans in their flight,
The dullest sailer waring bravely now,
So gaily curl the waves before each dashing prow."

BYRON.

As Sir Gervaise Oakes' active mind was liable to such sudden mutations of thought as that described in the close of the last chapter, Greenly neither smiled, nor dwelt on the subject at all; he simply pointed out to his superior the fact, that they were now abreast of the Thunderer, and desired to know whether it was his pleasure to proceed any further.

"To the Carnatic, Greenly, if Sir Wycherly will have the goodness to shape his course thither. I have a word to say to my friend Parker, before we sleep to-night. Give us room, however, to look at Morganic's fancies, for I never pass his ship without learning something new. Lord Morganic's vessel is a good school for us old fellows to attend—hey! Greenly?"

"The Achilles is certainly a model vessel in some respects, Sir Gervaise, though I flatter myself the Plantagenets have no great occasion to imitate her, in order to gain a character."

"*You* imitate Morganic in order to know how to keep a ship in order!—Poh! let Morganic come to school to *you*. Yet the fellow is not bashful in battle neither; keeps his station well, and makes himself both heard and felt. Ah! there he is, flourishing his hat on the poop, and wondering what the deuce Sir Jarvy's after, now! Sheer in, Wychecombe, and let us hear what he has to say."

"Good evening, Sir Gervaise," called out the earl, as usual taking the *initiative* in the discourse; "I was in hopes when I saw your flag in the boat, that you were going to do me the favour to open a bottle of claret, and to taste some fruit, I have still standing on the table."

"I thank you, my lord, but business before pleasure. We have not been idle to-day, though to-morrow shall be still more busy. How does the Achilles steer; now her foremast is in its place?"

"Yaws like a fellow with his grog aboard, Sir Gervaise, on my honour! We shall never do any thing with her, until you consent to let us stay her spars, in our own fashion. Do you intend to send me Daly back, or am I to play first lieutenant myself, admiral?"

"Daly's shipped for the cruise, and you must do as well as you can without him. If you find yourself without a second astern, in the course of the night, do not fancy she has gone to the bottom. Keep good look-outs, and pay attention to signals."

As Sir Gervaise waved his hand, the young noble did not venture to reply, much less to ask a question, though there was not a little speculation on the poop of the Achilles, concerning the meaning of his words. The boat moved on, and five minutes later Sir Gervaise was on the quarter-deck of the Carnatic.

Parker received the commander-in-chief, hat in hand, with a solicitude and anxiety that were constitutional, perhaps, and which no consciousness of deserving could entirely appease. Habit, however, had its share in it, since, accustomed to defer to rank from boyhood, and the architect of his own "little fortune," he had ever attached more importance to the commendation of his superior, than was usual with those who had other props to lean on than their own services. As soon as the honours of the quarter-deck had been duly paid—for these Sir Gervaise never neglected himself, nor allowed others to neglect—the vice-admiral intimated to Captain Parker a desire to see him in his cabin, requesting Greenly and Wycherly to accompany them below.

"Upon my word, Parker," commenced Sir Gervaise, looking around him at the air of singular domestic comfort that the after-cabin of the ship presented, "you have the knack of taking a house to sea with you, that no other captain of the fleet possesses! No finery, no Morganics, but a plain, wholesome, domestic look, that might make a man believe he was in his father's house. I would give a thousand pounds if my vagabonds could give the cabin of the Plantagenet such a Bowldero look, now!"

"Less than a hundred, sir, have done the little you see here. Mrs. Parker makes it a point to look to those matters, herself, and in that lies the whole secret, perhaps. A good wife is a great blessing, Sir Gervaise, though you have never been able to persuade yourself into the notion, I believe."

"I hardly think, Parker, the wife can do it all. Now there's Stowel, Bluewater's captain, he is married as well as yourself—nay, by George, I've heard the old fellow say he had as much wife as any man in his majesty's service—but *his* cabin looks like a cobbler's barn, and his state-room like a soldier's bunk! When we were lieutenants together in the Eurydice, Parker, your state-room had just the same air of comfort about it that this cabin has at this instant.

No—no—it's in the grain, man, or it would never show itself, in all times and places."

"You forget, Sir Gervaise, that when I had the honour to be your messmate in the Eurydice, I was a married man."

"I beg your pardon, my old friend; so you were, indeed! Why, that was a confounded long time ago, hey! Parker?"

"It was, truly, sir; but I was poor, and could not afford the extravagances of a single life. *I* married for the sake of economy, Admiral Oakes."

"And love—" answered Sir Gervaise, laughing. "I'll warrant you, Greenly, that he persuaded Mrs. Parker into that notion, whether true or not. I'll warrant you, he didn't tell *her* he married for so sneaking a thing as economy! I should like to see your state-room now, Parker."

"Nothing easier, Sir Gervaise," answered the captain, rising and opening the door. "Here it is, air, though little worthy the attention of the owner of Bowldero."

"A notable place, truly!—and with a housewife-look about it that must certainly remind you of Mrs. Parker—unless, indeed, that picture at the foot of your cot puts other notions into your head! What young hussy have you got there, my old Eurydice?—Hey! Parker?"

"That is a picture of my faithful wife, Sir Gervaise; a proper companion, I hope, of my cruise?"

"Hey! What, that young thing your wife, Parker! How the d—l came she to have you?"

"Ah, Sir Gervaise, she is a young thing no longer, but is well turned towards sixty. The picture was taken when she was a bride, and is all the dearer to me, now that I know the original has shared my fortunes so long. I never look at it, without remembering, with gratitude, how much she thinks of me in our cruises, and how often she prays for our success. *You* are not forgotten, either, sir, in her prayers."

"I!" exclaimed the vice-admiral, quite touched at the earnest simplicity of the other. "D'ye hear that, Greenly? I'll engage, now, this lady is a good woman—a really excellent creature—just such another as my poor sainted mother was, and a blessing to all around her! Give me your hand, Parker; and when you write next to your wife, tell her from me, God bless her; and say all you think a man ought to say on such an occasion. And now to business. Let us seat ourselves in this snug domestic-looking cabin of yours, and talk our matters over."

The two captains and Wycherly followed the vice-admiral into the after-cabin, where the latter seated himself on a small sofa, while the others took chairs, in respectful attitudes near him, no familiarity or jocularity on the part of a naval superior ever lessening the distance between him and those who *hold subordinate commissions*—a fact that legislators would do well to remember, when graduating rank in a service. As soon as all were placed, Sir Gervaise opened his mind.

"I have a delicate piece of duty, Captain Parker," he commenced, "which I wish entrusted to yourself. You must know that we handled the ship which escaped us this morning by running down into her own line, pretty roughly, in every respect; besides cutting two of her masts out of her. This ship, as you may have seen, has got up jury-masts, already; but they are spars that can only be intended to carry her into port. Monsieur de Vervillin is not the man I take him to be, if he intends to leave the quarrel between us where it is. Still he cannot keep that crippled ship in his fleet, any more than we can keep our prize, and I make no doubt he will send her off to Cherbourg as soon as it is dark; most probably accompanied by one of his corvettes; or perhaps by a frigate."

"Yes, Sir Gervaise," returned Parker, thoughtfully, as soon as his superior ceased to speak; "what you predict, is quite likely to happen."

"It *must* happen, Parker, the wind blowing directly for his haven. Now, you may easily imagine what I want of the Carnatic."

"I suppose I understand you, sir;—and yet, if I might presume to express a wish—"

"Speak out, old boy—you're talking to a friend. I have chosen you to serve you, both as one I like, and as the oldest captain in the fleet. Whoever catches that ship will hear more of it."

"Very true, sir; but are we not likely to have more work, here? and would it be altogether prudent to send so fine a ship as the Carnatic away, when the enemy will count ten to six, even if she remain?"

"All this has been thought of; and I suppose your own feeling has been anticipated. You think it will be more honourable to your vessel, to keep her place in the line, than to take a ship already half beaten."

"That's it, indeed, Sir Gervaise. I do confess some such thoughts were crossing my mind."

"Then see how easy it is to rose them out of it. I cannot fight the French, in this moderate weather, without a reinforcement. When the rear joins, we shall be just ten to ten, without you, and with you, should be eleven to ten. Now, I confess, I don't wish the least odds, and shall send away somebody;

especially when I feel certain a noble two-decked ship will be the reward. If a frigate accompany the crippled fellow, you'll have your hands full, and a very fair fight; and should you get either, it will be a handsome thing. What say you *now*, Parker?"

"I begin to think better of the plan, Sir Gervaise, and am grateful for the selection. I wish, however, I knew your own precise wishes—I've always found it safe to follow them, sir."

"Here they are, then. Get four or five sets of the sharpest eyes you have, and send them aloft to keep a steady look on your chap, while there is light enough to be certain of him. In a little while, they'll be able to recognise him in the dark; and by keeping your night-glasses well levelled, he can scarcely slip off, without your missing him. The moment he is gone, ware short round, and make the best of your way for Cape la Hogue, or Alderney; you will go three feet to his two, and, my life on it, by day-light you'll have him to windward of you, and then you'll be certain of him. Wait for no signals from me, but be off, as soon as it is dark. When your work is done, make the best of your way to the nearest English port, and clap a Scotchman on your shoulder to keep the king's sword from chafing it. They thought me fit for knighthood at three-and-twenty, and the deuce is in it, Parker, if you are not worthy of it at three-and-sixty!"

"Ah! Sir Gervaise, every thing you undertook succeeded! You never yet failed in any expedition."

"That has come from attempting much. My *plans* have often failed; but as something good has generally followed from them, I have the credit of designing to do, exactly what I've done."

Then followed a long, detailed discourse, on the subject before them, in which Greenly joined; the latter making several useful suggestions to the veteran commander of the Carnatic. After passing quite an hour in the cabin of Parker, Sir Gervaise took his leave and re-entered his barge. It was now so dark that small objects could not be distinguished a hundred yards, and the piles of ships, as the boat glided past them, resembled black hillocks, with clouds floating among their tree-like and waving spars. No captain presumed to hail the commander-in-chief, as he rowed down the line, again, with the exception of the peer of the realm. He indeed had always something to say; and, as he had been conjecturing what could induce the vice-admiral to pay so long a visit to the Carnatic, he could not refrain from uttering as much aloud, when he heard the measured stroke of the oars from the returning barge.

"We shall all be jealous of this compliment to Captain Parker, Sir Gervaise," he called out, "unless your favours are occasionally extended to some of us less worthy ones."

"Ay—ay—Morganic, you'll be remembered in proper time. In the mean while, keep your people's eyes open, so as not to lose sight of the French. We shall have something to say to them in the morning."

"Spare us a night-action, if possible, Sir Gervaise! I do detest fighting when sleepy; and I like to see my enemy, too. As much as you please in the day-time; but a quiet night, I do beseech you, sir."

"I'll warrant you, now, if the opera, or Ranelagh, or a drum, or a masquerade, were inviting you, Morganic, you'd think but little of your pillow!" answered Sir Gervaise, drily; "whatever you do yourself, my lord, don't let the Achilles get asleep on duty; I may have need of her to-morrow. Give way, Wychecombe, give way, and let us get home again."

In fifteen minutes from that instant, Sir Gervaise was once more on the poop of the Plantagenet, and the barge in its place on deck. Greenly was attending to the duties of his ship, and Bunting stood in readiness to circulate such orders as it might suit the commander-in-chief to give.

It was now nine o'clock, and it was not easy to distinguish objects on the ocean, even as large as a ship, at the distance of half a league. By the aid of the glasses, however, a vigilant look-out was kept on the French vessels, which, by this time, were quite two leagues distant, drawing more ahead. It was necessary to fill away, in order to close with them, and a night-signal was made to that effect. The whole British line braced forward their main-yards, as it might be, by a common impulse, and had there been one there of sufficiently acute senses, he might have heard all six of the main-top-sails flapping at the same instant. As a matter of course the vessels started ahead, and, the order being to follow the vice-admiral in a close line ahead, when the Plantagenet edged off, so as to bring the wind abeam, each vessel did the same, in succession, or as soon as in the commander-in-chief's wake, as if guided by instinct. About ten minutes later, the Carnatic, to the surprise of those who witnessed the man[oe]uvre in the Achilles, wore short round, and set studding-sails on her starboard side, steering large. The darkest portion of the horizon being that which lay to the eastward, or, in the direction of the continent, in twenty minutes the pyramid of her shadowy outline was swallowed in the gloom. All this time, la Victoire, with the Druid leading and towing, kept upon a bowline; and an hour later, when Sir Gervaise found himself abeam of the French line again, and half a league to windward of it, no traces were to be seen of the three ships last mentioned.

"So far, all goes well, gentlemen," observed the vice-admiral to the group around him on the poop; "and we will now try to count the enemy, to make certain *he*, too, has no stragglers out to pick up waifs. Greenly, try that glass; it is set for the night, and your eyes are the best we have. Be particular in looking for the fellow under jury-masts."

"I make out but ten ships in the line, Sir Gervaise," answered the captain, after a long examination; "of course the crippled ship must have gone to leeward. Of *her*, certainly, I can find no traces."

"You will oblige me, Sir Wycherly, by seeing what *you* can make out, in the same way."

After a still longer examination than that of the captain, Wycherly made the same report, adding that he thought he also missed the frigate that had been nearest le Foudroyant, repeating her signals throughout the day. This circumstance gratified Sir Gervaise, as he was pleased to find his prognostics came true, and he was not sorry to be rid of one of the enemy's light cruisers; a species of vessel that often proved embarrassing, after a decided affair, even to the conqueror.

"I think, Sir Gervaise," Wycherly modestly added, "that the French have boarded their tacks, and are pressing up to windward to near us. Did it not appear so to you, Captain Greenly?"

"Not at all. If they carry courses, the sails have been set within the last five minutes—ha! Sir Gervaise, that is an indication of a busy night!"

As he spoke. Greenly pointed to the place where the French admiral was known to be, where at that instant appeared a double row of lights; proving that the batteries had their lanterns lit, and showing a disposition to engage. In less than a minute the whole French line was to be traced along the sea, by the double rows of illumination, the light resembling that which is seen through the window of a room that has a bright fire, rather than one in which lamps or candles are actually visible. As this was just the species of engagement in which the English had much to risk, and little to gain, Sir Gervaise immediately gave orders to brace forward the yards, to board fore-and-main tacks, and to set top-gallant-sails. As a matter of course, the ships astern made sail in the same manner, and hauled up on taut bowlines, following the admiral.

"This is not our play," coolly remarked Sir Gervaise; "a crippled ship would drop directly into their arms and as for any success at long-shot, in a two-to-one fight, it is not to be looked for. No—no—Monsieur de Vervillin, show us your teeth if you will, and a pretty sight it is, but you do not draw a shot from me. I hope the order to show no lights is duly attended to."

"I do not think there is a light visible from any ship in the fleet, Sir Gervaise," answered Bunting, "though we are so near, there can be no great difficulty in telling where we are."

"All but the Carnatic and the prize, Bunting. The more fuss they make with us, the less will they think of them."

It is probable the French admiral had been deceived by the near approach of his enemy, for whose prowess he had a profound respect. He had made his preparations in expectation of an attack, but he did not open his fire, although heavy shot would certainly have told with effect. Indisposed to the uncertainty of a night-action, he declined bringing it on, and the lights disappeared from his ports an hour later; at that time the English ships, by carrying sail harder than was usual in so stiff a breeze, found themselves out of gun-shot, on the weather-bow of their enemies. Then, and not till then, did Sir Gervaise reduce his canvass, having, by means of his glasses, first ascertained that the French had again hauled up their courses, and were moving along at a very easy rate of sailing.

It was now near midnight, and Sir Gervaise prepared to go below. Previously to quitting the deck, however, he gave very explicit orders to Greenly, who transmitted them to the first lieutenant, that officer or the captain intending to be on the look-out through the night; the movements of the whole squadron being so dependent on those of the flag ship. The vice-admiral then retired, and went coolly to bed. He was not a man to lose his rest, because an enemy was just out of gun-shot. Accustomed to be man[oe]uvring in front of hostile fleets, the situation had lost its novelty, and he had so much confidence in the practice of his captains, that he well knew nothing could occur so long as his orders were obeyed; to doubt the latter would have been heresy in his eyes. In professional nonchalance, no man exceeded our vice-admiral. Blow high, or blow low, it never disturbed the economy of his cabin-life, beyond what unavoidably was connected with the comfort of his ship; nor did any prospect of battle cause a meal to vary a minute in time or a particle in form, until the bulk-heads were actually knocked down, and the batteries were cleared for action. Although excitable in trifles, and sometimes a little irritable, Sir Gervaise, in the way of his profession, was a great man on great occasions. His temperament was sanguine, and his spirit both decided and bold; and, in common with all such men who see the truth at all, when he did see it, he saw it so clearly, as to throw all the doubts that beset minds of a less masculine order into the shade. On the present occasion, he was sure nothing could well occur to disturb his rest; and he took it with the composure of one on *terra-firma*, and in the security of peace. Unlike those who are unaccustomed to scenes of excitement, he quietly undressed himself, and his head was no sooner on its pillow, than he fell into a profound sleep.

It would have been a curious subject of observation to an inexperienced person, to note the manner in which the two fleets man[oe]uvred throughout that night. After several hours of ineffectual efforts to bring their enemies fairly within reach of their guns, after the moon had risen, the French gave the matter up for a time, shortening sail while most of their superior officers caught a little rest.

The sun was just rising, as Galleygo laid his hand on the shoulder of the vice-admiral, agreeably to orders given the previous night. The touch sufficed: Sir Gervaise being wide awake in an instant. "Well," he said, rising to a sitting attitude, and putting the question which first occurs to a seaman, "how's the weather?"

"A good top-gallant breeze, Sir Jarvy, and just what's this ship's play. If you'd only let her out, and on them Johnny Crapauds, she'd be down among 'em, in half an hour, like a hawk upon a chicken. I ought to report to your honour, that the last chicken will be dished for breakfast unless we gives an order to the gun-room steward to turn us over some of his birds, as pay for what the pigs eat; which were real capons."

"Why, you pirate, you would not have me commit a robbery, on the high seas, would ye?"

"What robbery would it be to order the gun-room to *sell* us some poultry. Lord! Sir Jarvy, I'm as far from wishing to take a thing without an order, as the gunner's yeoman; but, let Mr. Atwood put it in black and white."

"Tush!" interrupted the master. "How did the French bear from us, when you were last on deck?"

"Why, there they is, Sir Jarvy," answered Galleygo, drawing the curtain from before the state-room window, and allowing the vice-admiral to see the rear of the French line for himself, by turning half round; "and just where we wants 'em. Their leading ship a little abaft our lee-beam, distant one league. That's what I calls satisfactory, now."

"Ay, that *is* a good position, Master Galleygo. Was the prize in sight, or were you too chicken-headed to look."

"I chicken-headed! Well, Sir Jarvy, of all characters and descriptions of *me*, that your honour has seen fit to put abroad, this is the most unjustest; chickens being a food I never thinks on, off soundings. Pig-headed you might in reason call me, Sir Jarvy; for I *do* looks arter the pigs, which is the only real stand-by in a ship; but I never dreams of a chicken, except for *your* happetite. When they was eight on 'em—"

"Was the prize in sight?" demanded Sir Gervaise, a little sharply.

"No, Sir Jarvy; she had disappeared, and the Druid with her. But this isn't all, sir; for they does say, some'at has befallen the Carnatic, she having gone out of our line, like a binnacle-lamp at eight bells."

"Ay, *she* is not visible, either."

"Not so much as a hen-coop, Sir Jarvy! We all wonders what has become of Captain Parker; no sign of him or of his ship is to be found on the briny ocean. The young gentlemen of the watch laugh, and say she must have gone up in a waterspout, but they laughs so much at misfortins, generally, that I never minds 'em."

"Have you had a good look-out at the ocean, this morning, Master Galleygo," asked Sir Gervaise, drawing his head out of a basin of water, for, by this time, he was half-dressed, and making his preparations for the razor. "You used to have an eye for a chase, when we were in a frigate, and ought to be able to tell me if Bluewater is in sight."

"Admiral Blue!—Well, Sir Jarvy, it *is* remarkable, but I had just rubbed his division out of my log, and forgotten all about it. There *was* a handful of craft, or so, off here to the nor'ard, at day-light, but I never thought it was Admiral Blue, it being more nat'ral to suppose him in his place, as usual, in the rear of our own line. Let me see, Sir Jarvy, how many ships has we absent under Admiral Blue?"

"Why, the five two-deckers of his own division, to be sure, besides the Ranger and the Gnat. Seven sail in all."

"Yes, that's just it! Well, your honour, there *was* five sail to be seen, out here to the nor'ard, as I told you, and, sure enough, it may have been Admiral Blue, with all his craft."

By this time, Sir Gervaise had his face covered with lather, but he forgot the circumstance in a moment. As the wind was at the north-west, and the Plantagenet was on the larboard tack, looking in the direction of the Bill of Portland, though much too far to the southward to allow the land to be seen, his own larboard quarter-gallery window commanded a good view of the whole horizon to windward. Crossing over from the starboard state-room, which he occupied *ex-officio*, he opened the window in question, and took a look for himself. There, sure enough, was visible a squadron of five ships, in close order, edging leisurely down on the two lines, under their top-sails, and just near enough to allow it to be ascertained that their courses were not set. This sight produced a sudden change in all the vice-admiral's movements. The business of the toilet was resumed in haste, and the beard was mowed with a slashing hand, that might have been hazardous in the motion of a ship, but for the long experience of a sailor. This important part of the operation was scarcely through, when Locker announced the presence of Captain Greenly in the main cabin.

"What now, Greenly?—What now?" called out the vice-admiral, puffing as he withdrew his head, again, from the basin—"What now, Greenly? Any news from Bluewater?"

"I am happy to tell you, Sir Gervaise, he has been in sight more than an hour, and is closing with us, though shyly and slowly. I would not let you be called, as all was right, and I knew sleep was necessary to a clear head."

"You have done quite right, Greenly; God willing, I intend this to be a busy day! The French must see our rear division?"

"Beyond a doubt, sir, but they show no signs of making off. M. de Vervillin will fight, I feel certain; though the experience of yesterday may render him a little shy as to the mode."

"And his crippled ship?—Old Parker's friend—I take it *she* is not visible."

"You were quite right in your conjecture, Sir Gervaise; the crippled ship is off, as is one of the frigates, no doubt to see her in. Blewet, too, has gone well to windward of the French, though he can fetch into no anchorage short of Portsmouth, if this breeze stand."

"Any haven will do. Our little success will animate the king's party, and give it more *éclat*, perhaps, than it really merits. Let there be no delay with the breakfast this morning, Greenly; it will be a busy day."

"Ay—ay, sir," answered the captain in the sailor's usual manner; "*that* has been seen to already, as I have expected as much. Admiral Bluewater keeps his ships in most beautiful order, sir! I do not think the Cæsar, which leads, is two cable's-length from the Dublin, the sternmost vessel. He is driving four-in-hand, with a tight rein, too, depend on it, sir."

At this instant, Sir Gervaise came out of his state-room, his coat in his hand, and with a countenance that was thoughtful. He finished dressing with an abstracted air, and would not have known the last garment was on, had not Galleygo given a violent pull on its skirts, in order to smooth the cloth about the shoulders.

"It is odd, that Bluewater should come down nearly before the wind, in a line ahead, and not in a line abreast!" Sir Gervaise rejoined, as his steward did this office for him.

"Let Admiral Blue alone, for doing what's right," put in Galleygo, in his usual confident and sell-possessed manner. "By keeping his ships astern of hisself, he can tell where to find 'em, and we understands from experience, if Admiral Blue knows where to find a ship, he knows how to use her."

Instead of rebuking this interference, which went a little further than common, Greenly was surprised to see the vice-admiral look his steward intently in the face, as if the man had expressed some shrewd and comprehensive truth. Then turning to his captain, Sir Gervaise intimated an intention of going on deck to survey the state of things with his own eyes.

CHAPTER XXVII.

"*Thou* shouldst have died, O high-soul'd chief!
In those bright days of glory fled,
When triumph so prevailed o'er grief,
We scarce would mourn the dead."

MRS. HEMANS.

The eventful day opened with most of the glories of a summer's morning. The wind alone prevented it from being one of the finest sun-risings of July. That continued fresh, at north-west, and, consequently, cool for the season. The seas of the south-west gale had entirely subsided, and were already succeeded by the regular but comparatively trilling swell of the new breeze. For large ships, it might be called smooth water; though the Driver and Active showed by their pitching and unsteadiness, and even the two-deckers, by their waving masts, that the unquiet ocean was yet in motion. The wind seemed likely to stand, and was what seamen would be apt to call a good six-knot breeze.

To leeward, still distant about a league, lay the French vessels, drawn up in beautiful array, and in an order so close, and a line so regular, as to induce the belief that M. de Vervillin had made his dispositions to receive the expected attack, in his present position. All his main-top-sails lay flat aback; the top-gallant-sails were flying loose, but with buntlings and clew-lines hauled up; the jibs were fluttering to leeward of their booms, and the courses were hanging in festoons beneath their yards. This was gallant fighting-canvass, and it excited the admiration of even his enemies. To increase this feeling, just as Sir Gervaise's foot reached the poop, the whole French line displayed their ensigns, and *le Foudroyant* fired a gun to windward.

"Hey! Greenly?" exclaimed the English commander-in-chief; "this is a manly defiance, and coming from M. de Vervillin, it means something! He wishes to take the day for it; though, as I think half that time will answer, we will wash up the cups before we go at it. Make the signals, Bunting, for the ships to heave-to, and then to get their breakfasts, as fast as possible. Steady breeze—steady breeze, Greenly, and all we want!"

Five minutes later, while Sir Gervaise was running his eye over the signal-book, the Plantagenet's calls were piping the people to their morning meal, at least an hour earlier than common; the people repaired to their messes, with a sort of stern joy; every man in the ship understanding the reason of a summons so unusual. The calls of the vessels astern were heard soon after, and one of the officers who was watching the enemy with a glass, reported that he thought the French were breakfasting, also. Orders being given to the officers to employ the next half hour in the same manner, nearly everybody was soon engaged in eating; few thinking that the meal might probably be their last. Sir Gervaise felt a concern, which he succeeded in concealing, however, at the circumstance that the ships to windward made no more sail; though he refrained from signalling the rear-admiral to that effect, from tenderness to his friend, and a vague apprehension of what might be the consequences. While the crews were eating, he stood gazing, thoughtfully, at the noble spectacle the enemy offered, to leeward, occasionally turning wistful glances at the division that was constantly drawing nearer to windward. At length Greenly, himself, reported that the Plantagenet had "turned the hands-to," again. At this intelligence, Sir Gervaise started, as from a reverie, smiled, and spoke. We will here remark, that now, as on the previous day, all the natural excitability of manner had disappeared from the commander-in-chief, and he was quiet, and exceedingly gentle in his deportment. This, all who knew him, understood to denote a serious determination to engage.

"I have desired Galleygo to set my little table, half an hour hence, in the after-cabin, Greenly, and you will share the meal with me. Sir Wycherly will be of our party, and I hope it will not be the last time we may meet at the same board. It is necessary every thing should be in fighting-order to-day!"

"So I understand it, Sir Gervaise. We are ready to begin, as soon as the order shall be received."

"Wait one moment until Bunting comes up from his breakfast. Ah! here he is, and we are quite ready for him, having bent-on the signal in his absence. Show the order, Bunting; for the day advances."

The little flags were fluttering at the main-top-gallant-mast-head of the Plantagenet in less than one minute, and in another it was repeated by the Chloe, Driver, and Active, all of which were lying-to, a quarter of a mile to windward, charged in particular with this, among other duties. So well was this signal known, that not a book in the fleet was consulted, but all the ships answered, the instant the flags could be seen and understood. Then the shrill whistles were heard along the line, calling "All hands" to "clear ship for action, ahoy!"

No sooner was this order given in the Plantagenet, than the ship became a scene of active but orderly exertion. The top-men were on the yards, stoppering, swinging the yards in chains, and lashing, in order to prevent shot from doing more injury than was unavoidable; bulwarks were knocked down; mess-chest, bags, and all other domestic appliances, disappeared *below*,[3] and the decks were cleared of every thing which could be removed, and which would not be necessary in an engagement. Fully a quarter of an hour was thus occupied, for there was no haste, and as it was no moment of mere parade, it was necessary that the work should be effectually done. The officers forbade haste, and nothing important was reported as effected, that some one in authority did not examine with his own eyes, to see that no proper care had been neglected. Then Mr. Bury, the first lieutenant, went on the main-yard, in person, to look at the manner in which it had been slung, while he sent the boatswain up forward, on the same errand. These were unusual precautions, but the word had passed through the ship "that Sir Jarvy was in earnest;" and whenever it was known that "Sir Jarvy" was in such a humour, every one understood that the day's work was to be hard, if not long.

"Our breakfast is ready, Sir Jarvy," reported Galleygo, "and as the decks is all clear, the b'ys can make a clean run of it from the coppers. I only wants to know when to serve it, your honour."

"Serve it now, my good fellow. Tell the Bowlderos to be nimble, and expect us below. Come, Greenly—come, Wychecombe—we are the last to eat—let us not be the last at our stations."

"Ship's clear, sir," reported Bury to his captain, as the three reached the quarter-deck, on their way to the cabin.

"Very well, Bury; when the fleet is signalled to go to quarters, we will obey with the rest."

As this was said, Greenly looked at the vice-admiral to catch his wishes. But Sir Gervaise had no intention of fatiguing his people unnecessarily. He had left his private orders with Bunting, and he passed down without an answer or a glance. The arrangements in the after-cabin were as snug and as comfortable as if the breakfast-table had been set in a private house, and the trio took their seats and commenced operations with hearty good will. The vice-admiral ordered the doors thrown open, and as the port-lids were up, from the place where he sat he could command glimpses, both to leeward and to windward, that included a view of the enemy, as well as one of his own expected reinforcements. The Bowlderos were in full livery, and more active and attentive than usual even. Their station in battle—for no man on board a vessel of war is an "*idler*" in a combat—was on the poop, as musketeers, near the person of their master, whose colours they wore, under the ensign of their prince, like vassals of an ancient baron. Notwithstanding the crisis of the morning, however, these men performed their customary functions with the precision and method of English menials, omitting no luxury or usage of the table. On a sofa behind the table, was spread the full dress-coat of a vice-admiral, then a neat but plain uniform, without either lace or epaulettes, but decorated with a rich star in brilliants, the emblem of the order of the Bath. This coat Sir Gervaise always wore in battle, unless the weather rendered a "storm-uniform," as he used to term a plainer attire, necessary.

The breakfast passed off pleasantly, the gentlemen eating as if no momentous events were near. Just at its close, however, Sir Gervaise leaned forward, and looking through one of the weather-ports of the main-cabin, an expression of pleasure illuminated his countenance, as he said—

"Ah! there go Bluewater's signals, at last!—a certain proof that he is about to put himself in communication with us."

"I have been a good deal surprised, sir," observed Greenly, a little drily, though with great respect of manner, "that you have not ordered the rear-admiral to make more sail. He is jogging along like a heavy wagon, and yet I hardly think he can mistake these five ships for Frenchmen!"

"He is never in a hurry, and no doubt wishes to let *his* crews breakfast, before he closes. I'll warrant ye, now, gentlemen, that his ships are at this moment all as clear as a church five minutes after the blessing has been pronounced."

"It will not be one of our Virginian churches, then, Sir Gervaise," observed Wycherly, smiling; "*they* serve for an exchange, to give and receive news in, after the service is over."

"Ay, that's the old rule—first pray, and then gossip. Well, Bunting, what does the rear-admiral say?"

"Upon my word, Sir Gervaise, I can make nothing of the signal, though it is easy enough to make out the flags," answered the puzzled signal-officer. "Will you have the goodness to look at the book yourself, sir. The number is one hundred and forty."

"One hundred and forty! Why, that must have something to do with anchoring!—ay, here it is. 'Anchor, I cannot, having lost my cables.' Who the devil asked him to anchor?"

"That's just it, sir. The signal-officer on board the Cæsar must have made some mistake in his flags; for, though the distance is considerable, our glasses are good enough to read them."

"Perhaps Admiral Bluewater has set the private, personal, telegraph at work, sir," quietly observed Greenly.

The commander-in-chief actually changed colour at this suggestion. His face, at first, flushed to crimson; then it became pale, like the countenance of one who suffered under acute bodily pain. Wycherly observed this, and respectfully inquired if Sir Gervaise were ill.

"I thank you, young sir," answered the vice-admiral, smiling painfully; "it is over. I believe I shall have to go into dock, and let Magrath look at some of my old hurts, which *are* sometimes troublesome. Mr. Bunting, do me the favour to go on deck, and ascertain, by a careful examination, if a short red pennant be not set some ten or twelve feet above the uppermost flag. Now, Greenly, we will take the other cup of tea, for there is plenty of leisure."

Two or three brooding minutes followed. Then Bunting returned to say the pennant *was* there, a fact he had quite overlooked in his former observations, confounding the narrow flag in question with the regular pennant of the king. This short red pennant denoted that the communication was verbal, according to a method invented by Bluewater himself, and by means of which, using the ordinary numbers, he was enabled to communicate with his friend, without any of the captains, or, indeed, without Sir Gervaise's own signal-officer's knowing what was said. In a word, without having recourse to any new flags, but, by simply giving new numbers to the old ones, and referring to a prepared dictionary, it was possible to hold a conversation in sentences, that should be a secret to all but themselves. Sir Gervaise took down the number of the signal that was flying, and directed Bunting to show the answering flag, with a similar pennant over it, and to continue this operation so long as the rear-admiral might make his signals. The numbers were to be sent below as fast as received. As soon as Bunting disappeared, the vice-admiral unlocked a secretary, the key of which was never out of his own possession, took from it a small dictionary, and laid it by his plate. All this time the breakfast proceeded, signals of this nature frequently occurring between the two admirals. In the course of the next ten minutes, a quarter-master brought below a succession of numbers written on small pieces of paper; after which Bunting appeared himself to say that the Cæsar had stopped signalling.

Sir Gervaise now looked out each word by its proper number, and wrote it down with his pencil as he proceeded, until the whole read—"God sake—make no signal. Engage not." No sooner was the communication understood, than the paper was torn into minute fragments, the book replaced, and the vice-admiral, turning with a calm determined countenance to Greenly, ordered him to beat to quarters as soon as Bunting could show a signal to the fleet to the same effect. On this hint, all but the vice-admiral went on deck, and the Bowlderos instantly set about removing the table and all the other appliances. Finding himself annoyed by the movements of the servants, Sir Gervaise walked out into the great cabin, which, regardless of its present condition, he began to pace as was his wont when lost in thought. The bulk-heads being down, and the furniture removed, this was in truth walking in sight of the crew. All who happened to be on the main-deck could see what passed, though no one presumed to enter a spot that was tabooed to vulgar feet, even when thus exposed. The aspect and manner of "Sir Jarvy," however, were not overlooked, and the men prognosticated a serious time.

Such was the state of things, when the drums beat to quarters, throughout the whole line. At the first tap, the great cabin sunk to the level of an ordinary battery; the seamen of two guns, with the proper officers, entering within the sacred limits, and coolly setting about clearing their pieces, and making the other preparations necessary for an action. All this time Sir Gervaise continued pacing what would have been the centre of his own cabin had the bulk-heads stood, the grim-looking sailors avoiding him with great dexterity, and invariably touching their hats as they were compelled to glide near his person, though every thing went on as if he were not present. Sir Gervaise might have remained lost in thought much longer than he did, had not the report of a gun recalled him to a consciousness of the scene that was enacting around him.

"What's that?" suddenly demanded the vice-admiral—"Is Blue water signalling again?"

"No, Sir Gervaise," answered the fourth lieutenant, looking out of a lee port; "it is the French admiral giving us another weather-gun; as much as to ask why we don't go down. This is the second compliment of the same sort that he has paid us already to-day!"

These words were not all spoken before the vice-admiral was on the quarter-deck; in half a minute more, he was on the poop. Here he found Greenly, Wychecombe, and Bunting, all looking with interest at the beautiful line of the enemy.

"Monsieur de Vervillin is impatient to wipe off the disgrace of yesterday," observed the first, "as is apparent by the invitations he gives us to come down. I presume Admiral Bluewater will wake up at this last hint."

"By Heaven, he has hauled his wind, and is standing to the northward and eastward!" exclaimed Sir Gervaise, surprise overcoming all his discretion. "Although an extraordinary movement, at such a time, it is wonderful in what beautiful order Bluewater keeps his ships!"

All that was said was true enough. The rear-admiral's division having suddenly hauled up, in a close line ahead, each ship followed her leader as mechanically as if they moved by a common impulse. As no one in the least doubted the rear-admiral's loyalty, and his courage was of proof, it was the general opinion that this unusual man[oe]uvre had some connection with the unintelligible signals, and the young officers laughingly inquired among themselves what "Sir Jarvy was likely to do next?"

It would seem, however, that Monsieur de Vervillin suspected a repetition of some of the scenes of the preceding day; for, no sooner did he perceive that the English rear was hugging the wind, than five of his leading ships filled, and drew ahead, as if to meet that division, man[oe]uvring to double on the head of his line; while the remaining five, with the Foudroyant, still lay with their top-sails to the mast, waiting for their enemy to come down. Sir Gervaise could not stand this long. He determined, if possible, to bring Bluewater to terms, and he ordered the Plantagenet to fill. Followed by his own division, he wore immediately, and went off under easy sail, quartering, towards Monsieur de Vervillin's rear, to avoid being raked.

The quarter of an hour that succeeded was one of intense interest, and of material changes; though not a shot was fired. As soon as the Comte de Vervillin perceived that the English were disposed to come nearer, he signalled his own division to bear up, and to run off dead before the wind, under their top-sails, commencing astern; which reversed his order of sailing, and brought le Foudroyant in the rear, or nearest to the enemy. This was no sooner done, than he settled all his top-sails on the caps. There could be no mistaking this man[oe]uvre. It was a direct invitation to Sir Gervaise to come down, fairly alongside; the bearing up at once removing all risk of being raked in so doing. The English commander-in-chief was not a man to neglect such a palpable challenge; but, making a few signals to direct the mode of attack he contemplated, he set fore-sail and main-top-gallant-sail, and brought the wind directly over his own taffrail. The vessels astern followed like clock-work, and no one now doubted that the mode of attack was settled for that day.

As the French, with Monsieur de Vervillin, were still half a mile to the southward and eastward of the approaching division, of their enemy, the Comte collected all his frigates and corvettes on his starboard hand, leaving a clear approach to Sir Gervaise on his larboard beam. This hint was understood, too, and the Plantagenet steered a course that would bring her up on that side of le Foudroyant, and at the distance of about one hundred yards from the muzzles of her guns. This threatened to be close work, and unusual work in fleets, at that day; but it was the game our commander-in-chief was fond of playing, and it was one, also, that promised soonest to bring matters to a result.

These preliminaries arranged, there was yet leisure for the respective commanders to look about them. The French were still fully a mile ahead of their enemies, and as both fleets were going in the same direction, the approach of the English was so slow as to leave some twenty minutes of that solemn breathing time, which reigns in a disciplined ship, previous to the commencement of the combat. The feelings of the two commanders-in-chief, at this pregnant instant, were singularly in contradiction to each other.

The Comte de Vervillin saw that the rear division of his force, under the Comte-Amiral le Vicomte des Prez, was in the very position he desired it to be, having obtained the advantage of the wind by the English division's coming down, and by keeping its own luff. Between the two French officers there was a perfect understanding as to the course each was to take, and both now felt sanguine hopes of being able to obliterate the disgrace of the previous day, and that, too, by means very similar to those by which it had been incurred. On the other hand, Sir Gervaise was beset with doubts as to the course Bluewater might pursue. He could not, however, come to the conclusion that he would abandon him to the joint efforts of the two hostile divisions; and so long as the French rear-admiral was occupied by the English force to windward, it left to himself a clear field and no favour in the action with Monsieur de Vervillin. He knew Bluewater's generous nature too well not to feel certain his own compliance with the request not to signal his inferior would touch his heart, and give him a double chance with all his better feelings. Nevertheless, Sir Gervaise Oakes did not lead into this action without many and painful misgivings. He had lived too long in the world not to know that political prejudice was the most demoralising of all our weaknesses, veiling our private vices under the plausible concealment of the public weal, and rendering even the well-disposed insensible to the wrongs they commit to individuals, by means of the deceptive flattery of serving the community. As doubt was more painful than the certainty of his worst forebodings, however, and it was not in his nature to refuse a combat so fairly offered, he was resolved to close with the Comte at every hazard, trusting the issue to God, and his own efforts.

The Plantagenet presented an eloquent picture of order and preparation, as she drew near the French line, on this memorable occasion. Her people were all at quarters, and, as Greenly walked through her batteries, he found every gun on the starboard side loose, levelled, and ready to be fired; while the opposite merely required a turn or two of the tackles to be cast loose, the priming to be applied, and the loggerhead to follow, in order to be discharged, also. A death-like stillness reigned from the poop to the cock-pit, the older seamen occasionally glancing through their ports in order to ascertain the relative positions of the two fleets, that they might be ready for the collision. As the English got within musket-shot, the French ran their top-sails to the mast-heads, and their ships gathered fresher way through the water. Still the former moved with the greatest velocity, carrying the most sail, and impelled by the greater momentum. When near enough, however, Sir Gervaise gave the order to reduce the canvass of his own ship.

"That will do, Greenly," he said, in a mild, quiet tone. "Let run the top-gallant-halyards, and haul up the fore-sail. The way you have, will bring you fairly alongside."

The captain gave the necessary orders, and the master shortened sail accordingly. Still the Plantagenet shot ahead, and, in three or four minutes more, her bows doubled so far on le Foudroyant's quarter, as to permit a gun to bear. This was the signal for both sides, each ship opening as it might be in the same breath. The flash, the roar, and the eddying smoke followed in quick succession, and in a period of time that seemed nearly instantaneous. The crash of shot, and the shrieks of wounded mingled with the infernal din, for nature extorts painful concessions of human weaknesses, at such moments, even from the bravest and firmest. Bunting was in the act of reporting to Sir Gervaise that no signal could yet be seen from the Cæsar, in the midst of this uproar, when a small round-shot, discharged from the Frenchman's poop, passed through his body, literally driving the heart before it, leaving him dead at his commander's feet.

"I shall depend on you, Sir Wycherly, for the discharge of poor Bunting's duty, the remainder of the cruise," observed Sir Gervaise, with a smile in which courtesy and regret struggled singularly for the mastery. "Quarter-masters, lay Mr. Bunting's body a little out of the way, and cover it with those signals. They are a suitable pall for so brave a man!"

Just as this occurred, the Warspite came clear of the Plantagenet, on her outside, according to orders, and she opened with her forward guns, taking the second ship in the French line for her target. In two minutes more these vessels also were furiously engaged in the hot strife. In this manner, ship after ship passed on the outside of the Plantagenet, and sheered into her berth ahead of her who had just been her own leader, until the Achilles, Lord Morganic, the last of the five, lay fairly side by side with le Conquereur, the vessel now at the head of the French line. That the reader may understand the incidents more readily, we will give the opposing lines in the precise form in which they lay, viz.

Plantagenet		le Foudroyant
Warspite		le Téméraire
Blenheim		le Dugay Trouin
Thunderer		l'Ajax
Achilles		le Conquereur.

The constantly recurring discharges of four hundred pieces of heavy ordnance, within a space so small, had the effect to repel the regular currents of air, and, almost immediately, to lessen a breeze of six or seven knots, to one that would not propel a ship more than two or three. This was the first observable phenomenon connected with the action, but, as it had been expected, Sir Gervaise had used the precaution to lay his ships as near as possible in the positions in which he intended them to fight the battle. The next great physical consequence, one equally expected and natural, but which wrought a great change in the aspect of the battle, was the cloud of smoke in which the ten ships were suddenly enveloped. At the first broadsides between the two admirals, volumes of light, fleecy vapour rolled over the sea, meeting midway, and rising thence in curling wreaths, left nothing but the masts and sails of the adversary visible in the hostile ship. This, of itself, would have soon hidden the combatants in the bosom of a nearly impenetrable cloud; but as the vessels drove onward they entered deeper beneath the sulphurous canopy, until it spread on each side of them, shutting out the view of ocean, skies, and horizon. The burning of the priming below contributed to increase the smoke, until, not only was respiration often difficult, but those who fought only a few yards apart frequently could not recognise each other's faces. In the midst of this scene of obscurity, and a din that might well have alarmed the caverns of the ocean, the earnest and well-drilled seamen toiled at their ponderous guns, and remedied with ready hands the injuries received in the rigging, each man as intent on his own particular duty as if he wrought in the occupations of an ordinary gale.

"Sir Wycherly," observed the vice-admiral, when the cannonading had continued some twenty minutes, "there is little for a flag-officer to do in such a cloud of smoke. I would give much to know the exact positions of the divisions of our two rear-admirals."

"There is but one mode of ascertaining that, Sir Gervaise—if it be your pleasure, I will attempt it. By going on the main-top-gallant-yard, one might get a clear view, perhaps."

Sir Gervaise smiled his approbation, and presently he saw the young man ascending the main-rigging, though half concealed in smoke. Just at this instant, Greenly ascended to the poop, from making a tour of observation below. Without waiting for a question, the captain made his report.

"We are doing pretty well, now, Sir Gervaise, though the first broadside of the Comte treated us roughly. I think his fire slackens, and Bury says, he is certain that his fore-top-mast is already gone. At all events, our lads are in good spirits, and as yet all the sticks keep their places."

"I'm glad of this, Greenly; particularly of the latter, just at this moment. I see you are looking at those signals—they cover the body of poor Bunting."

"And this train of blood to the ladder, sir—I hope our young baronet is not hurt?"

"No, it is one of the Bowlderos, who has lost a leg. I shall have to see that he wants for nothing hereafter."

There was a pause; then both the gentlemen smiled, as they heard the crashing work made by a shot just beneath them, which, by the sounds and the direction, they knew had passed through Greenly's crockery. Still neither spoke. After a few more minutes of silent observation, Sir Gervaise remarked that he thought the flashes of the French guns more distant than they had been at first, though, at that instant, not a trace of their enemy was to be discovered, except in the roar of the guns, and in these very flashes, and their effect on the Plantagenet.

"If so, sir, the Comte begins to find his berth too hot for him; here is the wind still directly over *our* taffrail, such as it is."

"No—no—we steer as we began—I keep my eye on that compass below, and am certain we hold a straight course. Go forward, Greenly, and see that a sharp look-out is kept ahead. It is time some of our own ships should be crippled; we must be careful not to run into them. Should such a thing happen sheer hard to starboard, and pass *inside*."

"Ay—ay—Sir Gervaise; your wishes shall be attended to."

As this was said, Greenly disappeared, and, at the next instant, Wycherly stood in his place.

"Well, sir—I am glad to see you back safe. If Greenly were here now, *he* would inquire about his *masts*, but *I* wish to know the position of the *ships*."

"I am the bearer of bad news, sir. Nothing at all could be seen from the top; but in the cross-trees, I got a good look through the smoke, and am sorry to say the French rear-admiral is coming down fast on our larboard-quarter, with all his force. We shall have him abeam in five minutes."

"And Bluewater?" demanded Sir Gervaise, quick as lightning.

"I could see nothing of Admiral Bluewater's ships; but knowing the importance of this intelligence, I came down immediately, and by the back-stay."

"You have done well, sir. Send a midshipman forward for Captain Greenly; then pass below yourself, and let the lieutenants in the batteries hear the news. They must divide their people, and by all means give a prompt and well-directed *first* broadside."

Wycherly waited for no more. He ran below with the activity of his years. The message found Greenly between the knight-heads, but he hurried aft to the poop to ascertain its object. It took Sir Gervaise but a moment to explain it all to the captain.

"In the name of Heaven, what can the other division be about," exclaimed Greenly, "that it lets the French rear-admiral come upon us, in a moment like this!"

"Of that, sir, it is unnecessary to speak *now*," answered the commander-in-chief, solemnly. "Our present business is to get ready for this new enemy. Go into the batteries again, and, as you prize victory, be careful not to throw away the first discharge, in the smoke."

As time pressed, Greenly swallowed his discontent, and departed. The five minutes that succeeded were bitter minutes to Sir Gervaise Oakes. Beside himself there were but five men on the poop; viz., the quarter-master who tended the signals, and three of the Bowlderos. All of these were using muskets as usual, though the vice-admiral never permitted marines to be stationed at a point which he wished to be as clear of smoke, and as much removed from bustle as possible. He began to pace this comparatively vacant little deck with a quick step, casting wistful glances towards the larboard-quarter; but though the smoke occasionally cleared a little in that direction, the firing having much slackened from exhaustion in the men, as well as from injuries given and received, he was unable to detect any signs of a ship. Such was the state of things when Wycherly returned and reported that his orders were delivered, and part of the people were already in the larboard-batteries.

CHAPTER XXVIII.

"And oh, the little warlike world within!
The well-reeved guns, the netted canopy,
The hoarse command, the busy humming din.
When at a word, the tops are manned on high:
Hark to the boatswain's call, the cheering cry!
While through the seaman's hand the tackle glides,
Or school-boy midshipman, that, standing by,
Strains his shrill pipe, as good or ill betides,
And well the docile crew that skilful urchin guides."

BYRON.

"Are you quite sure, Sir Wycherly Wychecombe, that there is not some mistake about the approach of the rear division of the French?" inquired the vice-admiral, endeavouring to catch some glimpse of the water, through the smoke on the larboard hand. "May not some crippled ship of our own have sheered from the line, and been left by us, unknowingly, on that side?"

"No, Sir Gervaise, there is *no* mistake; there *can* be none, unless I may have been deceived a little in the distance. I saw nothing but the sails and spars, not of a single vessel, but of *three* ships; and one of them wore the flag of a French rear-admiral at the mizzen. As a proof that I was not mistaken, sir, there it is this minute!"

The smoke on the off side of the Plantagenet, as a matter of course, was much less dense than that on the side engaged, and the wind beginning to blow in eddies, as ever happens in a heavy cannonade, there were moments in which it cast aside the "shroud of battle." At that instant an opening occurred through which a single mast, and a single sail were visible, in the precise spot where Wycherly had stated the enemy might be looked for. It was a mizzen-top-sail, beyond a question, and above it was fluttering the little square flag of the rear-admiral. Sir Gervaise decided on the character of the vessel, and on his own course, in an instant. Stepping to the edge of the poop, with his natural voice, without the aid of a trumpet of any sort, he called out in tones that rose above the roar of the contest, the ominous but familiar nautical words of "stand by!" Perhaps a call from powerful lungs (and the vice-admiral's voice, when he chose to use it, was like the blast of a clarion) is clearer and more impressive, when unaided by instruments, than when it comes disguised and unnatural through a tube. At any rate, these words were heard even on the lower deck, by those who stood near the hatches. Taking them up, they were repeated by a dozen voices, with such expressions as "Look out, lads; Sir Jarvy's awake!" "Sight your guns!" "Wait till she's square!"

and other similar admonitions that it is usual for the sea-officer to give, as he is about to commence the strife. At this critical moment, Sir Gervaise again looked up, and caught another glimpse of the little flag, as it passed into a vast wreath of smoke; he saw that the ship was fairly abeam, and, as if doubling all his powers, he shouted the word "fire!" Greenly was standing on the lower-deck ladder, with his head just even with the coamings of the hatch, as this order reached him, and he repeated it in a voice scarcely less startling. The cloud on the larboard side was driven in all directions, like dust scattered by wind. The ship seemed on fire, and the missiles of forty-one guns flew on their deadly errand, as it might be at a single flash. The old Plantagenet trembled to her keel, and even bowed a little at the recoils, but, like one suddenly relieved from a burthen, righted and went on her way none the less active. That timely broadside saved the English commander-in-chiefs ship from an early defeat. It took the crew of le Pluton, her new adversary, by surprise; for they had not been able to distinguish the precise position of their enemy; and, besides doing vast injury to both hull and people, drew her fire at an unpropitious moment. So uncertain and hasty, indeed, was the discharge the French ship gave in return, that no small portion of the contents of her guns passed ahead of the Plantagenet, and went into the larboard quarter of le Téméraire, the French admiral's second ahead.

"That was a timely salute," said Sir Gervaise, smiling as soon as the fire of his new enemy had been received without material injury. "The first blow is always half the battle. We may now work on with some hopes of success. Ah! here comes Greenly again, God be praised! unhurt."

The meeting of these two experienced seamen was cordial, but not without great seriousness. Both felt that the situation of not only the ship, but of the whole fleet, was extremely critical, the odds being much too great, and the position of the enemy too favourable, not to render the result, to say the very least, exceedingly doubtful. Some advantage had certainly been obtained, thus far; but there was little hope of preserving it long. The circumstances called for very decided and particularly bold measures.

"My mind is made up, Greenly," observed the vice-admiral. "We must go aboard of one of these ships, and make it a hand-to-hand affair. We will take the French commander-in-chief; he is evidently a good deal cut up by the manner in which his fire slackens, and if we can carry him, or even force him out of the line, it will give us a better chance with the rest. As for Bluewater, God only knows what has become of him! He is not here at any rate, and we must help ourselves."

"You have only to order, Sir Gervaise, to be obeyed. I will lead the boarders, myself."

"It must be a general thing, Greenly; I rather think we shall all of us have to go aboard of le Foudroyant. Go, give the necessary orders, and when every thing is ready, round in a little on the larboard braces, clap your helm a-port, and give the ship a rank sheer to starboard. This will bring matters to a crisis at once. By letting the fore-sail fall, and setting the spanker, you might shove the ship ahead a little faster."

Greenly instantly left the poop on this new and important duty. He sent his orders into the batteries, bidding the people remain at their guns, however, to the last moment; and particularly instructing the captain of marines, as to the manner in which he was to cover, and then follow the boarding-party. This done, he gave orders to brace forward the yards, as directed by Sir Gervaise.

The reader will not overlook the material circumstance that all we have related occurred amid the din of battle. Guns were exploding at each instant, the cloud of smoke was both thickening and extending, fire was flashing in the semi-obscurity of its volumes, shot were rending the wood and cutting the rigging, and the piercing shrieks of agony, only so much the more appalling by being extorted from the stern and resolute, blended their thrilling accompaniments. Men seemed to be converted into demons, and yet was there a lofty and stubborn resolution to conquer mingled with all, that ennobled the strife and rendered it heroic. The broadsides that were delivered in succession down the line, as ship after ship of the rear division reached her station, however, proclaimed that Monsieur des Prez had imitated Sir Gervaise's mode of closing, the only one by means of which the leading vessel could escape destruction, and that the English were completely doubled on. At this moment, the sail-trimmers of the Plantagenet handled their braces. The first pull was the last. No sooner were the ropes started, than the fore-top-mast went over the bows, dragging after it the main with all its hamper, the mizzen snapping like a pipe-stem, at the cap. By this cruel accident, the result of many injuries to shrouds, back-stays, and spars, the situation of the Plantagenet became worse than ever; for, not only was the wreck to be partially cleared, at least, to fight many of the larboard guns, but the command of the ship was, in a great measure, lost, in the centre of one of the most infernal *mêlées* that ever accompanied a combat at sea.

At no time does the trained seaman ever appear so great, as when he meets sudden misfortunes with the steadiness and quiet which it is a material part of the *morale* of discipline to inculcate. Greenly was full of ardour for the assault, and was thinking of the best mode of running foul of his adversary, when this calamity occurred; but the masts were hardly down, when he changed all his thoughts to a new current, and called out to the sail-trimmers to "lay over, and clear the wreck."

Sir Gervaise, too, met with a sudden and violent check to the current of his feelings. He had collected his Bowlderos, and was giving his instructions as to the manner in which they were to follow, and keep near his person, in the expected hand-to-hand encounter, when the heavy rushing of the air, and the swoop of the mass from above, announced what had occurred. Turning to the men, he calmly ordered them to aid in getting rid of the incumbrances, and was in the very act of directing Wycherly to join in the same duty, when the latter exclaimed—

"See, Sir Gervaise, here comes another of the Frenchmen close upon our quarter. By heavens, *they* must mean to board!"

The vice-admiral instinctively grasped his sword-hilt tighter, and turned in the direction mentioned by his companion. There, indeed, came a fresh ship, shoving the cloud aside, and, by the clearer atmosphere that seemed to accompany her, apparently bringing down a current of air stronger than common. When first seen, the jib-boom and bowsprit were both enveloped in smoke, but his bellying fore-top-sail, and the canvass hanging in festoons, loomed grandly in the vapour, the black yards seeming to embrace the wreaths, merely to cast them aside. The proximity, too, was fearful, her yard-arms promising to clear those of the Plantagenet only by a few feet, as her dark bows brushed along the admiral's side.

"This will be fearful work, indeed!" exclaimed Sir Gervaise. "A fresh broadside from a ship so near, will sweep all from the spars. Go, Wychecombe, tell Greenly to call in—Hold—'Tis an English ship! No Frenchman's bowsprit stands like that! Almighty God be praised! 'Tis the Cæsar—there is the old Roman's figure-head just shoving out of the smoke!"

This was said with a yell, rather than a cry, of delight, and in a voice so loud that the words were heard below, and flew through the ship like the hissing of an ascending rocket. To confirm the glorious tidings, the flash and roar of guns on the off-side of the stranger announced the welcome tidings that le Pluton had an enemy of her own to contend with, thus enabling the Plantagenet's people to throw all their strength on the starboard guns, and pursue their other necessary work without further molestation from the French rear-admiral. The gratitude of Sir Gervaise, as the rescuing ship thrust herself in between him and his most formidable assailant was too deep for language. He placed his hat mechanically before his face, and thanked God, with a fervour of spirit that never before had attended his thanksgivings. This brief act of devotion over, he found the bows of the Cæsar, which ship was advancing very slowly, in order not to pass too far ahead, just abreast of the spot where he stood, and so near that objects were pretty plainly visible. Between her knight-heads stood Bluewater, conning the ship, by means of a line of officers, his hat in his hand, waving in encouragement to his own people, while Geoffrey Cleveland held the trumpet at his elbow. At that moment three noble cheers were given by the crews of the two friendly vessels, and mingled with the increasing roar of the Cæsar's artillery. Then the smoke rose in a cloud over the forecastle of the latter ship, and persons could no longer be distinguished.

Nevertheless, like all that thus approached, the relieving ship passed slowly ahead, until nearly her whole length protected the undefended side of her consort, delivering her fire with fearful rapidity. The Plantagenets seemed to imbibe new life from this arrival, and their starboard guns spoke out again, as if manned by giants. It was five minutes, perhaps, after this seasonable arrival, before the guns of the other ships of the English rear announced their presence on the outside of Monsieur des Prez's force; thus bringing the whole of the two fleets into four lines, all steering dead before the wind, and, as it were, interwoven with each other. By that time, the poops of the Plantagenet and Cæsar became visible from one to the other, the smoke now driving principally off from the vessels. There again were our two admirals each anxiously watching to get a glimpse of his friend. The instant the place was clear, Sir Gervaise applied the trumpet to his mouth, and called out—

"God bless you—Dick! may God for ever bless you—*your* ship can do it— clap your helm hard a-starboard, and sheer into M. des Prez; you'll have him in five minutes."

Bluewater smiled, waved his hand, gave an order, and laid aside his trumpet. Two minutes later, the Cæsar sheered into the smoke on her larboard beam, and the crash of the meeting vessels was heard. By this time, the wreck of the Plantagenet was cut adrift, and she, too, made a rank sheer, though in a direction opposite to that of the Cæsar's. As she went through the smoke, her guns ceased, and when she emerged into the pure air, it was found that le Foudroyant had set courses and top-gallant-sails, and was drawing so fast ahead, as to render pursuit, under the little sail that could be set, unprofitable. Signals were out of the question, but this movement of the two admirals converted the whole battle scene into one of inexplicable confusion. Ship after ship changed her position, and ceased her fire from uncertainty what that position was, until a general silence succeeded the roar of the cannonade. It was indispensable to pause and let the smoke blow away.

It did not require many minutes to raise the curtain on the two fleets. As soon as the firing stopped, the wind increased, and the smoke was driven off to leeward in a vast straggling cloud, that seemed to scatter and disperse in the air spontaneously. Then a sight of the havoc and destruction that had been done in this short conflict was first obtained.

The two squadrons were intermingled, and it required some little time for Sir Gervaise to get a clear idea of the state of his own ships. Generally, it might be said that the vessels were scattering, the French sheering towards their own coast, while the English were principally coming by the wind on the larboard tack, or heading in towards England. The Cæsar and le Pluton were still foul of each other, though a rear-admiral's flag was flying at the mizzen of the first, while that which had so lately fluttered at the royal-mast-head of the other, had disappeared. The Achilles, Lord Morganic, was still among the French, more to leeward than any other English ship, without a single spar standing. Her ensigns were flying, notwithstanding, and the Thunderer and Dublin, both in tolerable order, were edging away rapidly to cover their crippled consort; though the nearest French vessels seemed more bent on getting out of the *mêlée*, and into their own line again, than on securing any advantage already obtained. Le Téméraire was in the same predicament as the Achilles as to spars, though much more injured in her hull, besides having thrice as many casualties. Her flag was down; the ship having fairly struck to the Warspite, whose boats were already alongside of her. Le Foudroyant, with quite one-third of her crew killed and wounded, was running off to leeward, with signals flying for her consorts to rally round her; but, within less than ten minutes after she became visible, her main and mizzen-masts both went. The Blenheim had lost all her top-masts, like the Plantagenet, and neither the Elizabeth nor the York had a mizzen-mast standing, although engaged but a very short time. Several lower yards were shot away, or so much injured as to compel the ships to shorten sail; this accident having occurred in both fleets. As for the damage done to the standing and running rigging, and to the sails, it is only necessary to say that shrouds, back and head-stays, braces, bowlines and lifts, were dangling in all directions, while the canvass that was open exhibited all sorts of rents, from that which had been torn like cloth in the shopman's hands, to the little eyelet holes of the canister and grape. It appeared, by the subsequent reports of the two parties, that, in this short but severe conflict, the slain and wounded of the English amounted to seven hundred and sixty-three, including officers; and that of the French, to one thousand four hundred and twelve. The disparity in this respect would probably have been greater against the latter, had it not been for the manner in which M. des Prez succeeded in doubling on his enemies.

Little need be said in explanation of the parts of this battle that have not been distinctly related. M. des Prez had man[oe]uvered in the manner he did, at the commencement of the affair, in the hope of drawing Sir Gervaise down upon the division of the Comte de Vervillin; and no sooner did he see, the first fairly enveloped in smoke, than he wore short round and joined in the affair, as has been mentioned. At this sight, Bluewater's loyalty to the Stuarts could resist no longer. Throwing out a general signal to engage, he squared away, set every thing that would draw on the Cæsar, and arrived in time to save his friend. The other ships followed, engaging on the outside, for want of room to imitate their leader.

Two more of the French ships, at least, in addition to *le Téméraire* and *le Pluton*, might have been added to the list of prizes, had the actual condition of their fleet been known. But, at such moments, a combatant sees and feels his own injuries, while he has to conjecture many of those of his adversaries; and the English were too much occupied in making the provisions necessary to save their remaining spars, to risk much in order to swell an advantage that was already so considerable. Some distant firing passed between the Thunderer and Dublin, and l'Ajax, le Dugay Trouin, and l'Hector, before the two former succeeded in getting Lord Morganic out of his difficulties; but it led to no material result; merely inflicting new injuries on certain spars that were sufficiently damaged before, and killing and wounding some fifteen or twenty men quite uselessly. As soon as the vice-admiral saw what was likely to be the effects of this episode, he called off Captain O'Neil of the Dublin, by signal, he being an officer of a "hot temper," as the soldier said of himself at Waterloo. The compliance with this order may be said to have terminated the battle.

The reader will remember that the wind, at the commencement of the engagement, was at north-west. It was nearly "killed," as seamen express it, by the cannonade; then it revived a little, as the concussions of the guns gradually diminished. But the combined effect of the advance of the day, and the rushing of new currents of air to fill the vacuums produced by the burning of so much powder, was a sudden shift of wind; a breeze coming out strong, and as it might be, in an instant, from the eastward. This unexpected alteration in the direction and power of the wind, cost the Thunderer her foremast, and did other damage to different ships; but, by dint of great activity and careful handling, all the English vessels got their heads round to the northward, while the French filled the other way, and went off free, steering nearly south-east, making the best of their way for Brest. The latter suffered still more than their enemies, by the change just mentioned; and when they reached port, as did all but one the following day, no less than three were towed in without a spar standing, bowsprits excepted.

The exception was *le Caton*, which ship M. de Vervillin set fire to and blew up, on account of her damages, in the course of the afternoon. Thus of twelve noble two-decked ships with which this officer sailed from Cherbourg only two days before, he reached Brest with but seven.

Nor were the English entirely without their embarrassments. Although the Warspite had compelled le Téméraire to strike, she was kept afloat herself with a good deal of difficulty, and that, too, not without considerable assistance from the other vessels. The leaks, however, were eventually stopped, and then the ship was given up to the care of her own crew. Other vessels suffered of course, but no English ship was in as much jeopardy as this.

The first hour after the action ceased, was one of great exertion and anxiety to our admiral. He called the Chloe alongside by signal, and, attended by Wycherly and his own quarter-masters, Galleygo, who went without orders, and the Bowlderos who were unhurt, he shifted his flag to that frigate. Then he immediately commenced passing from vessel to vessel, in order to ascertain the actual condition of his command. The Achilles detained him some time, and he was near her, or to leeward, when the wind shifted; which was bringing him to windward in the present stale of things. Of this advantage he availed himself, by urging the different ships off as fast as possible; and long before the sun was in the meridian, all the English vessels were making the best of their way towards the land, with the intention of fetching into Plymouth if possible; if not, into the nearest and best anchorage to leeward. The progress of the fleet was relatively slow, as a matter of course, though it got along at the rate of some five knots, by making a free wind of it.

The master of the Chloe had just taken the sun, in order to ascertain his latitude, when the vice-admiral commanded Denham to set top-gallant-sails, and go within hail of the Cæsar. That ship had got clear of *le Pluton* half an hour after the action ceased, and she was now leading the fleet, with her three top-sails on the caps. Aloft she had suffered comparatively little; but Sir Gervaise knew that there must have been a serious loss of men in carrying, hand to hand, a vessel like that of M. des Prez. He was anxious to see his friend, and to hear the manner in which his success had been obtained, and, we might add, to remonstrate with Bluewater on a course that had led the latter to the verge of a most dangerous abyss.

The Chloe was half an hour running through the fleet, which was a good deal extended, and was sailing without any regard to a line. Sir Gervaise had many questions to ask, too, of the different commanders in passing. At last the frigate overtook le Téméraire, which vessel was following the Cæsar under easy canvass. As the Chloe came up abeam, Sir Gervaise appeared in the gangway of the frigate, and, hat in hand, he asked with an accent that was intelligible, though it might not have absolutely stood the test of criticism,—

"Le Vice-Admiral Oakes demande comment se porte-il, le contre-amiral, le Vicomte des Prez?"

A little elderly man, dressed with extreme care, with a powdered head, but of a firm step and perfectly collected expression of countenance, appeared on the verge of le Téméraire's poop, trumpet in hand, to reply.

"Le Vicomte des Prez remercie bien Monsieur le Chevalier Oake, et désire vivement de savoir comment se porte Monsieur le Vice-Amiral?"

Mutual waves of the trumpets served as replies to the questions, and then, after taking a moment to muster his French, Sir Gervaise continued—

"J'espère voir Monsieur le Contre-Amiral à dîner, à cinq heures, précis."

The vicomte smiled at this characteristic manifestation of good-will and courtesy; and after pausing an instant to choose an expression to soften his refusal, and to express his own sense of the motive of the invitation, he called out—

"Veuillez bien recevoir nos excuses pour aujourd'hui, Mons. le Chevalier. Nous n'avons pas encore digéré le repas si noble reçu à vos mains comme déjeuner."

The Chloe passing ahead, bows terminated the interview. Sir Gervaise's French was at fault, for what between the rapid, neat, pronunciation of the Frenchman, the trumpet, and the turn of the expression, he did not comprehend the meaning of the *contre-amiral*.

"What does he say, Wychecombe?" he asked eagerly of the young man. "Will he come, or not?"

"Upon my word, Sir Gervaise, French is a sealed language to me. Never having been a prisoner, no opportunity has offered for acquiring the language. As I understood, you intended to ask him to dinner; I rather think, from his countenance, he meant to say he was not in spirits for the entertainment."

"Pooh! we would have put him in spirits, and Bluewater could have talked to him in his own tongue, by the fathom. We will close with the Cæsar to leeward, Denham; never mind rank on an occasion like this. It's time to let the top-gallant-halyards run; you'll have to settle your top-sails too, or we shall shoot past her. Bluewater may take it as a salute to his gallantry in carrying so fine a ship in so handsome a manner."

Several minutes now passed in silence, during which the frigate was less and less rapidly closing with the larger vessel, drawing ahead towards the last, as it might be, foot by foot. Sir Gervaise got upon one of the quarter-deck guns, and steadying himself against the hammock-cloths, he was in readiness to exchange the greetings he was accustomed to give and to receive from his friend, in the same heartfelt manner as if nothing had occurred to disturb the harmony of their feelings. The single glance of the eye, the waving of the hat, and the noble manner in which Bluewater interposed between him and his most dangerous enemy, was still present to his mind, and disposed him even more than common to the kindest feelings of his nature. Stowel was already on the poop of the Cæsar, and, as the Chloe came slowly on, he raised his hat in deference to the commander-in-chief. It was a point of delicacy with Sir Gervaise never to interfere with any subordinate flag-officer's vessel any more than duty rigidly required; consequently his communications with the captain of the Cæsar had usually been of a general nature, verbal orders and criticisms being studiously avoided. This circumstance rendered the commander-in-chief even a greater favourite than common with Stowel, who had all his own way in his own ship, in consequence of the rear-admiral's indifference to such matters.

"How do you do, Stowel?" called out Sir Gervaise, cordially. "I am delighted to see you on your legs, and hope the old Roman is not much the worse for this day's treatment"

"I thank you, Sir Gervaise, we are both afloat yet, though we have passed through warm times. The ship is damaged, sir, as you may suppose; and, although it stands so bravely, and looks so upright, that foremast of ours is as good as a condemned spar. One thirty-two through the heart of it, about ten feet from the deck, an eighteen in the hounds, and a double-header sticking in one of the hoops! A spar cannot be counted for much that has as many holes in it as those, sir!"

"Deal tenderly with it, my old friend, and spare the canvass; those chaps at Plymouth will set all to rights, again, in a week. Hoops can be had for asking, and as for holes in the heart, many a poor fellow has had them, and lived through it all. You are a case in point; Mrs. Stowel not having spared you in that way, I'll answer for it."

"Mrs. Stowel commands ashore, Sir Gervaise, and I command afloat; and in that way, we keep a quiet ship and a quiet house, I thank you, sir; and I endeavour to think of her at sea, as little as possible."

"Ay, that's the way with you doting husbands;—always ashamed of your own lively sensibilities. But what has become of Bluewater?—Does he know that we are alongside?"

Stowel looked round, cast his eyes up at the sails, and played with the hilt of his sword. The rapid eye of the commander-in-chief detected this embarrassment, and quick as thought he demanded what had happened.

"Why, Sir Gervaise, you know how it is with some admirals, who like to be in every thing. I told our respected and beloved friend, that he had nothing to do with boarding; that if either of us was to go, *I* was the proper man; but that we ought both to stick by the ship. He answered something about lost honour and duty, and you know, sir, what legs he has, when he wishes to use them! One might as well think of stopping a deserter by a halloo; away he went, with the first party, sword in hand, a sight I never saw before, and never wish to see again! Thus you see how it was, sir."

The commander-in-chief compressed his lips, until his features, and indeed his whole form was a picture of desperate resolution, though his face was as pale as death, and the muscles of his mouth twitched, in spite of all his physical self-command.

"I understand you, sir," he said, in a voice that seemed to issue from his chest; "you wish to say that Admiral Bluewater is killed."

"No, thank God! Sir Gervaise, not *quite* as bad as that, though sadly hurt; yes, indeed, very sadly hurt!"

Sir Gervaise Oakes groaned, and for a few minutes he leaned his head on the hammock-cloths, veiling his face from the sight of men. Then he raised his person erect, and said steadily—

"Run your top-sails to the mast-head, Captain Stowel, and round your ship to. I will come on board of you."

An order was given to Denham to take room, when the Chloe came to the wind on one tack and the Cæsar on the other. This was contrary to rule, as it increased the distance between the ships; but the vice-admiral was impatient to be in his barge. In ten minutes he was mounting the Cæsar's side, and in two more he was in Bluewater's main-cabin. Geoffrey Cleveland was seated by the table, with his face buried in his arms. Touching his shoulder, the boy raised his head, and showed a face covered with tears.

"How is he, boy?" demanded Sir Gervaise, hoarsely. "Do the surgeons give any hopes?"

The midshipman shook his head, and then, as if the question renewed his grief, he again buried his face in his arms. At this moment, the surgeon of the ship came from the rear-admiral's state-room, and following the commander-in-chief into the after-cabin, they had a long conference together.

Minute after minute passed, and the Cæsar and Chloe still lay with their main-top-sails aback. At the end of half an hour, Denham wore round and laid the head of his frigate in the proper direction. Ship after ship came up, and went on to the northward, fast as her crippled state would allow, yet no sign of movement was seen in the Cæsar. Two sail had appeared in the south-eastern board, and they, too, approached and passed without bringing the vice-admiral even on deck. These ships proved to be the Carnatic and her prize, le Scipion, which latter ship had been intercepted and easily captured by the former. The steering of M. de Vervillin to the south-west had left a clear passage to the two ships, which were coming down with a free wind at a handsome rate of sailing. This news was sent into the Cæsar's cabin, but it brought no person and no answer out of it. At length, when every thing had gone ahead, the barge returned to the Chloe. It merely took a note, however, which was no sooner read by Wycherly, than he summoned the Bowlderos and Galleygo, had all the vice-admiral's luggage passed into the boat, struck his flag, and took his leave of Denham. As soon as the boat was clear of the frigate, the latter made all sail after the fleet, to resume her ordinary duties of a look-out and a repeating-ship.

As soon as Wycherly reached the Cæsar, that ship hoisted in the vice-admiral's barge. A report was made to Sir Gervaise of what had been done, and then an order came on deck that occasioned all in the fleet to stare with surprise. The red flag of Sir Gervaise Oakes was run up at the foreroyal-mast-head of the Cæsar, while the white flag of the rear-admiral was still flying at her mizzen. Such a thing had never before been known to happen, if it has ever happened since; and to the time when she was subsequently lost, the Cæsar was known as the double flag-ship.

CHAPTER XXIX.

"He spoke; when behold the fair Geraldine's form
On the canvass enchantingly glowed;
His touches, they flew like the leaves in a storm;
And the pure pearly white, and the carnation warm,
Contending in harmony flowed."

ALSTON.

We shall now ask permission of the reader to advance the time just eight-and-forty hours; a liberty with the unities which, he will do us the justice to say, we have not often taken. We must also transfer the scene to that already described at Wychecombe, including the Head, the station, the roads, and the inland and seaward views. Summer weather had returned, too, the pennants of the ships at anchor scarce streaming from their masts far enough to form curved lines. Most of the English fleet was among these vessels, though the squadron had undergone some changes. The Druid had got into Portsmouth with *la Victoire*; the Driver and Active had made the best of their way to the nearest ports; with despatches for the admiralty; and the Achilles, in tow of the Dublin, with the Chloe to take care of both, had gone to leeward, with square yards, in the hope of making Falmouth. The rest of the force was present, the crippled ships having been towed into the roads that morning. The picture among the shipping was one of extreme activity and liveliness. Jury-masts were going up in the Warspite; lower and top-sail-yards were down to be fished, or new ones were rigging to be sent aloft in their places; the Plantagenet was all a-tanto, again, in readiness for another action, with rigging secured and masts fished, while none but an instructed eye could have detected, at a short distance, that the Cæsar, Carnatic, Dover, York, Elizabeth, and one or two more, had been in action at all. The landing was crowded with boats as before, and gun-room servants and midshipmen's boys were foraging as usual; some with honest intent to find delicacies for the wounded, but more with the roguish design of contributing to the comforts of the unhurt, by making appeals to the sympathies of the women of the neighbourhood, in behalf of the hurt.

The principal transformation that had been brought about by this state of things, however, was apparent at the station. This spot had the appearance of a place to which the headquarters of an army had been transferred, in the vicissitudes of the field; warlike sailors, if not soldiers, flocking to it, as the centre of interest and intelligence. Still there was a singularity observable in the manner in which these heroes of the deck paid their court; the cottage being seemingly tabooed, or at most, approached by very few, while the grass at the foot of the flag-staff was already beginning to show proofs of the pressure of many feet. This particular spot, indeed, was the centre of attraction; there, officers of all ranks and ages were constantly arriving, and thence they were as often departing; all bearing countenances sobered by anxiety and apprehension. Notwithstanding the constant mutations, there had been no instant since the rising of the sun, when some ten or twelve, at least, including captains, lieutenants, masters and idlers, had not been collected around the bench at the foot of the signal-staff, and frequently the number reached even to twenty.

A little retired from the crowd, and near the verge of the cliff, a large tent had been pitched. A marine paced in its front, as a sentinel. Another stood near the gate of the little door-yard of the cottage, and all persons who approached either, with the exception of a few of the privileged, were referred to the sergeant who commanded the guard. The arms of the latter were stacked on the grass, at hand, and the men off post were loitering near. These were the usual military signs of the presence of officers of rank, and may, in sooth, be taken as clues to the actual state of things, on and around the Head.

Admiral Bluewater lay in the cottage, while Sir Gervaise Oakes occupied the tent. The former had been transferred to the place where he was about to breathe his last, at his own urgent request, while his friend had refused to be separated from him, so long as life remained. The two flags were still flying at the mast-heads of the Cæsar, a sort of melancholy memorial of the tie that had so long bound their gallant owners in the strong sympathies of an enduring personal and professional friendship.

Persons of the education of Mrs. Dutton and her daughter, had not dwelt so long on that beautiful head-land, without leaving on the spot some lasting impressions of their tastes. Of the cottage, we have already spoken. The little garden, too, then bright with flowers, had a grace and refinement about it that we would hardly have expected to meet in such a place; and even the paths that led athwart the verdant common which spread over so much of the upland, had been directed with an eye to the picturesque and agreeable. One of these paths, too, led to a rustic summer-house—a sort of small, rude pavilion, constructed, like the fences, of fragments of wrecks, and placed on a shelf of the cliff, at a dizzy elevation, but in perfect security. So far from there being any danger in entering this summer-house, indeed, Wycherly, during his six months' residence near the Head, had made a path that descended still lower to a point that was utterly concealed from all eyes above, and had actually planted a seat on another shelf with so much security, that both Mildred and her mother often visited it in company. During the young man's recent absence, the poor girl, indeed, had passed much of her time there, weeping and suffering in solitude. To this seat, Dutton never ventured; the descent, though well protected with ropes, requiring greater steadiness of foot and head than intemperance had left him. Once or twice, Wycherly had induced Mildred to pass an hour with him alone in this romantic place, and some of his sweetest recollections of this just-minded and intelligent girl, were connected with the frank communications that had there occurred between them. On this bench he was seated at the time of the opening of the present chapter. The movement on the Head, and about the cottage, was so great, as to deprive him of every chance of seeing Mildred alone, and he had hoped that, led by some secret sympathy, she, too, might seek this perfectly retired seat, to obtain a moment of unobserved solitude, if not from some still dearer motive. He had not waited long, ere he heard a heavy foot over his head, and a man entered the summer-house. He was yet debating whether to abandon all hopes of seeing Mildred, when his acute ear caught her light and well-known footstep, as she reached the summer-house, also.

"Father, I have come as you desired," said the poor girl, in those tremulous tones which Wycherly too well understood, not to imagine the condition of Dutton. "Admiral Bluewater dozes, and mother has permitted me to steal away."

"Ay, Admiral Bluewater is a great man, though but little better than a dead one!" answered Dutton, as harshly in manner as the language was coarse. "You and your mother are all attention to *him*; did *I* lie in his place, which of you would be found hanging over my bed, with pale cheeks and tearful eyes?"

"*Both* of us, father! *Do* not—*do* not think so ill of your wife and daughter, as to suppose it possible that either of them could forget her duty."

"Yes, *duty* might do something, perhaps; what has duty to do with this useless rear-admiral? I *hate* the scoundrel—he was one of the court that cashiered me; and one, too, that I am told, was the most obstinate in refusing to help me into this pitiful berth of a master."

Mildred was silent. She could not vindicate her friend without criminating her father. As for Wycherly, he would have given a year's income to be at sea; yet he shrunk from wounding the poor daughter's feelings by letting her know he overheard the dialogue. This indecision made him the unwilling auditor of a conversation that he ought not to have heard—an occurrence which, had there been time for reflection, he would have taken means to prevent.

"Sit you down here, Mildred," resumed Dutton, sternly, "and listen to what I have to say. It is time that there should no longer be any trifling between us. You have the fortunes of your mother and myself in your hands; and, as one of the parties so deeply concerned, I am determined *mine* shall be settled at once."

"I do not understand you, father," said Mildred, with a tremour in her voice that almost induced the young man to show himself, though, we owe it to truth to say, that a lively curiosity *now* mingled with his other sensations. "How can I have the keeping of dear mother's fortunes and yours?"

"*Dear* mother, truly!—*Dear* enough has she proved to me; but I intend the daughter shall pay for it. Hark you, Mildred; I'll have no more of this trifling—but I ask you in a father's name, if any man has offered you his hand? Speak plainly, and conceal nothing—I *will* be answered."

"I wish to conceal nothing, father, that ought to be told; but when a young woman declines the honour that another does her in this way, *ought* she to reveal the secret, even to her father?"

"She *ought*; and, in your case, she *shall*. No more hesitation; name *one* of the offers you have had."

Mildred, after a brief pause, in a low, tremulous voice, pronounced the name of "Mr. Rotherham."

"I suspected as much," growled Dutton; "there was a time when even *he* might have answered, but we can do better than that now. Still he may be kept as a reserve; the thousand pounds Mr. Thomas says shall be paid, and that and the living will make a comfortable port after a stormy life. Well, who next, Mildred? Has Mr. Thomas Wychecombe ever come to the point?"

"He has asked me to become his wife, within the last twenty-four hours; if that is what you mean."

"No affectations, Milly; I can't bear them. You know well enough what I mean. What was your answer?"

"I do not love him in the least, father, and, of course, I told him I could not marry him."

"That don't follow *of course*, by any means, girl! The marrying is done by the priest, and the love is a very different thing. I hope you consider Mrs. Dutton as my wife?"

"What a question!" murmured Mildred.

"Well, and do you suppose she *loves* me; *can* love me, now I am a disgraced, impoverished man?"

"Father!"

"Come—come—enough of this. Mr. Thomas Wychecombe may not be legitimate—I rather think he is not, by the proofs Sir Reginald has produced within the last day or two; and I understand his own mother is dissatisfied with him, and *that* will knock his claim flat aback. Notwithstanding, Mildred, Tom Wychecombe has a good six hundred a year already, and Sir Reginald himself admits that he must take all the personal property the late baronet could leave."

"You forget, father," said Mildred, conscious of the inefficacy of any other appeal, "that Mr. Thomas has promised to pay the legacies that Sir Wycherly *intended* to leave."

"Don't place any expectations on that, Mildred. I dare say he would settle ten of the twenty thousand on you to-morrow, if you would consent to have him. But, now, as to this new baronet, for it seems he is to have both title and estate—has *he* ever offered?"

There was a long pause, during which Wycherly thought he heard the hard but suppressed breathing of Mildred. To remain quiet any longer, he felt was as impossible as, indeed, his conscience told him was dishonourable, and he sprang along the path to ascend to the summer-house. At the first sound of his footstep, a faint cry escaped Mildred; but when Wycherly entered the pavilion, he found her face buried in her hands, and Dutton tottering forward, equally in surprise and alarm. As the circumstances would not admit of evasion, the young man threw aside all reserve, and spoke plainly.

"I have been an unwilling listener to a *part* of your discourse with Mildred, Mr. Dutton," he said, "and can answer your last question for myself. I *have* offered my hand to your daughter, sir; an offer that I now renew, and the acceptance of which would make me the happiest man in England. If your influence could aid me—for she has refused my hand."

"Refused!" exclaimed Dutton, in a surprise that overcame the calculated amenity of manner he had assumed the instant Wycherly appeared— "Refused Sir Wycherly Wychecombe! but it was before your rights had been as well established as they are now. Mildred, answer to this—how *could* you— nay, how *dare* you refuse such an offer as this?"

Human nature could not well endure more. Mildred suffered her hands to fall helplessly into her lap, and exposed a face that was lovely as that of an angel's, though pale nearly to the hue of death. Feeling extorted the answer she made, though the words had hardly escaped her, ere she repented having uttered them, and had again buried her face in her hands—

"Father"—she said—"*could* I—*dare* I to encourage Sir Wycherly Wychecombe to unite himself to a family like ours!"

Conscience smote Dutton with a force that nearly sobered him, and what explanation might have followed it is hard to say; Wycherly, in an under-tone, however, requested to be left alone with the daughter. Dutton had sense enough to understand he was *de trop*, and shame enough to wish to escape. In half a minute, he had hobbled up to the summit of the cliff and disappeared.

"Mildred!—*Dearest* Mildred"—said Wycherly, tenderly, gently endeavouring to draw her attention to himself, "we are alone now; surely—surely—you will not refuse to *look* at *me*!"

"Is he gone?" asked Mildred, dropping her hands, and looking wildly around. "Thank God! It is over, for this time, at least! Now, let us go to the house; Admiral Bluewater may miss me."

"No, Mildred, not yet. You surely can spare me—me, who have suffered so much of late on your account—nay, by your *means*—you can, in mercy, spare me a few short minutes. Was *this* the reason—the *only* reason, dearest girl, why you so pertinaciously refused my hand?"

"Was it not sufficient, Wycherly?" answered Mildred, afraid the chartered air might hear her secret. "Remember *who* you are, and *what* I am! Could I suffer you to become the husband of one to whom such cruel, cruel propositions had been made by her own father!"

"I shall not affect to conceal my horror of such principles, Mildred, but your virtues shine all the brighter by having flourished in their company. Answer me but one question frankly, and every other difficulty can be gotten over. Do you love me well enough to be my wife, were you an orphan?"

Mildred's countenance was full of anguish, but this question changed its expression entirely. The moment was extraordinary as were the feelings it engendered, and, almost unconsciously to herself, she raised the hand that held her own to her lips, in a sort of reverence. In the next instant she was encircled in the young man's arms, and pressed with fervour to his heart.

"Let us go"—said Mildred, extricating herself from an embrace that was too involuntarily bestowed, and too heartfelt to alarm her delicacy. "I feel certain Admiral Bluewater will miss me!"

"No, Mildred, we cannot part thus. Give me, at least, the poor consolation of knowing, that if *this* difficulty did not exist—that if you were an orphan for instance—you would be mine."

"Oh! Wycherly, how gladly—how gladly!—But, say no more—nay—"

This time the embrace was longer, more fervent even than before, and Wycherly was too much of a sailor to let the sweet girl escape from his arms without imprinting on her lips a kiss. He had no sooner relinquished his hold of the slight person of Mildred, ere it vanished. With this characteristic leave-taking, we change the scene to the tent of Sir Gervaise Oakes.

"You have seen Admiral Bluewater?" demanded the commander-in-chief, as soon as the form of Magrath darkened the entrance, and speaking with the sudden earnestness of a man determined to know the worst. "If so, tell me at once what hopes there are for him."

"Of all the human passions, Sir Jairvis," answered Magrath, looking aside, to avoid the keen glance of the other, "hope is generally considered, by all rational men, as the most treacherous and delusive; I may add, of all denominations or divisions of hope, that which decides on life is the most unsairtain. We all hope to live, I'm thinking, to a good old age, and yet how many of us live just long enough to be disappointed!"

Sir Gervaise did not move until the surgeon ceased speaking; then he began to pace the tent in mournful silence. He understood Magrath's manner so well, that the last faint hope he had felt from seeking his opinion was gone; he now knew that his friend must die. It required all his fortitude to stand up against this blow; for, single, childless, and accustomed to each other almost from infancy, these two veteran sailors had got to regard themselves as merely isolated parts of the same being. Magrath was affected more than he chose to express, and he blew his nose several times in a way that an observer would have found suspicious.

"Will you confer on me the favour, Dr. Magrath," said Sir Gervaise, in a gentle, subdued manner, "to ask Captain Greenly to come hither, as you pass the flag-staff?"

"Most willingly, Sir Jairvis; and I know he'll be any thing but backward in complying."

It was not long ere the captain of the Plantagenet made his appearance. Like all around him, the recent victory appeared to bring no exultation.

"I suppose Magrath told *you* all," said the vice-admiral, squeezing the other's hand.

"He gives no hopes, Sir Gervaise, I sincerely regret to say."

"I knew as much! I knew as much! And yet he is easy, Greenly!—nay, even seems happy. I *did* feel a little hope that this absence from suffering might be a favourable omen."

"I am glad to hear that much, sir; for I have been thinking that it is my duty to speak to the rear-admiral on the subject of his brother's marriage. From his own silence on the subject, it is possible—nay, from *all* circumstances, it is *probable* he never knew of it, and there may be reasons why he ought to be informed of the affair. As you say he is so easy, would there be an impropriety in mentioning it to him?"

Greenly could not possibly have made a suggestion that was a greater favour to Sir Gervaise. The necessity of doing, his habits of decision, and having an object in view, contributed to relieve his mind by diverting his thoughts to some active duty; and he seized his hat, beckoned Greenly to follow, and moved across the hill with a rapid pace, taking the path to the cottage. It was necessary to pass the flag-staff. As this was done, every countenance met the vice-admiral's glance, with a look of sincere sympathy. The bows that were exchanged, had more in them than the naked courtesies of such salutations; they were eloquent of feeling on both sides.

Bluewater was awake, and retaining the hand of Mildred affectionately in his own, when his friend entered. Relinquishing his hold, however, he grasped the hand of the vice-admiral, and looked earnestly at him, as if he pitied the sorrow that he knew the survivor must feel.

"My dear Bluewater," commenced Sir Gervaise, who acted under a nervous excitement, as well as from constitutional decision, "here is Greenly with something to tell you that we both think you ought to know, at a moment like this."

The rear-admiral regarded his friend intently, as if inviting him to proceed.

"Why, it's about your brother Jack. I fancy you cannot have known that he was ever married, or I think I should have heard you speak of it."

"Married!" repeated Bluewater, with great interest, and speaking with very little difficulty. "I think that must be an error. Inconsiderate and warm-hearted he was, but there was only one woman he *could*, nay, *would* have married. She is long since dead, but not as *his* wife; for that her uncle, a man of great wealth, but of unbending will, would never have suffered. *He* survived her, though my poor brother did not."

This was said in a mild voice, for the wounded man spoke equally without effort, and without pain.

"You hear, Greenly?" observed Sir Gervaise. "And yet it is not probable that you should be mistaken."

"Certainly, I am not, gentlemen. I saw Colonel Bluewater married, as did another officer who is at this moment in this very fleet. Captain Blakely is the person I mean, and I know that the priest who performed the ceremony is still living, a beneficed clergyman."

"This is wonderful to me! He fervently loved Agnes Hedworth, but his poverty was an obstacle to the union; and both died so young, that there was little opportunity of conciliating the uncle."

"That, sir, is your mistake. Agnes Hedworth was the bride."

A noise in the room interrupted the dialogue, and the three gentlemen saw Wycherly and Mildred stooping to pick up the fragments of a bowl that Mrs. Dutton had let fall. The latter, apparently in alarm, at the little accident, had sunk back into a seat, pale and trembling.

"My dear Mrs. Dutton, take a glass of water," said Sir Gervaise, kindly approaching her; "your nerves have been sorely tried of late; else would not such a trifle affect you."

"It is not *that*!" exclaimed the matron, huskily. "It is not *that*! Oh! the fearful moment has come at last; and, from my inmost spirit I thank thee, my Lord and my God, that it has come free from shame and disgrace!"

The closing words were uttered on bended knees, and with uplifted hands.

"Mother!—dearest, dearest mother," cried Mildred, falling on her mother's neck. "What mean you? What new misery has happened to-day?"

"*Mother!* Yes, sweet one, thou art, thou ever *shalt* be my child! This is the pang I have most dreaded; but what is an unknown tie of blood, to use, and affection, and to a mother's care? If I did not bear thee, Mildred, no natural mother could have loved thee more, or would have died for thee, as willingly!"

"Distress has disturbed her, gentlemen," said Mildred, gently extricating herself from her mother's arms, and helping her to rise. "A few moments of rest will restore her."

"No, darling; it must come now—it *ought* to come now—after what I have just heard, it would be unpardonable not to tell it, *now*. Did I understand you to say, sir, that you were present at the marriage of Agnes Hedworth, and that, too, with the brother of Admiral Bluewater?"

"Of that fact, there can be no question, madam. I and others will testify to it. The marriage took place in London, in the summer of 1725, while Blakely and myself were up from Portsmouth, on leave. Colonel Bluewater asked us both to be present, under a pledge of secresy."

"And in the summer of 1726, Agnes Hedworth died in my house and my arms, an hour after giving birth to this dear, this precious child—Mildred Dutton, as she has ever since been called—Mildred Bluewater, as it would seem her name should be."

It is unnecessary to dwell on the surprise with which all present, or the delight with which Bluewater and Wycherly heard this extraordinary announcement. A cry escaped Mildred, who threw herself on Mrs. Dutton's neck, entwining it with her arms, convulsively, as if refusing to permit the tie that had so long bound them together, to be thus rudely torn asunder. But half an hour of weeping, and of the tenderest consolations, calmed the poor girl a little, and she was able to listen to the explanations. These were exceedingly simple, and so clear, as, in connection with the other evidence, to put the facts out of all doubt.

Miss Hedworth had become known to Mrs. Dutton, while the latter was an inmate of the house of her patron. A year or two after the marriage of the lieutenant, and while he was on a distant station, Agnes Hedworth threw herself on the protection of his wife, asking a refuge for a woman in the most critical circumstances. Like all who knew Agnes Hedworth, Mrs. Dutton both respected and loved her; but the distance created between them, by birth and station, was such as to prevent any confidence. The former, for the few days passed with her humble friend, had acted with the quiet dignity of a woman conscious of no wrong; and no questions could be asked that implied doubts. A succession of fainting fits prevented all communications in the hour of death, and Mrs. Dutton found herself left with a child on her hands, and the dead body of her friend. Miss Hedworth had come to her dwelling unattended and under a false name. These circumstances induced Mrs. Dutton to apprehend the worst, and she proceeded to make her arrangements with great tenderness for the reputation of the deceased. The body was removed to London, and letters were sent to the uncle to inform him where it was to be found, with a reference should he choose to inquire into the circumstances of his niece's death. Mrs. Dutton ascertained that the body was interred in the usual manner, but no inquiry was ever made, concerning the particulars. The young duchess, Miss Hedworth's sister, was then travelling in Italy, whence she did not return for more than a year; and we may add, though Mrs. Dutton was unable to make the explanation, that her inquiries after the fate of a beloved sister, were met by a simple statement that she had died suddenly, on a visit to a watering-place, whither she had gone with a female friend for her health. Whether Mr. Hedworth himself had any suspicions of his niece's condition, is uncertain; but the probabilities were against it, for she had offended him by refusing a match equal in all respects to that made by her elder sister, with the single exception that the latter had married a man she loved, whereas he exacted of Agnes a very different sacrifice. Owing to the alienation produced by this affair, there was little communication between the uncle and niece; the latter passing her time in retirement, and professedly with friends that the former neither knew nor cared to know. In short, such was the mode of life of the respective parties, that nothing was easier than for the unhappy young widow to conceal her state from her uncle. The motive was the fortune of the expected child; this uncle having it in his power to alienate from it, by will, if he saw fit, certain family property, that might otherwise descend to the issue of the two sisters, as his co-heiresses. What might have happened in the end, or what poor Agnes meditated doing, can never be known; death closing the secret with his irremovable seal.

Mrs. Dutton was the mother of a girl but three months old, at the time this little stranger was left on her hands. A few weeks later her own child died; and having waited several months in vain for tidings from the Hedworth family, she had the surviving infant christened by the same name as that borne by her own daughter, and soon came to love it, as much, perhaps, as if she had borne it. Three years passed in this manner, when the time drew near for the return of her husband from the East Indies. To be ready to meet him, she changed her abode to a naval port, and, in so doing, changed her domestics. This left her accidentally, but fortunately, as she afterwards thought, completely mistress of the secret of Mildreth's birth; the one or two others to whom it was known being in stations to render it improbable they should ever communicate any thing on the subject, unless it were asked of them. Her original intention, however, was to communicate the facts, without reserve, to her husband. But he came back an altered man; brutal in manners, cold in his affections, and the victim of drunkenness. By this time, the wife was too much attached to the child to think of exposing it to the wayward caprices of such a being; and Mildred was educated, and grew in stature and beauty as the real offspring of her reputed parents.

All this Mrs. Dutton related clearly and briefly, refraining, of course, from making any allusion to the conduct of her husband, and referring all her own benevolence to her attachment to the child. Bluewater had strength enough to receive Mildred in his arms, and he kissed her pale cheek, again and again, blessing her in the most fervent and solemn manner.

"My feelings were not treacherous or unfaithful," he said; "I loved thee, sweetest, from the first. Sir Gervaise Oakes has my will, made in thy favour, before we sailed on this last cruise, and every shilling I leave will be thine. Mr. Atwood, procure that will, and add a codicil explaining this recent discovery, and confirming the legacy; let not the last be touched, for it is spontaneous and comes from the heart."

"And, now," answered Mrs. Dutton, "enough has passed for once. The sick-bed should be more quiet. Give me my child, again:—I cannot yet consent to part with her for ever."

"Mother! mother!" exclaimed Mildred, throwing herself on Mrs. Dutton's bosom—"I am yours, and yours only."

"Not so, I fear. Mildred, if all I suspect be true, and this is as proper a moment as another to place that matter also before your honoured uncle. Come forward, Sir Wycherly—I have understood you to say, this minute, in my ear, that you hold the pledge of this wilful girl to become your wife, should she ever be an orphan. An orphan she is, and has been since the first hour of her birth."

"No—no—no," murmured Mildred, burying her face still deeper in her mother's bosom, "not while *you* live, *can* I be an orphan. Not now—another time—this is unseasonable—cruel—nay, it is not what I said.'"

"Take her away, dearest Mrs. Dutton," said Bluewater, tears of joy forcing themselves from his eyes. "Take her away, lest too much happiness come upon me at once. My thoughts should be calmer at such a moment."

Wycherly removed Mildred from her mother's arms, and gently led her from the room. When in Mrs. Dutton's apartment, he whispered something in the ear of the agitated girl that caused her to turn on him a look of happiness, though it came dimmed with tears; then *he* had his turn of holding her, for another precious instant, to his heart.

"My dear Mrs. Dutton—nay, my dear *mother*," he said, "Mildred and myself have both need of parents. I am an orphan like herself, and we can never consent to part with you. Look forward, I entreat you, to making one of our family in all things, for never can either Mildred or myself cease to consider you as any thing but a parent entitled to more than common reverence and affection."

Wycherly had hardly uttered this proper speech, when he received what he fancied a ten-fold reward. Mildred, in a burst of natural feeling, without affectation or reserve, but yielding to her heart only, threw her arms around his neck, murmured the word "thanks" several times, and wept freely on his bosom. When Mrs. Dutton received the sobbing girl from him, Wycherly kissed the mother's cheek, and he left the room.

Admiral Bluewater would not consent to seek his repose until he had a private conference with his friend and Wycherly. The latter was frankness and liberality itself, but the former would not wait for settlements. These he trusted to the young man's honour. His own time was short, and he should die perfectly happy could he leave his niece in the care of one like our Virginian. He wished the marriage to take place in his presence. On this, he even insisted, and, of course, Wycherly make no objections, but went to state the case to Mrs. Dutton and Mildred.

"It is singular, Dick," said Sir Gervaise, wiping his eyes, as he looked from a window that commanded a view of the sea, "that I have left both our flags flying in the Cæsar! I declare, the oddness of the circumstance never struck me till this minute."

"Let them float thus a little longer, Gervaise. They have faced many a gale and many a battle together, and may endure each other's company a few hours longer."

CHAPTER XXX.

"Compound or weakness and of strength,
Mighty, yet ignorant of thy power!
Loftier than earth, or air, or sea,
Yet meaner than the lowliest flower!

Margaret Davidson.

Not a syllable of explanation, reproach, or self-accusation had passed between the commander-in-chief and the rear-admiral, since the latter received his wound. Each party appeared to blot out the events of the last few days, leaving the long vista of their past services and friendship, undisfigured by a single unsightly or unpleasant object. Sir Gervaise, while he retained an active superintendence of his fleet, and issued the necessary orders right and left, hovered around the bed of Bluewater with the assiduity and almost with the tenderness of a woman; still not the slightest allusion was made to the recent battles, or to any thing that had occurred in the short cruise. The speech recorded at the close of the last chapter, was the first words he had uttered which might, in any manner, carry the mind of either back to events that both might wish forgotten. The rear-admiral felt this forbearance deeply, and now that the subject was thus accidentally broached between them, he had a desire to say something in continuation. Still he waited until the baronet had left the window and taken a seat by his bed.

"Gervaise," Bluewater then commenced, speaking low from weakness, but speaking distinctly from feeling, "I cannot die without asking your forgiveness. There were several hours when I actually meditated treason—I will not say to my *king*; on that point my opinions are unchanged—but to *you*."

"Why speak of this, Dick? You did not know yourself when you believed it possible to desert me in the face of the enemy. How much better I judged of your character, is seen in the fact that I did not hesitate to engage double my force, well knowing that you could not fail to come to my rescue."

Bluewater looked intently at his friend, and a smile of serious satisfaction passed over his pallid countenance as he listened to Sir Gervaise's words, which were uttered with his usual warmth and sincerity of manner.

"I believe you know me better than I know myself," he answered, after a thoughtful pause; "yes, better than I know myself. What a glorious close to our professional career would it have been, Oakes, had I followed you into battle, as was our old practice, and fallen in your wake, imitating your own high example!"

"It is better as it is, Dick—if any thing that has so sad a termination can be well—yes, it is better as it is; you have fallen at my *side*, as it were. We will think or talk no more of this."

"We have been friends, and close friends too, for a long period, Gervaise," returned Bluewater, stretching his arm from the bed, with the long, thin fingers of the hand extended to meet the other's grasp; "yet, I cannot recall an act of yours which I can justly lay to heart, as unkind, or untrue."

"God forgive me, if you can—I hope not, Dick; most sincerely do I hope not. It would give me great pain to believe it."

"*You* have no cause for self-reproach. In no one act or thought can you justly accuse yourself with injuring *me*. I should die much happier could I say the same of myself, Oakes!"

"Thought!—Dick?—Thought! You never meditated aught against *me* in your whole life. The love you bear *me*, is the true reason why you lie there, at this blessed moment."

"It is grateful to find that I have been understood. I am deeply indebted to you, Oakes, for declining to signal me and my division down, when I foolishly requested that untimely forbearance. I was then suffering an anguish of mind, to which any pain of the body I may now endure, is an elysium; your self-denial gave time—"

"For the *heart* to prompt you to that which your feelings yearned to do from the first, Bluewater," interrupted Sir Gervaise. "And, now, as your commanding officer, I enjoin silence on this subject, *for ever.*"

"I will endeavour to obey. It will not be long, Oakes, that I shall remain under your orders," added the rear-admiral, with a painful smile. "There should be no charge of mutiny against me in the *last* act of my life. You ought to forgive the one sin of omission, when you remember how much and how completely my will has been subject to yours, during the last five-and-thirty years,—how little my mind has matured a professional thought that yours has not originated!"

"Speak no more of 'forgive,' I charge you, Dick. That you have shown a girl-like docility in obeying all my orders, too, is a truth I will aver before God and man; but when it comes to *mind*, I am far from asserting that mine has had the mastery. I do believe, could the truth he ascertained, it would be found that I am, at this blessed moment, enjoying a professional reputation, which is more than half due to you."

"It matters little, now, Gervaise—it matters little, now. We were two light-hearted and gay lads, Oakes, when we first met as boys, fresh from school, and merry as health and spirits could make us."

"We were, indeed, Dick!—yes, we were; thoughtless as if this sad moment were never to arrive!"

"There were George Anson, and Peter Warren, little Charley Saunders, Jack Byng, and a set of us, that did, indeed, live as if we were never to die! We carried our lives, as it might be, in our hands, Oakes!"

"There is much of that, Dick, in boyhood and youth. But, he is happiest, after all, who can meet this moment as you do—calmly, and yet without any dependence on his own merits."

"I had an excellent mother, Oakes! Little do we think, in youth, how much we owe to the unextinguishable tenderness, and far-seeing lessons of our mothers! Ours both died while we were young, yet I do think we were their debtors for far more than we could ever repay."

Sir Gervaise simply assented, but making no immediate answer, otherwise, a long pause succeeded, during which the vice-admiral fancied that his friend was beginning to doze. He was mistaken.

"You will be made Viscount Bowldero, for these last affairs, Gervaise," the wounded man unexpectedly observed, showing how much his thoughts were still engrossed with the interests of his friend. "Nor do I see why you should again refuse a peerage. Those who remain in this world, may well yield to its usages and opinions, while they do not interfere with higher obligations."

"I!"—exclaimed Sir Gervaise, gloomily. "The thought of so commemorating what has happened, would be worse than defeat to me! No—I ask no change of name to remind me constantly of my loss!"

Bluewater looked grateful, rather than pleased; but he made no answer. Now, he fell into a light slumber, from which he did not awake until the time he had himself set for the marriage of Wycherly and Mildred. With one uncle dead and still unburied, and another about to quit the world for ever, a rite that is usually deemed as joyous as it is solemn, might seem unseasonable; but the dying man had made it a request that he might have the consolation of knowing ere he expired, that he left his niece under the legal protection of one as competent, as he was desirous of protecting her. The reader must imagine the arguments that were used for the occasion, but they were such as disposed all, in the end, to admit the propriety of yielding their ordinary prejudices to the exigencies of the moment. It may be well to add, also, to prevent useless cavilling, that the laws of England were not as rigid on the subject of the celebration of marriages in 1745, as they subsequently became; and that it was lawful then to perform the ceremony in a private house without a license, and without the publishing of banns, even; restrictions that were imposed a few years later. The penalty for dispensing with the publication of banns, was a fine of £100, imposed on the clergyman; and this fine Bluewater chose to pay, rather than leave the only great object of life that now remained before him unaccomplished. This penalty in no degree impaired the validity of the contract, though Mrs. Dutton, as a woman, felt averse to parting with her beloved, without a rigid observance of all the customary forms. The point had finally been disposed of, by recourse to arguments addressed to the reason of this respectable woman, and by urging the necessity of the case. Her consent, however, was not given without a proviso, that a license should be subsequently procured, and a second marriage be had at a more fitting moment, should the ecclesiastical authorities consent to the same; a most improbable thing in itself.

Mr. Rotherham availed himself of the statute inflicting the penalty, as an excuse for not officiating. His real motive, however, was understood, and the chaplain of the Plantagenet, a divine of character and piety, was substituted in his place. Bluewater had requested that as many of the captains of the fleet should be present as could be collected, and it was the assembling of these warriors of the deep, together with the arrival of the clergyman, that first gave notice of the approach of the appointed hour.

It is not our intention to dwell on the details of a ceremony that had so much that was painful in its solemnities. Neither Wycherly nor Mildred made any change in their attire, and the lovely bride wept from the time the service began, to the moment when she left the arms of her uncle, to be received in those of her husband, and was supported from the room. All seemed sad, indeed, but Bluewater; to him the scene was exciting, but it brought great relief to his mind.

"I am now ready to die, gentlemen," he said, as the door closed on the new-married couple. "My last worldly care is disposed of, and it were better for me to turn all my thoughts to another state of being. My niece, Lady Wychecombe, will inherit the little I have to leave; nor do I know that it is of much importance to substantiate her birth, as her uncle clearly bestowed what would have been her mother's property, on her aunt, the duchess. If my dying declaration can be of any use, however, you hear it, and can testify to it. Now, come and take leave of me, one by one, that I may bless you all, and thank you for much undeserved, and, I fear, unrequited love."

The scene that followed was solemn and sad. One by one, the captains drew near the bed, and to each the dying man had something kind and affectionate to say. Even the most cold-hearted looked grave, and O'Neil, a man remarkable for a *gaité de c[oe]ur* that rendered the excitement of battle some of the pleasantest moments of his life, literally shed tears on the hand he kissed.

"Ah! my old friend," said the rear-admiral, as Parker, of the Carnatic, drew near in his customary meek and subdued manner, "you perceive it is not years alone that bring us to our graves! They tell me you have behaved as usual in these late affairs; I trust that, after a long life of patient and arduous services, you are about to receive a proper reward."

"I will acknowledge, Admiral Bluewater," returned Parker, earnestly, "that it would be peculiarly grateful to receive some mark of the approbation of my sovereign; principally on account of my dear wife and children. We are not, like yourself, descended from a noble family; but must carve our rights to distinction, and they who have never known honours of this nature, prize them highly."

"Ay, my good Parker," interrupted the rear-admiral, "and they who have ever known them, know their emptiness; most especially as they approach that verge of existence whence the eye looks in a near and fearful glance, over the vast and unknown range of eternity."

"No doubt, sir; nor am I so vain as to suppose that hairs which have got to be grey as mine, can last for ever. But, what I was about to say is, that precious as honours are to the humble, I would cheerfully yield every hope of the sort I have, to see you on the poop of the Cæsar again, with Mr. Cornet at your elbow, leading the fleet, or following the motions of the vice-admiral."

"Thank you, my good Parker; that can never be; nor can I say, now, that I wish it might. When we have cast off from the world, there is less pleasure in looking back, than in looking ahead. God bless you, Parker, and keep you, as you ever have been, an honest man."

Stowel was the last to approach the bed, nor did he do it until all had left the room but Sir Gervaise and himself.

The indomitable good-nature, and the professional nonchalance of Bluewater, by leaving every subordinate undisturbed in the enjoyment of his own personal caprices, had rendered the rear-admiral a greater favourite, in one sense at least, than the commander-in-chief. Stowel, by his near connection with Bluewater, had profited more by these peculiarities than any other officer under him, and the effect on his feelings had been in a very just proportion to the benefits. He could not refrain, it is true, from remembering the day when he himself had been a lieutenant in the ship in which the rear-admiral had been a midshipman, but he no longer recollected the circumstance with the bitterness that it sometimes drew after it. On the contrary, it was now brought to his mind merely as the most distant of the many land-marks in their long and joint services.

"Well, Stowel," observed Bluewater, smiling sadly, "even the old Cæsar must be left behind. It is seldom a flag-captain has not some heart-burnings on account of his superior, and most sincerely do I beg you to forget and forgive any I may have occasioned yourself."

"Heaven help me, sir!—I was far, just then, from thinking of any such thing! I was fancying how little I should have thought it probable, when we were together in the Calypso, that I should ever be thus standing at *your* bed-side. Really, Admiral Bluewater, I would rejoice to share with you the remnant of life that is left me."

"I do believe you would, Stowel; but that can never be. I have just performed my last act in this world, in giving my niece to Sir Wycherly Wychecombe."

"Yes, sir;—yes, sir—marriage is no doubt honourable, as I often tell Mrs. Stowel, and therefore not to be despised; and yet it *is* singular, that a gentleman who has lived a bachelor himself, should fancy to see a marriage ceremony performed, and that, too, at the cost of £100, if any person choose to complain, just at the close of his own cruise! However, men are no more alike in such matters, than women in their domestic qualities; and I sincerely hope this young Sir Wycherly may find as much comfort, in the old house I understand he has a little inland here, as you and I have had together, sir, in the old Cæsar. I suppose there'll be no co-equals in Wychecombe Hall."

"I trust not, Stowel. But you must now receive my last orders, as to the Cæsar—"

"The commander-in-chief has his own flag flying aboard of us, sir!" interrupted the methodical captain, in a sort of admonitory way.

"Never mind that, Stowel;—I'll answer for his acquiescence. My body must be received on board, and carried round in the ship to Plymouth. Place it on the main-deck, where the people can see the coffin; I would pass my last hours above ground, in their midst."

"It shall be done, sir—yes, sir, to the letter, Sir Gervaise not countermanding. And I'll write this evening to Mrs. Stowel to say she needn't come down, as usual, as soon as she hears the ship is in, but that she must wait until your flag is fairly struck."

"I should be sorry, Stowel, to cause a moment's delay in the meeting of husband and wife!"

"Don't name it, Admiral Bluewater;—Mrs. Stowel will understand that it's duty; and when we married, I fully explained to her that duty, with a sailor, came before matrimony."

A little pause succeeded, then Bluewater took a final and affectionate leave of his captain. Some twenty minutes elapsed in a profound silence, during which Sir Gervaise did not stir, fancying that his friend again dozed. But it was ordered that Bluewater was never to sleep again, until he took the final rest of the dead. It was the mind, which had always blazed above the duller lethargy of his body, that buoyed him thus up, giving an unnatural impulse to his physical powers; an impulse, however, that was but momentary, and which, by means of the reaction, contributed, in the end, to his more speedy dissolution. Perceiving, at length, that his friend did not sleep, Sir Gervaise drew near his bed.

"Richard," he said, gently, "there is one without, who pines to be admitted. I have refused even his tears, under the impression that you felt disposed to sleep."

"Never less so. My mind appears to become brighter and clearer, instead of fading; I think I shall never sleep, in the sense you mean. Whoever the person is, let him be admitted."

Receiving this permission, Sir Gervaise opened the door, and Geoffrey Cleveland entered. At the same moment, Galleygo, who came and went at pleasure, thrust in his own ungainly form. The boy's face betrayed the nature and the extent of his grief. In his mind, Admiral Bluewater was associated with all the events of his own professional life; and, though the period had in truth been so short, in his brief existence, the vista through which he looked back, seemed quite as long as that which marked the friendship of the two admirals, themselves. Although he struggled manfully for self-control, feeling got the better of the lad, and he threw himself on his knees, at the side of his bed, sobbing as if his heart would break. Bluewater's eye glistened, and he laid a hand affectionately on the head of his young relative.

"Gervaise, you will take charge of this boy, when I'm gone," he said; "receive him in your own ship. I leave him to you, as a very near and dear professional legacy. Cheer up—cheer up—my brave boy; look upon all this as a sailor's fortune. Our lives are the—"

The word "king's," which should have succeeded, seemed to choke the speaker. Casting a glance of meaning at his friend, with a painful smile on his face, he continued silent.

"Ah! dear sir," answered the midshipman, ingenuously; "I knew that *we* might all be killed, but it never occurred to me that an admiral could lose his life in battle. I'm sure—I'm sure you are the very first that has met with this accident!"

"Not by many, my poor Geoffrey. As there are but few admirals, few fall; but we are as much exposed as others."

"If I had only run that Monsieur des Prez through the body, when we closed with him," returned the boy, grating his teeth, and looking all the vengeance for which, at the passing instant, he felt the desire; "it would have been *something*! I might have done it, too, for he was quite unguarded!"

"It would have been a very bad *thing*, boy, to have injured a brave man, uselessly."

"Of what use was it to shoot you, sir? We took their ship, just the same as if you had not been hurt."

"I rather think, Geoffrey, their ship was virtually taken before I was wounded," returned Bluewater, smiling. "But I was shot by a French marine, who did no more than his duty."

"Yes, sir," exclaimed the boy, impatiently; "and *he* escaped without a scratch. *He*, at least, ought to have been *massacred*."

"Thou art bloody-minded, child; I scarce know thee. *Massacred* is not a word for either a British nobleman or a British sailor. I saved the life of that marine; and, when you come to lie, like me, on your death-bed, Geoffrey, you will learn how sweet a consolation can be derived from the consciousness of such an act; we all need mercy, and none ought to expect it, for themselves, who do not yield it to others."

The boy was rebuked, and his feelings took a better, though scarcely a more natural direction. Bluewater now spoke to him of his newly-discovered cousin, and had a melancholy satisfaction in creating an interest in behalf of Mildred, in the breast of the noble-hearted and ingenuous boy. The latter listened with respectful attention, as had been his wont, until, deceived by the tranquil and benevolent manner of Bluewater, he permitted himself to fall into the natural delusion of believing the wound of the rear-admiral less serious than he had supposed, and to begin to entertain hopes that the wounded man might yet survive. Calmed by these feelings, he soon ceased to weep; and, promising discretion, was permitted by Sir Gervaise to remain in the room, where he busied himself in the offices of a nurse.

Another long pause succeeded this exciting little scene, during which Bluewater lay quietly communing with himself and his God. Sir Gervaise wrote orders, and read reports, though his eye was never off the countenance of his friend more than a minute or two at a time. At length, the rear-admiral aroused himself, again, and began to take an interest once more, in the persons and things around him.

"Galleygo, my old fellow-cruiser," he said, "I leave Sir Gervaise more particularly in your care. As we advance in life, our friends decrease in numbers; it is only those that have been well tried that we can rely on."

"Yes, Admiral Blue, I knows that, and so does Sir Jarvy. Yes, old shipmates afore young 'uns, any day, and old sailors, too, afore green hands. Sir Jarvy's Bowlderos are good plate-holders, and the likes of that; but when it comes to heavy weather, and a hard strain, I thinks but little on 'em, all put together."

"By the way, Oakes," said Bluewater, with a sudden interest in such a subject, that he never expected to feel again, "I have heard nothing of the first day's work, in which, through the little I have gleaned, by listening to those around me, I understand you took a two-decker, besides dismasting the French admiral?"

"Pardon me, Dick; you had better try and catch a little sleep; the subject of those two days' work is really painful to me."

"Well, then, Sir Jarvy, if you has an avarsion to telling the story to Admiral Blue, I can do it, your honour," put in Galleygo, who gloried in giving a graphic description of a sea-fight. "I thinks, now, a history of that day will comfort a flag-hofficer as has been so badly wounded himself."

Bluewater offering no opposition, Galleygo proceeded with his account of the evolutions of the ships, as we have already described them, succeeding surprisingly well in rendering the narrative interesting, and making himself perfectly intelligible and clear, by his thorough knowledge, and ready use, of the necessary nautical terms. When he came to the moment in which the English line separated, part passing to windward, and part to leeward of the two French ships, he related the incident in so clear and spirited a manner, that the commander-in-chief himself dropped his pen, and sat listening with pleasure.

"Who could imagine, Dick," Sir Gervaise observed, "that those fellows in the tops watch us so closely, and could give so accurate an account of what passes!"

"Ah! Gervaise, and what is the vigilance of Galleygo to that of the All-seeing eye! It is a terrible thought, at an hour like this, to remember that nothing can be forgotten. I have somewhere read that not an oath is uttered that does not continue to vibrate through all time, in the wide-spreading currents of sound—not a prayer lisped, that its record is not also to be found stamped on the laws of nature, by the indelible seal of the Almighty's will!"

There was little in common between the religious impressions of the two friends. They were both sailors, and though the word does not necessarily imply that they were sinners in an unusual degree, neither does it rigidly imply that they were saints. Each had received the usual elementary education, and then each had been turned adrift, as it might be on the ocean of life, to suffer the seed to take root, and the fruit to ripen as best they might. Few of those "who go down to the great deep in ships," and who escape the more brutalizing effects of lives so rude, are altogether without religious impressions. Living so much, as it were, in the immediate presence of the power of God, the sailor is much disposed to reverence his omnipotence, even while he transgresses his laws; but in nearly all those instances in which nature has implanted a temperament inclining to deep feeling, as was the case with Bluewater, not even the harsh examples, nor the loose or irresponsible lives of men thus separated from the customary ties of society, can wholly extinguish the reverence for God which is created by constantly dwelling in the presence of his earthly magnificence. This sentiment in Bluewater had not been altogether without fruits, for he both read and reflected much. Sometimes, though at isolated and distant intervals, he even prayed; and that fervently, and with a strong and full sense of his own demerits. As a consequence of this general disposition, and of the passing convictions, his mind was better attuned for the crisis before him, than would have been the case with most of his brethren in arms, who, when overtaken with the fate so common to the profession, are usually left to sustain their last moments with the lingering enthusiasm of strife and victory.

On the other hand, Sir Gervaise was as simple as a child in matters of this sort. He had a reverence for his Creator, and such general notions of his goodness and love, as the well-disposed are apt to feel; but all the dogmas concerning the lost condition of the human race, the mediation, and the power of faith, floated in his mind as opinions not to be controverted, and yet as scarcely to be felt. In short, the commander-in-chief admitted the practical heresy, which overshadows the faith of millions, while he deemed himself to be a stout advocate of church and king. Still, Sir Gervaise Oakes, on occasions, was more than usually disposed to seriousness, and was even inclined to be devout; but it was without much regard to theories or revelation. At such moments, while his opinions would not properly admit him within the pale of any Christian church, in particular, his feelings might have identified him with all. In a word, we apprehend he was a tolerably fair example of what vague generalities, when acting on a temperament not indisposed to moral impressions, render the great majority of men; who flit around the mysteries of a future state, without alighting either on the consolations of faith, or discovering any of those logical conclusions which, half the time unconsciously to themselves, they seem to expect. When Bluewater made his last remark, therefore, the vice-admiral looked anxiously at his friend; and religion for the first time since the other received his hurt, mingled with his reflections. He had devoutly, though mentally, returned thanks to God for his victory, but it had never occurred to him that Bluewater might need some preparation for death.

"Would you like to see the Plantagenet's chaplain, again, Dick?" he said, tenderly; "you are no *Papist*; of *that* I am certain."

"In that you are quite right, Gervaise. I consider all churches—*the* one holy *Catholic* church, if you will, as but a means furnished by divine benevolence to aid weak men in their pilgrimage; but I also believe that there is even a shorter way to his forgiveness than through these common avenues. How far I am right," he added, smiling, "none will probably know better than myself, a few hours hence."

"Friends *must* meet again, hereafter, Bluewater; it is irrational to suppose that they who have loved each other so well in this state of being, are to be for ever separated in the other."

"We will hope so, Oakes," taking the vice-admiral's hand; "we will hope so. Still, there will be no ships for us—no cruises—no victories—no triumphs! It is only at moments like this, at which I have arrived, that we come to view these things in their proper light. Of all the past, your constant, unwavering friendship, gives me the most pleasure!"

The vice-admiral could resist no longer. He turned aside and wept. This tribute to nature, in one so manly, was imposing even to the dying man, and Galleygo regarded it with awe. Familiar as the latter had become with his master, by use and indulgence, no living being, in his estimation, was as authoritative or as formidable as the commander-in-chief; and the effect of the present spectacle, was to induce him to hide his own face in self-abasement. Bluewater saw it all, but he neither spoke, nor gave any token of his observation. He merely prayed, and that right fervently, not only for his friend, but for his humble and uncouth follower.

A reaction took place in the system of the wounded man, about nine o'clock that night. At this time he believed himself near his end, and he sent for Wycherly and his niece, to take his leave of them. Mrs. Dutton was also present, as was Magrath, who remained on shore, in attendance. Mildred lay for half an hour, bathing her uncle's pillow with her tears, until she was removed at the surgeon's suggestion.

"Ye'll see, Sir Gervaise," he whispered—(or "Sir Jairvis," as he always pronounced the name,)—"ye'll see, Sir Jairvis, that it's a duty of the faculty to *prolong* life, even when there's no hope of *saving* it; and if ye'll be regairding the judgment of a professional man, Lady Wychecombe had better withdraw. It would really be a matter of honest exultation for us Plantagenets to get the rear-admiral through the night, seeing that the surgeon of the Cæsar said he could no survive the setting sun."

At the moment of final separation, Bluewater had little to say to his niece. Ho kissed and blessed her again and again, and then signed that she should be taken away. Mrs. Dutton, also, came in for a full share of his notice, he having desired her to remain after Wycherly and Mildred had quitted the room.

"To your care and affection, excellent woman," he said, in a voice that had now sunk nearly to a whisper—"we owe it, that Mildred is not unfit for her station. Her recovery would have been even more painful than her loss, had she been restored to her proper family, uneducated, vulgar, and coarse."

"That could hardly have happened to Mildred, sir, in any circumstances," answered the weeping woman. "Nature has done too much for the dear child, to render her any thing but delicate and lovely, under any tolerable circumstances of depression."

"She is better as she is, and God be thanked that he raised up such a protector for her childhood. You have been all in all to her in her infancy, and she will strive to repay it to your age."

Of this Mrs. Dutton felt too confident to need assurances; and receiving the dying man's blessing, she knelt at his bed-side, prayed fervently for a few minutes, and withdrew. After this, nothing out of the ordinary track occurred until past midnight, and Magrath, more than once, whispered his joyful anticipations that the rear-admiral would survive until morning. An hour before day, however, the wounded man revived, in a way that the surgeon distrusted. He knew that no physical change of this sort could well happen that did not arise from the momentary ascendency of mind over matter, as the spirit is on the point of finally abandoning its earthly tenement; a circumstance of no unusual occurrence in patients of strong and active intellectual properties, whose faculties often brighten for an instant, in their last moments, as the lamp flashes and glares as it is about to become extinct. Going to the bed, he examined his patient attentively, and was satisfied that the final moment was near.

"You're a man and a soldier, Sir Jairvis," he said, in a low voice, "and it'll no be doing good to attempt misleading your judgment in a case of this sort. Our respectable friend, the rear-admiral, is *articulo mortis*, as one might almost say; he cannot possibly survive half an hour."

Sir Gervaise started. He looked around him a little wistfully; for, at that moment, he would have given much to be alone with his dying friend. But he hesitated to make a request, which, it struck him, might seem improper. From this embarrassment, however, he was relieved by Bluewater, himself, who had the same desire, without the same scruples about confessing it. *He* drew the surgeon to his side, and whispered a wish to be left alone with the commander-in-chief.

"Well, there will be no trespass on the rules of practice in indulging the poor man in his desire," muttered Magrath, as he looked about him to gather the last of his professional instruments, like the workman who is about to quit one place of toil to repair to another; "and I'll just be indulging him."

So saying, he pushed Galleygo and Geoffrey from the room before him, left it himself, and closed the door.

Finding himself alone, Sir Gervaise knelt at the side of the bed and prayed, holding the hand of his friend in both his own. The example of Mrs. Dutton, and the yearnings of his own heart, exacted this sacrifice; when it was over he felt a great relief from sensations that nearly choked him.

"Do you forgive me, Gervaise?" whispered Bluewater.

"Name it not—name it not, my best friend. We all have our moments of weakness, and our need of pardon. May God forget all *my* sins, as freely as I forget your errors!"

"God bless you, Oakes, and keep you the same simple-minded, true-hearted man, you have ever been."

Sir Gervaise buried his face in the bed-clothes, and groaned.

"Kiss me, Oakes," murmured the rear-admiral.

In order to do this, the commander-in-chief rose from his knees and bent over the body of his friend. As he raised himself from the cheek he had saluted, a benignant smile gleamed on the face of the dying man, and he ceased to breathe. Near half a minute followed, however, before the last and most significant breath that is ever drawn from man, was given. The remainder of that night Sir Gervaise Oakes passed in the chamber alone, pacing the floor, recalling the many scenes of pleasure, danger, pain, and triumph, through which he and the dead had passed in company. With the return of light, he summoned the attendants, and retired to his tent.

CHAPTER XXXI.

"And they came for the buried king that lay
At rest in that ancient fane;
For he must be armed on the battle day,
With them to deliver Spain!—
Then the march went sounding on,
And the Moors by noontide sun,
Were dust on Tolosa's plain."

MRS. HEMANS.

It remains only to give a rapid sketch of the fortunes of our principal characters, and of the few incidents that are more immediately connected with what has gone before. The death of Bluewater was announced to the fleet, at sunrise, by hauling down his flag from the mizzen of the Cæsar. The vice-admiral's flag came down with it, and re-appeared at the next minute at the fore of the Plantagenet. But the little white emblem of rank never went aloft again in honour of the deceased. At noon, it was spread over his coffin, on the main-deck of the ship, agreeably to his own request; and more than once that day, did some rough old tar use it, to wipe the tear from his eyes.

In the afternoon of the day after the death of one of our heroes, the wind came round to the westward, and all the vessels lifted their anchors, and proceeded to Plymouth. The crippled ships, by this time, were in a state to carry more or less sail, and a stranger who had seen the melancholy-looking line, as it rounded the Start, would have fancied it a beaten fleet on its return to port. The only signs of exultation that appeared, were the jacks that were flying over the white flags of the prizes; and even when all had anchored, the same air of sadness reigned among these victorious mariners. The body was landed, with the usual forms; but the procession of warriors of the deep that followed it, was distinguished by a gravity that exceeded the ordinary aspects of mere form. Many of the captains, and Greenly in particular, had viewed the man[oe]uvring of Bluewater with surprise, and the latter not altogether without displeasure; but his subsequent conduct completely erased these impressions, leaving no other recollection connected with his conduct that morning than the brilliant courage, and admirable handling of his vessels, by which the fortunes of a nearly desperate day were retrieved. Those who did reflect any longer on the subject, attributed the singularity of the course pursued by the rear-admiral, to some private orders communicated in the telegraphic signal, as already mentioned.

It is unnecessary for us to dwell on the particular movements of the fleet, after it reached Plymouth. The ships were repaired, the prizes received into the service, and, in due time, all took the sea again, ready and anxious to encounter their country's enemies. They ran the careers usual to English heavy cruisers in that age; and as ships form characters in this work, perhaps it may not be amiss to take a general glance at their several fortunes, together with those of their respective commanders. Sir Gervaise fairly wore out the Plantagenet, which vessel was broken up three years later, though not until she had carried a blue flag at her main, more than two years. Greenly lived to be a rear-admiral of the red, and died of yellow-fever in the Island of Barbadoes. The Cæsar, with Stowel still in command of her, foundered at sea in a winter's cruise in the Baltic, every soul perishing. This calamity occurred the winter succeeding the summer of our legend, and the only relieving circumstance connected with the disaster, was the fact that her commander got rid of Mrs. Stowel altogether, from that day forward. The Thunderer had her share in many a subsequent battle, and Foley, her captain, died rear-admiral of England, and a vice-admiral of the red, thirty years later. The Carnatic was commanded by Parker, until the latter got a right to hoist a blue flag at the mizzen; which was done for just one day, to comply with form, when both ship and admiral were laid aside, as too old for further use. It should be added, however, that Parker was knighted by the king on board his own ship; a circumstance that cast a halo of sunshine over the close of the life of one, who had commenced his career so humbly, as to render this happy close more than equal to his expectations. In direct opposition to this, it may be said here, that Sir Gervaise refused, for the third time, to be made Viscount Bowldero, with a feeling just the reverse of that of Parker's; for, secure of his social position, and careless of politics, he viewed the elevation with an indifference that was a natural consequence enough of his own birth, fortune, and high character. On this occasion,—it was after another victory,—George II. personally alluded to the subject, remarking that the success we have recorded had never met with its reward; when the old seaman let out the true secret of his pertinaciously declining an honour, about which he might otherwise have been supposed to be as indifferent to the acceptance, as to the refusal. "Sir," he answered to the remark of the king, "I am duly sensible of your majesty's favour; but, I can never consent to receive a patent of nobility that, in my eyes, will always seem to be sealed with the blood of my closest and best friend." This reply was remembered, and the subject was never adverted to again.

The fate of the Blenheim was one of those impressive blanks that dot the pages of nautical history. She sailed for the Mediterranean alone, and after she had discharged her pilot, was never heard of again. This did not occur, however, until Captain Sterling had been killed on her decks, in one of Sir Gervaise's subsequent actions. The Achilles was suffered to drift in, too near to some heavy French batteries, before the treaty of Aix-la-Chapelle was signed; and, after every stick had been again cut out of her, she was compelled to lower her flag. His earldom and his courage, saved Lord Morganic from censure; but, being permitted to go up to Paris, previously to his exchange, he contracted a matrimonial engagement with a celebrated *danseuse*, a craft that gave him so much future employment, that he virtually abandoned his profession. Nevertheless, his name was on the list of vice-admirals of the blue, when he departed this life. The Warspite and Captain Goodfellow both died natural deaths; one as a receiving-ship, and the other as a rear-admiral of the white. The Dover, Captain Drinkwater, was lost in attempting to weather Scilly in a gale, when her commander, and quite half her crew, were drowned. The York did many a hard day's duty, before her time arrived; but, in the end, she was so much injured in a general action as to be abandoned and set fire to, at sea. Her commander was lost overboard, in the very first cruise she took, after that related in this work. The Elizabeth rotted as a guard-ship, in the Medway; and Captain Blakely retired from the service with one arm, a yellow admiral. The Dublin laid her bones in the cove of Cork, having been condemned after a severe winter passed on the north coast. Captain O'Neil was killed in a duel with a French officer, after the peace; the latter having stated that his ship had run away from two frigates commanded by the *Chevalier*. The Chloe was taken by an enemy's fleet, in the next war; but Captain Denham worked his way up to a white flag at the main, and a peerage. The Druid was wrecked that very summer, chasing inshore, near Bordeaux; and Blewet, in a professional point of view, never regained the ground he lost, on this occasion. As for the sloops and cutters, they went the way of all small cruisers, while their nameless commanders shared the usual fates of mariners.

Wycherly remained at Wychecombe until the interment of his uncle took place; at which, aided by Sir Reginald's influence and knowledge, and, in spite of Tom's intrigues, he appeared as chief mourner. The affair of the succession was also so managed as to give him very little trouble. Tom, discovering that his own illegitimacy was known, and seeing the hopelessness of a contest against such an antagonist as Sir Reginald, who knew quite as much of the facts as he did of the law of the case, was fain to retire from the field. From that moment, no one heard any thing more of the legacies. In the end he received the £20,000 in the five per cents, and the few chattels Sir Wycherly had a right to give away; but his enjoyment of them was short, as he contracted a severe cold that very autumn, and died of a malignant fever, in a few weeks. Leaving no will, his property escheated; but it was all restored to his two uterine brothers, by the liberality of the ministry, and out of respect to the long services of the baron, which two brothers, it will he remembered, alone had any of the blood of Wychecombe in their veins to boast of. This was disposing of the savings of both the baronet and the judge, with a very suitable regard to moral justice.

Wycherly also appeared, though it was in company with Sir Gervaise Oakes, as one of the principal mourners at the funeral obsequies of Admiral Bluewater. These were of a public character, and took place in Westminster Abbey. The carriages of that portion of the royal personages who were not restrained by the laws of court-etiquette, appeared in the procession; and several members of that very family that the deceased regarded as intruders, were present incog. at his last rites. This, however, was but one of the many illusions that the great masquerade of life is constantly offering to the public gaze.

There was little difficulty in establishing the claims of Mildred, to be considered the daughter of Colonel Bluewater and Agnes Hedworth. Lord Bluewater was soon satisfied; and, as he was quite indifferent to the possession of his kinsman's money, an acquisition he neither wished nor expected, the most perfect good-will existed between the parties. There was more difficulty with the Duchess of Glamorgan, who had acquired too many of the notions of very high rank, to look with complacency on a niece that had been educated as the daughter of a sailing-master in the navy. She raised many objections, while she admitted that she had been the confidant of her sister's attachment to John Bluewater. Her second son, Geoffrey, did more to remove her scruples than all the rest united; and when Sir Gervaise Oakes, in person, condescended to make a journey to the Park, to persuade her to examine the proofs, she could not well decline. As soon as one of her really candid mind entered into the inquiry, the evidence was found to be irresistible, and she at once yielded to the feelings of nature. Wycherly had been indefatigable in establishing his wife's claims—more so, indeed, than in establishing his own; and, at the suggestion of the vice-admiral—or, admiral of the white, as he had become by a recent general promotion—he consented to accompany the latter in this visit, waiting at the nearest town, however, for a summons to the Park, as soon as it could be ascertained that his presence would be agreeable to its mistress.

"If my niece prove but half as acceptable in appearance, as my *nephew*, Sir Gervaise," observed the duchess, when the young Virginian was introduced to her, and laying stress on the word we have italicised—"nothing can be wanting to the agreeables of this new connection. I am impatient, now, to see my niece; Sir Wycherly Wychecombe has prepared me to expect a young woman of more than common merit."

"My life on it, duchess, he has not raised your expectations too high. The poor girl is still dwelling in her cottage, the companion of her reputed mother; but it is time, Wychecombe, that you had claimed your bride."

"I expect to find her and Mrs. Dutton at the Hall, on my return, Sir Gervaise; it having been thus arranged between us. The sad ceremonies through which we have lately been, were unsuited to the introduction of the new mistress to her abode, and the last had been deferred to a more fitting occasion."

"Let the first visit that Lady Wychecombe pays, be to this place," said the duchess. "I do not command it, Sir Wycherly, as one who has some slight claims to her duty; but I solicit it, as one who wishes to possess every hold upon her love. Her mother was an *only* sister; and an *only* sister's child must be very near to one."

It would have been impossible for the Duchess of Glamorgan to have said as much as this before she saw the young Virginian; but, now he had turned out a person so very different from what she expected, she had lively hopes in behalf of her niece.

Wycherly returned to Wychecombe, after this short visit to Mildred's aunt, and found his lovely bride in quiet possession, accompanied by her mother. Dutton still remained at the station, for he had the sagacity to see that he might not be welcome, and modesty enough to act with a cautious reserve. But Wycherly respected his excellent wife too profoundly not to have a due regard to her feelings, in all things; and the master was invited to join the party. Brutality and meanness united, like those which belonged to the character of Dutton, are not easily abashed, and he accepted the invitation, in the hope that, after all, he was to reap as many advantages by the marriage of Mildred with the affluent baronet, as if she had actually been his daughter.

After passing a few weeks in sober happiness at home, Wycherly felt it due to all parties, to carry his wife to the Park, in order that she might make the acquaintance of the near relatives who dwelt there. Mrs. Dutton, by invitation, was of the party; but Dutton was left behind, having no necessary connection with the scenes and the feelings that were likely to occur. It would be painting the duchess too much *en beau*, were we to say that she met Mildred without certain misgivings and fears. But the first glimpse of her lovely niece completely put natural feelings in the ascendency. The resemblance to her sister was so strong as to cause a piercing cry to escape her, and, bursting into tears, she folded the trembling young woman to her heart, with a fervour and sincerity that set at naught all conventional manners. This was the commencement of a close intimacy; which lasted but a short time, however, the duchess dying two years later.

Wycherly continued in the service until the peace of Aix-la-Chapelle, when he finally quitted the sea. His strong native attachments led him back to Virginia, where all his own nearest relatives belonged, and where his whole heart might be said to be, when he saw Mildred and his children at his side. With him, early associations and habits had more strength, than traditions and memorials of the past. He erected a spacious dwelling on the estate inherited from his father, where he passed most of his time; consigning

Wychecombe to the care of a careful steward. With the additions and improvements that he was now enabled to make, his Virginian estate produced even a larger income than his English, and his interests really pointed to the choice he had made. But no pecuniary considerations lay at the bottom of his selection. He really preferred the graceful and courteous ease of the intercourse which characterized the manners of James' river. In that age, they were equally removed from the coarse and boisterous jollity of the English country-squire, and the heartless conventionalities of high life. In addition to this, his sensitive feelings rightly enough detected that he was regarded in the mother-country as a sort of intruder. He was spoken of, alluded to in the journals, and viewed even by his tenants as the *American* landlord; and he never felt truly at home in the country for which he had fought and bled. In England, his rank as a baronet was not sufficient to look down these little peculiarities; whereas, in Virginia, it gave him a certain *éclat*, that was grateful to one of the main weaknesses of human nature. "At home," as the mother-country was then affectionately termed, he had no hope of becoming a privy councillor; while, in his native colony, his rank and fortune, almost as a matter of course, placed him in the council of the governor. In a word, while Wycherly found most of those worldly considerations which influence men in the choice of their places of residence, in favour of the region in which he happened to be born, his election was made more from feeling and taste than from any thing else. His mind had taken an early bias in favour of the usages and opinions of the people among whom he had received his first impressions, and this bias he retained to the hour of his death.

Like a true woman, Mildred found her happiness with her husband and children. Of the latter she had but three; a boy and two girls. The care of the last was early committed to Mrs. Dutton. This excellent woman had remained at Wychecombe with her husband, until death put an end to his vices, though the close of his career was exempt from those scenes of brutal dictation and interference that had rendered the earlier part of her life so miserable. Apprehension of what might be the consequences to himself, acted as a check, and he had sagacity enough to see that the physical comforts he now possessed were all owing to the influence of his wife. He lived but four years, however. On his death, his widow immediately took her departure for America.

It would be substituting pure images of the fancy for a picture of sober realities, were we to say that Lady Wychecombe and her adopted mother never regretted the land of *their* birth. This negation of feeling, habits, and prejudices, is not to be expected even in an Esquimaux. They both had occasional strictures to make on the *climate*, (and this to Wycherly's great surprise, for *he* conscientiously believed that of England to be just the worst in the world,) on the fruits, the servants, the roads, and the difficulty of procuring various little comforts. But, as this was said good-naturedly and in pleasantry, rather than in the way of complaint, it led to no unpleasant scenes or feelings. As all three made occasional voyages to England, where his estates, and more particularly settlements with his factor, compelled the baronet to go once in about a lustrum, the fruits and the climate were finally given up by the ladies. After many years, even the slip-shod, careless, but hearty attendance of the negroes, came to be preferred to the dogged mannerism of the English domestics, perfect as were the latter in their parts; and the whole subject got to be one of amusement, instead of one of complaint. There is no greater mistake than to suppose that the traveller who passes *once* through a country, with his home-bred, and quite likely *provincial* notions thick upon him, is competent to describe, with due discrimination, even the usages of which he is actually a witness. This truth all the family came, in time, to discover; and while it rendered them more strictly critical in their remarks, it also rendered them more tolerant. As it was, few happier families were to be found in the British empire, than that of Sir Wycherly Wychecombe; its head retaining his manly and protecting affection for all dependent on him, while his wife, beautiful as a matron, as she had been lovely as a girl, clung to him with the tenacity of the vine to its own oak.

Of the result of the rising in the north, it is unnecessary to say much. The history of the *Chevalier's* successes in the first year, and of his final overthrow at Culloden, is well known. Sir Reginald Wychecombe, like hundreds of others, played his cards so skilfully that he avoided committing himself; and, although he lived and eventually died a suspected man, he escaped forfeitures and attainder. With Sir Wycherly, as the head of his house, he maintained a friendly correspondence to the last, even taking charge of the paternal estate in its owner's absence; manifesting to the hour of his death, a scrupulous probity in matters of money, mingled with an inherent love of management and intrigue, in things that related to politics and the succession. Sir Reginald lived long enough to see the hopes of the Jacobites completely extinguished, and the throne filled by a native Englishman.

Many long years after the events which rendered the week of its opening incidents so memorable among its actors, must now be imagined. Time had advanced with its usual unfaltering tread, and the greater part of a generation had been gathered to their fathers. George III. had been on the throne not less than three lustrums, and most of the important actors of the period of '45, were dead;—many of them, in a degree, forgotten. But each age has its own events and its own changes. Those colonies, which in 1745 were so loyal, so devoted to the house of Hanover, in the belief that political and religious liberty depended on the issue, had revolted against the supremacy of the parliament of the empire. America was already in arms against the mother country, and the very day before the occurrence of the little scene we are about to relate, the intelligence of the battle of Bunker Hill had reached London. Although the gazette and national pride had, in a degree, lessened the characteristics of this most remarkable of all similar combats, by exaggerating the numbers of the colonists engaged, and lessening the loss of the royal troops, the impression produced by the news is said to have been greater than any known to that age. It had been the prevalent opinion of England—an opinion that was then general in Europe, and which descended even to our own times—that the animals of the new continent, man included, had less courage and physical force, than those of the old; and astonishment, mingled with the forebodings of the intelligent, when it was found that a body of ill-armed countrymen had dared to meet, in a singularly bloody combat, twice their number of regular troops, and that, too, under the guns of the king's shipping and batteries. Rumours, for the moment, were rife in London, and the political world was filled with gloomy anticipations of the future.

On the morning of the day alluded to, Westminster Abbey, as usual, was open to the inspection of the curious and interested. Several parties were scattered among its aisles and chapels, some reading the inscriptions on the simple tablets of the dead which illustrate a nation, in illustrating themselves; others listening to the names of princes who derived their consequence from their thrones and alliances; and still other sets, who were wandering among the more elaborate memorials that have been raised equally to illustrate insignificance, and to mark the final resting-places of more modern heroes and statesmen. The beauty of the weather had brought out more visiters than common, and not less than half-a-dozen equipages were in waiting, in and about Palace Yard. Among others, one had a ducal coronet. This carriage did not fail to attract the attention that is more than usually bestowed on rank, in England. All were empty, however, and more than one party of pedestrians entered the venerable edifice, rejoicing that the view of a duke or a duchess, was to be thrown in, among the other sights, gratuitously. All who passed on foot, however, were not influenced by this vulgar feeling; for, one group went by, that did not even cast a glance at the collection of carriages; the seniors of the party being too much accustomed to such things to lend them a thought, and the juniors too full of anticipations of what they were about to see, to think of other matters. This party consisted of a handsome man of fifty-odd, a lady some three or four years his junior well preserved and still exceedingly attractive; a young man of twenty-six, and two lovely girls, that looked like twins; though one was really twenty-one, and the other but nineteen. These were Sir Wycherly and Lady Wychecombe, Wycherly their only son, then just returned from a five years' peregrination on the continent of Europe, and Mildred and Agnes, their daughters. The rest of the family had arrived in England about a fortnight before, to greet the heir on his return from the *grand tour*, as it was then termed. The meeting had been one of love, though Lady Wychecombe had to reprove a few innocent foreign affectations, as she fancied them to be, in her son; and the baronet, himself, laughed at the scraps of French, Italian, and German, that quite naturally mingled in the young man's discourse. All this, however, cast no cloud over the party, for it had ever been a family of entire confidence and unbroken love.

"This is a most solemn place to me," observed Sir Wycherly, as they entered at the Poets' corner, "and one in which a common man unavoidably feels his own insignificance. But, we will first make our pilgrimage, and look at these remarkable inscriptions as we come out. The tomb we seek is in a chapel on the other side of the church, near to the great doors. When I last saw it, it was quite alone."

On hearing this, the whole party moved on; though the two lovely young Virginians cast wistful and curious eyes behind them, at the wonders by which they were surrounded.

"Is not this an extraordinary edifice, Wycherly?" half whispered Agnes, the youngest of the sisters, as she clung to one arm of her brother, Mildred occupying the other. "Can the whole world furnish such another?"

"So much for hominy and James' river!" answered the young man, laughing—"now could you but see the pile at Rouen, or that at Rheims, or that at Antwerp, or even that at York, in this good kingdom, old Westminster would have to fall back upon its little tablets and big names. But Sir Wycherly stops; he must see what he calls his land-fall."

Sir Wycherly had indeed stopped. It was in consequence of having reached the head of the *ch[oe]ur*, whence he could see the interior of the recess, or chapel, towards which he had been moving. It still contained but a single monument, and that was adorned with an anchor and other nautical emblems. Even at that distance, the words "RICHARD BLUEWATER, REAR-ADMIRAL OF THE WHITE," might be read. But the baronet had come to a sudden halt, in consequence of seeing a party of three enter the chapel, in which he wished to be alone with his own family. The party consisted of an old man, who walked with tottering steps, and this so much the more from the circumstance that he leaned on a domestic nearly as old as himself, though of a somewhat sturdier frame, and of a tall imposing-looking person of middle age, who followed the two with patient steps. Several attendants of the cathedral watched this party from a distance with an air of curiosity and respect; but they had been requested not to accompany it to the chapel.

"They must be some old brother-officers of my poor uncle's, visiting his tomb!" whispered Lady Wychecombe. "The very venerable gentleman has naval emblems about his attire."

"*Do* you—*can* you forget him, love? 'Tis Sir Gervaise Oakes, the pride of England! yet how changed! It is now five-and-twenty years since we last met; still I knew him at a glance. The servant is old Galleygo, his steward; but the gentleman with him is a stranger. Let us advance; *we* cannot be intruders in such a place."

Sir Gervaise paid no attention to the entrance of the Wychecombes. It was evident, by the vacant look of his countenance, that time and hard service had impaired his faculties, though his body remained entire; an unusual thing for one who had been so often engaged. Still there were glimmerings of lively recollections, and even of strong sensibilities about his eyes, as sudden fancies crossed his mind. Once a year, the anniversary of his friend's interment, he visited that chapel; and he had now been brought here as much from habit, as by his own desire. A chair was provided for him, and he sat facing the tomb, with the large letters before his eyes. He regarded neither, though he bowed courteously to the salute of the strangers. His companion at first seemed a little surprised, if not offended at the intrusion; but when Wycherly mentioned that they were relatives of the deceased, he also bowed complacently, and made way for the ladies.

"This it is as what you wants to see, Sir Jarvy," observed Galleygo, jogging his master's shoulder by way of jogging his memory. "Them 'ere cables and hanchors, and that 'ere mizzen-mast, with a rear-admiral's flag a-flying, is rigged in this old church, in honour of our friend Admiral Blue, as was; but as is now dead and gone this many a long year."

"Admiral of the Blue," repeated Sir Gervaise coldly. "You're mistaken, Galleygo, I'm an admiral of the white, and admiral of the fleet in the bargain. I know my own rank, sir."

"I knows that as well as you does yourself, Sir Jarvy," answered Galleygo, whose grammar had rather become confirmed than improved, by time, "or as well as the First Lord himself. But Admiral Blue was once your best friend, and I doesn't at all admire at your forgetting him—one of these long nights you'll be forgetting *me.*"

"I beg your pardon, Galleygo; I rather think not. I remember *you*, when a very young man."

"Well, and so you mought remember Admiral Blue, if you'd just try. I know'd ye both when young luffs, myself."

"This is a painful scene," observed the stranger to Sir Wycherly, with a melancholy smile. "This gentleman is now at the tomb of his dearest friend; and yet, as you see, he appears to have lost all recollection that such a person ever existed. For what do we live, if a few brief years are to render our memories such vacant spots!"

"Has he been long in this way?" asked Lady Wychecombe, with interest.

The stranger started at the sound of her voice. He looked intently into the face of the still fair speaker, before he answered; then he bowed, and replied—

"He has been failing these five years, though his last visit here was much less painful than this. But are our own memories perfect?—Surely, I have seen that face before!—These young ladies, too—"

"Geoffrey—*dear* cousin Geoffrey!" exclaimed Lady Wychecombe, holding out both her hands. "It is—it must be the Duke of Glamorgan, Wycherly!"

No further explanations were needed. All the parties recognised each other in an instant. They had not met for many—many years, and each had passed the period of life when the greatest change occurs in the physical appearance; but, now that the ice was broken, a flood of recollections poured in. The duke, or Geoffrey Cleveland, as we prefer to call him, kissed his cousin and her daughters with frank affection, for no change of condition had altered his simple sea-habits, and he shook hands with the gentlemen, with a cordiality like that of old times. All this, however, was unheeded by Sir Gervaise, who sat looking at the monument, in a dull apathy.

"Galleygo," he said; but Galleygo had placed himself before Sir Wycherly, and thrust out a hand that looked like a bunch of knuckles.

"I knows ye!" exclaimed the steward, with a grin. "I know'd ye in the offing yonder, but I couldn't make out your number. Lord, sir, if this doesn't brighten Sir Jarvy up, again, and put him in mind of old times, I shall begin to think we have run out cable to the better end."

"I will speak to him, duke, if you think it advisable?" said Sir Wycherly, in an inquiring manner.

"Galleygo," put in Sir Gervaise, "what lubber fitted that cable?—he has turned in the clench the wrong way."

"Ay—ay, sir, they *is* great lubbers, them stone-cutters, Sir Jarvy; and they knows about as much of ships, as ships knows of them. But here is *young* Sir Wycherly Wychecombe come to see you—the *old* 'un's nevy."

"Sir Wycherly, you are a very welcome guest. Bowldero is a poor place for a gentleman of your merit; but such as it is, it is entirely at your service. What did you say the gentleman's name was, Galleygo?"

"Sir Wycherly Wychecombe, the *young* 'un—the *old* 'un slipped the night as we moored in his house."

"I hope, Sir Gervaise, I have not entirely passed from your recollection; it would grieve me sadly to think so. And my poor uncle, too; he who died of apoplexy in your presence!"

"*Nullus, nulla, nullum.* That's good Latin, hey! Duke? *Nullius, nullius, nullius.* My memory *is* excellent, gentlemen; nominative, *penna*; genitive, *pennæ*, and so on."

"Now, Sir Jarvy, since you're veering out your Latin, *I* should likes to know if you can tell a 'clove-hitch' from a 'carrick-bend?'"

"That is an extraordinary question, Galleygo, to put to an old seaman!"

"Well, if you remembers *that*, why can't you just as reasonably remember your old friend, Admiral Blue?"

"Admiral of the blue! I do recollect *many* admirals of the blue. They ought to make me an admiral of the blue, duke; I've been a rear-admiral long enough."

"You've *been* an admiral of the blue *once*; and that's enough for any man," interrupted Galleygo, again in his positive manner; "and it isn't five minutes since you know'd your own rank as well as the Secretary to the Admiralty himself. He veers and hauls, in this fashion, on an idee, gentlemen, until he doesn't know one end of it from t'other."

"This is not uncommon with men of great age," observed the duke. "They sometimes remember the things of their youth, while the whole of later life is a blank. I have remarked this with our venerable friend, in whose mind I think it will not be difficult, however, to revive the recollection of Admiral Bluewater, and even of yourself, Sir Wycherly. Let *me* make the effort, Galleygo."

"Yes, Lord Geoffrey," for so the steward always called the quondam reefer, "you does handle him more like a quick-working boat, than any on us; and so I'll take an hopportunity of just overhauling our old lieutenant's young 'uns, and of seeing what sort of craft he has set afloat for the next generation."

"Sir Gervaise," said the Duke, leaning over the chair, "here is Sir Wycherly Wychecombe, who once served a short time with us as a lieutenant; it was when you were in the Plantagenet. You remember the Plantagenet, I trust, my dear sir?"

"The Plantagenets? Certainly, duke; I read all about them when a boy. Edwards, and Henrys, and *Richards*—" at the last name he stopped; the muscles of his face twitched; memory had touched a sensitive chord. But it was too faintly, to produce more than a pause.

"There, now," growled Galleygo, in Agnes' face, he being just then employed in surveying her through a pair of silver spectacles that were a present from his master, "you see, he has forgotten the old Planter; and the next thing, he'll forget to eat his dinner. It's *wicked*, Sir Jarvy, to forget *such* a ship."

"I trust, at least, you have not forgotten Richard Bluewater?" continued the Duke, "he who fell in our last action with the Comte de Vervillin?"

A gleam of intelligence shot into the rigid and wrinkled face; the eye lighted, and a painful smile struggled around the lips.

"What, *Dick*!" he exclaimed, in a voice stronger than that in which he had previously spoken. "*Dick!* hey! duke? *good, excellent Dick?* We were midshipmen together, my lord duke; and I loved him like a brother!"

"I *knew* you did! and I dare say now you can recollect the melancholy occasion of his death?"

"Is Dick *dead?*" asked the admiral, with a vacant gaze.

"Lord—Lord, Sir Jarvy, you knows he is, and that 'ere marvel constructure is his monerment—now you *must* remember the old Planter, and the County of Fairvillian, and the threshing we guv'd him?"

"Pardon me, Galleygo; there is no occasion for warmth. When I was a midshipman, warmth of expression was disapproved of by all the elder officers."

"You cause me to lose ground," said the Duke, looking at the steward by way of bidding him be silent: "is it not extraordinary, Sir Wycherly, how his mind reverts to his youth, overlooking the scenes of latter life! Yes, *Dick is* dead, Sir Gervaise. He fell in that battle in which you were doubled on by the French—when you had le Foudroyant on one side of you, and le Pluton on the other—"

"*I remember it!*" interrupted Sir Gervaise, in a clear strong voice, his eye flashing with something like the fire of youth—"I remember it! Le Foudroyant was on our starboard beam; le Pluton a little on our larboard bow—Bunting had gone aloft to look out for Bluewater—no—poor Bunting was killed—"

"Sir Wycherly Wychecombe, who afterwards married Mildred Bluewater, Dick's niece," put in the baronet, himself, almost as eager as the admiral had now become; "Sir Wycherly Wychecombe *had* been aloft, but was returned to report the Pluton coming down!"

"So he did!—God bless him! A clever youth, and he *did* marry Dick's niece. God bless them *both*. Well, sir, you're a stranger, but the story will interest you. There we lay, almost smothered in the smoke, with one two-decker at work on our starboard beam, and another hammering away on the larboard bow, with our top-masts over the side, and the guns firing through the wreck."

"Ay, now you're getting it like a book!" exclaimed Galleygo exultingly, flourishing his stick, and strutting about the little chapel; "that's just the way things was, as I knows from seeing 'em!"

"I'm quite certain I'm right, Galleygo?"

"Right! your honour's righter than any log-book in the fleet. Give it to 'em, Sir Jarvy, larboard and starboard!"

"That we did—that we did"—continued the old man earnestly, becoming even grand in aspect, as he rose, always gentleman-like and graceful, but filled with native fire, "that did we! de Vervillin was on our right, and des Prez on our left—the smoke was choking us all—Bunting—no; young Wychecombe was at my side; he said a fresh Frenchman was shoving in between us and le Pluton, sir—God forbid! I *thought*; for we had enough of them, us it was. There she comes! See, here is her flying-jib-boom-end—and there—hey! Wychecombe?—*That's* the *old Roman*, shoving through the smoke!—Cæsar himself! and there stands Dick and young Geoffrey Cleveland—*he* was of your family, duke—there stands Dick Bluewater, between the knight-heads, waving his hat—*HURRAH!*—He's true, at last!—He's true, at last—*HURRAH! HURRAH!*"

The clarion tones rose like a trumpet's blast, and the cheering of the old sailor rang in the arches of the Abbey Church, causing all within hearing to start, as if a voice spoke from the tombs. Sir Gervaise, himself, seemed surprised; he looked up at the vaulted roof, with a gaze half-bewildered, half-delighted.

"Is this Bowldero, or Glamorgan House, my Lord Duke," he asked, in a whisper.

"It is neither, Admiral Oakes, but Westminster Abbey; and this is the tomb of your friend, rear-admiral Richard Bluewater."

"Galleygo, help me to kneel," the old man added in the manner of a corrected school-boy. "The stoutest of us all, should kneel to God, in his own temple. I beg pardon, gentlemen; I wish to pray."

The Duke of Glamorgan and Sir Wycherly Wychecombe helped the admiral to his knees, and Galleygo, as was his practice, knelt beside his master, who bowed his head on his man's shoulders. This touching spectacle brought all the others into the same humble attitude. Wycherly, Mildred, and their children, with the noble, kneeling and praying in company. One by one, the latter arose; still Galleygo and his master continued on the pavement. At length Geoffrey Cleveland stepped forward, and raised the old man, placing him, with Wycherly's assistance, in the chair. Here he sat, with a calm smile on his aged features, his open eyes riveted seemingly on the name of his friend, perfectly dead. There had been a reaction, which suddenly stopped the current of life, at the heart.

Thus expired Sir Gervaise Oakes, full of years and of honours; one of the bravest and most successful of England's sea-captains. He had lived his time, and supplied an instance of the insufficiency of worldly success to complete the destiny of man; having, in a degree, survived his faculties, and the consciousness of all he had done, and all he merited. As a small offset to this failing of nature, he had regained a glimmering view of one of the most striking scenes, and of much the most enduring sentiment, of a long life, which God, in mercy, permitted to be terminated in the act of humble submission to his own greatness and glory.

[1] Suffren, though one of the best sea-captains France ever possessed, was a man of extreme severity and great roughness of manner. Still he must have been a man of family, as his title of *Bailli* de Suffren, was derived from his being a Knight of Malta. It is a singular circumstance connected with the death of this distinguished officer, which occurred not long before the French revolution, that he disappeared in an extraordinary manner, and is buried no one knows where. It is supposed that he was killed by one of his own officers, in a rencontre in the streets of Paris, at night, and that the influence of the friends of the victor was sufficiently great to suppress inquiry. The cause of the quarrel is attributed to harsh treatment on service.

[2] The writer believes this noble-minded sailor to have been the late Admiral Sir Benjamin Caldwell. It is scarcely necessary to say that the invitation could not be accepted, though quite seriously given.

[3] In the action of the Nile, many of the French ships, under the impression that the enemy *must* engage on the *outside*, put their lumber, bags, &c., into the ports, and between the guns, in the larboard, or *inshore* batteries; and when the British anchored *inshore* of them, these batteries could not be used.